MADE FOR LOVING

Angus's heart thundered, his mind and body totally consumed with need for the beauty in his arms. He pressed firm hands to her back, bringing her soft curves into perfect alignment with his harder planes. Aye, this lass with her secret had been made for him, molded to him as none before. Birdi's compassion, her foibles enchanted him.

His tongue played across hers in shameless abandon, stroking, tasting, and teasing. When she mewed deep in her throat, a feeling like lightning flashed through him. She then arched, pressing closer, and he rolled instinctively.

Good God, the woman was made for loving.

BOOK YOUR PLACE ON OUR WEBSITE AND MAKE THE READING CONNECTION!

We've created a customized website just for our very special readers, where you can get the inside scoop on everything that's going on with Zebra, Pinnacle and Kensington books.

When you come online, you'll have the exciting opportunity to:

- View covers of upcoming books
- Read sample chapters
- Learn about our future publishing schedule (listed by publication month *and author*)
- Find out when your favorite authors will be visiting a city near you
- Search for and order backlist books from our online catalog
- Check out author bios and background information
- Send e-mail to your favorite authors
- Meet the Kensington staff online
- Join us in weekly chats with authors, readers and other guests
- Get writing guidelines
- AND MUCH MORE!

Visit our website at
http://www.kensingtonbooks.com

A Rogue in a Kilt

Sandy Blair

ZEBRA BOOKS
Kensington Publishing Corp.
http://www.kensingtonbooks.com

ZEBRA BOOKS are published by

Kensington Publishing Corp.
850 Third Avenue
New York, NY 10022

All Kensington titles, imprints and distributed lines are available at special quantity discounts for bulk purchases for sales promotion, premiums, fund-raising, educational or institutional use.

Special book excerpts or customized printings can also be created to fit specific needs. For details, write or phone the office of the Kensington Special Sales Manager: Kensington Publishing Corp., 850 Third Avenue, New York, NY 10022. Attn: Special Sales Department. Phone: 1-800-221-2647.

Zebra and the Z logo Reg. U.S. Pat. & TM Off.

First Printing: December 2004
10 9 8 7 6 5 4 3 2 1

Printed in the United States of America

To Becca:
Thank you for providing so much joy in my life.

For Alex:
May all your wishes come true.

Acknowledgments

The author would like to thank:

Hilary Sares, editor par excellence, whose steadfast encouragement and support turned a dream into a reality bound between two beautiful covers;

Paige Wheeler, agent extraordinaire, who was the first to believe in this story;

Lisa Hanes for falling in love with Duncan;

Scott Blair, husband without peer, who took me from castle to castle and carried mountains of research books up winding staircases with a minimal amount of *humphing*;

Dearest friends Julie Benson, Suzanne Welsh, Jane Graves, and Lorraine Heath whose enthusiastic support and goading kept me going and gave me the courage to compete.

Acknowledgements

Chapter 1

Loch Ard Forest, Scotland
September, 1410

Angus MacDougall, astride his charger, ducked but not fast enough. The lashing pine bough caught him firmly on the back of the head. He cursed as he rubbed the welt. "I swear if a fair and fulsome lady isna offered to me at Beal Castle, I'm stealing the first winsome lass that crosses my path."

But then he couldn't. He'd pledged to bring home a lady, a chatelaine.

Worse, he didn't want a wife. Had never wanted a wife. He liked taking his pleasure when the opportunity presented itself, then kissing the lass goodbye without fashing about her and home. Nor was he fit company for man or beast after battle. So why on earth had he bragged to his liege that he could take to wife any fair lady he chose—in three months' time, no less?

His best friend, Duncan MacDougall, had countered, "Ye braggart, I'll wager ye canna find such a lass by the Samhain solstice. If ye can, I'll hand over the keys to Donaliegh. If ye fail, ye forfeit six months' wages."

Angus's heart had stuttered. "Ye'll make me liege of Donaliegh?" Once a Stewart holding, Donaliegh hadn't had a true liege lord in years, not since Dumont's death.

'Twas by now in serious disrepair, but to be his own man . . . a laird.

"And Albany has approved this?" With their boy-king held in the Tower of London, the lad's uncle, the Duke of Albany, now held sway over all.

"Aye, he has. But fair warning, yer lady must be a willing one and able to take on the responsibilities of Donaliegh."

Angus had smiled into his cup. Three long months to find an agreeable lady seemed reasonable, if not excessive.

He held out his hand. "Done!"

But now, with two months gone and himself yet again in enemy territory—there wasn't a way to get from east to west without going through some rival clan's holdings—he was no closer to his goal than he had been when he'd left Castle Blackstone.

He huffed. Did he not stand six feet and a hand high? Was he not brawn from top to bottom with sound teeth and a full head of hair? Was he not a skilled knight, his laird's confidant and right arm? What wasn't to like?

But then, he was also known as Angus the Blood, supposedly a man of fearsome, bloodthirsty habits—reputed to eat the livers of his enemies. It made him ill thinking his carefully cultivated and totally false reputation should now result in no Donaliegh and the loss of six months' wages. Ack!

He'd been traveling for weeks from keep to castle, climbing mountains and slogging through bogs, sleeping on brittle heather most nights, and the only lasses offered to him thus far had been either terrified of him, curt—if not outright insulting—or of questionable mind, the last being a decidedly stout woman with oddly slanted eyes, low ears, and the mind of a bairn.

God's teeth!

Another branch whipped back, this time clipping his cheek. Cursing, he dismounted and led his stallion toward a patch of ground sparkling in the moonlight, to what he hoped would be a wee pool of fresh water within the ever-deepening forest. "Ye've been a good lad, Rampage," he whispered, "hauling my sorry arse across the breadth of Scotland and halfway back on this foolish quest."

Breaking through the dense foliage and finding a dark glen free of inhabitants and with a freshwater pool, he loosened his horse's girth.

"Go eat." He smacked his mount's rump. He never bothered with shackles. Like all cattle, his loyal charger preferred company to being alone.

As Rampage trotted into verdant fodder, Angus squatted within the edge of the tree line, opened his sporran, and pulled out the remnants of the hard cheese and oatcakes he'd purchased in Kelso. "A meager supper for a man of sixteen stone."

Were he home he'd be feasting on white fish, roasted pork, potatoes, and the weeds Blackstone's Lady Beth called salad. He swore never again to disparage her weeds. Aye, he would, henceforth, eat every bite with a smile, for anything was better than grinding on what lay in his hands.

His supper eaten but with stomach still rumbling, he leaned against a rough pine and pondered the morrow. He had one letter of introduction left.

Was there a possibility some winsome lass lurked in Beal Castle? Mayhap a daughter or niece whom MacCloud was anxious to marry off? One who hadn't heard of Angus the Blood, one not necessarily fair but with wide hips and lots of good teeth? A lass of sound mind and a quiet, accommodating disposition, one who knew how to cook, keep house, and wanted bairns?

Now bairns he did want. He'd often wondered what it would be like to have a son or mayhap a bonnie daughter as he'd watched Duncan and Lady Beth's rambunctious bairns romp. And now he had serious need for children. He would soon have Donaliegh and needed an heir.

But not even for Donaliegh or heirs would he betroth himself to a handful like his best friend's ladywife.

Lady Beth was precisely what he didn't want. Castle Blackstone's chatelaine had far too much fire in her belly for his taste.

The one and only time he'd naysayed the lass—the night he'd banned her, a newcomer, from Duncan's room where he lay fevered—Angus had found his poke of sweeties in his throat. He shuddered and gave his balls a gentle pat, thankful they'd survived the day.

But to be fair, Lady Beth had been the first to wish him well on his bride quest; had in fact told him he looked dashing in his flame-colored tunic and polished mail as she handed him a wee book of sonnets. "Memorize a few of these," she'd whispered after kissing his cheek, "smile, and for God's sake, chew with your mouth closed." He'd laughed at the time.

He wasn't laughing now.

Despite smiling 'til his cheeks smarted, spouting poetic drivel 'til his head throbbed, and chewing most carefully 'til his teeth ached, he still lacked a proper lady to birth his bairns and keep Donaliegh's fires burning.

He blew out a lungful of air and rose to find his mount at the pool's edge. He clucked and Rampage's head came up, ears twitching. As the horse ambled toward him, sampling flowers along the way, Angus glanced skyward. A falling star streaked across the sky and his spirits rose.

"But most important," he murmured, his gaze on the star, "if I must take a wife, I lust for one who will not see scars or Donaliegh when she looks upon me, but will see"—he tapped his chest—"what lurks in here."

Birdalane woke with a start to find her heart thudding, her breast tingling, and moisture between her thighs. What on earth ailed her?

She placed a hand on her forehead. No fever. She placed a hand on her stomach. No upset there either. Yet the odd feelings persisted.

She stared at her wee croft's rafters and tried to recall her dream. Had it caused the chaos within her?

Dredging up the image of the huge faceless man, the odd tingling between her thighs and within her breast intensified. She gasped.

The yearnings!

Her mother had spoken of this. *Never tempt fate,* her minnie had warned. *Ever. Not even in your mind. Better to go without sleep than to dream such dreams,* she had preached. Aye.

Birdi jumped out of bed.

Pulling her woolen blanket tighter about her, she shuddered and opened the door. She heaved a sigh of relief at finding dawn breaking, the sky turning the color of heather. She didn't have to return to bed to wait out the sun and mayhap fall back to sleep, only to have the wretched yearnings return.

Her candles long gone, she let the door fall wide on its leather hinges, shed her blanket, and shivered into her soft cotton shift. Using water from the sheepskin pouch hanging by the door, she made quick work of her ablutions and slipped on her coarse green kirtle and threadbare apron. She reached for her slippers.

"Ouch!"

She yanked on the thick strand of hair caught in her apron strings. "What I wouldna give for a sharp pair of shears." Her shears—so dull they barely cut thread—were no match for the dark curls billowing below her waist, spirals that defied braiding and were forever getting caught in something. Picturing herself shorn like a villager's ewe, she chuckled and reached for a length of hide lacing.

Her hair secured, she brushed the supper crumbs she'd left scattered across the table into her apron, walked out her door, and settled on the willow chair her mother had crafted so many years ago. She flapped her apron, sat back, and waited for her company.

Several minutes passed and then, as expected, came the flutter of wings batting air.

Cooing puffs of white and gray landed at her feet. She held her breath, not daring to move, though she dearly wanted to kneel and touch the floating bodies. As the doves pecked at her crumbs she wondered, are doves soft? Softer than Hen?

Poor Hen. The speckled beastie hadn't survived the winter, had been caught in an ice storm, but she still resided with Birdi in spirit, her flesh having provided sustenance and her feathers a new pillow.

Birdi leaned forward to get a clearer view of the doves she'd been trying to tame all summer, the chair squeaked, and the doves took flight on frenzied wings.

"Ooh . . . cattle pies."

She was alone again. Through burgeoning tears she looked about her fuzzy world of green blobs, brown spikes, and great expanses of pale blue—a world she could see only by daylight, and then none too well. She twisted a loose lock around her finger. Another fair day loomed before her. Aye, and she should be thanking Mother of All.

She dashed the wetness from her cheeks with the heels of her hands and gave herself a good shake. She should be harvesting blackberries and grain for the coming winter before all the beasts and vermin ate them, not sitting here sniveling and feeling forlorn because she had no one to talk to.

With luck she might again spy Wolf as she roamed the woods and crept along the outer edges of the villagers' fields gathering wayward stalks of grain.

The moon had gone from new to full since last she'd seen Wolf, had last felt his soft tongue lick her cheek. It

still didn't seem possible three whole seasons had passed
since she'd discovered him in a hollowed log, a skinny pup
with an injured leg. Nursed back to health, he'd grown
quickly. But one night she'd awakened to howling, and
then he was gone.

How wonderful it would be to stroke his soft underbelly,
to have him tugging at her skirt in play again. Aye.

Heart lightened by the prospect of finding him again,
she went back into her croft and reached for her gathering
basket beneath the table. As she picked it up, her fingers
began to itch and tingle.

Ack! 'Twas the *need* returned.

She cursed and pushed the basket back under the table.
She no longer fought the need—the urge to create or
help—as she had as a bairn; she now kenned it would only
grow into a formidable distraction.

She plopped down onto her three-legged cuttie stool,
took a deep settling breath, and opened her mind. After a
moment she reached above the water-worn stones that
formed her ingleside—her hearth—for the basket containing her collection of woolen threads, scraps of cloth,
and trinkets. She pulled out her bone needle and, squinting, threaded it. Setting to work she muttered, " 'Tis a
wonder I get anything done."

An hour later, she studied her creation: a doll with
wood-button eyes and combed fleece hair dressed in a kirtle made from a scrap of linen. Now why had she made
this? She wasn't a bairn, nor had she one. She heaved a
sigh and added a blue ribbon to the doll's yellow hair.

Doll and gathering basket in hand, she headed for the
path that separated her world from that of the Macarthurs.
As the sun broke over the treetops, she caught the sweet
tang of decaying apples on the wind. Were there still
enough apples on branches to make the fight through the
brambles worthwhile? Mayhap. If not, she could still

gather windfalls, carve out what she could for herself, and dry the rest for Deer's winter.

Finally spying light green and gold flashing between the lean black lines of shadowed tree trunks, a sure sign the glen with its rutted path—to where, she didn't ken—and its old oak stump lay, she hurried on.

At the roadway's edge she hunkered down behind a dense hedge and listened.

Hearing only the twitter of birds, the whisper of wind in the long-needled pines above her, she gathered her courage and scampered across the clearing to the stump.

Wider than her arms could span, the ancient stump had served as a depository for gifts since her mother's time— for those Birdi left when the *need* struck and for the tributes she rarely received.

She placed the doll on the stump and retreated into the woods. To wait for the one who would come.

Before long she heard a whistled tune and then footfalls before hearing a lad's voice say, " 'Tis only one birthday, Meg. Ye'll have more, many more, and come yer twelfth, Ma and Da will give ye sweetcakes and, mayhap, the dolly."

She heard a sniff and a wee lass whine, " 'Tis a long way away . . . that day. What if I dinna want a dolly then? What if I'm too auld? I'd so lusted . . ."

The footsteps and sniffles grew louder before the lad said, "I ken 'tis hard lustin' and nay gettin', but Ma did make bread pudding."

The lass sniffed loudly. "Aye, 'twas that." The footsteps stopped and the lass gasped. "Oh, Jamie, Mama saw me greeting, saw my tears! What if she now thinks I'm ungrateful? Am I bound for hell?"

Birdi frowned. Hell? Where was hell?

The lad mumbled what sounded like a curse and told the lass, "Ye willna be going anywhere but home with me, ye wee imp."

He must have tickled her because she giggled. "Stop that!" Birdi heard the patter of running feet and a moment later a squeal.

"Jamie, come quick. Look!"

Running footsteps followed. The lass exclaimed, "'Tis a dolly, just as I lusted for, Jamie, with big brown eyes and hair of gold. And see, she even has a blue ribbon in her hair. But who could have—Jamie, do you think?" The lass's voice dropped to an awe-filled whisper. "Could the spae have placed it here?"

The spae, the wise healer. 'Twas better than some names Birdi had been called. Grinning—she now kenned why she'd made the doll—she backed farther into the trees. There wasn't a reason to stay and every reason to flee.

Birdi hoped the lass's parents would let her keep her gift, as she traveled deeper into the forest following the scent of apples.

Her skirt caught and pain pierced her knee. She rubbed her leg and squinted at the dark mass at her side. She'd found the thorny hedge protecting the apple tree. Or rather, it had found her.

Since there wasn't a chance of her climbing over it, she dropped to her knees. The beasties of the forest also wanted apples, and with luck she'd again find their trail through the brambles.

It took a while, but she found their path, an opening tall enough for her to travel through but only on her belly. Pushing her basket in before her, she crawled into the tunnel and prayed she wouldn't meet a boar coming the other way. Boars were the only beasts within the forest she feared. One, a great rutting bull, had gored her mother.

When she saw sunlight and a hint of bright green, she thanked Goddess and quickened her pace.

The apple tree stood alone in a patch of knee-high grass, its gnarled branches so weighted with fruit they touched the ground. She took a deep breath of sweet, tangy air and laughed. Tonight she would feast on apples and porridge.

A short time later—her basket and pockets full—she crawled back into the tunnel. Out the other end, she turned toward her croft. With her thoughts on coring and drying the fruit and gathering and hulling wheat, she startled, hearing a branch break on her left. She froze and tipped her head, strained to catch further discordant sounds.

Squish, squish, squish.

The fine hairs on her arms stood up. Was that the sound of pine needles cracking under a heavy foot? She spun, heart in her throat. No villager, surely, would dare enter her world.

They—adults and bairns alike—kenned the rules laid down long before she was born; if she was needed—if a villager was injured or ill—a family member need only stand at the edge of the forest and wish for her. She would, in due course, find her way to the one in need. Her healing done, often with barely a word exchanged, they would give her eggs or mayhap even a bag of fleece in tribute and she would take her leave.

She would then lie abed—often racked with fever or pain for days—always thankful she wouldn't have bairns. For no babe, no matter how loved, should be cursed with her gift of healing.

For with it not only came pain, but this awful blindness.

A branch snapped to her right. She spun and sniffed the air. Was it man or beast? She cursed the too-still air. Were there two or only one moving quickly? Which way should she run?

Goddess, help me!

The memory of her mother's tale—of once being caught out in the open—caused her heart to hammer. Birdi had been the result, a constant reminder of that painful day.

Never having had a father or brother—she had, in fact, been thankful she hadn't one trying to marry her off—

she now fervently lusted for a protector, someone who could see where she could not, who could warn her of danger where she sensed it not.

A firm hand clasped Birdi's shoulder.

She shrieked and lashed out. Fingers curled like talons, she swung wildly at her assailant as apples rolled beneath her feet, threatening to topple her.

The hand fell away as suddenly as it had landed. "Hush, Birdi, hush! 'Tis only I, Tinker."

"Tinker?" She wanted to smite him for startling her so. Short of breath, with her heart still skipping and thudding, she demanded, "What on earth were ye thinking . . . skulking up on me? I could have clawed yer eyes out!"

"Beggin' yer pardon, dear lady. 'Twasna my intent." Tinker's face suddenly loomed before her, scruffy and as dark as saddle leather. Buried within a myriad of comical folds sat two grass-green eyes, a bulbous nose, and a toothless grin. She tapped the tip of his nose. "Ah, 'tis ye."

"Aye, and I've a gift for ye."

"A gift?" She knelt, pulled her basket onto her lap, and started gathering her spilled apples. Tinker knelt to help. "Now why would ye bring me a gift, Tinker?"

"For saving me life is why." He looked about and told her, "That's the lot, lass. All yer apples are in the basket."

They stood and she laced her free arm through his. His coat, the one she'd patched and aired in the sun, once again smelled of wood-smoke and male sweat. "Taking care of ye was the least I could do after falling on ye." In truth she'd tripped over him—found him more dead than alive, his tools and trinkets gone—last Beltane. "Did the sheriff capture the curs who waylaid ye?"

Tinker snorted. "Nay, and I dinna expect he ever will, what with the number of ruffians about. Nettles all. 'Tis good that ye keep to the woods, lass."

"I havena a choice. 'Tis all I ken and trust." She'd been told the world beyond her woods held castles, princes, and miraculous colored glass, but that it also held untold horrors. Like priests in black gowns, her mother had warned, who burned the likes of her on pyres.

"Tell me," he said, pulling a thick twig from her hair, "what have ye been about that ye're covered in mud?"

She held a flawless red apple out to him. "They hide behind a bramble hedge."

"Ah." Grinning, he snatched the fruit from her hand. "Thank ye."

"Come." She waved in the direction of her croft. "Sup with me. I want to hear about yer travels. Were yer in time for Sterling Fair?" He'd been on his way there when he'd been waylaid. As Tinker had mended, he'd filled her head with tales of fire-eaters, fearless knights, and elegant ladies dressed in gold. "Was there a puppet show and jugglers? Was there pork pies and music? Was there—"

"Whoa, lass." Around a bite of apple, he mumbled, "I would love to sup and answer yer questions, truly, but I canna take the time." He held out a large leather pouch. "I only came by to give ye this."

Taking the bag from his hand, Birdi struggled to keep her face placid. So many months had passed since last she'd supped with him, had spoken with someone who wasn't fearful of her.

Grinning, Tinker waved an impatient hand. "Open it, lass."

Masking her disappointment behind an understanding smile, she did as he bid and found a treasure trove: a yard of scarlet ribbon, a shiny silver buckle, a skein of deep green wool, and a foot-long length of lace.

"Oh my." Such prizes left her at a loss for further words.

Tinker's gnarled finger traced the raised stitches surrounding a delicate lace petal. "'Tis from Italia. The ladies of Edinburgh don such. Thought ye might find some use for it." He shrugged. "'Tisna something most about these parts find useful."

Tears welled behind Birdi's lashes, clouding what little vision she had. He lied. Anyone would treasure what she held in her hands. She reached out and stroked his whiskered cheek. "Thank ye."

Tinker ducked his chin and mumbled, " 'Tis the least I can do."

" 'Twas a favor ye did me." She treasured their brief time together. She hadn't had a friend before or since.

He patted her arm. "Be that as it may, I still thank ye." He craned his neck to look through the treetops. " 'Tis close to midmorn. I must take leave or I willna make Aberfoyle by gloaming." He took a final bite of apple, tossed the core, and then took her hands in his. "I truly wish ye well, lass."

"I wish ye the same." As he turned away, she asked, "When will ye be back?"

"Next summer, lass. I'll look for ye then."

Next summer? Her heart sank. Need a whole year pass before she could again stand close to someone, converse, or be touched? She heaved a sigh as her tears took shape. Apparently so.

She looked up to find him beyond sight and called "Take care, Tinker John."

When silence answered back, her tears spilled.

Birdi turned toward the heat of the sun and therefore her pool. Mayhap a bath would wash off not only the dirt coating her, but the melancholy now weighing her spirit down.

Angus rousted from a dreamless sleep when something wet brushed his ear. He lashed out with a clenched left fist, his dirk at the ready in his right.

Heart hammering, he rolled to his feet and found Rampage, legs splayed and ears pinned, staring at him as if he'd never seen a man before in his life. "God's teeth, horse! What the hell were ye thinking?"

Angus sheathed his dirk, shoved his hair out of his face, and settled on his haunches. His mount—head down, eyes still wary—stepped back. Angus held out his hand. "I didna mean to scare ye, ye big brute. Come."

Rampage twitched his bruised nose and blew out a derisive snort.

"Ah, come on, lad, I didna mean to clout ye." Realizing he'd best make amends quickly or he'd be playing catch-me-if-ye-can with his charger, Angus plucked a few tender shoots from the base of the nearest tree and held them out on an open palm. "Peace?"

Rampage, lips twitching, cautiously stretched out his neck to sniff the peace offering. Before Angus could catch his halter, Rampage's head jerked up and his ears angled toward the glen. As his nares flared trying to catch a scent, Angus heard a splash.

He jerked to his feet and yanked his claymore from its sheath. Hopefully, there were no more than three or four Macarthurs in the glen. Rampage nickered and pawed the earth, and Angus hushed him.

Until he kenned his enemy's number, he didn't need a hundred stone of charger tromping and snorting announcing his presence. A handful of Macarthurs he could handle. Fighting more would put his and Rampage's lives at risk.

Heart hammering, blood surging into tensed muscles, Angus crept to the forest edge aware Rampage slowly but quietly followed.

Finding only ripples rolling across the wee pool's surface, Angus's gaze raked the glen for intruders. It stood empty but for a few birds and butterflies. He blew out a breath. " 'Twas only a fish, ye bloody idiot." Feeling the fool, he also felt less guilt over accidentally clouting his mount, who'd started his blood racing for naught.

As Angus sheathed his claymore, the surface of the pool rippled again, this time with far larger waves. Blessed

Mother! What manner of fish could possibly make such a wake? Before he could ponder further, a dark shape broke the surface on the far side of the pool.

A woman—naked as the day she was born, as pale as a winter moon—rose like a phoenix to stand thigh deep in the water on the far shore.

Chapter 2

Angus immediately searched the area again, looking for the woman's husband, a guard. Finding none, his gaze returned to the lass.

Years of ingrained catechism demanded he cover his eyes and leave. Chivalry demanded he—a knight of girth and sword—at the very least rattle a bush and warn the fair lady of his presence, but he couldn't do either. The blood had drained from his head and limbs only to surge in his groin.

As the woman shed water from her rose-tipped breasts and slender arms with long, tapered hands, he drank in the sight. Not usually a man taken to fancy, he found himself envying the water, would have given his sword arm to sluice as the water did down the woman's glorious breasts and across the flat planes of her belly in such fashion.

He shifted his weight to accommodate the swelling beneath his kilt as she wrung water from her hair.

Black and glossy as a raven's wing, her locks immediately started to curl across the gentle swell of her hips. His fingers curled in like fashion, palms itching, wanting to grab fistfuls, imagining her hair caressing his chest and stomach as she sat astride him, her long, tapered thighs spread wide across his. Aye, 'twould surely be glorious.

She suddenly cocked her head, obviously listening. Not daring to breathe—much less move—he waited for her screech. When her gaze swept past him and she remained silent, he released his breath. The glare bouncing off the water had apparently masked him.

His eyes hungrily examined every inch of her as she waded to shore on long, slim legs and climbed the far bank. She then bent for something in the tall grass, and her bonnie round hurdies glistened in the sun like twin moons. He groaned aloud. The sight—more than any sane man could stare at without turning coddle-brained—made him bounce in response beneath his kilt.

Reluctantly, he dragged his gaze from her delicious bottom and looked about the glen once again. Where was her cur of a husband? How was it possible a wandering knight could stand and stare? Surely so lovely a lass had a husband. But then, mayhap she was widowed. The thought lightened his heart until he remembered upon whose land he stood. The Macarthur's. Ack!

As he pondered the dilemma, the lady shook out a shift. When she raised it over her head, Angus felt hard pressed not to yell *halt!*

He then squinted, sure he couldn't be seeing correctly. She held up not a gown of velvet or brocade with threads of silver and gold but a kirtle, course and dun. He blinked in disbelief as she pulled it over her head. So the lass wasn't of high birth after all. "Humph."

The possibilities for conquest—of a dalliance—yawned. He smiled, only to feel Rampage's great head butt his back. The horse nickered softly.

"Quiet, ye damn pest." He pushed on Rampage's deep chest and the horse obediently backed away. "Now, stay." Larger than most cattle and white atop that, Rampage had frightened many a warrior into soiling himself. His mere presence in the glen would likely frighten the wee lass to death. If not, then surely she'd flee, and he wouldn't have a hope of catching her. He was on the far side of the pool and she kenned the forest at her back.

Deciding he had nothing to lose and more than a hand-

ful to gain, he took a deep breath and stepped into the sunshine. To his utter surprise she smiled, quickly turned to
her right, and said something he couldn't hear. Her pace
quickened as she walked along the opposite shore. His
hopes soared. They would meet by the boulders, where the
reeds were thickest.

He then spotted movement in the tall grass just feet before her and halted. Was it her man lying in wait? To her
mate did she speak?

Nay. 'Twas something gray that crept on lowered
haunches in the tall grass toward the lass. Was it a lymer—
a dog? Hers or her liege lord's, and if so, why was it
skulking about like a—

My God, a wolf!

He wrenched his sgian dubh from beneath his arm. It
flew from his hand, his aim true.

A heartbeat later and to his horror the lovely lady
keened and dropped like a stone to her knees.

Birdi, her nose filled with the unaccountable scent of
blood, crooned as she ran frantic hands over Wolf. Had he
been fighting? Had he been caught in a villager's snare?
What ailed him? Why had he collapsed? Why did his chest
heave so?

Then her hands found the handle of a blade.

She gasped. How had this happened? Though her sight
was pitiful, she was certain he'd been coming toward her
with his bushy tail wagging, his pink tongue lolling, and
the next . . .

*How matters naught, fool! He'll die if you dinna do
something and quickly.*

She gripped the knife handle with both hands and
caused him to whimper. She leaned forward, a hair's
breadth from his magnificent pale ears. "Hush, sweet dautie, hush. Trust now as ye have in the past." Blinking away

the urge to greet for her friend, she rocked off her knees and into a squat, planting her feet wide to be sure she made firm contact with Mother. Holding her breath, she yanked the blade. It came loose; Wolf keened and then fell silent. Blood, scarlet as any sunset, bubbled up through his gash like a sacred spring. She pressed crossed palms to the wound to stem the flow. Painfully aware of the furious rhythm of his heart beating beneath her hands, she reached out to the powers surrounding her.

When familiar heat surged through her quaking limbs, her own heart finally slowed. She took a deep settling breath . . . . The power was again within her. All would now be well for her friend.

She closed her eyes and whispered, "Mother of All, I, Birdi, take upon myself this wound . . . ."

Chest heaving, Angus dropped to his knees beside the fallen, raven-haired woman. His bloodied sgian dubh lay in the grass at her side. His stomach turned.

How in God's name could this have happened? He threw a blade as accurate as any man and had for more years than he could recall.

Hands shaking, he cradled the woman in his lap, surprised by her slight weight. As his free hand skimmed over her kirtle, seeking the sticky wetness of blood, his peripheral sight caught something moving at the tree line.

Angus growled deep in his throat. The blasted wolf.

The beast slowed, looked over his shoulder at him, flattened his ears, and then bolted into the woods, his tail between his legs.

"Ye damn well best run, ye miserable—"

The woman in his arms moaned.

The wolf forgotten, Angus quickly resumed his search for her wound. He pulled her kirtle up, exposing her long slender thighs and rounded hips. What lay hidden within the dark curls at the apex of her thighs held no interest. He could only stare at the deep gash his knife had made at her waist.

Praying he'd not hit anything vital, he tore a strip from her kirtle hem—'twas cleaner than anything he had on—and wound the fabric about her waist to stem the blood's flow.

His gaze raked the woods for her croft, any place to shelter her and properly tend her wound. Finding not so much as a path, he cursed. Then he remembered he'd skirted a village not long before he settled to wait out the day. He let out a piercing whistle.

Rampage whinnied as he crashed through the tree line. His thundering hooves quickly ate up the distance between them. The minute he came to a prancing halt, Angus tapped his shoulder. "Down." The horse immediately obeyed, too well used to his master's weight in armor to bolt.

Angus then scooped the lady into his arms. She groaned loudly and his heart leapt for joy. "Lass, can ye hear me? Can ye open yer eyes?"

The woman's sweeping lashes slowly separated to reveal the most extraordinary eyes Angus had ever seen. The palest of blues, almost white, and outlined by dark rings, they reminded him of the ice mountains he'd once seen floating past the point of Cape Wrath. She blinked.

"Aaah . . ."

"Hush, lass, I will get ye to help."

"Nay . . . ." She then fainted again.

Cursing himself for an idiot, Angus clutched the pale lass to his heaving chest, tightened Rampage's girth as best he could with one hand, and then slipped a foot into the now low-slung stirrup.

Mounted, he clucked, and the horse rose. Angus turned Rampage toward his enemy's village.

Just minutes later and with the lady yet to reawaken, Angus pounded on the most outlying croft's door.

It opened immediately. "Aye, what do ye want?"

A shriveled man gazed out the portal, his eyes narrowed and cloudy as milk.

"A healer," Angus boomed, "for the lady."

"Go there." The querulous man pointed a shaking finger toward the big croft across the road.

"The one with ivy?" He didn't trust the blind man to know in which direction he pointed and had no time to go knocking door to door to find the right one.

"Aye, 'tis." With that the old man slammed his door shut.

"A welcomin' bastard," Angus growled and strode a hundred yards to the next croft.

A bairn opened the door. Her smile of welcome faded and her eyes grew round as sixpence as her gaze ran up his body. When it settled on the woman in his arms she screamed, *"Maaaa!"*

A wizen-faced woman came out of the shadowed interior to stand in the doorway. "What can I do for—"

The woman looked at the lady in his arms and immediately started shouting, "Away with ye! Out! Go!" She slammed the door in his face.

"What the . . ." He'd never met so surly a group in his life! His worry growing and his patience short, Angus strode to the next croft, the last before the road dropped down toward a valley and into the main village. When a man opened the door Angus growled, "This woman needs help. She'd been st—"

The door slammed in his face.

"Bloody hell!"

Angus raised a foot and kicked the door in. It crashed against the wall with such force the walls rattled and a chair fell over. He strode in. With his teeth bared, he glared at the occupants—a man, a frail woman, and two bairn—all huddled in the far corner of the croft's only room. "Will ye nay help this lady?"

In answer the adults silently shook their heads.

What ailed these people that they couldn't see the lass

was in sore need—that she could die? "Dressing! Get me dressing and poultice before I lose what little patience I have left to me."

The man waved frantically at his wife. She made the sign of the cross and, with the wee lass clutching her skirts, bolted to a chest. She pulled out a small crock and strips of sheeting. The woman then pushed the lassie toward her husband and cautiously approached Angus, her hands extended. "Here, sir knight. Take these with our blessings and go."

"Why willna ye help one of yer own?" He held out the woman in his arms. "She's but a wee lass." Surely, this wife kenned that he—a man—couldn't tend her? He had to leave her here.

"She isna a Macarthur and no one here will offer more than we," the man growled from the corner, his hands gripping his son's shoulders. "Take what my wife offers and go."

"Man, are ye blind? She needs help." Had Angus not been the cause of her injury, he would have dropped her on their rush pallet and walked out the door. But having been the cause, he could only grab the offered dressings. "May ye receive as ye give."

He stormed out. Spying an empty sheep pen at the far end of an adjacent field, Angus vaulted over the low-lying hedge with his mount following.

He kicked open the pen's gate and laid the woman in the hay. Muttering, "Heathens," he raised her skirt and removed the cloth he'd wrapped around her waist. He felt monumental relief finding no fresh blood. He'd expected gushes, given the jarring speed with which he'd carried her to the village.

He applied the greasy herb poultice the Macarthur woman had given him to the lady's gash and rewrapped her waist. He then sat back on his haunches and pondered his dilemma. He studied her face. After a minute, he ran a gentle finger along one jet-black winged eyebrow. And then her lips, so wide and full, they could break any man's heart. Ack.

"Who, lass, do ye belong to? Where will ye be safe?" He couldn't leave her here. Not after the reception they'd received. And why was there terror in the querulous man's eyes as he'd bidden him take the poultice and go? "Do ye belong to their enemy's liege lord, lass? Were ye lost when I found ye?" He heaved a sigh. One thing was certain. They couldn't tarry here. When word arrived at the Macarthur stronghold that a MacDougall rode among them, all hell would rain down on their heads.

Time to go.

He slipped both arms under his unwanted lady and stood. He'd been heading northwest, traveling through the upper lowlands toward Beal Castle, and couldn't change course. If he couldn't find her people on the way, then mayhap the MacCloud would ken whence the lass came, or at least take her in. Aye.

He mounted, settled the lady securely in his lap, and pressed his heels to Rampage's flanks.

As they reached the last of the village's fields the gangly lad he'd seen in the croft stepped out from behind a copse of pine. Sweating—his gaze darting along the road—the lad held out a cloth bundle. "Sir knight, 'tis for the spae, tribute for the dolly."

Angus scowled. What spae and what dolly? "Lad, out of my way."

"Please, sir." The lad hopped from foot to foot as he held out the bundle. "'Tis only barley, sir, but all I have to offer." His gaze again darted toward the village hidden behind a copse. "Sir, convey our thanks, mine and Margaret's." The lad tossed the bag up and ran.

Catching it, Angus called, "Ye name, lad?"

The lad turned. "Jamie, m'lord."

"And this lady's?" He tipped his head, indicating the woman in his arms.

The youth shrugged. "I dinna ken, m'lord. No one does." He then disappeared.

Angus slipped the lad's gift into the bag tied behind his saddle. Why had the lad asked him to give the bundle to a spae? He kenned none. "Humph! These Macarthurs are a breed apart. Aye, and I'll be most relieved to be away." He pressed his heels to Rampage's flanks.

Laird Ian Macarthur glared at his farrier, Robbie Macarthur. "What the hell do ye mean he rode off with her? He, *who?*" He couldn't believe someone had had the audacity to capture his personal spae.

Robbie spun his cap in nervous hands. "I dinna ken his name, sire. Just that he's a knight."

"Describe him."

"Tall, brawn, dark-brown-haired, blue-eyed."

Laird Macarthur stopped pacing before Dunbar Castle's empty hearth. "Oh, for—What banner? What colors did he wear? What horse did he ride, ye idiot?"

Robbie had the sense to pale before his wrath.

"He wore gules—the color of blood, sire. His shield was quartered and bore a raised gauntleted fist. He rode a white charger."

Ian Macarthur's blood immediately drained from his head. "Did he bear a scar above the eyes?"

Robbie nodded. "Do ye ken him, sire?"

"Oh, aye. 'Tis I who put the scar on him." Ian ground his teeth as a searing heat began throbbing below his wrist, phantom pain from a right hand no longer there, thanks to the bastard Angus the Blood. Only MacDougall would dare cross into Macarthur territory—alone—and take his spae. Foolhardy and proud was Angus MacDougall and now it would be the man's downfall.

Reaching for his broadsword with the only hand left to him, he ground out, "Saddle the horses."

* * *

Birdi yawned, wondering why the lovely rocking had ceased. It had been most pleasant, being cradled in warmth, listening to the slow, steady heartbeat under her ear. . . .

Her eyes flew open.

A man—the largest she'd ever beheld—hovered over her as she lay on the ground.

She screamed.

His large, callused hand landed firmly on her mouth. "Hush, lass, I willna harm thee." He then looked about. In a deep, gravelly whisper he told her, "I am Angus Mac-Dougall. I found thee in a Macarthur glen."

Gael! He spoke not the language of her mother or the villagers but of *them*—the Canteran—the marauding Highlanders of which her mother had warned.

She clawed at his arms and tried to kick, to roll away, only to feel a fierce pain tear through her side. She gasped and froze in place. Stars! What had happened to her? She looked down, found her thighs bare and her kirtle up about her waist, a waist wrapped in white. Keening, she frantically tried to cover herself, the part—her mother had warned—where she would always be most vulnerable.

He pressed her shoulders to the soft earth. "The bleeding has stopped, lass, but dinna aggravate the wound with thrashing. Please."

"What?" Sunlight haloed the man hovering over her. She blinked eyes gritty from sleep in disbelief. He had shoulders thrice the width of hers and arms as thick as an elm's trunk. She couldn't discern his features, the sun keeping them in shadow, but could see the outline of shoulder-length hair the hue of wet river-rock, a few strands gleaming with a touch of amber. A chilling sweat broke out across her brow and her heart leapt as her ears strained, her gaze darted about. Her nose twitched in a futile effort to recognize where she was, who he might be. She took a deep, steadying breath and managed, "Where am I?"

"Ah, ye speak Scot." Using the same he told her,

"Where ye be, fair lass, can wait for later. What I need ken now is yer name and whence ye hail. We need find yer sept so they can care for ye properly."

"Sept?" What was this? She craned her neck to see beyond his mountainous form and found nothing but a small square block close to them, no doubt a sheep crib, and the rest just broad splotches of gold in all directions. She inhaled deeply and this time caught the scent of ripening havers—oats. She was in a field. In the open! Oh Goddess, *no!* Did this man plan to do to her what the other had done to Minnie?

Goddess help me! I dinna want a babe! Goddess, please! No!

Horror sent blood roaring into her every limb. Keening between pants, she clawed. Finding herself suddenly free, she scrambled backward. Brittle shafts of grain dug deep into her palms and feet as she tried to place as much distance as possible between herself and the man who would do her immeasurable harm.

He caught her ankle.

Squeaking in tight-throated terror, she kicked her other leg at his head only to have it trapped by a heavily callused hand, as well. Before she could scream he yanked her forward by the ankles and loomed over her on hands and knees, his long thick fingers managing to lace through hers and press her hands firmly into the earth by her head. His knees then locked onto her hips as he blocked out the sun. "Where," he asked in a soft growl "do ye think ye're goin' without so much as a by-yer-leave?" He dipped his head and sniffed.

She managed a scream this time but his mouth locked onto hers, smothering the sound. Her eyes flew wide in shock. What manner of predator was this? No weasel, no fox on the hunt did such. She stared into deep blue eyes and waited—her breath hitching, heart hammering at her ribs—waited for his mouth to slide from hers and settle on her throat. Waited for the pain, the crunch of bone, for her neck to snap.

Instead his lips softened, the pressure eased. She then felt the tip of his tongue stroke her bottom lip. Once. Twice. Just a lick, nothing more, yet a searing tingle raced down her spine. Her heart tripped. Was he tasting her? Testing her health and soundness as meat? *Oh Goddess, please!*

To her monumental relief he lifted his head. As he did, his hair swung around his face and the tips brushed her cheek. To her surprise his hair felt as soft as her own, mayhap more so. Yet she held her breath, didn't dare release the last one she might ever take.

"Ye, fair lass, are as sweet as I feared."

As *he* feared? She was the one about to be eaten alive! To be torn apart and then ground down between brilliant white teeth set in a menacingly square jaw. "No!"

In response, he released her hands and settled back on his haunches, his mountainous weight keeping her hips trapped. "Aye. Definitely too sweet to be running loose, lass." He sighed heavily. "I mean ye no harm, though 'twas I who felled ye and for that I humbly apologize; I meant only to save ye from the wolf."

Wolf! She'd forgotten poor Wolf. Dreading the answer, she asked, "Is he dead?"

"Nay. My blade missed him and struck thee." He ran agitated hands through his hair, pushing it off his face. "How I missed, I've yet to ken."

Her relief in learning Wolf survived was sorely dampened by his admission that he'd been the one who brought Wolf down. Her breath caught in her chest. This man killed without thought.

Angus ground his teeth, seeing fear and fresh tears erupt from behind the lass's heavily lashed, ice-blue eyes. Feeling the strong need for a stiff drink—a gallon of whiskey would do nicely—he brushed a callused thumb across her delicate cheek. She jerked. Dear God above, she did look the hizzie with her face all scarlet, her brow furrowed, and her teeth bared. He'd have laughed but for kenning it would only terrify her more. Many a brawny man had soiled his sarks when Angus laughed—and without being sat upon, though he was usually holding a blade to the bastard's throat. . . .

"Lass, 'tisna reason to fight me. None. I promise. Hush now." He moved to her side, but held tight to one hand. "There now. Better?"

"Aye."

As she took a few shuddering breaths, he looked at her side. Finding no fresh blood, he blew out a breath in relief. Now, to the matter at hand: finding out who she was and to whom she belonged. "What, lass, is yer name?"

She eyed him like a cornered timber-wolf; her magnificent, icy eyes narrowed, her straight nose twitching and sniffing as her head cocked ever so slightly, first this way, then that, as if listening for a rescuer. Or a means of escape. 'Twas a futile effort. He was not called Angus the Blood for naught.

Finally she murmured, "Birdalane."

Birdalane? Nay. She must have misunderstood him, for no mother with any sense would burden her bairn with such a sorrowful name, an endearment reserved for a babe without kith or kin. "Lass, I meant yer Christian name." He had to have her surname—her clan—if he was to be free of her and on his way.

She hiccupped and whispered, "Birdi?"

She sounded none too sure. "Birdi it is, then." Obviously he need take another approach. "And yer sire?"

She pressed her lips into a hard line. "Shame."

Shame? To his knowledge there wasn't a clan of that name. And she certainly couldna mean nairich—debasement. Surely. He studied her for a moment, then decided she'd coshed her head when she fell. She wasn't, after all, a stout lass. Aye, 'twas most likely a blow to the noggin that caused her current confusion. He resigned himself to being patient and asked, "Are ye in pain, Birdie?"

Her eyes grew round as an owl's. Aha. Had their roles been reversed he wouldn't have answered, either, for fear of giving his enemy another tool to use against him. "I shall take that as an aye, but fear not. I shall take ye to yer people."

If possible, she appeared more frightened and vehemently shook her head. "Nay! Please, sir, turn me loose."

"Did ye run away from home?" No doubt, intent on thwarting a liege who wanted to marry her to someone she found distasteful.

Her mouth dropped open. "Nay, ye took me from home!"

Humph! Well, time was fleeing. He'd already lost a day and couldn't very well go courting with the likes of her—an incredibly bewitching though thoroughly disheveled wench—at his side. Had he been closer to Blackstone he would have left her under Duncan's protection, but that wasn't an option. Staring at her lush lips once again, he heaved a resigned sigh for things that might have been.

She hiccupped as she nibbled her lower lip. "I have need of privacy."

He frowned before realizing why. "Ah, but are ye sure ye can manage on yer own?" She nodded like a sandpiper. He rose and offered his hand. She looked askance, and he couldn't help but grin. "I promise I willna bite."

Looking none too sure that he'd keep his word, she took his hand. He pulled her to her feet and pointed to the sheep crib. "Back there, lass, behind the hay. I'll stand guard at the gate."

She wobbled off, a hand clutched to her side. Mercy, even hobbling she was a sight for his travel-weary soul. Her hair billowed like gossamer jet about her hips and caused his hands to clench as they had when he'd first spied her by the pool.

He turned his back to her. With his gaze raking the valley for Macarthurs, his memory conjured up the image of her emerging like a mythical kelpie, dripping and glistening from the pool; recalled the delightful tilt of her rose-tipped breasts and the roundness of her very bonnie hurdies. Lord, she had the finest arse he'd ever seen, and he'd seen a good few in his nine-and-twenty years.

He fervently wished he could keep her.

And why couldn't he?

He wasna yet promised to another. He had no idea what awaited him at Beal Castle. For all he kenned, the available MacCloud lass would be another sorry sight. Or as crazed as the last lass offered to him. "Humph."

Too, his family did have a long history of reeving brides. Wasn't his own ma once a reluctant border bride? And look how well that turned out—his da had been chasing her skirts the day he died. Aye, there was something to be said for keeping with family tradition.

But then he'd wagered he could bring home a lady, a chatelaine for Donaliegh. And he was a man of his word. Grunting, he decided the only right thing to do was to keep with his plan. He looked into the shadows of the crib. An inordinate amount of time had passed; more, certainly, than was needed for a wee lass to hike her skirts and piss. Fearing she might have fainted, he ducked under the rafters and called her name. Getting no response, he peeked behind the hay pile.

She was gone.

Chapter 3

Out of breath, Birdi plopped down in the middle of her blurry gold world. She was lost. Just minutes from the sheep crib and hopelessly lost.

But, she reminded herself, so long as she breathed there was hope. But how would she find her way back to her croft when she could see only an arm's length before her? How could she find home without kenning how far she'd traveled or in which direction to go? But find home she would. She had to, or she'd surely perish. Or worse.

And time was working against her—the Canteran would soon realize she'd escaped.

She raised her face to the sky and closed her eyes. Arms extended, her palms to the sun, the salt from past tears coating her lips, she pleaded, "Goddess, please guide me home. Please. I'm so very frightened." She then began crooning the chant of entreaty Minnie had taught her so many seasons past, one she'd never imagined she would ever need.

"Birdeee! Where the hell are ye, lass?"

Oh no! She spun. Stalks thrashed and snapped behind and to her right. The Canteran was close and searching for her.

"Birdalane Shame! We havena time for games!"

Sweat broke out on her brow and trickled between her breasts. Her hands began to shake. Would it be safer to remain, crouched in shoulder-high oats, hoping the brute wouldn't find her, or to bolt? Chewing her bottom lip, she keened, "What to do, what to do?"

The Canteran made the decision for her, his footfalls sounding dangerously close. She rocked onto her hands and knees and scrambled as fast as she could through the slicing stalks, heading away from his voice.

Aaawooo! Her heart leapt as Wolf's howl echoed off hills and across the field. He'd found her! She jumped to her feet and spun, trying to catch his direction.

Aaawooo!

There! Wolf stood somewhere directly before her—away from the setting sun and the Canteran. She ran. Heart pumping at a furious pace, her legs raced through golden grain. She ran like she had never run in her life. "Thank you, Goddess, thank you, thank you, thank you."

"Birdi! *stop!*"

She ran blindly, tears of relief coursing down her cheeks, toward her howling savior, her pet. He would guide her home. Home.

"Birdi!"

Angus broke into a run. *God's teeth!* Could she not hear the damn wolf? Could she not see him pacing in nervous anticipation just a hundred yards before her?

Angus thundered through the waving, thigh-high havers, his lungs pulling in great gulps. If he didn't catch up with her she'd charge straight into the great beast's gaping jaws. Christ's blood!

He was fifty feet from her—just a few long strides from grasping her—when she screeched and disappeared.

Simply vanished.

"What the . . ." He couldn't believe his eyes. The wolf forgotten, he raced on and nearly fell into a glack. He swung his arms like windmills, righted, and stared into the previously unseen ravine. And there he found her, six feet below him—panting, her arms and legs spread like a spider's—clinging to a narrow sandstone shelf some twenty feet above a dried-out riverbed cluttered with back-breaking boulders.

He dropped to his belly.

Crawling over the ravine edge, he held out an arm. "Woman, reach up and grab hold of my hand."

To his utter amazement she shook her head. "I canna."

"Of course ye can, just let loose the rocks and reach."

"I canna see yer hand . . . dirt in my eyes."

Angus cursed, reached behind his back and shed his sword. He pulled his breacan feile from his shoulders, made a knot at one end, and lowered the wool over the edge. "Lass, take hold of the breacan feile and I'll pull ye to safety."

"Ye what?"

He racked his brain for her word. "The plaid, lass, grab hold of the plaid."

She waved an arm above her head, missing it by a foot. "I canna see . . . ."

"Oh, for—" He eased a wee bit more over the crumbling edge so the cloth hit her hand. "Grab hold, woman, before I fall over and join ye."

Thankfully, she did as he asked and he started pulling. She came to a standing position on the ledge and he grasped one of her wrists. "Birdi, let loose of the plaid and grab onto my hand with both hands."

"Nay, I dare not."

"Birdi, make haste!" She remained in mortal danger; the sandstone beneath her feet was crumbling at an alarming rate with every breath she took. "Lass, plea—"

Hhhhhheeee!

His mount's whinny, long and urgent, caused Angus to look up. Dust clouds rose along the main road.

The Macarthurs! Bloody hell.

Hissing through clenched teeth, he let loose his end of his breacan feile—mentally kissing his prized covering good-bye—and engulfed both her hands with his. With one jerk he brought her up and over the edge. To his amazement his precious cloth came with her. Panting, he pried her fingers from it. "Lass, so help me God, if ye ever do anything so foolish—"

Looking irate, Birdi scrambled to her feet and placed her hands on her hips. "'Twasna my intention to fall off a cliff!"

With an eye on the approaching Macarthurs, he snorted and pulled his claymore from its sheath, then let loose a piercing whistle. She jumped at his side. He grabbed her hand as Rampage—hooves flashing, nares wide and snorting—came thundering across the oats. As the horse came to a prancing stop a few yards before him, Angus began running. "Hie, lass!"

Dragging her feet, she whined, "Hie? Why?"

Without explaining, he grabbed her under the arms, hoisted her in one quick motion onto the saddle, and vaulted up after her. She squeaked in protest as he wrapped a tight arm around her waist and pressed his spurs into his mount's flanks. The horse lunged north toward safety.

Birdi screeched. Clutching the saddle horn with one hand, the Canteran's arm with the other, she prayed like she'd never prayed before in her life.

She was accosted by the wind at her front, the man's hard chest at her back, and by the horse at her bottom and thighs. Blood pounded in her ears, making it impossible to hear in a world of shapeless, blurring color.

She rarely traveled at a run for fear she'd crash into something—or fall—and here she was trapped on a beast quite obviously running amok.

Goddess, help me!

And where were they going? Was he taking her farther from home? She fervently hoped not. Would Wolf be able to foll—

She screeched, the sensation of falling flipping her stomach. The Canteran's arm tightened its hold on her just as she jerked forward and then back. Icy cold water stung her bare feet as the beast splashed through what sounded like a rock-strewn river. A heartbeat later her captor muttered, "Good lad," and clucked. She was then propelled upward in jarring fashion to the tune of the horse's hooves clicking and clacking as he climbed. She'd barely caught her breath, and the scent of pine and cedar, when the Highlander pushed her head to the side. She kenned why when she felt pine needles brush against her cheek and legs. More branches whipped past, thrumming in the wind. The man at her back cursed with almost as much frequency. And on it went.

After what seemed like a lifetime, the Canteran whispered, "Whoa," and the horse, heaving beneath her, slowed to a walk, its lathered sides radiating heat against her bare legs.

"We're safe now, lass."

"Aye? And from what are we safe?" Her captor wasn't simply daft but wode—stark raving mad.

His breath ruffled the hair lying against her cheek. "From the Macarthur, lass. Did ye not see him? He and a good dozen of his men—their blades waving, their faces scarlet with rage?" He chuckled, sending vibrations through her sweat-soaked back and into her chest.

"Where are we?" *Goddess, please let it be closer to home.*

"We're in Fraiser territory. They are'na exactly MacDougall friends but they are most certainly Macarthur enemies. Those behind us will be wise to give up the chase."

"Fraiser territory." This wasn't good. Nay. She kenned no Fraisers. She sniffed and caught . . . what was that? Sharp, clean, and making her need for water more acute? Something white flashed close overhead, issuing a raucous cry. She squealed as she ducked.

"Dinna fash, Birdi, the gulls willna harm ye. They only seek handouts."

She was none too sure he spoke the truth.

He brushed the hair from her cheek and asked, "Have ye not seen them before?"

"Nay." She couldn't see them now—could see only flashes of whirling white—so how could she have seen gulls before?

"They fly in from the sea seeking fresh water."

"Ah." Gulls were apparently some kind of bird. Their song wasn't the least pleasing, not like the doves and lave-rocks that occupied her forest. She flinched as another called out. "I dinna like it here. I want to go home."

"I would gladly take ye home, but I havna time." He pointed ahead. "We spend the night over yon. Ye canna see it from here, but there's a cave at the foot of the burn. Hopefully 'tis dry, but there isna telling. We've had rain enough to satisfy Noah."

She didn't care if this Noah he spoke of was satisfied or not, nor if this place he spoke of was dripping wet. She wanted off the horse and out of his arms. Now that they'd slowed—and she'd conquered her fright—she'd become very aware of the pain at her side and in her legs. Her stomach ached for lack of food and her mouth felt like a lichen-coated rock.

And as the horse ambled along the edge of the loch, clicking on shale and padding through grass, she'd become most uncomfortably aware of Angus the Canteran's thighs as they cradled hers, of his hand as it relaxed against her stomach, of his every breath as she leaned against him, too weary to hold herself upright any longer. Her awareness generated feelings that were uncomfortably akin to the yearnings she'd awakened with just this morn.

"If ye let me go I'll not say a word to the Macarthurs, I promise." She avoided them as much as possible anyway. "Please. I can find my own way."

He huffed at her back. "I doubt that ye can, lass. We're many miles from where I found ye."

"Many?"

"Aye, many."

Unsettled, Birdi looked up. The sky was turning to deep lavender. Soon the sun would burrow into its mountain bed and the world would again become a frightening place of blacks and grays. She'd have no way of kenning real from shadow, solid ground from crags. She'd be trapped wherever he placed her, without hope of escape until the sun rose again. But rise it would, and off she'd run if she survived the night.

The horse stopped and the Canteran slipped from behind her, leaving her sweat-soaked back to chill in the rising wind. She shivered.

He reached up, grabbed her under the arms, and hauled her off the horse only to hold her at eye level for a moment. Above eyes as blue as the midsummer sky, he bore a deep scar the shape and size of a hawk's footprint. *My stars! That blow must have hurt.* But what had made it and why had it left such a scar?

He suddenly frowned and lowered her to the ground. "There, lass, behind the big boulder you'll find the entrance to the cave."

Her gaze traced the length of his arm, but his arm was long. It faded to fuzz. She couldn't see his hand and had to guess the direction he likely pointed toward.

"Go. I'll be with ye shortly."

Dare she? All was in shadow, most of the color having already drained from this place. She could hear water roaring—crashing—before her, and to the right, could feel the spray on her face. What if she fell—

"Lass, go and see if we have place for a fire."

Fire. 'Twould be a good thing, given her hands and feet felt like ice. Hoping he'd come with her, she stalled. "But I canna start one without flint."

"I'll bring it, but first I need tend the horse. Go."

Defeated, she wrapped her arms around her waist and took a hesitant step, then a second, relieved to discover that she trod on solid ground. Needing him to find her way, and hating that she did, she stammered, "I need ken . . . where ye are taking me."

"Later, lass. Just go."

She took one hesitant step, another, and then startled, arms flailing, when he said in her ear, "For heaven's sake, lass, 'twill be morn before ye get there." He took her by the elbow and led her toward the roaring water. She stumbled and nearly fell before he huffed in exasperation and hauled her to his side. He guided her through high stones, stones far grander than she'd ever imagined possible. She reached out a shaking hand as she brushed past one and was surprised to find it warmer than the air. She craned her neck, stretched over his arm to better look at its gritty surface—to make sure she knew this stone should she pass it again—and was yanked back.

"Come on, lass, ye can mird to yer heart's content another time."

Mird? The man spoke such an odd tongue.

She was nearly made deaf by the roar of water and soaked by frigid spray and then just as quickly was surrounded by total darkness, trapped within blackness by a flowing sheet of roaring silver. "What . . . where am I?"

"'Tis the cave, lass. Have ye nay been in one before?"

Wide-eyed, heart bounding against her ribs, she shook her head. Why would she or anyone else want to be in one? Panicked, she sniffed the air for something familiar and caught the scent of old ashes. He'd spoken of fire. Would he now cook her? Had he taken her to his lair? *Oh, Goddess . . .*

She felt rather than saw him draw near and squeaked.

He huffed again. "Take yer ease, lass. Here, put this on." Something pressed her chest and she felt his plaid. She draped it around her shoulders as much for protection as warmth. "What shall ye eat?"

"Whatever I catch."

'Twas not what she wanted to hear. "Do ye like berries? I can gather berries." She could hear him moving but could not see him. "Mayhap some mushrooms? Or fiddle ferns? Fiddle ferns are good." It was well past the time for finding fiddle ferns but he might not ken that. "Do ye like dandelions? 'Tis verra good for yer liver." *Oh, please say "aye" to something.*

"Thank ye, but I prefer meat."

Ack! She stumbled back and hit a wall. Hands splayed against unyielding stone, she decided talking of food wasn't the wisest of things she could be doing. "Tell me of this Beal. Is it grand? Does it have colored glass? Why are ye going there?" *Talk to me, Canteran, so I can tell where ye are and what ye're thinking.* "Are ye to meet someone there? Is that why ye must make haste? Do they have fairs? I'd like to see a juggler . . . and a fire-eater. Personally, I can barely credit such, but if 'tis so, I should very much like to see them. Do ye ken a prince? Mayhap a king? And where exactly is Beal? Is it north or south of where ye found me?"

She continued on at a breakneck pace, asking question after question with barely a breath in between.

Angus rolled his eyes. Birdi's babbling was giving him a headache. Why he frightened her so was beyond kenning. Had he not saved her from certain death as she clung to the ravine wall? Had he not saved her from that butcher Macarthur? He'd not harmed her—well, not since his blade had brought her down—which he hadn't intended and had already apologized for. And that reminded him— he'd not looked at her wound in a good many hours. Was it infected? Was that why she blathered and shivered so? He'd have to check as soon as he got a fire going.

Hoping to reassure her he muttered, "There isna reason to fash, Birdi. I promise I willna harm thee."

To his amazement she kept on chattering like a crazed squirrel. Hauling off his chain-mail helm, he heartily wished she'd fall asleep as soon as humanly possible so he could have some peace and quiet.

He looked about the cave and found a pile of dry kindling at the back where the last traveler had left it for the next man to find. He grabbed an armful and set about laying the wood within the spent ashes in the center of the cave. He opened his sporran and pulled out a shaft of dry grass and his flint box. After much huffing and blowing he had a reasonable fire going and turned to find Birdi—head lolling to one side—sound asleep whilst still propped against the wall. Amazed, he cautiously approached. How could she do this?

He peaked behind her and found she was resting on a small outcropping of stone. "Humph!"

He could not leave her like this while he caught their supper. She'd likely fall and cosh her head again, and she was already brain-coddled enough as it was.

Seeing her grip had loosened on his breacan feile he slipped it from her hands and spread it before the fire. He then called her name. Getting no response, he went to her and lifted her into his arms. The poor wee lass. She'd become exhausted. How much from fright and how much from blood loss he couldn't ken. But she was safe now.

He laid her before the fire and covered her. Standing back he studied her face by firelight. Good graces, she was lovely. The finest woman he'd ever seen. Too bad he couldna keep her.

After tending Rampage and having caught and gutted two fish, Angus cut a sapling into two-foot lengths and returned to the cave, where he found Birdi as he'd left her, still sound asleep. He roasted the fish and then tried to wake her. She grumbled and curled into a ball. Deciding to leave her be, he ate one fish and wrapped the second in fresh reeds for her to find when she awoke.

Using his saddle for a pillow, he settled on the opposite side of the fire from her. Studying her fitful sleep he again pondered what to do with Birdalane Shame if he couldn't find her clan. Shame. What kind of a name was that? The lack of "Mac" before her surname meant she wasn't from an auld clan, which left him wondering if a new sept had formed. 'Twas possible. Look at the Fraisers, Mazies, and Montgomerys. Lord, there were more clans than a man could wave a sword at these days between the border and the North Sea. Ack!

As the fire died, he decided that, as awkward as it might be, he'd likely end up bringing Birdi to Beal Castle. There was no reason he couldn't woo his hoped-for bride, marry her, and settle Birdi all in one fell swoop. He and his bride could then set out for the coast, for Drasmoor and Blackstone, where he'd claim the keys to Donaliegh.

Pleased he had a workable plan, he yawned and noticed Birdi shivering. Bloody hell. He'd forgotten to check her wound. Hoping she wasn't down with fever he went to her.

He touched her cheek and was surprised to find it cold. He ran a cautious finger along the exposed part of her neck and found the same. Humph.

He could stay awake all night feeding the fire—and she might still remain cold—or he could wrap her in his own warmth and mayhap get a few hours of much-needed sleep himself. He opted for the latter. They had a long ride on the morrow.

He pulled back her covering and stretched out beside her. Resting his head on his arm, he cradled her into his chest. A minute later, he realized his mistake.

Chapter 4

The woman fit his body as if she were made just for him. He inhaled, filling his lungs with the scent of her, of female musk and the lingering scent of sunshine and grain.

It took all his willpower to keep his hand from slipping up from where it draped across her slim waist. Jaw clenched, he eased his hips back. What on earth had possessed him to think he could lie beside her and sleep? And what kind of an animal was he? The poor wee lass was injured, for heaven's sake. Ack!

Merciful Lord, keep an eye on yer fool else I shame the pair of us. Please.

Hoping it might help, he started reciting the rosary in his mind. In the middle of his tenth decade of Hail Marys, he drifted off, still aware and yet comforted by the steady rise and fall of Birdi's breathing beneath his hand.

Birdi woke with a start. Something warm lay next to her, purring in her ear. Not daring to move—fearing she'd next feel its claws—she cautiously opened her eyes. Her heart thudded. Nothing smelled or sounded familiar. She then caught sight of a blurry but gleaming wall of water and her mind flooded with memories of falling, of being terrified, and then being nearly whipped to death while racing through the forest on horseback.

With a certainty she'd never felt before in her life—

without touching, without sniffing—she kenned what lay at her back. It wasn't a large cat, as she'd initially feared, but him—the Canteran.

It hadn't been a nightmare after all.

Heart thudding, she cautiously peered over her shoulder. Aye, 'twas Angus, and he was still asleep. She held her breath. What should she do? Could she reach his sword before he did and demand that he bring her home? Or should she just bolt while she still had a chance? After giving both ideas a moment's thought, she knew neither would likely succeed. He was bigger and faster than she by a hundredfold. What was needed was stealth.

Her confidence bolstered by the many trips she'd taken around Macarthurs, Birdi slowly raised the heavy arm draped across her waist. With a held breath and at a pace to make any snail proud she eased out from under it and came to her knees. She rose and padded on silent feet toward the wall of water.

Dry sand changed to cold damp stone as she drew nearer. Throat parched, she extended a cupped hand. The force of the rushing water slapped her wrist back and made her gasp. Well!

She'd just have to drink from the river when she got to it. She sidled to the right with one hand extended, her right foot tapping before her to be sure she didn't fall off the ledge. She came to a wall of stone. No. She was sure he'd led her in this way. But then she'd been exhausted and upset by the gulls, so mayhap . . .

She held out her left hand and tapped her way across the ledge only to hit another wall. "No! This isna happening."

She slapped her hands over her mouth and looked over her shoulder, peered into the darkness but couldn't see him. She prayed she hadn't awakened him. At least, he wasn't looming behind her.

Frustrated, cold, and thirsty, she ran her hands over her chilled arms and realized her skin and clothing were wet.

She stepped back and water splashed her shoulder. She squeaked, spun, and held up a hand. Cool water filled her palm. She drank as fast as she could.

Her thirst finally satisfied, she wrung her hands. What to do?

It was now obvious she couldn't leave without his help. She looked into the blackness of the cave and saw a fuzzy red glow. There was no help for it.

She returned to the heat and the man.

Squatting by the remains of the fire she caught sight of a fish skeleton. She touched it with a tentative finger. What remained was flexible. It had been recently cooked and eaten. She then saw a reed packet and brought it to her eyes for closer inspection. To her delight it held a warm, cooked fish. Keeping her gaze on the black mass that was the Canteran, she bit into the fish with a vengeance.

As she ate she pondered.

She hated admitting it but she needed the man lying before her. She was far from home on unknown ground, and needed his sight.

Since he wouldn't return her, how could she find her way? Wolf had been left far behind.

Too bad this man wasn't kind, like Tinker. Her friend would gladly have taken her home. Tinker! Was there a chance she could contact Tinker? And how? She could write naught but her name. The Canteran might be able to write but he couldn't know of Tinker. Tinker kenned the exact location of her home. The Canteran didn't, and she had to keep it that way.

He caused the yearnings.

As she pulled the last of the delectable flesh from the bones, she could see faint blocks of gray and brown within the cave and more details of Angus the Canteran, still asleep, curled on his side before her.

Who is this man? What is he? She'd spent the entire day

with him and had only the impression of great size, strength, and eyes as blue as the summer sky.

She wiped her hands on the reeds, then her skirt, and inched around the fire. She came close enough to touch him, but not daring to, she sniffed. He still smelled of pine, fire smoke, and something surprisingly pleasant. Of what, she couldn't put a name to. She leaned closer. Finding his breathing still slow and deep, her confidence grew. She inched closer still. His odd metal shirt was gone and he now wore only a tunic. The fabric was thick and looked soft. She touched his cuff with a tentative finger. Aye, it was as she imagined and of a finer weave than the kirtle she wore. Costly, if she was any judge of such things. Her gaze shifted left over his narrow hips. Why did he not wear leggings as Tinker and the men of the village wore? She studied the grooves and rises of his heavily muscled thighs and lower legs. Hmm.

She eyed the silver hilt of the short dagger—the sgian dubh—poking out from beneath one of the leather thongs wrapped around his heavy calves. To have a blade like that! She wouldn't be in this position had she had such a weapon to defend herself with.

Her gaze shifted to the right, up his torso, taking measure of his hardness, of the massive amounts of sinew and muscle. He was so unlike her, so unlike Tinker. And he definitely smelled better than Tinker. She tipped her head to better examine his face and her hair fell into her eyes. With an impatient hand she raked it over her shoulder.

His jaw was dark, bristled with the shortest of dark hairs. Not something she'd want. Feeling decidedly braver than she had at the beginning—this Angus was a very sound sleeper—she fingered a lock of his shoulder-length hair. Aye, it was indeed as soft as a hen's down. She then saw his fine braids. She rolled one between her fingers. Did the secret to keeping hair braided lie not in the weave but in the volume braided? Hmm.

His brow, though badly scarred, was wide. His eyebrows were dark and arched like a hawk's wings in flight. His lashes were thick, lying still on high, broad cheeks. His narrow nose wasn't straight but not so crooked as to distract. She decided she liked it. Her gaze then settled on his wide and well-formed lips.

They'd muffled her cry and hid the tongue that had licked her, tasted her. And why? He hadn't bothered to take a bite out of her. He'd eaten fish instead. Had he found her not to his liking? Sour or bitter? For some reason, she felt insulted. Did he taste any better?

Birdi leaned ever closer, and Angus held his breath.

He'd awakened when she'd gasped, apparently realizing with whom she laid, and had readied to catch her if she tried to bolt, but she hadn't. She'd simply explored, drunk, eaten, and then to his amazement decided to explore him. As he watched through slitted eyes, he bit the inside of his cheek to keep from grinning as her beautiful face kept shifting from surprise to puzzlement and then back again as she gently touched and sniffed. Anyone would have thought she'd never been so close to a man as she fingered his hair and studied him inch by inch. When her gaze shifted to his face he was forced to close his eyes. He could feel her breath on his cheek and desperately wanted to see what she thought. Was she frowning or smiling? And more than anything in the world he wished to feel her mouth on his.

Her lips caressed his with no more pressure than a butterfly could muster. He held his breath wondering what she'd do next. To his utter amazement her tongue grazed his lips. He groaned.

As if by its own accord, his left hand slid to the back of her neck. He pressed her closer, parting her lips further. She gasped, and he swept in to discover she was more pliant and delicious than he—even in his most lustful moments—had imagined.

With heart and blood racing with expectation, he slipped his free hand about her waist. Before he could execute a roll, could get her beneath him, her hands slammed into his chest. Startled, his eyes flew open. The fear in her eyes made him set her free.

She scampered back, a hand on her lips.

Shit.

Sorely disappointed, Angus rocked up onto his knees. "Dinna fash, Birdi, I told ye I wouldna harm ye, and I'm a man of my word." He sighed, gave himself a shake, and pointed at the remains of her fish. "Are ye still hungry, lass?"

She shook her head hard and came to her feet, one hand coming to rest at her waist.

"How is yer wound?" She moved with ease and hadn't felt feverish when she'd kissed him, but then he'd been distracted.

"Fair. I dinna bleed anymore."

He rose and stretched, his hands pressing the cave's roof. "Good. We've a good distance to travel today if we're to make Beal by tomorrow's gloaming." And they'd be lucky to make it even then.

She wrung her hands and backed away. "I dinna want to go to Beal. I want ye to take me back to the glen."

"I ken that, lass, but I canna." The Macarthur was out for his blood, and even if the bastard wasn't, Angus hadn't the luxury of time.

Looking crestfallen, Birdi nodded. "They fear me."

He scowled, was about to ask what she meant, and noticed she was quaking like a birch in a high wind. "Ack, are ye cold again?" He shook out his breacan feile and handed it to her. "Here. Wrap this about ye."

She hesitated but finally took it. He reached into his sporran, withdrew the salve the Macarthur woman had given him, and handed it to her. "I'll go out and give ye a bit of privacy so ye can dress yer wound." With the sweet taste of Birdi still lingering in his mouth, he didn't need to be seeing her half naked. He'd likely tup her where she stood.

He turned to leave, and her nails dug into his right hand. Her eyes, as light as the water at her back, were wide. "Ye willna leave without me."

He pried her fingers loose and patted her hand. "Lass, I promise I willna." Humph! In the last day she'd tried to kick his teeth in, run from him, and kiss him, had pleaded for her release, and now she was begging him not to leave without him. Women! He wouldn't ever ken them, which was another reason he'd never wanted a wife. Ack!

Laden down with his saddle and mail, he strode between the boulders and out from behind the waterfall and down to the river, to Rampage.

Birdi, heart beating like a frightened rabbit's—praying he'd keep his promise, praying he wouldn't leave her to perish in this damp world behind a wall of water—remained rooted in place long after Angus the Canteran had disappeared into the shadows.

There is nothing I wouldna give to be able to move about as he did. Nothing.

And what on earth had possessed her to place her mouth on his? To taste him? Had it been the *need?* Her palms had itched. More surprising than her doing it was discovering his lips pleasingly pliant. She did as he had done, took a wee taste with her tongue and encountered his tongue, as soft as antler velvet, as sweet as any berry. A heartbeat later—before she could pull away—he'd taken control, held her firmly in place and his tongue had stroked hers. It caused heat to sear a path to her middle, swirl as his tongue did, then settle between her thighs. 'Twas only then did she recognize what he was doing—summoning the *yearnings*.

Yearnings far stronger, fiercer, than her dream had summoned.

She'd reared back in shock, her fingers flying to tingling lips, her mother's words echoing in her head. *The yearn-*

ings are evil, Birdi. They scramble yer mind and make ye wode.

Aye, Minnie. *Wode.*

She had to leave . . . had to go before it happened again. Before what happened to her mother happened to her.

The lesson learned: he took control. Quickly.

She pulled the plug on the jar of poultice and sniffed. It smelled of black currant, juniper, and willow. It would do for now.

She stripped the dressing from her waist. The gash hurt as a burn might, but that was to be expected. She applied the poultice, redressed her wound, and was struggling with the plaid, trying to re-drape it about her, when she heard footfalls behind her. She spun and clouted Angus the Canteran smack in the nose.

Oh, Goddess!

Hissing, he grabbed her hands in one calloused fist. "Lass, if ye dinna stop jumping every time I come up on ye, I'll be forced to truss ye up like a Michaelmas goose." He blew in obvious annoyance and hauled her toward the light. Pondering what a Michaelmas goose might be, she tripped. He stopped and eyed her from top to bottom.

"No wonder. Ye have the plaid on wrong, lass. 'Tis worn like this." He took it from her shoulders, made fast pleats of the middle, wrapped one end around her waist, had to do it again to take up more length, and then draped the remainder over her shoulder. "See? 'Tis easy." He then slipped the wide belt from his waist and carefully wrapped it around hers—twice—and still a half-length was left hanging. "Well, it will have to do. At least, ye'll stay warm."

He took her hand and led her out of the cave and into brilliant sunshine, into a day warmer than expected. He waved toward her right. "There, lass, there's a privacy bush, but be quick."

He turned away, and Birdi was left on her own to stumble over river rock in the direction he pointed. Why he was behaving so out of sorts was beyond kenning. She'd been the one attacked. She huffed, tripped, and her hair fell over her face. Muttering, she pushed it out of her eyes, took another step, and stumbled again. Grinding her teeth, she grabbed her skirt with both hands and, keeping her gaze locked on the slippery stones beneath her feet, she walked without further stumbling.

Straight into an elderberry bush.

Angus poked through the neck of his chain mail in time to see Birdi collide with the bush. He shook his head as she muttered and turned. A heartbeat later her head jerked back with such force he was surprised she didn't lose her footing. Before he could take a step, she reached back, wrenched a thick lock of hair free of a branch, and marched on again. Birdi Shame had to be the most accident-prone female he'd ever laid eyes on. Another reason the sooner he got her back to her clan the better.

When she made it behind the bush without further incident, he finished donning his armor and turned his attention to Rampage. The beast snorted and blew out his stomach as Angus tried to tighten the saddle girth. "Ack, lad, ye ken I'll win in the end, so why do ye put me through this aggravation every time I saddle ye?"

Angus looked over his shoulder and found Birdi at the churning river's edge washing her hands. "Birdi, get away from there! I dinna want to be fishing ye out of—"

Too late.

The watterlogged earth beneath her suddenly gave way and she fell into the river with a surprised screech, hands over her head.

Cursing and with his gaze locked on the place where she'd disappeared, he ran. A foot from where she'd fallen in, his right leg sank into sucking mud up to his shin. He windmilled his arms to keep from getting both legs trapped and landed on his rear. God's teeth!

He pulled free just as Birdi broke the surface, sputtering and flailing a good ten yards down stream.

His heart thudding, her cries for help only escalating his alarm, he ran along the bank. Good God, he hadn't realized how fast the current was here.

She swam, thrashed really, but in the wrong direction. He brought his hands to his mouth and shouted, *"Birdi! This way. Come this way!"*

She turned, her face as white as the churning water surrounding her, and started thrashing, blessedly in the right direction, but the current still hauled her downstream, farther away from him. Realizing he couldn't outrun her and praying she could stay afloat, he whistled.

As he tore off his mail, Rampage pounded up behind him. He mounted and kicked Rampage into a canter. They raced along the bank and around boulders. Birdi made some small progress toward shore but even more progress toward Loch Purdith—and, God help her, the traitorous waterfall that emptied into it. "Birdi! Keep swimming lass! I'm coming!"

God, please get me to her before she wearies and drowns or falls over that precipice. She willna survive it.

As he raced to catch her, the fast-flowing river hauled her at breakneck speed over and between boulders. Ack, the abuse she had to be taking. He could only pray she wouldn't hit her head before he reached her.

The river swung left and he lost sight of her for several painful seconds. He leaped over trees brought down by floods and rounded the bend. He released his breath. She was alive. Her arms still churned, though not with her past determination. Not good, not good.

He spotted a partially submerged, felled tree some fifty feet before her. "The tree, Birdi! Try to grab hold of the tree!"

Her right arm reached up and out but to the left.

"To yer right, Birdi, to yer right!" God, the woman would be the death of him.

To his monumental relief the current spun her and put her in direct line with the tree. He raced past her at a full canter, came abreast of the tree, and reined in. Rampage snorted and stomped as Angus slid to the ground and raced for the log.

Heart slamming against his ribs, his arms extended for balance, he ran along the slippery bark until it disappeared below water. He dropped to his knees and then straddled it. His elation—in getting ahead and in direct line with her—evaporated as he saw the huge whirlpool churning between them. Praying it wouldn't take her in the opposite direction, he stretched out and bellowed, "Birdi! Reach for me! Here!"

Birdi's heart leapt. Angus the Canteran was before her, somewhere, telling her to grab hold of his hand. Choking on frothing water, she raised a weary arm, and was suddenly jerked from below. She screeched. Her skirt, once billowing about her waist, was now wound tight about her legs. She couldn't kick or right herself as she spun. She bucked and clawed at the water pulling her down.

Goddess, help! Please, I'll be drowned!

Arms thrashing, she slid beneath the surface.

Chapter 5

Birdi awoke to the sounds of hissing Gael, to the feel of large hands pressing on her stomach. *Ah, 'tis him, the Canteran, Angus Mac . . .* she couldn't remember his other name. He pulled on her arms, up, down, up, down, pushed again on her stomach, and then spun her onto her face. Numb with cold, too tired to breathe, she didn't care. She'd never see her home again so what did it matter? The saddest part of this journey, apart from not seeing colored glass, was kenning that no one would grieve, would miss her.

He pressed on her back, up, down, up, down. He was squeezing the life out of her. Why? She was flipped again; the sun's glare now bore against her eyelids. It felt good. Warm. He pressed on her stomach again, this time it hurt, and suddenly she was choking, vomiting, and gasping.

Good Goddess, he was trying to kill her!

She tried to defend herself but found her arms were weighted down. Already breathless, she started coughing again. This time it tore, racked, inside her chest. And he wouldn't stop pounding on her back. Pound, pound, pound. If she had a rock and the strength she'd cosh him a good one. On the head.

Merciful Goddess, please. Please, make him stop.

"Birdi, lass, are ye all right? Can ye hear me?"

He hauled her onto his lap, raked the hair off her face, and ran a calloused hand over her mouth, wiping the spit-tle from her lips. He then cradled her to his powerful, heaving chest and began rocking.

Above the sound of his thudding heart she heard, "Lass, ye scared the *sheet* out of me."

Sheet? She would have to ask the meaning, later, when she had the breath. Panting and shivering, she had only enough strength to marvel at the heat pouring off the wet man who held her so close, his hands scrubbing her limbs and back in an effort to warm her.

She'd nearly drowned and he'd saved her. He and hale Mary. Another thing she need remember to ask about when her teeth stopped chattering, when she could speak without her throat feeling like she'd swallowed hot coals.

"Ack, Birdi, I swear ye'll be the death of me."

She'd be the death of him? 'Twould more likely be widdershins—the other way around—if his hands continued to chafe her skin as they did. But she didn't complain. Chafing was better than his unmerciful pounding.

"Lass, open yer eyes and look at me."

She did and found his face only inches away, well within her clearest range of vision. He was staring at her intently from eyes fairer than the midsummer sky, bluer than a jay's feather, fringed by long spiked lashes the color of wet bark. Truly lovely. Too bad they were frowning at her. Sadder still, they weren't hers. She did so dislike her eyes.

She'd seen them once in a looking glass when she'd been summoned to the Macarthur's keep. She hadn't realized until that moment that her eyes marked her as different. The Macarthurs—those few she'd seen—had eyes of smoky blue or green. Hers, alas, were the color of snow in shadow. It explained why the Macarthurs feared her so. Graces, her eyes had startled even her, spying them for the first time. So why didn't they frighten the Canteran?

"Ye're freezing, lass, I need build a fire."

Before she could say there wasn't need—the heat radiating from his chest was certainly warm enough—he sprang to his feet and carried her to his horse. Holding her in one arm with no apparent effort, he reached behind his saddle and pulled down a leather bag. He carried it and her back toward the waterfall.

He laid her down on a grassy spot in the sun, the place where the horse—a huge, slow-moving white blob to her burning eyes—grazed. Angus opened the bag and pulled out yard upon yard of deep green, shimmering cloth. He then—to her horror—started pulling up her kirtle.

She squeaked and slapped his hands. "Leave me be!"

"Not until I have ye out of these wet clothes. I dinna want ye catching the ague."

He again reached for her hem and she swatted his arms. "I can do it myself. Turn around."

Grumbling, he handed her the shimmering cloth and turned his back.

Teeth chattering, she pulled on her water-soaked sleeves and her arms came free. She glared at his broad back. The nerve of the man, thinking he could strip her without so much as a by-yer-leave!

She yanked her kirtle over her head and quickly wrapped the shimmering cloth over her nakedness.

Fearing Birdi didn't have the strength to manage on her own, Angus watched her out the corner of his eye. Her chilled skin was almost blue.

When she'd finished donning the velvet fabric he'd intended as a wedding present for his bride, he faced her. "Are ye feeling better?"

In response, she narrowed her incredible eyes at him and pressed her lush lips into a thin line. One hand slipped out of the yards of fabric. When she fingered the velvet, he grinned. Aye, she felt better. Feeling immeasurably better himself, he told her, "I'll leave ye to warm in the sun while I gather some firewood."

The wood gathered and lit by her side, he stripped down to his sark—something he normally didn't wear, liking the feel of air about his nether parts, but now wore in an effort to protect his groin while traveling through forest at night—and donned the second tunic he carried.

He then spread their clothing on a flat boulder to dry in the sun. Stomach growling, he sat down beside her. A healthy pink had returned to her lips and cheeks, and her hair, which she'd pulled from beneath the cloth in his absence, was again starting to billow about her waist in the faint breeze. "Are ye warm yet?"

She nodded.

Wondering if he dared leave her to catch something for them to eat, he murmured, "Ye scared me witless, lass."

"Myself, as well. Thank ye for saving me."

"No need. I'm happy I managed it." He rolled onto his side and propped himself up on one elbow, his back to the sun. He studied the scar encircling her right wrist. It looked like she'd been caught in a poacher's snare. "Lass, how did ye come to be alone in Macarthur's forest?"

She pulled the velvet closer. "Minnie died."

"My condolences on the loss of yer mother. And what happened to yer guards?"

She tipped her head, her brow crinkling. "We had no guards."

"None?" He couldn't believe her mother's stupidity, given how lovely her daughter was. "How long ago was this?"

She nibbled on her lip. "Ten summers past, mayhap more."

Ten summers? Nay! She'd misunderstood. His Scot, apparently, wasn't as good as he thought. "Your mother died when you were a bairn?"

"Aye, when I was so high." She held her hand a yard from the ground.

Nay. She couldn't possibly have survived on her own for so long. "But how did ye feed and clothe yerself at such an age?"

"Minnie had taught me. 'Twas her way. We had only each other, and so I learned before she died."

Still not believing his ears, he asked, "And how did she die?"

"A boar gored her." Birdi's eyes became glassy. "She didna die right away. She lingered. I tried to help her, tried to ease her pain as best I could, but the fever still took her." She again fingered the velvet and a tear slipped down her cheek. "I wonder at times why it happened when it did, before I had grown."

He brushed the lock that fluttered about her face over her shoulder. "Sometimes there isna reason why things happen as they do. All we can do is make the best of a bad situation, which ye apparently did." Though how she had was beyond his ken.

She plucked at the fabric covering her lap. "Like now."

He chuckled. "Am I so bad, lass?"

She looked at him, one corner of her lips quirking up. "Why do ye wear the metal shirt?"

Ah, so she still wasn't yet ready to admit he wasn't a complete ogre. "To keep from being injured in battle."

"Oh." She remained silent for a moment, then asked, "What is this called?" She patted his bride's wedding present.

"Velvet. Ladies wear gowns made of it." Yards and yards of it. Another reason he hadn't wanted a wife before now. The fabric Birdi fingered—now smudged with mud and liberally covered with pine needles—had been booty, a prize of war, from his campaign in France fighting for Louis against the Sassenach—the English dogs. He couldn't have gained it otherwise. Its value was more than he earned in a year.

"Where did ye live, lass? I didn't see a croft."

She eyed him warily for a moment. "I have a croft. The villagers built it long ago. I have a soft bed, a table, a cuttie stool, and a fire-ingle." She smiled for the first time and his heart stuttered. Dimples, lovely deep crevices, bracketed her lush mouth and even teeth. "And I have," she told him, "a down pillow, a posnet, and two kirtles as well."

She was so proud of so little his heart nearly broke.

As he pondered how she'd survived, her dimples disappeared. Her eyes narrowed and made a canny shift. To his amazement, she said, "Ye can have it all if ye'll bring me back to the glen."

Ah, cunning. He suppressed a grin. "If the matter were so simple, lass, I would, and without so grand a bribe, but it isna possible."

"But why is it not?" She looked about to cry.

As kindly as possible he told her, "Because it isna safe for such a lovely lass as ye to be alone. Ye could be set upon by rogues."

"Rogues?"

"Aye, shiftless men who rob and plunder."

"Ah."

He nodded. It was enough she understood some of the danger. He hadn't wanted to discuss the possibility of rape. He touched the scar on her right wrist and she immediately pulled her hand beneath the velvet. "How did ye come by the injury, lass?"

She looked away. "What means *sheet?*"

He gaped at her, heat infusing his face. "Umm . . . 'tisna a word a lady uses, Birdi."

"Why not? Ye did."

True, he had, and on more than one occasion, but . . . "'Tis a curse, lass. I wasna thinking clearly when I said it."

She frowned, then pointed to the raised and clenched fist and motto embroidered on his chest. "What means this?"

Accepting her reluctance to confide in him, he looked down to where Birdi pointed. "*Vincere aut mori.* It means 'to win or die.'"

"Oh." Birdi wobbled.

He steadied her and she managed a smile of thanks that

didn't reach her eyes. He couldn't blame her. Had he been in her position he'd have wobbled too. Poor lass.

He rose and checked their clothing. Finding the top layers reasonably dry, he turned them.

His stomach then growled. He opened his sporran and pulled out his fishing string with weighted bobber. "I'm going to try and catch more fish. Will ye be alright?"

She squinted at his hands. "Aye. Be careful ye dinna fall in."

He laughed for the first time since meeting Birdalane Shame. "Ye are a wonder."

She grinned in lopsided fashion. "Ye dinna ken the half."

Suspecting she might be correct, he ambled toward the outcropping of rock at the base of the waterfall. In short time he caught three small fish, cleaned them, and brought them back to the fire. As the fish roasted, juices dripped onto the flames and he eyed the straight column of smoke marking their exact location. Deciding they'd be wiser eating half-cooked fish, he stood and kicked sand into the flames.

"What are ye doing?"

"Now that ye are warm and dry there's nay need to call undue attention to ourselves. 'Tisna safe when we're not among friends."

Just as the fire snuffed out, Rampage whinnied in warning. Angus spun. Three riders were rounding the river's bend, riding hard in their direction.

The fine-tempered steel of his claymore sang as he pulled his broadsword from its sheath and yanked Birdi to her feet. "Hide, lass. Back to the boulders with ye. Now!"

"But—"

"Now, damn it. Run!"

Christ's blood. He stood alone with a half-naked woman at his back. A woman any one of these men would gladly hie off with given half a chance.

Chapter 6

Sword in hand, Angus assessed the three riders as they charged toward him.

The youngest, a youth of about five-and-ten years, small boned and well dressed, was nay doubt Fraiser's heir and of little threat. The men flanking him, however, were a different matter entirely. The elder of the two was of Angus's own height, bearded, a bit heavier and thankfully a good bit older than he. From the man's dress Angus took him to be a Fraiser captain. The younger, also a big man, wore Fraiser plaid but no jeweled brooch, no marks of distinction other than a nasty-looking battle scar across one cheek. He was simply a skilled warrior.

As they came to a prancing halt before him on shaggy ponies, the eldest guard demanded, "Who be ye and what business have ye on Fraiser land?"

Angus looked each in the eye. "I'm Angus MacDougall and have no business with the Fraisers. I'm just passing through on my way to Beal."

"More like eating yer way through," the younger of the two guards grumbled, pointing to the discarded fish. "And ye have nay doubt neglected to pay Fraiser the plaque-mail."

As they eyed him warily, Angus mentally cursed. The fines levied by some Highland chieftains for safe passage through their lands could be backbreaking. Would the lad try to increase his father's coffers by some exorbitant amount?

Before he could ask how much they wanted, the lad leaned toward the younger of the two guards, pointed toward Rampage, and whispered something.

Humph! If the lad thought he could take his mount he'd best rethink. Rampage would toss the lad into the river the moment he set a foot in a stirrup.

Sneering, the eldest Fraiser asked, "Why is it, MacDougall, yer horse has six legs?"

What? Angus snapped his head around. Rampage did indeed appear to be standing on six legs; four heavily muscled and feathery white limbs and two decidedly sleek, feminine ones.

Good God Almighty! Birdi had taken refuge behind his charger.

Angus sucked air through clenched teeth. Why couldn't the blasted woman do what she was told?

The youth called, "Lady, come out where we can see ye."

Angus bellowed, "Dinna ye dare, lass. Stay right where ye are." To the men, he said. "What do I owe for the rest and the fish?"

"Now what's yer hurry?" the younger guard asked. Grinning in what could only be called a lascivious manner, the man eyed Rampage's flanks and started inching his horse around to the left.

Kenning the man's intent, Angus grasped the hilt of his broadsword in both hands and swung the claymore in menacing fashion, arcing it right and left, making the metal sing in the wind. "Keep yer distance from her."

The older of the two guards, his sword at the ready, laughed and kicked his mount, angling to the right. "Have ye reived yerself a wife, MacDougall? Last I heard no decent lass would have Angus the Blood."

Angus narrowed his eyes. It had been too much to hope they wouldn't recognize him. "Since ye ken me, ye also ken what will happen if ye try to touch my woman. Ye'd best take what coins ye want and go."

The younger guard snickered. "Now is that hospitable, MacDougall?" He angled more to the left for a better view of Birdi. "Why will ye nay introduce us to yer woman? I'll wager she's quite fair above those lovely white thighs."

Blood roared into Angus's tensing muscles. There wasn't a way he could keep both men at bay if they flanked him. Had he been alone he would have charged the closest and drawn in the other. As it was he had only one choice.

Screaming *"Vincere aut mori!"* at the top of his lungs, he charged young Fraiser. Before the startled youth could react, Angus swung his blade in a mighty arc and caught the lad's pony across the chest with the flat of his blade. The lad and horse keened as they toppled.

The guards spun.

Shouting and cursing, they flew at Angus with their swords raised.

Angus leaped over the kicking pony, grabbed the scrambling lad by the hair, and slammed a fist into his jaw. The lad collapsed like a ragdoll in his hands. He pressed his blade to the unconscious youth's throat as the guards bore down on him. "One step closer," Angus yelled, "and the lad dies!"

The men reined in, exchanged glances, and growled deep in their throats. Shoulders hunched, eyes narrowed, they inched forward.

Angus yanked the lad's head back, exposing the blood he'd already let. The men's faces blanched.

"Aye, ye ken me." He nodded to his right. "Move over there and dismount . . . slowly." To Birdi, he bellowed, "On the horse, lass. Now!" *Please, God, have her make haste.* He had no desire to kill the Fraiser lad. To do so would make his father, Alex Fraiser—a fierce chieftain—a bloodlust enemy of both Angus and his clan. To bring war down on innocent MacDougall heads was unthinkable. Those at Blackstone meant more to him than life itself.

Wondering what was taking Birdi so long, Angus slid his gaze from the frustrated Fraisers to his agitated horse snorting and pawing the earth.

He cursed.

All he saw were dangling feminine feet and a mound of deep green velvet lying beneath his horse's hooves.

Chapter 7

Birdi couldn't recall ever being more furious in her life. Hissing "Sheet, sheet, sheet," she clawed at the saddle as Angus's horse pranced.

Her initial terror—of being discovered by heavily armed strangers—had dissolved as quickly as a puff of smoke listening to their and Angus the Canteran's conversation.

Now, not only was she naked—thanks to the blasted horse stepping on the velvet and yanking it from her body as he shifted this way and that, thwarting her efforts to climb upon him—but the Canteran had done the unthinkable.

He'd called her his woman!

He hadn't, apparently, been satisfied with taking her from her home and tearing through miles of forest with her. Oh no! He had to claim her—*aloud*—before Goddess and two strangers! Twice!

She was now handfast to Angus MacDougall.

Oh, aye, she kenned handfasting all right. Two summers before her mother passed, she'd brought Birdi to the annual Beltane gathering—the last Birdi ever attended—where a young man and woman became handfast. Minnie had explained it all in depressing detail.

Did Angus the Canteran think her an idiot?

When she got to him—if she ever got to him—she'd give him what for. Oh, yes, she would! Thanks to his obstinacy, she no longer had a roof over her head, hadn't food nor clothing, and now no freedom.

She was his for a year and a day.

Holding onto the stirrup for dear life with one hand, she slapped the horse's side. "Halt, ye blasted beast!"

To her amazement the animal froze in place.

Sputtering her limited list of profanities, most of which referred to cattle droppings, she grasped the leather dangling from the saddle with both hands and hauled herself up, hand over hand. When her foot caught the stirrup, she sprang into the saddle. Relief flooded her. She took a deep breath, wondering how one steered the beast so she could drive it toward home after she rode over Angus the Canteran.

A whistle pieced the air, and the snorting horse lunged forward, its neck arched, hooves flashing. Birdi yelped and grabbed onto the saddle pommel for dear life.

As the beast closed on its master, Birdi silently cursed it, the strangers, and Angus MacDougall.

She came to an abrupt halt. Hair billowing about her, she straightened, took a deep breath, and heard a collective gasp. Metal clanged as it fell to the ground.

Eyes blazing, she turned in the direction of the sound and hissed, "What are ye staring at?"

One man to her right murmured, "Merciful Mother of God," and backed away.

Humph!

The saddle suddenly shifted beneath her and Angus Mac-Dougall engulfed her. As his arm clasped her waist and the horse bolt forward, he laughed, "Ye are a wonder, lass."

Ha! Wonder or not, she would have a word with him as soon as she could breathe again; his arm had a death grip on her. Not only had he declared them handfast, he'd left her clothes and the costly velvet behind. The man was totally wode!

After an interminable reckless ride, they came to rest beneath a treed canopy where the shadows felt cool and the air hung heavy with the scent of sap and fern. Birdi asked, "Are we now safe?"

Angus shifted behind her and dropped to the ground. "Aye, lass, for now."

Raking hair out of her eyes, she muttered, "Thank ye, stars." She'd had her fill of strange feelings—of odd flutters and heat—as they rode.

Initially, the Canteran's calloused hand had grasped her waist in a tight hold, but as the miles passed and the danger ebbed, their pace had slowed, and his grip had relaxed. With every jolt of the horse, every dip in the trail, his broad palm and long blunt fingers shifted. And his touch was far more disturbing than any of her dream-induced yearnings had ever been.

Aye, and the feel of his hard thighs and chest brushing her naked thighs and back . . .

Ack!

The sooner they parted ways, the better.

Angus grasped Birdi's waist.

As tempting as it was to press her naked to his chest, he held Birdi out at arm's length. The moment her feet hit the ground she wrenched free of his hold. Looking fit to kill, she stomped off some ten feet, then turned to face him.

He sighed. With her hands strategically placed, jet curls shifting ever so slightly over her breasts and barely masking the dressing about her waist, Birdalane Shame was a sight to behold.

And if he lived to be a hundred years old he wouldn't ever forget the stunned expressions on the Fraisers' faces as she rode up on them, as naked as the day she was born, her incredible, icy blue eyes blazing fury.

They wouldn't likely forget it, either.

Grinning, Angus started pulling off his tunic.

Birdi growled, "Now what do ye think ye're doing?"

"Getting me shirt off so ye have somethin' to wear."

The feel of her satin-smooth skin had nearly driven him insane over the last mile.

She tapped an impatient foot. "You, sir, are stark raving

wode! How dare ye claim me as yours? How dare ye take me to wife without my consent? I'll not have it! I willna, do ye hear!"

Angus gaped at her. "What on earth are ye blathering about?"

Birdi snarled deep in her throat. "Did ye or did ye not tell three strangers I was yer woman?"

"Aye, but—" The implication hit him like a gauntleted fist to the chest. *Oh, my God!*

He and Birdi were handfast.

When the Fraisers had asked if he'd taken a wife, he hadn't denied it. Had called her *my woman*. The fact that he'd done so to protect Birdi mattered naught.

But he couldn't take Birdalane Shame to wife. He had to marry a lady—a gentlewoman—to get Donaliegh! God's teeth!

Birdi shook her fist at him. "I want this undone. I willna be handfast . . . . Nay, I willna."

Aye, he wanted it undone, as well, but how? Thanks to his stupidity she was now his for a year and a day. *Oh, my God.* And his priest upon hearing this would naturally insist he sanctify the union within the Blackstone's kirk . . . .

Oh, my God!

As if reading his mind, she hissed, "Ye will take us to the sacred well and undo this, Angus MacDougall!"

He eyed her warily, his mind racing through the folklore and tales he'd heard as a youth, trying to recall a story of nullifying a handfasting. "Undo this how?"

Birdi huffed. "We need go to a sacred well, repeat three times that we dissolve this union, and then drink the water. 'Tis all, and this . . . this farce becomes a thing of the past."

"Are ye sure, lass, 'tis all that we need do?" *Please say aye.*

Birdi bit into her lower lip. "Mayhap there is more to the ceremony, but 'twill be enough for me."

Thank God.

"Consider it done." Angus pulled out of his shirt and held it out to Birdi. "Here, put this on before ye catch yer death." *Or I catch ye up by yer bonnie hurdies, spread yer legs, and make ye mine in truth before God.*

Consummating their erroneous handfasting would be equivalent to a life sentence if his priest learned he had. And hear it, he would. If not through another priest—the men in black had a network of spies that put even the Sassenach king's agents to shame—then he would through a wandering minstrel. Angus the Blood had proved rich fodder for many a bard's witty but oft-barbed tongue.

Birdi snatched his shirt from his hand and made quick work of donning it. As it settled around her calves, she asked, "Then 'tis agreed?"

"Aye, lass, 'tis agreed. I dinna want to be handfast to ye either." He'd lose all if he remained attached to Birdalane Shame. "Now where is this well?"

Birdi's furious expression shifted to one of open-mouthed surprise. "What do ye mean, 'where's this well?' 'Tis you who ken where we are. 'Tis you who should ken where the well is!"

"How should I ken such a place?" Humph! Good Lord, what was the woman thinking?

Birdi stomped a foot. "Are ye a blithering heathen, then?"

Teeth grinding with indignation, Angus closed the distance between them in three quick strides. He puffed out his chest as he loomed over her, hands on hips. "Nay, I'm a Catholic, if 'tis any of yer concern, so there's nay reason for me to be kenning where some superstitious lot's sacred well is!"

Birdi gaped at him. "Superstitious lot? Why ye—"

She punched him in the gut.

Had she turned yellow and flown away, he couldn't have been more surprised. Here she was nearly naked and all of five feet and a bit, and she had the audacity to hit Angus the Blood in anger.

He laughed, great barks rolling out of his chest like thunder.

Birdi, wide-eyed, scrambled backward.

His arm shot out and caught her. "Now where do ye think ye're going? Ye'll be staying with me until we undo this. I willna be losing Donaliegh because of ye."

She tried to wrench free. "What care I for some Donaleigh?" She slapped the hand that held her wrist. "Ye dinna need me. Ye can go to the well by yerself, say the words, and I'll swear—if asked—that I did the same. Truly, I will. Just please let me go."

Tears pooled in her lovely eyes.

Ack! He snaked a hand about her waist and pulled her into his chest. Here she was greetin' and carrying on and she'd done naught but catch his attention as she took a bath in a glen.

He brushed the hair from her face. "Lass, hush, there isna reason to fash, but we have to straighten this out. Together."

With her palms pressed to his naked chest, she shuddered and sniffed. He kissed the top of her head, and then with a finger lifted her chin. Lord, she was breathtaking with her cheeks all flushed with righteous indignation and her eyes glittering like melting ice in the sun. Were she a lady, he'd never let her go, no matter how she pleaded— would, in fact, drive her to distraction with his efforts to win her heart just as his da had successfully wooed his mother—but given their current circumstances . . .

"Lass, we have to dissolve this union and havena much time to do it." Word of his handfasting could get to Beal before he did. "We need ride as fast as possible to the nearest village, to Ardlui. There we'll seek out a midwife." Seeing her brow crease, he amended, "A howdie-wife." Most were reported to practice the auld religion. "She should ken where the nearest well of which ye speak lies. Agreed?"

Birdi nodded and he silently thanked the Blessed Virgin. Donaliegh was still within his grasp if they made haste.

"Are ye hungry, lass?" They hadn't the time to snare a rabbit or hunt berries, but if she was hungry . . .

Birdi shook her head. The last thing she wanted was food. Her stomach felt so gnarly she feared she'd likely toss anything she ate.

Her every move was being controlled by another, one far bigger than she, who kenned the area and had the advantage of sight. As she loathed her own helplessness, another thing disturbed her.

She had very sound reasons for not wanting to be handfast to Angus the Canteran. She didn't want him getting her with child. But why was *he* so opposed to their union?

He didn't fear her. Was Mary the cause? The woman was certainly on his mind enough. Given the man's size and preference of horse, Birdi easily pictured Angus's hale and hearty Mary: a big, solid woman with honey-colored hair and breasts the size and shape of beehives. She snorted. It certainly explained why he hadn't accosted her, had let her be even while she slept. By comparison, Angus MacDougall no doubt found her—Birdi—lacking.

Ack! She shook hard. The man was making her wode. What did she care if he found her lacking? The sooner she got away from him the better. Aye. And to do so she would have to phrase her message to Tinker in such a way that the auld man would have nay choice but to do her bidding. Just as she, at the moment, had nay choice but to do Angus MacDougall's.

"Are ye ready, lass?"

Birdi looked up to find Angus dressed in sparkling scarlet. She blinked in surprise and eased closer. "My word." The open, waist-length coat he now wore had great, puffy slit sleeves and was threaded with argent—silver. Buff-colored trews covered his legs.

Angus cleared his throat. "'Tis my courting costume. I'd have given it to ye to wear but as ye ken, it canna close."

He had a point. The magnificent coat showed off his equally magnificent chest for the world to see. "'Tis lovely . . . the coat, I mean."

"Humph." He held out a hand. "Shall we go?"

Robbie Macarthur, tired and parched, reined in and waited for his brother to pull alongside at the crossroad.

They'd been ordered into enemy territory by the Macarthur and charged with bringing home the spae. Their chieftain kenned they were not only brawn and skilled swordsmen but thorough.

The way leading west was little more than a deer path heading up into rugged terrain; the way heading north was a wagon road—flatter and regularly traveled. "What think ye?" Robbie asked as he brought his water bag to his mouth. "Continue north as ordered or turn west?"

They'd followed MacDougall's tracks as far as they could—before the bastard took to the gravel-strewn riverbeds, where they'd lost him—and were now deep in enemy territory and a day's ride south of Crianlarich.

Fegan stroked his pony's sweating neck. "My gut says we need turn west toward Ardlui. Though rugged, it cuts the distance, but . . ."

"Aye, but . . ."

Their liege had ordered them north, convinced Angus the Blood would take the spae the easiest and therefore the fastest route to Drasmoor and Castle Blackstone. Mac-Dougall had, after all, raced off due north, and their liege believed he'd continue north to Crianlarich, then head west across the top of Loch Awe toward Oban. From there he'd have a fast ride south to safety.

"Macarthur has a point. Carrying the spae before him and despite the horse's might, the Blood willna court trouble. If his horse slips up yon and the spae falls . . ."

"Aye, she'll be of little use to him dead."

Robbie grunted. " 'Tis agreed then. We turn right."

Kicking their ponies into a gallop, Fegan grumbled, "With any luck, his charger will come up lame, and we'll catch them by dawn."

At the north end of Loch Lomond, Birdi murmured, "What's burning?"

Scowling at the suspicious black columns rising above the treetops ahead of them, Angus muttered, "I dinna ken."

They scrambled up a steep, shale-strewn incline and came to rest on its tree-lined crest. Angus cursed. On the opposite shore of River Dochart only charred ruins remained of the village Ardlui.

Birdi whispered, "What's happened?"

Angus tightened his hold on Birdi as he kicked Rampage's sides. "We willna ken that until we get there."

Fording the river proved easier than he'd expected, with the water running low. As they scrambled up the west bank, Angus's gaze raked the mass devastation. "Merciful Mother . . ." Not one croft remained intact. Maimed, blood-soaked bodies—men, women, and bairns—lay everywhere.

The bloody bastards.

He carefully scanned the area for the butchers of Ardlui as he eased an agitated Rampage into the village. Finding the place stone quiet, he reined in, dismounted—silently cursing himself for not retrieving his chain mail—and pulled Birdi to the ground. "Stay by my side. Whoever did this appears to have fled, but . . ."

Angus reached for the pewter-and-bronze hilt of his claymore. He hauled the broadsword from its sheath in one fluid motion and then took Birdi's hand. "We need check to see if any have been left alive." When Birdi said nothing, he glanced down and found her white as snow, staring at a pool of blood at her feet. He wrapped an arm around her waist and eased her away. "Come, lass, we need seek the living, nay fash over the dead."

Eyes stinging and noses burning from the fetid smoke, they went from charred croft to charred croft—most still too hot to enter—and found no one alive.

On the far left of the village they found a croft with its roof burned away but the door still intact. Angus let loose of Birdi's hand. Praying someone had survived the carnage—might have found refuge in a root cellar or inglenook—he threw his weight against the door and it fell off its leather hinges and crashed to the floor. Inside, he found the charred remains of a lad of mayhap six years huddled in a corner. Throat tight, Angus again cursed the cowards who could take an innocent's life.

What manner of men were these savages?

Outside he found Birdi, some twenty yards from where he'd told her to stay put, keening as she knelt beside an ashen young woman whose throat had been slashed. As he approached, Birdi looked up. Flooding tears had made white tracks down her soot-coated cheeks.

"I . . . I canna do anything," Birdi keened. " 'Tis too late. She's cold."

He raised Birdi by the arms and pulled her into his side. " 'Tis naught anyone can do, lass." The damage had been done hours ago.

Shaking in his arms, deathly pale, she asked, "But . . . but why? Why would someone do this?" Her head turned left then right. "Death is everywhere. And the stench—"

Her head suddenly snapped back to the left. "There! Do ye hear it?"

Angus, his sword arm already tensing, looked about. "Hear what?"

She pulled free. As she took off at a near run, her hands out before her, she cried, "I'm coming! I'm coming!"

Staring after her, Angus cursed. He never should have brought Birdi into this smoldering hell.

Like any warrior, he'd grown accustomed to the sights and smells of death and destruction—God knew he'd caused enough himself—but had given no thought to the fact that gentler folk weren't steeled to it.

Hearing voices where there were none—in a manure pile, no less, for that appeared to be where she was heading—could mean only one thing. Birdalane Shame had lost her mind from the horror of it all.

He raced after her.

Heart thudding, palms itching, Birdi stumbled into a head-high mound of manure. Her nerves were afire, the *need* upon her in full force. Someone was frightened, in pain, but alive. But where? She spun, trying to catch the wee sound she'd heard just moments ago. "Where are ye?"

To her relief the mewing came again, this time low and directly before her. She dropped to her knees and frantically clawed into the warm, decaying mound. Within a heartbeat her fingers found a piece of wool. She clawed faster, deeper, and uncovered a blanketed bundle. She pulled it free as Angus came around the mound.

"Birdi, stop."

Paying no heed, she whipped the blanket open and found the pudgiest, most beautiful babe she'd ever laid eyes on. It blinked up at her, opened its toothless mouth, and wailed like a banshee.

At her back Angus muttered, "I dinna believe it."

Birdi scooped the babe into her arms. "Hush, dautie, hush." To Angus she said, "His mother must have hidden him. He's alive. 'Tis wondrous!"

Angus helped her to her feet, and Birdi checked the babe for injuries. Satisfied the wee, howling creature was sound, she cradled him to her chest. The babe immediately tried to rout at her breast. "Ack, the poor wee bit is hungry."

Angus scratched his head and looked about. "Aye, but whoever did this reived all the cattle so there isna milk to be had. Can we give him some water?"

Birdi jiggled the wailing babe. "Aye. Do ye think ye can find a bucket?" The babe needed a good wash.

Angus dutifully nodded and turned. A moment later she heard a chicken's frantic clucking, and pounding footsteps. Something whooshed past, the chicken screeched, and all fell silent.

"We've sup," Angus called to her.

"Grand." The babe was still howling and couldn't eat chicken.

Angus shouted, "Put yer wee finger in its mouth."

"But my hands are filthy."

Something dropped with a soft thud and Angus, now at her back, murmured, "Give 'im here." He took the babe with sure hands and the yowling immediately stopped. Birdi craned her neck to see what he'd done and found the babe sucking Angus the Canteran's wee finger, soot and all.

Oh, well.

She asked, "What now?"

"We get something in this wee one's belly and then secure the dead."

"Secure the dead?"

"Aye, in what's left of the barn. There are just too many slain for me to bury." He looked none too happy about the task as he bent and picked up what he'd dropped. 'Twas, she saw, a bright-feathered rooster.

Birdi cautiously followed Angus down the village road to the river's edge. With her gaze locked on his broad back, she stumbled over an auld man, his face a mask of agony and his chest a gaping wound. Hand over her heart she murmured, "Blessed Mother of All."

Ten feet later she tripped again, this time over a woman her own age. Birdi bent, closed the woman's vacant eyes, and without thought righted the basket at her side. It contained folded linens. The poor lass had been doing a simple chore when the butchers had cut her down. How could anyone be so cruel . . . so heartless?

Minnie had had her faults—too many to count—but she'd been right about one matter; this world beyond the glen was nay for the likes of her.

At the river's edge Angus handed her the babe and a bucket. "Tend the wee one while I tend to the dead."

Cradling the fussing babe she murmured, "Be careful."

He surprised her by stroking her cheek. "Are ye all right, Birdi?"

She wasn't, not in the least, but she said, "Aye. Go and do what needs be done."

"If ye see or hear anything untoward, yell, and I'll come at a run."

She looked down at the babe in her arms. "He's too young to be orphaned."

Angus lifted her chin and looked into her eyes. "There is never a good age to be orphaned, but ye managed and so shall he."

With that Angus left and Birdi settled on the bank. Using her fingers, she nervously dripped water into the babe's gaping mouth. He grimaced at the taste, but soon grew accustomed and eventually sucked on her fingers. As he did, her heart raced with the flush of maternal success. Caring for a babe wasn't so hard after all.

As the babe suckled she studied his almost white curls, wee perfect fingers, and dimpled arms. Warmth—the likes of which she'd never experienced before—filled her. He was such a bonnie lad. One who, with the proper guidance and love, could grow up to be a good man.

She heaved a sigh. Who would care for this precious bairn?

Something bleated in Birdi's ear.

"Ack!" She jumped nigh a foot, startling the babe.

As she soothed him with pats on the back, Angus chuckled. "Look what I found hiding in the barn . . . . A nanny goat. 'Twas probably too fast for the bastards to catch." He grunted in satisfaction as he tied it to a nearby post. "We now have milk for our wee lad."

Birdi edged closer to study the gray, shaggy beast. It stank and had horizontal slits in its eyes. Horrified that Angus expected her to place the precious babe against one of the beast's teats, she clutched the babe tightly to her chest. "Ye canna be serious?"

"Aye."

She shook her head and inched away.

Angus made a thick "humphing" sound in the back of his throat. "Have ye not milked a goat before?"

"Nay." She'd never even seen one before. Oh, she'd heard one a time or two when she'd been summoned to the village, but—

" 'Tis easy. Watch." Angus squatted and placed the bucket between the bleating beastie's legs. He reached under the nanny with both hands and grumbled, "Starting at the top, ye squeeze yer fingers down, like so. Do one hand, then the other." Hearing a rhythmic *squish, squish, squish*—milk hitting the bottom of the bucket—Birdi heaved a relieved sigh. Angus hadn't expected her to put the babe to a teat, after all. Just take the milk out of the goat. That she could do.

Angus placed the bucket beside her. "This should do for now. Once the babe is satisfied, ye can lay him down and milk the goat again." He rose and left her to flounder on her own.

With a good bit of fussing and choking, the babe finally drank his fill of goat milk. When he fell asleep in her arms, Birdi rose and sought out the basket she'd tripped over.

The dead woman's body was gone but the basket

remained. Propping it against her free hip, Birdi moved out of the path of the drifting, acrid smoke. Settled in the shade of what turned out to be an old elm, she went through the basket's contents and found scraps of soft linen, a wee tunic, a man's shirt, an apron, and a kirtle. Tears welled in her eyes. The woman whose eyes she'd closed might well have been the babe's minnie.

Ack, ye poor laddie.

Birdi, at least, had had her mother until she was of an age where she could feed and tend herself. And she had memories. Most had faded away but some still remained. If asked, she could still describe her mother. Black-headed, green-eyed, and thin. Painfully thin.

She made a pallet on the bottom of the basket with the shirt and apron and then laid the babe down to examine him more fully. Ugh, the poor wee thing was filthy.

The babe finally tended—'twas indeed a laddie—she stared at the gray-and-brown lump that was the goat. " 'Tis now yer turn."

The goat—apparently no happier than she about the prospect of milking—bucked and pulled at its rope each time Birdi placed the bucket beneath it. After a sixth try, her patience snapped. She grabbed the beast by the ears, glared into its evil-looking eyes, and hissed, "If ye dinna want to be stew in the next few minutes, ye nasty creature, ye'd best heel." To her utter amazement the nanny froze.

"Humph."

She set the bucket beneath the nanny again and gingerly reached for one of its swollen teats. Milking, she discovered, wasn't as easy as the Canteran claimed.

After innumerable grumbled curses, Birdi finally got out enough milk for the babe's next meal. Bucket in hand, she returned to the shade of the tree to find the babe, its thumb in its mouth, still fast asleep.

She settled beside him and stroked a pudgy arm. "What a lovely wee bit ye are . . . ." She didn't ken his name.

That wouldn't do. He needed a new name, one mayhap not as fair as his mother had given him, but one he could grow into. One that might bring good fortune. She discarded several she'd heard over the years—Ian, John, Peter, and Robbie—wanting something that better called to mind power, thoughtfulness, and grace.

She was pulled from her musing by now-familiar footsteps, and looked up to find a mass of scarlet before her. "Is all done?" she asked.

Angus, reeking of soot and the metallic stench of blood, collapsed at her side. "Aye. One and thirty now lie in the barn."

He'd laid the dead out with as much dignity as possible, said a prayer over them, and then nailed a makeshift cross to the propped door. Using a piece of charred wood, he'd written in Latin, *Herein lie the dearly departed of Ardlui, slain by unknown hands. May God have mercy on their souls.* He'd then signed his name.

Needing to touch something vital, alive, Angus reached into the basket and stroked the wee one's pudgy arms. "I canna help but wonder what would drive a man to commit such horrors. I've fought for my clan and for my king— killed more men than I have fingers to count on—but never have I slain a bairn or woman. Good God, I dinna ken this."

Birdi placed her hand over his. "Angus, at least this one still lives and we need be thankful for that."

Angus blinked in surprise. Birdi had tried to console him and had finally called him by name. Feeling inordinately pleased, though why he should be he didn't ken, he turned his attention back to the charred ruins of Ardlui. "We need leave this place. 'Tisna safe."

"I'll be most glad to go." Birdi lifted the sleeping babe from the basket and settled him on her shoulder. Handing Angus a bundle, she whispered, "They're nappies. We need also take the goat."

Angus came to his feet and heaved a resigned sigh. He now had only a fortnight and a week to find a pagan howdie-wife and a sacred well, break a handfast, find a home for a wee orphan, find one for Birdi, court a wife, and beat it back to Blackstone. All while hauling a fractious goat.

God help him.

An hour later, Birdi—still fretting over what would become of the babe in her arms—heard soft cooing in the trees to her right. Did her doves still come to her croft looking for crumbs? Had the titmice taken over her bedding and grain stores? Had her precious apples already started to rot?

"Angus, where is yer home?"

"The village of Drasmoor."

"And where is this?" Tinker hadn't mentioned it.

"On the west coast, on the Firth of Lorne."

" 'Tis far?"

"Aye, six days' ride away."

"Ah, and do ye pass Aberfoyle to get there?" 'Twas where Tinker had said he was heading.

"Nay. Aberfoyle is far to the north, and we're headed west."

"Oh." 'Twas not what she wanted to hear. "Have ye a croft in this Drasmoor?" Mayhap if he did have one, he'd understand her craving for her home.

"Nay, I live in Castle Blackstone at the pleasure of my liege, Duncan MacDougall, and his wife."

"Oh." This man at her back must be of some import. This could be good or bad. "Tell me about this castle."

"Blackstone rests on a wee island in Drasmoor Bay. My liege started construction some ten years back, shortly after the plague swept through our village and a vast number of our clan perished. He built Blackstone on an isle so that should the plague return, he could keep our sept safe."

Sept—Angus had used the word before. It seemed to mean clan.

Birdi had trouble picturing an entire clan living under one roof. Wouldn't the women be at each others' throats over what cooked in the inglenook? "How many are in your clan—sept?"

"At last count, there were over one hundred."

She craned her neck to look at him. "Ye must be sleeping twenty to a bed!" She'd have no part in that!

Angus—his blue eyes suddenly sparkling, crinkles forming at the far corners—chuckled. "Nay, most live in the village of Drasmoor or up in the hills. Just a few, like myself and the Silversteins, live with our liege and his family in Blackstone."

"Oh." She tore her gaze from his nicely shaped lips just as Rampage bucked and the goat bleated. Kenning what would happen next, she tightened her grip on the sleeping babe.

Angus kicked Rampage in the side for the umpteenth time; the horse snorted, frog-hopped, and then trotted a few jarring steps before settling again into a sedate walk.

All back to normal, she asked, "And what does this castle look like?" She hoped Angus the Canteran had Tinker's talent for painting pictures in her mind.

"'Tis big—takes up most of the isle—and is square and made of dark gray granite. It appears black in the rain."

She waited, hoping for more. When he remained silent she arched her neck and frowned up at him. "And the inside?"

He scratched his chin. "'Tis like most castles. There's a bailey, a well, barracks for the unwed men, a kirk, sheds for the cattle, a smithy."

Birdi heaved an exasperated sigh. "Inside, where the people live, MacDougall."

"Oh. In the keep there's a great hall with fireplaces at either end. We eat there. Above are storage rooms and sleeping quarters."

When Angus fell silent again, Birdi fought the overwhelming urge to clout his ears scarlet. "Is there colored glass and tapestries within?" Tinker's descriptions had made her heart race with the desire to see and touch all that Tinker had. "Are there shimmering golden chalices and huge pewter plates? Are there argent-backed mirrors? Is there a great stuffed elk on the wall?" Angus the Canteran was a pitiful storyteller.

He chuckled. "Blackstone isna so wealthy that it has colored glass and chalices of gold, but there are mounted heads and horns aplenty, and 'tis bonnie now that Lady Beth has come."

Ah. "And this Lady Beth? Is she fair?"

Before he could answer, their horse bucked, the goat bleated, and Angus again cursed and kicked. When they were moving again, she murmured, "Lady Beth."

Birdi had met only one lady, the Macarther's wife, and hadn't liked the brittle woman who took her frustrations out on those beneath her. After tending a lass of only twelve years with a lashed and festering back, Birdi had decided ladies were on level with boars. Something one kept a healthy distance away from.

"Ah, Lady Beth. She isna particularly fair of visage, not like ye, but she has a heart as big as a keep."

Birdi blinked in surprise. He was obviously taken with the lady, respected her, and if her ears weren't mistaken Angus thought she—Birdi—fair! But how? She was filthy; she stank, and hadn't combed her hair in three days. Minnie had been right about another matter . . . . Men were strange creatures. But this one was strange in a most interesting way. She need learn more.

"And what do ye do at the castle?"

"I command and train warriors at the lists, in sword play, and in defense."

"Sounds far grander and more exciting than my life."

He chuckled and she again felt vibrations—pleasant and alarming—ride down her spine.

"Nay," he told her, "most nights I'm so weary I fall into me bed face first."

Birdi smiled at that. He was a dedicated leader of men. 'Twas good, but his soldiering put him at great risk. She fingered the scar on her right wrist, recalled the second time she'd been called to the Macarthur's side, and decided mayhap she should give the matter of Angus MacDougall and the babe more thought.

Four hours later, Angus, frustrated beyond all civility, reined into a small grove that bordered the west bank of Loch Lomond. Through gritted teeth he growled, "We'll spend the night here."

He slid to the ground and reached for Birdi and the babe. Just as his hands encircled her waist, the goat bleated and Rampage, ears pinned, let fly a hoof. This time the goat landed with a mighty splash in the loch. Water flew, the horse immediately shied, and a hoof slammed down on Angus's toes.

He rammed a shoulder into his mount. "Ye bloody idiot, git off me!"

Eyes ringed in white, Rampage backed, and Angus set Birdi down. "So help me God, if I survive this . . ."

As the goat scrabbled out of the water Birdi asked, "Are ye alright?"

Angus growled deep in his throat. "Nay, and I may never be again."

They'd made only five miles' progress to the next village thanks to the blasted goat and the babe's constant need for attention. Angus was tired, filthy, hungry, and physically frustrated, thanks to Birdalane Shame's fine hurdies grinding into his groin for three whole days. "Tend to the babe."

Birdi nibbled at her lower lip. "As ye lust."

As I lust? "Humph!"

Had he had his druthers, the babe, Birdi, and the blasted goat would be off his hands this instant.

Matters couldn't get worse.

Grumbling, he grabbed the goat's tether and tied the stinking waterlogged animal to a tree. He unsaddled his idiot mount and then set about cutting small boughs to make a pallet for Birdi and the babe under a low-branched pine. He then filled their water bag and checked Rampage's hooves for stones. A crippled horse was the last thing he needed right now.

Finally satisfied all was in readiness for the night, he hauled their supper out of his saddlebag, returned to Birdi and the sleeping babe, and was pleasantly surprised to find that Birdi had covered the pine boughs he'd cut with a thick layer of pine needles. They'd now sleep a good six inches off the cold ground in relative comfort.

"Here." He held out a meaty chicken leg.

She took it and grinned. "Where did ye find this?"

Mollified by her deeply dimpled smile and the thought of a comfortable bed, he sat down beside her and muttered, " 'Tis the rooster."

She took a bite. " 'Tis wonderful, but I didna see ye cook him."

"While I tended to Ardlui's dead, he cooked in one of the smoldering fires."

"Ah, very clever of ye."

"Thank ye." He finished his chicken leg in two bites, and tore into the breast meat. "I've been hungrier, but I swear I've never tasted fairer chicken."

Birdi chuckled. "I've been wondering how ye've been managing to stay alive on what little food we've had."

He hastily swallowed his meat. "I didna mean to starve ye, lass."

She shook her head. "Ye havena. I've lived on far less for a lot longer. 'Tis just yer size that had me pondering."

He grinned. "Ah. I have been known to down a fair-sized hog when the mood strikes." Seeing she'd finished her chicken leg—she was indeed hungry—he tore off another piece of breast meat and handed it to her. "I'm sorry ye had to see all the death in Ardlui. Ye did well . . . finding the babe and tending him as ye have." She had been surprisingly calm.

Birdi looked down at the babe lying between them. "'Tis easy. He's the fairest wee bit." She took another bite of meat. "I've been thinking and have decided to keep him."

Aghast, Angus stared at Birdi as the remains of the rooster dropped into his lap. "Ye what!"

"Sssh, ye'll wake him."

Angus rocked onto his knees. Either Birdalane Shame had finally lost her mind, or he had. Deciding it had to be her, he collected the fallen meat. "Ye canna keep him. Ye've seen what can happen to women and bairns that *have* protection . . . . They can still become prey. Ye'd be defenseless."

"But the babe and I willna be defenseless." She smiled, flashing her glorious dimples at him. "We have ye . . . for a year and a day."

Chapter 8

"Ye *canna* be serious!" Angus, chest puffed out and his meal apparently forgotten, loomed over Birdi with his hands clenched on his hips.

The babe whimpered and she lifted him into her arms. "I most certainly am." She'd given the matter a great deal of thought. Had been consumed by it all afternoon.

Mother of All, apparently kenning Birdi wouldn't willingly give birth for fear her babe would come into the world as blind and as sensitive to others' pain as she, had taken pity.

She'd seen how Birdi had managed on her own, and kenned Birdi had the skills to survive. And kenning Birdi's devotion—mayhap even her loneliness and how much love lay dormant within her—she'd given Birdi the perfect gift. A babe who would grow into a perfect man . . . with a little guidance from Angus the Canteran. Mother did, after all, love things in pairs.

Of course, the Canteran would have to sleep on a pallet until he could craft a bed for himself, and he'd have to change his manner of livelihood so they'd remain safe and whole, but . . .

Birdi sighed contentedly.

Pacing before her, Angus growled, "I canna believe this!"

"Sssh, ye'll be frightening Wee Angus."

"*Ack!* And she's named him after me." He threw wide his arms. "Merciful Mother—"

"'Tis quite fitting, since ye helped me find him." Birdi decided it might be best to leave the rest of her reasoning for later. Angus MacDougall did appear a wee bit upset.

"Birdi—lass, we've already agreed on a course. We willna be changing it."

"Aye, we agreed, but 'twas before we found the babe." And before Mother of All had interceded. "Dinna fash, Angus, all this—ye finding me and me finding the babe— has happened for a reason."

"Aye, to drive me totally wode." He dropped to his knees beside her and raked his hands through his thick, wavy hair. "Lass, I ken yer fondness for the laddie, I truly do. He's fair and sweet, but he isna yours to keep. Nor am I."

Birdi frowned in confusion. "Why not? Wee Angus's minnie is dead, as is his da, for all we ken. Ye are strong and have proved kind." She felt heat rise in her cheeks at that admission and looked down at the tunic covering her lap. His tunic, one that still carried the enticing scent of him. "I'll make a good wife. I am—if ye'll forgive my immodesty—quite clever with a needle, and resourceful, so why isna this best for all concerned? Bring us back to my croft, and we can live—"

"Birdi, stop!" Angus rose and put his back to her. "I'm sorry, lass, though ye be fair—fairer than any lass I've ever seen—I need marry another. I was on my way to Beal Castle to court her when I found ye. I've pledged my word, Birdi, and I mean to keep it." He faced her, the setting sun placing him in shadow. "We *will* dissolve this handfasting as soon as possible. With that done, ye willna have anyone to keep the bairn safe, so we must find a home for him."

Birdi's mouth dropped open as something painful seared its way from her middle and encircled her heart. Angus was promised to another? 'Twas it the hale and hearty

Mary? Nay, this couldn't be! Mother of All wouldn't have done this to her. Not after all she'd endured.

With the threat of tears burning at the back of her throat, Birdi held her head high and stroked the sleeping babe's fingers. Angus was wrong. She need only prove it to him.

She had to. She had too much to lose, otherwise.

As dawn broke, turning the hills across the loch a deep violet, Angus opened his eyes. They felt gritty for lack of sleep after listening to Birdi's muffled sobs and the babe's repeated wailing the better part of the pitch-black night.

Today should have found him at Beal Castle. But was he there? Nay.

He took a deep, settling breath and let his gaze slowly drift over the curves and swells of the beautiful woman who had started his slide into disaster. If only their circumstances were different . . .

Birdi reclined on her side facing him; her head nestled in the crook of her arm, her black lashes fanning out over high smooth cheeks, her knees touching his thighs, and between Angus and Birdi—trapped and protected—lay Wee Angus blowing bubbles and playing with his fingers.

Merciful Mother of God, what have I gotten myself into?

He still couldn't believed she'd named the babe Angus.

The bairn, apparently thrilled to have finally caught someone's attention, cooed at him and kicked his legs.

Without thought Angus held out a finger. "And what are ye so delighted about so early of a morn?" The babe drew Angus's finger toward his mouth, his eyes crossed, and Angus grinned. Ah, the nipper was hungry, though how he could be after slurping milk half the night was a mystery.

He decided to let Birdi sleep. He could feed a babe. Mayhap if she rested, Birdi would see matters more clearly.

His way.

He rolled away and Birdi, mumbling in her sleep, drew the babe into her chest. As she did, a lock of her hair fell over her shoulder. Wee Angus squealed in delight. He had a fistful. Having wished he could do the same, Angus muttered, "I envy ye, laddie. Truly."

Only a few minutes later, with the goat milked and his horse saddled, Angus returned to the pallet to find Birdi still asleep and Wee Angus chewing contentedly on glossy black curls.

After easing the hair out of the child's mouth and fists, Angus picked the lad up and grabbed a clean nappy from the supply Birdi had garnered, along with a clump of moss.

He settled on a patch of grass at the loch's edge.

It took more effort than expected—the feisty wee imp was intent on rolling every which way but right—but Angus managed to get the lad's bottom covered with a moss-lined nappy.

With the babe draped over an arm, he slopped the dirty nappy in the water, then flung it over a tree branch. "Time to eat," he told the babe. On his way to the fractious goat, he tossed Wee Angus into the air. The babe squealed in delight; Angus grinned and did it again. "Someday," he whispered, "I hope to have a bairn or two as bonnie as ye."

A half hour later, sitting cross-legged in the grass with the contented babe in his lap, Angus asked, "What will become of ye, lad?"

There wasn't a way Birdi could keep the laddie, kind and motherly as she was. The lad couldn't grow properly eating as he had for the last two days. They'd have to find a wet-nurse for him. And the laddie needed a roof over his head. They'd been lucky; last night's ponderous thunderheads had passed without dropping a bit of rain, but more was likely to come, and he didn't want the lad catching the ague.

Examining the babe's perfect pink fingers and nails, Angus admitted, "Wee Angus, ye've put me in a bind."

"Good morn."

Angus looked up to find Birdi, her hair braided, standing at his shoulder. As she reached over him to pet the bairn, Angus caught the irresistible scent of warm woman. Bent as she was it would have taken little effort to pull her mouth down to his. "Good morn."

She nodded and asked the babe, "And how are ye this fine morn?"

In answer Wee Angus smiled as if Birdi had put the sun in the sky for his sole enjoyment.

Ack. The sooner he separated them the better. Rising, he said, "We've goat milk. Otherwise, I need to fish."

"Thank ye, but I dinna feel hungry."

Angus huffed. Birdi had eaten as hungrily as he for three days, so her lack of hunger didn't bode well. She was apparently still fashing over his refusal to let her keep the babe and no doubt planning to use her womanly wiles to convince him he was wrong. As if he ever was. "We'd best get ready to ride, then."

He handed the babe to Birdi, collected their baggage, and tethered the goat behind the snorting and agitated Rampage.

Mounted, he headed south, for Inveruglas. With any luck, the clan would have a midwife who knew of a sacred well—one close at hand—and she might even ken a wet-nurse for the wee one and the whereabouts of Birdi's clan, the Shames. If his luck held, he could then ride hard for Cairndow and Beal Castle, where his bride might wait.

He clucked, Rampage let fly an ill-aimed hoof at the goat, it bleated, and they were on their way.

An hour later Wee Angus filled his nappy.

Birdi gasped. The stench was enough to bring a bull to his knees. "Angus, please, we need stop before I lose my breath."

Angus—leaning back, she noted, as far as his saddle

would allow—muttered, "Aye, I suppose there isna hope for it. Up ahead 'tis a grassy spot."

None too soon he reined in and jumped from the horse. Birdi handed the babe down. Angus, his visage scrunched, held the cooing lad out at arm's length. "How can ye stand yerself, laddie?"

Birdi, grinning, started to slide off the horse on her belly. Halfway down, her tunic caught on the stirrup. As she continued her slide, the tunic rose, leaving her backside exposed to the breeze off the water. Feet finally planted on Mother, she wrenched her tunic free, turned, and found Angus blushing.

As he shifted a bit, Birdi felt heat rush into her cheeks. "Ye've seen it before, Angus." Men were such odd creatures. "Give the babe here."

Clean nappy and moss in hand, she marched with as much dignity as possible to the edge of the loch.

Birdi had just finished tying a new nappy on Wee Angus's clean bottom when she heard lowing and the ring of a cowbell. She spun and found great, light brown masses heading to the water's edge only yards to her right.

A woman called, "Hello."

Birdi scooped Wee Angus into her arms. Heart thudding, she murmured, "Hello."

The woman drew closer, and Birdi was taken by surprise. The woman smiled broadly at her. Tinker had been the only one ever to smile at her in such a fashion. Well, Angus had as well, but only a time or two. Of late he'd been fractious at best.

"I'm Kate, and this," the woman turned a bit and raised an arm, "is my sister Margie."

Birdi, unaware until that moment that there were two women, saw a tall green mass moving toward her.

"I'm Birdi."

Kate came closer and stroked Wee Angus's arm. "And who is this?"

Birdi admired Kate's bright red curls, then noticed the lass's rosy skin bore the ravages of the pox. Poor thing. "'Tis Wee Angus."

The sister, Margie, then tickled the babe, and Birdi saw that this woman was a bit older and definitely fairer than the first, and though she petted Wee Angus, her focus was over Birdi's shoulder.

Her brilliant green eyes bright with curiosity, Margie whispered, "Please tell me that beautiful man standing beside the charger is yer brother."

Beautiful man? Humph! Aye, Angus was more comely than any man Birdi had ever seen before, but . . .

"'Tis my man, Angus MacDougall." Birdi felt decidedly uncomfortable watching the lass's gaze rake Angus's body. Why, she couldna fathom, but uncomfortable she was and she wanted the woman to stop her hungry perusal.

The pretty woman said, "Not *the* Angus MacDougall . . . the one they call Angus the Blood?" The admiration remained on her visage as she made a delicate shudder. "My oh my, aren't ye the brave lassie."

Feeling defensive—she'd heard one of the Fraisers call him Angus the Blood as well, but in less admiring tones— Birdi lifted her chin. "Nay, he's . . . kind."

"Hmm, he certainly looks kind."

When the woman ran her tongue across her lower lip as Wolf had whenever he spied Hen, Birdi found herself hard pressed not to snatch the pretty woman bald-headed.

Jaws clenched, Birdi squared her shoulders. "We must take our leave. 'Twas good meeting ye." She turned and ran smack into Angus's chest.

Cradling her bruised nose as Angus steadied her, Birdi mumbled, "I didna ken ye were there."

Angus snaked an arm around her waist and bowed his head to the two women. "Good day, ladies."

Birdi caught a new tone in Angus's voice, looked up,

and was alarmed to see admiration in his eyes as he studied the pretty sister, Margie. Humph!

And Margie still hadn't pulled her gaze from Angus's broad chest. Aye, 'twas a fine chest to be sure—hard and well muscled—but how rude!

Red-headed Kate mumbled, "Good day, sir," to Angus, then tugged on her sister's arm. "Margie, we need go. Now!"

As Kate hauled her sister away, Birdi heaved a relieved sigh.

Angus murmured, "I found some berries. We need eat and go ourselves."

Arm about her waist, Angus guided a thoughtful Birdi to a grassy knoll overlooking the loch.

As they sat he heard the call of a falcon and looked up. The geld circled twice, folded its wings, and then dove for its unsuspecting prey. 'Twas a good sign. Had danger been riding hard their way, the bird would have sought safer hunting ground. He turned his attention back to the remains of their midday meal and saw that—despite being given ample time and the choicest fish and berries—Birdi had barely touched either. But he should be thankful for small blessings; Birdi's determined, straight-mouthed grimace had softened.

She cleared her throat. "I need ask ye something."

"Ask."

"Are ye honest . . . forthright?"

Unaccustomed to having his integrity questioned, Angus straightened. "Aye, absolutely."

She nodded, apparently pleased with the answer, and asked, "Why do they call ye Angus the Blood?"

It had been too much to hope she hadna heard the Fraiser call him that. " 'Tis a name I've cultivated to protect my clan."

She scowled. "How can a name protect them?"

Angus hesitated. Had she not asked for honesty, he'd have tempered his words, kenning she still feared him; but then, they'd soon be at Inveruglas. Better she hear the story from him than from them. "I am reported to eat the livers of the men I kill in battle. My reputation has caused many a man to flee me rather than risk being eaten should he fall."

Birdi blanched. "Nay!"

"Aye. 'Tis false, of course—I dinna even like liver—but it serves a purpose. Few tread on MacDougall land without good cause. And those that do ken they'd best behave or risk losing a body part to me."

Birdi worried her bottom lip as she gave his answer some thought. "Then why did ye taste me? In the field and again in the cave?"

Angus frowned, then realized she was referring to his kisses, and grinned. "I wasna tasting, but kissing."

"Explain *kissing*."

Never in his wildest dreams had he ever imagined so luscious a woman asking that. He chuckled. "What do ye need explained?"

"The why of it." She twisted the hem of his tunic. She'd refused to don the dead woman's kirtle he'd confiscated for her from Ardlui. "This kissing feels odd to start, ye ken?"

"Aye, but I find it pleasantly odd. Do ye?" He could only hope.

"Aye, but why did ye do it?"

Tread gently, laddie. "Men and women kiss when they feel a craving for each other or when they want to display affection. Just like mothers kiss babes because they love them."

Birdi ruminated on his words for several minutes. "So . . . if I kiss the babe, I'm tellin' him I love him?"

"Aye." Had she never been kissed before? What manner of mother had she? Good God Almighty.

Birdi's forehead scrunched. "So ye kissed me because ye love me?"

Ack. "I kissed ye because ye have a winning way about

ye, because ye are soft in all the right places, and because ye have a mouth any man would want to taste."

"Hmm." She wrenched several blades of grass out of the patch at her feet and started braiding them. "Would ye like to kiss me again?"

What do ye say now, MacDougall? Answer honestly and mayhap cause her to bolt, or lie and regret it for the rest of yer life? Ack.

"Aye, I would."

Chin tucked, she whispered, "Ye may, then."

His heart jolted. Before she could change her mind he leaned across the sleeping babe and placed his right hand on her neck. Using his thumb he raised her chin so he could look into her incredible, icy eyes. He saw no indecision or fear, only curiosity. He drew her closer still, and their mouths made gentle contact.

Her lips, though still, were as soft and pliant as he recalled. Now kenning she was totally unschooled in the matters of men and women, he took his time, increasing the pressure. After a moment he nibbled her lower lip and she gasped, giving him ready access to the sweet, moist confines of her mouth. He eased in and heated blood roared into his groin. Her tongue was as soft as a rose petal. She tasted of berries. Seeing her eyes close, he closed his own and stroked the interior of her mouth for just another moment, savoring her lush interior. He felt her tongue explore his for too short an interval, and then reluctantly pulled away.

To his relief, she sighed, opened her eyes, and then blushed a rosy hue. She cleared her throat, then asked, " 'Tis done?"

"Aye." It had taken all his willpower to pull back, to keep from delving deeper into her in the hopes of chasing away the rest of her reservations, but that wouldn't have been fair to her and certainly not fair to him. 'Twas bad enough he'd have to live with this memory—of what might have been—for a lifetime.

Please, Blessed Mary, let the lass at Beal be worth this sacrifice, or I willna be able to live with myself.

Birdi, her color still high, brushed a few tresses from her face—the ones he'd inadvertently pulled from her braid—and cleared her throat. "Very well."

"Have ye any other questions?"

"Mayhap, later."

Coming to his feet—and hoping she hadn't noticed the swelling within his trews—he said, "Ye best make use of yon bushes. We willna be stopping again 'til we reach Inveruglas."

Birdi took the hand he offered and came to her feet.

Angus studied the gentle sway of her hips as she made her way through the tall grass. Lord, she was one fine woman. She then stumbled over a rock the size of a sow—one any fool could see—and he frowned. He kenned he kissed well—had been told so on more than one occasion—but his kiss certainly couldn't have unsettled her so much that she couldn't see a boulder, could it?

A moment later he found himself wincing as Birdi, her gaze on the ground, nearly knocked herself senseless on a heavy, low-slung pine bough. As she rubbed her forehead and grumbled something, he scowled. She continued on, but this time with a hand out before her. She walked slowly, straight toward a head-high boulder gleaming nearly white in the glare of the afternoon sun. When her hand made contact, she turned left. A moment later she slipped behind a bush.

Something wasn't right.

As he waited, he ruminated over the last three days and the manner in which Birdi moved.

When she reemerged from the bushes, he scrutinized her every step. She followed the exact path she'd taken up to the bush, only this time she paused a few feet before the sow-sized stone. Instead of tripping over it, this time she cautiously skirted it, and then continued toward him. She smiled—despite the red welt on her forehead—as she reached for Wee Angus.

Feeling like a lead yoke had just been dropped onto his shoulders, Angus slowly rose. He patted Rampage's thick neck, then reached into his saddlebag and withdrew the last of his bride gifts, a three-yard roll of white satin ribbon.

With a heavy heart, he held his bride gift out in the palm of his hand—only five feet from Birdi's nose. "I found an apple. One of the lasses must have dropped it. Would ye like it?"

Birdi, babe in her arms, shook her head as she smiled at him. "It looks good, but nay. Ye can have it."

Angus's heart stuttered. The beautiful and resourceful Birdalane Shame was as blind as a mole.

Ian Macarthur, having no appetite for anything but news of his missing spae and the bastard MacDougall, shoved his untouched trencher away.

His men had been on the hunt for two days and should have found them by now. How long could it take to find one wee woman and a bastard knight?

He still couldn't believe she was gone. Not after what he'd done to ensure she was as powerful as possible, more so than her bitchy dame. Were it not for his efforts, the one who called herself Birdi would never even exist. How dare she do this to him?

And when he got his hands on MacDougall, the man would wish he'd never been born. Aye, he'd not simply kill the bastard; he'd take Angus the Blood apart, joint by joint, limb by precious limb.

Relishing the agony MacDougall would suffer, he reached for his tankard, found it empty, and threw it across the room. The three women clearing the tables scattered like startled chickens before him.

"God's teeth! Need I do everything myself? Fetch me more ale, woman!"

The stoutest of them—he thought she might be the smitty's wife—muttered, "Aye, my lord."

He did not care for the sullen look she gave him as she passed to do his bidding, but looked away rather than call her to task. His hold on the clan was already tentative at best. He needn't go looking for trouble.

Since the Campbells had forced the Macarthurs off their lands and out of Dunstaffnage Castle during his father's time, little had gone right for his sept.

His coffers empty, depleted of warriors, his father had been given little say in what lands his sept would then control. His father was told to occupy this place and built a meager keep. Unfortunately for Ian, his father's heir, the clan still wasn't content. The Macarthurs were bred for the sea; they were fishermen and smugglers, not shepherds and farmers. And the land was nay better suited to tilling and harvesting, either. It generated little beyond what they consumed, so he had no ready source of revenue. And there were taxes to pay and tithes. He'd had little to draw men to him.

Until he'd discovered the spae.

With her at his beck and call, he remained fit and could guarantee the health of a strong man and his family in return for his fealty. In a life filled with pestilence and war, that was no small matter.

And now she was gone—like his right hand. He had only one man to blame.

Chapter 9

As they entered the village of Inveruglas, Birdi looked over her shoulder. "What now troubles ye?" Angus—having spent the day clarifying his position on giving the babe away and breaking the handfast—was now unusually quiet.

"I dinna ken, but something isna right here." He paused before a stone building with a thatched roof and dropped to the ground. "Wait here. I need check something." He took several steps, then turned. "I mean it, Birdi, dinna get off that horse."

"As ye lust." Good stars, he was getting testier by the hour. Had it something to do with their kiss?

Aye, she, too, had found it disturbing, but in a new and wondrous way. Minnie had called yearnings evil, but what if Birdi'd misunderstood her mother? How could something so pleasant and warming possibly be evil? Birdi huffed. This not kenning and having no other woman to ask would be the death of her.

She caught the scent of roasting meat on the faint breeze, and her stomach growled. "Do ye ken this family?"

Mayhap they had something she could use to better feed the babe. Might even offer a bit of meat. She'd been foolish refusing food earlier, and now had a pounding head.

"Nay, 'tis a hostiel—an inn."

Ah, Tinker had spoken of inns, large crofts that people could—for a coin—find refuge in for a night or two. The possibility of spending the night with a real mattress beneath her and a fire at her feet brought her a small measure of comfort.

After Angus disappeared through the inn door, Birdi shifted her attention to her surroundings. The village's thatched cottages were close to one another, stout brown blobs strung along the wide roadway. Dark green—what she kenned to be forest—loomed behind them. Before the crofts and to her left still lay Loch Lomond, a wide swatch of glistening black. Before meeting Angus she hadn't kenned lochs could be so grand.

Hearing feet scamper, she turned toward the sound. A woman yelled, "Ye'd best hie, Willie, or ye'll be getting yer bottom blistered." A child answered, "Comin'!" and then all fell silent again but for a dog barking at a distance.

A moment later a familiar tightness encircled her heart and her hands began to itch.

Ack! 'Twas the *need* again. In no mood to heed it, she muttered, "Sheet." She liked the hiss and tension of Angus's word on her tongue. Aye, 'twas a good word, *sheet*.

"Sheet, sheet, sheet." It expressed her frustration with Angus MacDougall and her reluctance to heed the *need* very well indeed.

But Angus was right about one thing. Something was definitely wrong here.

There should be clatter, more comings and goings of clan folk. More than just a mother, a bairn, and a few dogs barking. Why were there no bairns at play, no women laughing as they gossiped, as there had been on the few times she been in the Macarthur's village? From what little she'd gleaned during her visits to her neighbors—and despite the Macarthur's being an unhappy and not particularly caring man—his clan was boisterous, the village noisy.

Aye, something was very wrong here.

* * *

Angus hunched to get through the inn door. Finding himself in an anteroom he pushed through the next door and was greeted by raised voices, one shouting, "The man's a berserker, and I willna pledge me fealty to the likes of him, no matter what he threatens!"

Forty or so clansmen were packed into the low-beamed room. A stout, flame-headed man finally noticed him and yelled, "Welcome, sir!"

All fell silent.

"Good day."

Hands on broad hips, the man asked, "Who be ye and what can we do for ye?"

Angus assessed the room's occupants: all were men, some young, some auld; most were flushed. A few shifted their hands from their lead tankards to the hilts of their dirks while they awaited his response.

"Sir Angus MacDougall, on my way to Beal Castle. I recently passed through Ardlui and am disturbed by what I found there."

Angus wasn't sure if it was the mention of his name or mention of Ardlui that started the shouting match once again, but start it did. Above the din, someone slammed a tankard on a table and demanded silence. All heads turned to the barrel-chested, white-haired gentleman sitting in the corner. He rose and the men parted.

Coming abreast of Angus the gentleman said, "I'm Connor Fraser, leader here, and you, sir, if I'm not mistaken, are the infamous Angus the Blood. Aye?"

Angus's gaze quickly slid around the room; all the occupants now had their hands on dirks. With effort, he kept his hands loose and at his sides. "Aye, sir, I am, and 'tis a pleasure to make yer acquaintance."

The older man took his time eyeing Angus from forelock to shoes. "I kenned yer father, fought beside him at Sterling." He then grunted. "He was a fine and honorable man."

Some of the tension eased out of Angus's shoulders.

"Aye, that he was, sir. I still miss him." Had for nigh on a decade now.

Connor Fraiser asked, "What news do ye bring from Ardlui?"

" 'Tis gone. All are dead and the place is naught but ash and burnt timbers."

The room exploded. Everyone was shouting, most were cursing. One man bellowed, "The bloody bastard!" Fraiser held up his arms. "Quiet! All of ye! Now!"

The room slowly quieted, though grumbling could still be heard in the far corners of the plastered and beamed room.

Fraiser, his voice gruff and commanding, declared, "We need ask this man what he saw, then we can make plans to deal with the Gunn."

Angus's jaw muscles twitched. " 'Tis the Gunn ye've been having troubles with?"

The Gunns were a notoriously unruly lot, had been since the dawn of time; the clan supposedly descended from the Pictish tribes of long ago. He didn't doubt their reported heraldry, given their taste for war.

"Aye, they've been driven south and are trying to reestablish a fife here through coercion and force. We've already lost three men fighting their efforts."

Angus blew out a breath. "That explains it." In great detail, he told the men what he'd found in Ardlui and how he'd dealt with the bodies.

Fraiser, in turn, assigned three men to travel north to bury the dead. "And take the priest with you." Grumbling, "I'm weary of trippin' over him," Fraiser waved Angus to a seat.

Uneasy about leaving Birdi unguarded, Angus said, "My lady awaits me outside. I need bring her and the babe in." Not until he'd said the words did he realize he'd claimed Birdi yet again. God's teeth!

Fraiser nodded. "Please, she's most welcome."

"Is there stabling available for my horse?" The goat could be tied to a fence post if need be.

"Aye, just to the rear."

Angus turned and a glassy-eyed man of about twenty years blocked his path. He tensed when the man placed a hand on his shoulder.

"Are ye certain about Ardlui? My brother . . ." Tears welled in his eyes.

Angus relaxed. "I'm verra sorry, but there wasna a man left alive."

The man took a deep, shuddering breath in an apparent effort to harness his grief, then moved away.

Mentally cursing the beasts that had inflicted such pain, Angus stepped outside.

Birdi had slipped back in the saddle so she could bounce Wee Angus between her thighs. As he approached them, Birdi planted a smacking kiss on the babe's cheek. Wee Angus gurgled and returned the favor with a sloppy kiss of his own.

Shaking his head, Angus said, "We'll rest here for a wee bit." He'd yet to query anyone about a wet-nurse or a sacred well. As he reached for Birdi he noticed her palms were red. "What's wrong with yer hands?"

Scratching, Birdi mumbled, " 'Tis nothing. Did ye learn what's wrong here?"

He lifted her from the saddle and set her on the ground. "Aye, another clan is trying to move into the area by force. The men inside believe they destroyed Ardlui."

As he guided her toward the inn's door—he didn't trust she'd find it on her own—Birdi asked, "But why would they slaughter when all they need do is ask permission to stay? There's more than enough land about."

Angus rolled his eyes. Birdalane Shame wasn't only as blind as a bat, but as naive as the bairn in her arms. How she'd managed to survive this long was beyond kenning.

"Land is power, Birdi, both political and financial. Whoever holds sway over this loch controls the water and a primary food supply for hundreds. Men have been known to kill for less."

Birdi shook her head and muttered, "Minnie was right again. Men are fools."

He grinned. She had a point. Here he was, risking his future to see her and the babe safe, and for what? A kiss and an opportunity to see gratitude in winter-blue eyes.

Birdi, scrubbing her free palm against her tunic, entered the inn. Hearing the deep growl of angry men all talking at once, her stomach flipped, then quivered. She couldn't tell how many were before her in the dark close space, but decided there were definitely too many.

When Angus took her elbow and tried to guide her farther into the room, she balked. "Nay, I need stay by the door . . . should the babe cry." *Or I need bolt.* If she went any deeper into the room she'd likely get trapped.

"As ye lust." He left her for a moment, then returned with a stool. "Sit. I'll find us some food."

Birdi only nodded, too agitated by the *need* and by the boisterous crowd to trust her voice. When she sensed Angus had moved away, she snaked out a hand to the right. Feeling a breeze seeping along a thin space, she relaxed a bit. Angus had placed her stool next to the door.

With one fear—of being trapped—managed, she tried to ease the heavy feeling within her chest with deep breaths, but the *need* continued to grow. Someone was crying out for help, needed her, but she couldn't help. Not now. She had to stay well. She had to care for the babe and she had precious little time to convince Angus she was right and he was wrong about her keeping the babe and their handfasting.

Angus MacDougall was nothing like she'd been taught to expect. After their initial encounter, he'd been kind for the most part. When he wasn't being totally considerate of her, he'd been only grumbly, more angry or impatient with himself than with her. Too, when he did smile it was as if a candle had been lit behind his eyes. They were so bright and warming, like a fire at gloaming. She sighed.

She had so little time and so much to accomplish.

Birdi started bouncing Wee Angus on her lap as she easily imagined the three of them living within her croft, Angus hunting, Birdi tending a small garden, and Wee Angus growing tall and strong at her knee. Quite pleased, she kissed his cheek and gave voice to the song she'd heard a villager sing so long ago.

Dance tae yer daddy
Ma bonnie laddie
Dance tae yer daddy, ma bonnie lamb!
An ye'll get a fishie
In a little dishie
Ye'll get a fishie whan the boat comes home.

Drooling, Wee Angus chuckled, and Birdi's heart soared. "Ah, so ye liked that, did ye?" She stood him on her lap and kissed his cheek.

"Ye have a pleasing voice."

Startled, Birdi looked over Wee Angus's head to find a white-headed man with very sad eyes kneeling before her. Heat infused her cheeks. "Thank ye."

Holding a gnarled finger out for Wee Angus to grasp, the man murmured, "My grandson enjoyed that ditty as well. His name was Brion . . . Brion Frasier. He would have been one year come Christmas."

When Birdi frowned in confusion, he said a bit louder, "Christmas, the holiday close to Samhain."

"Aye." Birdi still had no idea what Christmas entailed, but Samhain, the midwinter solstice, was one of her days to pay homage to Goddess.

Something deep inside warned not to ask the next obvious question, but the words came anyway. "What happened to the babe?"

"He died of a chest flux just three days past. We—his parents and I—kenned it could happen . . . . He was born frail so we'd been warned it could, but we still were'na prepared for it. He was so sweet and . . ."

A tear slid down the elder's face as he struggled to restrain the sob. Birdi's heart wrenched in sympathy. Suspecting he was the source of the deep, grieving *need* tormenting her, she asked, "How are ye faring?"

The man shrugged. "As well as an auld man can when he outlives bairns."

"And his parents?"

"Parent. Collin . . . the babe's da . . . he was killed in a skirmish with the Gunns two days ago."

Stunned that the man shouldered such great loss, Birdi touched his wet cheek. Aye, he ached with bone-deep grief, but to her great surprise his grief wasn't the one calling out, reaching for her. This man was ready for death, awaited it, would have welcomed it. "I'm so verra sorry for yer losses, sir."

"Thank ye, but I didna come over to ye to garner sympathy. I spoke with yer man, MacDougall. He tells me ye are seeking a wet-nurse for the babe, and my Kelsea has milk . . . ." He took a deep, shuddering breath. "I dinna ken if she'll agree, but . . ."

Birdi stopped listening. A fearful dread scurried through her blood. Her breath caught and her palms began to sweat. Her heart and mind were screaming *nay* so loudly she could hear nothing else.

She hauled Wee Angus off her lap and clutched him to her chest.

Nay, Goddess! He belongs to me! Mother of All, you gave him to me! Tears welled in Birdi's eyes as fire tore at her throat.

The old man stroked Wee Angus's cheek as tears once again flooded his eyes. "We can ask her."

Birdi shook her head, then jerked, hearing Angus say, "I

think we need ask, Birdi. I'm sorry, lass, but ye ken the babe canna grow as he should living on goat milk dripped from yer fingers."

She tried to focus on Angus through watery eyes. "I canna . . . I need time . . . ." The rest stuck in her throat.

She wanted to tell him she had a lifetime of untapped love to give this bairn and so much to teach him—about Goddess and chants—and so much to share—where the apples hid, how to find the softest flax, when to hunt for elderberries . . . . But the words simply wouldn't take shape.

Angus knelt beside her. "Come, lass. I ken this is hard, but ye must do it for the babe's sake." Taking her by the elbow, he brought her to her feet.

Birdi, the struggling babe clutched to her chest, looked about the comfortable earthen-floored room she stood in. It smelled of recently roasted meat, tallow candles, and peat fire, but how she came to be in the room, she could not have said.

The man with white hair motioned to his left. "Come, Kelsea's in here."

Unwilling, but kenning she must, Birdi took a deep breath and placed one foot forward. She dragged the other after it. To her dismay, Angus whispered words of encouragement at her back as he followed them. She tried to shut them out.

At a doorway she heard the old man say, "Kelsea dear, we have company."

Birdi stepped over the threshold and became vaguely aware she stood on a slate floor. By the light of a single window, its shutters thrown wide, she saw a large dark shape in the center of the room, assumed it to be the woman's bed, and eased toward it.

When she received no greeting, Birdi leaned forward to better glean the woman.

Kelsea Fraiser was very young, mayhap three or so summers younger than Birdi herself, yet looked to be fourscore or more older, particularly around her teary sable eyes. As she sat up in bed, lax hands in her lap, her freckle-dusted skin was pale, her cheeks drawn, and her lips as dry and cracked as an old oak's bark.

With pain searing the back of her throat—she now kenned whence the clawing *need* had come—Birdi reluctantly held Wee Angus out in shaking hands. "He's hungry, and I havna milk to give. Will ye nurse him?"

The widow Kelsea looked at Wee Angus for a moment, and, visage unchanged, turned her head toward the window.

Birdi set Wee Angus down on the bed and reluctantly reached for the woman's hand. The moment their hands touched, raw, unbridled anguish rushed through Birdi's chest, closed off her air, and chilled her blood. Stars floated before her eyes as her heart stuttered. Body shaking, she released the woman's hand.

Kelsea was willing herself to die. She couldn't take the pain of losing both her husband and her bairn any more. With that realization Birdi's mind filled with her mother's dying words: *Beware! When the blood curse comes another may come with it. If it does, they'll try to use ye as they have me, for their own ends. Spit in their eye, little birdalane. Spit in their eye.*

Birdi—awash with resentment, anger, and now fear, kenning Goddess had betrayed her—nonetheless said to Angus, "Take her into the other room and set her in the chair." She couldn't do what needed to be done standing on slate.

Tears sluicing down her cheeks, Birdi stepped back so Angus could lift the widow into his arms.

I'm sorry, Minnie, but I canna heed ye, even kenning what is to come. Though Goddess kenned she wanted to ignore this call so badly her bones felt brittle with the aching need to run.

She reluctantly followed the men into the sitting room. Once the widow Kelsea was settled, Birdi turned to Angus. "Go, both of you."

The grandfather started sputtering, "But I dinna—"

Years of deep-seated fear then coupled with her current despair. Birdi growled, *"Do as I say."*

Angus eyed her warily for only a moment, then took the auld man by the arm. " 'Tis women's work they're about. We men best take our leave."

When she heard the door close, Birdi took a deep, settling breath and tried to steel herself.

Slowly she spread the woman's thighs, stepped between them, and laid her precious Wee Angus in the woman's flaccid hands. The bairn, trapped as he was between them, would be safe as she did what needed to be done.

Feet firmly planted on Mother, she looked into Kelsea's eyes. Terror stared back at her. " 'Tis nay reason to fear," she whispered, "only reason to hope."

Accepting the babe would belong to another, that she now had nay reason to hope for or protect herself, Birdi placed one shaking hand behind the woman's neck and the other on her forehead. Voice cracking, aware her heart was already fracturing, she whispered, "Goddess, Mother of All, I beg to take upon myself this woman's pain and grief, to ease her heart . . . to mend her spirit. Please . . . though ye must see me as unfit"—she choked on a sob—"please help her."

She then closed her eyes and waited for what would come.

The babe would no longer be hers to cherish, and Angus the Canteran would soon leave as well. Minnie's voice rang in her ears. *Luckless birdalane, ye're fated to be alone.*

Chapter 10

As the auld man calmly cleaned his nails with a gleaming sgian dubh, Angus, his gaze locked on the Fraiser's door, paced—six strides right, six strides left. "How long can it possibly take to put a wee laddie to breast?"

Birdi had been inside for well on to an hour now, and something inside Angus's head had been chafing in warning every minute of it. He never ignored such warning in battle and was hard pressed to keep ignoring it now.

Malcolm Fraiser shrugged. "Kelsea's breasts were bound after our Brion passed. Mayhap it takes time to get milk flowing again?"

"Aye." But his gut said 'twas more than that.

The door latch finally clicked and he heaved a sigh of relief. "Thank God."

When the door opened, he was startled to see not Birdi but the Fraiser woman, her cheeks now touched with a bit of pink and in her arms, sucking contentedly at her breast, Wee Angus.

"Where's Birdi?"

"Come." Kelsea stepped aside so they could enter.

Angus came to an abrupt halt just inside the door.

Birdi—so pale he could see the vessels carrying her life's blood pulsing from across the room—sat on the floor before the chair the Fraiser woman had once occupied, grieving as if her heart would break. 'Twas as if Birdi and Kelsea had crawled inside each other's skin, or mayhap exchanged souls, which made nay sense at all. "Merciful Mother of God!"

He rushed to her, scooped her onto his lap, and cradled her to his chest. "What the hell happened to her?"

Instead of answering, the Fraiser woman squatted and took Birdi's tear-streaked chin in her hand. As they stared at each other, he could almost feel an understanding pass between them. That, he didn't like.

Kelsea kissed Birdi's cheek and then rose. As she adjusted the babe in her arms, she murmured, "I dinna ken, sir." She then sat in the chair, her attention directed toward the babe.

Unaccustomed to being thwarted, he growled and lifted Birdi's chin with a gentle finger and stared into her tearing eyes. Seeing only desolation and grief, his skin crawled with apprehension. "Lass, what ails ye? What can I do?"

" 'Tis naught ye can do, Angus."

She shuddered and he pulled her closer.

Her answer wasn't acceptable. Not so long as he drew breath. There had to be something he could do. Spying Malcolm Fraiser he said, "Bring her some mulled wine, mead, I dinna care what, so long as it's warm."

Brow furrowed, Fraiser answered, "Aye, right away."

As he shuffled off Angus called after him, "And a blanket. She's freezing."

Wee Angus gurgled into the ensuing silence, and the Fraiser woman lifted him onto her shoulder. Pounding gently on his back, she asked, "Does this precious laddie have a name?"

Before Angus could give it, Birdi's nails dug deep into his arm with surprising strength. She took a shuddering breath—one he felt clean into his gut as he held her.

"Nay," Birdi whispered, "ye need choose one for him."

The corners of Kelsea's lips lifted ever so slightly. "Aye, but I must think hard." She put the babe to her other breast and stroked his cheek. "It must be perfect to compensate for all he's been through."

Birdi murmured, "Aye," and pressed her face into Angus's shoulder, which did naught to muffle her next sob.

He never should have asked about a wet-nurse, and sure as hell shouldn't have brought Birdi here. *Ack! Birdi, lass, I'm so sorry. Had I kenned . . .*

Fraiser came back into the room bearing steaming tankards, a blanket, and a tin of shortbread. He knelt before Angus. "I brought mead for ye as well."

"Thank ye."

Angus wrapped the blanket about Birdi, then held a tankard to her lips. "Lass, drink this."

She took a sip, choked, and pushed it away. He forced more on her, until he was satisfied she'd consumed a good half pint. 'Twould make her sleepy, and sleep, he'd decided, might prove the best medicine for whatever ailed her. She certainly hadn't had much sleep since they'd found the babe.

Fraiser cleared his throat. "Since Collin's death, Kelsea's been staying here. Why don't ye spend the night in Kelsea's croft? I'll take ye, 'tis only a short walk away, the first one just beyond the kirk. I'll bring some sup to ye after a wee bit."

Kelsea murmured, "Aye, please do. There's peat for a fire by the inglenook and ye'll find the bed comfortable." Her gaze shifted from Angus to Birdi, who now appeared to be asleep. "And please, have her choose a gown and whatever else she might need from the wooden chest at the foot of the bed. Anything at all may be hers."

" 'Tis most generous of ye."

Kelsea shook her head. " 'Tis yer wife who is generous. I willna ever be able to repay her kindness."

Fraiser held the door open as Angus—with Birdi in arms—angled his way into the one-room croft. Two sturdy chairs, one with rockers, sat before an ingle-side made from smooth river-rock. A pile of aged peat lay on the hearth. A waxed pine table and two cuttie stools stood to the right, and a large pine bed to the left. Alongside the bed stood an empty, polished oak cradle.

Angus laid Birdi on the fine feather mattress, pulled the blanket about her, and turned to find Fraiser lighting the fire. "I thank ye for offering yer daughter's home to us for the night. Birdi wouldna have been comfortable at the inn." He'd noticed she'd been anxious earlier when surrounded by strangers and couldn't imagine how she'd respond in her current state.

Fraiser rose and dusted off his hands. "Ack. 'Tis our pleasure. And ye're right; the men over yon will be arguing half the night trying to decide what to do about the Gunn and his lot. Yer ladywife wouldna get any rest."

As Fraiser walked to the door, Angus said, "Ye should take the cradle with ye. Wee . . . the wee one will need it."

And Birdi need not see it. She'd likely greet until her generous heart was reduced to the size of a shriveled plum.

Fraiser picked up the cradle. Looking from it to Birdi as she lay pale and still, his eyes grew glassy. "Take good care of her. What she did today . . ." His voice cracked and faltered. Using the heels of his hands he scrubbed the wetness from his eyes. "I'll come by in a few hours with yer sup."

After Fraiser took his leave, Angus dropped the wooden bar over the door.

Standing bedside the bed, he whispered, "What happened to ye behind that door, lass?"

He'd left her fashing but hale and the Fraiser woman looking about to waste away. An hour later he found the reverse, and it frightened him.

He lay down beside her and cradled her in his arms, her head resting on his chest. He brushed a strand of hair from her forehead. Rolling the curly tip between his fingers, he recalled the first time he'd set eyes on her, how he'd imagined burying his fists in her hair.

"Do ye have any idea how much I want ye, Birdalane Shame? And despite yer being a bit willful and painfully proud." He sighed, examining the bruise in the middle of her forehead. "Ye should have told me about yer wee secret, lass . . . that ye canna see but a yard ahead of ye. Aye. It might have saved ye a few bonks on yer beautiful head."

And just as she wanted Wee Angus and couldn't keep him, he wanted but couldn't keep her. And the kenning made something deep inside his chest ache with regret.

" 'Tis a sorry state we've got ourselves in, Birdi, my love. A truly sorry state."

He'd asked Fraiser if he kenned the Shame clan. The man said he'd never heard mention of them. Angus then asked after the location of a sacred well. Fraiser shook his head. He suggested Angus ask in Cairndow.

If a well wasn't to be found there, they'd have to ride north, around the northern tip of Loch Fyne, then ride south to Inveraray, all of which would eat up precious time. Ack. Would Birdi be up to the ride, given her current state?

Birdi, mumbling incoherently, stretched. As she pressed against him, he felt the soft compression of a breast against his chest. A second later her left leg fell across his thigh and settled between his legs, her knee close to his groin. Two days ago he'd have killed to get her in the same position. Now, his heart only ached for her. Her brow then furrowed, and he stroked her back as gently as possible. What manner of goblins would dare chase such a lovely lass in her sleep?

The darkness parted.

Birdi crept closer to the clatter of wood beating on wood. The village bairns were back playing sword-fight at the edge of the golden field.

She kenned better than to show herself—her mother had warned repeatedly she'd come to harm if she did—but the lads sounded so happy. What harm could there be in just listening to them? They were, after all, just bairns about her age.

As she ducked behind a tall weed patch one lad bragged, "My da can flatten yer da any time he chooses, Will Macarthur."

"Nay, ye braggart, my da's a smitty, the strongest in the realm. He can whip yer da in thrice."

She heard a scuffle and an "Ooow" before one of the lads, keening, ran away.

"Ack, Robbie," the other called as he followed, "I didna mean to bloody yer nose!"

Disappointed—kenning they wouldn't likely return this day—Birdi turned for home, her mind ablaze with a dozen questions for her mother.

She found her before their croft. "Minnie, who's my da?"

Grinding a pestle, separating oat from husk, her mother grumbled, "Ye dinna have one."

Birdi's heart tripped at her lie. She'd spent enough time spying on the villagers to ken everyone had one. She stomped a foot. "Tell me about my da."

Minnie rounded, startling her, fists on hips. "Shame's yer sire; my shame, his shame, and yours for asking about matters that are none of yer concern and best forgotten." Minnie's face loomed large as she clamped a rough hand on Birdi's shoulder. "Ye are never to ask again. Do ye ken?"

Quaking, Birdi squeaked, "But—"

The resounding slap caught Birdi off guard. Cheek and eyes stinging, she keened, "Aye, Minnie, never again."

"Now fetch me more water from the pool and be quick about it, or ye'll not be having yer oats for sup." She then slapped Birdi's bottom, sending her in the direction of the *water bag. Birdi fell. Stars flashed; bright white wee suns in a field of black.*

Then total darkness returned.

"Minnie! Where are ye, Minnie?" Birdi—her heart quaking against her ribs, her palms and back sweaty and frigid—moved cautiously within the darkening woods. The sun, having slipped behind the hills, left only unfathomable shadows before her.

Minnie had never been gone this long. Never, in her eight summers.

Feeling her way along the path that led to the road separating her world from that of the villagers, Birdi called out again. The bushes to her right rattled and she jumped. Hands at her throat, readying to scream, she heard the frantic flapping of wings.

She blew out a breath, scrubbed at the tears clouding her vision only to have more form, and resumed her search. Minnie loathed greeting, but Birdi couldn't help it. The dark terrified her and her feet and ears were already aching with the cold. *"Minnie! Where are you?"*

Birdi had checked everywhere: the pool, the mushroom patch, the traps, even the edges of the fields, and still no Minnie. Where could she be?

An awful tightening seized her chest. Had Minnie left her? Had she been so angered by Birdi's questions about her da that she'd up and left?

Birdi stumbled down the path leading to the ancient stump, the only place left to look. *"Oh, Goddess, please, I'll be a good bairn, I promise. Please, please, dinna let it be true. Please, Goddess, please help me find my minnie."*

Birdi heard a sob. *"Minnie? Minnie!"*

Hands outstretched, she ran toward the dark shape lying before her on a bed of fallen leaves.

Minnie lay curled on her side on the path. Birdi dropped to her knees and pushed her mother's graying, disheveled

*hair off her face. "Minnie, what's wrong?" As her mother
groaned, Birdi noticed she knelt in wetness and caught the
unmistakable scent of blood, metallic and dry at the back
of her throat. "Oh, Minnie . . ." Squinting, Birdi then saw
that her mother's hands clutched her blood-soaked kirtle
at the waist.*

In a breathy whisper, Minnie said, "A boar . . . help me."

*It took all Birdi's strength to get Minnie onto her feet. As
they wavered and fell, Minnie kept saying, "Dinna . . . let
them . . . ken I'm gone."*

*Birdi struggled under her mother's weight. "I willna,
Minnie, but dinna fash. Ye'll be all better come morn. I
promise."*

*Knees and hands bleeding from repeated falls, sick to
her stomach with apprehension, Birdi got Minnie into their
croft and onto her bed. All she'd learned at her mother's
knee, the herbs and tonics, the poultices she'd pulled from
Minnie's bag, all the prayers she'd been taught, Birdi then
put to full use.*

*As dawn broke on the fourth day, Birdi, bleary eyed from
lack of sleep and hours of greeting, dropped to her knees.
"Come, Goddess, please, and make her well. I canna do
this alone. I'm too wee and dinna ken enough. Please
come and help me."*

*Minnie now took only one breath to Birdi's six, each
sounding like a rattling seed-pod. Her lips were so cracked
they bled despite the salve Birdi applied; her skin was so
hot Birdi feared she'd cook. But the worst was Minnie's silence. Desperate for one word—even a curse—as the sun
turned the room's whitewashed clay walls a dull pink,
Birdi shook her mother's shoulders. "Minnie, wake up.
Wake up!"*

*To her horror, Minnie took a single, rattling breath and
went completely silent.*

*Birdi collapsed onto her mother's still chest. "Nay! Min-
nie, wake up! Ye're scaring me, Minnie, wake up!"*

Her mother would be angry . . . . Birdi was taking too long to make her better, but that would be all right. It would. She could shout—even thrash Birdi all she wanted—because she'd be better and that was all that mattered. Aye, that was all that mattered. "Goddess, Mother of All, can ye hear me? Make Minnie talk to me. Now please. Please. Please. Please."

"I canna . . . breathe . . . . Minnie. I'm so scared . . . Minnie, Minnie . . . aaaaaah!"

A hand brushed her cheek. "Sssh, love, ye're safe. 'Tis only a dream, Birdi. Hush."

Birdi fought her way through her throat-seizing blackness in search of the source of the soothing words. The deep, burring voice, the smell, the heat surrounding her meant safety. She took a shuddering breath and finally managed to open her eyes.

Breath hitching, she whispered, "Angus."

"Aye." He wiped the wetness from her cheeks. "I didna mean to wake ye, but ye were deep in a nightmare, and none too happy about it."

Feeling the fool—her heart still beating at a frantic pace—she struggled to sit. "I'm sorry, I dinna—"

"Sssh, we all have them." He pulled her into his side, holding her close with an arm. "'Tis naught to be ashamed of. Are ye better now?"

Taking another shuddering breath, deciding there was no harm in taking comfort just this once, she relaxed against him. "Aye, much better."

He smiled. "Ye had me fashing for a moment."

"Sorry."

"Do ye have these terrors often?"

"Nay." Only whenever she healed another. She'd then wake so parched and hoarse she'd wonder if she'd screamed the night away.

He gently stroked her back. "Would ye like to talk about it? Mayhap it will make them go away for good."

" 'Tis naught but an old memory." She yawned, deciding it must be time to feed Wee Angus. Then the day's events crashed down upon her with the swiftness of a giant tree felled by lightening. A great, racking sob escaped before she could grab hold of it.

Her wee precious babe was gone.

"Ack, lass, sssh." Angus rolled onto his side and drew her closer. As she buried her face into the massive warm muscles of his chest, he kissed the top of her head. "Have ye ever seen a dolphin, love?"

She shook her head, unable to speak as she tried to cope with the pain squeezing the life out of her.

In a voice barely above a whisper he told her, "They're wondrous creatures—part fish, part man, according to legend. Gray and white, slick and smooth as polished steel, they roam the seas in herds of tens, leaping and gliding as if they hadna a care in the world.

" 'Tis a good omen when they frolic about a man's boat. They occasionally whistle as they keep pace with ye, their wide mouths smiling. Aye, they're verra fine, have been known to save drowning men by keeping them afloat with their powerful snouts and fins until help could arrive.

"When I was a lad of eight years—the year my minnie died—a lone mother dolphin and calf came into Drasmoor Bay. Since this had never occurred before it caused quite a stir. Some claimed 'twas a good omen. Others claimed 'twas a sign something dreadful had happened or was about to happen at sea. 'Twasna until a few brave souls rowed out to greet her that the truth was kenned.

"The babe with her had been attacked, and from the look of the wounds, by a fearsome shark or whale.

"Much fashing then ensued about what to do to help them. Since the fishing was poor within the bay, some men went out to sea each day and hauled back fish for the mother. Women concocted salves made of lanolin so they wouldna dissolve in the salty sea when applied to the babe's raw wounds. Being a bairn myself, and a bit fanciful at the time, I could do little but go out and watch the elders tend them, pray, and give the pair names. I named the mother Bigly, for she was indeed beautiful, and the wee one Dautie, for all thought of him with great affection. Days passed.

"Then one morn I awoke to the news the babe hadna made it through the night. Lass, I greeted 'til my heart nearly broke."

Birdi opened her eyes to find tears glistening in Angus's. So he'd loved and lost, too—his minnie and the dolphin all in one year. He understood.

She traced the gentle curves of his lips with a finger. Then to her own surprise she stretched a bit so they were face to face and kissed him. Softly, just as he had kissed her.

As she pulled away he smiled and cleared his throat. "Bigly left and life went on," he told her. "Then one morn we awoke to a trumpeter's blast. We all raced out to see what was amiss—we were having our fair share of troubles with the Bruce at the time—and found Auld Brian jumping and shouting on the shore looking fit to be tied.

"To our amazement, there, out in the harbor—bobbing and arching between Castle Blackstone and shore—was Bigly, the mother we'd all come to care about.

"I was simply beside myself with joy and scrambled into the first boat launched. We rowed out to greet her, and discovered she'd come to show us something—her new bonnie calf. He was a lighter gray than the other and bigger, his smiling mouth clicking and clacking at a pace so fast I could barely distinguish one from the other."

Angus brushed the loose strand from her face and kissed her ever so gently. "Ye'll have another in time, love, as bonnie as yer foundling, but one of yer heart and blood that no one can ever take away."

He silently studied her, no doubt hoping she would nod in agreement.

He cared that she ached near beyond breathing, but he didn't—couldn't—ever ken her deepest heartache: that all he'd promised would never come to pass. She was cursed . . . a near-blind spae.

Lusting she could share her grief, but kenning she never would, she nodded for his sake.

He squeezed her a wee bit. "That's the lass." He then whispered, "I dinna ken what transpired while ye were alone with Kelsea Fraiser, but I do ken ye are beyond any doubt the bravest and most generous woman I've ever met. I'm verra glad I ken ye, Birdalane." He stroked her cheek. "I mean that sincerely."

She fell in love with Angus MacDougall at that moment; heart, mind, and essence, she toppled. Seeking the warmth and strength radiating from him, she reached up and placed a hand behind his neck as he had once done to her and drew his mouth to hers.

He groaned into her mouth as she parted her lips. A heartbeat later he took control, his kiss searing a path deep into her being. Heat flashed in her belly, and miraculously, the pain squeezing her chest eased. Light-headed and breathless, she gave in to the heart-warming sensations and need she hadn't words to describe.

Chapter 11

Angus's heart thundered, his mind and body totally consumed with need for the beauty in his arms. He pressed firm hands to her back, bringing her soft curves into perfect alignment with his harder planes. Aye, this lass with her secret had been made for him, molded to him as none before. Her compassion, her foibles enchanted him.

His tongue played across hers in shameless abandon, stroking, tasting, and teasing. When she mewed deep in her throat, lightning flashed through every vessel and organ he owned. She then arched, pressing closer, and he rolled instinctively.

He settled above her, his weight on his arms. As his hips gently rocked, pressing his swollen need between her quaking thighs, heat radiated off her with an intensity that nearly took his breath away.

Good God, the woman was made for loving.

He buried one hand deep into her luxurious hair just as he had dreamed of doing for four long days. He stroked her cheek. The soft press of her heaving breasts against his chest called to him and he gently slid his lips across her satin jaw, nibbling here and there as he eased down toward the glorious prize awaiting his eager hands and mouth. She smelled of babe and grass, of lust and woman, of all any man could ever want as her breath caught in uneven pants. His lips grazed along the column of her long slender neck, licking at her pulse, stroking that tender place above her collarbone. To his delight, her flushed skin pebbled and quivered. Her blood thundered under his fingers as they caressed her throat. *Aye, lass, yer heart bounds as mine does.*

He nuzzled at the edge of the gaping tunic she wore—his—and her hands fluttered up his ribs. *Do ye ken, lass, what I want to do—nay, need do—to satisfy the hunger ye've stirred in me?*

His mouth had no difficulty finding the delicious, high swells he sought. Each quivered with mesmerizing delicacy with each hot lick. Ack, and the cloth hid the best. He could see in his mind's eye the deep rose-tipped crests that lurked lower still, with nipples now ridged and straining against the fabric that once had covered his chest.

His right hand slid up and over her delicate ribs. Cupping one soft swell with the palm of his hand, he groaned and eased lower, his lips seeking the hard nubs making wee tents in the fabric. *Ack, she's more than any man could ever hope to have.* Hands buried deep in his hair, Birdi mewed her approval. Good God Almighty, he wanted her, ached with tight painful need.

As his free hand slid down her thigh, seeking the hem of her covering, he heard a faint knocking at some great distance. Dismissing it, he turned his attention to her other breast. Drawing the tip into his mouth through the fabric, he heard her gasp and felt her back arch, giving him better purchase. "Aye, lass. 'Tis the way."

He sucked again and her legs wrapped about his waist. Her hips lifted, pressing moist heat into his bare stomach. "Oh, Birdi."

She was panting now, anxious for what she didn't ken, but he did. Oh, aye, he most certainly did.

Panting through gritted teeth, he shifted his weight to better lift the tunic blocking his access to the rose-tipped breasts he craved. He wanted her naked.

Claim her, something deep within ordered.

As the tunic rose above her waist, a hard rap sounded. "MacDougall, I've yer sup!"

Ack! Not now, man. I'm about to—

Ah, shit!

He was about to tup the stuffing out of the woman he'd craved for days and thereby consummate the handfasting he'd sworn to break. God's teeth! What was he thinking?

And there it was . . . the truth. He hadn't been thinking past comforting her, not at all. His brain had deserted his head and run to his bag o' sweeties.

He reluctantly eased the tunic back down over Birdi's hips. Heart still beating at a breakneck pace, he reluctantly rolled onto his back.

As the knocking on the door resounded around the croft yet again, he blew out a frustrated breath and pulled Birdi into his side. He brushed a lock from her forehead. "I'm sorry, lass, but Fraiser's apparently determined to feed us or ken the reason why."

And thank God.

The man would never ken he'd unwittingly saved Angus the Blood's sorry arse and Birdi's virtue, but Angus did, and would never forget it.

Birdi—her cheeks flushed, her gaze a bit unfocused—ran a slow hand across the fine hairs on his heaving chest. "But I dinna want food, Angus."

Sorely tempted to ask what she did want, he thought better of it. He'd likely give it to her, pledge or no pledge, Donaliegh; or no Donaliegh; for something beyond lust—beyond compassion—whispered *mine!* whenever he held her gaze.

"Aye, I ken, love—more than ye'll ever know—but we'd best let the man in before he breaks down the door."

And they sure as hell couldn't spend the night together in this bed. He'd best sleep on the floor.

Birdi, lower lip caught between small even teeth, nodded. Using his chest as a fulcrum, she sat up. Fingers splayed like the teeth of a comb, she pushed the hair off her face and looked about as if confused.

Guilt rippled in his gut. "Are ye all right, lass?"

She shrugged as she contemplated his question. "More befuddled than anything, I think." When the pounding started again, she murmured, "Mayhap ye best let the man in."

Angus rolled out of bed, painfully aware of the swollen tightness pressing against his belly. Raking his hands through his hair, he took his time getting to the door.

Fraiser, arms nigh on to overflowing, greeted him with a smile. "Good eve."

Angus, a full head taller, grunted and waved the man in.

Fraiser headed for the table. "I'd have let ye sleep, but experience has taught me these fish pies are best eaten hot." He chuckled. "My Kelsea may be fair on the eye but she's rough on a man's gut, though God kens she tries." He dropped the basket of singed pies on the table along with a round loaf of dark bread and a crock of honey. A pitcher of ale followed with a loud thunk. "If ye're still hungry after all this, just shout. There's more, more's the pity."

Fraiser turned as Birdi stood. "And how are ye feelin', lass?"

Birdi managed a brittle smile. In truth, she felt awful, like she'd been hauled through brambles feet first, then trounced upon. Her skin felt too tight, still tingled with the memory of Angus's hands and mouth. Her belly still churned—with what, she didn't ken—but churn it did, while her heart felt like a lodestone in the middle of her chest. "A bit better, thank ye."

"Good. My Kelsea's been fashin' somethin' awful about ye."

Birdi only nodded. She wanted to cry, *as goes yer daughter's joy, so goes my anguish,* but she couldn't. She never had and never would let those she healed ken what helping them did to her.

" *'Tis yer burden alone to bear,*" Minnie had warned on her deathbed, *"should ye, too, have the gift. 'Tis yer penance."*

Birdi took a deep, shuddering breath, wanting but unable to ask after Wee Angus; kenning that if she did the fragile wall—the levee Angus had somehow created with his kisses—would break and the mind-bending pain still lurking within her would rush out and wreak havoc once again.

Fraiser eyed the dwindling fire and threw a few blocks of peat into it. He then turned and smiled. "I'll take my leave now and let ye eat. If ye need anything, ye'll find me at home."

When he left, Birdi held her breath, anxious to ken what Angus would next do. Would he take her in his arms again, reinforcing the levee he'd built? She could only hope and pray to Goddess that he would.

Angus cleared his throat and then pulled out a chair, indicating she should sit. She did, wondering why he appeared so uncomfortable. He found two cups, then sat across from her, broke the bread, put food before her, and started eating.

All without touching her, without saying a word. Confused, she reached for his hand, and he snatched it away, but not before she sensed his inner need for withdrawal.

Stinging pain erupted within her chest; though all too familiar, it hurt far more than usual. Appetite gone, she swallowed the thickness burning at the back of her throat and folded her hands in her lap. What had she done or said that he now wanted to keep his distance from her? Had it been her kiss? Had it been her refusal to ask after Wee Angus? If she asked him what was the matter, he'd no doubt deny anything was wrong, just as the villagers always did when she'd found the courage to ask. Finding the room suddenly stifling, fearing she'd start to greet and never stop, she pushed back her chair and rose. Without thought she held out her hands, seeking the door she kenned to be at her back.

"Where are ye going?"

Ah, he speaks. "Out."

Chapter 12

When the door slammed in his face and Birdi, back rigid, disappeared into the night, Angus jumped to his feet. What had he done? Said? Ack, women!

He wrenched open the door, expecting to find Birdi standing before the croft, back to the door, arms folded across her chest, mouth in a firm line, as he'd seen Lady Beth pose whenever she was really annoyed with Duncan. Instead he found naught.

His own annoyance forgotten, he strode out and scanned the road for her. Nothing. No Birdi, just black and gray shadows that came and went under the light of a reiver's moon. One—thanks to fast-roaming clouds—that offered just enough light to see where one set a foot down, but not enough to be seen by.

Where the hell had she gone? He shivered as the wind kicked up off the loch, pictured what she wore, and cursed again.

She kenned no one here but Kelsea and her da . . . . *'Tis it. She went to see Wee Angus. And she will, nay doubt, catch the flux in the process.* He strode toward Fraiser's croft.

The trail of peat-rich smoke rising from the Fraiser chimney, the warm light peeking out from behind closed shutters, eased his mind considerably. At least she was warm. He knocked.

Fraiser answered. "MacDougall, come in. Come in. We

were just talking about ye." He smiled as the door swung wide.

Angus, feeling the idiot for fashing for no reason, stepped over the threshold. His gaze swept the room. Finding only Kelsea and the babe by the inglenook, his heart stuttered. He told himself to remain calm—that Birdi had to be close at hand—but his hands began to sweat.

"Has Birdi come by?"

Fraiser's brow furrowed. "Nay. I havena seen her since I brought yer sup. Why?"

"My apologies for disturbing ye."

Angus left a bemused Fraiser and Kelsea in his wake and raced to the Boar's Head Inn. He couldn't imagine why she'd go there, but it was the only other place he could think of that she was even the least familiar with, would feel comfortable walking about given her limited sight.

Back hunched, he pushed through the first and second doors and came to an abrupt halt. The tavern room was still crowded with shouting and grumbling men, the air heavy with the scent of sweat and stale ale, but it held no Birdi. Cursing, he shouldered his way through the crowd, ignoring the men who hailed him, hoping she'd sought refuge—from what, he still didn't ken—in the back of the room where the shadows were deepest.

No Birdi.

He'd run out of logical places to look, and the clan's talk of the marauding Gunns did naught to relieve his anxiety.

Should he raise the alarm, send the men out looking? She'd pitch a hissy if she'd simply gone to relieve herself. *Ah, that's it.* He blew out a breath. *She's not gone, but only relieving herself.*

He turned to go and came nose to nose with Ian MacKay, an auld friend and knight he hadn't seen in years, not since they fought side by side in Burgundy.

Ian clapped a firm hand on Angus's shoulder. "Mac-

Dougall, ye auld charger! What the hell are ye doin' this far south?"

Angus grinned. Ian hadn't aged a day. He was still as handsome as ever. "Looking for my ladywife. I seemed to have misplaced her."

Ian laughed and heads turned. They always did. As big and brawn as Angus himself, Ian sounded like thunder. "I had heard ye were on the hunt."

Good God, did every soul in the realm ken what he was about? "And what are ye doing here?" Angus asked. "Last I heard, ye were breaking virgin hearts in every alcove ye could find in Edinburgh Castle."

"Aye, and in the attic as well, but unfortunately Albany tired of losing the competition for the fairest lasses, and sent me on this damn mission."

"What mission?"

Ian threw an arm around Angus's shoulder and leaned toward his ear. "Not here."

Angus nodded. Politics and intrigue were Ian's bread and butter. The dirtier the better, and the less said in public the better, as well. When Ian tried to guide him to a far corner, Angus remained rooted. "I'm sorry, Ian, but now isna the time. I need find Birdi."

"Birdi, huh?" Deep dimples slowly formed on either side of the scoundrel's mouth as he studied Angus's visage. "I'll come with ye then. I need meet her."

As they stepped into the chilled night, Ian said, "Start at the beginning. How did ye come by this lass?"

Kenning Ian was discreet if naught else and needing a sane head to fathom what he no longer could, Angus muttered, "This insanity all started with a wager. I was . . ."

Chapter 13

Birdi squatted on the gravel that skirted Loch Lomond, wrapped her arms about her knees, and hunched her shoulders against the biting wind. With wet cheeks stinging, she stared into the glossy blackness lapping the shore before her.

'Twould be easy. Just step in and end it all. No more pain, no more fashing about food for another winter. No more loneliness.

But could she drown? She'd been a swimmer since birth without a soul teaching her how.

She heaved a shuddering sigh. Mayhap 'twas not the best of ideas. She'd likely bob to the surface like an apple in a wash bucket. But she couldn't keep going on like this day after day, year after year, filled with such angst and pain. Seeing loathing—or worse, indifference—for her in others' eyes. Against her will, her mind conjured up Angus as he sat across from her at the table, and her heart again felt his pulling back, his putting up a wall of restraint, and her tears spilled.

Not since her first encounter with Lady Macarthur—when Birdi had gone to the castle shortly after her mother's death seeking comfort and aid—had she felt such pain as she did now, had she realized how truly odd she was.

"Oh, Angus, why had ye not shut me out before I'd grown so fond of ye?"

"Fond of him, are you?"

"Aaaack!" Birdi jumped and fell backward, her arms flailing over the water.

A stranger—as tall and brawn as her Angus—reached out and grabbed her by the waist. He hauled her close, restraining her clawing hands. "Easy now, lass. I mean ye nay harm."

The clouds chose that moment to part, and moonlight lit the face of the man crushing Birdi to his chest. Her breath caught and her mouth fell open. Never in her life had she seen such a glorious countenance. The man appeared to be made of *or,* golden headed and golden skinned.

"I'm Angus's friend, and ye must be the lost Birdi."

Made mute by such an astonishing sight, she could only blink like an owl in response. She wasn't lost, she wanted to tell him—not in the usual sense, at least. And he kenned Angus?

"I'm Ian MacKay, knight of girth and sword, defender of the faithful, and most definitely at yer service." He smiled, displaying deep dimples, and slowly shifted his gaze from her face to her chest, where it lingered for some unfathomable reason.

She swallowed to clear the thickness that had suddenly taken root in her throat. "Umm . . . I'm Birdi."

He loosened his hold on her, but kept one hand at her waist. " 'Tis indeed a pleasure to make yer acquaintance, Birdi." He then guided her toward a before-unseen boulder. "Sit and tell me why such a lovely lass is sitting here in the dark fashing over my thoughtless friend."

Birdi twisted her fingers in her lap. "He isna thoughtless, not in the least. He's verra kind. He's just . . . he . . . ah, *sheet.*"

MacKay, to her shock, reared back and roared. His thunderous laugh echoed across the water as if before a gale. So astounding was it, she expected lightning to follow.

As he gained control of himself, he chuckled. "Ah, my friend has chosen well." He then squatted on his haunches before her and took one of her hands in a huge, calloused paw. Holding it gently, as if her hand were a fragile egg, he said, "Now tell me what all this greeting and fashing is about. I might be able to help. I've known yer querulous and stubborn man the better part of my life."

Birdi stared into the stranger's now solemn, wide-set eyes and something deep within her broke.

In a rush of stammered words, in a flood of tears, she spilled out her greatest fears regarding Angus Mac-Dougall. She told the stranger how he'd found her, how she'd feared him until he'd saved her in the river, about the accidental handfasting, how he'd held her and kissed her, about the babe she'd had to give up, and how now she felt certain she'd lost Angus. All in one heaving breath.

She then fell silent, shuddered, and waited. For what, she didn't ken; all was beyond hope, of that she was certain.

Ian MacKay silently studied Birdi MacDougall.

He'd already heard Angus's version of events—seriously abridged, he now realized—as they'd left the inn together. When they'd entered the croft and not found Birdi, his friend had panicked. They'd split up, Angus taking the back hills, he the loch shore, to hunt for her.

He'd not been the least surprised when Angus's Birdi spewed forth so much information. Women instinctively did so the moment he offered comfort. 'Twas apparently his gift. And now, having heard her version of events, he decided he'd never in all his twenty-nine years ever met such a woman.

Without affectation, she'd held nothing back as she told her tale of woe, though a good part he hadn't quite kenned—likely due to her racing, breathless delivery—but she hadn't tried to engage his sympathy and hadn't dissembled, placing the blame on his friend. She had, in fact, taken all the blame onto herself, though why she had he certainly couldn't imagine—from what he could garner, his friend was behaving like an idiot—but one thing was quite clear. This incredibly beautiful woman was heart and soul, head over heels, in love with Angus MacDougall.

The lucky bastard.

And he could help her. He had the skills. After all, he wasn't called "The Thief" by disgruntled men the breadth and length of Scotland for naught.

And he had the time. He wasn't in any great hurry to find out whether the rumors about the Campbell were true—whether his friend was in fact in league with the Sassenach king, as Albany suspected. He blew out a breath.

Mayhap, if he did do this good deed for Angus's lady-wife, he too might be blessed with a woman so guileless and pure of heart someday. He snorted. He should live so long.

His decision made, he smiled the smile that made half the lasses in Scotland quake at the sight of him. "Well now, Birdi, I can see yer side and where ye might need a wee bit of help to set MacDougall's head and heart on the right path." He patted her hand, noting with surprise her calluses. *Ah, she isna afraid of hard work.* More the better. Donaliegh would need such a chatelaine. Last he saw it, the place was bordering on ruin.

But before he could help her, he had to extract a promise from her. "Will ye trust me to work in yer and Angus's best interest? And promise not to misconstrue my intent by what I might say or do to bring yer MacDougall to heel?" He didn't fear he'd steal her heart from his friend—she loved the fool beyond measure—but feared his upcoming antics could raise her ire. Something that, he suspected from her straight-backed pose and unflinching gaze, he'd be wise to avoid.

She sniffed as she thought his request over. After a bit she said, "Aye, I promise, but ye willna harm him." Her unique, pale eyes narrowed as she leaned toward him. "Should he come to harm—"

"Whoa, Birdi." He'd been right. Her fragile beauty hid a spitfire, not some fear-filled featherbrain despite her atrocious name. "I promise, dear lady, he'll come to no harm, though he may wish me dead before I'm through."

She gave that some thought, then asked, "What need I do?"

He smiled. "Just be yerself."

Birdi nodded. As she pulled her hand from his, Angus MacDougall growled, "I see ye found her."

Ian winked at Birdi, rose, and offered her his hand. As she came to her feet, the Thief of Hearts asked his friend, "MacDougall, have ye ever known me *not* to find the fairest and most fulsome woman in town?"

Chapter 14

Angus growled deep in his throat. "Nay, I havena." Which was precisely what had his nerves on edge.

Congratulating himself on his restraint, he took Birdi's hand from Ian's arm and placed it on his own. With an eye on Ian he asked Birdi, "Are ye all right, lass?"

"Aye, just cold."

He pulled Birdi closer and saw that her cheeks were damp and her extraordinary long lashes spiked. "Ye've been greeting." He spun toward Ian. "What have ye done to her?"

Ian huffed. "MacDougall, open yer eyes. She *was* greeting when I found her. She wasna greeting when *you* found her."

Unable to argue with that bit of truth, Angus felt a pang of guilt. Birdi had been upset when she'd left the croft. The moment he got her inside again, he'd discover why. As he turned toward the croft, he saw Birdi cast a wary glance over her shoulder at his friend. Good. Apparently, her inability to see clearly had made her immune to Ian's impressive countenance and charms. Thank God.

To Ian he said, "Thank ye for finding her. I'm sure ye have pressing business to attend so I'll bid ye good night."

Instead of saying good night, Ian responded, "Actually, I've naught to do at present."

Birdi, to Angus's consternation, asked, "Have ye supped, sir?"

Ian grinned at her. "Nay, my lady, I've not."

"Then join us. We've more than enough." Birdi looked up at Angus. "He is yer friend, so 'tis only fitting, aye?"

What could he say? No? Let the idiot find his own food. "Aye, Birdi, 'tis fitting." Kenning but not caring that he sounded reticent—for his friend's presence would delay his finding out why Birdi had been sitting in the cold, fashing—he grumbled, "Come on then."

Had Angus not heard Ian's laugh echoing off the loch moments ago, he'd still be out scouring the hills for Birdi. When had the man planned to call him and let him ken he'd found Birdi? After he'd worked his wily ways around her? He wouldn't have put it past the bastard.

Angus hurried Birdi across the roadway, pushed open the croft door, and settled her in a chair before the table. After retrieving a blanket and wrapping it about her, he threw more peat on the fire. "Are ye warming, lass?"

Birdi, her brow furrowed for some reason, looked up at him. "Aye."

Kelsea Fraiser's croft felt unaccountably tight to Angus as Ian took a place opposite Birdi at the table.

He distributed a fish pie to each of them.

Angus picked at his pie and took a bite. Fraiser's warning that his Kelsea's pies were best "eaten hot" hadn't been spoken in jest. Now cold, they tasted like charred embers. He only poked at his pie as he watched, through narrowed eyes, Birdi's expression shift from surprise to delight as she listened to Ian's story of the current court jester.

His appetite gone, Angus pushed the remains on his trencher aside. "What business are ye on for Albany?"

Ian cast a quick glance back at Birdi as he pushed his own trencher away. "'Tis better not spoken—"

"Have nay fear. My ladywife willna ken nor care of whom ye speak."

Ian thought on that a moment, then said, "I'm on my way to Dunberg. Albany suspects the Campbell of conspiring with the Sassenach. Apparently, two agents were caught just this side of the border carrying detailed sketches of Edinburgh Castle's battlements and those of Sterling's." He hesitated, looked at Birdi for a moment, then turned his attention back to Angus. "After many hours below-stairs one agent finally made mention of Dunstaffnage before he . . . passed."

Birdi frowned. "The poor man died?"

"Aye."

Angus, his gaze on Ian, murmured, "The water there is verra bad, lass. Flux isna uncommon."

Birdi nodded sagely. "Then you should tell them to boil the water, particularly if the cows come to it."

She then finished off her fish pie in two quick bites, patted her stomach, and sighed contentedly. When she looked up and found them both staring at her, she smiled. "The pies are very fine, nay?"

Eyes averted, Ian and Angus reached for the bread and mumbled "Aye, verra." That was enough. They both started laughing.

Birdi huffed. "What may I ask do ye find so humorous?"

Both muttered, "Nothing," and reached for their ale.

Birdi then mumbled, "Minnie was right," and began licking her fingers.

Not trusting himself to continue watching her and not laugh again, Angus said, "I canna believe the Campbell is involved in such treachery."

The Campbell had once been father-in-marriage to Duncan, Angus's liege lord. Allies, the MacDougalls had fought shoulder to shoulder with the Campbells.

Ian downed his ale. "Nor I, but what Albany wants investigated, I investigate."

Her third pie finished, Birdi asked, "Who is Albany?"

"The Duke of Albany is our rightful king's uncle," his friend told her.

"Ah. You should tell him to boil his water as well."

Ian frowned at Angus and arched a brow in question.

Wanting to say, *Aye, she truly is this naive, and ye'd best keep yer dimples and friggin' hands to yerself,* Angus shrugged. "So how long do ye have to get to Dunstaffnage and back?" The sooner the Thief of Hearts was away the better.

"As long as I can possibly take." Ian poured himself more ale and then filled their tankards. "I've no stomach for anything that smacks of personal enmity."

"How so?"

"The Campbell isna the only one who's been questioning Albany's delay in ransoming our laddie out of Sassenach hands, but he is one of the loudest. Too, no one but the execu—Albany's man—heard any mention of Dunstaffnage before the man died. I find that rather convenient."

"Aye, 'tis."

If war was pending, then the sooner Duncan kenned it, the sooner stores could be laid in at Blackstone, and the sooner the sept could prepare. Angus didn't need another pressing reason to hurry this bride-quest along, but there it was. Ack.

Birdi yawned broadly, then pushed back her chair. "If ye'll pardon me, I'm verra tired. Sir MacKay—"

Ian rose and took Birdi's hand in his. As he placed a kiss on her knuckles, he murmured, "Good night, my lady, and please call me Ian."

Blushing—her gaze on her hand where he'd kissed her—Birdi murmured, "Ian, please feel free to make yerself comfortable by the hearth this night." To Angus she said, "I'll sleep next to the wall."

Made speechless by her invitation to Ian without so much as a by-yer-leave from him, Angus gaped after Birdi's lithe form as she glided the eight feet to the bed. She dove under the covers. A moment later a naked arm poked out and her tunic flew the length of the bed and landed on the floor. Merciful Mother. She was naked as a newborn jay . . . and in a room with two burly men she barely kenned!

The woman needed a keeper.

As she settled on her side, her back to them, Angus hissed, "Shit."

"Not what I was thinking, but I do envy yer dilemma."

Growling, Angus slowly turned, his eyes narrowing. Ian, grinning, nodded toward the table, indicating Angus take a seat. "A hard choice, my friend; sleep by me or that luscious bit." He sighed.

Angus, gut churning, settled in the chair Birdi had vacated. "Take a care."

Pouring ale, Ian murmured, "Ack, ye wound me."

Angus snorted. "Have ye given thought to the Shame clan?" If anyone kenned them it would be Ian. An agent of the king—in truth, Albany—Ian had spent the last five years within the halls of power.

"Aye, and canna recall ever hearing of them. Mayhap her sire was Sassenach. Shame sounds like something they'd choose."

"Humph." Not what he needed to hear. If she was indeed English, then he had but two choices. Bring her back to her glen, which didn't set well—what with the Macarthur there—or bring her home to Blackstone, and he couldn't imagine his bride taking that well.

"Do ye happen to ken a sacred well?"

Ian took a swig before answering, "Aye."

Hope surging, Angus asked, "Where?"

"South of Kelso."

"God's teeth, man, 'tis on the other side of the realm. I meant one close at hand."

Ian shrugged. "There's the one in the hills above Drasmoor, in the place we romped as bairns. Remember? Those about call it the Glen of Tears."

His friend was referring to a spring within MacDougall

territory, days away and miles from Beal Castle. "'Tis none closer?"

Ian shrugged. "There may well be, but I dinna ken such." After a moment he leaned forward and whispered, "Tell me the truth. Is she really as . . . innocent as she appears?"

Angus snorted. "More than ye'll ever ken." *A great deal more.*

"Then yer Birdi is most unusual." Ian rubbed his jaw, his gaze speculative as he studied Birdi's back. "Aye, and in a most decidedly refreshing way."

Fists clenched, Angus leaned forward. "Ye'll be keeping yer charms to yerself, if ye ken what's good for ye. I'll not see her hurt."

Jaw muscles twitching, Ian hissed back, "Friend, ye remind me of that dog in the manger. Ye canna eat the hay, dinna even want to lie in it, but ye willna to let the cow have it. Why is that?"

Why? Because he did want the damn hay, wanted to eat until he was glutted, ready to burst. Wanted to wallow in it, roll in it. He wanted Birdalane Shame with an intensity that bordered on pain. He just couldn't have her. Not and keep his word. Not and get Donaliegh. To be his own man for the first time in his sorry life.

Ian shook his head, his expression saying, *Ye're pathetic,* and then yawned. He rose. "Well, what shall it be then? The floor or the bed? I'll take whichever ye dinna want."

Angus, his teeth aching from the pressure of his clenched jaws, went to the bed. Eyes glaring, he faced his friend, stripped, and climbed in beside his naked Birdi. "Dinna forget to put out the candle."

He'd get no sleep this night.

Coming out of the last croft he could find, Fegan Macarthur raked his gaze the length of Crianlarich village, looking for his brother. Spying Robbie exiting the last croft to the west, he ran toward him. "Anything?"

"Nay, no one has seen hide or hair of the Blood, his horse, or our spae."

Fegan blew out a breath and cursed. "My instincts were right. We should have turned west. What now? I say we backtrack."

They'd wasted precious time heading north following their liege's orders; they and their mounts were exhausted, and the Macarthur was, nay doubt, at home readying to lop off a head.

His brother raked his hands through his unkempt hair and looked at the moon. It was already halfway through its arc toward the western mountains. "We eat, then head south. We havena time for sleep, but they, thinking they do, will. If the fates are kind, we'll catch up with them by sunset tomorrow."

Fegan, greatly relieved, nodded. The sooner they were done with this business the sooner he'd be home, spae in hand. His Mary's houghmagandie was due to start at any time, and he didn't want his wife birthing without the spae. He'd die if he lost his Mary. Aye, he would.

Birdi awoke to the comforting sound of Angus's guttural purring and with the warm weight of a relaxed but heavy arm about her waist. In her sleep, she'd rolled and thrown a leg over one of his powerful thighs. Her head rested on Angus's shoulder, and her right hand, fingers splayed, threaded through the fine, dark, curling hairs glazing his slowly rising and falling chest.

A week ago, she'd have screeched finding herself in such a position with a naked man. Now, she could only stare in awe at the powerful chest beneath her hand.

Goddess, he is most glorious, is he not?

But like Wee Angus, not for her to keep, unless Ian the

Golden Man had worked some magic during the night. And she seriously doubted he had.

She'd watched Angus carefully yesterday as they three ate the wondrous pies together by candlelight.

Angus had appeared agitated, though he'd been less withdrawn. He'd touched her, had covered her with a blanket, but 'twas not the same as kissing and fondling. She'd come to the conclusion he'd only behaved in a caring manner so as not to appear rude before his friend. Aye. And though they'd whispered—had thought her asleep—she'd heard him ask his friend about the sacred well.

He could break the handfasting for all she now cared, but he would do it without her. She'd spent a good part of the night thinking about how she could find her way home, before falling into a fitful sleep, and now—thanks to Kelsea—she'd have the means.

A pounding at the door made Angus jerk upright, his left arm reaching for his sword. He then realized where he was, that no danger lurked, and blinked down at her. When his gaze shifted from her face to her breasts, he groaned deep in his chest and scrambled out of bed. Hauling the covers up to her chin, he growled, "Good morn."

Seriously doubting it was—he'd again raised the invisible barrier between them—she murmured, "Morn."

Pounding sounded again and she heard Ian roll over and grumble, "Get the hell away."

"Angus, where is hell?" Mayhap she could find it. She'd heard the Macarthur bairns speak of it, so therefore it had to be close to her glen.

He blinked at her. "Ye dinna ken hell?"

"Nay. Should I?"

He shook his head and continued donning his clothing. "'Tis where the sinners go."

Sinners. Another clan she didn't ken. "'Tis far, this hell?"

He strode to the door, grumbling, "Dinna fash about it, Birdi. Ye'll not see it."

Ha! She'd see about that. If he wouldn't tell her, then she'd ask Ian. Surely he kenned it. After all, he was well traveled and had spoken of it.

The door opened and sunlight flashed across the room, making her squint. She heard Kelsea say, "Good morn. I've brought a wee something to break yer fast."

She stepped into her croft and came to an abrupt halt. Arm extended, she asked, "Who's that?"

Angus yawned. "A friend. He's harmless."

"Ah."

Apparently unfazed, she moved to the right and Birdi heard something thud on the table. Her nose then caught the scent of fresh bread, and if she wasn't mistaken, the irresistible aroma of hot blood sausage. Her stomach growled. Kelsea Fraiser was beyond doubt the most generous of women—not only had she given them her home for the night, she continued to share her fine food. Aye, and though it hurt her pride to admit it, Angus had been right in one matter. Wee Angus would reap great benefits having such a mother. She—Birdi the spae—could never have supplied such, though she certainly would have tried her very best. The admission caused a great pain to bloom in her chest, and her desire for food evaporated.

"Birdi?"

She looked up to find Kelsea standing beside the bed. "How are you feeling this morn?"

"Verra well, thank ye." She took a great breath, steeling herself. "And the wee one? How is he?"

Kelsea beamed as bright as the sun at her back. "He's splendid. This morn he suckled 'til I thought he'd turned me wrong side to, and then promptly fell back to sleep." She cast a look over her shoulder, then leaned forward to whisper, "I've something for ye." She slipped a folded piece of paper into Birdi's hand.

Birdi, heart stuttering, buried it beneath the covers. "Thank ye."

"Nay, I thank ye, though I pray ye have no need of the missive." Kelsea then straightened and in a clear voice asked, "So, have ye decided what ye must take from the chest?"

"Huh?"

Kelsea muttered, "Men," and moved to the foot of the bed, where she opened the chest. She pulled out yards of fabric, gave them a good shake, and then spread them out.

Birdi gasped. "My word!" The brocades and silks upon her lap were beyond description. When she heard a soft whistle, she looked up to find Angus looking over Kelsea's shoulder.

"I was a Lindsey," she told them, "before I fell in love with Collin." She stroked the vivid green silk and sighed. "I've not donned them since I left court ten years past. I didna want anyone thinking I was putting on airs."

Angus fingered the eight-inch hem on one gown. "And ye snubbed custom and took his name, though Lindsey is more auspicious, that speaks to yer relationship to the king."

She shrugged. "Collin was a proud man, proud to be a Fraiser, and I was proud of him."

Not kenning what they spoke of, still mesmerized by the rich weaves between her fingers, Birdi murmured, "I canna—"

"Ye must," Kelsea interjected. "Ye are now Lady Mac-Dougall, wife of a knight. Ye need look the part. Besides, they'll just fall to ruin if left in the chest. The argent strands need the warmth and oils from yer skin to stay supple." She held one gown to Birdi's chest, then the other, frowned, and then reached into the chest again, this time retrieving a mass of vivid blue. She shook that gown out and placed it against Birdi's chest. After cocking her head this way and that, she finally smiled. "That's the one. Makes yer lovely eyes glow."

Birdi could barely catch her breath. Not only was she fondling riches beyond her wildest imaginings, but Kelsea had called her horribly odd eyes lovely. Tears threatening, throat so raw she could barely swallow, Birdi fingered the three dense rows of pearls trimming the blue gown's scoop-necked bodice.

The gowns had been put away when Kelsea Fraiser had fallen in love with a man and wanted bairns, and now, they were coming out because she, Birdi, was giving up a bairn and a man she loved. Within Goddess's world, all, apparently, did cycle like the seasons. Even gowns.

She took a deep, shuddering breath and murmured, "I canna possibly—"

"Aye, ye can and ye will, or I'll lock the door and not let ye leave until such time as ye agree."

Angus drew Kelsea's hand to his lips. His voice sounded thick as he murmured, "Thank ye, my lady. Should ye ever need a strong arm . . ."

Kelsea smiled and patted his hand. "Sir, ye need only do what's in yer best interest and that will be payment enough."

The dark shape Birdi kenned to be Ian MacKay cleared its throat. "My lady, Ian MacKay at yer service." He bowed and took Kelsea's hand as Angus had. As he straightened, he said. "'Tis verra generous of ye." Turning his attention to Birdi, he said, "Aye, I agree with Lady Fraiser's choice. The blue is a perfect complement."

"Since we all agree," Kelsea said. "You gentlemen must eat and go. We women have work to do."

Ian growled, "Will ye please stop pacing and sit. Ye're giving me and yer horse a headache."

Angus glared at his friend and continued to wear a rut before the Fraiser croft. "What on earth is taking so long?"

The sun was already high in the sky. Too, he recollected only too vividly what had happened the last time he'd left Birdi alone with Kelsea.

"She's fine," Ian assured him. "Ye ken it takes hours for a woman to primp."

"Humph!" Birdi didn't primp. She woke, ate, made quick ablutions, and they were off. 'Twas, in truth, one of her finest qualities. She didn't fret about her appearance as so many women did. In that and in her endurance, she was very much like a man. Casting a glance at Ian, he modified the thought to *most men*. How Ian had managed to look ready for court after too much ale and too little sleep upon a dirt floor was beyond kenning, but shine he did like a new gold sovereign. "Humph!"

The door suddenly swung wide and Angus came to an abrupt halt. Standing before him stood not the orphan waif Birdalane Shame, but a fairy-tale princess gleaming bright in the midday sun. Cheeks scrubbed pink, lush lips berry-red, dressed in a gown of blazing blue and argent, her glorious raven hair caught up in twin argent cowls on either side of her flawless face and secured by a wide pearl headband, her shoulders draped in lush silver fox and vivid blue brocade, Birdi was quite simply . . . breathtaking. "Merciful Mother of God."

And he was going to the gallows.

First for the lust now surging through his veins—there had to be a canon law against such volume somewhere—and second for the fact that by royal decree no woman of his could don even cat fur, much less what Birdi now wore. He didn't earn the prerequisite thousand pounds sterling per year.

Aye, he'd hang—by either church or Crown decree—but hang he would, for he wasn't about to tell lovely Birdi to take a damn thing off. She'd earned it.

Ian's voice broke through his ruminating. ". . . ye take a man's breath away, my lady, and happy he dies, basking in yer fair and fulsome glow, so—"

Angus shouldered his friend aside. "Go die elsewhere, fool."

He took Birdi's hand and brought it to his lips. "The moon this day outshines the sun."

Truer words he'd never spoken. They came from the book of sonnets Lady Beth had given to him, words intended for another woman, but spoken from the heart to his accidental bride. With that realization came fear; should he continue to seek the sacred well, something deep in his bones warned he might well be giving up more than he could ever hope to gain.

He shook off the depressing thought and cleared his throat. "We need take our leave, Birdi." He bowed to Kelsea. "Lady Fraiser, ye have my heartfelt gratitude."

In return she touched his cheek and murmured, "God's speed." To Birdi she whispered, "Thank ye for saving my life, dear Birdi. I promise to love the babe with all my heart, and when he's auld enough, I'll speak of thee, so he'll ken how fortunate we are."

Birdi, eyes glassy, silently hugged Kelsea, then turned—her back stiff and straight, her countenance as smooth as glass—toward Rampage. Angus followed, kenning this wasn't a good sign.

"Are ye all right, lass?"

She took a stuttering breath. "She named him Collin."

Birdi then placed her hands on his shoulders. Angus hoisted her up and into the saddle, his gut suddenly churning. With a heavy heart he accepted that Birdi might in time forgive him for taking her away from her home, but never would she forgive him for giving away the bairn.

He turned to bid farewell to Ian, only to find his friend mounting his horse. "I bid ye well on yer trip to Dunberg," Angus said.

A grin spread over Ian's handsome countenance as his gaze raked Birdi. "No need. I've decided to keep ye company."

"The Blood and the spae were here." Robbie Macarthur held out the charred piece of wood he'd found near a ruined barn to his brother. It bore the name "Angus Mac-Dougall." Had he been party to what had happened in Ardlui? As well trained as Robbie was in swordplay, the thought made him shudder. He asked his brother, "Well?"

Fegan, scowling, shook his head. "The crofts were too far apart for the fires to be accidental." They'd found a fresh burial site with forty-odd names and fresh wolf tracks between the warm and smoldering crofts. "I dinna believe MacDougall did this on his own. Mayhap the Fraisers are at war. If they're fighting among themselves, we need move cautiously. But if it's clan against clan . . ."

Aye, they'd best learn quickly with whom the Fraisers fought . . . and hopefully it wasn't with the Macarthur or any of their allies. "How much farther to the next village?"

Fegan studied the cloud bank easing over the western horizon. "If the weather holds, we'll be in Inveruglas by sup."

The thought made Robbie's mouth water. They hadn't had a decent meal in days. "Then let's go."

They kicked their mounts' sides.

At Tarbot, no one kenned a sacred well, so they galloped on, heading due west with one eye to the sky, the other watching for trouble, namely the Gunns.

On the far side of the forest, at a wee clutch of crofts called Rest and Be Thankful, where the ground again rose to meet the looming lead-bellied clouds above, they broke bread with a herder and his wife and asked again about a sacred well. Neither kenned one, and on they rode.

On the outskirts of Cairndow Ian said, "We willna make Inveraray by nightfall."

"Aye, I'm painfully aware of that."

In fact, Angus felt ill with his awareness of time and distance. He had only a fortnight left before he need be back at Blackstone—less, if he wanted to warn Duncan about impending troubles—and their progress had been slowed by steep paths, crags, and forest getting to Cairndow, the last hamlet on their way to Inveraray. Had he been alone he would have risked an all-night ride, but he had Birdi's safety and new finery to consider.

Riding into Cairndow—the men's gazes sweeping the area for trouble—Angus grumbled, "If there isna an inn, mayhap a family will offer Birdi a pallet. You and I can always bed down in a stable." He wasn't about to spend another night lying next to luscious Birdi.

Ian put a hand on his shoulder. "I'll tend to it, may get it cheaper." He grinned, flashing his famous dimples, and wiggled a brow. Angus laughed for the first time in hours. "Go on with ye."

Birdi, sitting sidesaddle thanks to her new voluminous skirts, murmured, " 'Tis going to rain soon."

"Aye." Drawn by the repetitive sound of metal clanging on metal, Angus turned left and found a sizeable stable. "Good eve, smitty."

The blacksmith, flame-headed and barrel-chested, wiped the sweat from his eyes with the back of a thick hand. As he shouldered his massive hammer, he eyed Rampage from ears to hooves. "What can I do fer ye, sir?"

"Have ye stabling for two cattle?"

The man looked behind them. "I see only one."

"My friend seeks an inn."

He snorted. "Most likely full, 'tis market day." He then shifted his gaze to Birdi. As he took her measure he rubbed his jaw. "For two bodles apiece yer cattle can pasture yon." He pointed over his shoulder to a fenced paddock containing three mud-caked ponies.

Angus gritted his teeth. The stable was nigh on to empty. 'Twas obvious the man intended to gouge him, and he had little choice but to allow it if he intended to stay dry this night. "Three bawbees for three stalls with fresh hay."

The man chuckled and held out his hand. "Done."

Angus routed around in his sporran, pulled out the coins—each the equivalent of an English penny—and dropped them into the man's calloused paw. Angus rolled his eyes when the man bit into the coins.

At least their horses would be dry and safe, and he and Ian would have someplace to lay their heads.

A loud shout went up and Birdi jerked, nearly toppling out of the saddle. He steadied her.

Eyes wide, she stuttered, "What was that?"

"No need for alarm. 'Tis most likely some game the folks are cheering about. 'Tis market day."

Biting her lower lip, she asked, "Game? What means this?"

Good Lord, the woman had led a sheltered life. "Games are play. Where bairns or men vie with each other for sport or prizes, sometimes winning a coin or a cake, mayhap a goose. Depends on the game and what's offered." He dismounted and reached for her waist. "Would ye like to go see?"

"Aye . . . well, mayhap." Birdi nibbled on a fingernail. "I'm nay sure."

He smiled down at her as he took her elbow. "Ye'll enjoy it. Come, we need find Ian, anyway."

Birdi clung to Angus's arm as the sounds of men and animals engulfed her. She kenned not the number swirling about, but sensed she'd never been among so many in her life.

As Angus led Birdi along the road, frantic chickens clucked to her right and goats bleated to her left. A woman yelled, "Hot pies, hot pies, two fer a bodle!" Another shouted, "Fresh Partan! Poke 'em!" Birdi stopped and bent before a wicker stall and found a litter of wee hogs. Now why on earth would someone want these? A man scooped up a squealing pink blob and held it out to her.

Over the cacophony, he shouted, "A healthy gryce, m'lady. Just a penny!"

She forced a smile and shoved Angus with her elbow, pushing him away from the wode granger before they caught whatever ailed the poor man.

A moment later a bundle of blue cornflowers appeared under her nose. She jumped back.

"A gowpen of blavers for the lady, sir? Goes with her gown, they do. Only a bodle to a knight as fine as yerself."

Angus chuckled at her side. "Would ye like them?"

Staring open-mouthed at the wizened flower man, dressed in more colors than Birdi could lay name to, she shook her head. What strange people! And the Macarthurs had the ballocks to call *her* odd? Humph!

A great shout rang out and Angus craned his neck to look over the crowd. "Come, they're having a cattle pull."

"A what?" He grinned down at her, light sparking in his eyes. Good graces, the man was handsome—beyond handsome when he smiled like this.

"Men hook their horses with chains tail to tail and the strongest wins. There's bound to be wagering. Come. We'll likely find Ian there. The man's yet to miss an opportunity to fatten his purse."

She could do naught but murmur, "As ye lust." She was confused beyond endurance, yet some wee voice deep within shouted, *Drink it in. Dinna miss a thing.*

At the far end of the village, at the edge of a great field, they found Ian as Angus had predicted.

Coming alongside, Angus asked, "Which has yer coins?"

Ian chuckled. "The bay with the white feet."

Birdi could see naught but two brown blobs slowly shifting on a field of dusty green.

"Did ye find an inn?" Angus yelled over the shouting crowd.

"Aye, and a bed for yer lady, though the price comes dear."

Angus nodded as if expecting the answer. He then leaned toward Ian and whispered something. As Ian answered in like manner, Birdi heard a *meow* and felt a soft brush against her ankle. She squatted and found a ball of dark gray fluff with four white paws staring up at her with bright green eyes. Excitement bloomed in Birdi's chest. "Now aren't ye the bonniest."

Meoow.

She'd always wanted a cat; had hoped in vain to receive one in tribute since the first time she'd stroked the soft fur of a fat, complacent one in a Macarthur croft seasons ago. Hands shaking, Birdi reached for the kitten, but it scampered away. Not to be thwarted, she followed, dodging peddlers as she went. The kitten meowed again and she turned left, following the sound. She continued on, taking note as she always did of how many steps she took in each direction, so she could find her way back to Angus when she caught her prize, the kitten.

As she approached the entrance of a narrow, shadowed lane, her palms began to itch. Along with the annoying prickle came a heavy feeling deep within her chest.

Ack, not again. Not now.

While in her glen, she'd been called upon by the Macarthurs mayhap once a full moon, often less. Since leaving it, she'd been assaulted by *need* thrice in as many days, and disliked it intensely. If this kept up she'd be naught but raw skin and bones in a fortnight. She scratched her palms again and strained to hear the kitten.

Nothing. But the *need* was making itself known. Aye, and with increasing intensity.

Though disappointed about losing her kitten, Birdi heaved a resigned sigh, took a cleansing breath, and then focused. She'd get no peace unless she heeded the *need,* and she did so want to enjoy this place, and mayhap find the kitten. With any good fortune at all—and she thought she was overdue for some—the *need* would be easily tended as it had been when she'd made the dolly.

She turned into a lane. As she neared the end she heard

a woman's keening. She leaned forward as she slowly approached what appeared to be a large, brown mound.

As she drew near, it moved. Startled, she shied. When nothing further happened and the keening continued she edged closer. To her horror, 'twas not a pile of discards but a woman in rags, and in her arms lay a flaccid, pot-bellied babe.

"Help me."

Birdi squatted before the thin woman with hollow black eyes and touched her shoulder. "I will, but I need to ken more. How has this come to pass? Where is yer husband?"

The woman looked at the babe in her arms. "Died these three months past."

Never . . . ever . . . tend a stranger who counts the passages of the moon in Marches and Mays. Those that do are pledged to the black-gowned priests. They'll bring ye down . . . will do their utmost to smite ye.

Birdi reached out and placed a tentative finger on the wooden cross hanging from a bit of dirty yarn around the woman's neck. 'Twas the priest symbol. Like the one Lady Macarthur wore. This frail woman before her was indeed a follower.

Birdi took a steadying breath. *I'm sorry, Minnie, I canna turn my back on her. I ken too well this pain she suffers. Aye, only too well.*

Birdi kicked off her shoes and planted her feet firmly on Mother of All. Her heart bounding within her chest, she dreaded what would follow. "Ye must trust as ye have never trusted before, and pledge to keep our wee secret."

Chapter 15

With his gaze on the horse pull, Angus's thoughts were on Birdi and her reactions going through the market. Lord, 'twas like being a bairn again, seeing it again for the first time through her eyes. And Lord, was she funny. And her expression when she saw that litter of pigs was priceless. Aye, and the way people stared at her in awe! None would ever have guessed she wasn't a lady born. She carried herself straight and proud, smiled easily and often. And her laugh; it rang pure and clear, drawing the eye of every man within hearing. Aye, given a different set of circumstances—a different rearing—she would have made a perfect chatelaine for an ambitious man. Just the sight of her dressed in rich brocades was enough to steal a man's breath and make him weak at the knees. Aye, so why was he giving her up?

As he pondered the possibility of talking Lady Beth into training Birdi, he felt a drop of rain and turned to ask Birdi if she was ready to go.

She was gone.

Heart in his throat, he scoured the crowd. "Birdi!" Receiving no answer, he plowed his way through the tightly packed clansmen. "Birdi!"

Where the hell is she?

"What's amiss?" Ian stood at his back.

"Birdi's gone."

"Dinna fash. Something in the stalls probably caught her eye, and she's milling about there."

Angus quickened his pace, his head swinging right and left as he examined every doorway he passed. "Nay, she wouldna."

"Angus, she's a woman. Of course she would."

Teeth gritted, he hissed, "She wouldna, because she's blind."

Ian grabbed his arm and spun him. "She's *what?*"

Angus wrenched free and took off at a jog, claymore banging at his back. "Blind! Blind as a bat, as a burrowing mole, as blind as Lizzy's auld dog." Chest heaving, he came to an abrupt halt before the deserted market stalls. "God's teeth, where the hell could she have gone?"

Ian shrugged and looked about helplessly.

Angus gave the marketplace another quick scouring and growled, "Ye take the right, I'll go left. Bellow if ye find her."

As Angus ran he readily admitted to himself that he'd been frightened a time or two in his life, but never so often or to such a degree as he had been since meeting Birdalane Shame. And when he found her, he'd paddle her fine hurdies raw and blistered for the aggravation she was putting him through. Aye, and take great pleasure in the doing!

After checking every open doorway, he tore past the entrances of short mews off the main road one after the other, calling out her name. He'd raced past the last before the sight of vivid blue registered in his mind. He turned and raced back.

There, at the end of the mews, before a pile of rags and a closed stable door, squatted Birdi. He took a deep, settling breath, not trusting that he wouldn't grab her up by the hair and throw her over his knee. He didn't bother keeping the menace out of his voice as he growled, "Birdi?"

When she didn't respond he strode down the mews, and

found himself face to face with a pathetic-looking stranger, a woman the likes of which he hadn't seen since his time in France, when he'd boldly—and foolishly—toured the waterfronts, determined to drink himself into nightly stupors trying to forget all he had done in the name of king and country.

The frail, hollow-eyed woman held a babe in her lap, its fragile parchment skin the color of roasted pumpkin, its dark eyes sunken into a seemingly too-large head. Its legs called to mind those of storks. He kenned what ailed the bairn; he'd seen this child again and again after crops and cattle had been destroyed by war.

The babe was starving to death.

Birdi, head bent, tears streaming down her cheeks, ignored him. She was totally focused on the babe, one hand on its head, the other resting on the babe's bloated belly.

"Ack, Birdi, lass . . ."

She'd apparently found a babe to replace the one she'd lost. It wasn't uncommon for desperate women to offer their bairns up for sale. 'Twas often the only way to keep them alive.

He dropped to one knee. As he wrapped his arm around Birdi's shoulders, he heard her whisper, ". . . please, Mother of All, Goddess, please I beg thee," and his heart stuttered.

The blood drained from his head and he rocked back onto his haunches.

Oh my God. Birdi was pagan.

The bairn beneath her hands shivered. It opened its mouth and then wailed. Not strongly as a proper bairn might, but wail it did, its wee fists batting the falling mist. The mother, tears now streaming down her face, cooed and hushed the bairn as she cradled it to her chest.

Birdi wavered and fell against him. As he steadied her, he felt heat. My God, the woman was burning up, near to melting with raging fever. Had she touched the babe and contracted something?

His own shock forgotten, he tipped up her chin to see her face and a cold sweat exploded across his chest. Birdi's magnificent eyes were now as vacant as the bairn's had once been, staring skyward, unblinking. "Birdi! For God's sake answer me. Can ye hear me?"

"Give her . . . coins."

Angus scooped Birdi into his arms. He had to get her inside, get water into her, get food into her, do something. As he rose, she clawed at his chest with surprising strength. "The coins. All . . . will be . . . for naught . . . if the babe canna suckle."

In no mood to argue—not willing to examine what he'd heard while sweat careened down his back and chest, with blood hammering in his ears—he tossed the frail woman a fistful of coins. He then turned. The woman called "Bless ye!" as he ran with Birdi toward the main roadway.

As he rounded the corner he saw Ian emerge from a nearby building. "Ian!"

His friend came at a run, took one look at Birdi, and asked, "My God, man, what happened to her?" His hand reached for his dirk. "I'll kill the son of a whore."

"I dinna ken, but we need get her inside." The mist had turned to an all-out rain.

"This way." Ian raced ahead some thirty feet to the only two-story building on the now muddy roadway. He held the door wide as Angus angled Birdi through the doorway.

Following behind, Ian ordered, "Up the stairs. Second door."

The whitewashed room, its low ceiling made lower by thick round beams, held only a bed and a chair. 'Twould serve. It was warm and dry, the two things Birdi most needed.

Having had to hunch to get through the doorway, Angus

remained stooped as he crossed the room to the sturdy-looking, pine-post bed. He lowered Birdi onto thin ticking.

Leaning over his shoulder, Ian asked, "What can I do?"

Angus ran a shaking hand over the stubble on his jaw. *Think, man! Think!* What had Lady Beth done when Duncan lay at death's door with a raging fever? He pictured the sickroom, pictured Beth greeting over his friend, and it all came back.

"Fetch a bucket of cold water and rags."

"But she's—"

"Dinna argue, man, just do it!"

As Ian reached for the door, Angus amended, "And broth, hot broth."

His friend gone, Angus looked down at Birdi. Her cheeks were flushed, her body still. Her breathing was shallow and uneven. Merciful Mother of God! What was wrong that she'd sickened so quickly? And what had she done or given to that babe?

Having no answers and in desperate need to do something, he knelt at Birdi's side and started to undress her. He pushed off her cape and struggled with the pearl band about her head until he realized it was secured to the cauls. He pulled pins, got her headdress off, and her hair cascaded around her. He then studied her gown. Seeing no opening in the front, he rolled her onto her side and found no opening in the back. "Sheet!" he huffed. "Over the head then."

He shoved the weighty brocade up to her waist. That done, he hauled her to his chest, pulled her arms free, and yanked the two-stone weight over her head. Wondering how she'd borne so much without slumping, he tossed the gown onto the floor and carefully lowered Birdi back onto the mattress. She now wore only a thin cotton shift over her snow-white, pebbled skin.

The door burst open, and instinctively Angus wrenched

out his dirk. Seeing Ian, he muttered, "Ye scared the sheet out of me."

"Sorry." Ian dropped a bucket beside the bed and handed him a fistful of rags. "The broth will be ready in a moment."

"Thank ye."

Looking as fashed as Angus felt, Ian asked, "What else can I do?"

"Stand guard below." Pagans were about as welcome these days as the plague, and that woman Birdi spoke with had worn a cross.

"Has she spoken? Told ye what happened?"

Angus shook his head. "Not yet. I need tend to her now. Let none above stairs, and keep your ears open." He studied Birdi. "The moment her fever breaks, we're leaving. I'll let ye know when to make ready the horses."

Ian scowled. "Ye canna be serious. It's pouring."

Aye, and with any luck the rain would keep most inside and word wouldn't spread as fast as he feared. "We ride, rain or nay rain."

Muttering under his breath, Ian stomped out the door and down the stairs.

Angus soaked a rag in frigid water. Wringing it out, he whispered, "Ye are a one for keeping secrets, lass." He shook his head as he wiped her brow. "What on earth will I do with ye now?"

He wiped her down with water, limb by limb. As he wiped the filth from her feet he wondered what had become of her delicate silver shoes. He tossed the dirty rag and reached for another, and started again with her face.

An hour later, Birdi's fever still raged. At his wits' end, he decided to soak all of her, front and back, and to hell with preserving her modesty. He pulled her into his arms and pulled up her shift.

His jaw went slack as he stared over her shoulder at her back. Scars—the likes of which he hadn't seen even on friends, warriors—made lace out of her marble-white skin. Someone had taken a lash to her!

He laid her down and something deep in his gut tightened. *Oh my God.* More scars marred the front of her. Fine, raised lines ran across her right shoulder, upper left arm, and left thigh. With a faint heart he dragged his gaze to her left side. The wound he'd caused had healed surprisingly well. 'Twas now only a wee, faint, red line, but it, too, would eventually leave a scar. "Ack, lass, ye'll never ken how much I regret hurting ye."

He soaked another rag. As he scrubbed, he prayed. He would learn what had happened to her later.

Ian sat on the bottom step, his claymore across his lap. The fifteen men in the public room cast the occasional wary glance in his direction as he put a finer edge on his blade with a whetstone, but none spoke directly to him, though most, he suspected, talked of him. And of his friends above stairs.

Most in the room were cairds—tinkers—or herders come to Cairndow just for market day. They'd be leaving as soon as the sky cleared. Given the wind, that wouldn't be long. And thank God. His friend had lost all perspective, thinking they should ride out in weather like this with a fevered woman. Which did bode well, he supposed, in one respect.

Whether his friend kenned it or not, Angus MacDougall was taken with his lass. It made Ian's work—making Angus jealous and bringing him to the realization that he had his rightful bride already—that much easier.

And Birdi? She loved Angus, but he'd sensed a worrisome loss of patience within her. Why, he wasn't sure. The woman hadn't confided in him since doing so by the loch. That, too, he found disturbing. Women normally sought him out to fash aloud and ask his opinions. Birdi, however, was keeping her own counsel. Not a good thing, from his perspective, though it made her more intriguing.

And he still couldn't believe Birdi was blind. He'd been with her for two days, and not once had she asked directions, run into something, or gotten lost. Until today.

He "humphed" deep in his throat, wondering how she was doing.

The door blew open and a drenched, rotund woman rolled over the threshold. Looking very agitated, she waddled over to the cluster of men in the far corner. As her plump arms waved, Ian watched the men's expressions. Alarm registered on every one.

A heartbeat later, all shouting, they all raced out the door.

Ian spit on his whetstone and again stroked the edge of his blade.

Hearing men shouting, Angus grabbed his broadsword and raced to the window. Bracing himself for the worst—finding the Gunns or raving villagers—he threw open the shutters.

To his monumental relief, people were running not toward the inn but away from it, pitchforks and scythes in hand. He rolled the tension out of his shoulders.

He turned toward Birdi and saw he'd knocked over the bucket in his haste to get to the window. No matter. He needed more cold water, anyway.

Though still fevered, Birdi now mumbled and occasionally thrashed. She was finally fighting her way out of her flaccid stupor.

He picked up the bucket and opened the door. Seeing Ian stationed at the base of the stairs, he called, "What was the racket about?"

Ian looked up. "A wolf has apparently helped himself to a few pullets."

"Good for him." Though he had no love for the beasts, at least this one had the sense to choose chickens instead of a bairn or sheep. "I need more water."

Ian climbed the stairs. "How is she?"

"Still fevered, but I suspect she's getting better. I've no real reason . . . . I just feel it in my bones."

Ian took the bucket. "Bones and guts never lie." As he started down the stair he asked, "Do ye want the broth now?"

Ack! He'd forgotten about the broth. Lady Beth swore by it, had shoveled bowls of it into his liege as he recovered. "Aye."

Ian mumbled, "Be right back," and Angus returned to the room to find Birdi, lips parched, curled in a shivering ball. "Merciful Mother!" He hauled her onto his lap and reached for her cape. He obviously had no intuitive bones. God, he loathed being in over his head.

Mayhap the village had a healer. He'd send Ian out to ask. It would leave them unguarded, but only for a short while. Surely he had the skill to hold off a mob intent on burning Birdi at the stake for a short while.

A minute later footsteps sounded on the stairs and Ian called, " 'Tis just me."

He came in and dropped the bucket at Angus's feet. His gaze immediately riveted on Birdi's exposed back. "My God, who did that to her?"

"I dinna ken, but I'll kill the bastard as soon as I find out." Angus shifted Birdi's cloak a bit to better mask her nakedness from Ian. "Is the broth ready?"

"Aye, the publican's wife is bringing it up along with some bread and cheese for ye."

"I need ye to quietly ask around after a healer. I've done all I can to help her—"

"Nay." Birdi, to his surprise, again croaked, "Nay." She then licked her lips. "Drink."

Relief flooded him.

Ian said, "I'll get it," spun, and nearly collided with the publican's wife, who stood gawking in the doorway. He took the tray from her hands, mumbled, "Thank ye, mistress," and closed the door on her.

"Here." He set the tray on the end of the bed and studied Birdi for a moment. "Do ye still want a healer?"

Angus, scowling, lifted Birdi's chin. He still didn't like her color, nor had she opened her eyes. For all he kenned she was speaking in her sleep. "Aye."

Birdi flopped a hand against his chest. "Nay, An . . . gus, please."

She kenned him. Hadn't spoken in her sleep after all. "As ye lust, lass, no healer, but ye need take some of this." He held the bowl of broth to her lips.

After watching Birdi swallow a bit, Ian murmured, "I'll leave ye be now. Call if ye need anything."

When the door closed, Angus whispered, "Woman, I dinna like fashing quite so often, not in the least. At the rate ye're going, I'll be white-headed by the time I'm thirty."

"How many . . ." she cleared her throat, "seasons are ye?"

"Nine-and-twenty."

Birdi managed a wee smile.

He kissed her hair, now damp and tangled as it cloaked her front. She still felt fevered. "I need cool ye off again."

He stood and laid her down. When her hands moved to cover the jet curls at the apex of her thighs, he shook his head. "'Tis naught I havena seen before."

Lids half closed, she whispered, "When a woman's sick, she isna well, and ye shouldna tease."

He grinned then and draped her cloak over her. "I still need to cool ye down." He dipped a rag in the water.

Her gaze—as cool as the water—never left his visage as his hands moved in gentle circles from her smooth face to the column of her neck and down onto her scarred arms.

Her top extremities cooled, he pushed the cloak down to her waist and found himself staring at the perfect twin globes with rose-frosted tips pointing straight at him.

God Lord, he hadn't had a problem earlier, had run cold water over them as if they were merely ant mounds. But now, she watched and . . .

Birdi, her skin pebbling, asked, "Why do ye hesitate?"

If she didn't ken, he had nay way of explaining it.

Careful not to touch her there, he pulled up the cloak and cleared his throat. "Roll onto yer side. I need do yer back." Retreat was often a man's only ally.

"As ye lust."

Aye, in the basest sense of the word.

Birdi rolled, putting her back to him. As his wide hands stroked her back with cold water, she shivered again. "I'm sorry lass, but this needs to be done or yer brain will fry." Or so Lady Beth had warned as she'd tended his friend in similar circumstances.

"Ye have gentle hands," Birdi told him.

"Thank ye." He glided over the fine crisscrossing lines on her back. "Birdi?"

"Hmm?"

"When did this happen?"

"What?"

"The marks on yer back?"

She rolled then, flat onto her back, and clutched the cloak to her chest as if it were body armor.

Understanding she felt embarrassment, he still wanted to ken, so he could beat the shit out of the one who'd done it, should the opportunity arise. "I ken it's hard, lass, but we need speak of it. 'Tisna right a lass should suffer such. The man needs to be punished."

She frowned. "'Twas nay a man, but a woman."

Oh, dear Lord. Her mother.

His blood ran cold, though he shouldn't have been taken by surprise. The woman had given Birdi an atrocious name, neglected to even kiss the lass, and now this. What manner of beast was she? Ack.

Realizing Birdi stared at him, he cleared his throat and placed a hand on her forehead. She felt cooler. Mayhap he wasn't so bad a physician after all. He raised her shoulders and reached for the bowl of broth. "Drink."

She wrinkled her nose. "I dinna like it."

"Who said ye were supposed to? Drink."

The bowl empty, he lowered her back to the thin lumpy mattress. Were she at Blackstone she'd be lying on thick ticking, her head resting on a down-filled pillow, and his woolly warm blankets would be smothering her.

And Castle Blackstone's priest would be hovering just outside the door. Ack.

Teeth chattering, drenched to the skin, Robbie Macarthur eased behind the smitty's stable. He grinned for the first time in days, seeing a huge white head draped over one of the stall doors. The MacDougall's charger. They'd finally caught up with the bastard and their stolen spae!

Dinna get too comfortable, lassie. Soon ye'll be heading south.

Chapter 16

Birdi awoke to cool sunshine. She sniffed the air. Winter was on its way. Turning to the light, she saw Angus stretch before the open window.

He'd come up behind her after the healing had been done, but she couldn't recall more. More importantly, had the woman kept their secret? What thoughts and questions now ran through his mind? And how many days had she been lying here? She had only scattered memories of broth, of freezing as Angus scrubbed her with careful hands, of his rocking her back to sleep whenever she woke screaming.

"Has the rain passed?"

Angus turned and smiled. "Aye." He came closer and knelt beside her. His chest was bare, and she longed to reach out and touch it.

Placing a hand on her forehead, he asked, "How do ye feel?"

"Like a cow sat on my chest." Seeing his brow furrow, she grinned. "Dinna fash, Angus. I'll be right as rain come the morrow. Did I miss sup?"

"Aye, several."

She groaned, suspecting as much, and tried to sit. Angus wrapped an arm about her and swung her legs over the side of the bed.

"Are ye hungry?"

"Aye." She could eat that cow. "Where is Ian?"

"Downstairs flirting with the help."

Relief flooded her. If neither Ian nor Angus had run off it meant Angus hadn't seen the healing and the woman she'd helped had kept her word. She hadn't spoken to any about what Birdi had done. Her secret was safe.

Wondering how the babe now fared, she raked her hands through the matted hair clinging to her face and her fingers caught. Knots. One of these days she really needed to find herself a good pair of scissors. Mayhap Tinker had some . . . .

The missive!

Her gaze raced around the room, looking for her gown. Seeing a huge splash of vivid blue against one wall, she pointed to it. "May I have my gown, please? I'm cold."

"Of course. I'm afraid it's a bit wrinkled."

Wrinkled, sminkled. Who cared, so long as the missive Kelsea had written still remained in the pocket?

When Angus laid it on the foot of the bed, she had all she could do to keep her hands in her lap. "Thank ye."

"Do ye need help?"

"Nay." She cleared her throat. "I meant nay, thank ye, I can manage on my own."

He grinned. "Then I'll leave ye to it and go find us something to eat."

The moment the door closed, Birdi yanked the gown onto her lap and frantically searched through fold after fold. When one hand slipped into a deep pocket and touched paper, she heaved a relieved sigh. She cautiously pulled the missive out and unfolded it. Within still lay a golden coin—enough, Kelsea had told her, to send the missive to Tinker.

She brought the letter close to her eyes and squinted at the inked squiggles. Oh, how she wished she could read.

"Ye have no need to ken such, so stop nagging me."

"But the bairns in the village do." She'd watched them

use sticks to write in the earth. Had crawled on her belly
out into the open after they'd left to study their marks.

"Aye, and what good has it done them, or me, for that
matter?" A hand caught Birdi's ear. "Now go and fetch
more berries or ye'll have naught come winter. Go."

Birdi sighed. Someday, she'd learn. How, she wasn't
sure, but someday she would.

She folded the paper around the coin and put it back in
her pocket, then donned the gown.

She was struggling with her hair when Angus knocked.
"Birdi? May I come in?"

She grinned. He'd seen her naked, bathed her, and now
he asked? Men. "Aye, come in."

The door swung wide. Angus carried a tray so laden
with food it had to weigh more than she did. He set it on
the bed. "After ye eat, we need talk."

Oh dear. "About what?" She suddenly had no appetite.

"About whether or nay ye're ready to ride. I'd like to
make Inveraray by gloaming tomorrow . . . but only if ye
feel up to it." He tore a piece from one loaf and handed it
to her. "If ye say nay, I'll ken."

Aye, he would, but he'd be none too happy about it. "I'm
well enough to ride."

"Are ye absolutely sure?"

"Aye." The sooner they left, the less likely she'd be exposed. The woman she'd helped had, after all, worn the
sign of the black-cloaked priests. Better to be out of sight
and out of mind, as Minnie had once warned.

They ate in silence after that. When Angus had had his
fill—two loaves, a mound of sausage, and three fish—he
dug into the pouch he wore before his nether region.
"Here."

Not kenning what he held, she silently reached out.
Finding a firm, bone comb in her hand, she squealed,
"Bless ye, Angus MacDougall!"

He grinned as she pulled her hair over her shoulder and struggled to run the comb through it.

After a moment Angus patted his lap. "Come here. Let me help."

Seeing no hope for it, Birdi reluctantly assumed the hair-combing position. She sat between his thighs with her back to him, as she had before her mother. She squeezed her eyes shut and clamped her jaws, readying for the yanking and pulling that would surely follow. If her knots couldn't be combed out, they'd be yanked out.

"Knots lead to mats and mats to lice, and we'll have none of that here."

Angus combed through the lock caught between his thumb and forefinger and smiled as it sprang back into a nice fat curl. He dropped it over her shoulder and gently separated another strand from the tangled mass. "The first time I saw ye, I lusted to run my hands through this hair."

"Ye did? Why?"

Angus grinned. "Simply because."

"Oh." She craned her neck and looked up at him, a frown marring her smooth forehead. "Ye are truly an odd one."

He laughed then. He'd been a bit melancholy all morning, kenning their time together was drawing to an end, and it felt good to laugh for a change. Foolish, aye, but there it was.

"I was thinking of cutting it all off."

He gave her hair a gentle tug and grumbled, "Dinna ye dare."

Birdi craned her neck again to look at him. Something troubling lurked in the deep recesses of her eyes. When she didn't say anything but turned back around, he shrugged.

A knock sounded and Angus dropped a hand to his dirk. "Enter."

Ian stepped through the doorway, resplendent in gold and black. "Morn, Lady MacDougall. Good to see you looking so well." To Angus he said, "The publican needs ken if we'll be spending another night."

Ack! Why had Ian taken to calling Birdi Lady Mac-Dougall? It only reinforced their situation's futility. "Tell the man we'll be leaving shortly."

"I'll fetch the horses."

Only a few minutes later Angus ran a hand the length of Birdi's hair, grabbed a fistful as Wee Angus had, and brought it to his lips. Aye, there couldn't be any hair finer. He sighed, let it fall, and put his comb back in his sporran. "It's ready for ye to braid."

"Thank ye." Birdi stood, pulled the curling mass over one shoulder, and made quick work of weaving the strands together. He held out the argent cauls and pearl band.

"Nay. Can ye put them behind yer saddle in the bag?"

"Of course." He thought cauls a ridiculous affection, anyway. He helped her on with her cape. "Are ye ready?"

"Aye."

Downstairs, Angus found the publican waiting for him. As he handed over the coins, the fine hairs on the back of his neck stood. He turned to find a rough-looking man staring at Birdi. He couldn't blame him—she was lovely to behold—but something in the man's stance made Angus pull Birdi closer. With a hand on his dirk, he made haste out the door.

Fegan eased over to the window. Keeping to the shadows, he ruminated over the way the spae was dressed as he watched her and the Blood walk toward the stables. He hadn't seen the like in his life. Not even Lady Macarthur dressed in such finery. What was the bastard trying to prove? That he could steal anything he liked with impunity and parade it about? And why was he drawing attention to her? Every eye turned as they passed.

He gave himself a shake. It didn't matter. She wouldn't be the Blood's for more than an hour longer, anyway.

When his quarry rounded the corner he left the inn and ran across the street. Traveling behind head-high rowan, he made his way to his brother, who hid behind the stable.

When the road fronting Loch Fyne narrowed because of an outcropping, Angus kicked his mount ahead of Ian's. "Are ye growing tired, Birdi?"

"Nay."

"Humph." Birdi had been verra quiet since leaving the inn. He hoped it wasn't something he'd said, but then women were known to misconstrue a man's meaning at the oddest times. He'd seen Lady Beth do it often enough. Duncan's life was regularly at sixes and sevens without his having a hint as to why. Another reason Angus had shied away from wedded bliss for so many years. Women—no matter how loved—could drive sane men wode. Not that he loved Birdi.

He turned in the saddle to ask Ian if he'd won anything at the contest and saw two horsemen coming up on them fast, claymores drawn. He shouted in warning and Ian spun to look behind him.

Angus kicked Rampage around the boulders at a canter. Birdi, startled, asked, "What's wrong?"

"Trouble." Without explaining further, he lowered Birdi by an arm to the ground. He wrenched his sgian dubh from his leg lacings and pressed it into her hand. "Hide behind these boulders, up and to yer right. Climb as high and as quick as ye can."

Birdi grabbed his stirrup. "But why? What's happening?" The answer came by way of Ian shouting and steel clanging on steel.

"Hide, Birdi, now!"

The moment Birdi ran clear he turned Rampage on his hind legs and dug in his spurs.

As he came abreast of the fight, Ian toppled, a scarlet fountain spewing from his right shoulder.

Angus's battle cry tore from his throat as he swung his claymore at the man who'd felled Ian, then drove Rampage into the other rider. A battle veteran, his charger reared. Hooves flailing, he landed—all one hundred stone of him—on the pony's haunches. The pony screeched as it collapsed under the weight, unseating its rider. Angus swung his claymore again and caught the rising man on the side of his neck. He felt the resistance of bone as blood arced like a crimson rainbow. The man fell without issuing a sound. The second rider stared wide-eyed at his fallen companion for just a heartbeat, then spun and kicked his pony into a gallop, back to whence he'd come. Angus kicked Rampage in turn and followed.

He caught up with the rider at the next bend. Tall to start and better mounted, Angus had little trouble knocking the man off his horse. As the warrior crashed to the roadway, his shaggy mount bolted. Angus reined in and slid to the ground.

The man scrambled to his feet, claymore weaving before him, as Angus approached on foot. Ian was by now dead and this one was the man responsible.

Panting, the man eased to the right as Angus moved left, his blade singing as it swept the air before him in fast arcs. Teeth clenched, Angus growled, "Why?" If the bastard had any sense he'd drop his sword and answer.

The man lunged, feigned left, and swung again. Angus countered, catching him with the tip of his blade. The man jumped back and looked at his torn sleeve. Defiance flashed in the man's eyes as a smirk curled one side of his mouth. "So ye are as good as they claim."

Christ's blood! Had these men killed Ian just so they could brag they'd taken on Angus the Blood?

He saw red.

Sword flailing, his mind went blank. His muscles and experience took over the fight.

When he came to his senses, the man he fought lay in a bloody heap on the roadway, an arm missing, his neck severed.

Angus bowed his head and saw his own chest and legs were covered in blood. His claymore slipped from his bloody hands as his head fell back.

"Aaaaahhh!"

Birdi's skin prickled as pure agony echoed off the loch and rebounded off the high hills at her back. Her throat went dry. "Angus!"

She scrambled down shale and onto the roadway. "Please, Goddess, please, please dinna let it be Angus."

Arms outstretched she ran, head and heart reeling with the certain knowledge someone had died. "Please Goddess, please, I'll do anything ye ask. Please, oh please."

She stumbled, righted herself, and ran on. A moment later she saw something large lying in the road before her. Deep red was everywhere, big splotches of it scattered over the dark earth and lighter gravel of the roadway. Panting, heart threatening to make good its escape through her heaving chest, she dropped to her knees before the man. Blank brown eyes stared back at her. Who was this? 'Twasna Angus!

Ack! She didn't care who the man was. Her Angus was out here somewhere and she had to find him. She scrambled to her feet, took a step, and fell, her foot caught in her hem. Furious, she wrenched her skirts up with both hands, got to her feet, and ran on only to land hard on her hands and knees.

Familiar gold and black filled her limited field vision. "Ian? Oh, Goddess, it's Ian!" She crawled beside him through a pool of blood, looking for a wound. She instinctively jerked away when her hand made contact with wet stickiness. His right shoulder was soaked in blood. Leaning over him, she ran hasty fingers along his neck. She found a pulse, but it was only like that of a wee rabbit's, too fast and weak for a man his size, not strong enough to sustain his life. Should she stay and try to save him or seek Angus? Shaking, she keened, "What to do, what to do?"

When he groaned, his *need* ripped through her, and the decision was made. "Ian, can ye hear me?" His head lolled toward her and stunning blue eyes stared back at her. Tears ran down his cheeks. "Tell . . . him . . . I'm . . . sorry." His eyes then closed and his jaw went slack.

"Nay!" She slapped his cheek and shouted, "Listen to me! Believe. Trust in me."

To her relief, he opened his eyes once again. They didn't appear to see, but 'twas enough. Would have to be.

She rocked back onto her feet and, squatting, pressed her crossed palms firmly to his shoulder, making him groan. Heart racing, she pleaded, "Mother of All, 'tis I, Birdi. Please, I beg thee, come, and give me the strength once again. Please, Mother, please." She closed her eyes, took a deep, cleansing breath, and waited for the tingling heat to rise, a sure sign the force was again within her.

Feeling it surge through the soles of her feet, her heart finally slowed. Aye, 'twas now time. "Mother of All, I, Birdi, take upon myself this wound so Ian may live." She then crooned the auld words, the secret words of thanks and praise.

When she sensed the task done, Birdi lifted her hands from Ian's shoulder, and felt, rather than saw, a shadow over her where none should be.

Battling the mind-bending pain surging through her, she looked up. Angus's stark white face stared back.

Arms slack at his side, he dropped to his knees beside her. "Nay."

Her heart breaking, kenning he'd witnessed it all, she whispered, "I feared ye'd hate me. If ye kenned . . ."

Her world turned black.

Angus, his eyes locked on the scarlet stain blooming across Birdi's shoulder, barely managed to catch her before her head hit the ground. "Merciful Mother of God, please tell me this isna happening."

Nay.

He had never given credence to the tales of cailleachs, brehons, and bandrui. Hell, he barely gave credence to Saint Brigid, the patron saint of the Highlands. Yet try as he may he couldn't deny what his eyes had seen and his ears had heard. And he didn't want to believe. He wanted Birdi to be normal, just an odd, orphaned beauty. No secrets, no powers, no fears. Normal.

Blood continued to spread across Birdi's chest as the wind rushed across the loch. He felt cold tracks slide down his cheeks. Was his beautiful Birdi now dying?

Please, God, no.

He looked at his fallen friend still lying in a pool of blood. His jerkin was slashed and soaked with blood, as was the once snow-white shirt beneath, yet as Ian looked back at him from clear blue eyes, his skin returned to almost normal color when not a moment ago it had been ashen. His expression was as shocked as Angus suspected his own now was.

"She's a cailleach."

Struggling into a sitting position, Ian nodded. "Aye. Now put pressure on her wound."

Why hadn't he thought of that?

He pressed his hand down on Birdi's shoulder, feeling wet warmth—Birdi's life—beneath his palm. His stomach roiled. Oh dear God, his poor wee Birdi. *Her being pagan wasn't bad enough, God? Ye had to make her a cailleach?* Ack!

Ian wavered a bit and put his hands down to brace himself. "Are the bastards dead?"

Angus nodded. "But it happened again. I saw ye lying here, thinking ye dead, and . . ."

He didn't explain further. Ian had seen him lose control—become a berserker—once before; they'd come upon a group of Hessians raping two French women years ago.

Ian nodded in understanding, apparently unfazed, and then looked about. "We need to dress her wounds. Where's my horse?"

Angus shrugged. If there was any logic left in the world the cattle were together. He whistled. A moment later Rampage thundered up the road with Ian's black gelding at his back.

Ian staggered to his feet, grabbed his mount's reins, and tied him to a tree. "He isna as cooperative as yer beast." Ian routed around in the bag behind his saddle and pulled out a fine silk shirt. As he walked back, he tore it into strips.

"Take her cape off, and let's see what we're dealing with."

Angus undid the clasp at Birdi's breast and slipped the cape from her shoulders. Above the gown's wide scoop neck, he saw the top of the weeping scarlet slash. With his gut feeling like it was full of glass shards, he eased her arms out of the brocade. Ian held Birdi upright and Angus lifted the gown over her slack body. He pushed the sheer cotton shift down, exposing the whole oozing gash, and shuddered. It was a good six inches in length. He could see bone.

Ian cleared his throat. " 'Tis not so bad."

Angus glared at his friend.

Together they cleaned the wound and bound Birdi about the chest and right shoulder. Her shift and gown back in place, Angus cradled her to his chest. As he rocked side to side with her, he said, "We're only a few miles from

Clachan. I ken a kirk there where we can seek shelter for the night."

"Good. Come morn, 'tis only a day's ride to Inveraray. We can seek refuge with the Duke of Argyll until she recoups." After a minute he added, "Ye need be thinking about riding straight for Blackstone."

Angus brushed the loose strands from Birdi's face. Looking at her, lusting with all his heart that she would open her eyes, he said, "We canna. First, it's an arduous trek and she's in nay condition to make it, and second, Blackstone has a zealot for a priest. He'll drive her wode in an effort to convert her." Why his liege hadn't tossed the fanatic glutton out of Drasmoor years ago was beyond Angus's kenning. "And if he ever saw her lay on hands . . ."

Ian flexed his injured shoulder. "Listen to me. We can take a boat across Loch Awe at Portsonchan, which will cut off a good two-days' ride, then head due west. As for Fat John, who says he need ken what she is?"

"Ye dinna think he'll grow suspicious when she doesna show for vesters? When she doesna confess before him? The man isna an idiot." Fat John had given Lady Beth headaches too numerous to count when she'd first arrived—and the woman was Christian and worldly, unlike his Birdi.

"We'll make excuses for her absence until we can come up with something else."

Angus grunted. Birdi still didn't ken the Holy Ghost from a kelpie—would nay doubt trip herself up within a week—and God only kenned what would happen then. Ack. "How is yer shoulder?"

"Ye willna believe it." He shrugged off his jerkin and opened his shirt lacings for Angus to see.

Ian's wound—identical to the one Birdi now bore—was miraculously on the mend.

Though beyond belief, Angus no longer wondered how Birdi had come by her many scars.

Rising, he growled, "Let's get out of here."

Their footsteps echoed throughout Clachan kirk's frigid nave as Angus and Ian walked toward the altar. Ian, dirk in hand, murmured, " 'Tis empty."

Angus shifted Birdi in his arms. "Thank God." Birdi had been crying out in her sleep, much as she had after she'd tended Kelsea and the babe she'd found in the mews. There'd be no explaining it to a stranger. "Make a pallet for her there." He nodded toward the raised dais.

Ian snatched the cloth from the marble altar, hauled down a tapestry hanging to the right of a shallow alcove, and pulled the cushions from three tall, heavily carved chairs stationed to the left of the altar. After he'd laid them out, Angus lowered Birdi and covered her with Ian's breacan fiele. He then sat next to her and took her cool hand in his. He turned it over and rubbed a thumb over the calluses dotting her palm.

"Ye havena had an easy time of it, have ye, lass?"

And matters were likely to get worse. Ian was right. They need make for Blackstone. Castle Blackstone was an isle fortress. Ensconced within its walls, Birdi couldn't come to harm again. More importantly, she'd never be alone again. The priest he would deal with in some way.

And what of his wager with Duncan, and the lass who waited at Beal? He hissed through clenched teeth. Mayhap, if he looked pathetic enough—if he raised his wager to a full year's salary—Duncan would concede to giving him another fortnight to bring home a proper chatelaine bride. If Duncan would, he—Angus the Blood—might still be able to gain Donaliegh and his chiefship. And if he failed . . . hell, he'd already grown accustomed to starving.

He ran a finger along Birdi's lush lower lip. But to make it all work, he had to prepare her.

"Ian, find me some holy water."

Birdalane Shame was about to be baptized into the One True Faith.

Chapter 17

Birdi sat, shoulders sore, in a tall chair by a warm fire in a small, darkly paneled room. She pulled the soft blanket about her and warily eyed Angus as he spread their supper of bread and fish before them.

She'd been told when she awoke just an hour ago that they were now in Inveraray, in the home of a man named Argyll. Unable to tolerate the suspense any longer, she asked, "Are ye angry with me?"

"Nay. Mayhap disappointed ye didna trust me enough to confide in me, but not angry. Ye did, after all, save Ian's life."

Aye, there was that. "Thank ye for taking care of me. Again." He'd been most solicitous, despite her keeping him awake for two nights running as she raved and thrashed.

He pulled an angle iron out of the fire and stuck it in the tankard he held. A moment later he handed her warmed ale and honey. "Ye're welcome, but ye ken I canna tolerate any more secrets. Ye need be honest with me. And I want yer promise ye'll stop doing whatever it is ye do to bring yerself to harm."

" 'Tis not as if I seek the sick and dying, Angus." When the *need* came, it came, and there wasn't a thing she could do about it.

"I willna pretend to ken any of this, but I do ken ye do

it with a pure heart. Unfortunately, too many willna look upon yer . . ." He waved his hands in a helpless gesture.

"Healing?" she offered.

"Aye, healing, with the favor I view it."

"Ah." No great surprise there, she supposed. The Macarthurs feared her, so why wouldn't others? "And now what?"

He knelt before her so his eyes were level with hers and took her hands in his. She sighed. He had such lovely hands, broad and warm with such bonnie long fingers. Calloused, they held hers gently and made her feel safe.

"I'm taking ye home."

Her eyes grew wide. "Ye're taking us back to the glen?" She threw her arms about his neck. "Oh, thank ye, thank ye!" She kissed him then, hoping her lips could express the pure joy she felt within. Oh, she truly loved Angus the Canteran, and he obviously loved her. He wasn't angry after kenning what she truly was, had even called her pure of heart. Aye, she loved her Angus. They could live together . . . .

To her surprise, he gently pried her arms away.

"Birdi, we willna be going to yer glen, but to my home, Castle Blackstone."

"Oh." Disappointment landed with a thud in her chest. Like a hot coal it burned a hole within her breast. "But why?"

He cleared his throat. "With my people ye'll be safe and willna ever be alone again."

"I see." Her throat burned, realizing she'd misunderstood. He didn't feel as she did, didn't experience the same joy at their touching, listening to the other speak. He didn't want her, but only felt obligated to keep her safe.

Feeling much akin to how she'd felt handing over Wee Angus to Kelsea, she clasped her hands in her lap. "Ye dinna ken how it is, Angus. Yer clan will take one look at me and turn away just as the Macarthurs do."

He placed his hands on either side of her face. "Birdi, they willna, because I'll teach ye what ye need ken to be one of them."

"But my eyes . . ."

He frowned. "What about them?"

"They'll ken me—what I am—by my eyes."

"Birdi, though unique, yer eyes are beautiful. So bonnie, in fact, my heart nearly stopped the first time I saw them."

She shook her head, not believing a word, for if his heart had nearly stopped, he'd feel as she did. He'd be taking her home, and they'd share her croft and swim and . . .

"Birdi, ask Ian. Ye trust him. He'll tell ye the same."

She studied his eyes, so wondrously blue and kind. Poor man, he did believe what he said, but she kenned better. She'd seen her truth in a looking glass.

Forcing a smile, she asked, "What need I learn?"

He suddenly grinned. "That's the brave lass." He kissed the tip of her nose, then rose. Pacing, he said, "First, ye need ken manners. We are, after all, in the house of a duke. We can deal with prayers and the like later."

As he droned on, pacing and gesturing before her, Birdi patted her pocket. Aye, 'twas still there, her missive to Tinker. She'd post it on the morrow. Tonight and until Tinker could come for her, she need only humor the handsome Canteran who apparently still loved his hale Mary.

Beneath the flight of circling and squawking gulls, Angus led Birdi, dressed in a borrowed gown—hers was still having the blood washed out of it—through the streets of Inveraray. As he described the fishing boats and catches, explained the local lore, he watched men watch her.

He hadn't wanted to take her out, but she'd insisted, claiming she needed to buy a necessity. Never having lived with a woman, but kenning they had odd rituals and a monthly flow they called "the flowers," he thought better of arguing with her. Besides, if she traveled about and none shouted, *Witch!* she might finally believe she wasn't so visibly different from her peers. Unfortunately, she was lovely and people did stare—but then, she didn't notice, being so blind.

Stopping before a shop bearing a sign with a thistle, he handed her a coin. "This should get whatever ye need. I'll wait by the door. Should ye have any trouble, any at all, just call."

Biting her bottom lip, Birdi mumbled, "Thank ye." She then took a deep breath, squared her shoulders, and, chin high, entered the shop. He smiled. No one would ever ken she wasn't a lady of high birth.

After a few minutes she came out carrying two sugarplums.

"Did ye get what ye needed?"

She handed him one of the sweets and three bodles. "I did what I need do. Can we go back to the keep now?"

What was amiss? Why didn't she appear happy after her first successful barter? "Are ye sure? They have a market ye might enjoy."

"I'm sure."

"Verra well." He placed a hand at her waist and turned her up the hill. As they passed an alehouse a bawdy female voice called, "Drop her home and come back to me, handsome!"

Birdi grew roots in the roadway. Frowning, she asked, "Who's that?"

"Just a paikie."

"A what?"

He leaned forward so she could hear him over the woman's continued catcalls, the gulls, and the rumbling wagons. "A trull, ye ken, a prostitute."

Birdi nodded and pursed her lips. "And what is she to ye?"

"Nothing, I assure ye." He reached for her elbow, but

Birdi wrenched free and stomped over to the trull before he realized what she was about.

Hands on hips, her gaze raked the brassy-throated woman. "Ye have a bonnie gown, mistress, but yer mouth doesna do it justice."

The paikie assumed the same stance, a smirk gracing her hard-worn face. "And who might ye be, calling my mouth into question?"

Angus sidled up to Birdi and took her elbow, well aware people had stopped to listen. "Come on, Birdi. We need go."

Birdi shook off his hand. To the woman she hissed, "His ladywife, and I'll thank ye to keep yer thoughts to yerself."

"Oh, will ye now?"

"Aye, or I'll cut ye from gullet to tail, slip ye from yer skin and nail it on my door. Then I'll tan yer sorry hide—"

Angus yanked Birdi off her feet and spun. Carrying her in one arm, he strode up the hill. Over his shoulder, he called, "Our pardon, madam."

When he thought it safe, he set her down and, using a firm hand, hustled her along. Aware people still watched them he hissed, "God's teeth, Birdi. Ye dinna engage her ilk."

"But she's one of those . . . she spreads the . . . I canna remember the name. Ye ken, the one where yer poker gets full of pus and near falls off."

"Ack, Birdi! Ye canna be speaking of pokers and pus, not in public at any rate. Come."

He couldn't believe she even kenned the ailment grand-gore, let alone talked about it. Ack! The sooner he got her home and started shoving some solid catechism down her throat, the better off they'd both be. The woman had absolutely no sense of public decorum.

Angus frowned as Birdi, glassy eyed, held the prayer book he'd given her with the reverence a minion might give the Pope's staff. She obviously liked his gift, so why didn't she open it?

Biting her lower lip, she finally admitted, "I canna read."

"Ah." He rubbed his jaw for a moment and then smiled. " 'Tisna a problem. Ye have a quick mind. Ye can commit to memory what ye need ken."

"Oh?"

"Just repeat after me . . . . Our Father who—"

She blinked like an owl. "Ye ken my father?"

He grinned. "Nay, Birdi, 'tis only a prayer. Just repeat it. Our Father who art in heaven . . ."

"Our Father who art in heather."

"Nay *heather,* Birdi, hea-ven."

"Where's heaven?"

"In the sky, beyond the stars."

"There's something beyond the stars?"

Accepting it would be a long night, Angus assured her, "Aye, Birdi, a magical place full of angels—winged people of great spirit."

"Ah."

He smiled. This might not be so difficult after all. "Hallowed be thy name."

"What name?"

"God's."

"What god?"

Where the hell was silver-tongued Ian when he needed him? "Our God, yours and mine. Everyone's."

"I dinna ken him. Now, Mother of All, Goddess, I ken. She's all power—"

"Birdi, just listen and repeat."

She huffed and slouched in her chair. "As ye lust."

"Thy kingdom come, thy will be done, on earth as it is in heaven . . . ."

Looking petulant, her lower lip pouched out, she repeated the phrase.

"Very good. Now . . . Give us this day our daily bread."

"Give us this day our daily bread."

"And forgive us our debts as we forgive our debtors."

"Ye have debts?"

He squeezed the bridge of his nose in an effort to ease the pain building behind his eyes. "No, Birdi. It means to forgive those who injure ye."

She snorted, but repeated the phrase.

". . . and lead us not into temptation, but deliver us from evil, amen."

When she'd repeated that, he asked, "Would ye like me to say it again—all at once this time—so ye can better learn it?"

"Nay, I ken it just fine." She sighed, propped an elbow on the armrest, and rested her chin in her hand. "Our Father in heaven with the hallowed name—which Angus has neglected to mention—thank ye for the day and bread. Forgive the debts and debtors. Lead us away from temptation and evil, amen." She heaved a mournful-sounding sigh. "What means *amen?*"

Good God. "Amen means the end."

His, by the sound of things. Could he pass off her strange phrasing as a regional oddity? "Would ye mind trying another?" Mayhap she could get this one right.

She sighed. "I suppose. I've naught better to do."

He forced a smile, and considered the Hail Mary. 'Twas short and easy enough, but mayhap it would be better if he taught her something more encompassing, one she could recall should Blackstone's priest—or anyone else, for that matter—question her about doctrine. Settling on the Apostles' Creed, he said, "This one is long but verra important. Are ye ready?"

She sighed, her elbow still on the armrest, her chin still in her hand. "Aye."

"Repeat after me . . . . I believe in God, the Father Almighty, creature of heaven and earth . . ."

"Nay, nay, nay." Birdi held up a hand and straightened.

"Ye must have it wrong. Goddess made earth, *is* earth in fact. In the beginning . . ."

Angus was no longer listening.

The throbbing pain behind his eyes, the one that now pulsed with the rhythm of a farrier's hammer on steel, made it impossible. He slowly dropped to the sheepskin rug at Birdalane Shame's feet and reached for her tankard. He drained it and reached for the flagon. He'd been wrong in assuming it would be a long night. He'd yet to mention Christ, the Immaculate Conception, or the Resurrection, and he could already tell 'twas, in fact, going to be a verra, verra long night if they survived it at all.

The flagon emptied, he wondered where Argyll hid his whiskey.

Ian sat to the left of the Duke of Argyll, whiskey in hand, before the great hall's blazing fire, watching the duke's wooden-sword-wielding bairn torment the guards and a pair of gray lymers, their great heads tucked beneath equally great paws, while the ladies sat at a distance in apparent oblivion, their needles flashing through embroidery hoops.

He caught one green-eyed beauty shyly eyeing him from beneath the wide brim of her headdress as she labored. He smiled back, arched an eyebrow in question, and as expected she giggled and ducked her chin, her cheeks glowing bright red. Ah, virgins. Lovely to look at, but nay to touch.

He sighed, feeling both comfortable and envious of those in the hall. There was definitely something to be said for living within a keep with kith and kin. Ye didn't have to fash about private agendas and subterfuges, nor spend a fortune to look the part of a courtier when all ye really wanted to wear was a coarse shirt, yer breacan feile, and naught else.

He'd not seen his home—the lands in the far north-west—in five years, not since becoming an agent for the Duke of Albany.

Aye, the glamour of being at court, of traveling to the continent, had definitely waned, but 'twas a sacrifice he would continue to make willingly. First, to assure his sept remained secure within their holdings despite their frequent confrontations with their neighbors, the Earls of Caithness and Sutherland; and second, to keep Scotland safe until their true king returned. Though given what he now kenned of Albany, Ian wouldn't be holding his breath as he waited.

Argyll cleared his throat. "MacDougall's ladywife is verra quiet, and such an odd name . . . Birdi."

"'Tis MacDougall's pet name for her. She can be a bit flighty."

Despite Angus's obvious annoyance, Ian had introduced Angus and Birdi as husband and wife, since Birdi had no chaperone. The blood on their clothing he'd explained away by stating he'd been wounded and that Birdi had been soiled while tending him. The lie not only garnered sympathy for the fair and fulsome woman but elevated Birdi's status.

"And who is her sire?" Argyll asked.

Ah. Argyll wanted to ken what alliances Birdi and Angus's union may have formed. Ian yawned, feigning disinterest. "Her father was a lowland sheriff of little note who died many years past. She came with no dowry to speak of. Her gown was a wedding gift from the Mac-Dougall." He shrugged. "I fear my friend made an alliance of the heart rather than one of the purse. But ye can't fault the man—one need only take one look at Lady Mac-Dougall to ken his reason."

Argyll snorted. "Aye, she is most definitely fair, but dinna be as foolish as yer friend. Remember, ye canna eat beauty, nor will it defend yer holdings."

Relieved his lies wouldn't be challenged—having Argyll for an enemy could prove disastrous to all of them—Ian promised, "When the time comes, I shall heed yer advice."

"Do." After taking a sip of his ale, Argyll said, "Now tell me what ye hear of our jailed laddie and the Gunn."

The Macarthur growled deep in his throat. His best swordsmen—good men both—were dead? " 'Tisna possible," he growled at the man he'd sent to hunt the brothers down after growing impatient for word about his kidnapped spae.

"Aye, sire, they are." The messenger cast a quick glance at Mary Macarthur, heavy with child, greeting for all she was worth by the fire. Nodding in her direction, he whispered, "Beheaded, sire." He shuddered and said in a normal tone, "I buried them and brought back their swords and ponies for their families."

The Macarthur, not giving a wee bawbee what the man did with the damn swords and ponies, bit down on his tongue. 'Twouldna do to appear frazzled before the clan. "The MacDougall and the spae, man."

"I dinna ken where exactly, sire, but they were heading west. 'Twas an hour out of Cairndow that I found Robbie and Fegan."

Nay doubt the Blood and his spae were heading toward Drasmoor and Castle Blackstone. To his captain Macarthur he said, "Get the weaponry ready. I want every man over the age of five-and-ten armed and ready to ride at dawn."

He'd have MacDougall's head on a spike before the next full moon if he had to lop it off himself.

As the sky beyond the window started to lighten to soft lavender, Angus shifted on the uncomfortable pallet he'd made from the bedcovering and opened his eyes. Birdi lay on her side in the big bed their host had intended for both of them to share, her face as serene as a newborn babe's. Came from sleeping with a clear conscious, he supposed. He envied her. He couldn't recall the last time he'd slept through the night.

And what was he to do about Birdalane Shame?

She'd learned the Apostles' Creed, not well, but had committed the broad points to memory. But she wouldn't concede in any fashion or form that God—and not Goddess—had crafted the world.

Getting her to ken the Immaculate Conception and Resurrection had been easy—she had similar beliefs in her own faith—but getting her to understand the Crucifixion of Christ had been a nightmare. No way was she going to accept an all-powerful father's deliberately allowing his son—one he claimed to love—to die on a cross. They'd gone around and around on that singular point for most of the night. He'd finally admitted defeat when she'd suggested we hang God on a cross and see how he likes it.

His head started to throb just thinking about it.

To make matters more untenable, they—he and Ian—had declared Birdi his wife before the Duke of Argyll, which meant there was absolutely no way Father John couldn't hear about it. He'd raise bloody hell and insist on a kirk ceremony. Ack.

He might as well kiss Donaliegh and his chiefship goodbye. And all because he saw a fair maiden rise out of the water like a mythical kelpie and wanted her.

Hell, he still wanted her. *Just look at her.* She was not only stunningly beautiful, but funny, irreverent—and lusty, if their one bout of lovemaking was any indication. And he could still taste her, still feel the texture of her skin at the tips of his fingers, could still smell the sweet scent of grass and woman that emanated off her.

Ack, what to do?

One thing was certain. This was the absolute last time he would ever let his poke-a-sweeties rule his head.

Seeing Birdi's eyes open, he murmured, "Good morn."

"Morn." She cleared her throat. "Frog," she told him. "Minnie said they crawl in if ye sleep with yer mouth open." She stretched and yawned. "Though how one got all the way up here is beyond kenning." She rolled into a sitting position, her shoulders and arms exposed, her bandage evident, the sheet clamped in a fist at the junction of her high breasts. "How was yer sleep?"

"Wonderful."

"I'm hungry. Do ye think anyone is awake below stairs?"

Angus rolled up and onto his feet. Pouring water into a washbowl, he said, "I'll wager we can find some griddle cakes."

"Oow!" She beamed at him, dimples making crags in her cheeks.

He grinned. "Ye like havers, huh?"

"Oh, aye. They're best right after hulling, but I'll eat them any time." She bounded out of bed, her front covered, her backside jiggling ever so slightly, obviously enjoying the freedom and air.

She would definitely be the death of him.

Birdi settled beside him to watch his ablutions, stretching her mouth this way and that as he shaved.

Staring at his blade, she asked, "Why do ye do that?"

"I'm told ladies prefer a clean-shaven man."

She gave that some thought. "It does appear cleaner." She ran a careful hand down his cheek. "Feels nicer, too."

He had all he could do to keep from grabbing her wrist and planting a kiss on her palm. "Ah, the lady does apparently prefer a clean-shaven man."

"Am I a lady?"

"Of course."

"Because we're handfast?"

"In part."

Her brow furrowed. "What will I become when ye break the handfast?"

Ah . . . when *he* broke the handfast, huh? "Ye will still be a lady but not Lady MacDougall. Ye'll be Mistress Shame."

"Nay!" She jumped off the chair and went to the open window. Voice cracking, she declared, "I willna bare the shame of my . . . consepshin . . . as my name. She's dead. So is he, for all I ken. Let the ghost lie."

Frowning, he dropped the toweling he'd been using to dry his hands. He walked to her and, taking her by the shoulders, turned her to face him. "Birdi, what are yer talking about? Isna ye clan name Shame?"

"I dinna have a family, so how can I have such?"

Unease made mush of his already abused gut. "Birdi, when I asked ye who yer sire was ye told me Shame."

"Aye, 'twas what *she* said." A tear shimmered on the cusp of her thick lashes. In a low tone she hissed, "'Shame's yer sire, his shame, my shame, and now yer shame for asking.'" The tear toppled as a dewdrop might off the bend of a rose petal and made its slow way down one cheek. He caught it on the tip of his finger, where it sat like a liquid diamond.

He suddenly felt very ill. "Ye poor birdalane."

"Aye, 'twas exactly what she called me."

Birdi might as well have shoved a knife in his gut and twisted it. Merciful Mother of God. Her mother hadn't even had the decency to name her. If she'd been alive he would have strangled the woman right then and there and taken great pleasure in the doing.

He kissed her forehead. "Today you must choose a new and special first name. One as beautiful as ye." His arm about her waist, he walked back to the water bowl. "After yer ablutions, we'll eat. As we ride we'll think of yer new name. We'll get Ian to help."

And from this day forward Birdi would bear the last name of MacDougall, and he'd slit the throat of any man who claimed she hadn't the right.

Birdi sniffed. "I would like that."

"Verra good. Now turn, so I can unwrap this bandage."

In Castle Blackstone's great hall, Duncan MacDougall, laird of all he surveyed, smiled.

"What are ye grinning about?"

He looked up and found his ladywife, Katherine Elizabeth MacDougall Pudding MacDougall—Beth to those who loved her—leaning over his shoulder. Good God, he was a lucky man. He'd found her in a fractured coach one stormy night, and believing her to be the woman Albany intended for his fourth bride, Duncan had immediately married her. By the time he discovered the astonishing—and at the time horrifying—truth, that she was a woman of the future transported back in time by the wedding ring she now wore, he had already lost his heart to her, and his life had forever changed. The three bairns that romped about his feet were but a small measure of the many ways.

She bent down and kissed his cheek. "Well?"

"I just received a missive from my cousin Kelsea Lindsey Fraiser," he said.

"That's nice. What did she have to say?"

Chapter 18

Since the missive was written in French and his dear wife couldn't get her mind around the language, Duncan read aloud, "My most revered cousin, I write on behalf of a most astonishing woman named Birdi, who believes this missive is addressed to a person of her acquaintance named Tinker. If you are reading this I must assume your captain-at-arms Angus MacDougall has not seen the light and is behaving the fool."

Beth laughed.

Trying not to laugh himself, Duncan continued, "He obviously loves Birdi, and she, I assure you, is much in love with him. Their circumstances are, however, most different and difficult. Birdi is, in a word, extraordinary, both in visage and in heart, but she is not one of us, not of the gently bred. I beg you to look kindly upon her should she arrive on your threshold. She has done me a great service, one I will never be able to repay in this lifetime. She is truly pure goodness and more than a match for your Angus. If you please, your humble servant, Kelsea Lindsey Fraiser."

Beth curled in the chair across from him. "My, my, it seems your scheme worked. Our Angus has finally found himself a woman."

"Aye, but all isna apparently going well, else we wouldna have received this."

"Could it be because ye charged him with—Duncan

Thomas MacDougall! Stop pulling yer sister's hair or ye'll find yerself sitting in a corner."

"Humph!" Why could she not just clout the wee beastie on the side of his head as he did and be done with it? But nay. His ladywife had to torture their poor son for an hour, making the wee laddie sit in a corner where he fretted and grumbled for all to hear.

If he lived to be one hundred years, he'd never ken his ladywife's odd ways.

Beth turned her attention back to him. "What was I saying? Ah . . . Angus. Could it be that you charged him with finding a chatelaine but he didn't—that in your cousin's words, he found one that's not 'one of us?' "

"Mayhap. He does take pride in keeping his word." He sighed. "When I forced him into the wager, I just wanted him to find a worthy wife. I was weary of seeing envy in his eyes every time he watched the Silversteins, or you and me. He was lonely and too proud—"

"And stubborn."

"And too stubborn," he conceded, "to admit it. And I only insisted on a chatelaine because I didna trust him not to grab the first lass he came upon. He does crave a lairdship with a passion most men dinna expend even on their wives."

Beth grinned and patted her swollen belly. "Unlike one handsome laird I could mention."

Ack, 'twasna his fault Beth was a delicious handful in bed. "Humph!"

Beth rose. "I'd best get started getting a room ready." She put her hands on the small of her back and arched. "I don't move like I used to."

Duncan came to his feet and wrapped his arms about her. "Have I ever told ye how lovely ye are?" How she could think herself plain was beyond kenning.

Beth blushed to a rosy hue as she always did whenever he mentioned her appearance. "Go on with ye." She kissed him and waddled off carrying his seed, his legacy, snug within her hips. God, he loved her.

He cleared his throat. Now to make sure Angus experienced the same mind-befuddling existence.

Riding ahead of them down the slippery shale slope, Ian called over his shoulder, "Belinda!"

Angus, leaning back as far as the saddle would allow, asked, "What say ye? 'Tis fair."

Birdi, leaning back as well, shook her head. "Nay."

The men had already suggested hundreds of names, mayhap as many names as there were stars below heaven, and still none felt right to her. And they were now only a few miles from Angus's Drasmoor. She could already smell change in the air. Something tangy, not unlike the breeze off Inveraray, yet different, stronger, foreign, not unlike the man who held her. And she needed a name before she met his people.

She now kenned, to her shame—ack, she loathed that word—that she'd never been given a true one. She'd only assumed one. She huffed. "More, tell me more."

Angus yawned. "Meg, Peg, Margaret."

"Ye've said those before."

Ian called, "Florence, Paris, Roma."

Angus laughed. "Dinna listen to him. He's desperate."

Somehow, finding a name for her had turned into a challenge between the men. How, she didn't ken, but she suspected they did it only to keep awake. They hadna stopped but to relieve themselves or eat in more than a day.

"Mckensie," Ian called.

Angus huffed, "Nay. Mckensie MacDougall has far to many 'mc' sounds. Every time she says it people will think she's clearing the back of her throat."

He did have a point.

And she couldn't get over Angus's offering her his sire-name. She would be a MacDougall for life, no matter what awaited her in Drasmoor. So grand a gift she had no way of repaying.

Drasmoor. She didn't want to reach it. All would change. She'd lose the ease of being herself. The last three days—though hard on her back and bottom—had been a warm poultice on her heart and mind. Angus and Ian had even teased her about her power. Well, 'twasna really her power but Goddess's streaming through her, but they didn't care. They teased anyway. And to ken they really believed a god from some faraway place where sand became mountains—she'd like to see them before they fell—controlled the moon, the sun, and what grew about them. So verra strange.

As they came over the crest of a high ridge, Angus pointed over her shoulder. "Look, Birdi, your new home. Drasmoor and Castle Blackstone."

She shoved the hair whipping about her face in a stiff wind—one that carried the scent of peat, fish, and sea— aside. A mass of blue and green beyond all kenning loomed before her. More disturbing was seeing from her great height that it went on forever. Throat tightening, she realized that here she truly could get lost and might never be found.

They rode downhill, up, and down again and finally broke out of the forest. Angus slowed Rampage just as she heard dogs barking, cattle lowing, bairn laughter, and shouts—all she'd come to associate with a busy village.

"This is Drasmoor," Angus whispered.

As they followed Ian's horse, boisterous people ran up and greeted them using words Birdi didn't ken. She did her best to smile, despite the frantic thundering of blood in her ears.

Here the brown blobs—shapes she kenned to be crofts—were spaced too far apart, the smell of horse and fish was too strong. And then she saw a tall dark shape looming at a distance before her, nearly black against the bright blue she now kenned to be the sea. Fearing the answer, she pointed. "What is that?"

Angus pushed the hair off her ear and whispered, " 'Tis Castle Blackstone."

Ack! 'Twas surrounded by sea, water that didn't lie flat like her pool but moved as if alive. Oh, Goddess . . .

Before she could garner her courage she was lifted into a boat. When it rocked beneath her, she squealed and grabbed hold of the sides for dear life.

Angus steadied her. "Easy, Birdi. All's well."

"Nay! 'Tis far from well."

He chuckled as he sat and pulled her onto his lap. "There's nothing to fear, love. The sea's calm."

Oh, Goddess! 'Tis calm? Ooooh . . .

The boat shifted again as men joined them. She looked about. "Where's Ian?"

"He's tending the horses. Not to worry, he'll catch the next boat."

Too soon they were moving, rocking up and down to the rhythm of wood beating water and men grunting. Unable to do anything else, she squeezed her eyes shut and huddled into Angus's warm chest. She didn't like this, not at all.

Mother of All, 'tis I, Birdi. I ken ye're busy but ye need listen. I'm in great danger. I'm in a boat . . . .

Angus lifted Birdi's chin. "Ye can open yer eyes now. We're here."

"Oh." She straightened and looked up. " 'Tis bigger than I feared."

Angus stood and took her hand. " 'Tis a good-sized fortress, but there's naught to fear." He guided her to the side of the boat. "I'll lift ye up and onto the quay, but stay where I put ye. I dinna want to be fishing ye out of the sea."

She nodded like a sandpiper. "Aye."

When her feet hit solid ground, she froze in place, apparently not daring to bat an eyelash. Ah, Birdi.

Angus bounded onto the quay and took her arm. "Are ye ready to go inside?"

She looked none too sure, but took a deep breath and lifted her chin. "Aye."

"Good lass." Angus then took his own deep breath. He'd yet to figure out a way to tell his liege about the mess he'd gotten himself into without sounding the idiot.

But 'twas good to be home for the first time in months. He'd missed the camaraderie of his friends, and God kenned how much he'd missed Lady Beth's kitchen.

As they crossed the interior bailey, Birdi's head cocked right, then left, as she tried to identify the sounds, her lips moved soundlessly. She was, he kenned, counting her steps.

He opened the lower bailey door for her. "Take hold of the rope near yer left hand . . . . Good, now pay close heed. The steps are curved and bend to the right as ye climb. I'm right behind ye."

Birdi made slow and steady progress, her skirts in her right hand. "Why do they curve so?"

"So that should we come under siege the attackers willna be able to wield their swords within the stairwell."

"Oh."

At the top of the stairs he pushed on the heavy oak door, took Birdi's elbow, and guided her into Blackstone's thirty-foot-long great hall. Seeing his liege and lady standing before the left-hand fireplace, he turned Birdi in their direction.

"Something smells wondrous," Birdi murmured.

He smiled down at her. Wee Mistress Oatcakes didn't ken the half.

His smile vanished when he looked up and realized he

already stood before Duncan. He bowed. "My lord and lady."

Duncan's gaze roamed Birdi from tip to toe, then back again. "Welcome home, Angus. I see ye found what ye were looking for."

Nay exactly. "My lord, my lady, may I present Lady MacDougall of Loch Ard Forest. Lady MacDougall, this is my liege, Duncan MacDougall, and his honorable wife, Lady Beth."

Birdi, to his amazement, executed a graceful curtsey. Had he been asked to execute the same maneuver, he'd have fallen flat on his face, such was his current agitation.

Lady Beth came forward and took Birdi's hand from his arm. "I'm so verra pleased to make yer acquaintance. Come, we need leave these two alone so they can chat. I'll show ye to yer room."

As Lady Beth led her away, Birdi sent a silent plea to him over her shoulder.

" 'Tis well, Birdi, fear naught. I'll be there in just a moment."

Duncan snorted. "Not if I have anything to say about it." Motioning for Angus to take Lady Beth's chair, he said, "Sit and tell me about this Birdi. Ye have exquisite taste, by the way."

Angus groaned. "First I need whiskey." Lots of it.

Duncan caught the eye of a passing clanswoman. "Mistress, whiskey for our friend and one for yer liege. Tall ones."

Grinning, the woman dipped a curtsey. "As ye lust, sire." To Angus she said, " 'Tis good to have ye home, Angus."

"Thank ye, Kari."

Whiskey half drunk, Angus said, "All isna as I lusted, Duncan. I bragged I could bring home a lady of high birth, and I've failed. Birdi isna as she appears to be." He took another swing of the water of life. "One morn, deep in

Macarthur territory, I awoke to a splash in a nearby glen and found this woman arising from a pool . . . ."

Birdi found herself in the room Lady Beth had assigned to her and Angus. " 'Tis lovely, my lady." And it was, from what little she could see standing by the door.

"Please call me Beth. Duncan and Angus are such good friends it would be silly for ye to call me 'my lady' while they called each other by first names. May I call you Birdi?"

Birdi wrung her fingers, lusting with all her might that she'd already found the perfect name. "I willna be Birdi much longer."

"Oh?"

"Aye, Angus says I can choose any name I lust, but I havena found the right one as yet, but ye may call me Birdi until such time as I do find one."

"Well, I think that's a grand plan."

Birdi heaved a relieved sigh and wandered about the room slowly so as not to trip. What she could see and feel of it so far, she found most pleasing. The high poster bed was much like the one at the duke's home, but broader. She couldn't see the far side. Chests sat at the foot and one sat beneath a window with a deep sill. It was currently open but could be covered by thick wooden shutters. A fire burned to her left as she faced the door. She sniffed but couldn't catch the scent of Angus; but then he'd been gone a long while. "Is this Angus's room?"

Beth moved to sit on the end of the bed. "Nay, 'tis a special room reserved for special guests. The garderobe is just to the left."

A garden robe? She'd ask Angus when to wear it. She didn't want to appear the fool before his friend. Inching closer to Lady Beth so she might better study her, Birdi ran a hand across the honey-colored fabric on the bed. Ah, rich and deep, like the cloth Angus had left behind at the waterfall. Such a waste. " 'Tis lovely velvet."

"Thank you. Here." Lady Beth thumped the mattress. "Come sit beside me."

Birdi sat. Mmm, very soft, more so than even the duke's bed.

Taking one of Birdi's hands, Lady Beth smiled. "Do tell. How did ye meet our handsome Angus?"

Oh, nay. Nay, nay, she wouldn't be relating that tale. "He is handsome."

"Aye, he is."

As Lady Beth waited, Birdi racked her brain for something to say other than *he almost killed my wolf and I bled all over him*. When her stomach growled, she murmured, "I like oats. And Angus cooks fish verra well." She looked about helplessly. "I would like to learn how to make Lady Fraiser's fish pies. They were verra good."

Beth grinned. "Ah, ye're hungry. I do apologize. I'll see to it immediately while ye freshen up."

She was hungry. "Thank ye. Angus has told me ye are a fine cook."

"That's nice to hear. In truth, I just prepare foods that make men happy."

"Ye do?" If she could cook the foods that made Angus happy, mayhap he might grow fond of her and forget his hale Mary and her beehive breasts. "Might ye teach me?"

"I'd love to." Lady Beth stood and checked the water in the pitcher. "Oh, it's already cold. I'll have the lass fetch some warm water for ye."

"Nay, 'tis fine." Curious why this woman didn't speak as the others, Birdi garnered her courage and asked, "Are ye a stranger here as well?"

"Aye, as a matter of fact I am." She patted her belly, a good seven moons swollen with child. "I've been here three years."

"And are ye happy here?"

"Happier than I've ever been in my life." She stroked Birdi's cheek. "Ye will be as well. Angus is a good man." She walked to the door. "By the way, ye have lovely eyes."

Birdi tried to draw breath but nothing happened. As the room spun, she wondered what ailed the people of this clan that they didn't ken a spae's evil eyes when they saw them.

"Birdi? Sweetie, can ye hear me? Shit!"

Something cold and wet pressed Birdi's forehead and she opened her eyes. Lady Beth hovered over her, concern clearly etched on her oddly pretty visage. Wondering why she should garner such sympathy, Birdi looked down and saw she sat on the floor, propped against Lady Beth. Embarrassed to her toes, she struggled to stand.

Lady Beth pressed her shoulder—thankfully, her uninjured one. "Sit for just another moment."

She wiped Birdi's face and hands before looking deep into her eyes. "Are ye feeling better?"

Birdi nodded, still amazed the woman didn't screech.

"Let's forget about ablutions and such and get something in yer belly, shall we?"

"Aye, I'd like that."

"Good." She helped Birdi to her feet. Hand at her elbow, Lady Beth guided her back to the greatroom.

The moment she entered the warm room, the men came to their feet. Lady Beth handed her off to Angus and reached for a bell. A heartbeat later she was sitting at Angus's right on a raised platform at the opposite end of the room, her back to a warm fire, and a mountain of food before her, most of which she didn't recognize.

When she hesitated, Angus murmured, "Roast pork and applesauce, ye'll love it. That," he pointed to a pile of greens, some of which she did recognize, "is salad. Verra good as well."

"And this?" She pointed to a mound of brown cubes sitting next to the meat.

"Roasted potatoes with rosemary. Yum." He reached for a small metal pitcher and poured brown water over the meat. "Bon appetit."

"Huh?"

"Eat." With that, he dug into his trencher with both hands. Birdi, hungrier than she'd been in a great while and still shaky, sampled her first mouthful. Salty, crispy, *oh my word*. She had definitely died and gone to Angus's heaven.

She couldn't get the meat into her mouth fast enough. Lusting for four hands, she found Angus grinning at her. She smiled back but didn't stop eating. Lady Beth might ring her bell and then the delicious food would disappear.

When she scraped the last of her bread through the last of her brown juice, she leaned back, folded her hands over her well-stuffed middle, and sighed. To no one in particular she said, " 'Twas verra good."

The laird of Castle Blackstone hooted with laughter, startling her. "Ye've met yer match, my friend, at least at the table."

When Angus chuckled, Birdi relaxed again, deciding she might like it here, after all.

Angus stood, pulled her chair back, and whispered, "We now retire to the other end of the room while the table is cleared."

She took his outstretched hand. "As ye lust." Being a lady definitely had its benefits: good food, bonnie gowns, a comfy bed above stairs, and someone else to clear the table. She could live like this.

She was halfway across the long room, her hand resting on Angus's strong arm, when a door to the right squeaked and a dark shape moved toward her.

"Good day, MacDougall, Lady MacDougall," the dark shape said. "And who is this?"

As the man moved closer, Angus's liege said, "Father John, may I present Lady MacDougall. Lady MacDougall, this is . . ."

Birdi's heart stopped. Cold sweat erupted beneath her arms and across her brow. She saw only a black hood, black gown, and a large wooden cross. *Beware of the priests in black gowns who burn the likes of ye on pyres.*

"Aaaaahhhh!"

Arms out, elbows locked, she rammed the hooded specter of her nightmares. After knocking him backward, she bolted out the door. Tripping and stumbling down the circular stairs, she keened, "Oh, Goddess, please, please help me!"

They'd fattened her up to eat!

And she'd never forgive Angus. Such deceit was beyond . . . beyond . . .

At the bottom of the stairwell, Birdi slammed against a clansman coming in. She slapped him out of the way and raced straight ahead. Fifty steps, just fifty steps to get out of this dreadful place. *Run straight and ye'll ken the arch.*

Heart slamming against her ribs, hands before her, she ran, mouth wide—sucking in as much life-giving air as Goddess would allow. Halfway across the bailey she realized she'd forgotten to start counting. *Just go,* an inner voice bellowed, *and you'll find the sea. Just go!*

Aye, better to drown than be burned alive.

Nay, she wouldn't drown. She swam like a fish.

Running through the arch, ignoring the shouts and pounding footfalls rising behind her, she sent a final sacred prayer to Goddess, asking for the sea to welcome her, a stranger.

Without hesitation she ran straight into the heaving white foam roaring at the end of the stone walkway.

As the bone-breaking cold engulfed her, knocked the breath from her chest, she felt the sea grab hold and pull her to its bosom. She kicked with all her might and rose, but something kept trying to pull her back down. Her arms clawed at the water, her left strong, and her right almost useless. Why had she not stripped before plunging? *Oh, Goddess. Help!*

She kicked furiously, until her legs screamed for reprieve. Finally she felt the top of her head break through a wave and into the sun, but then—before she could grab a breath of air—she slipped down. She stopped fighting then. She was simply too wee to break free.

As the sea spun her in its liquid embrace, she confided to Goddess, *Ah. I ken now. I live as a stranger in yer land and shall now die a stranger in yer sea. So sad, but somehow so fitting.*

Chapter 19

Angus scowled in confusion for only a second before taking off after Birdi. As he raced through the open doorway he heard Lady Beth ask, "What the hell just happened?"

A good question. He wanted to ken as well. One thing was certain. Something had terrified Birdi. He hadn't heard such a keen, seen such horror on a woman's face since his time in France.

He bound downed the stairs, taking them three at a time. "Birdi, halt!"

Pushing open the lower door, he again heard her keening. He saw her then; arms outstretched, jet curls billowing behind her like huge black wings, she raced toward the raised portcullis. "Birdi! Wait!"

When she didn't stop but raced on, he cursed and ran after her. *Merciful Mother of God, if she doesna stop she'll run right off the end of the quay.*

To his horror, just as he set foot on the quay, she did precisely that. She never hesitated; never looked back, just ran straight into the sea.

"Nooo!" ripped from his throat.

He tore off his heavy jerkin as he ran, then dove into the pounding surf after her.

Cold knocked the breath out of him and he kicked to the surface. Bobbing at the top, he spun. *"Birdi!"* Oh, Christ, *please, I beg ye, help me find her.* He couldn't see for the tears and brine. *"Birdi!" She can't drown, please don't let her drown. "Birdi!"*

Something dark floated just beneath the green waves to his right. He dove.

There she floated like a dark angel; arms extended, eyes closed, black curls resembling silk flotsam as she hovered in her blue gown.

Lungs aching, he grabbed her under the arms and kicked for the sun.

He broke the surface, gasped, and lifted Birdi higher, thrusting her head out of the water. It lolled backward. "Ye canna be doing this twice, Birdi. Wake up!" Kicking to stay afloat, he shook her. "I willna have it, ye hear!" She coughed then, spewing seawater like a whale. She gasped a few times, coughed again, and opened her eyes. With the next breath she screeched.

"Birdi, 'tis me."

"Nay!" She fought, arms flailing, teeth bared like those of a trapped she-wolf.

"Birdi, for God's sake." He had all he could do to keep both of them above the waves surging toward the boulders. Pinning her arms and still kicking frantically to keep them both afloat, he asked, "What the hell has fashed ye so?"

Gasping, she yelled, "I willna, I willa be burned. Let me drown!"

"Drown? Birdi—" He had to suck more air or they both would perish. "Listen, no one is going to burn, I promise. I love ye and willna let that happen."

She froze then. Just gaped at him. "Ye love me?"

There it was. He did love Birdi, didn't want to, didn't ken the how or why of it, but aye, he did love his Birdi.

Good-bye, Donaliegh.

"Aye, Birdi, I love ye, I do."

"Oh Angus!" She threw her arms about his neck, sinking them both.

God, she felt good as her tongue sought his, cold and

frightened as she was. Cold and exhausted as he was, for that matter.

He kicked and surfaced and, keeping a tight hold on her, made for the quay. Hearing shouts, he looked up and found Duncan and Ian reaching for them. Dozens of clansmen stood at their backs.

Duncan, having the longest reach, caught Birdi and heaved her up and onto the quay. Ian grabbed his shoulders and hauled him up and over the boulders. On solid ground again, arms shoving, anxious to get to Birdi, he bellowed, "Out of my way!"

Angus found her in Beth's arms, Duncan's cloak wrapped about her, her pale skin nearly blue. Begging Beth's pardon, he scooped her into his arms. "Are ye all right?" The woman would be the death of him.

Teeth clicking like a squirrel's, she whispered, "I'm sorry, but I thought—*aaaaahhh!*"

Her magnificent eyes bulged like a frog's as she continued to screech and point to those leaning toward them.

"What? What has ye fashing?"

Birdi clawed at Angus's chest. "Get him away!"

He raked the crowd, not kenning, looking for a Macarthur, a Gunn, someone or something that wasn't right. "Who? What?"

She gasped, "The priest!"

Not kenning but willing to do anything so long as she stopped keening, he shouted, "Remove Fat John. Now!"

Duncan ordered, "Ian, take Father John back to the keep." Ian, scowling, grabbed the rotund priest's arm.

The priest sputtered and fumed as Ian, saying something about his needing mead, dragged him away.

Lady Beth grinned. Their gluttonous friend would be out cold in some storage room within the hour.

She caught Kari's eye. "Mistress, run ahead and stoke the fires in Angus's room." As the woman took off at a run Beth yelled, "And ready a bath!"

She took Duncan's arm and they followed Angus and his lady into the keep. In a whisper, Beth asked, "Do ye ken why she fears him?"

Duncan leaned toward her to avoid being overheard. "Aye, Birdi has every reason to fear Father John. She's nay doubt heard tales of cumberendra."

"Of what?"

"Church-ordered burnings at the stake. Witches usually, but heretics, as well. Birdi is a pagan healer."

"You're not serious?"

He nodded and slowed, letting those who traveled behind them pass. Finally alone with her, he whispered, "I've lusted to rid myself of Fat John for years. Now, more so than ever. If he remains, Angus will nay doubt leave, and that I willna have." He huffed. "My problem now lies in getting Fat John to leave of his own accord. I canna boot him out, as much as I'd like. The bishop would be here in a heartbeat, threatening excommunication and raising tithes."

Hmm. Beth had wanted to rid herself of the priest since arriving at Blackstone. The man—intent on converting her—was still harassing her, but not until today did she realize her husband wanted him gone as much as she did. Splendid!

She patted Duncan's arm. "Dear, just leave it to me."

Angus, freshly clothed and with his hands full, shouldered open the door to his new room and found Birdi up to her neck in warm water.

She peeked over the rim of Beth's huge tub. "Is he still here?"

Angus shook his head, dropped the flagon of hot mead and the tankards on the fireside table, and then knelt beside her. He reached for the fragrant rose soap bobbing on the water, a gift from Beth. "He's in the west wing. Ian willna let him out."

"All right, but so long as he's about I must stay in here."

His poor wee Birdi. He lathered the soap in his hands and murmured, "Sit."

When she did, knees bent and clutched to her chest, he eased the bubbles across the lace scars on her back. "Now, why didna ye tell me ye feared priests? I'd have kept him from ye."

She hunched her shoulders. "I thought . . . I feared . . . I didna ken if—"

"If I was in league with the priest?"

She squeaked, "Aye." Blushing, she admitted, "But I didna ken ye loved me. I was sure ye loved Mary and I—"

"Whoa. Mary who?"

"Hale Mary, the one ye whisper to when ye're most fashed. Ye ken. The one with honey hair and beehive breasts."

Oh my God. He couldn't help it. He started to laugh. The more detail he added to the image the harder he roared. He was in tears, gasping, by the time Birdi slapped his arm.

Looking indignant, she asked, "What, may I ask, do ye find so humorous?"

He wiped his cheeks with the backs of his soapy hands. "Love, do ye remember the tale of the Blessed Virgin and the Immaculate Conception?"

Birdi narrowed her eyes at him. "How could I not? Ye kept me up half the night making sure I would."

Because she looked so splendidly indignant, because it felt so good to be home, because she loved him and he loved her, because he'd lost Donaliegh and his chiefship and there wasn't a damn thing he could do about it but laugh, he laughed again, this time until it hurt.

Birdi, apparently deciding he'd lost his mind, huffed and sank beneath the bubbles.

She ran out of breath about the same time he caught his.

He reached for her and pulled her into his arms. "Birdi, I do love ye so."

"Good, because I do too, though why I should when ye poke jest at—"

He silenced her rebuke with his lips. She sighed and opened her mouth to him, her arms encircling his neck. He dove heart-first into Birdi's sweet moist richness.

As her tongue made its first tentative exploration across his, he rose, hauling her out of the water, and pressed her to him. His hands slid up her spine, memorizing every detail of the warm slick flesh, then slid down and lingered on her fine hurdies, enjoying the fullness. Wanting more, needing her to ken his need, he grasped her deliciously round bottom and pressed her into his swollen groin. She growled deep in her throat and raised a leg, wrapping it around his. Ah, she wanted him as he did her. No question.

The room was warm, but not anywhere near as warm as the blood surging through his limbs. He wanted her, all of her, and there wasn't a reason on earth why he shouldn't consummate their union.

He carried her to the wide, four-poster canopied bed. She mewed and reached for him as he pulled away.

"Patience." He ripped the clothes from his body and dropped down beside her. Heart racing, he drew her to his chest. As his lips slid down the smooth flesh of her neck, seeking the ultimate prize, the nipples of her well-formed breasts, he whispered, "Ye'll now be mine in truth, Lady MacDougall."

Breathily she whispered, "How so?"

He didn't bother to answer. She'd find out soon enough.

Chapter 20

Birdi groaned deep in her throat as Angus's tongue lapped the side of her right breast, as his hips pressed against her thighs. She wanted . . . wanted, oh, she didn't ken what she wanted, but 'twas something verra important. His strong hand then cupped her breast and his tongue edged closer to the peak.

Aye, aye.

When he latched on as babe might, something deep within her hips caught fire, and she groaned yet again. She arched to give him better access and dug her nails into his back to pull him closer. *Oh Goddess, thank ye.*

When he groaned, "Aye, lass, 'tis the way," her heart soared. He kenned this deep need within her, this terrible need to be touched and held, cared about for the first time in her life. He would quench her thirst. She was certain of it. More importantly, she was sure she would never get enough.

Angus felt certain he'd die from pure joy, so luscious was the feel of Birdi beneath his hands and mouth. When she threw a leg over his thigh he pulled her into his hips and slid a hand down her backside, seeking the secret place he longed to occupy. Was it warm and wet enough yet? *Please, God, let it be so.*

He moved a tentative finger forward and it slid into delicious moist heat. She moaned into his mouth as slick woman's dew coated his finger and eased his passage. *Oh, aye, 'tis blessedly ready.* He tried a second, wanting to in-crease her pleasure, and found her tight. Far too tight, he realized, for a man his size. Ack!

Birdi was still a virgin.

'Twas logical, given her past, but what to do now? He hadn't had one before. He'd tupped more women than he had digits, but never a virgin. No decent man did.

While he pondered, she groaned and slid a hand over his hip. As she explored his hurdies with a light touch, he tried counting the nails in the shutters.

When her hand delved deeper and caressed his balls, his mind screamed, *Just get on with it. She is, after all, willing and needy.*

Aye. He closed his eyes, and ran the tip of a second fin-ger through her slickness. Hoping to keep her mind on his mouth, he nibbled on her lower lip. As his tongue plunged into her sweet mouth, his finger did the same below. She gasped. He slid his fingers out just a wee bit, then pressed forward again, imitating the movement his swollen need would soon take. To his relief, she moaned and pressed her hips against his hand. He did it again with the same result but this time her hips continued to rock.

"Do ye like that?"

Panting, eyes half open and unfocused, she whispered "Aye."

In an effort to stretch her, he spread his fingers a wee bit more with each movement of her hips. When she groaned and murmured, "More," he rolled and settled between her thighs, his weight on his arms.

Her hips tipped up to greet him, and she moaned, "More, Angus, please."

Angus wanted more as well. "Aye, lass." He rubbed his tip against her, mixing his fluids with hers, and then with one hand under a fine hurdie to hold her secure, he pressed forward. She stiffened when he met minimal resistance.

Birdi, suddenly wide-eyed, whispered, "What happened?"

"Sssh, 'tis all done. From here on 'tis only pleasure."

Brow furrowed, she didn't appear convinced.

Their gazes locked, he grinned and slowly eased out, then back into her. God, her eyes were as clear and deep as a freshwater pool. He could drown in their depths and die a happy man.

He lowered his mouth to hers and again tasted the mint she'd sampled on the biscuits she'd eaten. He withdrew and eased forward again. This time her hands slid into his hair. Birdi then took over their kiss and pressed her hips into him. *Ah, sweet lass, now ye ken.*

As his pace increased, so did Birdi's. Then suddenly she flew past, her breath hitching, her eyes glazed. She grabbed onto his arse and rocked, fingers digging in deep. *Oh, Birdi.*

He'd been with some robust women, but none like this. She wanted, and she wanted now. He increased the depth of his thrusts, sliding over her, the fine hairs of his chest brushing her nipples so they stood high and proud. *Come on, Birdi, come on.*

She shattered then; keening his name, her back arched, her legs stiffened, and her nails dug deep into his hips as she reached for the stars.

He waited for her final spasm to pass then growled, "Mine." He rocked into her fully. Once, twice, and then he exploded into the deep, potent richness of Birdi Mac-Dougall.

Panting, he opened his eyes. Birdi was watching him, wonder gracing her lovely features. "I didna hurt ye, did I?" He hoped not. The last few minutes were a blur.

She ran a tentative finger along his lower lip. "Oh nay. 'Twas wondrous, truly." She then smiled and asked, "Can we do it again?"

He laughed and rolled with her clutched to his chest.

* * *

Late that night in the solar, Katherine Elizabeth Mac-Dougall gazed into her small, silver-backed looking glass. Satisfied with her artistry, she cleared her small dressing table of her homemade make-up and brushes. She then swept the telltale dusting of soot from its surface and snuffed all but one candle.

She crawled between the cool sheeting and pulled the bed drapes behind her loose, which would throw her in shadow. She fluffed her pillows, picked up her book, and settled in for a long wait. All was in readiness.

To her surprise, the knock came quickly. Their resident priest—a man who served others only to better serve himself—was apparently more fashed about Birdi's reaction to him than she'd realized. Good. His distraction would work to her advantage. Schooling her features into what she hoped to be an expression of hopeless despair, Lady Beth moaned, "Come in."

Father John poked his head through the doorway. "My lady, I come at yer husband's request, but I must also speak to ye as well about Sir MacDougall's ladywife."

As he hurried toward the bed, Beth eased forward just a bit so he could catch a glimpse of the red spots marring her face through the artfully applied—if she did say so herself—faint dusting of ash by the light of the candle.

He came to a screeching halt five feet from the bed, his hand flying to his mouth. She could hear him mumbling "Oh, mercy, 'tis black plague."

She held out a hand to him, which he ignored, so she dropped it. "Father, I ken I havena been verra receptive to yer past attempts to bring me to the One True Faith, but as ye can plainly see all is suddenly changed. As ye can imagine, my husband is most distressed."

Father John nodded with the rapidity of a woodpecker. Good. "I'm so glad ye ken our dilemma." Brows tented, she offered him a wee smile, one she hoped conveyed how gracious she thought him for not bolting out the door like he no doubt itched to do. "The MacDougall asks two things of ye. First, 'tis my husband's lust and mine that ye provide me with daily instruction so I might be properly prepared and receive the blessed sacraments, and . . ."

Eyes as wide as the top of a tankard, he took a step back. "And?"

"And ye say naught about what ye see when ye come to me each day." She wrung her hands. "Panic is like forest fire. Once started, it's impossible to stop. We canna let that happen here. Duncan will, out of necessity, quarantine us together on this island as soon as the food stores arrive tomorrow morning. Then with yer guidance we—locked in together—shall pray, and hopefully, my illness willna spread to all within the keep."

Without any apparent movement, Father John had somehow managed to get his back to the door. Lowering her voice an octave, she asked, "Do I have yer word? Does my husband?"

He reached behind him, a frantic hand searching for the handle and latch. "Of course, my lady. My lips are sealed."

She leaned back on her pillow. "Ye are so kind. Would ye tell my husband I'd like to see him now?"

Nodding, Father John bolted out the door as fast as his stout little legs could carry him.

Beth smiled.

The man would be on a boat before Duncan could mount the steps to the solar. By noon tomorrow he'd be halfway to Sterling spreading the news. That would keep the Gunns and any other clan set on causing problems at bay for hopefully a year. Her family would remain safe, Duncan would get his wish, Birdi would get hers, their whiskey production would stay on schedule, and she could have a babe in peace for a change. She sighed and rose. Not a bad night's work, all things considered.

Pouring water from the ewer into the washing bowl, she heard a plaintive cry bounce off Drasmoor's distant hills. Startled, she turned to the open window.

Aaaawooo rolled across the water once again.

Picturing her children at play in the upper fields just this morn, her skin pebbled and her blood ran cold. She slammed the pitcher on the table.

Duncan would get an earful as soon as he opened the door. He'd assured her no wolves had been seen in these parts for more than a decade.

Chapter 21

Angus stood on the parapet and stared down at Birdi where she sat facing out to sea, huddled at the end of the isle against the frigid November winds—arms about her legs, chin on her knees.

She'd been in Blackstone for three weeks and now something was fashing her near to death, and he didn't have an idea of what it might be. She refused to discuss it. More troubling was her refusal to make love.

Oh, she'd lie beside him each night, her head on his shoulder, her tears running down his chest, but then he'd awake in the middle of the night and find her curled in a ball before the fire. He'd carry her back to bed, but by morn, she'd be back on the floor again.

Her magnificent eyes were now ringed in black for lack of sleep, she was losing weight, and when she did smile it appeared so sad his heart nearly broke.

He'd had enough. Today his being the patient and considerate husband ceased. He would find out what was fashing Birdi or die trying.

He took the stairs two at a time down to the great hall. Crossing it, he nearly ran over Lady Beth. He righted her. "My pardon, Beth." He turned to go, and she grabbed his arm.

"Come, I need speak with ye."

"I'm sorry, but I need speak with Birdi."

She tightened her grip on his arm. "Do be kind. She's frightened about something."

"Humph! There's naught to be frightened about. I love her, she's safe here, has food and gowns." He took her hand from his arm. "If ye'll pardon me."

"Angus—"

He strode out and down the bailey stairs.

A moment later he stood at Birdi's back. She kenned his presence. He saw her tip her head. "We need talk."

"Not now."

He dropped down beside her. "Look at me."

She faced him, her cheeks chafed and scarlet from what the wind had done with her tears. "Oh, God, Birdi, ye canna go on like this. Please tell me what has ye so overwrought."

"Why? Ye canna change it."

"Change what? I dinna ken it. Mayhap I can." When she faced the sea again he growled in frustration. "Are ye homesick for yer glen? If so, we can visit it come spring when the snow leaves the passes." They'd be risking life and limb, but anything was better than this.

When she remained mute, he pulled her into his arms. "Birdi, ye're driving me wode here." He would definitely lose his mind if this kept up, if she wouldn't confide in him. Mayhap . . .

"Birdi, is it yer lack of finding a new name?"

She shook her head. "I've grown accustomed to the one I have."

Ack! So great was his frustration at that moment, had he been able to beat it out of her, he'd have been sorely pressed not to. "Tell me what I can do."

She looked at him, and fresh tears careened down her cheeks only to be shoved sideways by the wind before they could fall. "'Tis already done."

That's it! Teeth grinding, he scooped her into his arms and strode back toward the keep.

In the greatroom he called to Lady Beth, "My lady, come."

Understanding his liege's wife couldn't take many flights of stairs with ease, he strode toward the stairs that led to the kitchen one level below.

Waddling behind him, she asked, "Angus, what's amiss?"

"Just come, my lady."

They walked through the kitchen and into the windowless distillery. He set Birdi down on a stool and lit the candle. He then brought another stool in for Lady Beth. Settling her on it, he asked, "Are ye comfy?"

Obviously confused, Lady Beth said, "Aye, but—"

"Good, because ye two are going to stay in here until such time as Birdi tells ye what has her so fashed."

Birdi, face flushing, rose from her stool. "Ye canna be keeping us in here, Angus. She's eight moons gone with child!"

Hands on hips, Angus leaned forward so his nose touched Birdi's. "I can and I will, and no one will see hide nor hair of either of ye until I ken what the hell is going on."

He then spun and closed the door on their sputtering protests. The door barred, he leaned against it with his arms folded across his chest.

So there.

Birdi had never been more mortified or more depressed in her life. "I'm so sorry, Lady Beth."

Lady Beth reached out and patted her hand. "It's just Beth, remember?"

"Aye." Birdi sighed. Her life was in ruin, and she was making a ruin of everyone else's around her.

Beth eased her stool closer and wrapped an arm about Birdi's shoulders. "Ye ken he means to keep his word. We'll be in here forever if ye don't tell me what has ye so worried—fashed."

"But nothing I can say will make anything change."

Birdi was with child. Of that, she was certain. She would bring another like herself into the world. Blind and too sensitive to bear living. And if her minnie's prediction was correct, this babe cradled in her loins would be far more sensitive than she, just as she was more sensitive than her mother. Worse, she kenned no way to protect it. She couldn't even protect herself. Oh, why had she not thought before loving Angus?

"Birdi, please. Mayhap there is something we can do, or at least reassure ye about it. Ye must let us try to help ye."

"Do ye ken me, that I'm spae?"

"A healer, yes. Angus told us."

" 'Tis more, being what I am."

"I don't understand—ken."

Could this woman help? Nay, but mayhap spilling her woe might ease some of the pain girdling her chest, compressing it to the point where she could barely breathe. But where to begin?

"My mother was a healer and had the sight, but her skill was limited to kenning the root of a person's ailment. If she sensed someone had eaten a poison mushroom or such, she would give mustard and elder. If someone bled, she'd use stinging nettle and witch hazel or whatever else was best."

"Aye. Is this yer skill as well?"

"In part." Birdi looked at her palms, the place from where all healing flowed. "Through Goddess, I can lay hands to a wound and close it. I can touch a fevered brow and cool it."

"But isna that a good thing?"

"It would be if I didna feel their pain, but I do. Worse, with this gift comes blindness. I can see only but a yard before me."

"Oh, Birdi." Beth's arms tightened about her. "Honey, we don't care. Ye manage well enough. And we're here to help should ye need it."

Birdi's tears flowed. "But ye dinna ken. The babe will be stronger, blinder, and in so much pain."

"Babe? Birdi, ye're pregnant—with child?"

"Aye. 'Tis so awful."

Beth squeezed her. "Oh, sweetie, it's wonderful. Angus will be so happy."

She shook her head. "Nay, not when he realizes the child canna see." If Minnie was right, this child would be born totally blind. *Oh, and the pain it will experience . . . . Oh, Goddess.*

"Birdi, how much can ye see clearly?"

She held out her arm. "From my nose to here."

"And beyond that?"

She shrugged. "The world is just a mass of blurry blobs of color."

Beth grinned. "Sweetie, you're not blind. Ye're myopic." When Birdi frowned, she continued. "Near-sighted. Many people are. It's something that's fixed with . . ."

Beth then looked pensive. "I wonder if Duncan kens . . . . I need think on this a bit. Now, about yer power of healing, and mayhap the babe's. Have ye ever spoken to anyone besides your mother about it?"

"Just Angus and Ian."

"Nay, I meant have ye ever spoken to another healer?"

Birdi shook her head. "I dinna ken such." The last time she'd been to a gathering she'd been only a wee bairn. Mayhap a wise one would ken how to protect her bairn. If only . . .

"Then we must take ye to see Auld Maggie."

"Who?"

"The midwife, the shrine keeper."

Birdi couldn't believe her ears. "Ye have such here?"

Beth nodded. "Didn't Angus tell ye? We have a sacred spring and I forgot what else. Auld Maggie tends to it, so I never bother—"

Birdi threw her arms about Beth, nearly knocking her

off her stool. "Oh, thank ye! Thank ye, and thank ye, Goddess, as well." She jumped to her feet, a thousand questions forming that she need ask the cailleach. And she had a sacred wedding to plan. Handfasting was all well and good for her, but her child needed reassurance that he carried Angus's name by right. "We must go to the cailleach now. Right now."

Beth laughed. "As ye lust, but first we'll have to convince yer annoying husband to let us out."

Angus—relieved to his bones that Birdi had finally confided in someone and appeared somewhat brighter—watched Birdi bound up the stairs ahead of them. Taking Lady Beth by the elbow, he said, "Well?"

"Not yet."

"Ack, woman! I need ken."

"'Tis not my place to tell ye, Angus. All ye need ken right now is that we're going to see Auld Maggie."

"Whatever for?"

Beth patted his cheek. "She needs talk with the woman."

Hearing that didn't set particularly well. Auld Maggie, in his estimation, was a fraud. Though a competent midwife, Auld Maggie's healings were limited to curing colic and the like, something he could do with a good volume of veterinary precepts in hand—but if it made Birdi happy, if it kept the bloom in her cheeks, so be it.

As they entered the greatroom, Duncan said, "I see ye decided to let my ladywife out."

Angus grimaced. "I hadna any choice."

Duncan slapped a hand on his shoulder. "The next time, please inform me in advance so I can talk some sense into ye."

"Aye."

"So did ye find out what ails her?"

"Nay, but Beth did, and Birdi is definitely in better spirits. We're now off to see Auld Maggie."

"We who?"

"The three of us."

"Nay. Not Beth. She should be lying in, not being tossed about in a boat."

Angus held up his hands. "Ye ken what happened to me the last time I naysayed yer wench. Ye deal with her."

"I will." Duncan stomped off after his wife as Birdi came into the greatroom, her cape on and carrying a small bundle.

He took her bundle, wondering what it contained. "Will ye tell me now what had ye fashing?"

Birdi rose onto her toes and placed a hand behind his neck. He bent so she could kiss his lips.

"I'll speak with ye after I speak with the cailleach."

Angus grunted. If Auld Maggie was a cailleach, he was the king of Persia. "As ye lust. Come."

"But Lady Beth?"

Angus put a hand on Birdi's waist and guided her toward the bailey stairs. "She willna be coming. Duncan fears the trip will be too rough."

Birdi nodded. "Aye, 'tis better she stays. I dinna ken how long this will take, and she shouldna be tiring."

The sky was clear azure, the bay's waters calm, and the breeze offshore as they walked down the quay. The oar men would be fighting the wind to get them to shore but he hadn't reason to fash about Birdi being in the boat.

Ian, one arm about a bonnie lass, greeted them. "Where are ye going?"

"To Drasmoor. Birdi has to speak with someone."

"I'll come along. I need speak with ye before I bid ye goodbye." He kissed the lass soundly and bounded into the boat.

Just as he and Birdi settled on the middle thwart, Duncan called, "Halt!"

Angus couldn't help but chuckle, seeing Beth waddling toward them with Duncan slouching behind, his face mutinous and his arms full of pillows.

As Duncan jumped into the boat ahead of his wife, he growled, "One word, Angus, and ye'll spend the rest of the winter standing watch on Piety Ridge."

Jaw muscles straining, Angus murmured, "As my liege commands."

"Here." Duncan shoved the pillows at him. "Place them on a thwart while I help Beth in."

Once Lady Beth was settled, they pushed off. Through the entirety of the crossing Birdi kept one white-knuckled hand clasped on the boat's sheerplank and the other locked on Angus's arm, her lips moving in what he suspected were silent prayers.

Birdi yelped when the boat surged on a wave and a heartbeat later scraped bottom for a moment on Drasmoor's gravel shore. " 'Tis well, Birdi. We've landed."

"Oh." She released her death-grip on the side of the boat but kept one on his arm in the event he lied. Poor Birdi.

He couldn't imagine going through life as she did, suffering one jolting surprise after the other. No wonder she fashed.

He waited until Duncan had Beth on dry land before lifting Birdi up and out. Setting her on solid ground, he asked, "Are ye certain ye need do this?"

"Oh, aye, absolutely."

"Verra well." He placed her hand on his arm and led the way through the village and up a short incline. They crossed the wooden bridge stretched over a boulder-strewn burn and entered Auld Maggie's wee glen.

High on a ridge, the Macarthur slipped his blade from the MacDougall lookout's back and silently eased him onto the ground. He turned to his right and whispered to his second in command, "I believe that's the lot directly before us." They'd dispatched three. More guards lurked on either side but they'd be hard pressed to see them coming down the glack.

John whispered, "What now?"

The Macarthur drew a lungful of salt-laden air, something he'd sorely missed. "We wait till dark, then six and ten take two boats across. The rest stand guard and keep the cattle quiet." Wolf tracks were scattered all over the ridge.

"And the berserker?"

"I'll deal with him myself. Ye secure the spae, get her in the boat, and back to shore."

His captain grumbled. "As ye lust."

He kenned his friend wanted the privilege of killing MacDougall—Robbie and Fegan had been his brothers—but he had waited too long to do it himself. Macarthur's gaze settled on the occupants of the boat nearing the shore below them. "Well, I'll be damned. Look."

His captain squinted, then grinned. "'Tis our spae and the Blood."

"Now who said Highlanders werena accommodating?"

Birdi, hands sweating, froze before the door of Auld Maggie's wattle and stone hut. Inside might be the answers to her prayers. But what if the cailleach just shook her head and said she could do naught?

Beth came to her side. "Birdi, why do ye hesitate? Go inside."

"What if . . ." Birdi wrung her hands. "Where's Angus?"

Beth nodded to her right. "Over yon, talking with my husband and Ian."

Birdi looked in the direction Beth indicated and saw three tall shadows silhouetted against brilliant blue. *Oh, Goddess, I love this man. Please dinna let Minnie's prophecies be so. Please. For the babe's sake and for Angus's.*

Birdi finally squared her shoulders. Better to ken than not. "I'm ready."

Beth kissed her cheek. "I pray ye find the answers ye seek."

As Birdi raised her hand to knock, a wheezing voice called, "Come in, come in. I've been expecting ye."

Birdi's hopes soared as she pushed open the door.

Inside, the croft was dark and musky, the air heavy with the scents of sage, rosemary, and peat. Birdi took a cautious step forward and then another.

"To yer left, dearie." She turned and found a wizened woman half her height sitting in a willow chair much like the one her mother had crafted.

Straining to see, Birdi asked, "Were ye truly expecting me?"

Auld Maggie rose and took Birdi's hands in hers. As gnarled as the auld woman's hands were, Birdi was surprised to find them warm and strong.

"Nay," she cackled, "but those hereabouts expect me to say such, so I always do." She waved to a stool. "Sit."

Birdi's heart sank, and she pulled her hand from the woman's grasp. " 'Tis my mistake. I dinna . . ."

"Bairn, sit. I do ken that ye are more than I shall ever be, which is why I didna lie when ye asked."

"Oh." Feeling a bit better, Birdi sat, but on the edge of the chair should she need to bolt the four steps to the door.

"Now, why would such as ye be coming to me?"

Birdi folded her hands in her lap, deciding it would be best to just say and be done with it. "I'm with child and fear this babe will be born blind but with a gift far more potent than mine."

"Hmm. And why would ye believe such? Is this bairn's sire a spae such as yerself?"

"Oh, nay. Angus is just a man. Nay, I didna mean he's just any man. I meant—"

"I ken what ye mean, lass." Auld Maggie ruminated for a minute as she studied Beth. "Who told ye the babe would be born blind?"

"Minnie."

"And would she have been Rowena of Loch Ard Forest?"

Birdi's heart tripped. "How . . . Did ye ken my mother?"

"Aye, long ago." She shook her head in sad fashion. "'Tis nay wonder ye fash as ye do."

Birdi frowned. "Speak plainly." She'd loathed riddles since childhood. She also had too much at stake to waste time pondering.

"Yer mother was always odd, even by our standards. But after she fell in love with that Druid—"

Birdi cried, "What Druid?"

"Yer sire, lass, did she nay tell ye?"

"Nay. Tell me now."

Auld Maggie cocked her head and studied her for a moment. "As ye lust." She then settled back in her chair, her arms crossed beneath her shriveled breasts. "One day yer mother was out gathering grain and her leg got caught in a snare, the Druid's. He admitted he'd spied her on several occasions and had deliberately set the trap to catch her."

"But why?"

"He told her he was from Eire land, across the sea, and he'd never in his travels seen a more bonnie lass than she." The auld woman looked at her fire. "Ye ken our lives can be lonely, so it took nay great effort on his part to woo and tup her, all in short order. He was, according to yer mother, handsome beyond words." She turned her attention back to Birdi. "Given yer beauty I dinna doubt that he was. Since ye havena her eyes, ye must have his."

Birdi thought so as well. "And then what happened?" Why had her mother grown to hate?

"He left her when she began to show . . . with ye. He told her his darg was done—he'd planted his seed as he'd pledged. And then he just disappeared. Poof. Gone." Auld Maggie sighed. "Yer mother nearly lost her mind then. She loved the Druid as only a young woman could and now kenned he'd used her for his own purposes. She continued to come to the gatherings for a few more seasons, but she wasna as she once was. Then she stopped coming altogether. I often wondered what happened to her and ye."

"She was gored by a boar and died."

"Ah, and when was this?"

"When I was but a bairn."

"So who raised and trained ye?"

"No one. What do ye mean by *train?*"

Auld Maggie leaned forward, her eyes narrowed. "Pardon?"

"In what should I be trained?"

Frowning, Auld Maggie reached for her hand. "Tell me what ye ken."

Birdi shrugged and closed her eyes. "Yer hips and knees ache enough to bring ye to tears. Ye are ready to die, but dinna lust for it. Ye're waiting, waiting for—"

"Enough." Auld Maggie settled back in her chair. "What would ye do if I asked for yer help?"

Birdi described her way of healing.

"And then?"

"I'd find my bed and wait out the pain."

"As I suspected." Auld Maggie heaved a great sigh. "No wonder ye fash. Lass, there's nay need for ye to suffer so."

As the auld woman came to her feet, she grumbled, "At least she had the decency to teach ye about Goddess." She threw a block of peat on the fire, making sparks fly. "Birdi, there are ways to protect ye—"

A cry rang out, startling them both. Birdi came to her

feet. The door blew open and Lady Beth stumbled inside keening, *"Hide!"* The crash of steel on steel echoed off the walls of the croft before she slammed the door behind her. Panting, she threw her weight against Birdi. " 'Tis the Macarthur and his men."

"Angus!" Birdi pulled from Beth's embrace.

Beth latched on to her arm before Birdi could pull open the door again. "No! You can't go out there. Not now."

"But how many Macarthurs are there?"

Beth's eyes glazed. "Too many, but more of ours will come." She then prayed, "Please, God, let it be soon."

Auld Maggie scurried to the right. A moment later she pressed a small blade into Birdi's palm and long bone needles in Beth's. "Help me tip the table. Hie!"

Beth pulled on Birdi's arm. "Come, do as the woman asks."

Birdi nodded, her mind pleading, *Please, Goddess, please help Angus, please . . . .*

The shouting and clanging beyond the door escalated as Beth grabbed her end of the table. Just as they tossed the heavy plank onto its side, the sun's rays suddenly shot through the room. Over the women's screams a man of Birdi's height shouted, "The spae, grab her!"

Birdi raised her blade in defense, but a strong calloused hand grabbed her wrist and squeezed. Her fingers numbed, the blade fell as he jerked her forward.

The Macarthur captain hauled her, kicking and screaming, out of the croft. They'd not traveled three steps into the chaos when he grunted and suddenly arched. Beth had managed to drive her bone needles into the man's back. Wavering, he swung his left arm back in an effort to clout Beth, but Birdi jerked to the right, pulling the man with her. He growled deep in his throat as they fell. His grip loosened and Birdi wrenched free. She staggered to her feet and heard Beth scream, "Run, Birdi!"

Blood roaring in his ears, Angus pulled his gaze from

the Macarthur and saw Birdi plastered against the croft wall.

"Run!" ripped from his throat as his claymore flew in a low arc to counter the Macarthur's left-handed thrust. As the Macarthur spun with the impact, a less skilled but no less determined warrior charged him. Angus dispatched the man with a swift slice to the chest. To the right he saw Duncan do the same to another invader. He then heard pounding feet crossing the bridge. As the MacKay battle cry rent the air—Ian—a trumpet blasted in alarm. Thank God.

He focused again on the Macarthur liege only to find the man's gaze swinging toward Birdi. Angus bellowed, "Macarthur!"

The man refocused on Angus, his eyes gleaming black and his blade high in his left hand. Easing to his left, he made a come-hither movement with the steel-encased stump that had once been his right hand.

Their blades clashed. They pushed off and Angus swung right. The Macarthur countered with surprising dexterity.

Ah, he's been preparing.

Needing to get to Birdi, kenning the Macarthur's one arm wouldna be a match for his two, Angus gripped his blade with both hands. As he raised the claymore above his head, he saw something flash by to his left. He brought his blade down and the Macarthur staggered. He raised the claymore again with both arms for the killing blow and heard Birdi keen.

Startled and fearing the worst—that another Macarthur had grabbed her—he glanced left. To his horror, a huge wolf had Birdi by the hand. Haunches pulling, he was backing around the croft with her. Angus opened his mouth to shout and something tore through his middle.

He looked down in surprise to find the Macarthur's blade had gutted him. Something hot and furious then exploded in his chest.

Blind and deaf to all but the rage boiling within—that despite all, he still hadn't been strong enough to protect Birdi, that a sloth like the Macarthur should be his undoing—his blade fell on the grinning Macarthur chieftain. When the familiar sensation of steel tearing flesh and bone vibrated into his hands, he let loose the hilt and sank to his knees, his hands reaching for his gashed middle.

He looked down at the blood oozing through his fingers, but saw only Birdi being dragged away. *Ack, Birdi, please forgive me. I meant only to keep ye safe.*

As he toppled to his side, whispering, "Save Birdi," he saw the Macarthur lying before him, claymore still trapped in his chest.

At a great distance he heard voices. Someone rolled him and the sun warmed his cheek, then that, too, faded.

Forgive me, Birdi.

Chapter 22

Huddled within the dense brush behind Auld Maggie's croft, Wolf's great head clutched to her chest, Birdi reverently prayed for Angus's safety and for those she'd come to care about.

The Macarthur had come after her, and now innocent men were screaming and dying. Crying out for help. Were the cries those of the MacDougall, or Ian's? If so, she didn't ken how she could ever forgive herself. Or they forgive her. So much *need* now battered her head and chest; she fought to block them out. She would heed only one.

Wolf's head came up and he started to whine. As he pulled at her skirt she realized the sound of battle had ceased. *Oh, Goddess . . . .*

She then heard someone calling her name. She dashed the tears from her cheeks and rose but kept a hand on Wolf. Who had called her? The Macarthur? *Oh, Angus.*

"Birdi! Birdi!"

'Twas Lady Beth's husband! *Thank ye, Goddess, thank ye. But where is Angus?*

With one hand on the wall she ran back to the front of the croft, Wolf whining at her side.

Beth was the first to spy her. She screamed, "Wolf!"

Hand up, Birdi yelled, "Halt!" before someone could throw a blade as Angus once had. Wolf, ears back, snarled as if Birdi's life depended on it. "Sssh, 'tis alright. They're friends."

Wolf only snapped his jaws and growled louder.

Hoping she sounded calmer than she felt, she said, "No one move. Stand right where ye are. He willna harm me."

She heard a man's heavy breathing and looked right, her hope soaring. "Angus?"

A deep voice murmured, "Duncan."

Oh, nay. Why wasn't Angus the one coming to her? "Where's Angus?"

"Yon. Beth tends him."

She yelped, "Tends?" and Wolf began to growl again. She placed a hand on his head. "Sssh, dautie, sssh." To Duncan she said, "Bring me to him. Now." If Angus was injured, why hadn't he reached out to her? Why was the *need* not full upon her? What ailed him? Was he not awake?

Duncan took her shaking hand. With every step Birdi prayed. When they came to a halt, his voice cracked as he whispered, "Here he is."

Angus opened his eyes when he heard Birdi's strident keen, then felt her cool hands rush over him.

"Oh, Angus, nay!"

Fearing what would happen next, kenning he was dying, he choked out, "Get her away."

Lady Beth murmured, "But Angus—"

Eyes closing, accepting what must be, he again ordered, "Take her away!"

Duncan growled, "Let her help."

Angus whispered, "Get Ian."

His liege and lady didn't ken what would happen should Birdi be allowed to touch him. Angus had deliberately shaded the truth in an effort to ease Birdi's way into the clan. Only Ian kenned what would happen, and he would haul her away.

Duncan said, "Ian's with the men chasing the last of the

Macarthurs." He placed a hand on Angus's shoulder. "Let her help ye if she can. She loves ye."

Angus struggled to open his eyes. "Aye. 'Tis why she must go."

As the light and arguing voices faded and all turned black, Angus regretted not being able to tell Birdi a final time that he loved her. He then lusted he could see his Birdi's beautiful eyes just one more time before he died.

Birdi jerked with awareness. There. She felt it, the *need*. Aye, he called, but weakly. Heart hammering against her ribs, she ordered Duncan and Beth away, fearing if they touched Angus, Goddess wouldn't come. She pushed back Wolf where he lay by her side then squatted, her feet spread wide beneath her in firm contact with Mother of All.

Shadows moved and voices murmured in question all around her. "Only for ye, dearest Angus, would I give my life."

Birdi bent toward his ear. "Believe and trust in me." Praying his response wasn't truly necessary, she placed crossed palms upon his horrid wound and closed her eyes. Tears coursed down her cheeks as she pleaded aloud, "Mother of All, 'tis I, Birdi, and I beseech ye to come and help this man I love. Come, please, I beg ye." An interminable number of heartbeats passed before she felt tingling heat move up her legs. Her heart then slowed of its own accord, and her hands stopped shaking. Mother of All was again within her, and all would be well.

Birdi looked at the scar marring Angus's broad forehead and admired the fine shape of his lips and jaw a final time. Kenning full well what would happen and kenning even Auld Maggie could do naught to save her, she said, "I, Birdi, take upon myself this wound so that this man I love may live." As she waited for what would come, a strange calm settled over her. Her bairn would die with her, aye, but 'twas just as well. No bairn, no matter how loved or wanted, should have to suffer more than she already had—as surely it would.

Pain—worse than any she'd ever experienced—suddenly tore through her middle. Birdi doubled over. Unable to breathe, she then toppled. Loud gasps from those around her followed.

Strong arms hauled her up and cradled her. How kind. A gruff voice growled, "What the hell is happening?" She kenned the arms about her to be Duncan's. Oh, she hadn't meant to frighten him so.

As the agitated voices grew distant, she whispered, "Tell Angus . . . I loved him."

Angus reluctantly let go of Birdi's hand so Duncan and one of the oarsmen could carry Birdi up Blackstone's bailey stairs. As they entered the greatroom, he found Beth scrubbing her hands in hot water. She nodded toward the table while Birdi's wolf howled as if his heart were breaking on Drasmoor's shore. "Put her down there. Auld Maggie, get over here."

Dear God, how had this happened? Angus, pulled back from a black abyss, had opened his eyes and found his gut closed and Birdi stretched out across Duncan's arms, her middle bleeding and open like a smashed pumpkin.

Beth tore open the cloth bundles she'd prepared in the event of accident or war.

Angus, tears cascading down his still blood-smeared face, reached for Birdi's hand. "Can ye help her?"

"I'm sure as hell going to try." Lady Beth reached for her boiled cotton rags and began cleaning the edges of Birdi's huge wound. After muttering to herself about something called a hospual, Beth said, "Maggie, I'm going to need all the help I can get. Prayer, poultices, whatever else ye can offer."

The old woman, pale and apparently as shocked as the

rest of them, nodded and started crooning in a language Angus had never heard.

After a few minutes of watching Beth's hands shake every time the wolf howled, Angus growled, "Will somebody please shut that beast up or get him over here?"

He still couldn't believe the furry menace—what he now kenned to be Birdi's pet—had tracked them such a great distance.

Duncan ordered two men to take a boat across the bay. "Try feeding it. As a last resort fetch it back."

Recalling the farmers of Inveraray, Angus added, "Try giving it a chicken, a pullet."

Duncan then asked his wife, "What else can I do?"

"Keep the boiling water coming. Birdi's more likely to die from infection—festering—than blood loss."

'Twas also Angus's fear. Birdi's horrendous bleeding had, thankfully, already eased.

Finished with cleaning the wound, Lady Beth pulled silk threads and needles from her bundle. "Hold her tight."

Angus wrapped an arm about Birdi's shoulders and pressed his forehead to hers. Duncan moved to hold down her ankles.

When Birdi didn't so much as flinch with the first stitches, Angus's fear escalated.

After an hour Beth finally straightened. Birdi had a neat row of stitches—thirty in number—just below her waist. Now slathered in ointment and wrapped in boiled sheeting, Birdi was as tended as Beth's and Auld Maggie's skills could manage.

Lady Beth stepped back from the table. "Now all we can do is pray."

Angus murmured, "Thank ye."

Holding Birdi's flaccid hand, he bent his head. *Please, dear God, please help Birdi.*

He should have died. He'd have gone willingly and faced the fires of hell. Why hadn't she been willing to let fate take its course? Worse, he might never ken why. Her pulse only fluttered beneath his fingers. He didn't deserve her. If she survived, he would bring her back to her glen as she'd begged him to do on so many occasions. And if she so lusted it, he would stay with her. This time he *would* protect her.

Chapter 23

Feeling a flutter repeatedly rush across her fingers, Birdi wondered at the cause and opened her eyes. She smiled seeing Angus, his head level with hers. He had her hand firmly clasped in his near his lips, as he lay sound asleep facing her.

Mercy, he was handsome. Aye, as well as kind and brave. She studied his mouth as it hovered just a hair's breadth from her fingers. Oh, the sensations the man could conjure up with those beautiful lips were beyond description, beyond kenning. Wishing to feel their pliant texture, she started to roll onto her side. Piercing pain shot across her middle. She gasped. Merciful Goddess, what had happened to her? She pushed the cover back and found her stomach wrapped in sheeting from waist to hips. But how—?

It all came crashing back: going to see Auld Maggie, the Macarthur attack, the screaming and clash of steel on steel, and then Angus lying on the ground, his powerful body open and bleeding, destroyed.

She looked at him then and found him looking back through red-rimmed eyes. She smiled. Goddess had worked her magic again, and for some unfathomable reason had spared her as well. But then she did so love things in pairs. Birdi placed her hand low on her stomach. But then again, they'd be three, and she'd yet to tell him.

Birdi eased onto her side and brushed a lock of chestnut hair from his forehead. "Good morn."

"Until ye spoke I was afraid I was dreaming."

"Nay, ye're awake, and so, apparently, am I." She stroked his cheek. "How long this time?"

Angus stretched but kept hold of her hand. "Four verra long days."

Was he still angry? "Ye ken I had nay choice."

"Ah, but ye did, and why ye thought my life was of more worth than yer own is beyond kenning."

She sighed. How could she make him understand? "I love ye, Angus. Ye opened the world—the good and bad—to me. Ye kept me from drowning, fed me, protected me—"

"Nay, I didna protect ye—"

She placed a finger on his lips. "Hush. And ye showered me with more affection in just one phase of the moon than I've received in all my seasons. Ye are a worthy man who deserves to live, Angus. Whereas I . . ." She took a shuddering breath. "I am but a blind and feared spae. To be truthful, I didna ken I would survive . . . . but having done so, I do ken those below are now verra frightened of me." She hadn't seen the priest since the first day, but he'd no doubt be back. This time, torch in hand. She stroked his cheek. "I'll leave without being asked. Just ken I'll be leaving my heart behind." *And taking yer bairn, but he'll be well loved, I promise, so verra well loved.*

He brushed the tears from her cheeks. "Are ye through?"

She sniffed. "Aye."

"Good, because I'm not. First, ye are the most beautiful, most loving, most compassionate, and most obstinate woman I have ever met. Second, ye willna be going anywhere. Not without me, at least. Those below are nay fearful. They feel as I do. Third, I want to pledge to ye before God and man. I love ye, Birdi, and if the only way I can have ye is to bring ye back to yer croft and live among my enemies, so be it."

Birdi, realizing her mouth was agape, closed it. He couldn't mean it. Could he? And those below weren't crossing themselves day and night because she slept above? *Nay. This canna be.*

Someone knocked on the door. Angus, smiling, called, "Come in."

Auld Maggie poked her head around the door. "Has her fever broken yet?"

Angus grinned. "Ask her yerself."

"She's awake?" Auld Maggie shuffled over to the bed. "Ack, 'tis true, and look at ye. Yer eyes are as bright as new pennies. Praise Goddess."

"Aye," Angus muttered, "And Lady Beth's needlework."

Auld Maggie peeked beneath Birdi's dressings then clucked. "Ye're healing verra nicely. Better than I expected." She then put her hands on her hips. "Now, lassie, from here on out there'll be no more healing until ye learn to protect yerself. This bleeding and angst is totally unnecessary."

"'Tis?"

"Aye, 'tis. I was about to tell ye as much when the Macarthurs attacked. And ye'll nay be fashin' about yer babe. I have it on good authority—"

"What babe?" Angus, brow furrowed, sat bolt upright, looking back and forth between Auld Maggie and herself.

Birdi pulled the bedcovers up to her chin. Oh, Goddess. His visage was turning red. Never a good sign. "Our babe?"

"Our babe? Our babe! Ye're with child?"

She pulled the covers over her head. "Aye." *Oh, Goddess. He's going to kill me. I can tell.*

Through the heavy wool, Birdi heard Angus say, "Maggie, if ye excuse us, please? I need a word with my ladywife."

Birdi heard the door close.

A heartbeat later Angus said, "If ye dinna come out, I'm coming under there."

She peeked out. "I—"

"Is that what all yer fashing was about?"

"Aye."

Looking thunderous, he stood and walked to the window. "Ye didna want my bairn. Ye were willing to die kenning ye'd take it with ye."

"Ack! Angus, nay. I love ye and our bairn. 'Tis just . . . I thought . . ." *Just say it, Birdi. Get it over with.* "I kenned I might die when I laid my hands upon ye but I didna care. I love ye. Too, I was told any bairn I bore would be more sensitive and more blind than I. Had I died, our babe—one I would surely love—wouldna have been forced to suffer as I have for years on end. I didna want him to ken he wasna wanted. To reach out, hoping for affection or respect, only to be rejected. To live in a black world, not even my fuzzy one." A sob wracked her. "I ken that. All of it, and it hurts, Angus, it hurts so verra much some days I can barely breathe. So much so I have to force myself out of bed each—"

Angus's arms came around her. "Sssh, Birdi, sssh." He stroked her back as she continued to cry.

When she was able to speak, she whispered, " 'Twas nay from a lack of love or wanting, but from too much, that I did what I did."

He lifted her chin and looked into her eyes. "Birdi, I shall love our child, whether he sees or not, whether he's spae or not. He was conceived in love and will ken it so long as I breathe. And together we'll do the best we can to protect him from a world that may not be ready to accept him."

Studying his face, seeing tears hover within the deep blue she so loved, she whispered, "Aye, ye will."

"Aye." He gave her bottom a gentle pat. "So, now we need plan a wedding."

Birdi sniffed and grinned. "Aye. 'Twould be best to jump the bonfire at the Beltane celebration since it ensures luck and fertility, but we do seem to have plenty of both"—she patted her stomach—"so I suppose a wedding on Samhain will do."

For reasons Birdi couldn't quite fathom, Angus groaned.

Epilogue

And so it came to pass on the morning of the shortest day of the year, Samhain, that Angus and Birdi stood in Blackstone's great hall and pledged to love, honor, and obey 'til death did them part, before a traveling priest whom no one asked to remain, and the entire MacDougall clan.

When the ceremony was over, all raised their tankards to toast the newlyweds. Duncan, standing before a crowd anxious to start their feast, said, "Ladies and gentlemen, to the bride and groom." Cheers then rang off the rafters and fists thundered on tables. He raised his tankard again. "To Laird Angus MacDougall of Donaliegh and his lovely wife, Lady Elizabeth Birdi MacDougall."

Birdi preened. Aye, she'd finally chosen a name.

Angus, jaw slack, took the offered scroll and the keys from his liege's hands. "But ye said . . ."

Duncan threw his arm around his best friend. "All I ever wanted was for ye to find a woman who loved ye as much as my Beth loves me, and ye did."

Everyone ate, drank, and danced to the pipes and flutes until the sun began to set.

They then marched down to Blackstone's quay and got into their boats. The entire clan made their way across Drasmoor Bay and up into the hills to the sacred spring, where Auld Maggie, the shrine keeper, waited at the bonfire. Angus and Birdi again exchanged vows, drank from the sacred spring, and then joined hands and jumped into their future.

Duncan loaned Angus five stalwart soldiers to take with them to Donaliegh, since he didn't know the number or battle-readiness of the forces there. Angus tried to trap Wolf, but the beast would have no part of it, and in the end followed as he chose on foot.

Donaliegh was all they'd hoped for and all anyone would ever want to face in one lifetime, huge and run-down as it was.

Once the family were settled and the food stores and arms put away, Angus fashioned a leather collar for Wolf. Birdi painted it to match Angus's shield and attached it to Wolf's neck so all would ken he belonged to her. The clan was told not to harm him and to bring any complaints to their liege.

While Angus and the men labored, Birdi raised chickens, which she then turned loose in the high hills above Castle Donaliegh where Wolf roamed.

On Beltane day, Mistress Charlotte Rowena Prudence Katherine MacDougall—Birdi wanted to be sure the child never lacked for a name—came into the world in Donaliegh's warm solar.

She had her mother's black curls and dimples and her father's deep blue eyes, which pleased Birdi no end.

The babe grew as any healthy bairn should and played as any bairn might. Birdi and Angus were thrilled beyond measure that she could see as well as any and showed no sign of being highly sensitive to anyone's pain but her own.

All was as it should be until—at the tender age of two—Charlotte toddled out of the great hall and fell down the stairs leading to the bailey. What made the event so unusual was the fact that Birdi—she now had spectacles, the lenses having been made by a friend of Duncan's in Italia—and Angus both plainly saw that the staircase door was closed and latched when the bairn disappeared through it.

Wee Charlotte suffered only a few scrapes and bruises, but her parents have yet to recover.

EXPLORER'S GUIDE

PHILADELPHIA & AMISH COUNTRY

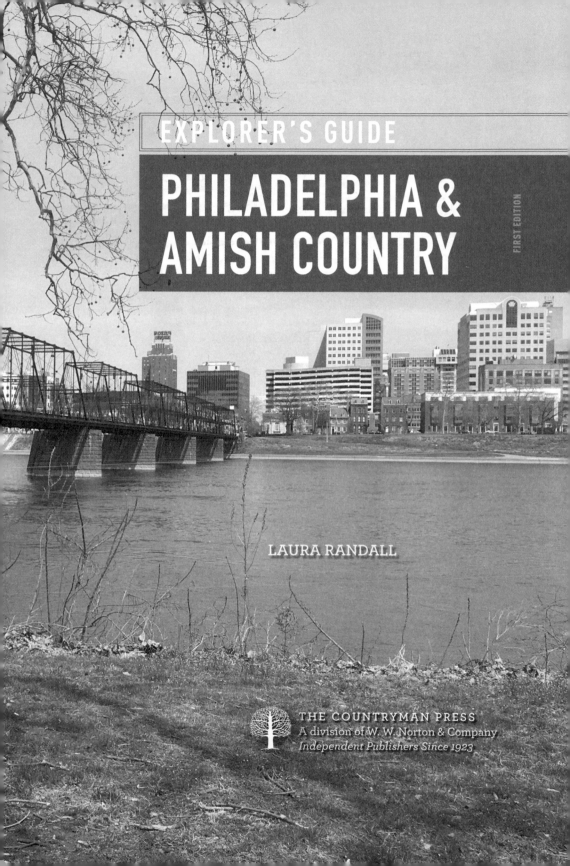

EXPLORER'S GUIDE

PHILADELPHIA & AMISH COUNTRY

FIRST EDITION

LAURA RANDALL

THE COUNTRYMAN PRESS
A division of W. W. Norton & Company
Independent Publishers Since 1923

Also available in the Explorer's Guide series:

Explorer's Guide Maine
Explorer's Guide Yellowstone & Grand Teton National Parks
Explorer's Guide Arkansas
Explorer's Guide Napa & Sonoma
Explorer's Guide New Mexico
Explorer's Guide Playa del Carmen, Tulum & the Riviera Maya
Explorer's Guide Vermont
Explorer's Guide Adirondacks
Explorer's Guide Buffalo & Niagara Falls
Explorer's Guide North Carolina's Outer Banks
Explorer's Guide North Florida & the Panhandle
Explorer's Guide Yosemite & the Southern Sierra Nevada
Explorer's Guide South Carolina
Explorer's Guide Austin, San Antonio & the Hill Country
Explorer's Guide Colorado
Explorer's Guide Cape Cod, Martha's Vineyard & Nantucket
Explorer's Guide Coastal Maine
Explorer's Guide Santa Fe & Taos
Explorer's Guide Sarasota, Sanibel Island & Naples

For information about permission to reproduce selections from this book, write to
Permissions, The Countryman Press, 500 Fifth Avenue, New York, NY 10110

For information about special discounts for bulk purchases, please contact
W. W. Norton Special Sales at specialsales@wwnorton.com or 800-233-4830

Manufacturing by Versa Press
Series book design by Chris Welch
Maps by Michael Borop (sitesatlas.com)
Production manager: Devon Zahn

Library of Congress Cataloging-in-Publication Data

Names: Randall, Laura, 1967– author.
Title: Philadelphia & Amish Country / Laura Randall.
Other titles: Philadelphia and Amish Country
Description: First edition. | New York, NY : The Countryman Press, [2020] |
Series: Explorer's guide | Includes index.
Identifiers: LCCN 2019055621 | ISBN 9781682684368 (pbk.) | ISBN 9781682684375 (epub)
Subjects: LCSH: Philadelphia (Pa.)—Guidebooks. | Amish Country (Pa.)—Guidebooks.
Classification: LCC F158.18 .R36 2020 | DDC 917.4804—dc23
LC record available at https://lccn.loc.gov/2019055621

The Countryman Press
www.countrymanpress.com

A division of W. W. Norton & Company, Inc.
500 Fifth Avenue, New York, NY 10110
www.wwnorton.com

10 9 8 7 6 5 4 3 2 1

For Bill and Rosemarie Randall

EXPLORE WITH US!

Welcome to *Explorer's Guide Philadelphia & Amish Country*, the definitive guide to Philadelphia and the large and diverse regions that surround it. It's the ideal companion for exploring the Brandywine Valley, Bucks County, Amish Country, Gettysburg, and the Pocono Mountains. Here you'll find thorough coverage of big cities and small towns, plus everything in between, with detailed listings of the best sightseeing, outdoor activities, restaurants, shopping, and B&Bs.

WHAT'S WHERE In the beginning of this book, you'll find an alphabetical listing of special highlights and important information that you may want to reference quickly. You'll find advice on everything from navigating the complicated state liquor laws to ordering cheesesteaks.

LODGING We've selected lodging places for inclusion in this book based on merit alone; we do not charge innkeepers for their inclusion. Please don't hold us or the respective innkeepers responsible for rates listed as of press time in 2019. Changes

KEY TO SYMBOLS

- ✐ **Child friendly**. The crayon denotes a family-friendly place or event that welcomes young children. Most B&Bs prohibit children under 12.
- ♿ **Handicapped access**. The wheelchair icon denotes a place with full ADA—Americans with Disabilities Act—standard access, still distressingly rare in these remote areas.
- ☂ **Rainy day**. The umbrella icon points out places where you can entertain yourself but still stay dry in bad weather.
- 🐾 **Pets**. The dog's paw icon identifies lodgings that allow pets—still the exception to the rule. Accommodations that accept pets may still charge an extra fee or restrict pets to certain areas, as well as require advance notice.
- 🎀 **Special value**. The blue-ribbon symbol appears next to selected lodging and restaurants that combine quality and moderate prices.
- 🍸 **Good bars**. The martini glass icon appears next to restaurants and entertainment venues that have them.
- 💍 **Weddings**. Listings with the ring symbol have the skill and capacity to host wedding ceremonies and receptions.
- ✪ **Author pick**. A unique place that the author believes is worth a special shout-out and is worth making an effort to go.
- ⚲ **Pool on site**.

are inevitable. At the time of this writing, the state room tax was 6 percent (plus an additional 1 percent in Philadelphia), and city and county room tax was 6 percent.

A general price range is given with lodging prices per room based on double occupancy.

KEY TO LODGING PRICES

$: Up to $75 per couple
$$: $76-$150 per couple
$$$: $151-$250 per couple
$$$$: More than $250 per couple

RESTAURANTS In most chapters, please note the distinction between Eating Out and Dining Out. By their nature, restaurants included in the Eating Out group are generally inexpensive. A range of prices is included for each entry.

Restaurant prices indicate the cost of a meal for two people, including an appetizer or sale, main course, and dessert.

KEY TO DINING PRICES

$: Up to $10
$$: $11-$25
$$$: $26-$40
$$$$: More than $40

Please send any comments or corrections to:

Explorer's Guide Editor
The Countryman Press
500 Fifth Avenue
New York, NY 10110

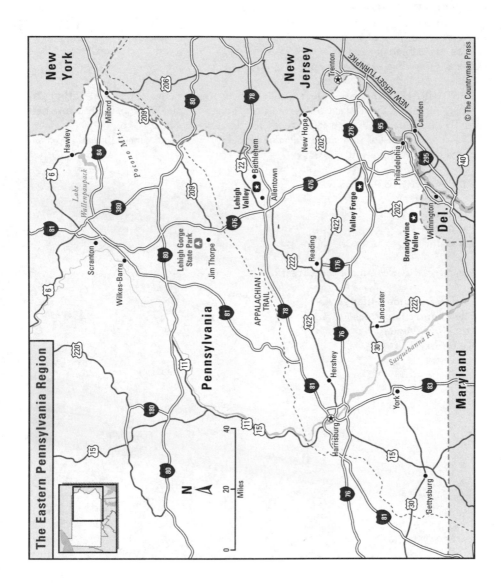

The Eastern Pennsylvania Region

New York

New Jersey

Pennsylvania

Maryland

Del.

© The Countryman Press

NEW JERSEY TURNPIKE

APPALACHIAN TRAIL

Pocono Mts.

Lake Wallenpaupack

Susquehanna R.

Lehigh Gorge State Park

Hawley
Milford
Scranton
Wilkes-Barre
Jim Thorpe
Bethlehem
Allentown
Lehigh Valley
New Hope
Trenton
Camden
Philadelphia
Wilmington
Brandywine Valley
Valley Forge
Reading
Lancaster
Hershey
Harrisburg
York
Gettysburg

N

0   20   40
Miles

220
6
81
84
380
6
80
180
15
111
11
15
206
209
209
22
476
476
80
78
15
81
76
81
81
78
222
422
422
176
202
476
95
276
295
40
202
202
222
30
83
30
76
208

CONTENTS

MAPS

ACKNOWLEDGMENTS

First, I want to send heartfelt appreciation to each business owner, docent, chamber of commerce member, historian, and park ranger who contributed information, offered assistance, and patiently answered my many, many questions about their towns and attractions. Your love for your jobs and the Keystone State is palpable and inspiring.

This book wouldn't have been possible without my network of friends and family who were always on hand to recommend and describe their favorite places to eat, stroll, shop, and sightsee around eastern Pennsylvania. Ayleen Stellhorn (Gettysburg, Harrisburg, and Lancaster), Deborah and Laine Kasdras (Berks County), Karen and Tom Condor (Harrisburg), Sherri Schmidt (Philadelphia), Lynn Williams and Tracey Molettiere (Southeastern Pennsylvania)—your tips and opinions are always spot-on and useful—here's to laughter and friendship.

Thanks and sincere appreciation must also go to my parents, Bill and Rosemarie Randall, for their tireless reconnaissance work, which in this book involved scouting out a country breakfast café on the back roads of Upper Bucks County, touring one of the only handbell makers in the world, and riding a tram through a former tire factory filled with nickelodeons, vintage cars, and animatronic clowns. The folks at The Countryman Press and W. W. Norton also deserve a shout for their editorial guidance and infectious enthusiasm for travel.

As always, thanks to John, Jack, and Theo Kimble for their willingness to visit parks, out-of-the-way museums, and Italian ice stands—not to mention test out every thrill ride at Hershey Park—with me at all hours of the day and night. Here's to a future of many more fun family adventures.

INTRODUCTION

With its abundant natural resources and central role in early American history, eastern Pennsylvania attracts a wide swath of travelers to its cities and rural towns. It is home to the Liberty Bell and Independence Hall, the country's second-largest Amish community and one of its biggest shopping malls, and more than 100 lakes, rivers, and state parks. Philadelphia may be the area's anchor and urban soul, but it is surrounded by miles of rolling green farmlands, forested mountains, and villages that haven't changed much since the King of England bequeathed the state to William Penn. Within an hour or two's drive from the city's center, you can tour a dozen historic battlefields, shop for antiques, go tubing along the Delaware River, visit a chocolate factory straight out of Willy Wonka, and eat chicken corn soup and chow-chow in an 18th-century farmhouse. The area really does offer something for everyone.

I am a native Pennsylvanian who grew up near Valley Forge National Historical Park and went to college within cannon-firing distance of the battlefields of Gettysburg. I spent summers cycling along the Schuylkill River, devouring lemon water ice at Rita's, cheering on the Phillies, and hiking and swimming in the Pocono Mountains. As an adult, I lived in a corner of a converted sugar mill in Old City, Philadelphia, just as the area was beginning to explode into the vibrant neighborhood it is today, and got married amid the B&Bs and quirky shops of New Hope, Bucks County. My husband and I chose to marry there because it represented to us an idyllic (yet accessible) place where our friends and family could kick back, explore at their leisure, and leave with a happy memory or two. In putting together a guide to the area for out-of-town guests, we coaxed local acquaintances into divulging their favorite haunts, walked the river towpath to check out the trails and views ourselves, and banged on doors of small Colonial inns.

I bring to this guide more than 20 years of experience as a travel writer and globe-trotter who appreciates a four-star dining experience as much as the discovery of a bargain hotel room that's as clean and attractive as the significantly more expensive chain place around the corner. I have traveled extensively, yet I still consider Pennsylvania home and return several times a year to see family and friends and get my fix of cobblestones, 18th-century architecture, and, yes, cheesesteaks. No matter what they tell you, they just aren't as good west of the Susquehanna.

You may notice that this guide devotes pages not just to the city of Philadelphia itself but also its outlying areas. The covered bridges of Bucks County and hex signs of northern Berks County will get as much attention as Constitution Hall and the Mummers Parade. I understand that visitors to the area are as interested in hiking a forest trail, hearing the Gettysburg Address at its original site, and shopping for Amish-made farm tables as much as they are in seeing the Liberty Bell, and I have applied that knowledge accordingly. This book is written for Pennsylvania residents who enjoy taking short excursions in their home state throughout the year, and it is written for those who own or rent vacation homes in places like the Pocono Mountains and want to gain a better understanding of their adopted neighborhoods. It's also written for American history lovers and for parents who want to introduce their children to names such as Hershey, Crayola, and Daniel Boone.

Most of all, however, this book aims to introduce eastern Pennsylvania's beauty and diversity to the many people who assume that the region is defined only by the nation's fifth-largest city. There is a whole idyllic and accessible side of eastern Pennsylvania that's also well worth a visit.

I welcome comments from readers offering updates and tips on their own favorite places to visit in Pennsylvania. Check out my blog (exploringpennsylvania.wordpress .com) for contact information, as well as my own updates and discoveries as I continue to explore the best the Keystone State has to offer.

WHAT'S WHERE IN PHILADELPHIA & BEYOND

AMISH COUNTRY Lancaster County is home to one of the country's largest Amish populations. They don't drive, but you will undoubtedly see them out and about in horse and buggy or walking to and from shops. Please respect their wishes and don't snap photos. The best ways to learn more about their culture and lifestyle are via buggy rides that wind through backcountry roads and farms or by joining an Amish family for dinner in their home, which can often be arranged by B&B owners.

ANTIQUES Quaint shopping districts abound in this part of the state. Serious antiques buyers flock to **Adamstown** near Reading, **Hawley** and **Honesdale** in the Pocono Mountains, and **Chadds Ford** and other small towns in the Brandywine Valley. You'll also find a good concentration of antiques shops in the Bucks County villages of New Hope, Lahaska, and Kintnersville.

CAVES There is nothing like a cave to make you feel your mortality, and eastern Pennsylvania has three fine ones that

AN ANTIQUES SHOP IN ST. PETERS VILLAGE NEAR FRENCH CREEK STATE PARK

are open to tourists. **Indian Echo Caverns** near Hershey is a favorite, and **Crystal Cave** and **Lost River Caverns** are the ones to hit if you're in the Reading/Kutztown area or the Lehigh Valley.

CHEESESTEAKS It's one word in Philadelphia and much of eastern Pennsylvania, and the favorite way to order it is with Cheez Whiz and fried onions. **John's Roast Pork** near the waterfront has been the king of the steak sandwich in recent years, garnering rave reviews of food critics, though many Philadelphians remain loyal to the two South Philadelphia institutions, **Pat's** and **Geno's**.

CIVIL WAR The Battle of Gettysburg yielded the largest number of casualties of any battle of the American Civil War and is often cited as the war's turning point. Today, thousands of Civil War buffs come to south central Pennsylvania to visit the solemn battlefield site and the countless other attractions that have sprung up around it. In Harrisburg, the **National Civil War Museum** takes pains to tell the story of the Civil War without taking sides. Numerous other smaller battles were also fought here in towns such as Hanover, Fairfield, and Carlisle.

CONVENIENCE STORES Once you get past the funny name, you'll realize that Wawa is the grande dame of convenience stores. If you're driving around the state and looking for a pick-me-up Tastykake or hoagie, this is the place to go. Everything here is fresh, the prices are reasonable, and the clerks are usually polite, if not downright friendly. Many branches

A COVERED BRIDGE IN LANCASTER COUNTY

sell gas at a discount, and the ATMs are surcharge-free. There are more than 500 Wawa stores in Pennsylvania, New Jersey, Delaware, and Maryland.

COVERED BRIDGES Forget the Bridges of Madison County—more than 200 covered bridges dot the Pennsylvania landscape between Philadelphia and Pittsburgh. Entire websites are devoted to their beauty and preservation. The places to find them in the eastern part of the state are Bucks County, especially the central and upper parts; Lancaster County; and the back roads of the Brandywine Valley.

DINERS Nobody does diners better than Pennsylvania, in my humble opinion. Expect homemade soups, hearty servings, efficient (if brusque) service, and low prices. It's hard to find a bad one in the state, but **Daddypops** in Hatboro (near the Bucks County line), **Saville Diner** in Boyertown, and **Hawley Diner** in the Pocono Mountains are three of the best.

FESTIVALS Eastern Pennsylvania loves a good party, especially if it involves Ben Franklin, fireworks, or green beer. Some of the state's best annual events can be found in small towns such as Kutztown (the **Kutztown Folk Festival**), Kennett Square (**Mushroom Festival**), and Bethlehem (**Celtic Classic Highland Games and Festival**). In Philadelphia, the feather-and-sequins **Mummers Parade** on New Year's Day is like no other costume parade you'll ever experience. Lancaster hosts the world's largest chicken BBQ in late summer at Long's Park, and Shawnee in the Pocono Mountains pays homage to the garlic bulb every Labor Day weekend.

FISHING A license is required to fish in Pennsylvania's rivers, lakes, and streams. For more information, go to www.pgc.state.pa.us. Another good source for the state's best fishing spots is www.paflyfish.com.

FLEA MARKETS They are rampant around here and offer terrific people-watching opportunities, not to mention the chance to buy such things as hand-made quilts and sticky buns. Two of the biggest and oldest are the **Green Dragon** near Lancaster and **Rice's** in New Hope.

Renninger's markets, with locations in Adamstown and Kutztown, and Root's Country Market in Manheim (Lancaster County) are also worth a special trip.

GAMBLING The state opened its first slot parlor in 2006; it now has 12 full-scale casinos in as many counties, with a 13th, Live!, slated to open in 2020 in Philadelphia's Stadium District. For updated info, go to www.visitpacasinos.com.

GARDENS Philadelphia and its outlying areas are home to dozens of world-class gardens. Head to **Longwood Gardens** in Kennett Square for seasonal perfection, or to **Chanticleer** in Wayne for a quiet meander. For a comprehensive list, download a passport with maps and descriptions of the area's public gardens at americasgardencapital.org (or pick up a hard copy at any of the featured properties). Adam Levine's *A Guide to the Great Gardens of the Philadelphia Region*

A FOUNTAIN AT LONGWOOD GARDENS IN THE BRANDYWINE VALLEY

(2007, Temple University Press) is also a great source for information on gardens in Pennsylvania, Delaware, and southern New Jersey.

HUNTING The forests and fields of Pennsylvania are open to hunting during established seasons. Common game species are deer, rabbit, pheasant, ruffed grouse, bear, squirrel, and waterfowl. Hunters are expected to follow the rules and regulations of the state game commission. For more information, go to pgc.state.pa.us or huntingpa.com.

ITALIAN ICE If you visit eastern Pennsylvania in the late spring or summer, chances are you'll see lines of people gathered at small stands selling Italian ices. Also called water ice, it's a dessert made from shaved ice and flavored with concentrated syrup (lemon is a favorite). **Rita's Water Ice** is a homegrown chain with stands throughout the state.

LIQUOR LAWS As anyone who has spent any time here knows, Pennsylvania has some of the most restrictive laws in the country concerning the purchase of alcohol. Ironically, Philadelphia also has more BYO restaurants than just about any other city. You can buy wine and spirits only in stores operated by the state-run Liquor Control Board. This book includes a BYO section at the end of each *Where to Eat* section to help you find Wine & Spirits stores in the area. For a complete list of stores in the state, go to lcb.state.pa.us.

MUSEUMS You'll find all kinds represented here, from the diverse offerings of the free **State Museum** in Harrisburg to niche facilities devoted to wood carving, 19th-century quilts, and Ben Franklin's inventions. Don't miss the **Mütter, Science History Institute** (formerly **Chemical Heritage**), or **Rodin Museums** if you're in Philadelphia. Elsewhere, the **Brandywine River Museum** and **Christian C. Sanderson Museum** in Chadds

WHOOPIE PIES FOR SALE AT A LANCASTER FARM STAND

Ford, **Dorflinger Glass Museum** in Honesdale, and **Wharton Esherick Museum** in Malvern are all worth a special trip. Children will love the huge **Please Touch Museum** in Philadelphia, the **National Canal Museum** and **Crayola Factory** in Easton, and the chocolate-themed attractions in **Hershey**.

PENNSYLVANIA DUTCH FOOD If you see chow-chow, chicken corn soup, or shoofly pie on a menu, chances are you're within spitting distance of Lancaster County. Chow-chow is a sweet and sour relish made from end-of-summer garden leftovers. Shoofly pie is a crumb-topped pie with a sticky molasses bottom. Other not-to-be-missed Pennsylvania Dutch delicacies: whoopie pie, an oversized cakelike Oreo, and funnel cake, fried dough topped with powdered sugar sold often at carnivals and festivals. The strong-of-stomach may also want to try scrapple, a pan-fried slab of cornmeal mush and pork byproducts, and "church spread," an Amish invention of corn syrup or molasses, marshmallow cream, and peanut butter.

RAILROAD Eastern Pennsylvania was a leader in rail travel during the 1800s, and today you will find many, many places here that celebrate that heritage. You can still view the rolling hills and farmland from restored passenger cars on the **Strasburg Rail Road**, the **Stourbridge Lion** in Honesdale, and **M&H Railroad** in Hummelstown. Train lovers of all ages also shouldn't miss the **Railroad Museum of Pennsylvania** in Strasburg or Scranton's **Steamtown National Historic Site**, which ranks among the best in the country.

SMOKING Smoking is prohibited in most public places and workplaces (except casinos) throughout the state.

SOFT PRETZELS You can have them for breakfast, tour factories that produce them by the ton, and watch them being hand-twisted by Amish grandmothers—all in a single day in the Reading or Lancaster areas. Life isn't complete until you have sampled a soft pretzel that's butter-brushed and fresh from the oven. **Philly Pretzel Factory** (phillypretzelfactory .com) has dozens of storefronts around the state turning out hand-twisted, hot-from-the-oven pretzels and specialty items like cheesesteak pretzels and spicy pretzel sausages.

STATE PARKS You'll find dozens of state parks in this part of the state; many offer camping, swimming, boating, hiking, and horseback riding options.

SOFT PRETZELS GALORE AT A PHILLY PRETZEL FACTORY STORE

MEASURING UP OUTSIDE THE ENTRANCE TO HERSHEY PARK

WATERFALLS The Pocono Mountains have some of the best cascades this side of Niagara. **Bushkill Falls** is probably the most famous, but there are also many free ones that are also worth a visit, including **Raymondskill Falls**, **Dingmans Falls**, and **Shohola Falls**.

WINERIES The state's wineries may be light years away from matching the Rhone or Napa Valleys in terms of quality, but its boutique wineries have significantly expanded and upgraded in recent years. Bucks County, Brandywine Valley, Lancaster, Gettysburg, and York County all boast serious wineries that often combine events and fun activities with tastings.

Promised Land in the Pocono Mountains, **French Creek** between Reading and Valley Forge, and **Nockamixon** in Upper Bucks County are a few favorites.

THEME PARKS With its wide appeal, reputation for cleanliness, and chocolate connection, **Hershey Park** dominates in this department. The state also has some smaller amusement parks that are worth a look: **Dutch Wonderland** in Lancaster is great for preschoolers, and **Knoebels** way up in Elysburg is known for its free admission, old-fashioned roller coasters, and good food. **Dorney Park & Wildwater Kingdom** in Allentown appeals to older kids with a relatively modest admission price that includes a large water park and a mix of roller coasters and thrill rides.

A WINERY ENTRANCE NEAR LANCASTER COUNTY

PHILADELPHIA

CENTER CITY

CENTER CITY WEST & UNIVERSITY CITY

INTRODUCTION

Ever since William Penn landed on its shores in 1682 and dubbed it the City of Brotherly Love, Philadelphia has been a place of contrasts. It gave the world Grace Kelly and Rocky Balboa. Its cheesesteak stands garner as much attention as its nationally acclaimed restaurants such as Vetri and Lacroix at the Rittenhouse. In Center City, sleek skyscrapers coexist next to neighborhoods of neat brick rowhouses where residents still throw block parties.

First and foremost, Philadelphia is the nation's birthplace, home to countless historic sites, pioneering architectural styles, and American firsts. It was here that the US Constitution and Declaration of Independence were signed, the first stock exchange opened, and the first urban planning experiment was set in motion. History is evident on just about every block, whether it's a plaque commemorating the Founding Fathers, an 18th-century Federal townhome, or a gravestone with the name FRANKLIN etched on it. It's here that you will find the country's oldest mint, art museum, post office, lending library, zoo, and continuously occupied public street.

Yet you don't have to be a history buff to visit Philadelphia. You will find things to enjoy if you like good food, soulful jazz, high-end shopping, and top-tier art museums. Philly, as it's often called, is home to top-notch restaurants, dozens of colleges, a terrific urban park larger than New York City's Central Park, and scores of restaurants, shops, hotels, and theaters. Reading Terminal Market, a massive indoor marketplace directly across from the Pennsylvania Convention Center and a few blocks from City Hall, unites locals and tourists alike with its fresh-cut flowers, vibrant produce, Amish-made breads and apple butter, and two-fisted pork sandwiches.

Observers and tourism officials like to say the city truly came into its own as a stand-alone travel destination in the late 1990s and early 2000s, with the openings of a 1 million-square-foot convention center, the $250 million Kimmel Center for the Performing Arts, two new sports stadiums, and the National Constitution Center. They have a point, but as someone who has spent time here since the 1970s, I like to think many of the right elements were in place long before that. The city, despite a host of urban problems like crime and graffiti that continue to this day, has always had good food, loud and loyal locals, and a walkable, easy-to-navigate downtown. It has always had Independence Hall, the Liberty Bell, and Ben Franklin's spirit.

First-time visitors should also expect experiences that they might not have elsewhere in the country, for better or for worse. You will hear "Yo!" more often than you can imagine. You will probably be called "hon," whatever your gender, by everyone from the curbside hot dog vendor to the stylish clerk at your boutique hotel. You may get snarled at, or at least a raised eyebrow, if you ask for anything but fried onions and Cheez Whiz on your cheesesteak ("Whiz with," or "Whiz without" is the local jargon for ordering with or without onions). And anyone who spends time at a sporting event here in which the hometown is losing will question why it deserves its City of Brotherly Love title.

The easiest and most satisfying way to see Philadelphia is to walk. It is laid out in a grid pattern of wide, straight streets that cross at right angles (thank you, Mr. Penn). Those in moderately good shape can walk or jog from the University of Pennsylvania campus all the way to the Delaware River via Walnut or Spruce Streets, passing by

Independence Hall, Washington Square Park, and many cobblestoned alleys along the way. Detour over a few blocks to the north and you'll find yourself climbing the steps of the Philadelphia Art Museum, where Rocky Balboa took his famous victory lap.

Philly is home to more than 100 neighborhoods. Center City is its core, anchored by City Hall and split to the east and west by Broad Street. South Philadelphia is home to multigenerational families, the bustling Italian Market, and some of the best trattorias around. The University of Pennsylvania's influence is strong amid West Philadelphia's corner stores and brownstones, while the Philadelphia Art Museum and other first-class museums dominate the Benjamin Franklin Parkway Area to the north. Much of the Historic District, including Independence Hall and the Liberty Bell, lies in or around Old City, a once-industrial area that has been transformed in recent years to a hip neighborhood with some of the city's best restaurants, nightlife, and art galleries. On the outskirts, Chestnut Hill, Germantown, and Manayunk have some of the city's best boutique shopping and examples of preserved 18th-century architecture.

Whatever your reason for visiting, Philadelphia is an important part of travel within the eastern Pennsylvania region, a place that can serve as a base for day or overnight trips to Gettysburg or Pennsylvania Dutch Country, or spark your interest in visiting them independently.

CENTER CITY

AREA CODE The area code for Philadelphia is 215.

GUIDANCE Independent Visitor Center (800-537-7676 or 215-965-7676; www
.phlvisitorcenter.com), Sixth and Market Streets, is a must for anyone visiting the Historic District. It's the place to pick up free timed tickets to Independence Hall, as well
as paid tickets to other attractions, plus it offers a café, gift shop, and a huge selection of publications and maps of the city and its surrounding counties. Volunteers and
National Park Service employees are on hand to answer questions. On the west side of
town, an information center in the east portal of **City Hall** (215-686-2840; Broad Street)
has local guides and brochures. Purchase tickets for City Hall tours here (see *To See*).
The staffed **Fairmount Park Welcome Center** at 16th Street and JFK Boulevard near
Love Park has park maps and other info. Both are open 9–5 weekdays.

GETTING THERE *By car:* Several major interstate highways lead through Philadelphia. From the north or south, take I-95 to I-676 (Vine Street Expressway), which cuts
right through Center City. From the west, I-76 (the Schuylkill Expressway) branches off
the Pennsylvania Turnpike and follows the river to South Philadelphia.
   By air: **Philadelphia International Airport** (215-937-6800) is about a 20-minute
drive from Center City and is served by all major airlines. The Southeastern Pennsylvania Transportation Authority (SEPTA) R1 line offers direct service between Center
City and the airport.
   By bus: **Greyhound** (800-231-2222; greyhound.com) and **Peter Pan** (800-343-9999;
peterpanbus.com) offer service between Philadelphia, New York, and dozens of major
cities, operating out of the Greyhound terminal next to Reading Terminal Market.
   By train: **Amtrak** stops at 30th Street Station on its Northeast Corridor route
between Richmond, Virginia, and Boston. SEPTA's R7 suburban train runs to Trenton,
New Jersey, where New Jersey Transit trains run to New York's Penn Station. The R7
stops at the Market Street East Station, about four blocks from Independence Hall.

GETTING AROUND SEPTA municipal buses run all over the city, though they can be
daunting for first-time visitors. The Market–Frankford Line is a rapid-transit line that
stops outside City Hall (Broad and Market) and near the University of Pennsylvania's
campus, ending in the city's far northwest corner. The purple **Phlash** bus (215-599-
0776; www.phillyphlash.com) runs a continuous loop between the city's major attractions, from Penn's Landing to the Parkway museums. Buses stop every 12 minutes at
designated purple lampposts and operate daily May–September and on weekends in
October and November. Cost is $2 a ride, or $5 for an all-day pass.

PARKING There is restricted metered parking available on the street throughout Center City. If you're spending the day, your best bet is to park in one of the many parking
garages in the city's historic area and near City Hall. The **Auto Park** at Independence
Mall (Sixth Street between Market and Arch), lets you enter Independence Visitor
Center without having to go outside. Convenient to both the Historic District and the

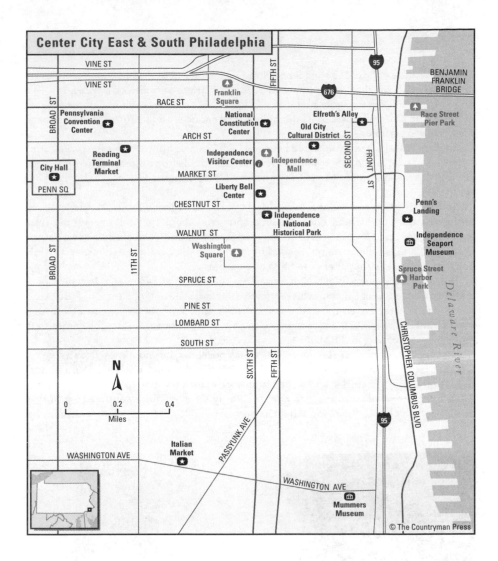

Center City East & South Philadelphia

VINE ST

VINE ST

RACE ST

Franklin Square

FIFTH ST

95

BENJAMIN FRANKLIN BRIDGE

BROAD ST

Pennsylvania Convention Center

National Constitution Center

ARCH ST

Elfreth's Alley

Old City Cultural District

SECOND ST

FRONT ST

Race Street Pier Park

Reading Terminal Market

Independence Visitor Center

Independence Mall

City Hall

PENN SQ

MARKET ST

Liberty Bell Center

CHESTNUT ST

Independence National Historical Park

Penn's Landing

Independence Seaport Museum

WALNUT ST

BROAD ST

11TH ST

Washington Square

Spruce Street Harbor Park

SPRUCE ST

PINE ST

LOMBARD ST

SOUTH ST

SIXTH ST

FIFTH ST

CHRISTOPHER COLUMBUS BLVD

Delaware River

N

0   0.2   0.4
Miles

PASSYUNK AVE

95

Italian Market

WASHINGTON AVE

WASHINGTON AVE

Mummers Museum

© The Countryman Press

convention center is the Philadelphia Parking Authority's **Auto Parking Plaza** (215-925-4305), 801 Filbert Street, which offers early-bird specials to cars entering before 10 a.m. For the best rates, go online to philapark.org/locator or Philadelphia.bestparking.com and type in the address of your destination.

WHEN TO GO Philadelphia's many museums, theaters, and shops make it a good place to visit year-round. The lines at many of its historic sites, such as Independence Hall and the Liberty Bell, tend to be shortest in January and February. If you prefer warmer weather and lots of activities, try to plan your visit in the summer, when Penn's Landing and the city's squares are alive with all kinds of entertainment and festivities.

✲ Neighborhoods

Old City. At the edge of Independence National Historical Park, Old City has its share of worthy historic sites, including Ben Franklin's grave and Elfreth's Alley. It's best known, however, for its lively nightlife and gallery scene, the result of a gentrification in the 1990s that transformed its dilapidated warehouses and factories into loft apartments and art studios.

Society Hill. This neighborhood between Old City and South Street is known for its preserved Federal and Georgian row homes and cobblestone streets. The only high-rises are three apartment towers designed by I. M. Pei in the 1970s to help revitalize the area.

South Street/Queen Village. South Street between 10th and Front Streets is a commercial strip of nightclubs, cheesesteak stands, and shops that sell everything from leather pants and Goth hair dye to antique armoires and Reeboks. To the south is Queen Village, a quieter neighborhood of narrow streets, antiques shops, and neighborhood BYO cafés that always seem to be buzzing.

Washington Square West. The sprawling neighborhood between Independence Hall and Broad Street contains the shopping districts of Jewelers' Row and Pine Street Antiques, several hospitals, and a mix of high-end restaurants, cheap electronics stores, and old taverns. It's also home to the city's small but thriving gay community and a handful of bars and B&Bs.

Waterfront/Columbus Avenue. Once a busy port area, it is now known for its warm-weather festivals and wide-open views of the Benjamin Franklin Bridge. Penn's Landing, several big-box stores, and a couple of huge river-view bars like Dave & Buster's are the main anchors, but it's also home to Philly treasures like John's Roast Pork, a family-owned cheesesteak stand that has been around for decades. Cherry Street Pier,

BEN FRANKLIN WATCHES OVER AN OLD CITY STREET

Spruce Street Harbor Park, and Blue Cross RiverRink are recent additions that have drawn even more people to the area. I-95 divides the waterfront from Old City and South Philadelphia, but there are two pedestrian bridges that lead to Penn's Landing.

✳ To See

MUSEUMS ♿ ⬆ 🔊 **Science History Institute** (215-925-2222; sciencehistory.org), 315 Chestnut Street. Open 10-5 Tuesday–Saturday; free. The periodic table has never looked so good. This small two-story museum showcases the impact of chemistry and life sciences on our lives in sleek exhibits that combine fine art and high-tech images with antique tools and professorial explanations. A cool and tranquil respite from the tourist-filled historic sites that surround it, this may be Old City's least-known free attraction.

⬆ **National Liberty Museum** (215-925-2800; libertymuseum.org), 321 Chestnut Street, Old City. Open daily, but hours vary throughout the year; $7-9 adults, $5 ages 13–21, $4 ages 5–12. This eclectic museum is dedicated to promoting the ideals of freedom and diversity. Exhibits include a showcase of glass sculptures by Dale Chihuly, memorials to America's Nobel Peace Prize winners, and a gallery featuring frank images and statistics on youth violence. Tucked away in a corner on the upper levels you will find John Lennon's handwritten lyrics to "Beautiful Boy."

⬆ **National Museum of American Jewish History** (215-923-3811; nmajh.org), 101 South Independence Mall East. Closed Mondays and most Jewish holidays; $15 adults, $13 seniors and ages 13–21. Let other museums effectively cover the Holocaust; this large five-story building on Independence Mall instead focuses on 350 years of Jewish life in the United States. There are films, interactive displays, and artifacts such as a pipe that belonged to Albert Einstein, a baseball glove owned by Sandy Koufax, and a Torah from colonial times. It's hard to take it all in in one visit.

⬆ **Mummers Museum** (215-336-3050; mummersmuseum.com), 1100 South Second Street (at Washington Avenue), South Philly. Open Wednesday–Sunday; $5. Philadelphia's version of Madame Tussaud's, featuring wax figures dressed in the feathered and spangled costumes that characterize the city's raucous New Year's Day parade. There's also an exhibit explaining the parade's history, as well as live string-band concerts in the summer. This is the way to experience the Mummers Parade without having to endure the cold weather or the smell of hops.

HISTORIC SITES ✪ ⬆ **Museum of the American Revolution** (215-253-6731; amrevmuseum.org), 101 South Third Street. Open daily; $21 adults, $13 ages 6–17. This newest addition to the Historic District opened in 2017 in the old visitor center space. The kid-friendly exhibits combine interactive activities with a rich collection of objects that span the entire war, including chiseled French and British swords and George Washington's preserved field tent, unveiled hourly in a climate-controlled environment theater. Other displays invite you to design your

A STATUE OF ALEXANDER HAMILTON IN THE LOBBY OF THE MUSEUM OF THE AMERICAN REVOLUTION

INDEPENDENCE HALL IN OLD CITY

own soldier uniform; sit under a version of the Boston "Liberty Tree," where stirrings of the revolution began; and witness a stirring digital re-creation of angry citizens in New York using ropes to pull down a statue of King George III.

Carpenter's Hall (215-925-0167), 320 Chestnut Street. Open 10–4 daily, closed Mondays and Tuesdays in January and February; free. This redbrick Georgian building was the original home of a guild of carpenters and architects and served as the site of the First Continental Congress in 1774. It was also the site of the nation's first bank robbery. On display are some of the original Windsor chairs on which the representatives sat, as well as displays of carpenters' tools and a parade float built to celebrate the ratification of the US Constitution. It's easy to miss with all the other historic sites around but worth seeking out.

✪ ❀ ♿ **Franklin Court** (215-965-2305), Market and Chestnut Streets between Third and Fourth. Fans of Ben Franklin won't want to miss this fascinating complex of buildings and exhibits that pay homage to the city's wittiest and most influential inhabitant. Enter through a brick archway on Market Street to a courtyard where Franklin's original house once stood, now outlined by a steel frame "ghost sculpture," designed by Pritzker Prize–winning architect Robert Venturi. The nearby underground museum displays Franklin's many inventions, plus fill-in-the-blank quote displays and an electronic version of Magic Squares, the Sudoku-like brainteaser he invented while sitting through debates at the Pennsylvania Assembly. On the way out, stop by Franklin's small printing office and bindery, 320 Market Street, and take a postcard to get hand-stamped at the B. Free Franklin Post Office two doors down.

❀ **Elfreth's Alley** (215-574-0560; elfrethsalley.org), Second Street between Race and Arch, Old City. This narrow block of 32 row homes built between 1728 and 1836 is believed to be America's oldest continuously occupied residential street. It is named for a blacksmith who once lived here alongside carpenters, pewter makers, and other

EXPLORING THE HISTORIC DISTRICT

Independence Hall (215-497-8974), Chestnut Street between Fifth and Sixth. Open 9–5 daily; free. If you have time to visit only one historic attraction in Philly, this is quite possibly the best choice. It's hard not to step inside and immediately sense the building's monumental significance and hear the echoes of "We the People" within its walls. Free guided tours of the restored Georgian building include a stop in the regal blue Assembly Room, where the Declaration of Independence was adopted in 1776 and the US Constitution was drafted in 1787. Artifacts on display include the "rising sun" chair used by George Washington during the Constitutional Convention and the silver inkstand used in the formal signing of the Declaration of Independence and the Constitution. Between March and December, all visitors must pick up free timed tickets at the Independence Visitor Center. The 30-minute tours run every 15 minutes, but they do fill up, especially during the summer months. Outside the hall, you can take a guided horse and buggy ride through the Historic District or grab a bench under a tree in Independence Square, site of the Declaration's first public reading.

Across the street sits the Liberty Bell Center (215-597-8974), Sixth and Market Streets, home to the 2,080-pound bronze bell that heralded the country's most significant achievements before cracking and becoming unusable in 1846. It's worth a brief stop, though it can be challenging to get a clear photo of the bell. Expect shoulder-to-shoulder crowds on weekends during the summer. It's free, but all visitors must pass a security screening. From April to October, the park hosts the "Lights of Liberty Show," an audio-visual spectacular that takes visitors into the heart of the American Revolution through hand-painted images projected onto the buildings around Independence National Historical Park, while a musical score composed for the show and performed by musicians of the Philadelphia Orchestra is played through special headphones. Get tickets at the visitor center.

PICK UP TOUR TICKETS AND GIFTS AT THE BUSTLING INDEPENDENCE VISITOR CENTER

THE ENTRANCE TO BEN FRANKLIN'S PRINTING OFFICE IN OLD CITY, NOW FRANKLIN COURT

craftspeople of the period. Today, all but two of the homes are privately owned and occupied. Nos. 124–126 constitute a small museum that offers 45-minute guided tours, perhaps to dissuade visitors from peeking into the windows of the other homes. It's open noon–5 Friday–Sunday starting in March or April; check the website for exact dates and tour times and fees. Many residents throw open their doors to the public every June (see *Special Events*).

Christ Church Burial Ground (215-922-1695), Fifth and Arch Streets. $3 adults. Throw a good-luck penny on Benjamin Franklin's gravestone, located within the brick walls of this small cemetery that also holds the remains of Franklin's wife Deborah and four other signers of the Declaration of Independence.

⊤ **Portrait Gallery** in the Second Bank of the United States (800-537-7676), 420 Chestnut Street. Open 11–4 Tuesday–Saturday; free. See the original portraits of the 18th-century luminaries you have been learning about at other historic sites in this magnificent Ionic-columned building. Highlights include George Washington's death mask and a small replica of Charles Willson Peale's natural history collection in the back.

⊤ **Masonic Temple** (215-988-1910), 1 North Broad Street. Admission charged for tours. This stunning Norman-style structure near City Hall was a meeting place for 28 Philadelphia-based Masonic organizations in the 18th century. Guided tours of the seven extravagantly decorated lodge halls are given daily. A small first-floor exhibit includes George Washington's Masonic apron, a fragment of mahogany taken from his coffin, and a collection of historic walking sticks.

✳ To Do

FOR FAMILIES ✐ ♿ ⊤ ✳ **National Constitution Center** (215-409-6600; constitution center.org), 525 Arch Street. Open daily except Thanksgiving, Christmas, and New Year's Day; admission charged. It's easy to spend several hours in this sleek and spacious building on Independence Square. Begin your visit in the theater, where a live costumed actor tells the "We the People" story with the help of 360-degree multimedia images, then head to the high-tech exhibit hall where interactive, in-depth displays will appeal to both novice history students and serious historians. Older kids will have fun reciting the presidential oath of office from a podium and donning the robes of Supreme Court justices before rendering their opinions of key cases. Don't miss Signers' Hall, featuring life-sized bronze statues of all 42 Constitution signers as they may have been seated or standing during the convention. The statue designers studied

A LANDMARK PIPE ORGAN

Macy's, in the fabled Wanamaker Building at Market and South 13th Streets, is home to the first and only pipe organ ever to be designated a National Historic Landmark. Its 28,000 pipes debuted in 1911 and still rattle the rafters of the grand old building two or three times a day, Monday–Saturday. Shows are at noon Monday–Saturday; 5:30 p.m. Monday, Tuesday, Thursday, and Saturday; and 7 p.m. Wednesday and Saturday. Many suburban Philadelphia kids have fond memories of getting dressed up and taking the train into the city to watch the annual Christmas Light Show in the courtyard atrium—a light and sound extravaganza of dancing reindeer and snowflakes accompanied by organ music. The shows run hourly from the day after Thanksgiving through December 25. For more information, visit wanamakerorgan.com or call the store at 215-241-9000.

each delegate's height, weight, and facial features and made them so realistic you may feel the urge to strike up a conversation with George or Alexander.

* **Money in Motion** at the Federal Reserve Bank (866-574-3727; philadelphiafed .org), Sixth and Arch Streets. Open Monday–Friday year-round and Saturdays throughout the summer; free. See a $10,000 bill, exchange old quarters for the latest ones, learn how to identify counterfeit bills, and test your knowledge of the US currency system via high-tech kiosks. Housed in the nation's first Federal Reserve Bank, this small, kid-friendly exhibit requires a full body scan of all visitors but is well worth a stop if you're in the vicinity of Independence Hall. Everyone is handed a small bag of shredded money on the way out.

* **Franklin Square** (215-629-4026; historicphiladelphia.org), Sixth and Race Streets. When the kids are about to wig out from history lesson overload, this 7.5-acre park is where you want to go. An easy walk from Independence Hall and Constitution Center, it features a carousel, playground, Philly-themed mini-golf, and vintage marble fountain with dancing water shows. The SquareBurger kiosk (215-629-4026) sells good burgers, breakfast tacos, and milkshakes; hours vary by season.

* **Penn's Landing** stretches along the Delaware River between Vine and South Streets and includes the spot where William Penn first arrived from England in 1682 aboard the ship *Welcome*. Once the center of Philly's maritime activities and a thriving commercial district, it's now a waterfront park with a promenade, outdoor events plaza, and nice views of the Benjamin Franklin Bridge. It's also home to **Independence Seaport Museum**, (215-413-8655; phillyseaport.org), with exhibits on the US Navy and life at sea in the 18th century. The museum also manages the USS *Olympia*, the oldest steel warship and only US vessel remaining from the Spanish-American War, and the USS *Becuna*, a submarine that patrolled the South Pacific during World War II. Admission to the museum includes tours of both ships. Just south of the museum is **Spruce Street Harbor Park,** a seasonal "urban beach," typically open mid-May–September, featuring tree-strung hammocks, food kiosks, and boardwalk-style games.

Penn's Landing can be accessed by walking across the pedestrian bridge at Walnut and Front Streets or by car via I-95 at the Columbus Boulevard exit.

�֍ Green Space

* ✪ **John Heinz National Wildlife Refuge** at Tinicum (215-365-3118; fws.gov/refuge /John_Heinz), 8601 Lindbergh Boulevard. Open daily; free. This 1,000-acre refuge

MUST SEE

MAGIC GARDENS Welcome to Philadelphia's kookiest and most endearing attraction. Artist Isaiah Zagar began tiling South Street in the 1960s with discarded factory porcelain and glass—and never stopped. The community stepped in to save the buildings from demolition in the 1990s, and the half-block complex is now run by a nonprofit group (with Zagar making frequent appearances to teach workshops and answer questions). Anyone can gape at the floor-to-ceiling-tiled courtyard from the street, but to fully experience this folk art masterpiece, you need to wander through the labyrinthine rooms, closets, and basement. Watch a movie (made by his son) on Zagar's life and technique, then wander some more. Trained guides lead tours of the buildings and nearby street murals most Saturday mornings. Magic Gardens (215-733-0390; www.phillymagicgardens.org), 1020 South Street, $10 admission ($5 ages 6–12). Open daily.

A VISITOR SOAKS UP THE INDOOR-OUTDOOR ARTWORK AT SOUTH STREET'S MAGIC GARDENS

is just a mile from Philadelphia International Airport. Once threatened by plans to reroute I-95, it was saved by local environmentalists and the late senator for whom it's named. It's a hidden gem with a variety of dog- and kid-friendly hiking and biking trails; you can also canoe or kayak (bring your own boat) in the largest remaining freshwater tidal marsh in Pennsylvania and fish in Darby Creek (a license is required for those 16 and older). Wildlife includes muskrats, fox, deer, turtles, and 280 species of birds. Pick up a map at the eco-friendly visitor center near the entrance and check out the nature exhibits before heading outside to explore.

Race Street Pier, Race Street at Delaware Avenue. Walk over the Market Street pedestrian bridge to Penn's Landing and follow the waterfront sidewalk north about 0.5 mile to reach the city's newest and coolest park. Designed by the team behind Manhattan's High Line park, it's now a cantilevered recreational space with grass,

A VIEW OF THE BEN FRANKLIN BRIDGE FROM RACE STREET PIER

trees, and benches with commanding views of the Ben Franklin Bridge. It's about a 20-minute walk from Old City.

✳ Outdoor Activities

BUS/BOAT EXCURSIONS Double-decker buses stop at more than 25 city attractions and let you explore the city at your own pace. Two commercial companies, **Big Bus** (215-389-8687; philllytour.com) and **Philadelphia Sightseeing** (215-922-2300; philadelphiasightseeingtours.com), depart from Fifth and Market Streets several times a day with similar 90-minute itineraries and accompanying guides providing commentary along the way. You can also hop on and off at any stop and purchase one-, two-, and three-day passes starting at $35 for adults and $12 for kids 4–12.

RiverLink Ferry (215-925-5465), Penn's Landing. Open May–September; fee charged. Ferries depart from Penn's Landing every hour and head across the river to the revitalized Camden, New Jersey, waterfront, where there's the USS *New Jersey* battleship and the kid-friendly Adventure Aquarium. The trip takes 15 minutes and offers terrific views of the Philly skyline. They also run express rides during, before, and after popular concerts at Susquehanna Bank Center.

Paddle Penn's Landing rents paddleboats, swan and dragon boats, and kayaks in front of the Independence Seaport Museum (211 South Columbus Boulevard).

BASEBALL The **Philadelphia Phillies** (215-463-1000; 1 Citizens Bank Way), 2008 World Series champs, play all their home games at the modern, fan-friendly Citizens Bank Park, which replaced Veterans Stadium in 2004. Ninety-minute tours are offered Monday–Saturday April–September, and Monday, Wednesday, and Friday the rest of the year; call for times and reservations.

BASKETBALL The **76ers** (215-339-7676; 3601 South Broad Street) play hoops at the Wachovia Center near Citizens Park. College basketball is big here: the **Drexel University Dragons** play at Daskalakis Athletic Center in University City (866-437-3935; Market Street between 33rd and 34th), while the **University of Pennsylvania's Quakers** play at the venerable Palestra (215-898-6151; 215 South 33rd Street).

HORSE-DRAWN CARRIAGES Led by guides in colonial garb, they wind their way through the Historic District on most days and evenings. Many local couples have become engaged during a romantic moonlit ride. Tours last anywhere from 15 minutes to an hour and cost $50–120 for up to four people. Carriages line up on Chestnut and Sixth Streets near Independence Hall most days and at South and Second Streets most evenings.

ICE SKATING Blue Cross RiverRink (215-925-7465), Columbus Boulevard at Market Street, offers daily public skating sessions and lessons late November–early March. In summer, it transforms into the city's only outdoor roller-skating rink.

✳ Lodging

HOTELS & INNS Alexander Inn (215-923-3535; alexanderinn.com), 12th and Spruce Streets. You can walk to Reading Terminal Market, the Broad Street theaters, and Old City historic sites from this efficient seven-story inn. It's often filled with a wide range of travelers who like the discreet European-style service, stylish rooms, and reasonable rates. A practical breakfast of yogurt, cereal, fruit, and boiled eggs is served daily in a dining room off the lobby. There's a tiny gym in the basement. Rooms $$.

🏌 **Omni Hotel** at Independence Park (215-925-0000; omnihotels.com), 401 Chestnut Street. History-minded visitors love the location of this sleek, multistory chain hotel near Independence Hall and Constitution Center. Other perks: a small indoor pool, spa and fitness center, and complimentary shoeshines. Request a room on an upper floor for great views of the city and ask about packages that include tickets to local attractions and valet parking. $$$.

Penn's View Hotel (215-922-7600; 800-331-7634; pennsviewhotel.com), Front Street. This small, family-owned hotel has a prime Old City location, elegant rooms, and dignified Old World vibe. The 27 rooms and suites are large and decorated in Colonial style; many have Jacuzzi tubs, fireplaces, or balconies. Try to snag one on the top floor facing the Benjamin Franklin Bridge. It's an easy walk to Independence Hall, Penn's Landing, and Old City's nightlife. One of the city's best wine bars is downstairs (see *Dining Out*). $$$, including continental breakfast.

Morris House Hotel (215-922-2446; morrishousehotel.com), 225 South Eighth Street, between Walnut and Locust Streets. This attractive 1787 Federal mansion was once home to Philadelphia mayor Anthony Morris. The 15 opulent rooms have modern amenities such as DVD players and complimentary wireless Internet access; extended suites in a separate wing have kitchens, living areas, and Jacuzzi tubs. Afternoon tea is served daily by a roaring fireplace or in the peaceful back garden. Children are welcome. This is one of the few nonchain hotel alternatives in this area of the city, and it's a good one. Rooms $$$, including continental breakfast. Parking in a garage across the street is extra.

🕯 **Loew's Philadelphia** (215-627-1200; loewshotels.com), 1200 Market Street. Yes, it's a chain that caters to convention crowds, but this 581-room hotel is housed in a beautiful art deco building and has many charms, including a large gym, friendly staff, and over-the-top pet services. The downside is that it's on a busy, characterless section of Market Street. $$$.

Lokal Hotel (267-702-4345; staylokal .com), 139 North Third Street, Old City. A recent addition to the Old City scene, this boutique hotel in a renovated walk-up has six loft suites with a sleek, industrial design and modern amenities like a coffee bar, in-room iPads, and high-speed Internet access. Check-in is deliberately "invisible" and via auto-mated code. Lokal also operates two penthouse suites with a courtyard in Fishtown. $$$.

BED & BREAKFASTS **La Reserve** (215-735-1137; lareservebandb.com), 1804 Pine Street. Centrally located in a residential neighborhood a few blocks from Ritten-house Square, this 19th-century town-home has six comfortable rooms, some with shared baths, and one efficiency apartment. Guests are encouraged to play the baby grand piano in the lobby or read in the elegant library. Parking is challenging around here, but there is a small discount at a nearby lot. $$–$$$, includes breakfast.

🍴 **Thomas Bond House** (215-923-8523; thomasbondhousebandb.com), 129 South Second Street. Ben Franklin probably didn't sleep in this 1769 townhouse, but he surely knocked back a few within its walls with Mr. Bond, his friend and a prominent local physician. Now owned by the National Park Service, it sits next to a parking garage and is surrounded by many of Old City's top bars and restaurants. The 12 rooms are decorated in Colonial style with four-poster beds, working fireplaces (in some rooms), and Chippendale period furniture; there are complimentary wines and cheeses in the evening and muffins at breakfast. It's not the most luxurious choice in the area, but it is a unique and affordable B&B option right in the heart of the city. $$.

✳ Where to Eat

DINING OUT 🍸 **Buddakan** (215-574-9440; buddakan.com), 325 Chestnut Street. Lunch Monday–Friday, dinner daily. Sit next to the city's most beautiful people and enjoy edamame ravioli or tuna carpaccio pizza under the watchful eye of a gargantuan golden Buddha. $$$–$$$$.

Chloe (215-629-2337; chloebyob.com), 232 Arch Street. Dinner Wednesday–Saturday. Reliable BYO near Elfreth's Alley that is ideal for a quiet romantic dinner. The menu is simple but creative—grilled Caesar salad, coffee-rubbed rib eye with house-made Worcestershire and herb-crusted cod with littleneck clams, wilted leeks, ramps, and lemon aioli. No reservations. $$$.

🍸 **City Tavern** (215-413-1443; city tavern.com), 138 South Second Street. Lunch and dinner daily. John Adams called it "the most genteel tavern in America." It still makes the most of the fact that the Founding Fathers dined here, catering to tour buses and having its servers channel Betsy Ross. The menu includes colonial classics such as cornmeal-fried oysters, West Indies pep-per pot soup, and turkey potpie. Yes, it has its own gift shop. $$$.

🍸 **Fork** (215-625-9425), 306 Market Street. This stylish bistro was one of the first upscale restaurants to open in Old City in the late 1990s and has outlasted many places that followed it. The hand-some dining room has a visible kitchen and a large, *Cheers*-like bar. Look for innovative dishes such as Sicilian cau-liflower steak with Marcona almonds and whole roasted duck with juniper honey glaze. There's also Saturday tea and Sunday brunch. Reservations recommended. $$$.

Kanella (215-922-1773), 1001 Spruce Street. This blue-awning Greek BYO garners frequent praise for its breakfasts and dinners, but don't expect a tourist-friendly Greek taverna menu; instead you'll find sheep cheese pan-fried in ouzo, falafel with tahini, and pork loin and seftalia kebabs. It typically closes for vacation in late August.

Mercato (215-985-2962; mercatobyob .com), 1216 Spruce Street. This is the place to go when you crave homemade papardelle or exquisite pork chop Milanese before a Broad Street theater performance and don't want to drive to South Philly. Cash only, BYO. $$–$$$.

Ⴤ **Panorama** (215-922-7800; pennsviewhotel.com/panorama), Front and Market Streets. This Old World Italian restaurant in the Penn's View Hotel is known for its legendary wine bar, which offers more than 150 wines by the glass, flight, or bottle. The food is traditional and reliably good, as is the service. All the pasta is homemade, and you may order appetizer sizes of any entrée. There's a divine triple-cream tiramisu for dessert. $$–$$$.

Talula's Garden (215-592-7787; talulas garden.com), 210 West Washington Square. Reservations are a must at this special-occasion eatery known for its fresh local ingredients, excellent cheeses, and homemade breads. Across the courtyard, **Talula's Daily** caters to a daytime crowd with espresso, pastries, and gourmet sandwiches, then turns into a sought-after supper club at night with a changing fixed-price menu. Reservations a must. $$–$$$.

Ⴤ **Vetri** (215-732-3478; vetricucina .com), 1312 Spruce Street. Closed Sundays. Marc Vetri's original 35-seat dining room provides one of the city's most sensational culinary experiences. The tasting menu might include a sweet onion crêpe with white truffle fondue, Swiss chard gnocchi with ricotta salata and brown butter, and dry-aged rib eye with spring onion. The 5,000-bottle wine cellar specializes in regional wines. Reservations required.

Zahav (215-625-8800; zahav restaurant.com), 237 St. James Place. Since its opening in 2008, Michael Solomonov's modern Israeli cuisine has been showered with accolades, including the Best Restaurant in America by the James Beard Foundation. The curated menu reflects Solomonov's love for Israeli-Mediterranean food and culture, with small plates such as caramelized fennel with whipped feta; kebabs grilled over coals; baked-to-order laffa bread; and hummus light years away from the supermarket varieties. The beverages are extraordinary, too: from pumpernickel- and caraway-infused Jim Beam rye to a nonalcoholic turmeric lime soda. Reservations (available 60 days in advance) are strongly recommended and disappear fast, but walk-ins with patience may eventually get a seat at the bar, where all the menu items are available. $$$.

SOUTH PHILLY

Fond (215-551-5000; fondphilly.com), 1617 East Passyunk Avenue. Le Bec Fin alum Lee Styer turns out salt- and sugar-cured pork belly, chicken liver mousse with pickled red onions, and malted chocolate ice cream with peanut butter ganache at this warm, yellow-walled café. BYO. $$.

Tre Scalini (215-551-3870; trescalini philadelphia.com), 1915 East Passyunk Avenue. Dinner Tuesday–Sunday. This veteran neighborhood BYO moved to bigger digs near Broad Street in 2010, but Franca DiRenza (now a nonna), is still the chef and the menu is still straightforward Italian inspired by her hometown of Molise. You can't go wrong with the homemade gnocchi or veal piccante. $$.

Villa di Roma (215-592-1295; villa diroma.com), 936 South Ninth Street. Lunch and dinner Tuesday–Sunday. For a true South Philly experience, head to this family-run "gravy" trattoria in the center of the Italian Market area. You'll forget about the no-frills ambiance and wagon-wheel chandeliers as soon as you whiff the oregano-spiked marinara sauce simmering in the kitchen or look at the

FISHTOWN

Not long ago, Fishtown was a working-class neighborhood of brick and brownstone homes near a notorious crime corridor. Today, it's one of Philly's hottest destinations, drawing a vibrant mix of millennials, hipster parents, and empty nesters to its restaurants, wine bars, yoga studios, and concert venues. It even has a luxury hotel, **Wm. Mulherin's Sons** (215-291-1355; wmmulherinssons.com)—four industrial chic units and an Italian bistro located in a former whiskey-blending facility. Other notable spots: Suraya (215-302-1900; surayaphilly.com), a morning-to-night Lebanese café and restaurant with a big, inviting courtyard; Frankford Hall (215-634-3338; frankfordhall.com), a massive indoor/outdoor German beer garden and community space; and Pizzeria Beddia (267-928-2256; pizzeriabeddia.com), the acclaimed pizza mecca that expanded in 2019 to include a bar and tables at 1313 North Lee Street.

Yet walk down its main artery of Frankford Avenue and you'll see that Fishtown has managed to retain an unpretentious Philly-style vibe. Johnny Brenda's and The Fillmore feature a consistently impressive and eclectic lineup of talented bands in relaxed spaces (see *Entertainment*). And when you can't get a table at Beddia, head to Pizza Brain (215-291-2965; pizzabrain .org) for a monster slice of excellent pizza and gelato. While you wait, you can take in the Guinness Book of World Records–sanctioned collection of pizza-related memorabilia, which includes clocks, action figures, posters, and album covers. It's a must-see Philadelphia destination, just like the neighborhood itself.

PIZZA BRAIN IN FISHTOWN FEATURES DISPLAYS OF PIZZA ART AND MEMORABILIA

reasonably priced menu. Regulars get misty-eyed over the fried asparagus in scampi butter; there are also steamed mussels marinara, spaghetti and meatballs, and sausage cacciatore. $$.

EATING OUT Brauhaus Schmitz (267-909-8814), 718 South Street. German beer hall in the heart of the South Street scene with a solid menu of bratwurst, crispy pork schnitzel, and Bavarian pretzels to die for. $$.

Dimitri's (215-625-0556; dmitris restaurant.com), 795 South Third Street, Queen Village. Dinner daily. This popular BYO two blocks off South Street is known for its fresh Greek-style seafood. It doesn't take reservations and you might wait up to 90 minutes for a table, but the food is worth it. Favorites include tender grilled octopus, pan-fried flounder, and an appetizer of marinated olives and hummus. To kill time when there's a wait, hang out at the bar at the New Wave Café across the street, where the staff will fetch you when a table is ready. Cash only. There's a second location at 944 North Second Street in Northern Liberties. $$$.

Jones (215-223-5663; jones-restaurant .com), 700 Chestnut Street. Restaurateur Stephen Starr's crowd-pleaser serves fried chicken and waffles, beef brisket, chocolate peanut butter pie, and imaginative cocktails a block from Independence Hall. $$.

Vietnam Restaurant (215-592-1163; eatatvietnam.com), 22 North 11th Street, Chinatown. Lunch and dinner daily. Good food, reasonable prices, and a relaxing wood paneling and bamboo ambiance. Try the crispy duck or anything that comes with a dipping sauce. Head upstairs to Bar Saigon for a Flaming Volcano or Mai Tai before dinner. There's also a branch in University City. $$.

Sabrina's Café (215-574-1599; sabrinas cafe.com), 910 Christian Street. Breakfast and lunch daily, dinner Monday–Saturday. Tucked into three cozy rooms

in a South Philadelphia row house, Sabrina's serves lunch and dinner but is best known for its good and hearty breakfasts. The weekend brunch menu might include challah French toast stuffed with cream cheese or a three-egg frittata. No reservations; expect a wait on weekends. BYO. There are branches at 1802 Callowhill Street in the Fairmount neighborhood and 227 North 34th Street in University City. $$.

Little Italy Pizza (215-922-1440; golittleitaly.com), 901 South Street. Stop here for a baked pizza roll or a bacon, chicken, and ranch slice before or after a night out on South Street. There's plenty of indoor seating. $.

COFFEE, SANDWICHES & DESSERT
The Bourse (215-625-0300), 111 South Independence Mall, is a gourmet food hall in a grand Victorian building on the site of the first US commodities exchange. It has undergone many transformations over the years, most recently as an upscale marketplace that offers Philadelphia staples like sticky buns and cheesesteaks as well as a global selection of poke bowls, Indian street food, and Chinese dumplings. There's also a branch of **Penzey's Spices** on the first floor and a craft brewpub and cocktail bar.

Bean Café (215-629-2250), 615 South Street. La Columbe coffee, art on the walls, and a vibe that encourages you to linger over your laptop or latte.

Cosmi's (215-468-6093), 1501 South Eighth Street, South Philly. Open daily. Folks line up for the cheesesteaks, which come with Whiz, long hots (peppers), broccoli rabe, and more at this tiny corner deli. There are also authentic hoagies (from prosciutto to veggie), chili, pizza fries, and just about every other deli standard on the menu. The only seating is a fold-up table and chair on the sidewalk outside. $.

Ishkabibble's (215-923-4337), 337 South Street. A popular spot for late-night cheesesteaks (the chicken versions are especially good), gravy fries, and water ice. Seating at the original locale is limited to a few bar stools or the curb out front, but there's also a sit-down version a block away, at 517 South Street, with the same menu and late hours. $.

Jim's Steaks (215-928-1911), 400 South Street. My personal favorite cheesesteak spot. Order on the first floor, watch the smooth line chefs assemble your sandwich, and bring it on up to the dining room, where you can watch the South Street scene unfold below. $.

John's Roast Pork (215-463-1951), 14 Snyder Avenue (near Columbus). Open Tuesday–Saturday. Outdoor seating only. Don't go for the ambiance, go for the excellent cheesesteaks, fried egg sandwiches, and hot pork sandwiches. $.

Old City Coffee (215-629-9292), 221 Church Street. Tucked off a cobblestone alley about three blocks from Independence Hall, this small shop serves the best coffee east of Broad Street; good pastries, too. There's an attached seating area and a few tables outside. There's also a branch at Reading Terminal Market.

Tartes (215-625-2510), 212 Arch Street. Tiny walk-up bakery in Old City with a couple of outside tables serving coffee, hand-rolled tarts, and some of the tastiest cookies around. Closed Sundays.

BYO Where to buy wine in Center City and South Philadelphia:

Wine & Spirits Shoppe (215-560-6900; 724 South Street) offers a wide selection of wines and liquors in the heart of the South Street scene. In Old City, just south of Market, is **State Liquor** (215-625-0906; 32 South Second Street). Closer to City Hall and the convention center is **State Liquor Super Store** (215-560-4381; 1218 Chestnut Street). You'll find a wine boutique with knowledgeable clerks inside the gourmet **Garces Trading Co.** complex (215-923-2261; 1111 Locust Street).

✻ Entertainment

MUSIC **The Fillmore** (215-309-0150; thefillmorephilly.com), 29 East Allen Street. Located in a big former metal factory in uber-hip Fishtown, this popular venue has three distinct spaces: a main stage hosting an eclectic lineup of live music, a smaller club within a club for up-and-coming bands and DJs, and a bar and lounge with global pub grub. In a nod to the iconic 1960s-era Fillmore in San Francisco, a refurbished Volkswagen bus in the lobby doubles as a gift shop.

Theatre of Living Arts (215-922-1011; venuetlaphilly.com), 334 South Street. Iconic music venue in the heart of South Street hosting up-and-coming performers in a no-frills, two-level setting.

MOVIES **Ritz 5** (215-925-7900; landmarktheatres.com), 214 Walnut Street, opened in 1976 and is one of the best places to see first-run art and independent films in Philly. **Ritz at the Bourse,** a couple of blocks away at 400 Ranstead Street, has an additional five screens, and the **Ritz East** at 125 South Second Street has two screens.

THEATER **Arden Theatre** (215-922-1122; ardentheatre.org), 40 North Second Street, stages classic and cutting-edge dramas, comedies, and children's shows. It has a slew of awards to show for its work and has been named Theatre Company of the Year four times by the *Philadelphia Inquirer*.

Forrest Theatre (215-923-1515; forrest-theatre.com), 1114 Walnut Street. The place to catch such touring Broadway productions as *Les Miserables* and *Hamilton*.

Lantern Theater (215-829-0395; lanterntheater.org), 10th and Ludlow Streets. "Impressively diverse in genre and style" is how one local paper describes the Lantern's selection of classic, modern, and original plays.

Walnut Street Theatre (215-574-3550; walnutstreettheatre.org), 825 Walnut Street, is the city's oldest theater, serving as the debut stage for Ethel Barrymore and Edwin Forrest. It often features big Broadway musicals on its main stage.

NIGHTLIFE The Old City and South Street areas are packed with nightspots that appeal to a variety of crowds.

Ⓨ **The Continental** (215-923-6069), 134 Market Street. Beautiful people sip espresso martinis and snack on tapas under olive-shaped halogen lamps in this diner-turned-cutting-edge-nightspot. Weekday happy hours feature $6 cocktails.

Nick's Old City (215-928-9411), 16 South Second Street. Cheap bar food, including ground-bacon burgers, plus beer bucket specials and karaoke on weekends.

Standard Tap (215-238-0630), 901 North Second Street, Northern Liberties. One of Philly's first craft brewpubs (with upscale snacks to match), it attracts a diverse crowd of artists, locals, and suits.

Sto's Bar (267-687-8653), 236 Market Street. Friendly sports bar in the heart of Old City with a wall of TVs, above-average pub fare, and every bar game imaginable. In spring and summer, there's a hopping beer garden with an outdoor bar and games.

CENTER CITY

Dirty Frank's (215-985-9600), 347 South 13th Street. Philly's finest dive bar, with a *Sopranos* pinball machine, darts, wood paneling, and cheap, strong drinks.

Ⓨ **McGillin's Old Ale House** (215-735-5562), 1310 Drury Street. Philly's oldest (and hardest to locate) pub is tucked in an alley between 13th and Juniper Streets. The brick-walled downstairs room is decorated with American flags, black-and-white cityscape photos, and framed liquor licenses that date back to the 1800s. The crowd tends to be young

and festive; there's karaoke on Wednesday nights.

Ⓨ **Woody's** (215-545-1893), 202 South 13th Street. Popular nightclub in the heart of Philly's small gay community. Theme nights include Latin music on Thursday and country line dancing on Friday.

✳ Selective Shopping

Philly has several quaint districts featuring a dozen or more stores that specialize in similar items. **Antiques Row** runs on Pine Street where you'll find shops selling grandfather clocks, estate jewelry, hand-carved cabinets, and more. **Jewelers' Row** is the place to go for discounted diamonds; its shops line a red-bricked block of Sansom Street between Seventh and Eighth Streets. In Old City, many art galleries stay open late on the first Friday of the month, when the area is a packed with art lovers and partyers (for more info, visit oldcitydistrict.org).

OLD CITY

Art Star Gallery and Boutique (215-238-1557; artstarphilly.com), 623 North Second Street. Whimsical jewelry, clothes, ceramics, and hostess gifts—most at reasonable prices. The shop orchestrates an art bazaar with live music at Penn's Landing every May and pop-up markets on summer weekends at Spruce Street Harbor Park and other locales. It also has a branch in The Bourse at Fifth and Market Streets.

Clay Studio (215-925-3453; theclaystudio.org), 139 North Second Street. Innovative selection of ceramic cups, bowls, vases, and tiles. There are all kinds of pottery-making classes and workshops for adults and kids.

Giovanni's Room (215-923-2960), 345 South 12th Street. The nation's oldest LBGT bookstore opened in 1973, taking its name from the James Baldwin novel. A historical marker outside the store acknowledges its role as a "refuge and cultural center at the onset of the modern lesbian, gay, bisexual, and transgender civil rights movement." Now run by the nonprofit Philly AIDS Thrift, it offers the best selection of gay, lesbian, bisexual, and transgender literature in the city, as well as a selection of clothing and gifts.

Scarlett Alley (215-592-7898), 241 Race Street, Old City. Stylish gifts for the person who has everything: designer cutting boards, ceramic bowls, cashmere robes, baby blankets, and much more.

Book Trader (215-925-0511; phillybooktrader.com), 7 North Second Street. A reader's haven of used books, comfy old chairs, and friendly cats, just up the street from Elfreth's Alley. There's an especially strong cookbook section, and no one cares how long you linger (except maybe the cats who want your chair).

MARKETS **Reading Terminal Market** (215-922-2317; readingterminalmarket .org), 12th and Arch Streets. Open 8–6 daily, though some stalls are closed on Sundays and the Amish-owned stalls are closed Sunday–Tuesday. This fabulous indoor collection of food, flower, and

SOFT PRETZELS ARE HANDMADE AT READING TERMINAL MARKET

produce stalls has been operating since 1893 on the lower level of the Reading Terminal, home to the largest single-arch train shed in the world. It's a great introduction to Philadelphia's flavors and people, and an excellent place to get a quick lunch if you're in the area. In the northwest corner, Amish women serve up scrapple, homefries, and eggs at the counter of the always-busy **Dutch Eating Place.** Across the way, you can take home Lancaster County baked goods such as whoopie pies, sticky buns, and shoofly pies, and sample soft pretzels still warm from the oven at Fisher's. Ice cream lovers won't want to miss **Basset's,** a venerable local ice cream company that serves the richest vanilla double dip around, and hungry omnivores should check out **DiNic's** for juicy roast pork sandwiches. Tucked in between the food stalls are vendors selling everything from used cookbooks to dried-flower arrangements. Saturday morning is the best time for people watching and finding all the stalls open, though expect shoulder-to-shoulder crowds if a convention is in town (the convention center and several large hotels are nearby).

Italian Market, Ninth Street between Washington and Christian, South Philadelphia. Closed Mondays. Anyone who has seen *Rocky* will remember the boxer's famous training run through this

OPERATING SINCE 1893, READING TERMINAL MARKET HOUSES A WIDE-RANGING COLLECTION OF FOOD, FLOWER, AND PRODUCE STALLS

A long with soft pretzels, cheesesteaks, pork roll, and Italian water ice, scrapple will go down in history as a beloved local food that sets the Philadelphia area apart from the rest of the planet. You will find it on the menus and breakfast platters of most diners around here: a pan-fried gray slice of cornmeal mush and pork by-product that has been made fun of by outsiders more often than Johnny Carson dissed the city of Burbank. In reality, it's no worse, and arguably tastier, than a hot dog when made properly—a crisp exterior and soft, creamy inside that tastes more like seasoned mashed potatoes than pig parts.

indoor-outdoor street market on his way to the steps of the art museum. It's loud, rude, chaotic, and fascinating—a mix of outdoor stalls offering fresh produce, live seafood, bootleg music, and T-shirts, and brick-and-mortar stores selling spices, cheeses, homemade ravioli, and pastries. Several Mexican taco stands and Vietnamese grocers have opened in recent years and added to the area's vibrancy. **Tallutto's** (215-627-4967), a legendary Italian gourmet shop known for its homemade pasta and imported meats, olive oils, and vinegars, anchors one end at 944 South Ninth Street, while **Fante's Kitchen Shop** (215-922-5557; 1006 South Ninth Street) is a chef's paradise of microplanes and cavatelli makers.

✳ Special Events

January: **Mummers Parade** (New Year's Day), Broad and Market Streets—raucous string-band parade that began in the 1700s and features thousands of men (and a few women) strutting and strumming their way up Broad Street in outrageous sequined and feathered costumes.

March: **Philadelphia International Flower Show** (first and second week), Pennsylvania Convention Center—the world's largest indoor flower show with elaborate exhibits, expert lectures, and culinary demos, all of which are centered around an annual theme like "Legends of Ireland" or "Islands of Hawaii."

June: **Fete Day** (first Saturday), Elfreth's Alley—residents of America's oldest continuously occupied street throw a block party and invite the public to partake of house and garden tours, live music, and crafts demonstrations (see *Historic Sites*).

July: **Independence Day Celebration** (July Fourth), Historic District—series of events that begins with the awarding of the prestigious Liberty Medal in front of Independence Hall and is capped by an evening concert and fireworks across town on the Benjamin Franklin Parkway.

September: **Fringe Festival** (fringearts .com)—cutting-edge performances by dancers, acrobats, actors, clowns, and performance artists on stages all over the city.

October: **Outfest** (first weekend), Spruce and Pine Streets between 11th and 13th—Philly's four-day pride festival has grown to be one of the largest in the world, with more than 150 vendors, performers, and community groups filling Midtown Village.

CENTER CITY WEST & UNIVERSITY CITY

GETTING THERE *By train:* **Amtrak** (800-USA-RAIL) stops at 30th Street Station on its Northeast Corridor route between Richmond, Virginia, and Boston. SEPTA's R7 suburban train runs to Trenton, New Jersey, where New Jersey Transit trains run to New York's Penn Station. The R7 stops at Suburban Station, about four blocks from Rittenhouse Square, and 30th Street Station.

GETTING AROUND **SEPTA** municipal buses run all over the city, though they can be daunting for first-time visitors. The Market–Frankford Line is a rapid-transit line that stops outside City Hall (Broad and Market) and near the University of Pennsylvania's campus, ending in the city's far northwest corner. The purple **Phlash** bus (215-599-0776; phillyphlash.com) runs a continuous loop between the city's major attractions, from Penn's Landing to the Parkway museums. Buses stop every 12 minutes at designated purple lampposts and operate daily May–September and on weekends in October and November.

✳ Neighborhoods

Logan Square anchors the northeast end of the Benjamin Franklin Parkway and is one of five original planned squares laid out on the city grid. Originally called Northwest Square, the park has a somewhat macabre history of being a site of public executions and burial plots until the early 19th century. In 1825, it was renamed Logan Square after Philadelphia statesman James Logan. Among the sites you'll find nearby are the Academy of Natural Sciences, the Franklin Institute, the Free Library of Philadelphia, and the Roman Catholic Cathedral Basilica of Saints Peter and Paul.

Rittenhouse Square. This affluent, pedestrian-friendly neighborhood takes its name from the tree-filled square that anchors it. It is named after David Rittenhouse, the astronomer and descendant of Philadelphia's first papermaker, William Rittenhouse, and home to many of the city's top restaurants, hotels, and shops. Walnut Street between Broad and 21st Streets is its commercial pulse, but don't be afraid to wander; the historic architecture along residential streets like Spruce and Delancey is delightful.

University City. This West Philly neighborhood got its start in the late 1880s, when the University of Pennsylvania moved across the Schuylkill River from Center City, though no one really referred to it by its current name until the 1960s. Life here still revolves around the Ivy League school, as well as nearby Drexel University. Though the area has struggled with blight and crime problems, you will find streets lined with beautiful old Victorian row homes, a luxury movie theater, national retailers, and many hip restaurants.

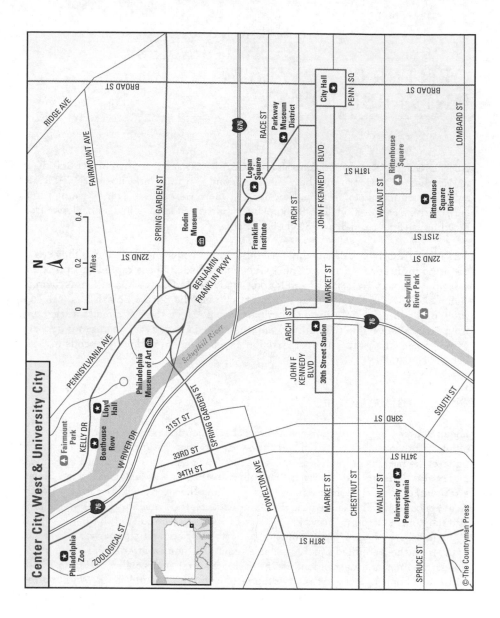

✳ To See

HISTORIC SITES Eastern State Penitentiary (215-236-3300; easternstate.org), 2124 Fairmount Avenue. Open daily April–November; admission charged. Willie Sutton and Al Capone were among the inmates who slept in the vaulted, skylighted cells of this 1829 prison, whose wagon-wheel design (and belief in reform through isolation) served as a model for dozens of other 19th-century prisons. Admission includes a 30-minute guided tour of the decrepit cellblocks (including Capone's), plus interesting details on life as an inmate. The prison's popular "Terror Behind the Walls" event,

EXCURSIONS

University of Pennsylvania, at 30th and Walnut Streets in West Philadelphia, is the city's oldest and most prestigious university. Founded by Benjamin Franklin and others in 1740, it boasts the nation's first medical, law, and business schools. While the neighborhood surrounding Penn has undergone a revitalization, the campus itself is worth a visit, whether you have a connection to it or not. Anyone may stroll across its attractive quadrangle and admire the Gothic-style buildings and centuries-old trees. Don't miss the three statues of Franklin on campus—one depicts the school's founder as a carefree teenager newly arrived from Boston, another as a portly statesman, and a third seated on a bench, engrossed in the *Pennsylvania Gazette*. Also worth checking out while here is the **University of Pennsylvania Museum of Archaeology and Anthropology** (215-898-4000; penn.museum; admission charged; kids 5 and under free), home to a 12-ton sphinx, Egyptian mummies, and other artifacts the university has acquired through 130 years of global expeditions. In 2017, it began its first major expansion in a century, adding a main entrance hall and large galleries showcasing a rich assortment of artifacts from the Middle East, Mexico, and Central America. Finally, art lovers should check out the latest exhibit at the **Institute for Contemporary Art** (215-898-5911; icaphila.org; 118 South 36th Street), which hosted the first-ever museum shows of Andy Warhol and Laurie Anderson. Closed Mondays and Tuesdays; free.

BENJAMIN FRANKLIN AND A FRIEND ON PENN'S CAMPUS

EXCURSIONS

WALKING PHILADELPHIA For several years when I lived in Los Angeles, I was a contributor to the arts and entertainment section of the *Philadelphia Daily News*. That meant interviewing actors and directors about their work and lives. If they had ever spent any time in Philly, I also would ask about their best memories of the city. Sarah Jessica Parker remembered a mime who performed near her dad's place at the old Headhouse Square, Nicolas Cage liked the pizza at **Tacconelli's,** and Elizabeth Banks has fond memories of catching a show at the **Theatre of Living Arts** after a dinner date in South Philly. All good stories, but my favorite answer came from Rick Yune, who played a villain in the James Bond film, *Die Another Day*. As a University of Pennsylvania student in the 1990s, he recalled his favorite running route: beginning at 40th and Chestnut in West Philly, east to the Delaware Avenue waterfront, then back. Whether you run, walk, or stroll it, it's a fantastic way to experience the city—32 blocks that take you by historic sites, beautiful old churches, unexpected murals, top restaurants, brick homes, and gates that lead to secret gardens or alleys. Take Walnut one way and follow Chestnut back past Independence Hall, Washington Square, and City Hall, or zigzag between them and other parallel streets such as Spruce or Pine. The grid layout means you'll never get lost (though you may have to share the sidewalk with many pedestrians in some places), and you'll end with a better sense of the city's eclectic mix of academia, history, and blue-collar pride.

heldsxs evenings in October, features five separate haunted houses, complete with howling prisoners and sadistic guards, and a DJ-hosted Monster Mash.

    ♿ ✎ ✪ **Fort Mifflin** (215-685-4167; fortmifflin.us), Hog Island and Fort Mifflin Roads (near Philadelphia International Airport). Open Wednesday–Sunday from March 1–December 15, other times by chance or special arrangement; admission charged. One of the greatest bombardments of the Revolutionary War took place here in 1777. About 400 American troops garrisoned at Fort Mifflin frustrated British naval

COSTUMED GUIDES OFFER CANNON- AND MUSKET-FIRING DEMONSTRATIONS AT HISTORIC FORT MIFFLIN

THE BLACKSMITH'S SHOP IS ONE OF THE OLDEST STRUCTURES ON THE GROUNDS OF FORT MIFFLIN

attempts to resupply their occupying forces in Philadelphia. Hundreds of men died and the fort was decimated, but the standoff allowed General George Washington and his troops time to arrive safely at Valley Forge and settle in for the winter. Also known as Mud Island, this multipurpose fort served as a federal prison during the Civil War and an ammunition depot during World Wars I and II. Costumed guides and interpretive signs are available to help navigate the grounds, and there are often cannon- and musket-firing demonstrations on weekends and holidays. It's out of the way compared to Philadelphia's other historic sites but an important stop on any Pennsylvania history tour. Combine it with a trip to the John Heinz Refuge (see *Green Space*) or stop here before or after a flight out of Philadelphia International Airport. Events are held on the grounds throughout the year, from a spring Renaissance Faire to after-hours paranormal programs.

⚓ ❋ **Edgar Allen Poe National Historic Site** (215-597-8780; nps.gov/edal), 532 North Seventh Street. Open Wednesday–Sunday; free. The 19th-century horror author penned *The Tell-Tale Heart, The Fall of the House of Usher*, and more in this small brick house north of Old City. Ranger-led tours include a trip to the basement that's said to be the inspiration for *The Black Cat*, and engaging anecdotes about Poe's writing habits and family. The National Park Service has deliberately left the rooms empty and the floorboards creaky, making the visit all the more creepy and reminiscent of the former resident. It's a little off the beaten path, but it's a must for Poe fans and literary buffs.

♿ ✏ **Laurel Hill Cemetery** (215-228-8200; thelaurelhillcemetery.org), 3822 Ridge Avenue, a national historic landmark whose tenants include astronomer David Rittenhouse, 40 Civil War–era generals, and six victims of the *Titanic* sinking. It's a peaceful place for a stroll or jog, with a bluff-side setting overlooking the Schuylkill River. Download its free mobile app for a self-guided tour, or take one of several guided tours that cover a wide range of themes, from ghosts and tree species to Egyptian symbolism. There are also yoga classes, movies, and concerts in the spring and summer. Check the website for details.

PHILADELPHIA'S CITY HALL IS THE LARGEST MUNICIPAL BUILDING IN THE UNITED STATES

  ♿ ♁ ❊ **City Hall** (215-686-2840), Broad Street. Tours Monday–Friday at 12:30; admission charged. This granite monolith in the center of town, capped by a 37-foot statue of William Penn, has the distinction of being the country's largest and most costly municipal building. It's also a beautiful example of Victorian architecture when it's not hidden by scaffolding. The 90-minute tour details the building's history, architecture, and sculpture, and includes a visit to the tower observation deck. Tours of only the observation deck, which affords one of the best panoramic views in the city, run every 15 minutes, 9:30–4. All tours leave from the information center near the east entrance.

MUSEUMS ♿ ✐ ♁ ❊ **Philadelphia Museum of Art** (215-763-8100), 2600 Benjamin Franklin Parkway. Closed Mondays; admission charged. Park in the garage for a fee or seek out a free space on the streets off the parkway. This grandiose Greco-Roman temple is America's third-largest art museum and home to more than 225,000 works of art, including important collections of Pennsylvania German and French impressionist paintings and 18th- and 19th-century furniture. The third floor features a stunning reconstructed Hindu stone temple that dates back to 1550, a medieval French cloister with a massive Romanesque fountain, and a cedar-thatched Japanese teahouse designed by Ogi Rodo and purchased by the museum in 1928.

    Allow for at least several hours to tour the 200 galleries; a nice spot to rest is the Resnick Rotunda in the European Art section, where masterpieces by Van Gogh, Cezanne, and Renoir surround benches and a gurgling fountain. If you don't have time to go inside, you can jog, Rocky-style, up the steps of the grand old building or just settle for posing next to a bronze statue of the Italian Stallion at the foot of the steps at the east entrance. The museum throws a big "Art after 5" cocktail party every Friday evening with live music, movie screenings, and mingling events. Across the street at 2501 Benjamin Franklin Parkway, the Ruth and Raymond G. Perelman Building has special exhibits, as well as the museum's photography and textiles collections. Food options include the elegant Granite Hill café or the busy cafeteria, which serves healthy (though expensive) lunches.

  ⛿ ✳ **Rodin Museum** (215-763-8100; rodinmuseum.org), Benjamin Franklin Parkway at 22nd Street. Open Tuesday–Saturday; admission charged. Home to the largest collection of Auguste Rodin sculptures outside France, including his most notable works, *The Thinker* and *The Burghers of Calais,* as well as drawings, prints, letters, and books. The museum reopened in 2012 after an extensive renovation refurbished most of the sculptures and returned them to their original locations when the museum opened in 1929. A visit to the small Beaux Arts building is a lovely, intimate experience, with many benches, a library, and gardens that invite lingering.

  ↑ **Rosenbach Museum & Library** (215-732-1600; zestocho.org), 2010 Delancey Place. Open Tuesday–Sunday; admission charged, free for kids 12 and younger. Bibliophiles will love the intriguing literary treasures found in this 1863 double townhouse off Rittenhouse Square: James Joyce's handwritten manuscript for *Ulysses,* a lock of Charles Dickens's hair, and Bram Stoker's notes and outlines for *Dracula,* to name a few. The owners and brothers, A. S. W. and Philip Rosenbach, were 19th-century art and book dealers; there are also personal letters penned by George Washington, the reassembled Greenwich Village living room of poet Marianne Moore, and more than 10,000 illustrations and manuscripts by Maurice Sendak. Tours are given several times a day.

  ⛿ ✳ **Pennsylvania Academy of Fine Arts** (215-972-7600; pafa.org), 118 North Broad Street. Closed Mondays; admission charged. An impressive collection of American paintings and sculpture by Benjamin West, Mary Cassatt, Thomas Eakins, Winslow Homer, and others housed in an exquisite Victorian Gothic building that served as the nation's first art museum and school. Next door, the contemporary Samuel M. V. Hamilton building displays works by Georgia O'Keeffe, Roy Lichtenstein, and Mark Rothko.

  ⛿ ✐ ↑ ✳ **The Mütter Museum** (215-560-8564; muttermuseum.org), 19 South 22nd Street. Open daily 10–5; admission charged. In 1858, Thomas Dent Mütter, a retired professor of surgery, donated his spectacular collection of cancerous tumors, skeletons, and other anatomic specimens and medical artifacts to the College of Physicians of Philadelphia. Today, they're on display in all their gruesome glory in several large rooms off the school's lobby. The 8-foot colon is always a jaw-dropper; you'll also find skeletons that demonstrate the lasting effects of corsets on the torso and a display of book bindings made out of human skin. A new Civil War medicine exhibit includes a piece of Lincoln assassin John Wilkes Booth's thorax and the dried, bloodied arm of Major Henry Rathbone, who was stabbed while trying to keep Booth from fleeing the Ford's Theatre. The small gift shop is chock-full of fun, macabre gifts such as cadaver soaps and crocheted skulls.

✳ To Do

FOR FAMILIES ✐ ↑ ✳ **Franklin Institute Science Museum** (215-448-1200; fi.edu), 222 North 20th Street. Open daily; admission charged. Kids and grown-ups alike will find many things to enjoy at this favorite Parkway attraction. Founded in 1824, it has a planetarium, an IMAX theater, and many hands-on exhibits that celebrate and teach the wonders of science, from sports to trains to Isaac Newton. A walk through the giant papier-mâché replica of a beating heart is a must—so is a stop in the Franklin Gallery, where you'll find many of Ben's own inventions and models, including his lightning rod and a reproduction of his bifocals.

A BUST OF BEN FRANKLIN LOOMS LARGE AT ONE LIBERTY OBSERVATION DECK

Academy of Natural Sciences (215-299-1000; ansp.org), 1900 Benjamin Franklin Parkway. Open daily; admission charged. Another Philly attraction that was the first of its kind (it's the nation's oldest natural history museum), this neighbor to the Franklin Institute is the place to go for dinosaurs and enormous mounted-animal dioramas. Future paleontologists can dig for fossils in Dinosaur Hall (weekends only) and mingle with live butterflies in a re-created rain forest.

One Liberty Observation Deck (215-561-3325; phillyfromthetop.com), 1650 Market Street. Admission charged. Panoramic views of the city from a 57th-floor observatory with touch-screen maps, a giant bust of Benjamin Franklin, and old-fashioned board games that encourage you to stay awhile.

Please Touch Museum (215-963-0667; pleasetouchmuseum.org), 4231 Avenue of the Republic. Open daily; admission charged. A magical interactive place for the under-8 set in the grand setting of Fairmount Park's Memorial Hall. Kids can float a boat down a miniature Schuylkill River, navigate a hedge maze and hall of mirrors, and launch rockets through spinning rings. Philadelphia-born parents will appreciate the preserved set and props from *Captain Noah and His Magical Ark,* a favorite TV show shot locally in the 1970s. It is $12 to park in the museum's lot, or there's usually plenty of street parking.

Smith Memorial Playground (215-765-4325; smithkidsplayplace.org), 33rd and Oxford Streets. Free. Open Tuesday–Sunday from April–October. The average plastic playground will never look the same again after you've taken the kids to this fabulous 6-acre space in east Fairmount Park just above Kelly Drive. There's a wooden slide, a giant spiderweb for climbing, and a three-story play mansion for kids 5 and under, full of toys, tricycles, and a kid-friendly kitchen.

SCENIC DRIVES A pleasant urban drive begins at the Museum of Art and follows Kelly Drive north past Boathouse Row. Turn right at Hunting Park Avenue and look for Laurel Hill Cemetery on the bluff to your left, cross Ridge Avenue, and then turn left onto Henry Avenue and follow it about a mile to 3901 Henry Avenue, site of the childhood home of Grace Kelly. Continue north on Henry Avenue about 3 miles past neighborhoods of brick and stone row houses and make a right onto Wise's Mill Road, which will bring you back into Fairmount Park. Follow the narrow, tree-lined road as it winds next to the Wissahickon River to the **Valley Green Inn** (215-247-1730), where you can have a leisurely lunch or brunch on its front porch overlooking the creek and bicycle path.

❋ Green Space

Bartram's Gardens (215-729-5281; bartramsgarden.org), 54th Street and Lindbergh Boulevard. Open daily except holidays. John Bartram planted what would become the nation's oldest living botanical garden here in 1728. It's a beautiful property despite its location in the middle of an industrialized neighborhood near the airport, with a board-walk trail, 15-acre meadow, and the world's oldest gingko tree. Guided tours of Bar-tram's original 1731 house and garden are available for $12 a person Thursday–Sunday from April–November; admission to the grounds is free. There's also a boat ramp with access to the Schuylkill River.

Clark Park (friendsofclarkpark.org), 43rd Street at Baltimore Avenue, University City. A life-sized bronze statue of Charles Dickens oversees 9 acres of welcome green space, trees, and a playground. In February the park throws a party in honor of Mr. Dickens's birthday; it also hosts outdoor movies, youth soccer, flea markets, and Shakespeare in the summer. There's a popular farmers' market on Saturday mornings and Thursday evenings from April–November.

Penn Park, 31st Street between South and Walnut Streets. The University of Penn-sylvania transformed an old post office parking lot into a lush 24-acre park beneath the Walnut Street Bridge, calling it a "gateway between Center City and West Phila-delphia." It has tennis courts, jogging paths, two athletic fields, and stellar views of the Philadelphia skyline.

Rail Park (therailpark.org), 1300 Noble Street. Philadelphia's version of New York's High Line, situated on two obsolete rail lines that used to serve Reading Terminal. Phase One opened in 2018, a quarter-mile stretch that includes bike trails, footpaths, native plants, and hanging benches supported by structural steel beams. There's a wheelchair-accessible entrance at Broad and Noble and a staircase on Callowhill between 11th and 12th Streets.

❋ Outdoor Activities

BICYCLING/RENTALS The **Schuylkill River Trail** is a paved bicycle and jogging trail that follows the Schuylkill River 23 miles from Center City to Norristown. A popular 9-mile loop for walkers, joggers, and cyclists begins at the art museum, runs north past Boathouse Row and up the east bank of the Schuylkill, crosses the river at Falls Bridge, and works its way back to the museum along the west side of the river.

Bike rentals are available at **Wheel Fun Rentals** (215-232-7778), 1 Boathouse Row, next to Lloyd Hall, or from **Fairmount Bicycles** (267-507-9370), 2015 Fairmount Avenue.

The city closes the 4-mile stretch of Martin Luther King Drive west of the Schuylkill River to vehicular traffic on weekends between April and October; it fills up fast with cyclists, runners, and in-line skaters.

FAIRMOUNT PARK

Covering 9,200 acres that resemble the shape of an elephant's head, Fairmount Park (215-683-0200; fairmountpark.org) is one of the nation's oldest and largest urban parks. It lines either side of the Schuylkill River from the Philadelphia Museum of Art north to Manayunk, then snakes west and north through the leafy Wissahickon Valley. You could spend days here and not cover all of its diverse attractions. Maps are usually available at Lloyd Hall, the modern two-story community center that has a café with limited hours and a bike rental outfit. The lower section (from Falls Bridge south to the art museum) is the part that's easiest to access from Center City. It includes Boathouse Row, a line of Victorian boathouses along Kelly Drive that is home to a group of amateur rowing clubs called the Schuylkill Navy. (East River Drive was renamed Kelly Drive in 1985 after local oarsman Jack, who also happened to be Grace Kelly's brother.) Each boathouse is decorated with strings of lights, creating a festive, gingerbread house–style display at night; I've passed Boathouse Row at night hundreds of times and never fail to be awed by the sight. Below is a collection of the lower park's best attractions. For information on the upper section of Fairmount Park, see *Chestnut Hill, Germantown & Manayunk* on page 57.

✐ ❄ Philadelphia Zoo (215-243-1100; philadelphiazoo.org), 3400 West Girard Avenue. Open year-round; admission charged. The country's oldest zoo is a compact 42 acres that is home to 1,800 species of animals, including polar bears, red pandas, camels, and two rare white African lions. Kids will love the swan boats and the free-flight Wings of Asia aviary. Its newest attraction is the Zooballoon, a hot-air balloon ride that gives you a bird's-eye view of the animals. Parking will set you back another $16.

Nearby is the Smith Civil War Memorial Arch, 4231 North Concourse Drive, which honors the state's Civil War heroes. At its base are the whispering benches, developed in a way that a whisper into the wall at one end will carry all the way to the other end. It's also a popular local spot to get engaged or steal a first kiss.

After the yellow fever epidemic in 1793, many city dwellers built country homes along the Schuylkill River to escape the heat and disease. Today, many of these Fairmount Park Mansions remain intact, and about a dozen are open several days a week for tours. The neoclassical Lemon Hill (215-235-1776; 7201 North Randolph Drive) in the park's eastern section was meticulously restored in 2005 and has three stacked oval rooms with curved doors and floor-to-ceiling Palladian windows. Strawberry Mansion (215-228-8364; 2450 Strawberry Mansion Drive), so named because it once served as a restaurant with a signature dessert of strawberries and cream, is known for its antique toy and doll collection and array of Federal and Empire furniture.

BOATING Rowing along the Schuylkill near Boathouse Row is reserved for trained athletes, but anyone can play spectator on the river's banks. From April through September, you can watch regattas on the Schuylkill River, which have been held for more than a century. Contact the **National Association of Amateur Oarsmen** (215-769-2068) or the **Boathouse Association** (215-686-0052) for a complete schedule of races.

FISHING You can fish for bass and catfish behind the Philadelphia Museum of Art at the **Water Works** pier, and along the river north of **Boathouse Row.** A required license, $12 for Pennsylvania residents or $27 for out-of-staters, can be obtained online at pa.wildlifelicense.com.

The park's most interesting and unsung mansion has got to be the **Ryerss Museum & Library** (215-685-0544; 7370 Central Avenue), about a 20-minute drive from Center City in the city's Fox Chase section. Robert Ryerss, president of the Tioga Railroad and an avid collector of Asian art and artifacts, scandalized society when he married his housekeeper eight months before he died and willed her his family's Italianate summer home with the stipulation that she eventually leave it to the city to run as a public museum. She did, but not before traveling around the world and adding to her husband's 25,000-piece collection with such treasures as an 11th-century Buddha from Japan and a Chinese papier-mâché puppet theater. Don't miss the family's beloved pet cemetery. Tours are free (Friday–Sunday), also at the behest of Mr. Ryerss.

Wissahickon Valley Park (215-685-9285) is part of the Fairmount Park system and stretches northwest along Wissahickon Creek past Chestnut Hill. It's home to breathtaking natural settings and some of the best hiking and biking trails in the city. Maps and free trail permits are available at the **Wissahickon Environmental Center** (215-685-9285, 300 Northwestern Avenue), located at the north corner of the park and a short drive from the Morris Arboretum. On the site of a former nursery, it's worth a stop alone for its huge wildlife mural, aquarium, and helpful staff.

Other top attractions include **Rittenhouse Town** (215-438-5711, 206 Lincoln Drive), the site of the first paper mill in North America, built in 1690 by William Rittenhouse (great grandfather of David, the scientist for whom Rittenhouse Square is named). By the late 18th century, the area grew into a small, self-sufficient community with more than 40 buildings. Today, seven buildings remain, including a barn that houses a papermaking studio and the original Rittenhouse family homestead and bakehouse. Pick up a self-guided walking map at the visitor center or download a map at rittenhousetown.org. Plan your visit for a weekend in the summer, when guided tours are given for a small fee. Even when the buildings aren't open, its creek-side setting just off Lincoln Drive is a pleasant place to read or let the kids run around.

Forbidden Drive is the park's top hiking, biking, and equestrian trail, a wide gravel road that parallels Wissahickon Creek. It has been closed to car traffic since the 1920s (hence the name) and begins off Lincoln Drive near Rittenhouse Town, winding 5 miles one way past WPA shelters from the 1930s, a covered bridge, and dense woodland to Northwestern Avenue at the city's limits. A local rite of passage is the elaborate Sunday brunch at the **Valley Green Inn** (215-247-1730; valleygreeninn.com), a full-service restaurant in a 19th-century hotel with a front porch that overlooks the trail. There's even a place to hitch your horses while you eat. It's a lovely place to relax and watch the parade of bikers, hikers, and nature lovers go by.

GOLF **Cobbs Creek Golf Club** (215-877-8707), 7200 Lansdowne Avenue, a well-maintained course on the northwest edge of the city, offers a challenging par-71 course.

HORSEBACK RIDING **Chamounix Equestrian Center** (215-877-4419; worktoride.net), 98 Chamounix Drive, Fairmount Park. Riding lessons are available Wednesday and Friday–Sunday from April–November.

ZIPLINING **Treetop Quest** (267-901-4145), 51 Chamounix Drive in Fairmount Park, offers a series of *American Ninja Warrior*–style obstacle courses linked by ziplines with varying challenge levels.

✳ Lodging

HOTELS & INNS **The Logan** (215-546-9000; theloganhotel.com), Logan Square. If you're looking to splurge on accommodations, this is the place to go. Overlooking one of the city's best public squares, it has 98 elegant and spacious rooms, luxurious marble bathrooms, and attentive service. The amenities are endless: plush bathrobes, twice-daily maid service, an indoor pool, fitness center, and TVs in the bathrooms. $$$$.

Sofitel (215-569-8300), 120 South 17th Street. Hip and businesslike at once, this 306-room hotel was once home to the Philadelphia Stock Exchange and is in a prime location near Rittenhouse Square's best bars and restaurants. The handsome rooms have cloudlike king beds and modern cherry wood furniture. $$$$.

Club Quarters (215-282-5000; clubquartershotels.com), 1628 Chestnut Street. The rooms are on the small side, but spotless and attractively decorated with mahogany furniture and colorful linens. There is also a small fitness center and 24-hour room service. The inviting lobby is stocked with magazines, comfy couches, and a help-yourself beverage area. Rooms $89–119 (weekday rates are more).

Hotel Palomar (215-563-5006; hotelpalomar-philadelphia.com) 117 South 17th Street. The hip boutique hotel near Rittenhouse Square has 230 rooms and suites that blend luxury with a bit of Zen (high-end Frette linens, free yoga products to borrow, evening wine hour). Pets are welcome at no extra charge. $$$–$$$$.

Independent Hotel (215-772-1440; theindependenthotel.com), 1234 Locust Street. The 24 rooms and suites in this historic hotel are comfortable, spacious, and art-filled and come with mini-fridges and microwaves. Other reasons to stay here: The service is excellent, and it tends to be quiet in spite of its location in the center of the theater district. A continental breakfast is included, though parking is not. The queen loft suite is ideal for families. $$$.

UNIVERSITY CITY

Inn at Penn (215-222-0200; theinnatpenn.com), 3600 Sansom Street. Just as the name implies, this 238-room inn caters to those with connections to the University of Pennsylvania, which sits just across the street. It is run by the Hilton chain but maintains an independent and polished academic air. Rooms are large and elegant and include coffeemakers, plush robes, and high-end bath amenities. There's also a fitness center, a restaurant, and a clubby lounge called the Living Room, where coffee, tea, and cocktails are served. $$–$$$.

Gables (215-662-1918; gablesbb.com), 4520 Chester Avenue. Built in 1889, this beautiful Victorian building with its wraparound porch and gardens is a less expensive and homier alternative to the big hotels surrounding Penn. It's near Spruce Street, about six blocks from Penn's campus. Many of the 10 rooms feature antique brass beds and fireplaces; two have shared baths. $$–$$$.

HOSTELS **Chamounix Mansion** (215-878-3676; philahostel.org), 3250 Chamounix Drive, Philadelphia. This 1802 country estate in Fairmount Park attracts a wide mix of frugal travelers for its leafy setting and close proximity to Center City. Each dormitory-style room has between four and 16 beds and little else. The elegant parlor in the main house, however, will make you feel like a privileged guest of the original owners. There are also laundry and kitchen facilities and Internet access. $.

✳ Where to Eat

DINING OUT **Audrey Claire** (215-731-1222), 20th and Spruce Streets. This terrific corner bistro near Rittenhouse

Square serves Mediterranean-influenced dishes such as roasted chicken with lemon and feta, and garlic-crusted rack of lamb. Don't miss the amazing selection of appetizers, especially the grilled flatbreads and spicy hummus. No reservations; be prepared for a long wait on weekends. BYO. $$.

℣ **Friday Saturday Sunday** (215-546-4232), 261 South 21st Street. This beloved restaurant transformed itself in 2017 into a hip, innovative force in the Rittenhouse Square restaurant scene. The menu mixes traditional plates like roast chicken and New York strip with bold new creations like chicken liver mousse with carmelized foie gras and date molasses. The cocktail menu at the downstairs bar is equally adventurous. $$$.

℣ **Nineteen** (215-790-1919), 200 South Broad Street. This 19th-floor restaurant in the Park Hyatt at the Bellevue has panoramic views of the city, fabulous cuisine, and an elegant dining room featuring a raw bar and a huge pearl chandelier. The menu emphasizes simple seafood and steaks, with such dishes as Boston codfish and chips, steak frites, and bouillabaisse with garlic aioli. The three-course café lunch is a good value. Don't miss the signature dessert: lemon-foam carrot cake served with cream cheese sorbet. $$$.

℣ **Osteria** (215-763-0920; osteriaphilly .com), 640 North Broad Street. Lunch Thursday and Friday, dinner daily. Marc Vetri's ode to rustic Italian country food in the Fairmount area. The food is indisputably spectacular: Go for the rigatoni with chicken liver, cipollini, and sage or the wood-roasted whole branzino, or keep things simple with a thin-crusted margherita pizza. $$–$$$.

℣ **Rouge** (215-732-6622), 205 South 18th Street. This stylish late-night bar and restaurant underwent a major renovation in 2019 and remains a mainstay of the Rittenhouse Square dining scene. Its patio is always hopping. The food tends to be American with a French influence: poached sea trout béarnaise with radish and caviar, tuna tartare, and pommes frites. Extensive wine list. $$–$$$.

℣ **Tria** (215-972-8742; www.triaphilly .com), 123 South 18th Street. Sleek and stylish, it's perfect for an after-dinner drink and light meal. The excellent wine list is longer than the menu, and the cheese list (ranked by stinky, approachable, stoic, and racy) is longer than an average grocery list. A fine selection of local and imported beers too. There is another location at Washington Square West. Dishes $.

UNIVERSITY CITY

℣ **White Dog Café** (215-386-9224), 3420 Sansom Street. This gourmet hub for social activists is Philadelphia's version of Berkeley's Chez Panisse. Its menu pushes locally grown and raised produce; you might find Kung Pao tofu with toasted peanuts and free-range Lancaster County chicken for dinner, and smoked salmon sandwiches with caper cream cheese for lunch. The piano parlor features live music on Friday and Saturday nights, and there are regular lectures and film events. $$–$$$.

℣ **Distrito** (215-222-1657; distrito restaurant.com), 3945 Chestnut Street. Lunch and dinner daily. Go for the modern Mexican cuisine (crab enchiladas, short-rib huaraches); stay for the superb margaritas and neon-hued party ambiance. Request the Volkswagen table even if you don't bring the kids. $$–$$$.

Vernick Food + Drink (267-639-6644; vernickphilly.com), 2031 Walnut Street. Award-winning chef Greg Vernick prepares simple, exquisite cuisine (shaved asparagus with manchego, organic Amish chicken with lemon and herb jus) in a bilevel brownstone with an open kitchen and a bar/lounge area. Reservations recommended but not required.

EATING OUT The Market at Comcast Center (215-496-1810), 1701 John F. Kennedy Boulevard. The tallest building in Philadelphia also boasts its fanciest food

FEDERAL DONUTS HAS FRIED CHICKEN AND MADE-TO-ORDER DONUTS

court. Sushi, crab cakes, croissants, and fresh fruit and produce are among your options. Don't leave without checking out the giant high-def video wall in the lobby. Rainy day tip: The building can be accessed underground from City Hall and Suburban Station. Across 18th Street is Comcast Technology Center, home to the estimable **Vernick Coffee Bar.** Sit at high-top communal tables and enjoy high-concept takes on oatmeal, egg-and-cheese sandwiches, and grilled romaine, plus a case of decadent pastries such as chocolate espresso scones and matcha green tea croissants.

⊽ **Monk's Café** (215-545-7005) 264 South 16th Street. Lunch and dinner daily. This narrow neighborhood tavern regularly wins "Best of Philly" awards for its huge Belgian beer selection. It also has swell burgers (beef and veggie), beer-braised mussels, and pommes frites served with bourbon mayonnaise. $$.

⊽ **Oyster House** (215-567-7683; oysterhousephilly.com), 1516 Sansom Street. Lunch and dinner served Monday–Saturday. Original owners rescued this Philly institution from disrepute in 2009 and turned it into a noisy, whitewashed palace to the bivalve. Expect sweet crab salad, classic snapper turtle soup, and entrées such as fisherman's stew and grilled halibut with polenta and piperade. It's the place to get lobster rolls in summer, and the daily Buck-A-Shuck Oyster Hour is great fun. $$–$$$.

Federal Donuts (215-665-1101; federaldonuts.com), 1632 Sansom Street. Hot, fresh donuts, strong coffee, and fried chicken (served from 11 a.m.). This is acclaimed Philadelphia chef Michael Solomonov's take on three essential comfort foods—and it works. They've since added za'atar fries and egg sandwiches to the simple menu. There are also branches on South Street, in West Philly, and other locales around the city.

✐ ⊽ **Pietro's Coal Oven Pizzeria** (215-735-8090), 1714 Walnut Street. This enduring trattoria serves thin-crust pizza with gourmet toppings like goat cheese and prosciutto, and a wide selection of pastas and salads. It's good for families looking for a reasonable meal in Rittenhouse Square. $$.

Di Bruno Bros. (215-665-9220), 1730 Chestnut Street. Lunch daily. This outpost of the Italian Market cheese shop has an upstairs café that's perfect for a quick gourmet lunch (try the Mamma Mia panini with prosciutto, fresh mozzarella, and roasted peppers). Afterward, browse the selections of imported olives, pâtés, and specialty cheeses. BYO. $.

UNIVERSITY CITY

Abner's (215-662-0100), 3813 Chestnut Street. If you need a cheesesteak fix west of Broad, this is the joint to seek out; it's usually packed with Penn students. $.

Saad's Halal Palace (215-222-7223), 4500 Walnut Street. It's a little off the beaten path (about five blocks west of Penn's campus) but a great find for a cheap, filling meal of falafel, shawarma, and other Middle Eastern dishes. $.

COFFEE

RITTENHOUSE SQUARE

La Colombe Coffee Roasters (215-563-0860), 130 South 19th Street. Open daily. No lattes, teas, or attitude—just fabulous house-blend coffee served in an art-filled room with large windows.

Good Karma Café (215-496-9003), 2319 Walnut Street. Penn students living in Center City fill up their carry mugs with fair-trade coffee before crossing the Schuylkill to West Philly.

BYO Where to buy wine west of City Hall:

Around Rittenhouse Square there are **Wine & Spirits** stores at 2040 Market Street (215-241-1497) and 1515 Locust Street (215-545-1112). In Spruce Hill near University City, there's a state store at 4301 Chestnut Street (215-823-6795).

✳ Entertainment

MUSIC & THEATER **Academy of Music** (215-893-1999), Broad and Locust Streets. One of the oldest opera houses in the United States and a gorgeous setting for performances by the Pennsylvania Ballet and Opera Philadelphia.

Ψ 占 **Chris' Jazz Café** (215-568-3131; chrisjazzcafe.com), 1421 Sansom Street. Decades-old jazz joint near City Hall. Cover charge $15–30.

占 **Curtis Institute of Music** (215-893-5261), 1726 Locust Street, Rittenhouse Square. This prestigious conservatory holds free student recitals every Monday, Wednesday, and Friday from October–May. Arrive early; seating is on a first-come basis.

Kimmel Center (215-790-5800; kimmelcenter.org), 260 South Broad Street. The city's newest performing arts center is home to the 2,500-seat Verizon Hall, where you can catch the Philadelphia Orchestra and other musical performances. Tours are given daily at 1 p.m.

Ψ **Natalie's Lounge** (215-222-5162), 4003 Market Street. This narrow, smoky jazz club in West Philly has hosted John Coltrane, Grover Washington Jr., and other jazz and blues legends. It's still going strong after 60 years.

占 **Philadelphia Film Center** (215-569-9700; www.princemusictheater.org), 1412 Chestnut Street. Musical theater—opera, cabaret, experimental—in a 450-seat movie palace.

占 Ψ **World Café Live** (215-222-1400), 3025 Walnut Street. This smoke-free club and restaurant near Penn is the best place in town to catch cutting-edge indie artists. A smaller upstairs stage features new and local talent.

DANCE **Philadanco!** (215-387-8200; philadanco.org). Long-running dance studio that is widely recognized as a leader in innovative modern dance rooted in African American traditions.

Check the website for a schedule of performances; you can sometimes catch a show at the Kimmel Center.

MOVIES **Cinemark University City** (215-386-9600), 40th and Walnut Streets. Six screens with stadium seating, showing first-run films.

Lightbox Film Center (215-387-5125; lightboxfilmcenter.org), 3701 Chestnut Street. The place for spaghetti westerns, John Carpenter triple features, and avant-garde cinema. The art house cinema is located inside International House, a longtime city hub for global arts, culture, and residential activities.

PFS Roxy Theater (215-923-6699), 2023 Sansom Street. You'll find two small screens, lower-than-average ticket prices, and a refreshing lack of multiplex sterility at this Rittenhouse Square institution.

NIGHTLIFE **Alma de Cuba** (215-988-1799), 1623 Walnut Street, Rittenhouse Square. Comfy chairs, dim lighting, and splendid pomegranate martinis make this two-level restaurant a worthy late-night stop if you're in Rittenhouse Square.

Y **The Bards** (215-569-9585), 2013 Walnut Street, Rittenhouse Square. An agreeable mix of barflies, professionals, and Penn graduate students share Guinness on tap and shepherd's pie at the long bar of this friendly Irish pub. Its weeknight happy hour is very popular, and there's live Irish music on Sunday evenings.

Y **Bob and Barbara's** (215-545-4511), 1509 South Street. Live jazz until 2 a.m. Friday and Saturday and a legendary Drag Night every Thursday.

Y **City Tap House** (215-662-0105; citytap.com), 3925 Walnut Street (in the Radian Building). Everything you'd want in a gastropub: 60 craft ales on tap, good grub (from burgers to striped bass), and future stockbrokers (Penn's Wharton School is next door). Regulars can keep

track of the beer they sample on cards that are then entered into an online database.

Y **Franklin Mortgage and Investment Co.** (215-467-2677), 112 South 18th Street. Perfectly executed cocktails in a subterranean speakeasy environment. Upstairs is what may be Philadelphia's only real-deal tiki bar. Try a classic Fogcutter or a Missionary's Downfall amid the bamboo, palm fronds, and leather banquettes.

Y **JG Domestic** (215-222-2363), 2929 Arch Street in Cira Center next to 30th Street Station. Iron Chef Jose Garces' farm-to-table restaurant has great happy hour specials between 4 and 6 p.m. weekdays. Phillies games. It's not an easy walk from Center City, but you can take the Frankford Line to 30th Street Station and walk from there.

Y **Jolly's Dueling Piano Bar** (267-687-1161; jollyspianobar.com), 1420 Locust Street. It's impossible not to have fun. Expect Billy Joel and Neil Diamond sing-alongs, sports on the TV, and lots of happy bachelorette parties.

Y **Misconduct Tavern** (215-732-5797), 1511 Locust Street. A favorite place to catch a Phillies game—or celebrate their win afterward with craft beers and blue cheese burgers.

Y **Pod** (215-387-1803), 3636 Sansom Street, University City. A college bar for students with trust funds (or at least some extra cash) and a taste for sake martinis and conveyor-belt sushi. Its futuristic all-white décor and hip sound system make this a fun alternative when you're not in the mood for the city's 19th-century beer taverns.

❋ Selective Shopping

Rittenhouse Square has a multistory **Barnes & Noble** store (215-665-0716) overlooking the north side, an **Apple Store,** and many upscale designer clothing and gift boutiques along Walnut Street, plus several hidden gems like

EXCURSIONS

CHESTNUT HILL, GERMANTOWN & MANAYUNK Chestnut Hill, Germantown, and Manayunk all lie outside Philadelphia's original boundaries and have a slightly suburban feel, each in its own distinctive way. Germantown sits the closest to Center City and was once one of Philadelphia's most affluent communities. Today it has a grittier feel and is less pedestrian friendly than its neighbors to the north, but its historical monuments are well preserved and among the finest and least crowded in the city, most notably the elegant and bullet-riddled **Cliveden** (215-848-1777; cliveden.org), at 6401 Germantown Avenue, site of the Battle of Germantown in 1777, and the **Johnson House** (215-438-1768; johnsonhouse.org), at 6306 Germantown Avenue, a 1768 Quaker home and Underground Railroad stop that is believed to have sheltered and fed Harriet Tubman and William Still as they guided hundreds of slaves to freedom.

Chestnut Hill is just a 10-minute drive north up Germantown Avenue, with its thriving main drag of boutique shops, sidewalk cafés, and attractive architecture. Once a farming community, it is now a sought-after address for many young Philadelphia families who like its easy access to Center City, wide tree-lined streets, and expansive **Wissahickon Valley Park,** part of the Fairmount Park system. It offers some of the best dining opportunities in the area, including the elegant **Mica** (267-335-3912; micarestaurant.com) at 8609 Germantown Avenue, and **McNally's Tavern** (215-247-9736) at 8634 Germantown Avenue, home of the Schmitter—a pumped-up version of the Philly cheesesteak that includes fried onions, tomato, salami, and Russian dressing. It's also home to **Morris Arboretum** (215-247-5777; morrisarboretum.org) and **Woodmere Art Museum** (215-247-0476; woodmereartmuseum.org), a stately mansion displaying works by Philadelphia-area artists such as N. C. Wyeth, Benjamin West, Daniel Garber, and Violet Oakley. **Wissahickon Valley Park** (215-685-9285) is part of the Fairmount Park system and stretches northwest along the Wissahickon Creek past Chestnut Hill.

Manayunk, a former textile-manufacturing center perched above the Manayunk Canal a bit farther north, has transformed its main street into a happening string of restaurants, loft apartments, boutiques, and tattoo parlors, though the hilly streets above it still have the feel of a tight working-class community. Its name is, fittingly, a Native American expression for "where we go to drink." If you like a lively night out that is sure to include young Yuengling-guzzling crowds and parking challenges, then this is the place for you. Fitness buffs might want to consider a daytime visit and pick up the **Manayunk Canal Towpath** off Main Street for a unique bike ride along a route that was originally used by mules pulling boats loaded with coal to textile mills lining the river. It connects with the paved, multiuse **Schuylkill River Trail** (schuylkillrivertrail.com), an ongoing project that stretches from Center City through Valley Forge National Park and beyond.

Joseph Fox Bookshop (215-563-4184; 1724 Sansom Street), an independent bookseller with a great architecture selection. Chestnut Street between 16th and 17th is home to the **Shops at Liberty Place,** where you'll find Nine West, J. Crew, and other upscale chains. Also worth a stop is **Bella Turka** (215-560-8733; 1700 Sansom Street) for unique and colorful jewelry and accessories from Turkey. There's also a branch in midtown at 113 South 13th Street.

In University City, **Sansom Common** (215-573-5290) at 36th and Sansom has dozens of specialty, fashion, music, book, and gift shops, including Urban Outfitters and Barnes & Noble, all catering to collegiate tastes.

In the Fairmount district near the art museum are two wonderful used bookshops: **Book Haven** (215-235-3226; 2202 Fairmount Avenue), two well-stocked stories across from Eastern State Penitentiary, and **Book Corner**, run by the

Friends of the Free Library (215-567-0527; 311 North 20th Street, behind the Central Library), a vast collection of used and nearly new books at low prices.

✳ Special Events

April: **Penn Relays** (last weekend), University of Pennsylvania, is America's first intercollegiate and amateur track event takes over Franklin Field. Besides the races, you'll find food stands, live music, and other activities around campus.

June: **Bloomsday** (June 16), Rosenbach Library, Rittenhouse Square—the home of James Joyce's original *Ulysses* manuscript—celebrates the famed literary holiday with Irish music, food provided by nearby pubs, and a series of readings by local celebrities on Delancey Place. Inside, there's a special exhibit of Joyce materials.

SOUTHEASTERN PENNSYLVANIA

THE MAIN LINE & VALLEY FORGE

THE BRANDYWINE VALLEY

THE MAIN LINE &
VALLEY FORGE

The Main Line is an affluent western suburb of Philadelphia comprising a handful of towns along or near US 30 (Lancaster Avenue). There are no skyscrapers or malls or industrial centers; what you'll find are mansions fit for European aristocrats, some of the country's top private colleges, and more families listed on the Social Register than just about anywhere else in the country.

The Main Line takes its name from the local rail line that has run between Center City, Harrisburg, and Pittsburgh since the 19th century. It includes all the towns with station stops between Center City and Malvern: Overbrook, Merion, Narberth, Wynnewood, Ardmore, Haverford, Bryn Mawr, and Paoli. Bala Cynwyd, Gladwyne, Radnor, Wayne, Villanova, and Malvern are also considered a part or adjacent to the Main Line and are mentioned in this chapter.

Many travel guides and articles mention the Main Line within context of Philadelphia, but it's a destination that increasingly deserves stand-alone coverage, with stellar shopping and restaurant options and exquisite public gardens. Despite a lingering *Philadelphia Story*–type snobbishness that borders on caricature, and golf and cricket clubs that ooze exclusivity, the area offers much to enjoy. Colleges such as Villanova and Bryn Mawr have excellent art galleries, gardens, and theaters that are open to the public, and its restaurants and delis are good enough to motivate Philadelphians to abandon the city for an afternoon or evening.

Just a few miles away from the Main Line is Valley Forge, an unincorporated part of Chester County that is best known for lending its name to the encampment of George Washington's Continental army during the winter of 1777–78. Its 3,600-acre national historic park is undoubtedly the area's most famous attraction, though the King of Prussia Mall, which claims to be the country's largest shopping mall, draws the most visitors and groupies each year (a whopping 22 million).

King of Prussia takes its name from a local 18th-century tavern called the King of Prussia Inn, which was named for the Prussian King Frederick II, possibly due to his support of George Washington during the American Revolution (another educated guess is the name was a way of attracting the German soldiers who were fighting nearby alongside the Americans). The tavern long ceased operating (it was moved from its original location in 2002 and is now home to the chamber of commerce), replaced by rampant commercial and residential development that grew up around the mall.

The Valley Forge area is close enough to Philadelphia to make it a reasonable day trip, but it has enough lodging, eating, and recreational options to spend a night or two. The King of Prussia Mall is a city unto itself, with hundreds of upscale stores and restaurants, and just down the road is a full-service casino that opened in 2012. Two of the Philadelphia area's most popular jogging and biking trails, the Perkiomen and Schuylkill River Trails, converge here. And a couple of villages within easy reach of Valley Forge, Skippack and Phoenixville, offer quaint small-town shopping and dining alternatives.

AREA CODE The western Main Line lies within the 610 area code. The eastern edge uses 215. The Valley Forge area lies within the 610 and 484 area codes.

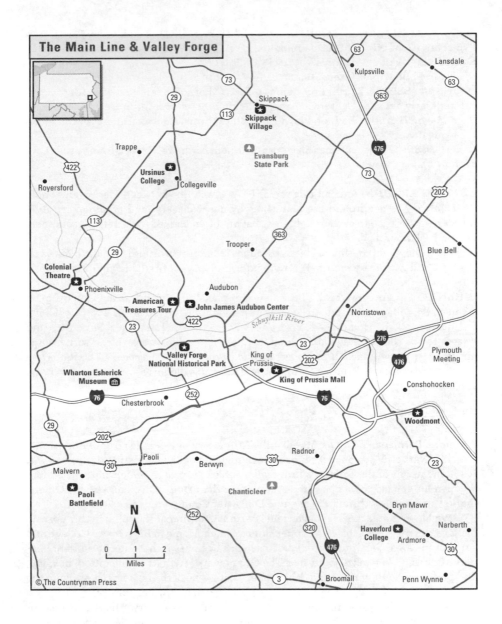

The Main Line & Valley Forge

Lansdale
Kulpsville
63
63
73
Skippack
29
113
Skippack Village
363
476
Trappe
Evansburg State Park
422
73
Ursinus College
202
Royersford
Collegeville
113
Blue Bell
Trooper
363
29
Colonial Theatre
Phoenixville
Audubon
American Treasures Tour
John James Audubon Center
Norristown
23
Schuylkill River
23
422
276
Valley Forge National Historical Park
King of Prussia
202
Plymouth Meeting
Wharton Esherick Museum
476
King of Prussia Mall
Conshohocken
76
252
76
Chesterbrook
Woodmont
29
202
Paoli
Radnor
23
Malvern
30
Berwyn
30
Chanticleer
Bryn Mawr
Paoli Battlefield
N
252
Narberth
320
Haverford College
Ardmore
30
0 1 2
476
Miles
© The Countryman Press
3
Broomall
Penn Wynne

GUIDANCE The Welcome Center at **Valley Forge National Historical Park** (610-783-1077; 1400 North Outer Line Drive) is one of the best sources for brochures and maps of the southeastern Pennsylvania area. For online information, go to mainlineneighbors .com, an independent website with good information on local events, parks, restaurants, and shopping.

GETTING THERE *By car:* US 30 (Lancaster Avenue) cuts an east–west route through the Main Line between Philadelphia and Paoli. From I-76 (the Schuylkill Expressway), exit at City Avenue for the eastern towns of Merion, Bryn Mawr, and Ardmore, and follow US 1 to US 30 west. For the western end of the Main Line and Valley Forge, take I-76 south to the King of Prussia interchange and follow US 202 south. From the Blue Route (I-476), exit at Villanova.

By air: **Philadelphia International** (215-937-6800) is the closest airport.

By train: **SEPTA's R5** rail line trains to Paoli/Thorndale (215-580-7800; septa.org) run regularly between Center City and the Main Line, with stops in Merion, Ardmore, Bryn Mawr, Villanova, Radnor, Wayne, and other towns. **Amtrak** trains also run along the same line.

By bus: **SEPTA** bus route has 44 stops in Merion, Ardmore, Narberth, and other Lancaster Avenue towns.

GETTING AROUND You can ride the SEPTA R5 rail line between Merion and Paoli. It's also easy to get around the Main Line by car. Lancaster and Montgomery Avenues are major east–west thoroughfares that are often choked with traffic; avoid them during rush hour if possible.

Free trolleys run continuous loops through Ardmore, Haverford, and Bryn Mawr on the first Friday of every month. For more information, visit firstfridaymainline.com.

WHEN TO GO Anytime, really. It's quietest on the Main Line in late July and August, when most college students are gone and residents have left for the Jersey Shore. Spring and fall are good times to visit Valley Forge National Historical Park; there are fewer crowds than in the summer, and its hills and meadows are ablaze with orange and yellow foliage in the fall and tall grass and wildflowers in the spring. The shops and restaurants of King of Prussia, Skippack, and Phoenixville thrive year-round.

✳ Towns & Villages

Ardmore. Formerly known as Athensville, Ardmore is only 3 miles from Philadelphia and, like Narberth (see below), tends to be more laid-back than other Main Line towns. It's home to one of the country's first malls, Suburban Square, which was turned into an open-air complex of shops and restaurants in the 1970s. It also has a good farmers' market selling everything from sushi to Lancaster County produce.

Bryn Mawr. Katharine Hepburn would fit right in dining or shopping in this upscale enclave, where ladies still wear proper suits to lunch. Home to Bryn Mawr College and some of the area's wealthiest citizens, it also has businesses that cater to student budgets and tastes, like pizza joints and The Grog tavern. With its train station, hospital, and proximity to Haverford and other colleges, it is one of the busiest towns along the Main Line; expect gridlock and allow plenty of time to find street parking.

Gladwyne. Gladwyne still feels like the quiet, walkable country village it was a century ago. Its center at the intersection of Youngs Ford and Righters Mill Roads, historically known as Merion Square, includes small shops and single or double houses that were once tenant housing for the laborers or mill workers of nearby Mill Creek Valley. It's home to several parks and historic mansions, including Woodmont Palace.

Narberth is a dinner-and-movie sort of place. Its pretty tree-lined downtown, centered around Narberth and Haverford Avenues, has many good restaurants, a historic one-screen movie theater, and hip boutiques and consignment shops that seem to always rate a "Best of Philly" award for something or other.

Wayne. Named after "Mad" Anthony Wayne, a brigadier general known for his insomniac ways, this lively town makes a good base for visiting both the Main Line and nearby Valley Forge, especially if you want a nonchain lodging option. It's home to the handsome Wayne Hotel and lovely Chanticleer pleasure garden. You can easily spend an afternoon shopping and eating in its downtown, which was glammed up in the 1990s and now includes lots of shops selling home furnishings and scented candles.

Phoenixville. This small town on the northwest edge of Valley Forge underwent a transformation in recent years from blue-collar steel town to parking-challenged urban neighborhood. Bridge Street, its main thoroughfare, is (so far, at least) a mix of art galleries, BYO bistros, old-time barber shops, and faded diners. Anchoring the downtown area is the restored Colonial Theater, famous for its role in the sci-fi film *The Blob*.

Skippack. Once a stop on a 1900s rural trolley route, Skippack added "Village" to its name in the 1990s, opened some antiques shops and nice restaurants, and waited for the people to come. They did, and now it is rarely described without the adjective quaint. It is a nice shopping alternative for those who aren't in the mood for the nearby King of Prussia Mall; it also has a great community theater and plenty of parking behind the shops that front busy Skippack Pike.

✳ To See

MUSEUMS & GALLERIES ☉ **Wharton Esherick Museum** (610-644-5822; whartonesherickmuseum.org), 1520 Horseshoe Trail Road, Malvern. Open March–December; one-hour tours on weekends; group tours weekdays. You'll never look at a piece of timber the same after visiting the studio and home of one of America's greatest and perhaps least appreciated woodworkers. Wharton Esherick was a Philadelphia-born artist who turned his attention to woodcraft after failing at a string of illustrating jobs. His stone-and-wood home and studio, just as he left it since his death in 1970, is on a crest overlooking Valley Forge—a hobbitlike wonderland of irregular plank floors, drop-leaf oak desks, sculptures, and hand-carved coat hooks. Three of the four levels are connected by a stunning spiral staircase made from massive pieces of red oak.

☂ **Philip and Muriel Berman Museum of Art** (610-409-3500; ursinus.edu/berman), 601 East Main Street, Collegeville. Closed Mondays; free. This small gem on the campus of Ursinus College features paintings and prints by Charles Willson Peale, Walter Baum, Andy Warhol, Roy Lichtenstein, and Susan Rothenberg; Japanese block prints; and Pennsylvania German artifacts such as almanacs, pottery, and quilts. An impressive collection of more than 40 outdoor sculptures peppers the liberal arts college campus, where J. D. Salinger studied for four months in 1938. Another literary nugget: John Updike's parents, Wesley and Linda, met here and married two years after graduating. The author donated his mother's writings to the college, and they are available for viewing at the Myrin Library.

☂ **Cantor-Fitzgerald Gallery** (610-896-1287), 370 Lancaster Avenue, Haverford. Open daily from September–May, weekdays from June–August; free. The founder of the Wall Street company helped finance this sleek gallery space in the Hurford Center on the campus of Haverford College. Exhibits change monthly and feature sculpture, photography, printmaking, and other media by professional artists.

HISTORIC SITES ☂ ✎ **John James Audubon Center at Mill Grove** (610-666-5593; johnjames.audubon.org), 1201 Pawlings Road, Audubon. Closed Mondays. Self-guided house tours for a small fee. Audubon lived in this rambling stone farmhouse when he first moved to America from Europe in the early 1800s; it was here that he started studying and painting the birds that would shape his career. Mill Grove attracts a fraction of the traffic that nearby Valley Forge National Historical Park does, but it's worth an hour-long stop. A sleek new visitor center and museum was added in 2019, with extensive birding exhibits such as a sound forest and digital flyway map. Situated on a hill with an inviting back porch overlooking Perkiomen Creek, the house is filled with original paintings and books by Audubon, including a complete four-volume set of *The Birds of America,* Audubon's famous portrayal of nearly 500 distinct species of birds. Picnic areas and 5 miles of hiking trails surround the house.

Woodmont Palace (610-525-5598), 1622 Spring Mill Road, Gladwyne. Tours are offered on Sundays from April–October; free. You have to see this massive French Gothic–style manor to believe it. Built by a local steel magnate in the 1800s, it's now home to the International Peace Mission Movement, a religious group founded in the early 20th century by an African American man who renamed himself Father Divine and claimed to be the embodiment of Jesus. His widow, known as Mother Divine, still lives in the manse and allows the public to tour the house or stroll the bucolic grounds one afternoon a week. Tours of the manor house take about an hour and include a visit to the "Shrine of Life" where Father Divine is buried. Modest dress is required (no shorts or sleeveless shirts).

Merion Friends Meetinghouse (610-664-4210), 615 Montgomery Avenue, Merion. One of the oldest Quaker meetinghouses in America, this 17th-century building counts William Penn among its worshippers. The cherry trees that dot its burying ground have a great backstory: Japanese and American horticulturalists planted them in the early 1900s as a test to ensure that the cherry trees Japan intended to give to Washington, DC, would survive the climate. They did, and they're still a beautiful sight in the spring. There are worship services on Sunday and rummage sales and art exhibits throughout the year.

Paoli Battlefield (ushistory.org/paoli), Wayne and Monument Avenues, Malvern. Open daily from mid-May–mid-October weekends from November–April. During the night of September 20, 1777, the British launched a surprise attack against General Anthony Wayne's troops that is now known as the Paoli Massacre. Using bayonets and swords, they killed between 50 and 100 men and wounded about 150 more. The battlefield is surrounded by development but has been preserved in its original form as woodland and farm fields. There is no visitor center, but an easy 0.5-mile walking trail leads you past interpretative signs and significant sites.

✻ To Do

FOR FAMILIES ✪ ⬆ ✐ **Stoogeum** (267-468-0810; stoogeum.com), 904 Sheble Lane (near Bethlehem Pike), Ambler. Open Thursday 10–3, and for group tours Monday–Wednesday and Friday; admission charged for adults; kids 12 and younger are free. Tough to believe, but this unassuming office building 30 minutes north of Philadelphia holds the largest public display of Three Stooges memorabilia in the world. Owner and founder Gary Lassin is president of the Three Stooges Fan Club and married to a grandniece of the Philadelphia-born Larry Fine; in 2004 he set about fashioning a museum dedicated to the legendary comedy trio out of the thousands of items he had accumulated over the years. The result is most *soitenly* fabulous, whether you're a fan or not. The crowds who fill the place when it's open are a nice mix of young and old—with everyone showing equal appreciation for the 1980s Stooges pinball machine, computerized *Stoogeology 101* exhibit (which urges participants to give Curly an eye poke to proceed), and old photos and comic books. The third floor is devoted to artwork of and by the Stooges. Check the website for updates.

A MAIN LINE PLEASURE GARDEN

Chanticleer (610-687-4163; chanticleergarden.org), 786 Church Road, Wayne. Open Wednesday–Sunday from April–October; admission charged; children under 12 free. Grounds stay open until 8 p.m. on Fridays in the summer. Hip meets elegant at this 35-acre estate and garden tucked into a tony neighborhood south of Lancaster Avenue. To give you a sense of its pedigree, the family residence of Hope Montgomery Scott, the Main Line heiress on whom Katharine Hepburn's character is reportedly based in *The Philadelphia Story*, is nearby. Once the estate of pharmaceutical mogul Adolph G. Rosengarten, it is now a pleasure garden with wisteria-draped arbors, a babbling brook, and rolling green hills. In the spring, fields surrounding the main house are awash with 150,000 white and yellow daffodils. There are few signs (plant lists are available in small, whimsical kiosks), and Adirondack chairs and stone couches with cushions are placed invitingly around the premises to take advantage of the lovely views. When the horticulturalists aren't tending to the flora and fauna, they are creating furniture, sculptures, and metal bridges for placement around the property. No child and few adults will be able to resist rolling down the lush sloping hillside near the main house (it's even encouraged). House and introductory garden tours are given at 11 a.m. Friday and Saturday for an additional charge. 🖉

GARDENS **Barnes Arboretum at St. Joseph's University** (610-660-2802; barnesfoundation.org/whats-on/arboretum), 41 Lapsley Lane, Merion. Free. Although much of the art once housed in the original mansion was moved to a new facility on the Benjamin Franklin Parkway, the lush arboretum and horticultural programs remained at the Main Line property, boasting more than 35 state champion trees and 2,500 varieties of woody and herbaceous plants. The peony and lilac collections date from the early 1900s. It's open to the public on weekends from May–August, with free guided tours at 1 p.m. and an audio guide for smartphones. Check website for exact dates and times.

Jenkins Arboretum (610-647-8870; jenkinsarboretum.org), 631 Berwyn Baptist Road, Devon. Open 8 a.m.–sunset daily. Elisabeth Phillippe Jenkins received part of this natural woodland property as a wedding present from her father in 1926. Her husband helped turn it into a public arboretum after her death in 1965. Now 46 acres, it is known for its big-leaved rhododendrons and evergreen azaleas, and usually hits its colorful peak from April to June. It has 1.2 miles of winding paved paths and a 2-acre pond framed by daylilies, wildflowers, and white pines. You'll come away from here with a newfound appreciation for leaves and twigs, since gardeners leave them where they fall to act as a sort of natural mulch.

Haverford College Arboretum (610-896-1101; haverford.edu/arboretum), 370 Lancaster Avenue, Haverford. Open daily dawn to dusk. Rolling lawns, a 3-acre pond, and hundreds of majestic old trees can be found in this small arboretum on the campus of Haverford College. A 2.2-mile walking and jogging nature trail circles the campus. Maps and self-guided brochures are available at the arboretum office near the main visitors parking lot.

✳ Outdoor Activities

BICYCLING The **Radnor Trail** is a paved 2.4-mile path with graded shoulders for walkers and horses. It begins at Radnor–Chester Road south of Lancaster Avenue and follows an old railroad line to Sugartown Road.

HISTORY & FITNESS AT VALLEY FORGE

Valley Forge National Historical Park (610-783-1077; nps.gov/vafo), 1400 North Outer Line Drive, Valley Forge. Free. Welcome center open 9–5 daily (until 6 p.m. in summer), grounds open year-round 6 a.m.–10 p.m. No battles were fought here, but this 3,600-acre property is considered a critical turning point of the Revolutionary War. It's where George Washington chose to settle his weary and ill-equipped army for the winter of 1777–78. Despite the fact that as many as 2,000 Continental soldiers (out of a total 12,000) died of hunger, disease, and frostbite while here, it's also where Washington, with the help of Prussian drill master Friedrich von Steuben, eventually shaped his beleaguered army into a force to be reckoned with that would go on to defeat the British. Today the area is marked by rolling hills and woodlands, earthen forts, reconstructed log cabins, towering war memorials, and miles of hiking and biking trails.

Begin your visit at the welcome center, where you can catch a short film and talk to National Park Service staffers about what's going on that day. The whole park and its highlights can be covered in a couple of hours by car (self-guided driving tours are available), or you may opt to take a ranger-led walking tour (offered three times daily in summer).

There are also daily narrated open-air trolley tours in summer and weekends in September and October, and after-hours picnics with actors playing George and Martha Washington and Continental soldiers. Call the welcome center for details.

One of the best ways to experience the park is by walking its well-maintained paths. Leave your car at the visitor center or the Washington Memorial Chapel on the north side of the park and pick up the easily accessible 5-mile loop trail. The chapel itself, built in 1917 and home to an active Episcopalian church, is worth a stop for its soaring stained-glass windows and hand-carved choir stalls. It also features a carillon of 58 bells that represent the US states and territories (concerts are held every Sunday and weekday evenings during summer) and the Justice Bell, a replica of the Liberty Bell that was used to promote the women's suffrage movement in the early 1900s.

Behind the chapel are a tiny used bookshop and a gift and snack shop that sells homemade soup, sandwiches, and shoofly pie for reasonable prices. From here you can pick up the main park trail for a short hike to the fields where Washington trained his army, and the Isaac Potts House (see below), one of the park's top attractions.

Valley Forge National Historical Park has several miles of moderate bike trails. City bikes for kids and adults are available for rent in the lower parking area of the welcome center between May and October.

The Schuylkill River Trail (schuylkillrivertrail.com) follows the river 25 miles west from Philadelphia's Fairmount Park, crosses through Valley Forge and Lower Perkiomen Valley Park, where it links with the 19-mile Perkiomen Trail, which continues west through the towns of Collegeville, Schwenksville, and Green Lane. Several bike shops near the route rent bikes or can offer guidance, including Bikesport (610-489-7300; 325 West Main Street, Trappe) and Indian Valley Bikeworks (215-513-7550; 500 Main Street, Harleysville).

FISHING The lower half of Little Valley Creek near Washington's headquarters at Valley Forge National Historical Park is stocked with brown trout and popular for fly-fishing, though all caught fish must be released back into the creek.

Skippack Creek is stocked with brown and rainbow trout March–Memorial Day

The area around the **Isaac Potts House**, which served as Washington's headquarters during that fateful winter, underwent a large renovation in 2007 that included restoring a 1911 train station near the house and adding exhibits aimed at better capturing the misery and pressure that permeated the encampment and Washington's state of mind, according to park officials.

With nearly 30 miles of moderate trails, Valley Forge is also a haven for bicyclists, equestrians, and walkers. On spring and summer evenings, the 5-mile Joseph Plumb Martin Trail, which begins on North Outer Line Drive near the welcome center and passes rows of log cabins, the **National Memorial Arch**, and the chapel, is filled with exercise hounds. The website has good downloadable trail maps.

THE ISAAC POTTS HOUSE SERVED AS GENERAL WASHINGTON'S HEADQUARTERS AT VALLEY FORGE DURING THE WINTER OF 1777

and warm-water fish such as smallmouth bass, catfish, and eel throughout the year. An accessible fishing dock is on Lewis Road in **Evansburg State Park** (see *Green Space*).

GOLF **Jeffersonville Golf Course** (610-539-0472), 2400 West Main Street, Jeffersonville. A well-maintained, 18-hole, par-72 municipal course designed by Donald J. Ross.

Pickering Valley Golf Club (610-933-2223), 450 South White Horse Road, Phoenixville. A no-frills yet challenging 18-hole course featuring 6,572 yards of golf from the longest tees with a par of 72.

HORSEBACK RIDING **Greylyn Farm** (610-889-3009; greylynfarm.com), Sugartown Road and Paoli Pike, Malvern. Private or group instruction in showing horses.

Red Buffalo Ranch (610-489-9707; redbuffaloranch.com), 1093 Anders Road, Collegeville. Leads one- to four-hour guided trail rides through adjacent Evansburg State Park (see also *Green Space*). They also give lessons to all levels of riders.

✳ Lodging

You'll find many chain hotels in St. Davids, near Radnor, and a few miles away in the King of Prussia area.

BED & BREAKFASTS ♂ **The General Warren** (610-296-3637; generalwarren .com), Old Lancaster Highway, Malvern. This historic inn off US 202 was a popular stage stop and Tory stronghold during the American Revolution. It has eight comfortable Colonial-style suites with sitting areas, private baths, and TVs. There's a well-regarded restaurant and tavern on the ground floor (see *Dining Out*). No children or pets. $$.

🔥 **Great Valley House** (610-644-6759; greatvalleyhouse.com), 1475 Swedesford Road, Valley Forge. Also near US 202 and a mile from Valley Forge National Historical Park, this 17th-century stone farmhouse has three guest rooms, each with quaint Victorian touches such as claw-foot bathtubs and canopy beds, as well as TVs, refrigerators, and wireless Internet access. The downstairs common areas are filled with owner Pattye Benson's collections of antique dolls, quilts, and vintage clothes from the late 1800s. Breakfast is served in the pre-Revolutionary kitchen in front of a walk-in stone fireplace. The 4 acres of grounds are a nice touch, and the tree-fringed swimming pool makes you feel like you are lounging at a friend's home. $$, two-night minimum on weekends with some exceptions.

HOTELS & INNS **Hotel Fiesole** (610-222-8009; hotelfiesole.net), 2046 Skippack Pike, Skippack. This attractive 16-room luxury inn is Skippack's only upscale lodging option. Located along its thriving main street, it was once a popular restaurant known as the Trolley Stop. All that's left is the original trolley, which now serves as a dining room for one of the hotel's three restaurants. Its rates are on the high side for this area, but rooms are large and have marble baths, flat-screen televisions, and sitting areas. Try to get one facing Perkiomen Creek. $$$.

🔥 **Radnor Hotel** (610-688-5800; radnorhotel.com), 491 East Lancaster Avenue (PA 30), St. Davids. A full-service, four-story hotel at the Main Line's west end near the Schuylkill Expressway and PA 30. Rooms are on the bland side, but the service and convenience get high marks from the business folks who frequent it. Rates drop considerably on the weekend. $$–$$$.

Wyndham (610-526-5236; brynmawr .edu/wyndham), 235 North Merion Avenue, Bryn Mawr. Housed in a quaint stone farmhouse that serves as Bryn Mawr's alumnae headquarters, this seven-room inn is one of the best lodging deals you'll find on the Main Line. Rooms are immaculate and decorated in a restrained Colonial style; all have private baths and include a continental breakfast. It's within walking distance of the Bryn Mawr train station and many shops and restaurants. Reserve early, as the inn often fills up fast with visiting parents and graduates; it closes for a week in November, three weeks in December, and a couple of weeks in August. $$.

Wayne Hotel (610-687-5000; waynehotel.com), 139 East Lancaster Avenue, Wayne. This four-story Tudor Revival building in the center of Wayne's shopping and restaurant district was a retirement home and synagogue before new owners bought it in 1985 and restored it to the handsome inn it was when it opened in 1906. Its 37 rooms and three suites have a Victorian feel with comfortable mahogany beds, lace curtains, and flowery wallpaper. Guests have access to a gym and seasonal swimming pool at the Radnor Hotel a few miles away. $$$.

French Creek Inn (610-935-3838; frenchcreekinn.net), 2 Ridge Road, near PA 23 and PA 724, Phoenixville. This family-owned budget motel has 22 large, sparsely furnished rooms with refrigerators, microwaves, and TVs. It's 5 miles to Valley Forge and 2 miles to Phoenixville's Main Street. $.

✳ Where to Eat

DINING OUT ⏦ **333 Belrose** (610-293-1000), 333 Belrose Avenue, Wayne. Lunch and dinner Monday–Friday, dinner Saturdays. This stylish restaurant has a contemporary American menu that features innovative seafood dishes such as sriracha-spiked tuna tartare, mussels bouillabaisse, and wood-grilled salmon with crab butter. There are good burgers, too, which come with garlic fries. The bar is often packed during happy hour. Extensive wine list. $$–$$$

Autograph Brasserie (610-964-2588), 503 West Lancaster Avenue, Wayne. The European-inspired menu includes steak frites with truffle fries and handmade pasta, and the atmosphere is both elegant and whimsical, with framed celebrity photos, albums, and instruments on the walls. $$$.

Blackfish BYOB (484-397-0888; blackfishrestaurant.com), 119 Fayette Street, Conshohocken. Closed Sundays and Mondays. Seasonal New American cuisine in a contemporary storefront on Conshohocken's main street. $$.

Mediterranean Grill, (610-525-2627), 870 West Lancaster Avenue, Bryn Mawr. Attractive BYO near the Bryn Mawr train station that is the go-to place for lamb kebabs, tahdeg (crispy rice and pita), oven-roasted baby eggplant, and all things Persian. Conveniently, there's a wine shop a few doors away (see *BYO*).

⏦ **Teresa's Café** (610-293-9909), 124 North Wayne Avenue, Wayne. This enduring James Beard Award–winning neighborhood bistro just off Lancaster Avenue serves gourmet pizzas, pastas, and Italian entrées such as veal medallions in a lemon-caper wine sauce and mushroom risotto. You can't go wrong with anything that comes with the house-made pesto. The restaurant has a full bar and an adjacent gastropub, **Teresa's Next Door,** serving sandwiches and mussels. $$.

⏦ **White Dog Café** (610-225-3700), 200 West Lancaster Avenue, Wayne. The first outpost of West Philadelphia's original with the same tasty, locally sourced food and typically long waits. The difference is the location (Main Line opulence instead of hip city townhouse) and people (country clubbers instead of college professors). The dog-themed art remains the same. $$.

Wyndham (610-526-5236; brynmawr.edu/wyndham), 235 North Merion Avenue, Bryn Mawr. Lunch Monday–Friday. Closed July and August and the last week of December. This small restaurant at the alumnae house of Bryn Mawr College exudes a "ladies who lunch" vibe, but it's open to anyone and well worth a visit if you're in the area. The buffet is a great value if it's available and includes a choice of soups, salads, and changing entrées. There are also à la carte dishes such as butternut squash salad, pecan-crusted chicken, and ground sirloin burgers. Try to get a table on the covered patio overlooking the lawn. You may bring your own wine for a small fee. $$.

PHOENIXVILLE

Black Lab Bistro (610-935-5988), 248 Bridge Street. Closed Mondays. The food is consistently fabulous at this upscale bistro near the Colonial Theatre. The dinner menu might feature braised short ribs, artichoke-crusted salmon, and pepper-seared ostrich fillet. Lunch includes butternut squash gnocchi, a lump crab omelet, as well as tasty sandwiches. BYO. No reservations are taken Friday and Saturday. $$.

Louette's BYO (610-924-9906; louettesbyo.com), 106 Bridge Street. This upscale rustic space stands out among the many pubs on Bridge Street. The changing menu of small plates may feature charred broccolini, house-made ramen, and hand-torn scallops with mustard jus.

Majolica (610-917-0962, majolica restaurant.com), 258 Bridge Street. Critically lauded BYO next door to the Black Lab. The seasonal French-inspired menu might include pastrami-cured salmon, veal sweetbreads with roasted radish and molasses butter, and duck cassoulet. For dessert, try the warm Nutella crêpes or spiced cardamom-coffee doughnuts. Six- and eight-course tasting menus are available on Wednesday, Thursday, and Sunday. $$.

KING OF PRUSSIA

♈ **Creed's Seafood and Steaks** (610-265-2550; creedskop.com), 499 North Gulph Road. This classy, old-school steakhouse is one of the few nonchain dining options in King of Prussia. It has been around since the early 1980s and continues to thrive, perhaps because of its impeccable service and a reliable menu that includes locally sourced rib eye, jumbo lump crabcakes, and a curated raw bar. $$$.

SKIPPACK

Mistral (610-222-8009), 2046 Skippack Pike. Dinner daily, Sunday brunch. This special-occasion restaurant in the Hotel Fiesole is elegant and inviting, with a stained-glass ceiling, white tablecloths, and a large fireplace. The northern Italian menu features a wide range of pastas, seafood, and meats, including braised rabbit, buffalo, and free-range chicken. A less expensive and abbreviated menu is available at the more casual **Bella Rossa** downstairs. $$$–$$$$.

Vallini (484-991-8738; valliniskippack .com), 4027 West Skippack Pike. Farm-to-table Italian BYO bistro showcasing house-made pastas and entrées such as veal Marsala and whole roasted branzino. The setting, in a converted house with an open kitchen, is cozy and welcoming.

EATING OUT Berwyn Pizza (610-647-6339), 1026 East Lancaster Avenue, Berwyn. The pizzas are very good, but it's the cheesesteak that wins the biggest raves. $.

Hymie's Delicatessen (610-554-3544), 342 Montgomery Avenue, Merion. You won't find much in the way of décor at this always-busy spot along a busy stretch of Montgomery Avenue, but you won't care once the food arrives. As much a diner as a deli, it serves amazing matzo ball soup, thin-sliced pastrami sandwiches with homemade coleslaw, and other deli staples. Breakfast is served all day. Expect a wait on weekends. $.

Minella's Diner (610-687-1575), 320 West Lancaster Avenue, Wayne. A popular 24-hour diner that serves breakfast all day and night. The huge menu includes everything you'd expect from a good diner: eggs every way, pancakes, burgers, salads, fried flounder, moussaka, and more. $–$$.

Tradestone Café (484-368-3096; tradestonecafe.com), 117 Fayette Street, Conshohocken. Open daily 6 a.m.–3 p.m. The coffee is La Colombe and the breads are baked in-house at this inviting daytime spot known for its gourmet sandwiches, soups, and pastries. $–$$.

PHOENIXVILLE

Nudy's Café (610-933-6085), 450 Bridge Street. Long-running breakfast and lunch spot offering a huge menu of diner staples, from build-your-own omelets to BLTs and hot roast beef sandwiches. $.

Steel City Coffee House (610-933-4043), 203 Bridge Street, Phoenixville. Everything you'd want in an independent coffeehouse: a loftlike space, four different special roasts on tap at any given time, and a wide selection of panini, salads, and scones. Coffee refills are free. For dessert, there are homemade cookies, frozen Snickers bars, and all kinds of ice cream variations (see also *Entertainment*).

SKIPPACK

TimeOut Sports Bar (484-991-8546), 4024 Skippack Pike. This casual hangout in the former Roadhouse locale serves wings and burgers and has a family-friendly vibe, with many TVs, shuffleboard, foosball, and arcade games. $.

Well Fed (484-584-0900), 4006 Skippack Pike. A modern diner with an old-fashioned counter and an all-day breakfast menu mixing old and new dishes, from creamed chipped beef on toast to omelets with prosciutto or house-made roast pork. $.

BAKERIES & FARMERS' MARKETS

Butterscotch Pastry Shop (610-827-0900), 406 Hollow Road, Birchrunville. Open Thursday–Sunday. Not long ago,

VINTAGE ROLLING PINS AND OTHER ANTIQUES FILL THE BUTTERSCOTCH PASTRY SHOP IN BIRCHRUNVILLE

BUTTERSCOTCH PASTRY SHOP SERVES DELECTABLE PASTRIES AND SANDWICHES IN A FORMER ANTIQUES STORE IN BIRCHRUNVILLE

this was an antiques shop owned by the beloved *Antiques Roadshow* host Richard Wright. In 2017, the owners of the acclaimed Birchrunville Store Café (see *Dining Out*) across the street turned it into a daytime showcase for exquisite desserts and sandwiches. It retains the warmth and charm of Wright's emporium, with a fireplace, custom wood tables, and décor that includes repurposed rolling pins, copper pipes, and tractor seats. Then there's the food: flaky croissants, light-as-air soufflés, and the signature butterscotch muffins. A changing roster of open-faced sandwiches and salads rounds out the lunch menu. I can't think of a better place to spend a cold Sunday morning, but things get even more inviting in springtime or early fall, when you can enjoy your coffee and treats outside on a table next to Birch Run Creek.

Hope's Cookies (215-660-9607), 1125 West Lancaster Avenue, Rosemont. This local bakery has a thriving business delivering preservative-free cookies to homesick college students. Fun flavors include caramel pecan, lemon cooler, White Russian, and chocolate raspberry.

Ardmore Farmers' Market (610-896-7560), Anderson and Coulter Avenues, Ardmore. This popular market in

Suburban Square includes indoor and outdoor dining areas and 20 vendors selling everything from hoagies and sushi to artisanal cheeses and African spices.

Lancaster County Farmers' Market (610-688-9856), 289 West Lancaster Avenue, Wayne. Open 8 a.m.–6 p.m. Wednesday and Friday, 8 a.m.–4 p.m. Saturdays. If you can't make it to Amish country, this large indoor market is the next best thing. It has more than a dozen stalls selling hand-rolled pretzels, fresh turkeys, wood-smoked hams, silk flower arrangements, and all kinds of seasonal produce. It's less frenetic and roomier than other indoor farmers' markets.

BYO Where to buy wine on the Main Line:

You'll find **Wine & Spirits** stores in Bryn Mawr at 922 West Lancaster Avenue (610-581-4560); in Wayne at 209 West Lancaster Avenue (610-964-6720); and in the Ardmore Plaza Shopping Center at 62 Greenfield Avenue (610-645-5010).

✳ Entertainment

MOVIES ❢ **Colonial Theatre** (610-917-1228; thecolonialtheatre.com), 227 Bridge Street, Phoenixville. A 1903 theater that was the site of *The Blob*'s last supper in the 1958 cult sci-fi film starring Steve McQueen. It was restored by a nonprofit group in the 1990s and now shows art and independent films as well as children's classics. Free tours are given at noon on the first and third Sundays of the month. Every July, the theater celebrates its 15 minutes of fame with a Blobfest (see *Special Events*).

Narberth Theater (610-667-0115), 129 North Narberth Avenue, Narberth. This classic art deco theater has added an additional screen and stadium seating and shows first-run films.

Reel Cinemas Anthony Wayne Theater (610-225-0980), 109 West Lancaster Avenue, Wayne. Another old theater divided into four screens showing first-run films. It's within walking distance of many shops and restaurants.

Bryn Mawr Film Institute (610-527-9898; brynmawrfilm.org), 824 West Lancaster Avenue, Bryn Mawr. Restored 1926 movie palace showing independent, documentary, art, and repertory films.

MUSIC **Steel City Coffee House** (610-933-4043; steelcitycoffeehouse.com), 203 Bridge Street, Phoenixville. This hip café turns into a happening place to hear live music on Friday and Saturday nights.

THEATER **Forge Theatre** (610-935-1920), 241 First Avenue, Phoenixville. Located in a former funeral home, this company has been staging Broadway and off-Broadway shows for more than 45 years. Ticket prices are quite reasonable.

People's Light and Theater Company (610-644-3500; peopleslight.org), 39 Conestoga Road, Malvern. This venerable theater group produces several plays per season, mixing world premieres, contemporary plays, and new approaches to classic texts like *Anne of Green Gables*. The main stage is in a beautifully restored 18th-century barn.

Villanova Theater (610-519-7474; www.theatre.villanova.edu), Lancaster and Ithan Avenues, Villanova. Villanova University's well-regarded theater department stages four shows a year, ranging from classic and contemporary plays to musicals.

NIGHTLIFE Main Line nightlife tends to cater to cash-strapped college students. You'll find plenty of beer and pool halls with happy hour deals.

The Grog Grill (610-527-5870), 863 West Lancaster Avenue, Bryn Mawr. A popular hangout for students from Bryn Mawr, Haverford, and Villanova, it's an amiable place to relax with a beer and a few friends. Families fill the upstairs nonsmoking dining room in the early evening.

THE LARGEST SHOPPING MALL ON THE EAST COAST

King of Prussia Mall (610-265-5727; kingofprussiamall.com), 160 North Gulph Road, King of Prussia. When I was a kid, my friends and I would brag to out-of-towners that this sprawling shopping complex was the biggest mall in the world, or at least it always seemed that way to us. It is the East Coast version of Mall of America—with a square footage equaling two Louisiana Superdomes and enough marble flooring to cover the entire flight deck of an aircraft carrier. For years, it operated as two separate complexes known as the Court and the Plaza, linked by an outdoor walkway. In 2016, the two complexes were connected permanently, and the mall is now four times its original size. It has eight department stores, three food courts, and more than 400 shops, including Bloomingdale's, Nordstrom, Charles Tyrwhitt, Hugo Boss, Lindt Chocolate, Sephora, and Forever 21. Nearly a quarter of its 25 million annual visitors are tourists. Serious shoppers could easily spend an entire weekend here. Lounge areas with charging stations, free WiFi, concierge desks, and free wheelchair rentals round out the "royalty for the day" experience. Check out the website or the mall's Facebook page (@KingofPrussiaMall) for seasonal events and sales. 🚹♿

McShea's (610-667-0510), 242 Haverford Avenue, Narberth. A friendly neighborhood pub with a large beer selection and a variety of nightly entertainment, including DJs, open-mic nights, and beer pong games.

Rusty Nail (610-649-6245), 2580 Haverford Road, Ardmore. Specializes in live original music from local bands. There's also satellite TV as well as pool tables and a late-night pub menu.

✳ Selective Shopping

SKIPPACK

Skippack Village, Skippack Pike, between Bridge Road and Ashland Drive. No chain stores or restaurants can be found on this two-lane road of unique boutiques, jewelers, cheese shops, and cafés. Many of the quaint cottages they operate out of were built in the 1700s. Don't miss the covered bridge built by Amish carpenters behind the parking lot next to Hotel Fiesole. Download a walking map at skippackvillage.com. The village even has its own theater, **Playcrafters** (2011 Store Road), which has been staging plays and musicals in a renovated barn since 1949.

ON OR NEAR LANCASTER AVENUE

Bryn Mawr Hospital Thrift Shop (610-525-4888), 801 County Line Road, Bryn Mawr. Closed Sundays. No thrift store junkie should miss this sprawling shop stocked with hand-me-downs from some of the area's richest neighborhoods. The main store sells furniture, jewelry, bric-a-brac, and women's clothing on three floors. Across the street are small shops for men's and children's clothing.

Suburban Square (610-896-7560; suburbansquare.com), Anderson and Coulter Avenues, Ardmore. This attractive outdoor mall is perhaps the best place around to immerse oneself in the Main Line lifestyle: Shop for dresses at Lily Pulitzer, handmade scarves at El Quetzal, and designer bikinis at Everything But Water. Then head over to the adjacent Ardmore Farmers' Market for Lancaster County meats and fresh produce.

Junior League Thrift Shop (610-896-8828), 25 West Lancaster Avenue. Closed Sundays. Frequently named by local papers as the best thrift store on the Main Line, this well-maintained store sells furniture, designer clothing, jewelry, toys, and books.

Main Point Books (610-254-9040), 116 North Wayne Avenue, Wayne. Well-organized independent bookstore in downtown Wayne with a curated selection of new books and a friendly vibe.

Eagle Village Shops (610-293-2012; eaglevillageshops.com), Lancaster Avenue and Eagle Road. A small complex of upscale independent shops, many specializing in home furnishings or women's clothing. It's east of downtown with a large parking lot.

⁂ Special Events

May: **Devon Horse Show** (last weekend and first weekend of June), Horse Show Grounds, Devon—the oldest and largest annual outdoor horse competition in the United States features more than 1,200 horses competing for prizes and a county fair with Ferris wheel rides, equestrian-themed crafts, and cotton candy.

June: **Main Line Jazz and Food Festival** (first weekend), Wayne—showcases some of the finest jazz performers in Philly, plus signature dishes from more than 20 Main Line restaurants. Visit mainlinejazz.com for information.

July: **Blobfest** (second weekend), Bridge Street, Phoenixville—this small town celebrates its prominent role in the 1958 film with a two-day festival of *The Blob* screenings, scene reenactments, a tinfoil hat contest, and a street festival.

August: **Philadelphia Folk Fest** (third weekend), Old Pool Farm, Upper Salford Township—John Prine, Bonnie Raitt, Arlo Guthrie, and the Decemberists are just a few of the famous artists who have performed at this country music bash, which celebrated its 55th anniversary in 2016. For more info, visit pfs.org.

December: **March-In of the Continental Army** (second or third weekend), Valley Forge National Historical Park—costumed soldiers reenact the Continental army's arrival in Valley Forge, followed by musket and artillery demonstrations. In mid-June, there's a similar march-out event marking the army's departure.

THE BRANDYWINE VALLEY

An easy drive from Philadelphia and Baltimore via I-95, the Brandywine Valley follows the Brandywine River from southeastern Pennsylvania into northern Delaware. Featuring dozens of excellent restaurants and some of the states' best B&Bs, it's a popular weekend getaway for Philadelphians and Washingtonians, though one could easily spend a week here and find plenty to do and see. This is where the Battle of Brandywine Creek was fought and a young French soldier named Lafayette made his auspicious military debut. It's where the du Pont family made its fortunes and built the extraordinary mansions and gardens that now draw millions of visitors. It's where Nelson Conyers (N. C.) Wyeth, one of America's top illustrators, got his start as an artist at Howard Pyle's Brandywine School of Illustration, and where his eccentric son, Andrew, and grandson, Jamie, took inspiration for their own acclaimed landscape and portrait paintings. Just over the state line in Delaware are the Hagley Museum and Library, the Nemours Mansion and Gardens, and Winterthur Museum, Garden, and Library.

The Brandywine Valley was an important paper-milling center in the 18th century, supplying paper to Ben Franklin's print shop in Philadelphia and throughout the colonies. William Penn's influence was prominent and can still be seen today in the many Quaker meetinghouses that dot the valley.

Today, US 1 and US 202 are two main routes that cut through the heart of the Brandywine Valley, each with its share of strip malls and chain hotels. But turn off these thoroughfares and you'll soon find yourself surrounded by rolling farmland, old gristmills, antiques shops, and arguably the best used bookstore in the country, Baldwin's Book Barn. Closer to the Maryland border west of Kennett Square is mushroom country, where nearly half of the country's mushrooms originate from greenhouses and special buildings that once grew carnations. It's also horse country—attracting breeders, trainers, and riding enthusiasts to its trails, rolling hills, and expansive pastures for nearly a century.

While the Brandywine Valley tends to be geared toward grown-up getaways, it has many kid-friendly places, such as Linvilla Orchards on the northern edge, Jimmy John's hot dogs, and the American Helicopter Museum and Treehouse World in West Chester.

GUIDANCE You'll find maps, history exhibits, and information on Philadelphia and surrounding areas at the **Chester County Visitor Center** (610-388-2900; brandywinevalley.com), Kennett Square. It's located just outside the gates of Longwood Gardens in a Quaker meetinghouse that once served as a stop on the Underground Railroad. In Chadds Ford just south of US 1, the **Brandywine Conference and Visitor Bureau** (610-565-3679; www.destinationdelco.com) has maps and brochures of Delaware County and other attractions and a helpful staff. In Delaware, the **Greater Wilmington Convention and Visitors Bureau** has two offices, downtown at 100 West 10th Street and in the Delaware Travel Plaza along I-95.

GETTING THERE *By air:* The center of the Brandywine Valley is about a 20- to 30-minute drive from **Philadelphia International Airport** (215-937-6800) via I-95. **Baltimore-Washington International Airport** is about 100 miles away, also via I-95.

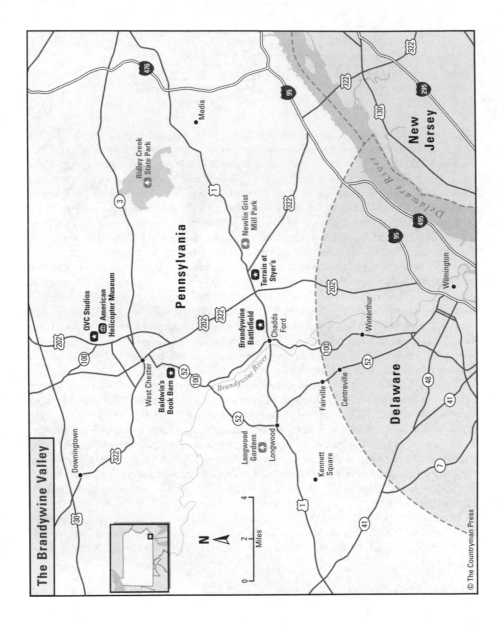

The Brandywine Valley

By car: I-95, via Philadelphia or Delaware, cuts to the west of the Brandywine; US 202 between West Chester and the Maryland border cuts right through it.

By train: The R3 line of the Southeastern Pennsylvania Transportation Authority, or SEPTA (215-580-7800; septa.org), runs regularly between Philadelphia's 30th Street Station and Media.

GETTING AROUND The easiest way to navigate the Brandywine Valley is by car. Try to avoid US 1 and US 202 during rush hour; both are popular truck routes that connect to I-95. US 30, which runs east–west above West Chester, is also a main route into Philadelphia and is best avoided at rush hour.

WHEN TO GO The fall and Christmas seasons are particularly attractive in the Brandywine Valley. Unlike some areas of eastern Pennsylvania, many of its attractions, including Longwood Gardens and Winterthur, stay open year-round. January and February bring a melancholy (but no less beautiful) starkness to the area and mean fewer crowds and lines. Winter is the perfect time to visit the Brandywine Valley Museum and pay homage to Andrew Wyeth's landscapes.

✳ Towns & Villages

Chadds Ford takes its name from a small stretch of the Brandywine Creek that was once forded by travelers and John Chads, who started a ferry business nearby to carry passengers when conditions were rough. US 1 passes right through town, making it a popular base for visiting the entire valley. It's home to the Brandywine Battlefield, the Brandywine River Museum, and many antiques shops and B&Bs.

Kennett Square. This hamlet at the west end of the Brandywine Valley calls itself "the mushroom capital of the world." Its pretty downtown includes many mom-and-pop shops and restaurants and is surrounded by rural B&Bs and farms that produce nearly half of the country's mushroom supply.

Media. The county seat of Delaware County, Media has a population of about 6,000 and an attractive main street with good restaurants, shops, an arts theater, Trader Joe's, and a small veterans museum. It's on the eastern edge of the Brandywine Valley and is connected to the Upper Darby section of Philadelphia by the 101 trolley, which runs down the middle of its main street.

West Chester. A settlement since 1692, this historic town of about 18,000 people has served as the Chester county seat since 1786. It is one of the largest towns in the Brandywine Valley and offers the widest options for dining, nightlife, and shopping. US 30 and 202 are busy thoroughfares that cross through or near the center, but it maintains an attractive and walkable downtown with shops, small cafés, and the area's best nightlife options. It is also home to a 130-year-old state college, West Chester University, and the QVC shopping network.

✳ To See

HISTORIC SITES ♿ **Brandywine Battlefield State Historic Park** (610-459-3342; brandywinebattlefield.org), US 1, east of Chadds Ford. Closed December–mid-March, except by appointment. The largest single-day battle of the Revolutionary War took place here on September 11, 1777, marking the first military action for a certain young Frenchman, the Marquis de Lafayette. Unfamiliar with the terrain, the Americans were outwitted and ultimately defeated by British troops. Perhaps for this reason the historic site doesn't get the attention or funding it deserves, but volunteers are happy to discuss the sequence of events and give you a sense of what colonial-era life was like. Watch a 20-minute video in the small visitor center, then take a driving or walking tour of the property and two modest farmhouses that served as headquarters for Washington and Lafayette. Every September, the park hosts a reenactment of the battle.

♿ **Nemours Mansion and Gardens** (302-651-6912; nemoursmansion.org), Powder Mill Drive (PA 141) and Alapocas Road, Wilmington, Delaware. Admission charged; reservations recommended. Open Tuesday–Sunday from May–December. Built by Alfred I. du Pont in 1910 for his second wife, Alicia Maddox du Pont, this 102-room French neoclassical mansion may be the most extravagant East Coast property you will ever visit. Its treasures include Marie Antoinette's musical clock, paintings from four centuries, a vintage car collection, iron gates that belonged to Henry VIII and Catherine the Great, and many more nods to the du Ponts' European roots. Plan to spend at least half a day here—tours begin with exhibits and a film about du Pont at the visitor center, then a bus takes you to the mansion for an intimate docent-led tour (groups are limited to six people), followed by about 45 minutes to independently roam the vast manicured gardens.

MUSEUMS ♿ ✍ ⵠ **Brandywine River Museum** (610-388-2700; brandywine.org), Chadds Ford. Open daily. Admission charged; student and senior discounts offered. This former 1800s gristmill on the banks of the Brandywine River houses works by three generations of Wyeths—N. C., Andrew, and Jamie—as well as such renowned illustrators as Howard Pyle, Maxfield Parrish, Reginald Marsh, and Theodor Geisel (Dr. Seuss). Plan to spend an hour in the galleries and another hour wandering the wildflower gardens and browsing the marvelous gift shop. From April–November, for an additional fee the museum offers one-hour docent-led tours of the nearby homes and studios of N. C. and Andrew, as well as Kuerner Farm, the 19th-century farmhouse and barn that inspired many of Andrew's paintings. They are all well worth the extra time and money. (See *Andrew Wyeth's Pennsylvania* on page 79.)

✍ ⵠ **Christian C. Sanderson Museum** (610-388-6545; sandersonmuseum.org), 1755 Creek Road, Chadds Ford. Admission charged. Open Saturday and Sunday from March–November. Another fascinating museum unique to the Brandywine Valley: Christian Sanderson was a local teacher and American history fanatic who happened to be close friends with his Chadds Ford neighbor, N. C. Wyeth. Sanderson's wide-ranging collection of letters, paintings, flags, and signs now fills every room of this country house and features original sketches and paintings by N. C. and a hauntingly beautiful portrait

CREEKSIDE CAFÉ AT THE BRANDYWINE RIVER MUSEUM

MUST SEE

ANDREW WYETH'S PENNSYLVANIA "I am working so please do not disturb. I do not sign autographs."

This sign greets visitors to Andrew Wyeth's former home and studio just up the road from the Brandywine River Museum. It's the first indication that much remains just as the artist left it after he died in 2009 at the age of 91: family photographs, his boyhood collection of toy soldiers, and old 16-mm prints of favorite movies such as *The Big Parade* and *Captain Blood*. In his modest studio, naturally lit by a huge north-facing window, brushes and easels are arranged as if Wyeth had just set them down, and sketches of animals and his signature stark landscapes hang or lie on the floor in various states of completion. The museum offers hour-long tours of Andrew's home/studio (separate from the admission fee) from April–November (there are also separate tours of N. C. Wyeth's home and studio and nearby

PAINTBRUSHES ARRANGED IN THE HOME STUDIO OF ANDREW WYETH

Kuerner Farm, inspiration for many of Andrew's paintings). Take one or all of the tours, then check out the Wyeth paintings on display at the museum armed with new insights on the creative processes of these great American artists.

ANDREW WYETH'S FORMER HOME AND STUDIO

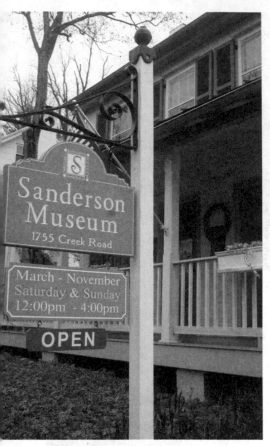

THE CHRISTIAN SANDERSON MUSEUM IN CHADDS FORD IS HOME TO A ROBUST COLLECTION OF HISTORICAL MEMORABILIA

of Sanderson by Andrew Wyeth. There's also a book owned by Benjamin Franklin, along with a lock of George Washington's hair, unexploded Civil War munitions, and much more. Pair this with a stop at the nearby Brandywine Battlefield—Sanderson helped it gain recognition as a state historic site.

      ᴅ ᕗ **American Helicopter Museum and Education Center** (610-436-9600; helicoptermuseum.org), 1200 American Boulevard, West Chester. Closed Mondays and Tuesdays; admission charged, with senior and student discounts. A tribute to the rotor-blade industry and its roots in southeastern Pennsylvania, this QVC neighbor displays more than 35 aircraft on its property, including the evacuation helicopter from TV's *M*A*S*H* and the V-22 Osprey currently used by the Marine Corps. Kids can climb in and take the controls of some of the aircraft; there's also a toddler area. Helicopter rides are available to the public on select weekends.

      ᕗ **Hagley Museum and Library** (302-658-2400; hagley.org), DE 141 between PA 100 and US 202, Wilmington, Delaware. Admission charged. Maybe it's the gunpowder connection, but the Hagley sometimes gets ignored amid the opulence of other du Pont estates in the area. In fact, it's a great place for families and for anyone curious about early American industry and how the du Ponts acquired their immense wealth. E. I. du Pont began producing black gunpowder on the site in 1802. The 230-acre complex along the Brandywine River includes massive stone mills, a waterwheel, and the du Ponts' first US home. Plan to spend at least half a day, if not longer. There's also a great little organic café on the premises.

✳ To Do

FACTORY TOUR ᕗ **Herr's Snack Factory Tours** (800-637-6225; herrs.com), 20 Herr Drive, Nottingham. Tours Monday–Friday. Free, but call ahead to guarantee a spot; production is sometimes closed on Fridays. This family-owned potato chip giant began with a 1938 panel truck, three kettles, and a couple of knives; now it processes 500 pounds of potatoes a day. Its free 45-minute tours begin with a film about the company's history, then lead you past front-row views of the potato chip– and pretzel-making process. The best part: fresh-out-of-the-oven chips to all visitors at the tour's end. The gift shop features every Herr's product imaginable, plus a half-price table.

INSIDE THE WORLD OF 24/7 SHOPPING

QVC Studios Tour (800-600-9900; qvctours.com), 1200 Wilson Drive, West Chester. Tours are offered on the hour daily between 10 and 4. How do those ankle bracelets and skin care systems pass muster with quality control experts? When is David Venable most likely to turn up in person? What is host Rick Domeier's favorite movie? Learn these and other facts about the fascinating world of round-the-clock shopping on QVC's popular daily tours. Friendly guides share behind-the-scene anecdotes and blooper videos (everything is live), then lead you past the color-coordinated product warehouse, the audio-visual computer nerve center, and an observation deck overlooking the various studio sets, where you might glimpse Venable, Marie Osmond, or other celebrity guests. No reservations are needed, but the tours are limited to 20 people and often fill up in the summer. A deluxe three-hour tour is given most Fridays; it's $100 a person and includes lunch in the QVC commissary, a visit to the green room where celebs chill before going on camera, and a tour of the workshop where sets are created. Tickets for some of the shows are available but require advance reservations; check the website for more information. Tours include a coupon to use in the well-stocked gift shop, and there's a small convenience store selling coffee, tea, and packaged snacks. ♿ ⬆

QVC TOURS INCLUDE TIME FOR SHOPPING

FOR FAMILIES ✐ **Linvilla Orchards** (610-876-7116; linvilla.com), 137 West Knowlton Road, Media. This 300-acre family farm has seasonal hayrides, a massive wooden playground, and animal-feeding areas featuring deer, sheep, goats, and emus. For parents there are fresh corn, peaches, and blackberries in the summer, apples and pumpkins in the fall, and fresh-baked pies year-round. There always seems to be a weekend festival celebrating whatever the current crop is. Expect big crowds every weekend in October.

✐ **Sugartown Strawberries** (610-647-0711; sugartownstrawberries.com), 650 Sugartown Road, Malvern. Pick your own strawberries beginning in May, or schedule a bird-watching tour with Farmer Bob (a.k.a. caretaker Robert Lange), who will explain the farm's diverse habitats and wetlands. There's a pumpkin patch, along with wagon rides and a hay-bale maze on October weekends.

✐ **Treehouse World** (484-329-7853; treehouseworld.com), 1442 Phoenixville Pike, West Chester. Kids leave the electronics behind at this unique forested wonderland. The treehouses are elaborate engineering feats with names and themes like Bluebeard (a three-level playground with a slide and rope bridges) and Train (an engine-to-caboose journey complete with a steam whistle). Other activities on the premises include ziplining and (closely supervised) tomahawk throwing.

SCENIC DRIVES For a terrific back road drive between West Chester and Chadds Ford, take Lenape Road (PA 52) south. You'll pass Baldwin's Book Barn on the right, where Adirondack chairs dot the lawn and a barn full of written treasures beckons. Continue on 52 as it veers south and turns into Creek Road, and follow that along the east side of the Brandywine River for another mile. You'll end up at US 1 near two of the area's best attractions, the Brandywine River Museum and the Christian C. Sanderson Museum.

WINERIES The Brandywine Valley has several wineries set on picturesque farmland and operating out of century-old buildings and barns. Visit www.bvwinetrail.org for information on events and a complete listing of wineries.

Black Walnut Winery (610-857-5566; blackwalnutwinery.com), 3000 Lincoln Highway (near the end of the US 30 bypass), Sadsburyville. The setting, a renovated 200-year-old barn with a deck and patio overlooking a landscaped pond, doesn't get much better than this. They also have a tasting room in Phoenixville.

Chadds Ford Winery (610-388-6221; chaddsford.com), 632 Baltimore Pike (US 1). One of the first large wineries to open in Chester County, this scenic estate sells a variety of wines, including chambourcin, syrah, and pinot noir, and has evolved into a true destination with daily tastings, cellar tours, wine-education classes, and live concerts and other events in the summer. It's just down the road from the Brandywine River Museum.

J. Maki Winery (610-286-7754; www.jmakiwinery.com), 200 Grove Road, Elverson. This lovely 32-acre estate in the far northern reaches of Chester County produces red and white varietals, plus award-winning champagnes and dessert ice wines. The tasting room is open Thursday–Monday.

Kruetz Creek Vineyards (610-869-4412), 553 South Guernsey Road, West Grove. Open Saturday and Sunday. Jim and Carol Kirkpatrick grow a dozen varieties of grapes on 8 acres of farmland southwest of Kennett Square. Free tastings, plus there's often live music on weekends throughout the year. They also run a cheery tasting room in downtown West Chester (610-436-5006; 44 East Gay Street), where you can bring your own food (BYOF) to go with your bottle or flight.

Va La Vineyards (610-268-2702; valavineyards.com), 8820 Gap Newport Pike, Avondale. Once a mushroom farm, this hillside winery now produces wines from field blends of northern Italian varietals that are roundly praised for their unique, fascinating flavors. Its cozy tasting room in a 19th-century barn offers tasting flights featuring current releases paired with locally sourced small plates. Regular hours are Friday–Sunday, with live music and other events sometimes scheduled.

✳ Green Space

⌔ **Brandywine Creek State Park** (302-577-3534), 41 Adams Dam Road, Wilmington, Delaware. Once a dairy farm owned by the du Pont family, this 933-acre park has 14 miles of trails, open meadows that encourage picnicking and kite flying, and plenty of recreational water activities such as fishing and canoeing. A nature center has maps, a gift shop, and an observation deck. Rocky Run is a popular 2-mile trail that winds along the creek and through pine forest and meadows. It begins at Thompson Bridge parking lot.

⌔ **Newlin Grist Mill Park** (610-459-2359), 219 South Cheyney Road. This small park off US 1 is home to several miles of trails and the oldest operating 18th-century gristmill in the state. The visitor center is located in a restored 1850s train station. The easy 1.5-mile Water Walk follows the west banks of Chester Creek past dense woodland, trout ponds, and a 300-year-old dam to the gristmill, then loops back around to the visitor center.

⌔ **Ridley Creek State Park** (610-892-3200), 1023 Sycamore Mills Road, Media. This 2,600-acre park has 12 miles of hiking, biking, and equestrian trails; 14 picnic areas; and fishing platforms. Its crown jewel is the **Colonial Plantation** (610-566-1725; colonialplantation.org), a working farm restored to its late 18th-century appearance. On weekends from April–November, there are costumed demonstrations of open-hearth cooking, food preservation, field plowing, and other chores of the era. Open Wednesday–Sunday; closed mid-December–March. Enter from West Chester Pike (PA 3). Be sure to check out the Belgian horses, Devon milking cows, and other animals that live on the property; they all represent the types of breeds that were around in the late 1700s.

✳ Outdoor Activities

BOAT EXCURSIONS/RENTALS The Brandywine River tends to be calm and meandering, perfect for self-guided canoeing and kayaking trips. **Northbrook Canoe Company** (610-793-2279; northbrookcanoe.com), 1810 Beagle Road in West Chester, rents one-person canoes and kayaks. Inner tubes are also available. Canoeing is also offered at **Brandywine Creek State Park;** call 302-655-5740 for fees and a schedule. **Wilderness Canoes** (302-654-2227) offers two- and four-hour canoe or tandem kayak trips down the Brandywine.

FISHING **Ridley Creek State Park** in Media and **Newlin Grist Mill Park** are two good spots for trout fishing. Anglers may also fish for smallmouth bass, bluegill, crappie, and trout at **Brandywine Creek State Park**. A fishing license and a trout stamp are required and can be obtained at any of the park offices (see *Green Space*).

TWO VERY DIFFERENT GARDENS

Two of the biggest attractions in the Brandywine Valley are Longwood Gardens in Kennett Square and Winterthur, about a 15-minute drive across the Delaware border. Both belonged to members of the du Pont family and have lush gardens and grand estates, and both are money and time well spent. They are also very different. Here's the rundown on each one. A tip: Don't ever, ever attempt to visit either property on Mother's Day.

Longwood Gardens (610-388-1000; longwoodgardens.com), 1001 Longwood Road. Established by Pierre S. du Pont, the former chairman of General Motors and a big fan of freely running water, Longwood Gardens resembles a formal 20th-century European pleasure garden, with its ornate marble fountains and shrubs clipped to perfection. Highlights include a conservatory that shelters 20 indoor gardens and 5,500 types of plants (changed to intimately reflect each season), a flower garden walk that blooms with thousands of tulips in the spring, and a main fountain garden with more than 350 water jets that soar as high as 130 feet. One of its newest additions is a restored 1930s pipe organ. At 10,010 pipes, it's the largest of its kind in the world; check the website for a concert schedule. For kids there's an indoor children's garden within the conservatory with bamboo mazes and plenty of water-based activities. The gardens stay open until 10 p.m. on Tuesday, Friday, and Saturday in the summer, when colorful illuminated fountain shows are accompanied by live orchestra music. The elaborate poinsettia display at Christmas draws big crowds, as does the Summer Concert Series, whose performers have included Keb' Mo' and Pink Martini.

Less than 10 miles away is Winterthur (302-888-4600; winterthur.org), 5105 Kennett Pike, the country estate of collector and horticulturist Henry du Pont until 1951. If Longwood is the proper Sorbonne-educated uncle, Winterthur (the h is silent) is its slightly nuttier and laid-back second cousin. Whimsical displays of wildflowers, azaleas, daffodils, and magnolia and quince trees surround the estate; inside exhibits include an entire wall of hanging Windsor chairs and a collection of unusual soup tureens. The marquee attraction here is the 175-room house, where the du Ponts lived and entertained for more than 20 years, which features their splendid collections of antique American furniture and other artifacts that were made in America between 1640 and 1860. The one-hour tours change throughout the year; a popular one is the "Elegant Entertaining" tour of the grand dining room, sitting rooms, and other public rooms. In December and early January, the "Yuletide" tour includes 18 festively decorated rooms and sells out quickly. Free trams run every few minutes from the visitor center through the gardens to the main house and often include banter from witty drivers.

GOLF **Broad Run Golfer's Club** (610-738-4410), 1520 Tattersall Way, West Chester. An 18-hole course with sloped fairways, deep bunkers, and three ponds on 370 acres of countryside.

Loch Nairn Golf Club (610-268-2234, lochnairn.com), 514 McCue Road, Avondale. An 18-hole public course with tree-lined fairways laced with streams, lakes, and ponds.

HIKING **Brandywine Creek State Park** (302-577-3534), 41 Adams Dam Road, Greenville, Delaware (see *Green Space*).

HORSEBACK RIDING At Ridley Creek State Park, **Hidden Valley Farms** (610-892-7260) operates a stable that offers private and group lessons. **Pony Island Stable** (610-764-6775; ponyislandstable.com) in Kennett Square offers lessons and training or practice rides for all levels.

✳ Lodging

INNS & MOTELS Brandywine River Hotel (610-388-1200; brandywinehotelpa.com), US 1 and PA 100, Chadds Ford. A European-style inn along busy US 1 that combines the amenities of a business hotel with homey bed & breakfast touches like afternoon tea and cookies. The 40 rooms and suites are handsomely decorated; many have queen or king beds, convertible sofas, and Jacuzzi tubs. A fitness center and cocktail bar are also on the premises. $$–$$$.

BED & BREAKFASTS ♂ Fairville Inn (610-388-5900; www.fairvilleinn.com), 506 Kennett Pike (PA 52). A longtime favorite for romantic weekend getaways, this pretty three-building complex is just above the Delaware border and five minutes from the Winterthur estate. The five rooms in the 1820s Federal residence have queen or king beds and private baths; there's also a carriage house with four rooms and two large and quiet suites, as well as a springhouse with four rooms with fireplaces and private decks that face a rolling meadow. Breakfast in the dining room is a lavish event: a buffet of fruit, yogurt, and pastries, plus a choice of three hot entrées. No children under 13. $$$; two-night minimum on Saturday.

♂ ♻ Faunbrook (610-436-5788; faunbrook.com), 699 Rosedale Avenue, West Chester. A classic B&B near West Chester University that masterfully blends 1880s history and décor with modern comforts such as WiFi, ultracomfortable beds, and central air. Each of the five rooms is unique and named after the children of the US congressman who owned the stately property in the late 1800s. Edith's Room on the third floor is a quiet haven of lace curtains and wicker; most of the rooms have unusually large private bathrooms with claw-foot tubs, perfect for a luxurious soak. A wraparound porch is framed by original wrought iron, and common rooms include a cozy mahogany-ceilinged den for afternoon wine or tea. Owner Lori Zytkowicz lives on the premises and serves an elegant breakfast (crème brûlée French toast is a specialty) in the dining room with fine china and candlelight. Baldwin's Book Barn is just a mile down the road. $$–$$$.

♻ Hamanassett (610-459-3000; hamanassett.com), 725 Darlington Road, Media. Owner Ashley Mon, who was raised in New Orleans, infuses this 1856 mansion with Southern charm and her exquisite taste in antique furniture and collectibles. It can be found at the top of a hill in a residential development a few blocks from US 1 near the Brandywine Battlefield. The seven rooms are spacious, with queen or king beds, large bathrooms, and top-quality linens. Be sure to check out Mon's antique toy collection and sip sherry amid the books and grand piano in the great room. Breakfast is a gourmet delight here, featuring such items as pesto pinwheel omelets and homemade crawfish bread. Themed cooking school packages ("Brandywine Bounty" and "Last Dinner on the *Titanic*") are also available some weekends. There's a two-bedroom carriage house behind the main house where kids and pets are allowed. $$$.

The Inn at Grace Winery (610-459-4711; 800-793-3892; gracewinery.com), 50 Sweetwater Road, Glen Mills. This 18th-century Quaker farmhouse and winery on 50 bucolic acres 2 miles off US 1 is now a luxurious bed & breakfast owned by Grace Kelly's nephew, Chris Le Vine, and his wife, Vicki. With seven handsome guest rooms, five kid- and pet-friendly cottages, a landscaped swimming pool, fitness center, and nature trail, it's geared toward anyone looking for a complete weekend escape with minimal use of the car keys. Horses and sheep roam the grounds. The royal blue master bedroom in the 1815 wing is a guest favorite, with its meadow views and large fireplace; the Dormer Room, a large exposed-brick attic room, served as an infirmary during the Civil War. The farm is a popular site for wedding receptions. $$$.

CAMPGROUNDS **KOA of West Chester** (610-486-0447; 800-562-1726), 1659 Embreeville Road, Coatesville. Open late March–early November. About 7 miles west of West Chester, this attractive property skirts the Brandywine River and has 28 tent sites, 75 RV sites, and 15 one- and two-room cabins. A large swimming pool, playground, and fishing pond are also on-site. $.

✳ Where to Eat

DINING OUT

WEST CHESTER

♈ **Dilworthtown Inn** (610-399-1390; dilworthtowninn.com), 1390 Old Wilmington Pike. Open daily for dinner. This restored 18th-century tavern may be the most romantic restaurant in the entire state. It seats 200 on any given night, but its three floors of separate candlelit dining rooms, many with walk-in fireplaces, make for an intimate and unique dining experience. The menu leans toward American with Asian influences, plus standbys such as châteaubriand for two, braised short ribs, and pan-seared scallops. The wine selection is excellent, with more than 800 vintages. Reservations strongly recommended. Jackets suggested for men. $$$–$$$$.

♈ **Blue Pear Bistro** (610-399-9812; bluepearbistro.com), 275 Brintons Bridge Road. Dinner Monday–Saturday. A modern, more casual alternative to the adjacent Dilworthtown Inn but with the same owners. There are USDA prime cheeseburgers, grilled Spanish octopus with smoked paprika aioli, and other upscale snacks. $$–$$$.

♈ **Limoncello** (610-436-6230; limoncellorestaurant.com), 9 North Walnut Street. Lunch and dinner daily. Gourmet pizzas and southern Italian cuisine are the specialty here. Its popular lunch buffet, served Monday–Saturday, includes a robust variety of salads, pasta, and meat dishes. Appetizers are half-price during weekday happy hours. Toasted, buttery limoncello cake with vanilla gelato is a featured dessert. $$.

High Street Caffe (610-696-7435), 322 South High Street. Lunch Tuesday–Friday, dinner daily. Lively local favorite known for its savory Cajun Creole dishes, such as jambalaya, étouffée, and blackened alligator. It also has a full-service bar but maintains its BYO policy Sunday–Tuesday. $$–$$$.

NEARBY

♈ **Fellini's Café** (610-892-7616; fellinis cafe.com), 106 West State Street, Media. Lunch and dinner daily. A festive Italian trattoria with Old Country wall murals, live opera music on Monday nights, and a huge selection of pastas. Daily specials might include pan-roasted sea bass or rib eye pizzaiola. $$.

♈ **Sovana Bistro** (610-444-5600; sovanabistro.com), 656 Unionville Road, Kennett Square. Lunch and dinner Tuesday–Saturday, dinner Sundays. Suave European bistro in the middle of horse country. Don't miss the thin-crust pizzas (date and chorizo, meatballs with ricotta). Other menu highlights: housemade pappardelle with wild boar Bolognese, and "under a brick" Amish chicken. The no-reservations policy can mean long waits on weekends. $$–$$$.

♈ **Taqueria Moroleon** (610-268-3066; taqueriamoroleon.com), 8173 Newport Gap Pike (PA 41), Avondale. Open daily for lunch and dinner. A popular Mexican restaurant near the Delaware border. Named after owner Isidro Rodriguez's hometown in Mexico, it manages to appeal to both foodies who praise its citrus-marinated skirt steak tacos, chiles rellenos, and rich seafood soup, and Saturday night diners who just want a strawberry margarita and Tex-Mex fajitas. No one should miss the Moroleón Molcajete, a mortar full of sizzling chicken, shrimp, beef, and cumin-scented chorizo in a pool of spicy tomatillo salsa. Be prepared for a wait on weekends, or take a seat at the boisterous bar. $–$$.

♥ **The Whip Tavern** (610-383-0600), 1383 North Chatham Road, Coatesville. Closed Tuesdays. Catch a Phillies game while you dig into bangers and mash, bubble and squeak, Welsh rarebit, or vinegar fries in this true-blood English pub and beloved local haunt. Expect to find plenty of local gentry at the bar, some still wearing breeches and polo shirts after a day of riding. $$–$$$.

EATING OUT ♂ ✿ **Hank's Place** (610-388-7061), Baltimore Pike at PA 100, Chadds Ford. Breakfast and lunch daily, dinner Tuesday–Saturday. A local institution known for its calories-be-damned breakfasts—shiitake mushroom omelets, eggs Benedict topped off with chipped beef, and crispy scrapple are a few favorites. Lunch and dinner include homemade meat loaf, chicken potpie, and macaroni and cheese with stewed tomatoes. Fun fact: Andrew Wyeth liked to have breakfast here. Cash only. $.

WEST CHESTER

♂ **Jimmy John's** (610-459-3083), West Chester Pike (US 202). Open daily for breakfast, lunch, and dinner. This institution on US 202 (*not* affiliated with the Chicago-based national chain) has been serving "pipin' hot sandwiches" to omnivores since 1940. The specialty is hot dogs, but you can also get burgers, cheesesteaks, and pork roll sandwiches, all for bargain prices. You can add bacon to anything for an extra 50 cents. Kids will love the electric trains that circle the dining area. $.

♥ **Kooma** (610-430-8980), 151 Gay Street. A lively bar scene and quality

sushi attract a young and hip crowd. The stir-fry dishes are also tasty. $$.

NEARBY

♂ ♥ **Buckley's Tavern** (302-656-9776), 5812 Kennett Pike, Centreville, Delaware. Patrons of this 19th-century watering hole include employees of Winterthur (it's right down the road), out-of-towners, and the ascot-wearing horsey set. The Southern-influenced menu features everything from wild mushroom calzone and burgers to shrimp, grits, and seared gaucho steak with sweet potato fries. Sunday brunch entrées, such as smoked salmon quiche and blueberry johnnycakes, are half-price for anyone wearing pajamas. The adjoining tavern is a lively local gathering place. $$.

Nomadic Pies (610-857-7600; nomadicpies.com), 132 West State Street, Kennett Square. Divine sweet and savory pies. Meet a friend for a slice of quiche or chocolate lavender, or order a whole steak and Gruyère to go.

Talula's Table (610-444-8255; talulastable.com), 102 West State Street, Kennett Square. Open daily 7–7. This gourmet food shop specializes in take-out foods such as exotic mushroom risotto and chicken potpie; you may also eat at the long table in the back. In the morning there are croissants, lemon ginger scones, sticky buns, and all kinds of coffee and tea. Its intimate Farm Table dinners for eight to 12 people, which take place after the market closes, are legendary and typically require reservations months in advance.

Station Taproom (484-593-0560; stationtaproom.com), 2017 West Lancaster Avenue, Downingtown. Two local beer connoisseurs run this snug and casual pub, which not surprisingly is known for its excellent beer selection and menu of global comfort dishes like smoked brisket and breakfast poutine. $$.

World of Beer (610-991-2863; worldofbeer.com), 102 Main Street,

Exton. Lively gathering spot right off US 30 at Exton Crossing serving classic tavern food and a huge selection of global brews. The patio, with couches, firepits, and games, is a huge draw in warm weather. $$.

CHOCOLATE The Brandywine Valley is known more for its mushroom production than its confectionaries, but here are three excellent chocolatiers that call Chester County home:

Eclat Chocolate (610-692-5206; eclatchocolate.com), 24 South High Street, West Chester. Truffles, caramels, and signature chocolates from master chocolatier Christopher Curtain. The handcrafted obsession bars are a treat, mixing dark chocolate with unique ingredients such as crushed Pennsylvania Dutch pretzels, porcini and thyme, and caramelized hazelnuts. Samples are usually available in the elegant, meticulously arranged shop on West Chester's main thoroughfare.

Neuchatel Chocolates (610-932-2706), 461 Limestone Road, Oxford. Open daily. The US headquarters of the Swiss chocolatier is located just off US 1 near Lincoln University. Its store sells truffles, buttercreams, and its signature Swiss Chips, local Herr's potato chips dipped in rich Swiss chocolate. There are also seasonal items like Neuchatel panettone.

Bevan's Own Make Candy (610-566-0581; bevansownmakecandy.com), 143 East Baltimore Pike, Media. A third-generation family-owned business, Bevan's is a nostalgia rush of vintage equipment, original family recipes, and small-town friendliness. Owner Randy Bevan uses many of the same processes and recipes that his grandfather did to turn out truffles, buttercreams, hand-rolled Easter eggs, and other treats.

FARM STANDS & VINEYARDS
Haskell's SIW Vegetables (610-388-7491), 4317 South Creek Road (PA 100), Chadds Ford. Open daily June–October. Sweet corn, melons, peppers, and dozens of varieties of heirloom tomatoes, all grown across the street at Hill Girt Farm.

The Woodlands (610-444-2192; thewoodlandsatphillips.com), 1020 Kaolin Road, Kennett Square. Closed Sundays. The retail store of the Phillips Gourmet Mushroom empire is in a restored 1820s farmhouse about a mile south of PA 1. You'll find every type of mushroom here, from plain white to oyster, plus pickled mushrooms, mushroom-centric cookbooks, and even mushroom freezer pops. There's also a 20-minute film about the process of growing mushrooms, as well as cooking demonstrations in the kitchen and specialty cooking classes. There are no public tours of the mushroom farms, but this is the next best way to learn more about this dominant southeastern Pennsylvania industry.

BYO Where to buy wine in the Brandywine Valley:

Collier's (302-656-3542), 5810 Kennett Pike, Centreville, Delaware, has a large selection of local and international wines, as does **Tim's Liquors** (302-239-5478), 6303 Limestone Road, Hockessin, Delaware. There's also a **Wine & Spirits** store (610-436-1706) at 933 Paoli Pike, West Chester. In Kennett Square, **Country Butcher Fine Food** (610-444-5980) sells wine from local wineries.

✳ Entertainment

MUSIC The Brandywine Valley isn't known for its active nightlife or live music scene. The best late-night options are in downtown Media or West Chester along Gay and High Streets, where stores stay open until 9 on the first Friday of every month.

Y **Brickette Lounge** (610-696-9656; brickettelounge.com), 1339 Pottstown Pike, West Chester. A fun bar and restaurant featuring live country bands and classic rock. There's karaoke on most

Fridays and line dancing on Tuesday and Thursday. No cover charge.

🍸 **Iron Hill Brewery** (610-738-9600), 3 West Gay Street, West Chester. This popular local brewery has live music some nights.

THEATER **Media Theatre** (610-891-0100; mediatheatre.org), 104 East State Street. A former vaudeville house that stages five Broadway shows a year and children's plays such as *Snow White* and *Robin Hood*.

✳ Selective Shopping

Terrain at Styer's (877-583-7724; shop terrain.com), 914 Baltimore Pike (PA 1), Glen Mills. The founders of Urban Outfitters are behind this unique home décor shop and nursery. It's an oasis of wine-barrel chandeliers, French birdcages, zinc fountains, teak furniture, and lavender plants in the middle of an ugly stretch of urban development and busy traffic. Leave time for lunch or dinner in the flower-filled greenhouse café.

CHADDS FORD

Brandywine River Antiques Market (610-388-2000; brandywineriverantiques .com), 878 Baltimore Pike, Chadds Ford. Closed Mondays and Tuesdays. Local antiques shoppers like this large, multivendor warehouse for its reasonable prices and wide selection of pottery, glass, books, and country and Victorian furniture. It's near the busy intersection of US 1 and PA 100 and right in front of the Brandywine River Hotel.

Brandywine View (610-388-6060; brandywineview.com), 1244 Baltimore Pike (US 1). Open Wednesday–Sunday. "Three floors, have fun!" is the standard greeting customers get when entering this large, eclectic emporium. Dive in and browse for Victorian ice cream molds, vintage signs, locally made candles, and more.

BIRDHOUSES FOR SALE AT TERRAIN AT STYERS

Pennsbury-Chadds Ford Antique Mall (610-388-1620), 641 East Baltimore Pike (US 1). More than 100 dealers selling everything from Civil War artifacts and vintage clothes to antique dolls and Oriental rugs. The upper level is open Thursday–Monday; the lower level is open Saturday and Sunday.

KENNETT SQUARE

McLimans (610-444-3876; mclimans .com), 940 West Cypress Street. Open Wednesday–Sunday. Two stories of used and antique furniture at reasonable prices. The current inventory can be viewed on the website, so you can browse before you go.

The Mushroom Cap (610-444-8484), 114 West State Street. Closed Sundays. This small store in downtown Kennett Square is devoted to the town's largest export. You'll find mushroom magnets, charm necklaces, and cookbooks, plus marinated mushrooms, mushroom pâté, and fresh-picked shiitake and whites from owner Kathi Lafferty's family farm.

There's a great little museum in the back with displays of tools, product labels, a miniature model of a mushroom house, and a video that explains how the crop is produced.

WEST CHESTER

Baldwin's Book Barn (610-696-0816; bookbarn.com), 865 Lenape Road (PA 100). Open daily 10 a.m.–6 p.m. This 19th-century Quaker-built dairy barn is now a book lover's utopia, with 300,000 used and rare books crammed into five floors of crooked shelves and creaky planked floors. William and Lilla Baldwin began their bookselling business in Delaware in 1934; they moved it across the state line to the stone barn in 1946. Their son Tom now runs the place, despite ongoing rumors that it is for sale. Begin your visit in the welcoming front room, where there's a large wood-burning stove and a sizable collection of antique maps and drawings, then just start wandering. Most sections are labeled—there's everything from fiction to old yearbooks to "books about books"—and you're more apt to find an out-of-print book on the Civil War than

THE FRONT ROOM OF BALDWIN'S BOOK BARN

a current best-seller (that's part of the charm). Chairs are thoughtfully positioned throughout the place (and Adirondacks are outside on the lawn) for those who feel like curling up with their finds. This is one of the best bookstores on the planet and is alone worth a trip to the Brandywine Valley.

QVC Outlet (610-889-3872), 245 Lancaster Avenue (in the Lincoln Court Shopping Center). One of a handful of outlets run by the shopping network. Everything is discounted, but the selection changes daily—one day you might find a treasure trove of 18-karat jewelry; another might feature Ellen DeGeneres handbags and Spanx undergarments. There's also a branch in Lancaster's Rockvale Square shopping center.

✳ Special Events

May: **Point-to-Point Steeplechase** (first Sunday), Centreville, Delaware—the social event of the season includes a parade of antique carriages, steeplechase racing, and tailgating on the elegant grounds of the Winterthur estate.

September: **Mushroom Festival** (first weekend after Labor Day), Kennett Square—the mushroom is the star of this two-day event featuring tours of local farms, a mushroom soup cook-off, an antiques and art show, and food offerings like pumpkin-mushroom ice cream. Also in September is the **Revolutionary Times at Brandywine** (second weekend), when costumed soldiers reenact the 1777 Battle of Brandywine at the battlefield site.

December: **Candlelight Christmas in Chadds Ford** (first weekend)—the Chadds Ford Historical Society (610-388-7376) sponsors a driving tour of fieldstone farmhouses, Victorian mansions, and other historic buildings decorated in 18th-century style.

BUCKS COUNTY

LOWER BUCKS

CENTRAL & UPPER BUCKS

INTRODUCTION

Situated in the southeastern corner of Pennsylvania and less than an hour's drive from Philadelphia, Bucks County has long been associated with old farmhouses, rolling green hillsides, and a peaceful, *Green Acres* way of life. It was one of three original Pennsylvania counties founded by William Penn in 1862 and takes its name not from the deer that still populate its forests and rolling hillsides, but from the Penn family's native village of Buckinghamshire, England. Its place in history was cemented on Christmas Day 1776, when George Washington rallied his troops to cross the Delaware River in Lower Bucks County in the middle of a fierce winter storm. The Continental army then headed downriver and surprised the British soldiers camping out in Trenton, New Jersey, marking a major turning point of the Revolutionary War.

The river dominates the county's east side and separates Bucks County from central New Jersey. A historic 60-mile towpath parallels the river between Bristol to the south and Easton in the Lehigh Valley. Once trod by mule teams pulling cargo-laden boats along the canal, the towpath is used today by walkers, joggers, bicyclists, and cross-country skiers. Ever since Dorothy Parker bought 40 acres in Pipersville and took up gardening in the 1930s, burned-out city dwellers have been coming to Bucks County, especially the central and northern parts, to decompress and listen to the grass grow. The area has been home to lyricist Oscar Hammerstein II, writers Pearl S. Buck and James A. Michener (who was raised in Doylestown), anthropologist Margaret Mead, and authors Stan and Jan Berenstain (famed for their *Berenstain Bears* children's books). Residential development over the past couple decades has changed the landscape of Central and Upper Bucks County (for the worse, if you ask any local who predates 1985), but the bucolic feel remains on its backcountry roads and in its quaint stone inns, and keeps visitors coming back again and again.

Just about every B&B here will claim that Washington slept, ate, tippled, soaked his feet, or hatched a battle in the very spot where you are standing. Quite often, they are right. Fortunately, many of the inns have been upgraded since the general's visits with luxuries such as indoor plumbing, 300-thread-count bed linens, and whirlpool tubs. The ones that remain on the rustic side often have their own appeal, like very reasonable rates and a chance to encounter the many "friendly" ghosts of soldiers and other Revolutionary War–era figures said to haunt the streets of New Hope and its vicinity.

Unlike Washington and his troops, many business owners in Bucks County have no interest in braving a freezing winter along the Delaware and shut down for the better part of January or February. I mention this whenever possible in the listings, but it's a good idea to call ahead during this slow time of year. Also note that heavy rains often lead to flash flooding in low-lying parts of the county, such as River Road and the New Hope area.

Bucks County has a total population of more than 630,000 and tends to be viewed in three parts: Lower Bucks, easily accessible via I-95, is the most urban of the three and home to Pennsylvania's second-largest casino, a *Sesame Street*–themed amusement park, and the many chain hotels that come with these attractions. Central Bucks has the hip riverfront village of New Hope and the brilliant museums and county-seat bustle of Doylestown. Upper Bucks remains largely rural and sleepy, with family-friendly campgrounds, old-fashioned general stores, and narrow, winding country roads that are perfect for Sunday drives but that you wouldn't ever, ever want to drive under the influence of anything stronger than a cup of tea.

It's tough to cover all three parts of Bucks County in one trip; the rural, two-lane roads that give much of the area its beauty also mean that drives can take two or three times longer than a map or online program suggests. For many visitors, that's part of the charm.

LOWER BUCKS

AREA CODE The entire Lower Bucks region lies within 215.

GUIDANCE Bucks County Conference and Visitor Bureau (800-836-2825; visitbucks county.com), 3207 Street Road, Bensalem. This shiny new center in the southeast corner of Bucks County is a good source of information for the entire region. Their annual visitor guide offers detailed listings of many of the area's attractions, lodging, and eating options.

GETTING THERE *By car:* I-95, via Philadelphia or Trenton, New Jersey, cuts right through the lower end of Bucks County. The Pennsylvania Turnpike has three exits for Bucks County: Exit 343 for PA 611 north (Doylestown), Exit 351 for US 1 north (Quakertown), and Exit 358 for US 13 north.

By train: SEPTA's R3 line (215-580-7800; septa.org) runs regularly between Philadelphia's 30th Street Station and Yardley; the R2 stops in Warrington.

By bus: SEPTA bus route 14 to Bensalem and Langhorne.

By air: Lower Bucks County is accessible from two major airports: **Philadelphia International** (215-937-6800) and New Jersey's **Newark International** (800-397-4636).

GETTING AROUND *By car:* The small towns of Yardley and Newtown are pedestrian friendly, but a car is your best way of getting around the south end of Bucks County. Major sights such as Pennsbury Manor, Sesame Place, and Washington Crossing are easiest to reach by car.

By foot: Lower Bucks County's many parks offer a variety of hiking trails for all fitness levels (see *Green Space*). For an urban walking experience, head to Newtown's Historic District. Many people like to walk the Delaware Canal towpath between Yardley and Washington Crossing, a 3-mile stretch.

WHEN TO GO The fall brings a riot of color to the area's forests and rolling hills, while December means a flood of lights and festivals in places such as New Hope, Peddler's Village, and Byers' Choice. If you plan to be here in early spring, check with local sources about the condition of roads and towns near the Delaware River, which is prone to flooding.

✳ Towns & Villages

Bristol. First settled in 1681, Bristol is one of the oldest towns in Bucks County and home to the venerable King George Inn, which claims to be the oldest continuously run inn in the country. The focal point of the town is a waterfront area near Mill and Radcliffe Streets, where you will find the King George, a number of stores and cafés, a theater, and a pretty waterfront promenade.

Newtown. This thriving town was the county seat from 1725 to 1813. Its Historic District, intersected by State and Washington Streets, is lined with many preserved colonial-era residences, taverns, and inns. Newtown sponsors a pedestrian-friendly

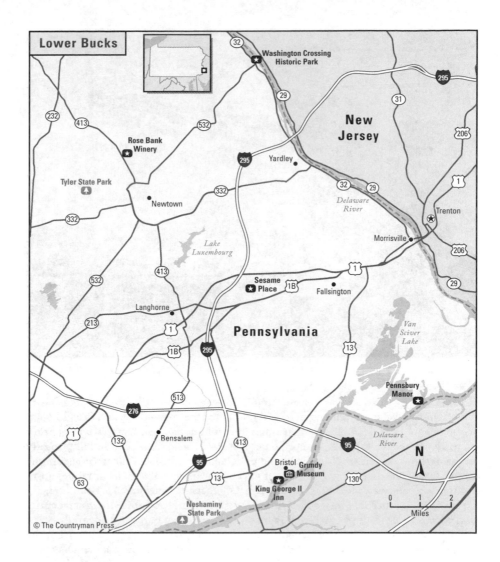

bash on the first Friday of the month, when many downtown shops and galleries stay open late.

Yardley. Anchored by a restored gristmill, this quaint town south of I-95 has several good restaurants, a man-made pond, and a pretty main street lined with trees and Victorian homes. It was a station for the Underground Railroad during the Civil War and is home to the family-owned Cramer's Bakery and the Yardley Inn. The Delaware River, bordering the town to the east, adds to its beauty.

✳ To See

HISTORIC SITES ♿ ✎ ♂ **Pennsbury Manor** (215-946-0400; pennsburymanor.org), 400 Pennsbury Memorial Road, Morrisville. Open Tuesday–Sunday; admission charged. As much as William Penn contributed to this state in name and philosophy,

DAD'S HAT, A RYE WHISKEY DISTILLERY, OPERATES OUT OF A FORMER WOOLEN MILL IN BRISTOL DAD'S HAT RYE

few sites or museums offer a window into his time here. That's why this 43-acre site, to which the Quaker governor and his family retreated to escape the "city life" and political mayhem of Philadelphia, is more than just an English gentleman's 17th-century country estate. The redbrick manor house that Penn designed and built fell into ruin in the early 1700s, but was reconstructed painstakingly by historical architects in the 1930s. It includes an herb garden, one of the state's largest collections of 17th-century furnishings, and views of the Delaware River. On weekends, costumed artisans demonstrate open-hearth cooking, woodworking, sheep shearing, and other trades and crafts of the time. Don't forget to check out Penn's personal sailing barge in a covered garage near the main house. Tours of the house are given several times each day during the summer and twice a day on weekends in winter. Perhaps because of its remote location, it is often blissfully uncrowded.

    ⚓ ☂ **Margaret R. Grundy Memorial Museum** (215-788-7891; grundymuseum.org), 610 Radcliffe Street, Bristol. The Grundys were a prominent Bucks County family and owners of a large woolen mills complex that thrived from the late 1800s through 1930. Their home is a preserved Victorian showpiece of finely carved woodwork, jeweled glass windows, and original belongings, including dresses and dance cards of Margaret Grundy. Admission is free and includes a guided tour of the interior and access to the gardens and adjacent library. Open Tuesday–Thursday and Saturday, April–December. The riverfront park on the property is open to the public year-round Monday–Saturday, and visitors are encouraged to picnic or just relax and enjoy the scenic views of the Delaware.

WINERIES Many of Bucks County's wineries started as hobbies or pipe dreams but have grown into serious producers of chardonnay, cabernet, and other drinkable wines, much to the pleased surprise of everyone involved. The historic buildings and peaceful rural settings of the properties are sometimes as enjoyable as the wines themselves. Some wineries are only open for tastings on weekends, while others are open daily. Check websites for specific hours or visit www.buckscountywinetrail.com for more information.

Bishop Estate Winery (215-249-3559; bishopestatepa.com), 2730 Hilltown Pike, Perkasie. A new addition to the Bucks County wine scene, this family-run operation makes 16 kinds of wines on its scenic 100-year-old farm in rural Central Bucks. It's open daily for tastings, and most weekends visitors are treated to live music in a relaxed setting with firepits. Sometimes there are food trucks, or you can bring your own food.

&. **Buckingham Valley Vineyards** (215-794-7188; pawine.com), 1521 PA 413, Buckingham (Central Bucks). Open Tuesday–Sunday. One of Pennsylvania's largest and oldest wineries was begun in the 1970s by two Penn graduates. The Forest family still runs the place, conveniently located between New Hope and Doylestown, offering a selection of wines from deep, oak-aged reds to dry whites, as well as self-guided tours. It's a laid-back environment, with self-service tastings and picnic tables that encourage lingering.

&. ♂ **Crossing Vineyards** (215-493-6500; crossingvineyards.com), 1853 Wrightstown Road, between Washington Crossing and Newtown (Lower Bucks). The Carroll family began selling wines in 2003 and regularly wins awards for its viognier and pinot noir. Set on a 200-acre estate, the facility has separate barrel and bottling rooms and a tasting room overlooking 15 acres of vineyards. It also serves as a community gathering place, with evening lectures, singles events, and "meet the winemaker" dinners.

&. **New Hope Winery** (215-794-2331; newhopewinery.com), 6123 Lower York Road. A music destination as much as a winery, this large property has a bar and restaurant, the Pour House, and hosts accomplished blues guitarists and singer-songwriters such as John Waite and Melissa Manchester. Wine is available during concerts.

&. ♂ **Rose Bank Winery** (215-860-5899; rosebankwinery.com), 258 Durham Road, Newtown (Lower Bucks). Even teetotalers will be charmed by this 1790 manor estate north of Newtown. Besides a winery, it's a sheep farm and a popular setting for weddings. Its specialty is a sweet wine made with New Jersey blueberries. Events, such as baby-goat yoga and handmade artisan markets, are held throughout the year. Check the website for details.

Wycombe Vineyards (215-598-9463; wycombevineyards.com), 1391 Forest Grove Road, Furlong. This family-owned vineyard produces classic vinifera and French hybrid varietals, dry whites, reds, and sweet dessert wines. The secluded property has picnic areas, a large deck, and a cozy, rustic tasting room that's open Friday–Sunday. The sangria slushies are popular in summer.

&. ♂ **Sand Castle Winery** (800-722-9463; sandcastlewinery.com), 755 River Road, Erwinna (Upper Bucks). The 11,000-square-foot main facility really looks like a sand castle. Ascend the winding road just above the Golden Pheasant Inn and sample Johannesburg riesling, chardonnay, cabernet, and pinot noir drawn from the surrounding vineyards.

VINEYARDS AT THE SAND CASTLE WINERY IN BUCKS COUNTY

GENERAL WASHINGTON CROSSES THE DELAWARE

Washington Crossing Historic Park (215-493-4076; www.washingtoncrossingpark .org), 1112 River Road, Washington Crossing. Open daily; free. Of all the Washington-slept-here places in Bucks County, this is the place history buffs will most want to witness. It was here that George Washington rallied his troops to cross the Delaware River in the middle of a fierce winter storm on Christmas Day 1776, surprising the British soldiers over in Trenton and resulting in one of the most significant battles of the Revolutionary War. Even on a gentle summer day, it's easy to stand at the spot where Washington's demoralized troops embarked on their 11-hour journey, gaze across the powerful river, and marvel at the determination it must have taken to pick up those oars. ✐ ♿ ☂

The park is spread out along River Road and home to several picnic areas, easy walking trails, and 13 historic buildings, including McConkey's Ferry Inn, the guard outpost where General Washington and his aides ate dinner and made plans prior to the crossing, and the Thompson-Neely House, a private home that served as a convalescent hospital in the winter of 1776 and 1777. Start at the visitor center on River Road north of PA 532, where you can watch a short film, pick up maps, and check out the digitally mastered photomural of Emanuel Leutze's famous painting, *Washington Crossing the Delaware* (staffers will grumble that New York's Metropolitan Museum of Art has the real thing). Just outside the visitor center is the stone marker that commemorates the spot where the troops crossed, as well as a 20th-century barn with several replica Durham boats that were used to transport soldiers, horses, and equipment across the river on that famous night.

A short drive north on River Road is **Bowman's Hill Tower**, a 125-foot tower that was built in 1931 as a monument to the Revolutionary War and offers sweeping views of the Delaware River Valley. It's open May–December, though the hours can be erratic. Guided tours include entrance to the tower and tours of McConkey's Ferry Inn and the **Thompson-Neely House**. Also worth a stop is the memorial grave site of 40 to 60 unknown soldiers who died during that bitter winter. It can be accessed via the Delaware Canal towpath east of the Thompson-Neely House.

Daily tours of the barrels and underground wine cellar are available. It's worth a stop for the views of the vineyards and Delaware River alone, and the upstairs art gallery is a hushed oasis of Bohemian glass and paintings by artists from Slovakia, the homeland of the winery's owners, Joseph and Paul Maxian.

Unami Ridge Winery (215-804-5545; unamiridge.com), 2144 Kumry Road, Trumbauersville (Upper Bucks). One of the smallest wineries in the county is located at its northwesternmost tip near Quakertown. It's a charming spot, however, where you can sip fine chardonnay on a patio overlooking the vineyard. Owners Jim and Kathy Jenks also produce scheurebe, riesling, cabernet franc, and pinot noir.

✻ To Do

FOR FAMILIES ✐ ♿ **Sesame Place** (215-752-7070; sesameplace.com), 100 Sesame Road, Langhorne. Open May–October; admission charged. If you catch this 14-acre theme park on a weekday or early in the day when the lines are manageable and the noise levels bearable, there is fun to be had. It's the first theme park in the world to be designated as a certified autism center and the only one featuring Elmo and his *Sesame Street* pals in live dance shows, a daily parade, and more than 28 different rides and water attractions that splash, climb, bounce, and twirl. Highlights include a Grover-led

The park is visited most often in December, when dozens of "soldiers" and a carefully selected General Washington cross the river in an annual reenactment of the event. The visitor center was expanded and modernized in 2012 and includes historical exhibits, a gift shop, and an exact replica of Emanuel Leutze's famous painting of George Washington crossing the Delaware River.

SITE WHERE WASHINGTON CROSSED THE DELAWARE RIVER

roller coaster; Cookie's Monster Land, filled with cookie-themed rides; and special opportunities to meet, greet, and eat with Elmo, Big Bird, and other friends.

Shady Brook Farm (215-968-1670; shadybrookfarm.com), 1 Stony Hill Road, Yardley. Pick your own peaches, raspberries, and apples at one of the last remaining working farms in Bucks County. The store and café sell raw milk, local organic beef, homemade ice cream, and all kinds of prepared foods. Seasonal events include summer wine fests on Friday nights, a pumpkin festival at Halloween, and a holiday light show in December.

GAMBLING **Parx Casino and Racetrack** (215-639-9000; parxcasino.com), 3001 Street Road, Bensalem. Dubbed a "racino" because it houses both a casino and thoroughbred horse racetrack, this five-story betting parlor 25 miles east of Philadelphia opened in late 2006 after the Pennsylvania Gaming Board voted to grant permanent casino licenses to six existing horse-racing facilities. It can't compete with Atlantic City's glitz and high-stakes jackpots, but local crowds fill up the parking lot on weekends and keep the 3,200 slot machines clanging. There are also electronic gaming tables (blackjack, poker, and roulette) and weekly poker tournaments. For sustenance, there's an upscale steakhouse, a deli, and a branch of the Philly crab house, Chickie's & Pete's. The adjacent racetrack hosts thoroughbred races year-round, including the $1 million Pennsylvania Derby over Labor Day weekend.

MUST SEE **STILL DISTILLING** Pennsylvania was once one of the biggest producers of premium rye whiskey in the world. Prohibition changed that, but a small distillery in an industrial corner of Bristol is trying earnestly to bring back the 200-year-old tradition. Cofounder and distiller Herman Mihalich named the company **Dad's Hat** in honor of his father's affinity for Stetson fedoras and old-school optimism. It sources its rye from local farms and operates out of a refurbished woolen mill a few blocks from the Delaware River. Its spirits are sold at taverns and stores; it also offers hour-long guided tours of the distillation and aging process on Saturdays, often led by Mihalich himself; reservations are required. The fee includes a whiskey-tasting session in a bar area right off the factory floor (215-781-8300; dadshatrye.com).

TOURS OF DAD'S HAT DISTILLERY INCLUDE LESSONS ON BARREL AGING DAD'S HAT RYE

Green Space

Churchville Nature Center (215-357-4005; churchvillenaturecenter.org), 501 Churchville Lane, Churchville. Open Tuesday–Sunday. Despite its proximity to busy roads and new housing developments, this 65-acre preserve is an oasis of wild gardens, dense woodland, and salt marshes, with 2 miles of hiking trails and a large picnic grove. There's also a visitor center, as well as a re-created Lenape Indian village with traditional wigwams and elm-bark wickiups (the Lenni-Lenape were the original residents of the Delaware River Valley).

Hortuculus Farm (hortuculusfarm.com), 60 Thompson Mill Road, Wrightstown. Open for self-guided tours May–October. Admission charged. Part of William Penn's original land grant, this 100-acre 18th-century farmstead features a 1793 house, two dairy barns, and 24 different gardens. A specialty "connoisseur's nursery" sells hard-to-find perennials, shrubs, annuals, and more, as well as tropicals, standards, and frame-grown specimens.

✔ ☀ **Neshaminy State Park** (215-639-4538), 263 Dunks Ferry Road, Bensalem. Neshaminy Creek meets the Delaware River at this 330-acre park just south of I-95. The short River Walk Trail has a wonderful view of the Philadelphia skyline and is a favorite trail for dog walkers. Pick up a brochure at the park office for more information on the estuary. There's also a swimming pool and picnic areas.

✔ ☀ **Tyler State Park** (215-968-2021), 101 Swamp Road, Newtown. Neshaminy Creek winds through this popular 1,700-acre park, which was once the estate of the Tylers, a wealthy farming family that developed one of the finest Ayrshire dairy herds in the county. It has 10 miles of hilly bike trails, seven picnic areas, playgrounds, and walking paths that lead past original stone buildings and the longest covered bridge in Bucks County. Not enough? You can also rent canoes, fish for carp and smallmouth bass, play disc golf, or walk the dog.

Tyler Formal Gardens (bucks.edu/discover/history/gardens), 275 Swamp Road, Newtown. Formal four-tier gardens on the campus of Bucks County Community College. It's a popular spot for wedding photos, but anyone can stroll the lovely grounds during the college's business hours.

✳ Outdoor Activities

GOLF **Makefield Highlands Golf Club** (215-321-7000; makefieldhighlands.com), 1418 Woodside Road, Yardley. An 18-hole, par-72 course featuring 7,058 yards of golf from the longest tees.

TENNIS **Frosty Hollow Tennis Center** (215-493-3646), New Falls Road, Levittown. Ten indoor public courts.

Bucks County Racquet Club (215-493-5556), Washington Crossing. Indoor and outdoor courts are open to the public by the hour.

Core Creek Tennis Center (215-322-6802), Woodbourne Road, Langhorne. Outdoor public courts.

✳ Lodging

Lower Bucks has more hotels than anywhere else in the county, though the majority tend to be chains catering to I-95 travelers. **Courtyard by Marriott** (215-945-8390), in Langhorne, is one of the closest hotels to Sesame Place and offers free shuttle service to the park for its guests. There are also some interesting, comfortable sleeping options for intrepid travelers who don't mind staying off the beaten path or sharing a yard with a potbellied pig.

BED & BREAKFASTS **Temperance House** (215-860-9975; temperancehouse .com), 5 South Street, Newtown. First opened as an inn in 1772, this red-shingled brick building in the heart of downtown Newtown has served as a gathering place for those fighting colonists' causes and a teetotaling restaurant whose hardest drink was lemonade. Today, "the Temp" is attached to a full-service bar and restaurant (see *Dining Out*) and has 11 unique rooms and suites with private baths that are modern and comfortable while retaining the inn's historic feel. Light sleepers might want to avoid the rooms facing State Street. $$.

☿ **Bridgetown Mill House** (215-752-8996; bridgetownmillhouse.com), 760 Langhorne-Newtown Road (PA 413), Langhorne. One of the few luxury lodging options in Lower Bucks County, this former gristmill property has five guest rooms, 8 acres of lawns and gardens, and a first-rate restaurant (see *Dining Out*). Kim and Carlos DaCosta bought the place in 1995 and spent three years converting it into a high-end bed & breakfast, preserving the Federal architecture that exemplifies many of Bucks County's historic rural estates. Rooms have four-poster canopy beds, private baths, and TVs, and include breakfast. Guests also have access to the library, solarium, formal dining room, sitting room, brick patio, and 0.25-mile jogging track that winds past Neshaminy Creek. $$$.

OTHER LODGING **Cottage at Kabeyun** (215-736-1213; www.buckscountycottage .com), 699 River Road, Yardley. Alfred and Emily Glossbrenner own this white-shingled riverfront cottage about 2 miles south of downtown Yardley. It's perfect for families or couples looking for a home-away-from-home getaway. The 700-square-foot cottage has one master bedroom, one bathroom, a full kitchen, and an office or second bedroom with a twin bed and pop-up trundle. The Gloss-brenners, who live next door, are on hand to answer questions and keep the place stocked with towels, fireplace logs, books, and other amenities. Another bonus: Access to the Delaware Canal towpath is 0.25-mile away. It sometimes books up for a month at a time, so reserve early if you can. A three-night minimum stay is usually required, with weekly rates available.

℘ **Ross Mill Farm** (215-322-1539; rossmillfarm.com), 2464 Walton Road, Rushland. Owners Richard and Susan Magidson call their farm north of Newtown the world's only boardinghouse for pet potbellied pigs. But they also let humans stay on the premises in a 17th-century cottage for the bargain price of $140 a night. The rustic cottage sleeps up to six people and has a full kitchen, working fireplace, and 30 surrounding acres that guests are welcome to share with the pigs. It's a great place

for families (though note that the upstairs bedroom can be accessed only via spiral staircase), and pets are welcome. Unlike the piggy spa, the cottage doesn't come with pool or daily maid service.

✳ Where to Eat

DINING OUT Ⓨ & **Bridgetown Mill House** (215-752-8996; bridgetown millhouse.com), 760 Langhorne-Newtown Road (PA 413), Langhorne. Dinner Tuesday–Saturday. This is a special-occasion restaurant worth the splurge; reservations are recommended. The wait staff dress in tuxedoes, tables are set with fine white linens and crystal stemware, and large picture windows framed in oak line the main dining room. The classic continental menu changes every three months; among the standouts are Prince Edward Island mussels in a white wine sauce and slow-cooked veal osso buco. There's also a summer tapas menu served on the expansive patio. $$$.

& **Charcoal** (215-493-6394; charcoal byob.com), 11 South Delaware Avenue, Yardley. Breakfast, lunch, and dinner Tuesday–Sunday. Breakfast and lunch at this riverfront café means simple diner fare: omelets, turkey burgers, and club sandwiches. Dinner, on the other hand, is bold and modern: Yardley hot chicken drizzled with cayenne caramel, coq au vin with carrot and horseradish caserecce, and rye radiatori with bacon Bolognese. Expect lots of nightly specials and whimsical gastro-science creations. Reservations are recommended at dinner. $$–$$$.

& Ⓨ **King George II Inn** (215-788-5536; kginn.com), 102 Radcliffe Street, Bristol. This 17th-century landmark was a stagecoach stop for travelers between New York and Philadelphia. Have a cocktail in the cozy, wood-paneled bar, then enjoy acorn squash ravioli or slow-roasted prime rib in a dining room with lovely views of the Delaware River. This beloved watering hole has had its ups and downs over the years but happily remains open. $$.

🍸 **Pineville Tavern** (215-598-3890), 1098 Durham Road, Pineville. Most everything on the menu shines here, from the spaghetti and meatballs to the kale salad, but it's the Million Dollar Burger (topped with onion jam and house-cured bacon) that wins awards and gets over-the-top raves. The tavern first opened in 1742, serving travelers along the old stagecoach route that is now PA 413. The dining rooms are warm and cozy, with beamed ceilings, stone walls, and a large antique bar. A big deck out back draws a fun crowd in the summer. Mondays are half-price burger nights and Wednesday is steak night, with $25 for select cuts or a $59 Peter Lugar–style porterhouse. $$–$$$.

🍸 **Temperance House** (215-860-9975), 5 South Street, Newtown. Bargain Tuesday–Thursday dinner specials (three courses for $18) keep this place buzzing on weekday evenings. The classic American menu includes filet mignon, New York strip steak, Guinness BBQ ribs, and pan-seared scallops and shrimp with sun-dried tomato risotto; the more casual tavern menu features roast pork sandwiches, crabcakes, and cheesesteak spring rolls. $$–$$$.

🍸 **Washington Crossing Inn** (215-493-3634), PA 32 and PA 532, Washington Crossing. Open daily for lunch, dinner, and late-night snacks. Not long ago, this 18th-century inn around the corner from the site of Washington's historic crossing was known more for its quirkiness—a parrot greeted patrons at the entrance and portraits of Elvis hung on the walls—than its culinary attributes. But the menu has been revamped and modernized, and it's a good choice if you like pomp and history with your meal. Dinner might be rack of lamb in pistachio crust, sesame tuna and tempura shrimp, or slow-roasted prime rib. Request a table in the inn's anteroom, a step-down former porch featuring murals of Bucks County's covered bridges. Staffers will tell you that General Washington ate one of his last

AN ANTIQUES-FILLED DINING ROOM IN THE HISTORIC PINEVILLE TAVERN

meals here before heading over to Trenton. $$$.

  ♿ ♼ **Yardley Inn** (215-493-3800; yardleyinn.com), Afton Avenue at River Road, Yardley. Lunch and dinner daily, Sunday brunch. Locals favor this circa-1890 restaurant across from the Delaware River for its classic modern décor, friendly environment, and an upscale menu that includes handmade ricotta cavatelli, and crispy cod in a smoky chowder broth. The reasonably priced bar menu features grass-fed burgers, salads, and a variety of tasty appetizers, including beet panzanella and pork belly lettuce wraps. Reservations are recommended on weekends. $$$.

EATING OUT ♦ ♿ ♼ **Bowman's Tavern** (215-862-2972), 1600 River Road, New Hope. A good place for a casual meal (crabcakes, hot roast beef sandwiches, Caesar salads, grilled pork chops) between New Hope and Washington Crossing. There's live music in the piano lounge every night; expect big crowds on weekends. $$–$$$.

  Daddypops Diner (215-675-9717), 232 North York Road, Hatboro. Open daily 6 a.m.–2 p.m. The stuffed French toast, crisp homefries, and low prices make up for indifferent service at this old-school diner near the Bucks County line. People drive miles for its house-made scrapple, which was featured on the Food Network's *Diners, Drive-Ins, and Dives*.

  Maryanne's Homestyle Cooking (267-589-6196), 1263 Woodbourne Road, Levittown. Familiar diner-style eats, plus specialty concoctions like bacon cheddar homefries and cinnamon French toast with homemade cannoli filling. It's open for breakfast and lunch and a short drive from Sesame Place.

  ♦ ♿ ♼ **Isaac Newton's** (215-860-5100; isaacnewtons.com), 18 South State Street, Newtown. The gourmet burgers and stellar selection of microbrews and Belgian-style beers keep this place buzzing every night. It's in a two-story building in the municipal parking lot behind State Street. The outside deck is a popular spot on summer evenings.

  Jack's Cold Cuts (215-639-2346; jackscoldcuts.com), 1951 Street Road, Bensalem. This New York–style deli near Parx Casino features 80 varieties of sandwiches (turkey with roasted peppers, hot brisket, roast pork and sauerkraut, and white fish salad, to name a few). Prices are reasonable. $.

  Jules Thin Crust Pizza (215-579-0111; julesthincrust.com), 300 Sycamore Street, Newtown. Open daily for lunch and dinner. This BYO is the place to go when you want your pizza with a dash of sophistication. The delicate pies are served on wood slabs with toppings such as fig jam, organic artichokes, and arugula. There are also branches in Doylestown, Ardmore, and Jenkintown.

  The Borough (215-788-9955), 1800 Farragut Avenue, Bristol. A welcoming neighborhood pub in downtown Bristol with reliably good comfort eats like hand-tossed pizza with house-made marinara, half-pound steak sandwiches, and cooked-to-order wings.

BYO Where to buy wine in Lower Bucks:
  Wine & Spirits stores are in Yardley at 635 Heacock Road (215-493-3182) and Morrisville at 229 Plaza Boulevard in Pennsbury Plaza (215-736-3127).

CAFÉS & BAKERIES Cramer's Bakery (215-493-2760), 26 East Afton Avenue, Yardley. Specialties at this venerable bakery include seven-layer cake, raisin bars, and pumpkin chocolate cookies. They also sell delicious German butter cake, a yeast-based cake with a pudding center that was a popular Philadelphia dessert until people started to realize its calorie count was higher than the state deficit.

  Colonial Farms (215-493-1548), 1108 Taylorsville Road (at PA 532), Washington Crossing. Pick up a ham and Brie sandwich or a sack of pastries at this gourmet market and bring a picnic to nearby Washington Crossing State Park.

Lochel's Bakery (215-773-9779; lochelsbakery.com), 57 South York Road, Hatboro. Closed Mondays. Stop here for a delicious cream-filled doughnut or cannoli cupcake. The cinnamon buns and French apple pie are also good, and the cakes are design masterpieces of buttercream icing and rosebuds.

Pretty Bird Coffee Roasters, (267-714-2800), 7 South Main Street, Yardley. Exquisite lattes, pastries, and gourmet sandwiches make this hip daytime spot stand out from the pack.

♪ ♿ **Zebra-Striped Whale** (215-860-4122), 12 South State Street, Newtown. Named after a children's book written by owner Shari F. Donahue, this inviting café serves micro-roasted coffee, frozen hot chocolate, and custom-made ice cream "whirlwinds" of candy, fruit, or nuts.

✳ Entertainment

MUSIC & NIGHTLIFE **Broken Goblet** (267-812-5653; brokengoblet.com), 2500 State Road, Bensalem. Known for its tea-infused ales, this hip brewery often hosts singer-songwriters on weekends. Check the website for a schedule.

Washington Crossing Inn (215-493-3634), PA 32 and PA 532. The piano bar features live performances (usually on the mellow side) every weekend and some weeknights.

Newtown Chamber Orchestra (215-968-2005; newtownchamberorchestra .org) performs at various sites throughout the area, including Bucks County Community College. Check website for details.

♿ **Xcite Center at Parx Casino** (888-588-PARX; parxcasino.com) in Bensalem hosts DJs and live performers such as Patti LaBelle and Reba McEntire. Check website for schedules.

Vault Brewing Company (267-573-4291; vaultbrewing.com), 10 South Main Street, Yardley. This cutting-edge brewpub features seasonal cuisine, an open view of its brewery, and live jazz every Friday and Saturday.

THEATER ♿ **Bristol Riverside Theatre** (215-785-0100; brtstage.org), 120 Radcliffe Street, Bristol. This restored 300-seat theater hosts professionally staged musicals, dramas, and art exhibits. Fun children's shows too.

Langhorne Players (215-860-0818; langhorneplayers.org) stages five dramas and comedies a season at the Spring Garden Mill at Tyler State Park. Past shows include *Marjorie Prime* and *The 39 Steps*.

Newtown Theatre (215-968-3859, thenewtowntheatre.com), 120 North State Street, Newtown. One of the nation's oldest movie theaters screens first-run films, plus several plays and musicals a year staged by the Newtown Arts Company. Lucky for us, the owners installed air-conditioning in 2002 for a gala screening of *Signs*, the M. Night Shyamalan movie that was filmed in and around Newtown.

✳ Selective Shopping

Another Time Antiques (215-788-3131), 301 Mill Street, Bristol. Fun-to-browse shop selling period lamps, vintage jewelry, and a large selection of furniture.

Bristol Amish Market (215-826-9971; bristolamishmarket.com), 498 Green Lane, Bristol. Open Thursday–Saturday. Food, furniture, and sheds are the specialties of this indoor market just off I-95. It's a great place to shop for handcrafted Shaker- and Mission-style tables and indulge in hand-rolled pretzels, apple cider doughnuts, and made-to-order hoagies at the same time.

The Shops at Carousel Village (carouselvillage.com), 591 Durham Road, Wrightstown. This charming complex of shops and kid-friendly attractions is worth its own special trip, or combine it with a meal at Pineville Tavern or a weekend tasting session at nearby Buckingham or Wycombe Vineyards. An antique carousel and mini-train operate on weekends. There's also a plant nursery, organic market, and several shops selling antiques, high-end shoes, and clothing. **OwowCow Creamery** also has a branch here.

Trainpops Attic (215-788-2014; trainpopsattic.com), 400 Mill Street, Bristol. This 6,000-square-foot emporium carries a full range of model trains and accessories, including HO-, N- and O-gauge tracks. The staff is knowledgeable and there's much to look at, even if you're not buying—from vintage photographs to up-and-running layouts.

Newtown Book and Record Exchange (215-968-4914; newtownbookandrecord .com), 102 South State Street. Looking for a Stephen King paperback or a 1960s Band of Joy LP? You just may find it at this well-organized storefront where owner Bobbie Lewis has been selling used books, records, and CDs for 30 years.

Touchstone Art Gallery (215-321-3285), 11 East Afton Avenue, Yardley. Unique crafts, jewelry, and ceramics by local artists near Cramer's Bakery.

✳ Special Events

August: **Middletown Grange Fair** (mid- to late August), Wrightstown fairgrounds— real country agricultural fair, with farm products, livestock judging, horse shows, and BBQ dinners.

October: **Crafts in the Meadow** (third weekend), Tyler State Park, Newtown— the Pennsylvania Guild of Craftsmen's biggest outdoor exhibition features more than 180 displays of paintings, sculptures, and other works, plus live music and fine foods.

December: **Reenactment of Washington's Crossing** (Christmas Day), Washington Crossing State Park—thousands of people gather on the banks of the Delaware to watch costumed volunteers re-create George Washington's historic boat ride across the icy river. The reenactment begins around 1 p.m. and finishes across the river in Titusville, New Jersey. Musket-firing ceremonies and speeches are held on both sides of the river. It's the cornerstone event of this park, and much time and consideration go into selecting the volunteer who portrays General Washington.

CENTRAL & UPPER BUCKS

AREA CODE The entire region lies within the 215 area code, except for the northern-most corner, which uses 610.

GUIDANCE New Hope Visitor Center (215-862-5030), 1 Mechanic Street. Open daily. Housed in New Hope's first city hall, school, and jailhouse, this is a great source for free walking maps, calendars, gallery schedules, and local newspapers. New Hope–emblazed mugs, shot glasses, tote bags, and snow globes are available for purchase. **Doylestown Business Alliance** (215-340-9988; www.discoverdoylestown.org), 17 West State Street, offers detailed walking maps and visitor guides.

GETTING THERE *By car:* I-95, via Philadelphia or Trenton, New Jersey, cuts right through the lower end of Bucks County. To get to points north, take the River Road/PA 32 exit and head toward New Hope. US 202 is also a good way to reach New Hope or Doylestown from the east.

By bus: **Trans-Bridge Lines** (800-962-9135; transbridgelines.com) operates daily bus service to Lambertville, New Jersey, from New York City and from Newark and JFK airports. The bus stops at Main and Bridge Streets in Lambertville, which sits just over the bridge from New Hope.

By train: SEPTA regional R5 line runs between Philadelphia's 30th Street Station and downtown Doylestown.

By air: Bucks County is accessible from two major airports: **Philadelphia International** (215-937-6800) and **New Jersey's Newark International** (800-397-4636). **Lehigh Valley International Airport** in Allentown (888-359-5842) is convenient to Quakertown and other villages in Upper Bucks County.

GETTING AROUND *By car:* The two-lane roads that link New Hope with Doylestown and other Central Bucks towns are easy to navigate and lined with antiques shops and farm estates. US 202 runs east–west across Central Bucks County, passing through the towns of New Hope, Lahaska, Doylestown, and Chalfont. PA 611 is the easiest way to reach Doylestown from Philadelphia and points west.

By foot or bicycle: **Delaware Canal State Park** (610-982-5560; www.dcnr.state.pa.us). The Delaware Canal runs parallel to the Delaware River and was used to transport coal and other cargo from inland Pennsylvania to Philadelphia and New York in the 19th century. Its 60-mile towpath makes a fine bicycle or walking route that runs between Bristol and Easton and passes through Washington Crossing, New Hope, and other river towns. Parking is easiest (read: free and unlimited) at **Washington Crossing Historic Park** (see page 98) and **Virginia Forrest Recreation Area** on River Road north of Centre Bridge. Many cyclists like to cross the bridges at Lumberville or Upper Black Eddy over to New Jersey, then take the Jersey-side towpath south back to Lambertville or Washington Crossing. An easy 8-mile loop begins in New Hope and follows the towpath north to Centre Bridge, then crosses over to Stockton, New Jersey, and takes the path south past an 18th-century gristmill to Lambertville and crosses the bridge back into New Hope. Sometimes the bridges are closed due to maintenance or flooding damage, so it's a good idea to check with the state park office before setting out.

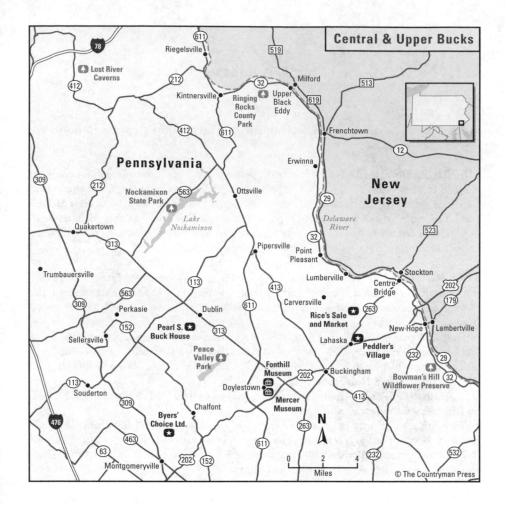

© The Countryman Press

✳ Towns and Villages

Doylestown. Driving west on US 202, you will find this bustling county seat. Alecia Moore (also known as Pink), James A. Michener, and Margaret Mead all spent their formative years here, and it is home to many excellent restaurants and museums. Courthouse and other office workers fill its streets on weekdays, but weekends and evenings bring more of a hip, urban feel.

Lahaska. This small town between New Hope and Doylestown is most often associated with Peddler's Village, a quaint shopping village that once housed a chicken farm known as Hentown. You'll also find a cluster of outlet stores directly across from Peddler's Village, along with several homegrown antiques shops.

Lambertville, New Jersey. This town of about 4,000 is an easy walk or drive from New Hope via a two-lane car and pedestrian bridge. Its wide streets are lined with Victorian-era homes, a few inns and B&Bs, and many independent shops and restaurants. It's easier to find free parking here than it is in New Hope. The Shad Festival in April is one of its biggest events of the year.

New Hope. Situated on a picturesque spot next to the Delaware River, this is perhaps the best known of Central Bucks County's tourist destinations. Gay and straight vacationers like the creative vibe of its downtown, with its hodgepodge of antiques shops, art galleries, open-patio bars, and Washington-slept-here B&Bs. Others find the packed sidewalks and lack of parking intolerable and prefer to seek out the country flea markets, horse farms, and lush parks that fringe the northern and western parts of town.

Lumberville. George Washington most decidedly did not sleep in this tiny Tory-sympathizing river town 7 miles north of New Hope. Named after the lumber mills that operated here in the late 1800s, it is today anchored by a general store, a footbridge that connects it with New Jersey, and the Black Bass Inn, a charming, if faded, 18th-century inn and restaurant still steeped in Tory memorabilia.

Point Pleasant. A few miles north of Lumberville, this river village was a popular fishing spot for the Lenape Indians; later its inns and taverns catered to the rafters and canalmen who transported goods along the Delaware River and Canal. Today it's home to Bucks County River Country and known for its recreational water activities. You'll also find a general store and shops selling garden accessories and antiques here.

Quakertown. This growing bedroom community serves both the Delaware Valley and the Lehigh Valley to the north. In the 18th century, it was home to a community of Welsh and German farmers, and these roots are evident today in the hex signs that decorate barns and the funnel cakes and chow-chow for sale at the local farmers' market. Its quaint downtown, centered around Broad and Main Streets, is a pleasant mix of historic buildings, mom-and-pop stores selling everything from Italian ice to antiques, and even an old-fashioned five-and-dime. Just as the southern part of Bucks County likes to tout its Washington-slept-here connections, Quakertown and its environs can't help but brag that the Liberty Bell slept there—at least for a night—on its way to its hiding place in the Lehigh Valley during the Revolutionary War.

✳ To See

MUSEUMS & HISTORIC SITES **Fonthill Castle** (215-348-9461; mercermuseum.org), 84 South Pine Street. Open daily for guided tours. Admission charged; a "Mercer experience" pass gets you into both Fonthill and the Mercer Museum. There's a bit of California's Hearst Castle in this imposing early-20th-century mansion, once the home of Henry C. Mercer, a wealthy Benjamin Franklin–like character. Just about every inch of the 44 rooms is covered with handcrafted, multicolored tiles; there are also 18 fireplaces, 32 stairwells, and 200 windows.

✐ ♿ ☂ **Mercer Museum** (215-345-0210; mercermuseum.org), 84 South Pine Street. Open daily. Admission charged. Henry Mercer believed that the story of human progress and accomplishments was told by the tools and objects that people used, and he set about collecting and preserving those tools with extraordinary perseverance. His exhaustive collection of blacksmith's anvils, ox yokes, apple grinders, whale oil lamps, and thousands of other items is on display on seven rambling stories of a medieval-like castle, which was designated a National Historic Landmark in 1985. Exhibits and tours geared toward kids ages three and up are held throughout the year. All the Doylestown museums mentioned here are worth a visit, but this would be my top choice if I had time to hit only one.

❂ **George Nakashima Woodworker** (215-862-2272; nakashimawoodworkers.com), 1847 Aquetong Road, New Hope. The renowned Japanese American woodworker passed away in 1990; his daughter Mira still lives and designs her own furniture on the

MY NEW HOPE

When my future husband and I sought a place in eastern Pennsylvania to get married, New Hope seemed like the perfect setting. Walkable streets, quaint inns to accommodate out-of-town guests, and a unique combination of history and artistic whimsy—all anchored by the mesmerizing Delaware River.

Much has changed since we wed at St. Martin of Tours on the hill above town. For one thing, the old stone church is now a community center and police station headquarters. Flooding over the years has wreaked havoc on access roads and caused some longtime businesses to close or relocate.

Yet the things that make New Hope such a popular weekend destination remain exactly as I remember them: the steel truss bridge that links New Hope to the equally picturesque town of Lambertville and makes such a pleasant sunset walk; the modern sculptures fronting 18th-century buildings such as the local library and Parry Mansion; the shops selling mystical potions, Indonesian masks, and sketches of the surrounding countryside; and the bed & breakfast owners who point out Underground Railroad tunnels beneath their homes one day and deliver cream cheese–stuffed French toast to your door the next.

A Dunkin' Donuts has taken over the fancy dress shop that long anchored the Bridge and Main Streets intersection. Ney Alley on the canal towpath, once a collection of art galleries and a meeting place for Pennsylvania impressionists like Edward Redfield, is now deserted save for a boxing gym.

But it's still the New Hope I fell in love with years ago, a place to wander and discover, or break bread and relax with friends for an hour or two. The river has tested the town's patience over the years, but it still has the ability to charm and comfort anyone who visits.

WEDGWOOD INN IS A QUAINT B&B IN THE HEART OF NEW HOPE

family's rural compound. The 14 buildings—all designed and built by the artist without plans—and grounds are open to the public on Saturday afternoon only. It's a rare chance to see Nakashima's masterpieces arranged in a domestic setting.

    ✦ ↑**Michener Art Museum** (215-340-9800; michenerartmuseum.org), 138 South Pine Street. Open Tuesday–Sunday, April–December; closed Tuesdays, January–March. Admission charged. Bucks County native son James Michener funded this small-but-notable art museum, which features changing exhibitions of Pennsylvania impressionist painters and other contemporary and historic artists from the area. Don't miss the Japanese-style reading room featuring furniture by renowned woodworker George Nakashima. There's also a small room dedicated to the Pulitzer Prize–winning author. It has the typewriter and desk on which Michener wrote *Sayonara* and *A Floating World,* and books, road maps, and records from his personal collection, including the complete works of Balzac given to him by his aunt when he was a boy. There's also information on his failed run for US Congress in 1962 and his extensive and meticulous research and writing process.

    ✎ **The Locktender's House and Lock 11** (215-862-2021), 145 South Main Street, New Hope. Open Monday–Friday. Boats can't go uphill or downhill, so Delaware Canal engineers installed 23 locks to raise and lower them on stretches of level water. Learn how they did this through this interpretive center's exhibits, murals, and artifacts.

    ↑ ♀ ✳ **Moravian Pottery and Tile Works** (215-345-6722), 130 Swamp Road, Doylestown. Open daily; admission charged. When he wasn't collecting artifacts or building castles, Henry Mercer designed tiles. Not just any tiles, as you will see on a visit to the Spanish-style building that served as his studio. These tiles were forged in three-dimensional relief and depicted scenes from folktales, the Bible, and Dickens novels. Tours run every 30 minutes and include a movie and the chance to observe full-time ceramicists, who continue to produce tiles according to Mercer's designs.

    ↑ **National Shrine of Our Lady of Czestochowa** (215-345-0600; zestochowa.us), 654 Ferry Road. Millions of people, including Pope John Paul II, have visited this sprawling Polish spiritual center since it opened in 1966. The grounds on the outskirts of Doylestown include a modern church with stained-glass panels that tell the history of Christianity in Poland and the United States, a huge cemetery, and a large gift shop. Some masses are in Polish. A cafeteria serves kielbasa, pierogi, and other authentic Polish fare on Sundays, or you can pick up frozen pierogi or paczki (jelly doughnuts) to take home. Its Polish American festival each September draws crowds from all over the state (see *Special Events*).

UPPER BUCKS COUNTY

Pearl S. Buck House (215-249-0100; psbi.org), 520 Dublin Road, Dublin. Guided tours Tuesday–Sunday; closed January and February. Admission charged. Pearl Buck used to say this house's solid stone walls and 1835 age symbolized her strength and durability. The author of *The Good Earth* and numerous other books lived with her family on this farmstead, known as Green Hills, from 1933 to 1973, and her gravesite sits just off the main driveway. The China-born Buck's love for Asia comes through in many of the rooms, which are decorated with Chinese screens, Chen Chi paintings, and a silk wall hanging given to Buck by the Dalai Lama. There is also a rich collection of Pennsylvania country furniture and a room dedicated to all of Buck's awards, including the Nobel and Pulitzer Prizes.

    Tobin Studios (610-442-5169), 530 California Road, Quakertown. A field of remarkable sculptures by artist Steve Tobin in an industrial area just off PA 309 near Quakertown's downtown. Tobin, known for steel-root and glass sculptures inspired by nature and science, works out of a 125,000-square-foot warehouse here, and anyone is welcome to stop by and view the giant abstracts that surround it.

✳ To Do

BICYCLE RENTALS The mostly flat 60-mile Delaware Canal towpath is popular with all levels of cyclists. **New Hope Cyclery** (215-862-6888; newhopecyclery.com), 404 York Road, rents every kind of bike and support item (closed Wednesdays). On the Jersey side, try **Cycle Corner of Frenchtown** (908-996-7712; thecyclecorner.com), 52 Bridge Street.

BOAT EXCURSIONS **New Hope Boat Rides** (215-862-2050), 22 North Main Street, New Hope. Captain Timothy Yates leads half-hour excursions on a Mississippi-style stern paddle-wheel pontoon boat. Rides leave roughly every 30 minutes on weekends, May–September. At Lake Nockamixon in Upper Bucks, **Nockamixon Boat Rental** (215-538-1340; www.nockamixonboatrental.com) rents canoes, motorboats, rowboats, sailboats, paddleboats, kayaks, and pontoon boats during the summer.

TUBING **Bucks County River Country** (215-297-5000; rivercountry.net), 2 Walters Lane, Point Pleasant. Open mid-May–October. This veteran river-outfitting operation offers rentals, plus two- to four-hour guided trips down the Delaware; all-day outings and season passes are also available.

    Delaware River Tubing (866-938-8823; delawarerivertubing.com), 2998 Daniel Bray Highway, Frenchtown, New Jersey, just across the Uhlerstown Bridge. The tubing and rafting rides include a free lunch or dinner at what may be the world's only swim-up hot dog stand.

SCULPTURES BY STEVE TOBIN AT HIS QUAKERTOWN STUDIO

VISITORS CAN BOARD ANTIQUE TRAIN CARS AT NEW HOPE'S VINTAGE STATION

FLY-FISHING The catch in the Delaware River includes shad in April, striped bass in May, and small- and largemouth bass in October. Gary Mauz (215-343-1720; flyfishingguideservice.com) has been fly-fishing along the Delaware for decades and offers half- or full-day excursions, plus lessons. Book early for summer outings.

FOR FAMILIES ✐ ⛾ **Giggleberry Fair** (215-794-8960; giggleberryfair.com), Peddler's Village, Doylestown. Open daily. Kids will love this indoor playground, with its wooden-horse carousel, three-story obstacle course, and discovery room for the under-5 set. The place can be quite loud on weekends, when birthday groups show up. A pass gets your child into all the attractions, but there's also an à la carte option.

✐ ⛾ **Bucks County Children's Museum** (215-693-1290; buckskids.org), 500 Union Square, New Hope. Closed Mondays; admission charged. Geared to the 8-and-under set, this hands-on kids' wonderland features a science-based tree house, simulated balloon ride, and archaeological dig in which kids may unearth replica historical items such as a Civil War bugle or a piece of the boat George Washington used to cross the Delaware. In another nod to the area's roots, there is also an old-fashioned general store, a post office, and a covered bridge.

✐ **New Hope and Ivyland Railroad** (215-862-2332; newhoperailroad.com), 32 West Bridge Street, New Hope. Open daily from late May–October, weekends only in winter and early spring. Beautifully restored vintage steam- and diesel-powered engines carry passengers between New Hope and Lahaska several times a day; professional uniformed conductors lend an old-school aura to the ride and take you back to the country's locomotive heydays. There are also storytelling theme rides for kids in the summer and wine-and-cheese-tasting rides for adults on some weekends.

A CAR AND PEDESTRIAN BRIDGE LINKING NEW HOPE AND LAMBERTVILLE, NEW JERSEY

FLYING **Van Sant Airport** (610-847-8320), 516 Cafferty Road, Erwinna. Bar and Dannie Eisenhauer offer rides in biplane barnstormers, plane and glider rentals, plus flight instruction.

GOLF **Fox Hollow Golf Club** (215 538-1920), 2020 Trumbauersville Road, Quakertown. Eighteen holes featuring 6,613 yards of golf from the longest tees for a par of 71.

    Four Seasons Golf Center (215-348-5575; fourseasonsgolf.net), 1208 Swamp Road (PA 313), Fountainville, has a driving range and two miniature golf courses.

HORSEBACK RIDING **Haycock Stables** (215-257-6271; haycockstables.com), 1035 Old Bethlehem Road, Perkasie. Trail rides through Lake Nockamixon are offered several times a day Tuesday–Sunday.

HUNTING About 3,000 acres are open to seasonal hunting and trapping at Nockamixon State Park. Common game are deer, pheasant, rabbit, and turkey.

GHOST TOURS **Adele Gamble** (215-343-5564; ghosttoursofnewhope.com) leads lantern-lit walking tours through New Hope every Saturday night at 8, June–November, for a per-person fee. She assures her charges that all her ghosts are friendly. Tours begin at the corner of Main and Ferry Streets.

SCENIC DRIVES A classic Sunday drive, the **Delaware River Loop** rambles along winding roads that hug the river and pass by dense woodlands, antiques stores, and inns that have hosted presidents and Founding Fathers. Begin in Pennsylvania near

Morrisville and follow PA 29 (River Road) north past Washington Crossing State Park. Stop in New Hope for some shopping or a stroll along the Delaware Canal towpath, then continue 7 miles to Lumberville, where the **Black Bass Hotel** (215-297-5770) serves a lavish brunch in a room overlooking the Delaware. Continue a few more miles north to Upper Black Eddy, where you can cross the truss bridge into Milford, New Jersey, and browse the antiques shops along Bridge Street. From Milford, head south along NJ 519 to NJ 29, which passes through the quaint riverfront towns of Frenchtown and Stockton, perhaps stopping at the **Lovin' Oven** just south of Frenchtown for maple oat pancakes or a turmeric elixir. At Lambertville, make a right on Bridge Street and cross back into New Hope. Cap the day with a drink or decadent dessert on the river-view deck of **The Landing** (215-862-5711). It can take as little as an hour or an entire afternoon to drive the loop, depending on how much eating and shopping you do along the way.

✳ Green Space

✎ ♿ ♂ **Bowman's Hill Wildflower Preserve** (215-862-2924; bhwp.org), 1635 River Road, between New Hope and Washington Crossing. Open 8:30–sunset daily; admission charged. Established in 1934 to preserve Pennsylvania's native flora and fauna, Bowman's Hill features more than a thousand species of plants and flowers, 26 walking trails, and a bird observatory. Some of the paths are wheelchair and stroller accessible. Guided wildflower walks are held every Tuesday and Sunday from April–October.

Gardens at Mill Fleurs (215-297-1000; thegardensatmillfleurs.com), 27 Cafferty Road, Point Pleasant. Closed Sundays; admission charged. Guided tours of an 18th-century gristmill property set on the wild banks of Tohickon Creek include homemade

THE DELAWARE CANAL TOWPATH DRAWS CYCLISTS AND WALKERS ON WEEKENDS

cookies and refreshments in an ice house pavilion. Open tours (no reservations required) are held on Saturdays from May–September. Check the website for details.

✎ ♿ **Peace Valley Park and Nature Center** (215-345-7860), 170 Chapman Road, Doylestown. A 1,500-acre park with a lake framed by rolling hills, 14 miles of walking trails, and a bird blind that is frequented by cardinals, woodpeckers, finches, and sparrows. The 6-mile, paved biking/walking trail around the lake is arguably the prettiest bike path in the county. Stop at the nature center at 170 Chapman Road for maps, birdseed, and information on guided hikes. At the north end of the park is **Peace Valley Lavender Farm** (215-249-8462; peacevalleylavender.com), where visitors may wander across violet-hued fields and witness how lavender is harvested and dried. Admission is free; the gift shop sells tough-to-resist soaps, oils, and sachets.

UPPER BUCKS COUNTY

✎ **Lake Nockamixon** (215-529-7300; dcnr.state.pa.us), 1542 Mountain View Road, Quakertown. This 5,300-acre park 4 miles east of Quakertown is a scenic and popular recreation spot for locals and nature-loving out-of-towners. Its centerpiece is a 1,450-acre reservoir that allows sailing, boating, windsurfing, and fishing (but no swimming). Surrounding the lake are picnic areas, several miles of biking and hiking trails, 20 miles of equestrian trails, and 10 modern log cabins (see *Lodging*). In the winter, this is a popular spot for ice skating, sledding, and cross-country skiing. There's also a great swimming pool overlooking the lake that's open to the public during summer.

✎ **Ringing Rocks Park** (215-757-0571), Ringing Rocks Road at Bridgeton Hill Road, Upper Black Eddy. Open daily. This has to be the only park around that encourages its visitors to pack hammers along with their picnic baskets and bird binoculars. That's because smack in the middle of it lies an 8-acre field of large boulders, many of which ring like bells when struck lightly with hammers. According to park history, these are diabase rocks that 175 million years ago were formed by fire and cooled underground, meaning they solidified at superfast speed. This put the bonds composing the rocks under a great deal of stress and, just like with the tightening of a guitar string, causes them to produce a high-pitched sound when tapped. Not surprisingly, this park is very popular with families, who can be seen trudging toward the boulder field on weekends like Snow White's dwarves going off to work. It's a bit challenging to find, so be sure to bring a good map.

Ralph Stover State Park (610-982-5560), 6011 State Park Road, Pipersville. This 47-acre park 2 miles north of Point Pleasant is best known for its sheer rock cliff and stunning views of Tohickon Creek and the dense woodland surrounding it. Experienced rock climbers may scale the 200-foot sheer rock face, but anybody can enjoy the safety-railed view from the top, thanks to a nearby parking area off Tory Road and a generous grant from the late James A. Michener. The park also has a pretty picnic area and a couple of short hiking trails. White-water kayaks and canoes may be launched from Tohickon Creek. The trails here link up with nearby Tohickon Valley Park, which is owned by the county.

Tohickon Valley Park (215-757-0571), Cafferty Road. Crowds flock to this park in late March and early November, when water flows from Lake Nockamixon to the north flow at a rate of 500 cubic feet per second and the normally staid Tohickon Creek turns into a raging white-water playground. It also has a playground, a trout-fishing stream, and tidy cabins that book up fast in the spring and summer (see *Lodging*). Its hiking and biking trails are among the most challenging in Bucks County and connect with Ralph Stover State Park.

✳ Lodging

INNS & MOTELS **Aaron Burr House** (215-862-2343; aaronburrbandb.com), 2998 North River Road. This inn is indeed named after the infamous gentleman who shot and killed Alexander Hamilton in one of colonial America's most famous duels. Burr fled here after the crime, but that may be the only nefarious thing about this cozy Victorian inn near the center of town. Host and trained chef Lisa Pretecrum has created a welcoming atmosphere. Each room is distinct, with artwork, antiques, and private bath; some have fireplaces and four-poster beds, and her gourmet breakfasts draw raves. $$$.

♿ **Doylestown Inn** (215-345-6610; doylestownhatteryinn.com), 18 West State Street, Doylestown. This elegant century-old inn in the center of town has 11 understated rooms with four-poster beds and jetted tubs. Premium rooms are larger, with turreted sitting areas and gas fireplaces. Its famous guests include Henry Ford, Pearl S. Buck, Dorothy Parker, Henry Fonda, and James Michener. **The Hattery and Still**, a modern bistro and bar, honors the inn's former roots as a hattery, cigar shop, and speakeasy with vintage touches such as wooden beverage boxes, ice chests, a peephole, and a player piano. $$$.

🍸 ♂ **Inn at Lambertville Station** (609-397-4400; lambertvillestation.com), 11 Bridge Street, Lambertville, New Jersey. This riverfront inn, just over the bridge from New Hope, has 45 antiques-filled rooms with nice views of the Delaware, but the high standard of service really sets it apart. Want to check in early or have breakfast delivered to your room? The staff will do everything they can to accommodate you. There's also an honor bar, a creek-side deck off the lobby, and wireless Internet access in every room. It's a popular spot for weekend weddings; guests who book a first-floor room should take note that the hallway serves as the main entrance path to the ballroom. $$$$.

Logan Inn (215-862-2300; loganinn .com), 10 West Ferry Street, New Hope. This three-story hotel, which fronts Main Street, opened in 1727 and is one of the longest continuously running inns in the country. Its 16 rooms are cozy, combining modern luxury with Colonial-style touches such as four-poster beds. Rumor has it that Room 6 is haunted by a former owner who lost the inn at a sheriff's sale. The ghost of Aaron Burr, who fled to New Hope after his famous duel with Alexander Hamilton, is also suspected of roaming the premises. The inn added an upscale New American restaurant and spa in recent years, and plans are in the works to add more rooms. Its large covered patio, with firepits and cabanas, draws lively crowds on summer weekends. $$$.

BED & BREAKFASTS **1870 Wedgwood Inn** (215-862-2570; wedgwoodinn.com), 80 West Bridge Street, New Hope. Innkeepers Carl and Nadine Glassman expertly oversee two renovated Victorian homes just a few blocks north of Main Street. The main house has front and back sitting porches and attractive rooms with intricate stenciling, brass ceiling fans, antiques, and queen or king beds; some have fireplaces, small private balconies, and sitting areas. Next door, the 1833 Umpleby House has eight handsome rooms and suites (the huge third-floor Loft Suite is a favorite). Enjoy breakfast on china and teacups in the Wedgwood's lace-curtained dining room or request it delivered to your room. It's one of the few B&Bs in the area to accommodate kids and dogs (in designated rooms). Guests have access to a beautiful hidden yard with a hammock and gazebos. $$-$$$.

♂ **Inn at Bowman's Hill** (215-862-8090; theinnatbowmanshill.com), 518 Lurgan Road. The rates are higher than many other area B&Bs, but you'll want for nothing at this secluded retreat a couple miles south of New Hope village, whether it's heated towel racks, multiple-jet showers, or vine-covered pergolas. The manicured grounds include a swimming pool, spa, and large outdoor deck. The traditional English breakfast is made with eggs from the inn's free-range hens. Last-minute specials are sometimes available. $$$$.

Porches on the Towpath (215-862-3277; porchesnewhope.com), 20 Fisher's Alley. Hidden away at the end of a quiet lane yet within walking distance of town, this two-story Federal house was once the home of "Pop" and Ethel Reading, who ran a popular sandwich shop out of it in the 1930s. The 10 rooms (four of which are located in a restored carriage house) have nice touches such as claw-foot bathtubs, antique furnishings, and French doors that open to shady porches or patios. A country breakfast is served each morning in the chandelier-lit dining room. Walkers and cyclists will appreciate the easy access to the canal towpath, but many guests prefer relaxing on the hotel's wide, inviting porches. $$–$$$.

UPPER BUCKS COUNTY

Black Bass Hotel (215-297-9660; black basshotel.com), 3774 River Road, Lumberville. George Washington most definitely did not sleep in this historic inn (the 1770s innkeeper was loyal to the British crown), but anyone who likes a little luxury (and very good food) with their history lessons will want to spend the night here. The nine suites were renovated and glammed up in 2008 with ornate beds, antique furniture, and flat-screen TVs; most have private balconies overlooking the river. $$$–$$$$; last-minute discounted rates are sometimes available. Breakfast in the riverfront dining room is included. There's also an excellent restaurant and tavern on the premises (see *Dining Out*).

1836 Bridgeton House (610-982-5856; bridgetonhouse.com), 1525 River Road, Upper Black Eddy. This riverfront B&B is the perfect antidote for stressed-out city dwellers looking to get away from it all. The only thing old about the place is the 1836 building; everything else, from the staff's attentiveness to the whimsical styles of the rooms, is as modern as it gets. All 12 rooms have private baths, televisions, plank floors, and feather beds. Many have private balconies and fireplaces. Guests may have breakfast in their rooms or next to a cooking fireplace in the dining room. There's also a private dock, along with an outdoor living room that's great for an afternoon of reading or lounging. $$$–$$$$.

Frog Hollow Farm (610-847-3764; froghollowfarmbnb.com), 401 Frogtown Road, Kintnersville. This intimate three-room inn is about 20 miles from Quakerstown. Petie's Room (named after the resident dog) is the showcase room, but the Cathedral Room is also lovely with its sunlit loft, exposed stone walls, and bathroom that overlooks the barn and sheep pasture. Sun tea or mulled cider is served on the outdoor deck every afternoon, and port is served in the reading room in the evening. Owners Patti and Mitch Adler can also arrange a dinner package at nearby Ferndale Inn, which includes a chauffeured ride in a restored 1931 Ford Coupe. $$$.

Galvanized America Inn and Art Gallery (610-766-7617; galvanizedamerica .com), 6470 Durham Road, Pipersville. A restored 1754 farmhouse with art-filled rooms and suites, and nice touches like a landscaped pool and firepit area. It makes a great base if you're looking to spend the weekend exploring the back roads and covered bridges of Bucks County. $$$.

Golden Pheasant Inn (610-294-9595; goldenpheasantinn.com), 763 River Road, Erwinna. Built as a mule-barge rest stop in the late 1800s, this luxury inn is located right on the Delaware Canal and a short walk from the Sand Castle Winery. Run by the daughters of longtime owners Michel and Barbara

Faure, it is known for its excellent French restaurant (see *Dining Out*). Its four water-view rooms were renovated and modernized in 2012; they include private marble baths with custom mosaics, luxury European linens, and flat-screen TVs. A hearty breakfast is included. $$$–$$$$; two-night minimum on weekends.

CAMPGROUNDS & CABINS

UPPER BUCKS COUNTY

Lake Nockamixon (888-727-2277), 1542 Mountain View Drive, Quakertown. Ten modern cabins that sleep six to eight people can be rented at weekly rates.

Colonial Woods Family Camping Resort (610-847-5808; colonialwoods .com), 545 Lonely Cottage Drive, Upper Black Eddy. Open mid-April–October. Known as the Four Seasons of campgrounds, this facility has 208 tent and RV hook-up sites, plus a swimming pool, playground, laundry facilities, stocked fishing lake, and air-conditioned community lodge. $.

Tohickon Family Campground (866-536-2267; tohickoncampground.com), 8308 Covered Bridge Drive, Quakertown. Full-service campground with more than 200 tent and hook-up sites, a swimming pool, and lots of free kid and adult activities. $.

✳ Where to Eat

DINING OUT Domani Star (215-230-9100; domanistar.com), 57 West State Street, Doylestown. Lunch Monday–Saturday, dinner daily. Bring your own wine to this boisterous awning-topped bistro down the street from the Doylestown Inn. There is little elbow room and the noise levels can be high, but the *cucina Italiana* by Chef Chris Oravec is consistently good. Highlights include handmade lasagna, veal Milanese, and crispy eggplant rollatini. A multicourse "Local's Menu" is available Tuesday–Thursday for $35. $$–$$$.

Ψ **Honey** (215-489-4200; honey restaurant.com), 42 Shewell Avenue, Doylestown. The lighting is soft and golden, while the menu is bold and modern at this cozy café run by two William Penn Inn alums. Dinner choices include black tea–glazed spare ribs, risotto cakes with chickpea caponata, and wild boar tenderloin with Burgundy snails, cremini mushrooms, and bacon; the drink menu showcases Pennsylvania craft beer and honey-infused cocktails. Save room for dessert: The fried apple pie with sour cream ice cream is the bee's knees. $$–$$$.

Slate Bleu (215-348-0222), 100 South Main Street, Doylestown. Closed Tuesdays. Excellent French-inspired fare and wines are served amid the original timber and exposed brickwork of a former livery.

LAMBERTVILLE, NEW JERSEY

Ψ **Anton's at the Swan** (609-397-1960), 43 South Main Street. Dinner Tuesday–Sunday. The food is very good and thoughtfully prepared, but it's the formal surroundings and exceptional service that you'll remember most about this 1870 hotel turned upscale restaurant. The simple menu includes sautéed halibut, grilled fillet of beef, and pan-roasted duck breast with air-dried cherries. The separate bar, with its pressed-tin ceiling, fireplace, and leather couches, is a must-stop before or after dinner for a perfect martini.

♿ **Hamilton's Grill Room** (609-397-4343; hamiltonsgrillroom.com), 8 Coryell Street. Broadway set designer and restaurateur Jim Hamilton (father of star Manhattan chef and author Gabrielle Hamilton) has been serving fresh seafood in a romantic canal-side setting for years. The menu changes daily but might include crab cheesecake, duck confit, or grilled halibut piccata. BYO. $$$.

Manon (609-397-2596), 19 North Union Street. Tiny French bistro that only locals seem to know about. The food (chicken in garlic-cream sauce, mussels in a tomato and herb broth) is consistently praised and the atmosphere dubbed authentically Provençal. BYO. No credit cards. $$$.

NEW HOPE/LAHASKA

&. ⴼ **Cock 'n Bull** (215-794-4051), Lahaska. This long-running flagship restaurant has been operating since Peddler's Village opened in 1962. It is known as much for its country-kitsch décor and themed Colonial dinners as its traditional American menu of chicken potpie and prime rib. Sunday brunch is an all-you-can-eat extravaganza of omelets, sausages, carved roasts, pancakes, and desserts. $$$.

Karla's (717-862-2612; karlasnewhope.com), 5 West Mechanic Street. Karla's open-air dining room is a lovely place to be on a warm summer night. The menu features a nice assortment of burgers, salads, and classic entrées such as soy-ginger glazed salmon and braised short ribs. Monday night is Local's Night, with a three-course menu and live guitar. There's a full bar as well as live jazz some evenings. $$–$$$.

ⴼ **The Landing** (215-862-5711; landingrestaurant.com), 22 North Main Street. Lunch and dinner daily. Known for its large deck overlooking the river, The Landing also has good food to match its primo views. Its all-day menu includes hot pastrami on rye, crabcake sliders, coconut shrimp on tostadas, and a long list of gourmet salads and appetizers. The extensive wine list changes frequently. In the cooler months, grab a table by the roaring fireplace. $$–$$$.

ⴼ ♂ **Marsha Brown** (215-862-7044; marshabrownrestaurant.com), 15 South Main Street. Lunch and dinner daily. Ecclesiastical roots meet culinary excellence at this Methodist church turned restaurant in the center of town. The menu specializes in prime beef and seafood, as well as Creole recipes from the New Orleans–raised owner's family stash. Reservations recommended. $$$.

✪ **Sprig and Vine** (215-693-1427; sprigandvine.com), 450 Union Square Drive. This upscale vegetarian restaurant has been a hit since it opened in the Union Square complex in 2010. Loyalists love the soft jazz, laid-back vibe, and creative menu with dishes such as purple sweet potato ravioli, miso-maple-mustard glazed tempeh with horseradish-cashew cream, and za'atar-grilled oyster mushrooms. Desserts are also excellent. $$.

UPPER BUCKS COUNTY

ⴼ **Black Bass Hotel** (215-297-9260; blackbassinn.com), 3774 River Road, Lumberville. The river views from the dining room and deck of this 18th-century inn are exquisite, and so is the cuisine served along with them. You'll find Charleston Meeting Street crab au gratin, butter-poached Maine lobster risotto, and grilled filet mignon with foie gras butter for dinner; there's also slow-cooked cassoulet and gourmet salads and sandwiches on the lunch and tavern menus. There is a prix fixe locals menu Monday–Wednesday and a lavish four-course Sunday brunch. Don't leave without checking out the tavern area: The pewter bar was imported from Maxim's of Paris, and there's plenty of Tory memorabilia on display. $$–$$$.

&. ⴼ **Golden Pheasant Inn** (610-294-9595; goldenpheasantinn.com), 763 River Road, Erwinna. Dinner Tuesday–Saturday, brunch Sunday. Blake Faure now runs the longtime French restaurant started by her father, Michel Faure, a former chef at Philadelphia's Le Bec Fin. It continues the tradition of classical French cuisine with a seasonal menu that features trout, venison, pheasant, and frog legs in an array of intensely flavored sauces. Sit in the modern glass-enclosed dining room or opt for the original Tavern Room, with its fireplace, antique chandeliers, and hanging copper pots and pans. $$$.

Ferndale Inn (610-847-2662; theferndaleinn.com), 551 Church Hill

THE CARVERSVILLE INN, BUILT IN 1813, IS NOW A CHEF-DRIVEN RESTAURANT

Road, at PA 611, Ferndale, 2 miles south of Kintnersville. Dinner Wednesday–Monday. This longtime restaurant is known for its top-notch service and traditional dishes such as clams casino, filet mignon, and scallops in lemon sauce. Packages available for guests of Frog Hollow B&B (see *Lodging*). The wine list includes selections from Sand Castle Winery. $$$.

Maize (610-257-2264; maizeonwalnut .com), 519 Walnut Street, Perkasie. Dinner Tuesday–Saturday. Chef Matthew McPhelin worked at the Rittenhouse Hotel's Lacroix before opening his own BYO bistro near Quakertown. The menu highlights local ingredients and changes daily; entrées might include shrimp with herbed grits and mushrooms or short ribs with braised cabbage. $$$.

EATING OUT

DOYLESTOWN

Y **Mesquito Grille** (215-230-7427), 128 West State Street. Open for lunch and dinner Wednesday–Monday. This unpretentious bar and restaurant serves the best Buffalo chicken wings outside of New York State, plus steaks, pork spare-ribs, and BBQ chicken. The beer menu boasts 150 different bottles and is available for take-out. Count on lots of sports on the widescreen TVs. $$.

Spuntino Wood Fired Pizzeria (215-340-7660; spuntinowoodfiredpizzeria .com), 22 South Main Street. Closed Mondays and Tuesdays. Top-notch wood-fired pizzas are the specialty of this popular BYO spot run by two brothers.

NEW HOPE

Duck Soup Café (215-862-5890; duck soupcafe.com), 6542 Lower York Road, in the Logan Square shopping center. Closed Mondays. Cash-only hideaway and local favorite known for its home-style breakfasts, soups, and delicious sandwiches such as open-faced eggplant and a BLT croissant. Dinner is served Friday only. $–$$.

Y **Villa Vito** (215-862-9936), 26 West Bridge Street. Lunch and dinner daily.

This long-running family-owned restaurant serves big salads and decent cheese-steaks and pastas, but the delicious thin-crust pizza makes it worth a visit. Try the white spinach or sausage. Dine on the shady backyard patio in the summer. $–$$.

☖ **Nektar** (215-862-2241), 8 West Mechanic Street. This polished eatery, which bills itself as a wine, beer, and whiskey bar, has floor-to-ceiling windows and a back deck overlooking a pretty creek and pedestrian bridge. It serves sophisticated pub grub such as truffle ravioli, steak tip flatbreads, and cheese and charcuterie plates. $$.

UPPER BUCKS

Bucks County Seafood (215-249-1295; buckscountyseafoodpa.com), 164 North Main Street, Dublin. Dine in on fresh conch chowder and rich crab cakes, or take home salmon steaks, red snapper, or scallops to throw on the grill. Crabs are available by the bushel in summer.

🖉 ♿ **Dublin Towne Diner** (215-249-3686), 133 North Main Street, Dublin. Open daily. Everything you want in a diner—low prices, gruff waitresses, and a salad bar big enough to satisfy a football team in training. For a real Pennsylvania breakfast, try the pork roll with eggs. $.

🖉 **Luberto's Brick Oven Pizza and Trattoria** (215-249-0688; lubertosbrickoven.com), 169 North Main Street, Dublin. Heaping portions and good, simple Italian food served in unfussy surroundings. Order the white mushroom pizza, eggplant Parmesan, or anything that comes with pink vodka sauce. It gets busy on weekends, but the tables turn fast. BYO. $$.

🖉 **Lumberville General Store** (215-297-9262), 3741 River Road, across the street from the Black Bass Hotel. This cozy and bright café is in a restored 1770 property that once operated as the town's general store and post office. Today it's a popular stop for weekend cyclists coming off the Delaware Canal towpath and anyone who wants to soak up a little history with a croissant or house-smoked salmon with scrambled eggs. At lunch, there are gourmet salads and smashed burgers. The Friday and Saturday supper club—a three-course menu that changes weekly—is legendary. Seatings start at 6 p.m.

CAFÉS & BAKERIES C'est La Vie (215-862-1956), 20 South Main Street, New Hope. If you're not staying in one of the area's many B&Bs, try this hidden riverfront spot for a morning croissant or cappuccino.

Factory Girl Bake Shop (267-740-2354; factorygirlbakeshop.com), 45 North Main Street, New Hope. Brioche doughnuts, salted caramel brownies, English muffin bread—you never know what Kimberly Scola might have on offer at her bright and tiny bakery. She also makes decadent wedding and birthday cakes.

Homestead Coffee Roasters (610-982-5121; homesteadcoffee.com), 1650 Bridgeton Hill Road, Upper Black Eddy. House-roasted coffee and simple breakfast and lunch fare in an 1880s general store beside the canal.

The Lucky Cupcake Company (267-544-5912), 74 Peddler's Village, Lahaska. From-scratch cupcakes in traditional and groundbreaking flavors such as maple bacon French toast and limoncello, plus cheesecakes, scones, and muffins.

Moo Hope Ice Cream (215-862-2050), 22 South Main Street, New Hope. This family-run outfit replaced the venerable Gerenser's, a longtime institution known for its unique ice cream, in 2014. The new owners have continued the tradition of serving up fun flavors like chocolate pudding crunch and pumpkin chip in a prime riverside location.

OwowCow Creamery (610-847-7070), 4105 Durham Road, Ottsville. Sinfully good ice cream shop near Nockamixon State Park with flavors such as chocolate jalapeño, pecan pie, and rosewater cardamom. There are also branches in Chalfont, Wrightstown, and Lambertville, New Jersey.

EXCURSIONS

CARVERSVILLE Once a Lenni-Lenape Indian gathering place, Carversville today is a classic Bucks County hamlet of 18th-century stone homes anchored by an old mill, a storybook stream, and a waterfall. A center of commerce in the 1700s, it was home to gristmills and a factory that made roram hats, fur-covered caps worn by Revolutionary-era boys. Today, the town claims toy historian Noel Barrett, a longtime host of PBS's *Antiques Roadshow*, as an enthusiastic resident. In 2013, chef Max Hansen took over the kitchen of the Carversville grocery and general store, a longtime gathering place for local gossip and grub. The kitchen is open Tuesday–Sunday for breakfast and lunch; don't be surprised to find a slew of bicycles parked out front on weekends and buff cyclists feasting on breakfast burritos or avocado toast. Across the way, the **Carversville Inn** (215-297-0900; carversvilleinn.com) serves an innovative Cajun-influenced lunch and dinner menu in formal 1813 surroundings. On the last Monday night of the month during the summer, the village runs underappreciated films like *Joe Versus the Volcano* on the side of the general store. To get to Carversville from River Road, head west on Fleecydale Road in Lumberville to the intersection of Aquetong Road. It's a beautiful though narrow and curvy ride that follows a tree-shaded stream.

🦞 **Vera's Country Café** (610-847-8372), 4203 Durham Road, Ottsville. Closed Mondays and Tuesdays. This quaint daytime diner above Nockamixon State Park serves delicious comfort eats, from French toast to shrimp quesadillas, at reasonable prices.

BYO Where to buy wine and spirits in Central and Upper Bucks:

In New Hope, try the **Wine & Spirits** store (215-862-4650) in Logan Square Shopping Center. Or drive across the bridge to the service-friendly **Phillip's Wine Shoppe** (609-397-0587) in Stockton, New Jersey, and browse their well-organized selection. In Ottsville, just south of Ferndale, there's a **Wine & Spirits** store at 8794 Easton Road (610-847-2472). In Peddler's Village, **Hewn Spirits** (267-544-0720; hewnspirits .com) sells small-batch bourbon and rum made at its Pipersville distillery; it also has a small bar for tastings and cocktails.

✳ Entertainment

MUSIC ⅄ **Great Barn Taproom** (215-803-1592), 12 West Mechanic Street, New Hope. Open Thursday–Sunday. Craft beer made in Bucks County is served in a pleasant setting with a patio overlooking the canal and Main Street bridge. Live music on weekends.

⅄ ✪ **John and Peter's** (215-862-5981; johnandpeters.com), 96 South Main Street, New Hope. A must-stop for music lovers, it has hosted Norah Jones, George Thorogood, and countless local, original acts. New owners took over from the eponymous founders in 2018, intent on upholding the joint's reputation as "the musical heart and soul of New Hope." Burgers, a tater tot bar, and other casual eats are served all day.

♿ ⅄ **Triumph Brewing Company** (215-862-8300; triumphbrewing.com), 400 Union Square, New Hope. This busy microbrewery stays open late with a varying entertainment slate of karaoke, acoustic guitar, and Texas Hold 'Em.

DANCING ⅄ **The Raven** (215-862-2081; theravennewhope.com), 385 Bridge Street, New Hope. A popular gay night spot any night of the week, this oak-paneled bar and restaurant transforms into a huge dance party Saturday and every other Thursday.

MOVIES **County Theater** (215-345-6789; countytheater.org), 20 East State

Street, Doylestown. Current independent releases screened in a restored 1938 art deco theater in the center of town. There are often weekday screenings of classic films and kids' movies on select Saturdays. The theater launched a major expansion in 2019 to upgrade its current facilities and add a third screening room.

THEATER ✪ **Bucks County Playhouse** (215-862-9606; www.bcptheater.org), Stockton Street, New Hope. Grace Kelly and Julie Harris made their theatrical debuts in this former gristmill in 1949 and 1964, respectively. Legendary as a summer theater stage for a litany of stars that included Helen Hayes, Zero Mostel, Dick Van Dyke, and Angela Lansbury, it has struggled over the years with debt and closure, but was renovated and reopened in 2012 with the help of a local nonprofit and hosts a roster of musicals, plays, and youth theater productions. Plans are also in the works for an affiliated inn and Jose Garces restaurant to open next door.

New Hope Arts Center (215-862-9606; newhopearts.org), Stockton Street. This artists' hub in the center of town hosts sculpture exhibits, film and theater festivals, and other community events.

UPPER BUCKS COUNTY

Sellersville Theatre (215-257-5808; st94 .com), Main and Temple Streets, Sellersville. This historic stage offers a wide and stellar range of live music and comedy shows, from Paula Poundstone to Richard Thompson.

♆ **Washington House** (215-257-3000; washingtonhouse.net), 136 North Main Street, Sellersville (next to the Sellersville Theatre). George Washington may have slept in this restored 18th-century inn; today it's known for its lively bar, which features free live music on select weekdays and regular wine and beer tasting events.

✳ Selective Shopping

New Hope's Main Street is lined with shops, some of which shout "tourist trap" from the tops of their refinished 18th-century eaves, but there are also many independent gems worth seeking out. The best discoveries come by exploring the alleys and roads that branch off the main strip, like Mechanic and Union Streets, or stopping at the many antiques shops along York Road (US 202) between New Hope and Buckingham. For a fun, old-fashioned shopping experience, head to downtown Quakertown, a mix of antiques shops, bookstores, bakeries, and cafés anchored by **McCoole's Red Lion Inn** (215-538-1776), 4 South Main Street. **Sine's 5 and 10 Cent Store** (215-536-6102), 236 West Broad Street sells bulk candy, toys, Christmas knick-knacks, and other items; a frozen-in-time lunch counter serves creamy milkshakes and homemade soups. The **Quakertown Farmers' Market** (215-536-4115), 201 Station Road, is a huge indoor-outdoor affair whose motto is "bargains are our business" and where more than 400 vendors sell everything from antique armoires and premium cigars to three-for-$1 toothbrushes.

Farley's Bookshop (215-862-2452), 44 South Main Street. An old-fashioned, independent bookshop in the heart of New Hope with more than 70,000 titles and a strong section on local culture and history, this shop is a must visit for anyone who loves to read.

Heart of the Home (215-862-1880), 28 South Main Street. The perfect place to shop for the person who has everything, this customer-centered shop sells elephant birdhouses, leaf-embossed leather handbags, porcelain teapots, and jewelry.

Integrity Studio (215-534-1500; integritystudio.com), 40 West Bridge Street. Open Saturday and Sunday, other days by appointment. Owner Carl Christensen is a photographer and woodcrafter who founded Integrity Studio to present his fine art photography of Bucks County landscapes in his handcrafted frames. He and his wife are active supporters of land conservation and charitable organizations in the region.

Love Saves the Day (215-862-1399), 1 South Main Street. This vintage toy and clothing shop closed its East Village store in 2008 but continues to operate its New Hope outpost. It is a browser's paradise of feather boas, comic books, Grateful Dead tie-dyes, and Betty Boop lunch boxes. It is a local institution.

LAMBERTVILLE, NEW JERSEY

The People's Store (609-397-9808), 28 North Union Street. Three floors of antique lamps and furniture, books, art displays, and vintage clothing.

Panoply Books (609-397-1145; panoplybooks.com), 46 North Union Street. Everything you'd want in a used bookstore: a diverse, offbeat collection, plus leather chairs and the occasional tribal artwork and silk rug for sale.

The Sojourner (609-397-8849; sojourner.biz), 26 Bridge Street. The ever-changing merchandise includes embroidered cottons from China, sterling silver jewelry from Mexico and Italy, and sapphire swirl lamps from Istanbul. You never know what exotic items owners Elsie and Amy Coss might bring back from regular trips abroad. It's also known for its large bead collection.

ELSEWHERE IN BUCKS COUNTY

Byers' Choice (215-822-0150; byerschoice.com), 4355 County Line Road, Chalfont. Closed Sundays and Mondays. It's Christmas all year at the headquarters of Byers' Choice, maker of handcrafted caroler figurines that are sold at specialty shops around the country. Here, you can shop for doe-eyed Kindles (elves), Christmas tree cookie molds, and red velvet Santas at the gift emporium and watch the company's 180 artists put the finishing touches on the figurines (weekdays only) at the Christmas Museum.

Cowgirl Chile Co. (215-348-4646), 52 East State Street, Doylestown. You can watch artists hand-etch the semiprecious metal jewelry at this fun shop. The A–Z charm collection is a favorite.

Craft Boutique at Moyer Farmhouse (215-716-3077), 308 North Main Street, Chalfont. A rambling and warm home full of personal, handcrafted gift items, many created by local artisans with Pennsylvania themes. There's even a freezer full of homemade soups in the kitchen area.

Doylestown Bookshop (215-230-7610), 16 South Main Street, Doylestown. A homegrown bookstore with a helpful staff, wide selection, and one of the most comprehensive collections of Berenstain Bears titles around. (The late authors, Stan and Jan Berenstain, lived nearby.)

ANTIQUES Serious antiques shoppers will want to check out the Upper Bucks County towns of Riegelsville and Kintnersville.

Antique Haven (610-749-0230), 1435 Easton Road, Riegelsville. A variety of antiques and collectibles, from vintage cocktail shakers and old books to late 19th-century furniture.

Allen's Antiques (610-749-0337), 668 Easton Road, Riegelsville. Open Friday–Sunday, or by appointment. A wide selection of general-interest antiques, plus special interest items like folk art, china, watches, and formal furniture. There's an "affordable" section of collectibles, tools, and attic finds in the back barn.

FLEA & FARMERS' MARKETS
The Market at DelVal (215-230-7170; themarketatdelval.com), 2100 Lower State Road, Doylestown. Open daily. An abundance of produce (and vinegars and honey and sausages) straight out of the

EXCURSIONS

Peddler's Village (215-794-4000; peddlersvillage .com), US 202 and PA 263, Lahaska. Inspired by the village of Carmel, California, this former chicken farm opened in 1962 with a handful of shops and one restaurant. It's now home to more than 60 boutiques and shops selling everything from books and toys to handcrafted clocks, lace lingerie, and soy candles. With its landscaped brick pathways and easy, free parking, it's a low-maintenance alternative to New Hope's busier streets. It plays host to many different events throughout the year, including a Strawberry Festival in May and a scarecrow-making contest in October. Several good dining options, such as **Hart's Tavern** and the ever-reliable **Cock 'n Bull,** make it easy to spend an entire day here, or make it a getaway with a stay on premises at the quaint **Golden Plough Inn. Skin 'n Tonic** (215-794-3966) is an excellent day spa in a charming old house on the complex.

adjacent 500-acre teaching farm. In the summer there's homemade ice cream from the college's creamery, as well as wine fests on Friday nights with live music.

Golden Nugget Flea Market (609-397-0811; gnmarket.com), 1850 River Road, Lambertville. Open 6 a.m.–4 p.m. Wednesday, Saturday, and Sunday. Roseville pottery, 1950s pinball machines, comic books, and vintage jewelry are some of the items you'll find at this indoor-outdoor market south of downtown Lambertville.

Rice's Sale and Market (215-297-5993; ricesmarket.com), 6326 Greenhill Road, New Hope. Open 7 a.m.–1:30 p.m. Tuesday year-round, and Saturday from March–December. Bargain hunters and avid collectors won't want to miss this 700-vendor market about 6 miles northwest of downtown New Hope. It began as a livestock auction in 1860 and evolved into an indoor-outdoor extravaganza of fresh produce, woodcrafts, antique furniture, Amish pastries, used CDs, and dried-flower arrangements. Those in the know skip Saturday and show up on Tuesday (the earlier the better), when all the vendors are present and accounted for.

❋ Special Events

January: **Winter Festival** (last weekend), New Hope and Lambertville, New Jersey—includes ice-carving demonstrations, a chili cook-off, children's theater performances, and a festive parade led by Mummers string bands. For more info, visit www.winterfestival.net.

April: **Shad Festival** (last weekend), Lambertville, New Jersey—riverfront bash that includes crafts displays, culinary tents, and live music, all in celebration of the silvery fish's spring appearance in the Delaware River.

May: **New Hope Gay Pride Festival** (third weekend), New Hope—street festival that attracts thousands of local and out-of-state visitors. **Arts Alive!** (third weekend), Quakertown—art exhibits, sidewalk sales, strolling performances, and cooking and glass-blowing demonstrations take over Quakertown's center.

July: **New Hope Film Festival** (second weekend), New Hope—screens features, short films, and documentaries from all over the world, with many of the filmmakers attending the events at New Hope Arts Center.

PENNSYLVANIA DUTCH COUNTRY

■

LANCASTER COUNTY/ AMISH COUNTRY

READING & KUTZTOWN

LANCASTER COUNTY/
AMISH COUNTRY

Lancaster County, about 65 miles west of Philadelphia, was settled in the early 1700s by the Amish, Mennonites, and the Brethren Anabaptist Christian communities who trace their roots back to 16th-century Europe. It is home to one of the country's largest Amish populations. The Amish are known for their plain dress, pacifism, and avoidance of modern conveniences such as electricity and cars. Most, however, have accepted, even embraced, the tourism industry that dominates the area, allowing visitors to eat dinner in their homes (for a small fee), selling their crafts and baked goods in commercial shops and out of their homes, and even leading and narrating buggy rides through the countryside.

The city of Lancaster is the county seat and hub of Lancaster County, with a population of more than 50,000 and an urban downtown with nifty attractions such as the Central Market and Fulton Opera House. The heart of Amish Country, however, lies east of here in the rural towns of Bird-in-Hand, Intercourse, and Paradise. This is where you'll find fourth-generation Amish farms, the largest concentrations of craft and quilt shops, hand-painted ROOT BEER FOR SALE signs, and large commercial operations, from buggy rides to F/X theaters, that are squarely aimed at tourists.

You don't have to spend much time in Lancaster County to realize tourism is the dominant industry. While the area still has an attractive rural backdrop of farms and rolling green hills, it is also home to dozens of souvenir shops, all-you-can-eat smorgasbords, and just about every chain motel in existence. I suggest that first-time visitors do some advance research and planning about Amish Country before heading there. If you wind up seeing the area from development-crazy Lincoln Highway (US 30), you may wonder what all the fuss is about and leave before ever sampling some of the state's tastiest soft pretzels or viewing the amazing selections of handcrafted Windsor chairs, farm tables, and quilts.

One of the best ways to enjoy the area is to slow your pace (don't honk when the horse and buggy trots along in front of you at 12 miles an hour, for instance) and follow the winding back roads as much as possible. It's difficult to get lost, and some of the best views, shops, and ice cream can be found away from the crowds and traffic.

Today, families from New York, Philadelphia, and the Washington, DC, area come to Lancaster to give their citified kids a chance to milk cows, romp through cornfields, ride in horse-drawn buggies, and climb around old steam engines. Bus tours are big, too, filling the area's family-style restaurants, biblical-themed theaters, and farmers' markets and auctions. Individuals and couples looking for a quiet getaway of antiques shopping and romantic dinners will also find that here—most notably in the quaint northern towns of Lititz and Ephrata.

AREA CODE Except for the southeastern edge, which uses 610, Lancaster County lies within the 717 area code.

GUIDANCE Mennonite Information Center (717-768-0807), 3551 Old Philadelphia Pike, Intercourse. Open Monday–Saturday from March–December; Friday and

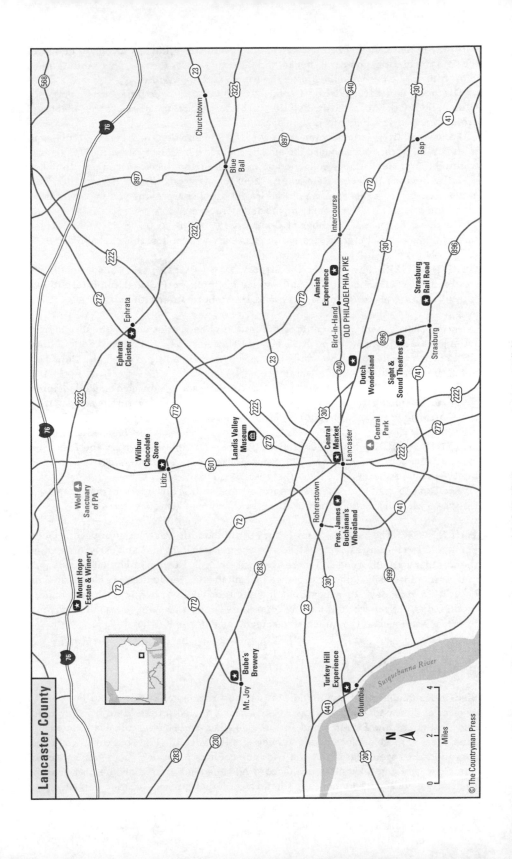

Lancaster County

560
76
23
322
Churchtown
897
340
30
897
Blue Ball
897
322
Gap
41
322
222
772
Intercourse
772
30
Amish Experience
Bird-in-Hand
896
272
Ephrata
Ephrata Cloister
OLD PHILADELPHIA PIKE
Strasburg Rail Road
322
23
896
Sight & Sound Theatres
340
Strasburg
76
222
Dutch Wonderland
741
Wilbur Chocolate Store
772
Landis Valley Museum
772
222
772
Central Market
30
772
Wolf Sanctuary of PA
Lititz
501
Lancaster
Central Park
222
222
Rohrerstown
141
272
Mount Hope Estate & Winery
72
72
Pres. James Buchanan's Wheatland
772
283
999
30
72
Bube's Brewery
23
Mt. Joy
Turkey Hill Experience
Susquehanna River
283
230
30
441
Columbia
30

N

0   2   4
Miles

© The Countryman Press

Saturday in January and February. Near Kitchen Kettle Village, it has maps and local tourist information, postcards, books, and fair-trade crafts for sale, plus exhibits and a short film on the faith and lifestyle of the Amish and Mennonites.

Discover Lancaster Visitor Center (717-299-8901; discoverlancaster.com), 501 Greenfield Road, Lancaster. Just off US 30, this large facility has restrooms, maps and brochures, and a staffed information desk.

Lancaster City Visitor Center (717-517-5718), 38 Penn Square, Lancaster. Look here in the building that once housed the old city hall for general city information, historic walking tours, and a unique collection of prints featuring the city's iconic buildings.

Lititz Springs Welcome Center (717-626-8981), 18 North Broad Street, Lititz. This center, located in a replica of an old railway station, can provide you with details on Lititz and other Lancaster County towns and attractions.

Northern Lancaster Chamber of Commerce (717-738-9010), 16 East Main Street, Ephrata. Maps, brochures, postcards, and more are available at this old train depot.

GETTING THERE *By air:* **Lancaster Airport** (717-569-1221), on PA 501 south of Lititz, has limited service. The nearest full-service airports are **Philadelphia International** (215-937-6800), about 65 miles away, and **Harrisburg International,** about 40 miles away.

By car: Three main thoroughfares run through Lancaster County. US 30 runs from Philadelphia's Main Line through the city of Lancaster, then west toward York County. US 222 runs north–south through Lancaster between Reading and the Maryland border. From Hershey, take US 322 east.

By bus: **Capitol Trailways** (800-333-8444) runs bus service to and from Philadelphia.

By train: **Amtrak** trains to Philadelphia and New York run several times a day from the Amtrak station (717-291-5080), 53 McGovern Avenue, Lancaster.

GETTING AROUND Most people drive between destinations within the Lancaster area. You can join the Amish and take a horse-drawn buggy ride around the back roads, but these tend to be leisurely tours that return you to the same place.

Red Rose Transit (717-397-4246; redrosetransit.com) runs buses all over Lancaster County. Pick up a schedule and tickets at the downtown visitor center.

WHEN TO GO The Lancaster area is busy throughout the year, with August and October attracting the largest crowds. Those in the know visit in May and early June, when the weather's usually good and there are fewer crowds. Keep in mind that many shops and restaurants, especially those owned by Amish and Mennonites, are closed on Sundays. It's a great day to see locals out and about on walks or buggy rides or attending hymn sings, but you won't find many commercial activities open, except at large tourist attractions such as the Amish Homestead and Kitchen Kettle.

✳ Cities, Towns & Villages

Bird-in-Hand. Despite a population of just 300 residents, Bird-in-Hand is home to several of Lancaster's biggest tourist attractions, including the Plain & Fancy Farm and Restaurant, the Bird-in-Hand Farmers' Market, and several midsized hotels and inns. Most of these are located along busy Old Philadelphia Pike, but the town is also surrounded by scenic farmland and two-lane country roads. It's about 5 miles east of Lancaster city and takes its name, according to legend, from a debate between two road surveyors about whether they should stay at their present location or push ahead to Lancaster. One of them supposedly responded: "A bird in the hand is worth two in the bush." So they stayed. One of the best things about Bird-in-Hand is its bake shop, a sticky bun and whoopie pie mecca that should not be missed.

Columbia. For a good look at a river town, drive out of Lancaster on US 30 West and take the last exit before you get to the Susquehanna River. Many parts of Columbia still show the grittiness of life along the river, but you'll also find antiques shops and some exceptional tourist spots. The Turkey Hill Experience shows how the county's famous ice cream is made; time ticks away at the fascinating National Watch and Clock Museum; and the Wright's Ferry Mansion offers a look at a Pennsylvania English Quaker house from the mid-1700s.

Ephrata. Considered a hub of northern Lancaster County, Ephrata (pronounced EH-fra-ta) was founded by Conrad Beissel, the German-born man who also started the town's famous religious cloister. Its name means "fruitful" in old Hebrew, and it has less of a tourist feel than other towns in the area. Besides the monastery, the town boasts a pedestrian-friendly downtown lined with shops, restaurants, and homes with wide front porches. It is also home to one of the area's largest and best farmers' markets, the Green Dragon, which features antiques and animal auctions, flea market finds, Pennsylvania Dutch food, and Doneckers, an upscale shopping complex, restaurant, and inn.

Intercourse. No one seems to know for sure how the town got its name, though it has certainly been the butt of countless jokes and postcards. One guess is that it stems from the town's location at the intersection of two busy roads, which also explains its earlier name, Cross Keys. This is perhaps Lancaster's busiest town and one that is heavily geared to tourists, though its dry goods and fabric stores also attract many local Amish and Mennonites. About 2 miles east of Bird-in-Hand, it's home to Kitchen Kettle shopping village, the People's Place Museum complex, plus dozens of independent quilt and crafts shops. Expect traffic, even gridlock, along this stretch of PA 340 most weekends.

Lititz. Founded as a Moravian community in 1756 and named after a castle in Bohemia, this town of about 9,000 people has one of the most charming main streets you'll ever find. It's about 6 miles north of Lancaster and makes a good base for a visit to Amish Country, with many good B&Bs, parks, independent shops, and restaurants. It is also home to one of the oldest pretzel bakeries in the nation, as well as the Wilbur Chocolate Store and Linden Hall, the country's oldest female boarding school. Many of its attractions and shops are within walking distance of one another.

Mount Joy. Located on Lancaster County's western edge, this town of 8,000

A FRONT PORCH IN LITITZ

I f you don't have much time to see a particular town in Lancaster County, plan your visit on a Friday night. Downtown Lancaster (visitlancastercity.com/first-friday) pulls out all the stops and the shops stay open late on the first Friday of the month. You'll find musicians playing on the street corners and artists at work in their studios. Many restaurants and breweries join the fun with special menu items and tastings. Lancaster County's smaller towns follow suit: Celebrate in Lititz on the second Friday of the month; Mount Joy and Columbia share the fourth Friday.

people can also be visited in context with trips to Hershey, Harrisburg, and York. It is home to several well-regarded farm-stay inns and B&Bs, and its revitalized main street has many antiques and gift shops and restaurants. You'll also find Bube's Brewery, a 19th-century brewery turned theme park of sorts, here.

Strasburg. Trains are the main theme in this village south of Lancaster, though it traces its roots back to 17th-century French hunters and traders who named it after the town of Strasbourg in France. Today, it's a small child's dream, with several different train-themed attractions and even a motel that lets you sleep in spiffed-up cabooses. Its anchor is the Strasburg Rail Road, which dates to 1832 and is touted as the oldest continuously operating public utility in the state. Strasburg is also home to Sight & Sound, a live theater company known for its biblical-themed stage extravaganzas. You'll notice that many of Strasburg addresses list only the street or route name, but it's nearly impossible to get lost here; almost everything is within throwing distance of PA 741 (Gap Road) and PA 896.

✷ To See

HISTORIC SITES **Ephrata Cloister** (717-733-6600; ephratacloister.org), 632 West Main Street (US 322), Ephrata. Open daily from March–December, closed Mondays in January and February; admission fee charged. Founded in 1732 by German-born Conrad Beissel, this somewhat radical religious community practiced celibacy and asceticism and was known for its calligraphy, a cappella music, and printing and bookbinding skills. Today, you can visit the cluster of preserved medieval-style buildings where its nearly 300 members lived, in a grassy area near downtown Ephrata. You may opt for a self-guided tour, but the guided tours (included in the admission price) include access to more buildings and insights into the austere lifestyle and habitat. Plan to spend about two hours here, and leave time to browse the gift shop.

Hans Herr House (717-464-4438; hansherr.org), 1849 Hans Herr Drive, Lancaster. Guided tours Monday–Saturday from April–November. Andrew Wyeth, a descendant of Herr, painted many pictures of this 1719 stone structure, which served as the first Mennonite meetinghouse in America and is considered the oldest structure in the county. The property also includes a blacksmith's shop and a replica Native American longhouse, inspired by the traditional eastern woodland construction used by Pennsylvania tribes between 1570 and 1770.

Julius Sturgis Pretzel Bakery (717-626-4354; juliusssturgis.com), 219 East Main Street (PA 772), Lititz. Pretzels come in all shapes and sizes, and the ones made by the Sturgis family still follow the recipes and some of the methods put in place in 1861. Although today's pretzels are made in a modern factory in Shillington, Pennsylvania, the original pretzel bakery, which was the first commercial pretzel bakery in America, is still open for business in Lititz. Twenty-minute tours end with a hands-on pretzel-twisting demonstration (you get to keep your creation). Expect short waits in the summer.

Wheatland (717-392-4633; lancasterhistory.org), 230 North President Avenue. Admission fee charged. James Buchanan was the only president to hail from Pennsylvania; he grew up in Mercersburg and attended Dickinson College in Carlisle. When he left the White House, he was widely criticized for failing to prevent the Civil War, but he found solace in this 1828 Federal house and lived there until his death in 1868. Costumed guides lead hour-long tours of the home, which contains many of Buchanan's original belongings. A separate museum on the grounds (included in tour admission) features rotating exhibits on Lancaster history from colonial days to the present, as well as presidential campaign materials and gifts Buchanan received during his presidency.

MAKING PRETZELS BY HAND AT A BAKERY IN LITITZ

MUSEUMS 🖉 ♿ ❄ **Landis Valley Museum** (717-569-0401; landisvalleymuseum.org), 2451 Kissel Hill Road, Lancaster. Open daily; admission charged. George and Henry Landis started a small museum in north Lancaster to exhibit family heirlooms in the 1920s; the state acquired it in the 1950s and expanded it into a 21-building village that showcases Pennsylvania German culture, folk traditions, decorative arts, and language. The best time to visit is in summer and early fall, when costumed clockmakers, tavern keepers, farmers, and others demonstrate their trades throughout the complex. The Weathervane gift shop sells beautiful handcrafted gifts and books on local history and farming.

🖉 **Demuth Museum** (717-299-9940; demuth.org), 120 East King Street, Lancaster. Open Tuesday–Sunday, closed January; donations accepted. Lancaster-born Charles Demuth was a master watercolorist known for his uniquely modernist renderings of the area's factories, grain elevators, and churches. This wonderful little museum was his childhood home and painting studio. It contains 40 original Demuth works, plus exhibits showcasing the work of artists who influenced him. There is also a lovely outside garden planted with flowers cultivated by the artist's mother, and the adjacent Demuth Tobacco Shop, the oldest operating tobacco shop in the country. You don't have to know Demuth's work to appreciate this quietly beautiful attraction. It's within walking distance of Central Market.

🖉 **Railroad Museum of Pennsylvania** (717-687-8628; rrmuseumpa.org), PA 741, Strasburg. Open daily from April–October; Tuesday–Sunday from November–March; admission charged. The main attraction of this train lover's mecca is the Rolling Stock Hall, home to four railroad tracks and two dozen preserved locomotive and passenger cars dating from 1875 to the 20th century. There are also displays of train tickets, art, uniforms, and tools; kids will love Stewart Junction and its hands-on electric train setups. It is directly across the street from the Strasburg Rail Road. The museum underwent a major overhaul in 2019, adding new exhibits, an updated diesel railcar simulator, and interpretive displays.

INTERCOURSE

American Military Edged Weaponry Museum (717-768-7185), 3562 Old Philadelphia Pike, Intercourse. Open Monday–Saturday from May–November; small admission fee charged. Military history buffs will want to check out the comprehensive collection of military knives on display, from swords and sabers to fencing bayonets and Ka-Bars. There are also displays of old recruiting posters and weapons and artifacts from the Spanish-American War, the Vietnam War, and Operation Desert Storm.

✻ To Do

✐ ⅄ **The Amish Experience** (717-768-3600; amishexperience.com), 3121 Old Philadelphia Pike (PA 340), Bird-in-Hand. This is ground zero for many visitors looking to expand their understanding of the Amish way of life. There's a an easy-to-digest multimedia show (complete with 3D sound and special effects) about an Amish family struggling with their teenage son's desire to leave the church, as well as guided tours of a replica of a typical Amish homestead. Combo deals are available; if you must do only one, take the house tour—guides are knowledgeable and full of anecdotes about the Amish lifestyle. Those who want to know even more may want to take the interactive Amish VIP tour, added in 2019, which brings a limited number of visitors to three Amish properties to chat with families and witness daily activities such as milking cows, woodworking, or making soap. Check the website for ticket information and a schedule: amishexperience.com/vip-tour.

↑ ◎ **Julius Sturgis Pretzels** (717-626-4354; juliussturgis.com), 219 East Main Street, Lititz. America's first pretzel bakery; 20-minute tours are $4 and end with a hands-on pretzel-twisting demonstration. Expect short waits in the summer.

✐ ⅄ ↑ **Lancaster Science Factory** (717-509-6363; lancastersciencefactory.org), 454 New Holland Avenue, Lancaster. Closed Mondays from Labor Day–Memorial Day; admission fee. The perfect place to take the kids on a rainy Sunday. They can build a truss bridge, learn about acoustics, and partake in dozens of impressively low-tech brain teasers and puzzles that require more thinking than button pushing. Recent additions include a makerspace classroom and a courtyard with a focus on environmental sustainability. It's next to the Cork Factory Hotel and a five-minute drive from Penn Square.

Mount Hope Estate and Winery (717-665-7021; mounthopewinery.com), 2775 Lebanon Road (PA 72), Manheim. Much more than a winery and vineyard, the mansion at Mount Hope was built and the formal gardens laid out in 1800 by Henry Bates Grubb, then updated to a Victorian style by Daisy Elizabeth Brooke Grubb in 1895. Today the mansion hosts not only tastings but also some of the area's most interesting events, including a murder mystery theater, holiday stories and carols, the Pennsylvania Renaissance Faire, and the Celtic Fling (*see Special Events*).

Spooky Nook Sports Complex (717-945-7087; spookynooksports.com), 2193 Spooky Nook Road, Manheim. Known simply as "The Nook" around town—"Spooky" is pronounced "spuk-ee"—this is the place to be if you need to get a workout in while you're on vacation or decide to catch one of the statewide or national sporting tournaments held here. More than a dozen regulation courts and fields are housed in this 700,000-square-foot facility and within the climate-controlled dome. Grab a day pass and spend some time conquering the 30-foot walls, the 15-foot boulder, and the crack, or work out in the fitness center's boxing ring, free weight area, cardio room, or track.

FOR FAMILIES ♂ ♿ **Dutch Wonderland** (717-291-1888; dutchwonderland.com), 2249 Lincoln Highway East, Lancaster. Open daily from mid-June–August, weekends in May, September, and early October; admission charged; two-day flex passes available. Beyond the flamboyant faux castle on US 30 lies a compact and very manageable amusement park targeted to the 12-and-under set. The 35 kid-friendly rides include kid-powered train cars, a double-splash log flume, a carousel, bumper cars, and paddleboats. It also has a fun water park (with lounge chairs for parents) and daily medieval-themed stage shows and princess story times. Don't miss Exploration Island, home to a dozen animatronic dinosaurs, fossil digs, and a gondola cruise. Discounted combo deals are available with Hershey Park, which owns Dutch Wonderland.

♼ **Lancaster Marionette Theatre** (717-394-8398; lancastermarionette.org), 126 North Water Street, Lancaster. This local puppet theater was founded by Robert Brock in 1990. Schedules and tickets can be found on lmt.yapsody.com, and every ticket includes a visit to the John Durang Puppet Museum and a backstage tour 20 minutes prior to the show. Past shows—for adults and kids alike—included *Sleeping Beauty, Sherlock Holmes, Here Comes Peter Cottontail,* and *Rumpelstiltskin.*

♂ **Strasburg Rail Road** (866-725-9666; strasburgrailroad.com), 301 Gap Road (PA 741), Strasburg. Open daily from mid-April–mid-October. Admission charged; kids are half-price. Take a 45-minute ride on a coal-powered 1860s-era steam locomotive though the rural countryside. Guides describe the railroad's history along the way.

♂ ♼ **National Toy Train Museum** (717-687-8976; nttmuseum.org), 300 Paradise Lane, Strasburg. Open Friday–Monday from May–October, weekends in April, November, and December; admission charged. Owned and operated by the Train Collectors Association, this is a splendid place to take kids before or after a ride on the nearby Strasburg Rail Road. Young and old train lovers will enjoy the displays of locomotives and cars from the 1800s to the present. It's next to the Red Caboose Motel (see *Inns & Motels*).

♂ **Cherry-Crest Farm Maze** (717-687-6843; cherrycrestfarm.com), 150 Cherry Hill Road, Ronks. Closed Sundays; admission charged. This 175-acre farm near Strasburg has hayrides, obstacle courses, animal feedings, and dozens of other kid-friendly activities, but it is best known for its giant cornfield maze, open Friday and Saturday, May–November.

SCENIC DRIVES Head south on PA 896 through the tiny town of Georgetown. The road is dotted with horse farms and small family farm stands selling fresh corn, tomatoes, and other produce; payment is often by the honor system. PA 741 near the village of Gap is also a scenic country drive and quieter alternative to busy PA 30; start at the historic clocktower on Middle Street in Gap, then continue west to **Fisher Farm Stand,** which boasts some of the best prices around for produce, shoofly pies, jams, and pickles. Then wander next door to the small quilt shop attached to a Mennonite home and browse the hand-stitched beauties.

TURKEY HILL EXPERIENCE

Milk a mechanical cow. Free dive into a rainbow ball pit. Create your own ice cream flavor, then make a commercial about it. Sample an Eagles Touchdown Sundae. This former silk mill is as much interactive indoor playground as it is examination of the general ice cream–making process (the Turkey Hill dairy farm is actually a few miles away). The plentiful samples of ice cream and iced tea are a nice touch. There's also a free exhibit on the ground floor about the area's dairy industry and river communities. The large Creamery café sells hard-to-find and seasonal flavors such as whoopie pie. Turkey Hill Experience (888-986-8784; turkeyhillexperience.com), 301 Linden Street, Columbia. Open daily; admission charged.

MILKING A COW AT THE TURKEY HILL EXPERIENCE

✻ Outdoor Activities

BASEBALL The **Lancaster Barnstormers** are part of the Atlantic League of Professional Baseball and play at **Clipper Magazine Stadium** (717-509-4487; lancasterbarnstormers .com), 650 Prince Street, near the heart of downtown. Despite its lack of affiliation with Major League Baseball, the team has a loyal local following and may be the only stadium in the country to sell whoopie pies in its snack bars.

BICYCLING The Lancaster area offers a labyrinth of winding country roads that are ideal for cycling. For a detailed list of trails and suggested rides, visit lancasterbikeclub .net. **Trek Bicycles** (717-394-8998; 117 Rohrerstown Road) on Lancaster's west side also has good maps and information on local trails and rents road and mountain bikes. **Intercourse Bikeworks,** (717-929-0327; intercoursebikeworks.com), with a branch in

Lititz, offers rentals and guided countryside tours that may end with dinner at an Amish family's home.

If you're planning to visit in August, sign up for the **Lancaster Bicycle Club's** Covered Bridge Classic (see *Special Events*), which features multiple rides up to 100 miles long. The routes wind through pristine Amish farmland and a handful of Lancaster County's 29 historic covered bridges.

BUGGY RIDES The competition is fierce for these horse-drawn backcountry rides, which usually last about 30 minutes and roam the countryside. Most places operate daily, except Sunday, from about 9 to 6, with prices starting at $15 for adults and $10 for kids, plus a tip for the driver (though the ones listed below often have discount coupons available on their websites). Trips are usually in an open-air family carriage that seats a dozen or so. Most of the drivers are local Amish or Mennonite men who welcome questions about their culture and lifestyles.

Aaron and Jessica's Buggy Rides (717-768-8828; amishbuggyrides.com), next to the Amish Experience in Bird-in-Hand,

CORN FOR SALE IN AMISH COUNTRY

offers four different backcountry tours led by Amish or Mennonite guides. They usually stop at an Amish farm, where you can buy produce and baked goods. Ever tourist friendly, they're also open most Sundays and allow pets on the ride.

Ed's Buggy Rides (717-687-0360; edsbuggyrides.com), PA 896, Strasburg. Across the street from the Sight & Sound Theatres, its guides lead you through the cornfields and back roads of southern Lancaster County.

AAA Buggy Rides (717-687-9962; aaabuggyrides.com) operates out of the Red Caboose Motel in Strasburg and Kitchen Kettle Village in Intercourse. It's open Sunday.

FISHING **Evening Rise Fly Fishing Outfitters** (717-509-3636), 1953 Fruitville Pike, Lancaster. A good source for supplies and information on local rivers and streams. In winter you can ice fish on Speedwell Forge near Lititz.

GOLF **Tanglewood Manor Golf Club** (717-786-2500; 866-845-0479), 653 Scotland Road, Quarryville. An 18-hole, par-72 course surrounded by rolling hills with two man-made ponds, plus putting and chipping practice greens. It's about 5 miles south of Strasburg.

Olde Hickory Golf Course (717-569-9107), 600 Olde Hickory Road, Lancaster. Nine holes to 1,600 yards with a par of 28.

Overlook Golf Course (717-569-9551), 2040 Lititz Pike, Lititz. Opened in 1928, this 18-hole public course measures 6,083 yards and has a par of 70. There's also a driving range.

A HORSE-DRAWN BUGGY RIDE ON LANCASTER'S COUNTRY ROADS AYLEEN GONTZ

Tree Top Golf Course (717-665-6262), 1624 Creek Road, Manheim. An 18-hole, par-65 course with rolling terrain, good for novices or accomplished golfers looking for a quick round.

Willow Valley Golf Course (717-464-4448), 2416 Willow Street Pike, Lancaster. Nine-hole, 2,300-yard course on 35 manicured acres.

HORSEBACK RIDING **Ironstone Ranch** (717-902-9791; ironstoneranch.com), Elizabethtown. Guided horseback and tractor rides on 10 miles of trails on an estate that includes an 1877 Gothic Revival–style barn, named the Star Barn for its star-shaped louvered ventilators. The barn hosts tours, farm-to-table events, and weddings. **Nookside Stables** (717-618-8178; nookside.com) in Manheim offers lessons and guided horseback rides on 46 acres, plus "adventure rides" that teach how to ride and handle a mount, then guide the horses through an obstacle course.

HUNTING **Middle Creek Wildlife Management Area** (717-733-1512), 100 Museum Road, Stevens. Public waterfowl hunting is permitted here during open hunting season, and special deer hunts are scheduled periodically; check with the visitor center for specific areas and rules.

TENNIS **D. F. Buchmiller Park** (717-299-8215), 1050 Rockford Road, Lancaster, has several public tennis courts. **Central Park** (717-299-8215) in Lancaster also has courts at 585 Golf Road.

ZIPLINING **Refreshing Mountain Retreat and Adventure Center** (717-738-1490; refreshingmountain.com) in Stevens offers three zipline courses for ages five and up, including one with an elevated obstacle course with a variety of challenges.

✳ Green Space

PARKS & REFUGES Central Park (717-299-8215), 3 Nature's Way (near PA 222 and PA 272), Lancaster. This 540-acre park along the Conestoga River has playgrounds, a skate park, easy biking and walking trails, a photogenic covered bridge, and an environmental center and library. Near the main entrance on Rockford Road, the hilltop Garden of Five Senses invites visitors to use all five senses to appreciate its abundant flowers, shrubs, and waterfalls.

Columbia Crossing River Trails Center (717-449-5607), 41 Walnut Street, Columbia. This new facility on the east bank of the Susquehanna is the southern starting point of the 14-mile Northwest Lancaster County River Trail and a launch area for powerboats and paddlecraft. Built at the foot of one of the Susquehanna River's arching bridges, it's also a beautiful spot for a picnic lunch. Restrooms and drinks are located inside; there is also an informative display about the history and geology of the river.

🖉 **Wolf Sanctuary of Pennsylvania** (717-626-4617; wolfsanctuarypa.org), 465 Speedwell Forge, Lititz. Wolves haven't made Pennsylvania home for the past hundred years, but here you'll find 40 wolves who have nowhere else to go. The sanctuary is open for guided tours Tuesday, Thursday, Saturday, and Sunday and often hosts special events such as full moon nights (for ages 16 and up) with bonfires and live music. Your admission fee and donations to this nonprofit help to provide food, shelter, and veterinary care. **Long's Park,** (717-735-8883; longspark.org), US 30 at Harrisburg Pike, Lancaster. A 71-acre park with a spring-fed lake, ducks, picnic pavilions, tennis courts, and a small petting zoo that's open from June–September. The playground, which resembles a big wooden castle, is as good as it gets for the younger set—tire swings, turrets, bridges, and lots of giddy children. The park hosts a summer outdoor music series, an arts-and-crafts festival, and the world's largest chicken BBQ every May (see *Special Events*).

Lititz Springs Park (717-626-8981), 15 North Broad Street. Owned by the Lititz Moravian Congregation, this charming 7-acre park is anchored by a replica of a 19th-century train depot (home to a visitor center) and has two playgrounds, benches, pedestrian paths, and a pretty stream. It's right next to the Wilbur Chocolate Store and within walking distance of many stores and restaurants.

Middle Creek Wildlife Management Area (717-733-1512), 100 Museum Road, Stevens. Run by the state game commission, this 6,254-acre refuge between Lititz and Reading has three picnic areas, a shallow lake for boating and fishing, and 20 miles of year-round hiking trails that traverse the property's varied habitats. Pick up a self-guided driving map at the visitor center off Hopeland Road in Kleinfeltersville, and check out the waterfowl display and hands-on children's area. Around late February or March, as many as 100,000 migrating snow geese flock to the refuge on their way north to Canada; it's a beautiful sight that draws gawkers from all over the state. Public waterfowl hunting is permitted here during open hunting season, and special deer hunts are scheduled periodically; check with the visitor center for specific areas and rules.

WALKS The flat and straight **Lancaster Junction Recreation Trail** runs just over 2 miles (one way), passing through acres of scenic farmland and following a shaded creek on its northern half. It's also great for biking and horseback riding. To get to the southern trailhead, take PA 283 west of Lancaster City to Spooky Nook Road and turn right on Champ Road. The trailhead is on the left at road's end. For a scenic view of the Susquehanna River, head to **Chickies Rock County Park** in Marietta. If you're looking for short, sweet, and wooded, head for the **Shenk's Ferry Wildflower Preserve.** The

DOG-FRIENDLY LANCASTER

Beau's Dream Dog Park at Buchanan Park (717-291-4841), 901 Buchanan Avenue, Lancaster. With one half for big dogs and the other half for little dogs, this Lancaster park is a win-win for canines and their humans. Dogs play on artificial turf and frolic on water pads while dog parents relax on shaded seats. Once a landfill, Noel Dorwart Park (408 Parklawn Court) in Lancaster is built on reclaimed land and offers a more outdoorsy experience, with dog-friendly walking trails featuring a stream and a trestle bridge (dogs must be leashed) and a play area (for unleashed dogs). The Lititz Farmers' Market, held Thursday nights from the start of growing season through October, welcomes leashed dogs, as does Kitchen Kettle Village in Intercourse. Human eateries in Lancaster that accommodate canines include Dalton's Doggie Deck at the Spring House Brewing Co. (717-984-2530; 209 Hazel Street), The Fridge (717-490-6825; 534 North Mulberry Street) and the Four54 Grill (717-390-2626; 454 New Holland Avenue).

OTTO THE DACHSUND ON THE LANCASTER JUNCTION RECREATION TRAIL RACHEL STELLHORN PHOTOGRAPHY

trailhead on Shenk's Ferry Road near Holtwood Dam can be a challenge to find, but keep your eyes open in early spring and you'll be rewarded with blooms from trillium, lady slippers, and other native wildflowers. The **Turkey Hill Overlook Trail,** combined with the Enola Low Grade Rail Trail, is a 6-mile loop along the river that starts and ends on River Road in Washington Boro and offers views of the river and nearby wind turbines.

✳ Lodging

BED & BREAKFASTS **Inn at Twin Linden** (717-445-7619; innattwinlinden.com), 2092 Main Street, Churchtown. This graceful 19th-century home is about 25 minutes from the tourist heart of Amish Country, but some might consider that a blessing. Housed in a historic mansion with gardens that back up to Mennonite farm fields, it has six rooms and two suites, all with feather beds and luxury linens, many with gas fireplaces and Jacuzzi tubs. The Polo and Churchtown Rooms and both suites face the back gardens and tend to get less street noise. A three-course breakfast is served in a dining room overlooking the back garden; almond croissant French toast is a specialty. $$.

Lovelace Manor (717-399-3275; lovelacemanor.com), 2236 Marietta Avenue, Lancaster. No children under

12. This beautiful 1882 home is about 5 minutes from Lancaster City and 15 to 20 minutes from outlying towns such as Strasburg and Bird-in-Hand. Named after the 17th-century poet Richard Lovelace (an ancestor of owner Lark McCarley), it has four spacious rooms decorated in soft beige and brown with private baths, 12-foot-high ceilings, a billiard and games room, and several sitting porches. An outdoor hot tub and 24-hour access to a pantry stocked with soft drinks and snacks are also available. Breakfast is an elegant affair served on china and crystal in the main dining room. $$$.

LITITZ

Alden House (717-627-3363; aldenhouse .com), 62 East Main Street, Lititz. Within walking distance of the shops and restaurants of downtown Lititz, this 1850s Federal home offers lower rates than many other local B&Bs. The six rooms and suites are heavy on antiques, curtains, and floral accents, with queen beds, private baths, and televisions; common areas include three porches and a back garden with a fish pond. Breakfast is a large and lavish affair featuring fruit, a main entrée (maybe French Acadian crêpes or three-egg omelets), breads and muffins, and desserts such as apple cake or lemon pudding. $$–$$$.

Swiss Woods (717-627-3358; 800-594-8018; swisswoods.com), 500 Blantz Road, Lititz. No children under 12. Surrounded by acres of landscaped gardens and countryside, this seven-room, Swiss-themed inn is considered one of the best B&Bs in the north Lancaster area. It's about 3 miles from downtown Lititz and has seven large rooms with private baths, goose down comforters, and natural woodwork. A favorite room is Lake of Geneva, which has a private balcony overlooking the gardens and Speedwell Forge Lake. Breakfasts are very good and might include baked oatmeal, quiche with garden herbs,

or cherry cobbler. Afternoon snacks might include cranberry cookies with brown-butter glaze, biscotti, or orange bundt cakes. $$$.

INNS & HOTELS Amish View Inn (717-768-1162; amishviewinn.com), 3125 Old Philadelphia Pike (PA 340), Bird-in-Hand. I normally would steer visitors away from hotels on traffic-heavy routes such as 340 and US 30, but this small 50-room hotel is an exception. It's adjacent to Plain & Fancy Farm and a good bet for families or anyone who wants to be right in the middle of all the buggy-ride and farm-stand bustle. The spacious rooms have mahogany-frame king beds, DVD players, and refrigerators, and include a huge breakfast of waffles and made-to-order omelets. The north-facing rooms overlook beautiful rolling green pastures. One- and two-bedroom suites have whirlpool tubs and fireplaces. An indoor pool, a Jacuzzi, and a fitness room are also on-site. $–$$$.

🛏 ♂ **Eden Resort and Suites** (717-569-6444; edenresort.com), 222 Eden Road, Lancaster. Kid-friendly amenities and a central location near US 222 and PA 272 make this large resort popular with families. The 285 rooms and suites are modern and comfortable, with refrigerators, coffeemakers, and flat-panel TVs. Amenities include indoor and outdoor pools, a kids' playground and water splash area, bocce court, and much more. $$$.

Cork Factory Hotel (717-735-2075; corkfactoryhotel.com), 480 New Holland Avenue, Lancaster. Lancaster was once the second-largest cork-producing city in the United States. One of its largest factories was turned into a luxury hotel in 2008 and is an ideal alternative for folks who prefer modern spaciousness over B&B quaintness or rustic farm stays. It's also a popular site for weddings and other events. The handsome rooms have one or two king beds, exposed brick walls, and enough space to practically accommodate an entire gymnastics team. It's right next to the Lancaster

Science Factory and an easy five-minute drive to Penn Square. On-premises dining options include the Cork & Cap restaurant and a bakery with an open kitchen and communal tables. $$$.

🎣 🛏 **Heritage Hotel** (717-898-2431; heritagelancaster.com), 500 Centerville Road, Lancaster. This large hotel is right off US 30 and makes a convenient base if you're spending a few days in Amish Country. The 166 traditional rooms are tidy and large, with one king or two queen beds. Formerly known as Sherwood Knoll, it is popular with bus tours and traveling sports teams. There's a small pool (plus a wading pool for kids). It's adjacent to Loxley's, a two-level bar and restaurant that caters to all tastes (from make-your-own pizzas for kids to prime rib and dry martinis for grown-ups). There's live music Wednesday and Saturday. It's also next door to the Dutch Apple Dinner Theater (see *Entertainment*). $$.

Hershey Farm Restaurant and Inn (800-827-8635; hersheyfarm.com), 240 Hartman Bridge Road (PA 896), Ronks. The closet hotel to Sight & Sound Theatres offers a wide variety of rooms, including suites and apartments for families and a rental space for large groups. Also on-site is a restaurant, a petting farm, a fishing pond, a farmers' market, a restaurant and smorgasbord, shops, and Amos, a rather large statue of an Amish man. Hotel guests can walk from the back of the inn's property to the front of Sight & Sound in about 10 minutes.

Lancaster Arts Hotel (717-299-3000; 877-208-5521; lancasterartshotel.com), 300 Harrisburg Pike, Lancaster. Gorgeous local artwork and 63 modern rooms and suites now fill this former tobacco warehouse near the center of downtown. It is one of the city's hippest spots, with a popular lobby bar and a clientele that could be straight out of Manhattan. All rooms have wine refrigerators, flat-screen TVs, and iPod docking stations. A continental breakfast is included and served in the stone-walled dining room or outside on the waterfall-serenaded patio. For dinner, don't miss the highly regarded John J. Jefferies restaurant (see *Dining Out*). $$$.

🛏 **Red Caboose Motel** (717-687-5000; redcaboosemotel.com), 312 Paradise Lane, Strasburg. The "rooms" in this motel next to the National Toy Train Museum are actual 25-ton N-5 cabooses, at least on the outside. The interiors have real beds, private baths, and flat-screen TVs; some have whirlpool tubs, fridges, and microwaves. This is a good value for families looking to stay near Strasburg's train attractions. A playground, a petting zoo, and a restaurant, Casey Jones', replicating a dining car with views of the countryside and trains rolling by. In summer, movies are screened on the side of the barn. $$.

🛏 **Harvest Drive Family Inn** (717-768-7186; 800-233-0176; harvestdrive .com), 3370 Harvest Drive, Intercourse. Surrounded by corn and alfalfa fields on a quiet road outside Intercourse, this family-owned motel has clean and basic rooms that sleep up to six people. There is a playground and Pennsylvania Dutch–style restaurant on the property. Rates drop considerably January–March and include breakfast. $–$$.

FARM STAYS More than 30 farms in or near Lancaster County offer "farm stays" to guests for rates of about $100 to $150 a night. They are usually a real treat for kids and a heck of a lot more interesting than staying in a chain motel on US 30. Most include a hearty breakfast (except on Sunday), plus activities such as hayrides and opportunities to help with milking cows and feeding chickens. The rooms tend to be comfortable but basic, often with shared baths. For a more comprehensive list, go to afarmstay.com.

Old Fogie Farm (717-426-3992; oldfogiefarm.com), 16 Stackstown Road, Marietta. This working farm on the county's western edge stands out for its charming yet modern rooms (with cable and air-conditioning) and the down-to-earth attitude of Tom and Biz Fogie ("We're not just a bunch of fluff"). Kids will love the wading pond, tire swing, and friendly yard pig. The Hayloft Family Suite has queen and trundle beds, a full kitchen, claw-foot tub, and deck overlooking the barnyard. Breakfast is extra, and there is a three-night minimum stay on holiday weekends. $$.

Rocky Acre (717-653-4449; rockyacre .com), 1020 Pinkerton Road, Mount Joy. You might call this the Four Seasons of farm stays, with its romantic Victorian-style rooms, all of which have air-conditioning and private baths. There is also a two-bedroom apartment that sleeps up to seven and a guest house with a full kitchen and private entrance. Located on a 550-acre dairy farm, it offers delicious multicourse breakfasts and plenty of recreational activities, from pony, train, and tractor rides to guided farm tours and a petting zoo. Owners Eileen and Galen Benner have been in the farm-stay business for more than 40 years. There is a two-night minimum on weekends. $$–$$$.

Verdant View Farm (717-687-7353; 888-321-8119; verdantview.com), 439 Strasburg Road, Paradise. This 118-acre Mennonite dairy farm is a quick drive or walk from most of Strasburg's train attractions. Kids will love watching the Strasburg train pass through the field behind the Ranck family farmhouse; they may also help milk the cows, feed the swans and geese, fish for bass and bluegills in the pond, and pet the many cats, sheep, and rabbits that call the farm home. Basic rooms in the farmhouse are on the second floor. Two have private baths and sleep up to four; a newly renovated first-floor suite includes a master bedroom, private bath, and a small room with bunk beds, perfect for families. A highlight is the optional breakfast (for an extra $5): a feast, usually led by Don or Ginnie Ranck, of yogurt, applesauce, French toast, eggs, toast, fresh milk, coffee, and good conversation. Farm

tours are open to anyone for a small fee: They might include homemade ice cream tastings and cheese-making demonstrations. $$.

CAMPGROUNDS & CABINS Flory's Cottages and Camping (717-687-6670; floryscamping.com), 99 North Ronks Road. Shaded, level grassy sites with electric, water, sewer, hook-ups. Tent sites $; cottages $$.

Beaver Creek Farm Cabins (717-687-7745; beavercreekfarmcabins.com), 2 Little Beaver Road (PA 896), Strasburg. Eight 2-bedroom cabins (and one single bedroom) on a lush farm property with a covered bridge, pond, and views of the countryside. $$.

Loose Caboose Campground (717-442-8429; theloosecaboosecampground .com), 5130 Strasburg Road (PA 741), Kinzers. Good option for families who plan to spend a lot of time in nearby Strasburg. It's on 26 forested acres with a children's playground, campfire sites, and picnic pavilions. $.

✦ **Spring Gulch Resort Campground** (717-354-3100; springgulch.com), 475 Lynch Road, New Holland. Huge, highly rated campground with 415 tent sites, cabins, and housing rentals; a day spa; two heated pools; fishing and swimming lakes; and a fitness center. Saturday to Saturday stays required in summer. Its popular Folk Festival the third weekend of May draws big crowds. $–$$.

✳ Where to Eat

Lancaster County restaurants often specialize in hearty Pennsylvania Dutch foods such as chicken potpie, pepper cabbage, and baked ham. You can also easily arrange to have dinner in an Amish family's home; many inn and B&B owners are happy to help set these up. It typically costs under $20 a person and features a multicourse, home-cooked Pennsylvania Dutch meal and genial conversation.

PENNSYLVANIA DUTCH SMORGASBORDS

These all-you-can-eat buffets are a staple of Lancaster County. Regular patrons debate passionately over which ones are the best and which ones should be left to stew in their canned sweet potatoes. Many of them are big enough to seat hundreds of diners, making them popular with bus tours. Most offer soup and salad bar, carving stations, many Pennsylvania Dutch dishes, and a wide selection of desserts. Selective or light eaters might want to avoid these buffets and stick with smaller à la carte establishments. For others, here are a few favorite standbys.

Shady Maple (717-354-8222), 129 Toddy Drive, East Earl. Closed Mondays. This huge complex along PA 23 began as a farm stand and has expanded into a small city with an 1,100-seat restaurant, grocery store, banquet hall, and stadiumlike parking. It gets consistent raves from buffet pros for its homemade fruit breads, wide selection of meats, seafood, vegetables, and hot and cold dessert bar. $.

Dienner's Country Restaurant (717-687-9571), 2855 Lincoln Highway, Ronks. Smaller than other smorgasbords, this homey diner is known for its fall-off-the-bone rotisserie chicken and low prices. It also offers à la carte items such as burgers and daily specials of meat loaf and chicken potpie. $.

Miller's (717-687-6621), 2811 Lincoln Highway East, Ronks. Breakfast, lunch, and dinner daily. This centrally located restaurant caters to bus tours and out-of-towners; it takes reservations and is one of the few smorgasbords to stay open on Sunday and to serve wine and beer. Its huge serve-yourself buffet features items such as top sirloin, baked ham with cider sauce, chicken potpie, and baked cabbage in cream sauce. The large dining room overlooks the countryside. $$.

Stoltzfus Farm Restaurant (717-768-8156), PA 772, Intercourse. Lunch and dinner Monday–Saturday from April–October; weekends in April and November. Meals are served family-style (no menu) at long tables and include a typical Pennsylvania Dutch menu of ham loaf, fried chicken, buttered noodles, chow-chow, and pepper cabbage. The sausage and other meats come from the family's adjacent butcher shop. No reservations. $$.

DINING OUT ⛾ **Bube's Brewery** (717-653-2056; bubesbrewery.com), 102 North Market Street, Mount Joy. Open daily for lunch and dinner. Alois Bube, a German immigrant, started this small brewery in the 1870s and later opened a hotel next door. Today the large complex is as much an indoor theme park as a restaurant and bar, with brewery tours, three different dining areas, a summer biergarten, gift shop, and live music from jazz trios to minstrel performances. Dine on a six-course, prix fixe, murder mystery dinner at Alois in the hotel portion, or head to the Catacombs, where costumed guides lead you on a tour of the cellars before your meal. Lunch and dinner are also available at the more casual Bottling Works on the original brewery site. The menu is as vast as the Lancaster County countryside; the baked tomato soup and grilled cheese with crabmeat are a couple of favorites. The house brews change often, but might include oatmeal stout, brown ale, and Hefeweizen. Did we mention there are ghost tours, too? Bottling Works $$, Alois $$$$, Catacombs $$$.

♿ ⛾ **Carr's** (717-299-7090; carrsrestaurant.com), 50 West Grant Street, Lancaster. Lunch and dinner Tuesday–Saturday, Sunday brunch. This upscale restaurant, renovated and expanded in 2017, is a great place to sample creative American dishes before a show at the Fulton Theatre. Owner and Chef Tim Carr is a Lancaster area native who uses organic and locally made or raised products, from cheese and mustard to free-range chickens, as often as possible. At dinner, try the wild mushroom ravioli or tenderloin medallions in a blue cheese red wine sauce. The downstairs dining room is inviting, with a large mural of a Parisian street scene and view of the restaurant's extensive wine collection. Lunch is a good value; a favorite is the open-faced meat loaf sandwich with hunter's sauce and fries. Reservations recommended. $$–$$$.

℣ **General Sutter Inn** (717-626-2115; generalsutterinn.com), 14 East Main Street, Lititz. Open daily; call for hours. The General Sutter has operated continuously since 1764 at the intersection of PA 501 and PA 772. Its formal restaurant offers a satisfying dinner menu that includes steak frites, jumbo lump crabcakes with jalapeño remoulade, and fettuccine with wild mushrooms, asparagus, mascarpone, and chive oil. There's also a less expensive tavern menu of house-made flash-fried pickles, fish-and-chips, sausage rolls, and a variety of sandwiches. The outdoor patio is a popular place during the summer. Tavern menu $; dinner entrées $$.

Himalayan Curry & Grill (717-393-2330), 22 East Orange Street, Lancaster. Excellent Indian fare and Nepali specialties such as chicken-stuffed momo dumplings and mustard fish curry with pickled radish.

℣ **John J. Jeffries** (717-431-3307; johnjjeffries.com), 300 Harrisburg Pike, Lancaster. Just about everything on the menu is locally raised and organic at this hip new eatery in the Lancaster Arts Hotel. The creative menu changes seasonally and might include wild-caught shrimp and grits, grass-fed beef meatballs with spring onion–tomato risotto, or vegetarian dosas with black-eyed peas, lentil, quinoa, and jasmine-rice crêpes. Desserts are simple and refreshing: classic lemon curd, blueberry-rhubarb sorbet, or dark chocolate pâté with crème anglaise. Reservations recommended. $$$.

℣ **Olde Greenfield Inn** (717-393-0668; thegreenfieldrestaurant.com), 595 Greenfield Road, Lancaster. Lunch and dinner Tuesday–Saturday, Sunday brunch. This restored 1790s stone farmhouse is regularly rated among the area's top romantic restaurants by local newspapers and magazines. Try to reserve a table in the intimate wine cellar. The American menu includes herb-grilled lamb tenderloin, filet mignon, and Black Angus short-rib cottage pie. A bar lounge offers live music on Wednesday nights. Reservations suggested. $$–$$$.

EATING OUT **Café Chocolate** (717-626-0123), 40 Main Street, Lititz. Besides a large assortment of desserts made from fair-trade chocolate, this cute café serves salads, crêpes, vegan soups, and savory mains such as hickory-smoked chicken and chili con chocolate. $.

Central Market (717-291-4723), 23 North Market Street, Lancaster. Open Tuesday, Friday, and Saturday. Seating is limited, but the delicious food and wide range of choices make this a terrific lunch spot if you're in the downtown area. Housed in a beautiful brick 1880s building, it is home to dozens of stalls selling everything from chicken corn chowder and Kunzler hot dogs to Greek salads, empanadas, and tomato pie. The wonderful Carr's restaurant has a stall, as do S. Clyde Weaver Meats, Maplehofe Dairy, and Long's Horseradish. I've never had a bad meal here; the best thing to do is just wander around until your stomach tells you to stop. And consider picking up some creamline milk, whoopie pies, and fresh-picked flowers on the way out. Some vendors do not take credit cards.

Country Table Restaurant (717-653-4745; countrytablerestaurant.com), Bake Shoppe and Deli, 740 East Main Street, Mount Joy. Closed Sundays. This western Lancaster County eatery has plenty of fans who say it serves the best Pennsylvania Dutch food in the county. For breakfast you might find cherry-baked oatmeal, sausage gravy over biscuits with homefries, and waffles with fresh blueberries. The lunch specials, which include soup, salad, and a sandwich such as ham, cheddar, and bacon on rye, are a good value. $.

Isaac's Deli (717-687-7699), Shops at Traintown, Gap Road (PA 741), Strasburg. You'll find a reliable selection of salads, soups, flatbread pizzas, and grilled sandwiches at this local kid-friendly chain with a pink flamingo mascot. For a unique twist, try any of the grilled soft-pretzel roll sandwiches. $.

Oregon Dairy Restaurant (717-661-6804; oregondairy.com), Oregon Pike (at US 222), Lititz. Big portions and hearty Pennsylvania Dutch platters make this a favorite of families. A train running around part of the dining room will keep the kids occupied until the food comes. Every breakfast platter comes with a hockey puck–sized doughnut and a glass of fresh milk, and there's a well-regarded lunch and dinner buffet on Friday and Saturday. À la carte dinner options include ham loaf, liver and onions, and chicken and waffles. Also on premises is a full-service supermarket, a terrific children's play area (complete with cow chutes and a milk carton slide), and an ice cream shop with plenty of patio seating. $.

Rachel's Café & Creperie (717-399-3515; rachelscreperie.com), 201 West Walnut Street, Lancaster. With a large new outdoor deck, this beloved restaurant now has room for its indoor diners to spread out as they relax and eat crêpes for every meal of the day. Smoothies, coffee, and salads come on the side. $.

Speckled Hen Coffee & Kitchen (717-288-3139; speckledhencoffee.com), 141 East Main Street, Strasburg. A welcoming coffee bar serving up grab-and-go cups of joe and worth-the-wait pour-overs, plus all-day breakfasts, hot and cold sandwiches, and Lapp Valley Farm ice cream. $

Strasburg Country Store and Creamery (717-687-0766; strasburg.com), Strasburg. Try this old-fashioned general store and café on the square for ice cream in crunchy waffle cones, drinks from a decades-old antique marble soda fountain, and creamy homemade fudge. For something more substantial, order soup and a salad, or try the Amish Rachel (Reuben's other half). $.

Tomato Pie Café (717-627-1762; tomatopiecafe.net), 23 North Broad Street, Lititz. Indoor and outdoor seating at one of the town's beautiful old homes lends serious charm to a delicious spot where vegans and omnivores can share table space with ease. There's also a full espresso bar (with dairy-free options) and creative menu items like white lavender mocha latte, coconut crunch pancakes, and kimchi tomato pie. Delicious fare for meat eaters and vegans alike. $.

BAKERIES & FARM STANDS Farm stands can be found all over Lancaster County on busy highways and rural backcountry roads. They often sell everything from fresh produce and poultry to root beer and homemade potato chips.

Bird-in-Hand Bake Shop (717-656-7947), 542 Gibbons Road, Bird-in-Hand. A terrific Mennonite-owned bakery known for its reasonable prices and whoopie pies, cinnamon raisin bread, and shoofly pies. A playground and petting zoo are outside for the kids.

Farmette Farms, Rothsville Road, Ephrata. Closed Sundays. This roadside Mennonite stand sells peaches, corn, tomatoes, and other seasonal produce at reasonable prices. There are always baked goods on hand, such as raisin bars and peach pie, and the nursery sells potted flowers, plants, and homemade peat moss. There's neither a phone nor an address, but it is less than a mile west of Main Street.

Fisher's Farm Stand, Strasburg Road, PA 741. Closed Sundays. Mennonite-owned roadside stand selling homemade jams, bread-and-butter pickles, produce, and pies at very fair prices. Next door is a quilt shop (in the basement of a home), with full quilts starting at $395 and children's-themed quilts starting at $155.

Lapp Valley Farm (717-354-7988), 244 Mentzer Road, New Holland. A Mennonite dairy farm that produces the best homemade ice cream in the region. There are also homemade waffle cones, hot cocoa in the winter, and a selection of cheese, butter, and eggs.

Miesse Chocolates and Ice Cream Parlor (717-392-6011), 118 North Water Street, Lancaster. This old-fashioned candy store and factory has been producing hand-dipped chocolates since 1875. A refurbished 12-foot soda fountain serves milkshakes, egg creams, and hand-dipped ice cream from Penn State's renowned Berkey Creamery.

FARMERS' MARKETS **Green Dragon Market and Auction** (717-738-1117; greendragonmarket.com), 955 North State Street, Ephrata. Open 9–9 Fridays. As the local saying goes: "If you can't buy it at the Green Dragon, it chust ain't fer sale." This venerable old market, about 4 miles north of downtown Ephrata, is a shopper's mecca of 400 growers and vendors selling fresh flowers, produce, wood furniture, handmade clothing and quilts, and more. Its two auction houses specialize in antiques and livestock, and are fun to watch even if you're not buying. When you get hungry, have a Pennsylvania Dutch meal at the five sit-down restaurants or grab a soft pretzel or sausage sandwich at the many snack stands. Plan to spend at least a couple of hours here, if not an entire afternoon.

Bird-in-Hand Farmers' Market (717-393-9674), PA 340 and Maple Avenue, Bird-in-Hand. Open Friday and Saturday from December–March; Wednesday–Saturday from July–October; and Wednesday, Friday, and Saturday from April–June and November. This small market gets a lot of bus-tour traffic because of its prime location on PA 340. Look for the usual assortment of crafts, produce, baked goods, and hand-rolled soft pretzels. It's owned by Good 'N Plenty Restaurant, which is nearby.

Root's Country Market and Auction (717-898-7811), 705 Graystone Road, Manheim. Open 9–9 Tuesday. Just off PA 72 between Lebanon and Lancaster, this always lively, family-run market has 200 vendors selling smoked meats, fresh and dried herbs, doll clothes, hand-painted wooden ducks, and furniture. For instant nourishment, visit the Amish food stalls for soft pretzels, homemade potato chips, and apple dumplings. Locals bide their time until the afternoon produce auction (starting at 1 p.m.), when there are great deals on seasonal fruits, vegetables, and flowers. An indoor-outdoor flea market with 175 vendors, also open Tuesdays, is just across the street.

✳ Entertainment

THEATER & MOVIES **Fulton Theatre** (717-397-7425; thefulton.org), 12 North Prince Street, Lancaster. A former roadhouse and vaudeville stage that now hosts symphony, opera, and Broadway shows. Scholars lead free programs and Q&A sessions about the current production a half hour before showtime.

American Music Theater (717-397-7700), 2425 Old Lincoln Highway East (US 30), Lancaster. Live concerts and original Broadway shows.

Dutch Apple Dinner Theatre (717-898-1900; dutchapple.com), 510 Centerville Road, Lancaster. Traditional Broadway favorites and comedy shows accompanied by a decent buffet dinner and ice cream bar in a tiered dining room. It's very popular with kids and seniors.

American Music Theater (717-397-7700; amtshows.com), 2425 Lincoln Highway East, Lancaster. Enjoy touring concerts and original shows in this 1,600-seat theater.

Magic Lantern Shows at the Plain & Fancy Farm Theater (717-768-8400), 3121 Philadelphia Pike, Bird-in-Hand. Highly entertaining shows at the Amish Experience that pay homage to the days

MUST SEE

SIGHT & SOUND You don't have to be a reader of the Bible to appreciate the epic Christian musicals staged each year by **Sight & Sound Theatres** (800-377-1277; sight-sound.com, 300 Hartman Bridge Road [PA 896], Ronks). Technology nerds and theater lovers alike are equally amazed and impressed by the extravagant shows, which use actors, live animals, music, and spectacular special effects to bring Bible stories to life.

Located just 8 miles southeast of Lancaster in the small farming village of Ronks, Sight & Sound draws nearly 1 million visitors to Lancaster County each year. That number is impressive by itself, but it becomes even more so when you consider that the average Sight & Sound show runs two to three times a day, Tuesday–Saturday year-round, to mostly sold-out audiences.

Visitors take their seats in a cavernous auditorium, with more than 1,200 seats on the floor and about 800 in the balcony. The show takes place before them—this is the theater lovers' part—on a 300-foot stage that wraps around the left and right sides of the auditorium. The enor-

SIGHT & SOUND THEATRES, KNOWN FOR ITS EXTRAVAGANT BIBLICAL-THEMED SHOWS AYLEEN GONTZ

when traveling showmen brought multiple characters and voices to life against a backdrop of music, sound effects, and sing-alongs.

Rainbow's Comedy Playhouse (800-292-4301; rainbowcomedy.com), 3065 Lincoln Highway East, Lancaster. Eat and laugh your way through a night of live comedy shows.

Bird-in-Hand Stage (717-455-3539; bird-in-hand.com/stage), 2760A Old Philadelphia Pike, Bird-in-Hand. Offers live musicals and magic shows.

Y **Zoetropolis Cinema + Stillhouse** (717-208-6572) 112 North Water Street, Lancaster. Art house films, live music, and a kitchen/bar serving creative small plates and cocktails.

SPECIAL EFFECTS PLAY A BIG ROLE IN THE SHOWS AT SIGHT & SOUND THEATRES AYLEEN GONTZ

mous cast (each role has three players) is elaborately costumed and includes not only adults and children, but also a full complement of animals that are cared for on-site. The action often spills into the aisles and cascades down from the ceiling.

The intricate sets tower some 40 feet above the stage and—here's the techy part—are backed by a 110-foot-wide, 30-foot-tall LED screen that seamlessly continues the landscape beyond the physical set. The screen is the largest of its kind in the world and comprises 1,200 smaller screens with 22 million pixels in each individual screen. While the movement of some set pieces is executed by hand, others, like boats that move across the stage, are coordinated by GPS.

Hershey Inn and Farm (see *Lodging*) is the closest hotel to the theater and is popular with traveling groups in town for the show. For a post-theater sweet treat, try the **Strasburg Country Store and Creamery** or the **Speckled Hen Café,** both in Strasburg (see *Eating Out*).

✳ Selective Shopping

Amish and Mennonites have created their own exquisite baskets, quilts, dolls, furniture, toys, wall hangings, and hex designs for centuries. You will find much of it for sale in stores along Old Philadelphia Pike in Intercourse and Bird-in-Hand, as well as PA 772 between Intercourse and Leola. Most shops are closed on Sundays. Two large outlet malls, **Rockvale** (717-293-9595), 35 South Willowdale Drive, and **Tanger** (717-392-7260), 311 Stanley K. Tanger Boulevard, can be found on US 30 in Lancaster near Dutch Wonderland. Tanger underwent a 13-acre expansion in 2017 and added

MUD SALES

Named for the soggy late-winter ground, mud sales are Amish-run auctions that have been a festive rite of spring in Lancaster County for nearly 50 years. Even if you're not in the market for the goods, which range from outdoor sheds to small crafts and handmade quilts, this is an ideal opportunity to mingle with the Amish at their most relaxed and natural, not to mention feast on hot buttered pretzels and roast pork sandwiches. Mud sales are held in small towns throughout the county, with proceeds going to local volunteer fire companies. They are usually held on Saturday in late February through early April and start around 8 or 9 a.m. Visit discoverlancaster.com or lancasterpa.com/mud-sales for more information and a current schedule.

25 new retail stores, including H&M and The North Face.

CANDLES & CRAFTS Moravian Mission Gift Shop (717-626-9027), 8 Church Square, Lititz. Open Friday and Saturday, March–December. Tucked behind the archives building on the square, this is the place to find Moravian crafts, books, etched glass, multicolored glass stars, and beeswax candles.

Old Candle Barn (717-768-3231), 3551A Old Philadelphia Pike, Intercourse. Don't be put off by its World War I Quonset hut appearance; this huge shop features an impressive variety of handcrafted candles, potpourri, and crafts. If you're here on a weekday, you can watch the candles being dipped and poured in the downstairs factory.

Weathervane Shop (717-569-9312), 2451 Kissel Hill Road, Lancaster. The gift shop at the Landis Valley Museum sells pottery, wooden cabinetry, linens, and folk art produced by the museum's own craftspeople.

QUILTS Many back roads have simple signs indicating places where quilts are sold; selection is often more limited than in the shops, but prices are usually lower.

Old Country Store (717-768-7171), 3513 Old Philadelphia Pike, Intercourse. Open daily. This pleasant shop has a knowledgeable sales staff and a wide selection of contemporary quilts. It also sells quilt fabrics at fair prices.

Quilt and Fabric Shack (717-768-0338), 3127 Old Philadelphia Pike, Bird-in-Hand. Quilts and wall hangings handmade by Amish and Mennonite women. They also carry a large selection of fabrics.

Smucker's Quilts (717-656-8730), 117 North Groffdale Road, New Holland. This family-run shop offers a variety of quilts, from traditional Amish varieties to contemporary designs. It also carries wall hangings, Amish clothes, toys, and other gift items.

FURNITURE E. Braun Farm Tables (717-768-7227; braunfarmtables.com), 3561 Old Philadelphia Pike, Intercourse. This family-owned company makes gorgeous farm tables, chairs, bed frames, and other furniture using wood salvaged from farm buildings from the late 1800s and 1900s.

SPECIAL SHOPS Aaron's Books (717-627-1990; aaronsbooks.com), 35 East Main Street, Lititz. Named after the owners' son, this welcoming family-owned store sells new and used books and fair-trade gifts and note cards; there's also a neat children's play area. It regularly hosts book groups and author readings and is a widely used community resource.

Caffeinated Bookworm (717-740-5120), 245 Centerville Road, Lancaster. This cozy used bookstore features a wide variety of used books in great condition, plus coffee, tea, help finding just the right read, and the occasional author visit.

Outback Toys (888-414-4705), 101 West Lincoln Avenue, Lititz. This might be the best shop for farm-themed toys in the world. The warehouse-sized space just north of town is full of kid-sized tractors, toy barns, Breyer horses, and all things John Deere. Staff members are knowledgeable and happy to help you find that limited-edition miniature Gleaner combine.

EPHRATA

Ten Thousand Villages (717-721-8400), 240 North Reading Road (PA 272). Closed Sundays. The original store of the fair-trade empire (its headquarters are nearby) has an ever-changing selection of handcrafted vases, baskets, batiks, stationery, and jewelry, plus heirloom-quality Bunyaad rugs hand-knotted in Pakistan. It often holds big sales to make room for new merchandise.

INTERCOURSE

Kitchen Kettle Village (717-768-8261), PA 340. Yes, it's contrived, but this shopping village is a fun one-stop destination of buggy and tractor rides, kettle corn stands, live music (on weekends), and about 30 shops selling everything from personalized teddy bears to hex signs and soft pretzels. The Jam & Relish Kitchen is a favorite stop for chow-chow, jams, jellies, and relishes; they are generous with samples. You can also get Lapp Valley Farms ice cream here (see *Bakeries & Farm Stands*).

Zook's Fabric Store (717-768-8153), 3535 Old Philadelphia Pike. This Amish variety store merged with Sauders Fabric to create a single superstore, carrying more than 16,000 bolts of fabric. It is considered one of the best places around to purchase high-quality quilting fabrics at reasonable prices.

✳ Special Events

May: **Sertoma Club Chicken Barbecue** (third weekend), Long's Park, Lancaster—the world's largest chicken BBQ (it's even in the *Guinness Book of World Records*) turns out more than 33,000 chicken dinners for a donation of $10 per person.

August: **Pennsylvania Renaissance Faire** (second weekend of August, then weekends through October), 2775 Lebanon Road, Manheim—one of the county's most popular events with lots of jousting knights, costumed wenches, and terrific interactive street performances. With 90 shows daily on 12 stages, microbrewed ales on tap, period food, and a Scotch egg–eating contest, it's impossible not to have a good time. **Covered Bridge Classic** (third weekend; coveredbridgeclassic .com), on the HACC campus, 1641 Old Philadelphia Pike, Lancaster—the Lancaster Bicycle Club plots routes covering 16, 34, 66, and 100 miles past beautiful scenery that includes Amish farmland and covered bridges.

September: **Ephrata Fair** (fourth weekend), downtown Ephrata—a huge country fair featuring carnival rides, live music, livestock competitions, and a street parade; don't miss the toasted cheeseburgers. **Whoopie Pie Festival** (second weekend; whoopiepiefestival .com), Hershey Farm Restaurant and Inn, Ronks—100 different flavors of this sweet Amish treat are showcased, along with craft vendors and music. **Liederkranz Oktoberfest** (third weekend; lancasterliederkranz.com), Lancaster—join the rest of the county and enjoy German beer and food at the oldest traditional Oktoberfest in the area.

October: **Lititz Chocolate Walk** (first or second weekend; lititzchocolatewalk .com), downtown Lititz—two dozen of the area's chocolatiers offer displays and demonstrations of their work around town.

READING & KUTZTOWN

bout 60 miles west of Philadelphia, Reading is the state's fifth-largest city, with about 81,000 residents. Once a major manufacturing center for hosiery and hardware, it was also the site of one of the nation's oldest and largest railroads, the Philadelphia and Reading. In the early 1970s, abandoned textile mills on the outskirts of town were developed to create one of the country's first outlet malls.

Despite struggles with crime and suburban flight, downtown Reading has seen a revitalization in the past decade with the opening of GoggleWorks, a hip complex of artists' studios, a large performing arts center, and a solid roster of good restaurants and bars. An interesting footnote: Reading was the actual setting (fictionalized as Mount Judge) in the Rabbit books by John Updike, who grew up in nearby Shillington and worked as a copyboy for the *Reading Eagle* in the early 1950s. Berks County figured prominently in many of the prize-winning author's novels and essays.

A few miles to the south of Reading, just across the Berks County line, you'll find Adamstown, a shopper's paradise of antiques stores and markets. To the city's north are winding country roads dotted with hex sign barns, historic hotels, and Pennsylvania Dutch diners.

Kutztown, also featured in this chapter, is about 20 miles to the northeast and more rural, with a rich Pennsylvania Dutch heritage. Founded around 1779 as Cootstown, which was later changed to Kutztown, it is home to a pretty and walkable downtown, Kutztown University, and a comprehensive museum on Pennsylvania Dutch culture and traditions. Every June and July, it hosts the Kutztown Folk Festival, a renowned nine-day celebration of all things Pennsylvania Dutch.

GUIDANCE **Greater Reading Convention & Visitors Bureau** (610-375-4085; 800-443-6610; visitpaamericana.com) has a visitor center in the GoggleWorks complex at 201 Washington Street. It's open Friday, Saturday, and the second Sunday of the month.

GETTING THERE *By air:* Major airports serving Reading and Kutztown are **Lehigh Valley International Airport** in Allentown (888-359-5842) and **Philadelphia International** (215-937-6800). **Reading Regional** (610-372-4666) offers limited service.

By car: From Philadelphia and points east, take I-76 to Exit 298 (Morgantown–Reading), then follow US 422 west to downtown Reading. To reach Kutztown from Reading, take US 222 to Old US 22 and head east. From Philadelphia, take I-476, the Northeast Extension of I-76 (the Pennsylvania Turnpike) to I-78/US 22 west.

GETTING AROUND **BARTA** (610-921-0601; bartabus.com) offers more than 20 bus routes in and around Reading that begin at the Berks Area Regional Transportation Authority (BARTA) Transportation Center downtown and run to FirstEnergy Stadium, Hamburg, and other towns.

WHEN TO GO Most of the antiques and collectors markets are open year-round. The country and hillsides surrounding Reading and Kutztown are ablaze in brown, yellow, and orange in October, adding a visual element to visits to the area's flea markets and

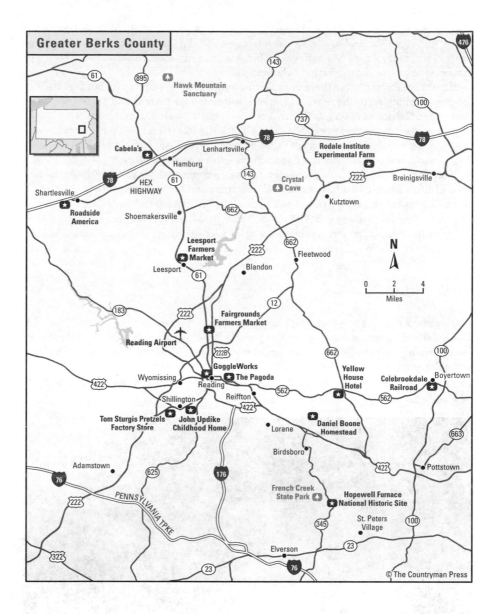

Greater Berks County

Hawk Mountain Sanctuary

Cabela's

Lenhartsville

Hamburg

HEX HIGHWAY

Shartlesville

Roadside America

Shoemakersville

Rodale Institute Experimental Farm

Crystal Cave

Kutztown

Breinigsville

Leesport Farmers Market

Leesport

Blandon

Fleetwood

N

0 2 4
Miles

Fairgrounds Farmers Market

Reading Airport

Wyomissing

GoggleWorks

The Pagoda

Reading

Reiffton

Shillington

Yellow House Hotel

Colebrookdale Railroad

Boyertown

Tom Sturgis Pretzels Factory Store

John Updike Childhood Home

Lorane

Daniel Boone Homestead

Birdsboro

Adamstown

PENNSYLVANIA TPKE

French Creek State Park

Hopewell Furnace National Historic Site

St. Peters Village

Pottstown

Elverson

© The Countryman Press

rural towns. Kutztown is at its best in late June and early July, when a Pennsylvania
Dutch folk festival is in high gear.

✳ Villages

Adamstown. Someone once said, "If it's old and American, chances are it's in Adamstown." This small town at the northeastern edge of Lancaster County describes itself
as Antiques Capital, USA. Indeed, it probably has more antiques shops and markets
than it does residents. (At last count, the population was 1,200.) A mile from the

Pennsylvania Turnpike, it's a shopper's paradise of junk stores, high-end antiques shops, consignment malls, and several massive Sunday-only flea markets. There are a few restaurants where you can fuel up between buying and browsing marathons but little else to amuse those who hate shopping.

Hamburg. Named after the city in Germany and framed by rural countryside and the Blue Mountains to the north, this place epitomizes the American small town. The opening of Cabela's in 2003, and with it several chain hotels and restaurants, changed its look and demographics a bit, but its main street, located on Old US 22, remains frozen in time, with family restaurants that date to the 1800s; a couple of old-fashioned, inexpensive hotels; a few antiques shops; and a five-and-dime store.

Shartlesville. Not far from Hamburg, this town urges visitors to "slow down the fast pace of life." Established in the 1800s by German and Swiss tradespeople, it's a good place to stop for an hour or two if you happen to be visiting Cabela's or making your way to or from Harrisburg and Allentown. You'll find here several Pennsylvania Dutch restaurants, homegrown vegetable stands, and Roadside America, an indoor miniature village and beloved landmark of sorts.

✳ To See

GoggleWorks (610-374-4600; goggleworks.org), 201 Washington Street, Reading. Open daily. Housed in a former safety goggle factory (hence the name) near downtown, this hip arts complex and community hub opened in 2005 as a place that lets artists create and display their work in public; you'll find everything from folk art and photography to lithographs and pottery represented, plus a glass-blowing facility,

A GIANT FIBERGLASS AMISH COUPLE GREETS VISITORS NEAR THE ENTRANCE OF ROADSIDE AMERICA

HEX HIGHWAY

Hex signs are an important part of Pennsylvania Dutch folk art, used to decorate barns and symbolizing good luck and good harvest. This approximately 22-mile drive follows part of the designated Dutch Hex Highway past many old barns and farmhouses decorated with the round and colorful signs, as well as past historic churches, small towns, and rural countryside. Begin in Shartlesville north of Reading and follow Old US 22 east through Shartlesville's frozen-in-time main street. In Hamburg, stop at Stoudt's Fruit Farm (610-488-7549) for some apples or nectarines, then continue to Lenhartsville, where you can examine the old hex signs on the Deitsch Eck Restaurant (610-562-8520; Old US 22) before dining on pork and sauerkraut or chicken potpie. From here, head north on PA 143 toward Kempton and turn left at Hawk Mountain Road. Continue another 7 miles through scenic farmland to Hawk Mountain Sanctuary (610-756-6961; 1700 Hawk Mountain Road) and spend the rest of the afternoon hiking the nature trails or watching raptors fly by at eye level. A complete map is available at hexsigntour.com. For more information on the history and meaning of hex signs, visit the Pennsylvania German Cultural Heritage Center on Kutztown University's campus (see *To Do*).

community makerspace, ceramics and photography studios, a movie theater, and a café serving creative global eats and drinks, which you can bring with you anywhere on the premises. Stop at the front desk for a map before setting off to explore. The best time to visit is the second Sunday of the month, when you'll find many of the artists at work in their studios, or the first Friday of the month, when some of the galleries host opening receptions for new exhibitions. Parking is ample and free.

Boyertown Museum of Historical Vehicles (610-367-2090; boyertownmuseum.org), 85 South Walnut Street; small admission fee charged. The theme is locally made vehicles of all kinds—from Charles Duryea's three-cylinder wagonette to pre-Harley motorcycles to a late 18th-century Kutztown sleigh. There's also a preserved roadside diner/decommissioned train car (the late Fegley's of Reading), which was moved by crane to the museum in 2003. You'll leave with a greater appreciation for the Reading area's important role in auto and wagon manufacturing. There is a good local farmers' market in the museum's parking lot every Saturday from June–October (with plenty of street parking).

Central Pennsylvania African American Museum (610-371-8739; cpaam.net), 119 North 10th Street, Reading. Open Wednesday and Friday 9:30 a.m.–12:30 p.m., Saturday 1–3 p.m.; $8 adults. The Underground Railroad was started not far from here by a Quaker farmer in Columbia, Pennsylvania. Reading's oldest black-owned church traces its history and displays all kinds of interesting African American art, antiques, books, and relics of slavery.

The Pagoda (610-375-6399; pagoda skyline.org), 98 Duryea Drive. The best

HISTORIC READING PAGODA HAS PANORAMIC VIEWS OF BERKS COUNTY

BUTTERFLIES AND BANK BARNS

In 1947, a man named J. I. Rodale started the Soil and Health Foundation on his small farm near Kutztown to promote his theory that healthy soil, not chemical fertilizer, is the basis for growing healthy food. Some call it the birth of the organic farming movement. Today, the 333-acre farm is home to the Rodale Institute Experimental Farm (610-683-1400; rodaleinstitute.org; 611 Siegfriedale Road, Kutztown), a research farm and educational center that is open to the public for self-guided tours and workshops. Start in the old stone schoolhouse, where books on gardening and cooking are for sale, along with locally made honey and jams. The self-guided walking tour begins here, too—wear sturdy walking shoes and be prepared to trudge through thick grass and woodland at times. This is not your average manicured garden tour but a window into a working, sustainable organic farm. You will pass garden beds bursting with cantaloupes and zucchini, compost windrows, bank barns, owl hollows, and patchwork-quilt fields of corn, alfalfa, wheat, and soybeans. In summer an unfathomable number of bugs and butterflies—plus the occasional herd of cows—will cross your path. The gift shop often sells healthy snacks and drinks—or bring a picnic lunch and have it on one of the picnic tables outside. Plant sales and gardening workshops are held throughout the year, and customized guided tours are available; visit rodaleinstitute.org for details. Closed Mondays.

CROPS AT RODALE EXPERIMENTAL FARM

views in the city can be found atop this seven-story traditional Japanese-style pagoda on Mount Penn. Built in 1906 by a local businessman, it was intended to be a luxury hotel but instead was sold to the City of Reading for $1. (Fun fact: John Updike modeled the Pinnacle Hotel after it in his Pulitzer Prize–winning book, *Rabbit, Run*). Visitors may climb (87 steps) to the observation deck for gorgeous views of the Berks County countryside and to admire the historic bell, cast in Japan in 1739 and shipped to Reading in 1907; a café serves drinks and light meals on Friday, Saturday, and Sunday afternoons. The drive up to the Pagoda is also noteworthy; in the 1900s, the steep, winding road was the final test for cars made by the Charles Duryea Power Co. If they didn't make it up to the top, they were sent back to the factory for retooling.

Reading Public Museum (610-371-5850; readingpublicmuseum.org), 500 Museum Road, Reading. Closed Mondays; admission charged. This multifaceted museum has a planetarium (with Friday night laser shows), an arboretum, and more than a dozen science, art, and history galleries displaying dinosaur fossils, Pennsylvania German artifacts, taxidermy-mounted animals, and more. The art collection includes works by such notables as Winslow Homer, Benjamin West, Milton Avery, John Singer Sargent, Edgar Degas, and local boy Keith Haring. Pretty Wyomissing Creek runs through the arboretum; plan a visit in the spring to see the cherry blossoms in bloom. On Sunday mornings, live music and breakfast ("Bagels, Bach, and Beyond") can be enjoyed in the atrium.

Pennsylvania German Cultural Heritage Center (610-683-4000), 22 Luckinbill Road, on the Kutztown University campus. Open 10–4 weekdays; free. The site of the annual Kutztown Folk Festival, this is also the place to go anytime for a crash course in Pennsylvania Dutch history, culture, and traditions. The museum offers thousands of 19th- and 20th-century artifacts, plus ancient farm equipment, a one-room schoolhouse, and reconstructed log homes.

✳ To Do

✪ ✎ **Berks County Heritage Center** (610-374-8839), 2201 Tulpehocken Road, Wyomissing. A complex of stone buildings, a cemetery, herb garden, and gristmill on the Union Canal, all dating back to the 1800s. It's also home to the must-see Gruber Wagon Works, a reassembled 1900s-era wagon manufacturer with original Conestoga wagons and thousands of the original tools used to build them. A National Historic Site, it is one of the few remaining places where you can witness the intricate work that went into making hayflats, wheelbarrows, and other specialty wagons of the era. A small fee gets you a thorough guided tour of both the C. Howard Hiester Canal Center, home to the largest collection of 19th-century canal memorabilia in the country, and the Wagon Works. Don't leave without checking out Wertz's Bridge, the longest single-span covered bridge in the state. Cars are not allowed on the bridge, but pedestrians are.

✎ **Hopewell Furnace National Historic Site** (610-582-8773), 2 Mark Bird Lane, Elverson. A huge iron furnace that supplied cannon and shot to the Continental army and navy is just one of the highlights of this unsung National Park Service site in the middle of French Creek State Park. The self-guided tour takes you past a barn that now shelters dozens of sheep, boarding houses once occupied by furnace workers, and the ironmaster's circa-1770 mansion. There's also an easy junior ranger program that kids can complete in an hour or two, along with access to the Horseshoe Trail, one of French Creek's best hikes. The best time to visit

HOPEWELL FURNACE NATIONAL HISTORIC SITE

MUST SEE

JOHN UPDIKE'S PENNSYLVANIA "That Pennsylvania—Lutheran or something, I don't know what it can be traced to—but there's something about it that makes it easy to write about."

Perhaps no other author spoke to Pennsylvania in his literature more than John Updike. Raised in the villages of Shillington and Plowville, he left to attend Harvard at 18 but often mined the local places and people of his youth for his books. Reading (pronounced RED-ing) was called Brewer or Alton in the prize-winning books *Rabbit, Run; Rabbit at Rest;* and *The Centaur,* and Shillington was often Olinger in *New Yorker* stories such as "Pigeon Feathers" and "A&P."

JOHN UPDIKE'S CHILDHOOD HOME IN SHILLINGTON

is weekends, when the furnace is sometimes lit and there are often blacksmithing and forging demonstrations. In September and October, visitors may pick apples from the 250 trees that surround the site for a small fee.

FOR FAMILIES ✒ **Crystal Cave** (610-683-6765; crystalcavepa.com), 963 Crystal Cave Road, Kutztown. Open daily from March–November; admission charged. Few kids from eastern Pennsylvania completed their childhoods without seeing Crystal Cave. It was discovered in 1871 by two Pennsylvania Dutchmen and has been a tourist attraction pretty much ever since. It's not unusual to see a few tour buses in the parking lot, but the entire complex still has a quiet, unhurried vibe. One-hour tours take you 125 feet below, where it's 54 degrees year-round and guides point out formations that resemble animals and rooms with names like the Bridal Veil (it was the site of Pennsylvania's first "cave wedding" in 1919). There's also a free geological museum; a shady mini-golf course; and a moderate nature trail that leads to a view of the surrounding

His childhood home sits on a tidy corner lot on Philadelphia Avenue in Shillington. After his death in 2009, the nonprofit John Updike Society purchased the house and spent years restoring it to Updike's time, furnishing it with original pieces donated by the author's children. It opened for guided tours in 2019; visitors may also follow a self-guided walking tour of Shillington that includes the writer's high school, local barber shop, and the site of the A&P that he captured in his short-story collection, *Pigeon Feathers*.

In Reading, a five-minute drive away, devotees will want to check out **Marvel Ranch,** a frozen-in-time diner, and **Jimmie Kramer's Peanut Bar,** where the author hung out while working as a copyboy for the *Reading Eagle*. Around the corner, the regal **Reading Public Library,** where he spent many hours as a boy with his nose in a book, holds a comprehensive collection of his writings, artworks, and other documents.

Updike's gravestone, carved by his son Michael, lies at **Plowville Cemetery** near his family farm. The marker, engraved with a poem and the author's grinning face framed by wings, sits

JOHN UPDIKE'S GRAVE IN PLOWVILLE

beside his parents' gravestones on a slight hilltop with views of the Pennsylvania countryside he knew and chronicled so remarkably well. For more information, visit johnupdikechildhoodhome.com.

valley. It seems to be in the middle of nowhere, but it's only about a 20-minute drive off I-78 or US 222.

✎ **Koziar's Christmas Village** (610-488-1110; koziarschristmasvillage.com), 782 Christmas Village Road, Bernville. Open evenings in November and December (call or check website for days and times); admission charged. Koziar's began in 1955 as a family's personal holiday display and has turned into one of the state's top Christmastime attractions. Millions of lights decorate an entire farm, and an indoor electric train display, appearances by Santa, and a reasonably priced gift shop selling ornaments and other 'tis-the-season decorations are also on hand. The view as you drive in over the hill is amazing.

✎ ⬆ **Roadside America** (610-488-6241; roadsideamericainc.com), 109 Roadside Drive, Shartlesville. Closed Tuesdays and Wednesdays; admission charged. Road kitsch doesn't get much better than this: a giant statue of a smiling Amish couple greets you near the entrance, and inside is a replica of "the American countryside

YUENGLING BREWERY

About 30 miles northwest of Kutztown sits the hilly former coal mining town of Pottsville, home to the oldest operating brewery in the United States. D. G. Yuengling & Son has been producing moderately priced beer since 1831 and is now owned by fifth-generation family members. Sometime in the past two decades, someone realized that everyone loves a good brewery tour and opened up the factory and its production lines to the public. The free tours last about an hour and are very hands-on and personal: You can peek inside the giant beer vats, ask questions of the knowledgeable guides, and walk inside the hand-dug caves that were used to store kegs of beer before refrigeration made things easier. In the taproom, visitors are treated to generous samples of the lager they just watched being made (nonalcoholic birch beer is also available). There is a gift shop, of course. This is one of finest free tours around and worth the detour if you are in the Poconos or Reading/Kutztown area. Tours are free and run Monday–Saturday from April–December, and Monday–Friday for the rest of the year. Expect big crowds (40 or more people) on Saturdays and most summer days; no reservations. For more information, visit yuengling.com or call 570-628-4890.

YUENGLING ICE CREAM AT THE FACTORY TOUR IN POTTSTOWN
AYLEEN GONTZ

STAINED GLASS CEILING AT THE YUENGLING BREWHOUSE
AYLEEN GONTZ

as it might be seen by a giant so huge he could see from coast to coast." This indoor miniature village draws *ooohs* and *aaahs* from its many fans (and eye rolls from some locals), but it's a truly unusual experience and worth a stop for anyone who likes a little old-fashioned fun with their road trips. You could easily spend an hour or two examining the tiny bake shops, churches, theaters, gas stations, and some 400 other buildings that make up the display—most kids love the buttons that let them ring church bells, operate steamrollers, and steer trains.

Daniel Boone Homestead (610-582-4900; danielboonehomestead.org), 400 Daniel Boone Road, Birdsboro. Open for tours Tuesday–Sunday. The famous frontiersman spent his adolescent years on this large farm east of Reading before his father moved the family to North Carolina. Not much data exists on his life back then, but the tour provides a thorough look at life in the 1700s. Set on more than 570 acres, it includes the original log house where Boone was born, a blacksmith shop, smokehouse, and circa-1810 sawmill. You don't have to take the tour to enjoy the property's two picnic areas, lake, and walking trails.

&. ✎ **Colebrookdale Railroad** (610-367-0200; colebrookdalerailroad.com), Washington and Third Streets, Boyertown. Beautifully restored century-old train cars take riders on two-hour excursions past some of the oldest iron-making sites in the US. Meals are available in the dining car, and themed outings, such as "Mother's Day Tea" and "Kentucky Derby Run," are held throughout the year.

✎ **Wanamaker, Kempton & Southern Railroad** (610-756-6469; kemptontrain.com), 42 Community Center Drive, Kempton. Train rides depart four times a day on Sundays in May and June, Saturday and Sunday in July, August, and October. One of the more reasonably priced locomotive joy rides on the Pennsylvania train circuit. Kids will want to check out the Schuylkill and Lehigh Model Railroad in the decommissioned coach behind the station.

WINERIES Berks County's wineries are relatively new to the state's tasting trail bandwagon. Many are located in the northern reaches of the county, surrounded by quiet countryside. They offer pleasant, low-pressure tasting experiences and regular themed weekends like "Wine and Chocolate." For a comprehensive list, visit berkscountywinetrail.com.

Setter Ridge Vineyards (610-683-8463; setterridgevineyards.com), 99 Dietrich Valley Road, Kutztown. Knowledgeable staff (likely a member of the Blair family) and a cozy tasting room framed by views of the Blue Mountains make this a standout. Pinot noir is a specialty. Children and leashed pets are welcome; there is plenty of open space.

Clover Hill Winery (610-395-2468; cloverhillwinery.com), 9850 Newton Road, Breinigsville. A veteran vintner by Berks County standards, it produces a variety of vintages, including an award-winning riesling and cabernet sauvignon. Its main tasting room is big and modern (some complain that it's too sterile), with windows overlooking vineyards. There's also a vineyard and tasting room in Robesonia, east of Reading.

Long Trout Winery (570-366-6443; longtroutwinery.com), 84 Fork Mountain Road, Auburn. Open Wednesday evening, Saturday, and Sunday. The wine itself is almost an afterthought at this mellow mountain winery, whose motto is WHERE THE WINE IS COOL AND HIPPIE CHICKS RULE. The tasting room is a shrine to the 1960s, and the PG-rated wine labels are a hoot. Tastings are free and generous. There are picnic tables to settle in and enjoy your purchase. There is also disc golf.

Pinnacle Ridge (610-756-4481; www.pinridge.com), 407 Old US 22, Kutztown. Hex signs decorate the renovated bank barn that houses the processing area and tasting room. Sparkling wines are a specialty, and its veritas and chambourcin vintages have a slew of awards from the Pennsylvania Farm Show.

✳ Outdoor Activities

BICYCLING The 23-mile loop around **Blue Marsh Lake** (610-376-6337), 1268 Palisades Drive, Leesport, was named one of America's top 10 bike trails by *Bicycling* magazine in the 1990s. It hasn't changed much since then, with a tight and twisting singletrack, short uphill climbs, and stellar views. The Union Canal Trail is also a cyclist favorite (see *Hiking*).

FISHING **Hunsicker's Grove** (610-372-8939), 9350 Longswamp Road, Mertztown, has a wheelchair-accessible dock and a pond stocked with fish. It hosts a popular children's fishing rodeo every May.

GOLF **Blackwood Golf Course** (610-385-6200), 510 Red Corner Road, Douglassville. Attractive and relatively undemanding 18-hole course with three tees to 6,403 yards.

Reading Country Club (610-779-1000), 5311 Perkiomen Avenue, Reading. This 18-hole course dates to 1923 and has gently rolling terrain and tree-lined fairways.

SIGN IN FRENCH CREEK STATE PARK

HIKING The 4.5-mile **Union Canal Trail** at Tulpehocken Creek Valley Park (610-372-8939; co.berks.pa.us/parks) is a perfect way to combine exercise with local history lessons. Start at **Stonecliff Recreation Area** and follow the path past old stone buildings and original locks dating back to the 1820s, when the canal was built. After about 2 miles you'll reach the **Berks County Heritage Center,** home to a sweet little museum about the state's canal history and Wertz's Covered Bridge, the longest surviving single-span covered bridge in Pennsylvania. The trail ends near the parking area for Blue Marsh Lake. Maps are available at the heritage center (see *To Do*).

Near French Creek State Park at the north end of **St. Peters Village**, a parking lot on the west side of St. Peters Road hooks up with a network of flat hiking trails in a pretty forested area notable for its many natural and quarry-generated boulders. There's not much signage, but trails begin near a small bridge on the northwest edge of the parking lot. You'll find plenty of dogs and kids here on weekends.

HORSEBACK RIDING **French Creek State Park** (see *Green Space*) has 8 miles of equestrian trails. The clearly marked Horseshoe Trail, which begins in Valley Forge, skirts the park's two lakes and continues to the Appalachian Trail near Harrisburg.

✳ Green Space

Blue Marsh Lake (610-376-6337), 1268 Palisades Drive, Leesport. Recreational hot spot north of Reading with good swimming, fishing, and boating opportunities. In summer, there are ranger-led hikes, bat programs, and stargazing events. Nature trails run near the water's edge (the Foxtrot Trail can be accessed from the swimming beach), while mountain bikers like Skinners Loop. There's a small fee to enter; more info is available at the visitor center.

French Creek State Park (610-582-9680), 843 Park Road, Elverson. Set amid picturesque farmland straddling Berks and Chester Counties, this 7,340-acre tree-filled park offers two lakes—Hopewell and Scotts Run—plus picnic areas, two disc courses, a campground, and 30 miles of hiking trails. You can fish for trout and bass and ride non-motorized boats in the lakes. Swimming isn't allowed, but there's a large public pool near Hopewell Lake. This is also a popular spot for orienteering, with a self-guided course that lets you locate markers in the park with the aid of a map and compass. Maps and other information are available at the park office. In the center of the park sits the lovely **Hopewell Furnace National Historic Site** (see *To Do*).

✳ Lodging

BED & BREAKFASTS **Overlook Mansion** (610-371-9173; overlookmansionbed andbreakfast.com), 620 Centre Avenue, Reading. Daphne Miller and Paul Strause are the friendly owners of this Second Empire mansion across from Centre Park in north Reading. The two large, high-ceilinged rooms have queen beds, televisions, WiFi, and refrigerators. Have breakfast delivered to your room or eat outside on the porch overlooking a garden. Miller, a reliable source of information on the area, also hosts theme weekends and events such as ghostly walking tours through the nearby Charles Evans Cemetery. $$$.

NEARBY

Land Haven (610-845-3257; landhaven bandb.com), 1194 Huff's Church Road, Barto. This comfortable B&B was once an 1870s general store, and owners Ed and Donna Land take care to honor its history. The five rooms are named after the original proprietors and have queen or king beds, private baths or showers, and a lovely mix of whimsical and antique décor. It also has an antiques store, a large library of old cookbooks (7,000 plus!), and special events such as cooking classes and live singer-songwriter concerts. It's about 18 miles from Reading. $$.

🐾 **Hawk Mountain Bed & Breakfast** (610-756-4224; hawkmountainbb.com), 221 Stone Valley Road, Kempton. This lodge, tucked in the scenic Stoney Run Valley and about 8 miles from the hawk sanctuary, has a large swimming pool and eight attractive rooms with queen beds, TVs, and private entrances and baths. Two deluxe rooms have fireplaces and Jacuzzi tubs. A full country breakfast of pancakes or waffles, sausage, and fruit comes with the rate, as do complimentary beverages (including Yuengling lager). $$–$$$; two-night minimum in September and October.

Main Street Inn (610-683-0401; kutztownmainstreetinn.com), 401 West

Main Street, Kutztown. Refurbished Victorian home one block from Kutztown University and six blocks from Renninger's Market. Attention to detail is owner Pam Corrado's specialty, from round-the-clock kitchen snacks and wine to exquisitely old-fashioned rooms with claw-foot bathtubs and gas fireplaces. No children under 12. $$.

Pamela's Forget-Me-Not (610-756-3398; pamelasforgetmenot.com), 33 Hawk Mountain Road, Kempton. The closest accommodations to Hawk Mountain Sanctuary, with four private romantic rooms in a country Victorian home. The Carriage House loft features a large deck and Jacuzzi, and sleeps up to six people, while the Honeymoon Cottage has a gas fireplace, two-person Jacuzzi, and deck. Owner Pamela Gyory is a gracious host and happy to share tips about the area (she got engaged on Hawk Mountain). A full breakfast (crêpes

with organic fruit and maple syrup are a specialty) is delivered to the outer rooms or served in the dining room or the wraparound porch. $$.

The Inn at St. Peters Village (610-469-2600), 3471 St. Peters Road, St. Peters. Six attractive antiques-filled rooms with private baths in a restored 19th-century building with a large deck overlooking pretty French Creek. There's a restaurant and bar on the premises (see *Nightlife*), and hiking trails, antiques shops, and a bakery nearby. $$$.

CAMPGROUNDS

Blue Rocks Family Campground (610-756-6366; bluerockscampground.com), 341 Sousley Road, Lenhartsville. It's about 11 miles to Hawk Mountain Sanctuary, with swimming pools, a fishing pond, lots of kids' activities, and hiking trails that access the Appalachian Trail. The highlight of the property is a glacier

HIKING TRAILS ALONG FRENCH CREEK NEAR ST. PETERS VILLAGE

EXCURSIONS

ST. PETERS VILLAGE This tiny Victorian-era village along French Creek once served as a company town of sorts for two rock quarries. The mines stopped operating years ago, but many of the 19th-century buildings have been restored and turned into charming places to eat, drink, and shop, and good hiking trails can be accessed from the north end of the village. The seven-room **Inn at St. Peters Village**, a former fox hunt club turned B&B, anchors the southern end of town (3471 St. Peters Road; 610-469-2600) and offers a full-service restaurant and bar. A few doors down is **St. Peters Bakery** (3441 St. Peters Road; 610-469-7501), a welcoming hub of quiche, breads, and cinnamon rolls with a fireplace and a deck overlooking the creek. Keep walking north and you'll find an ice cream shop (open in spring and summer) and a pinball arcade (3411 St. Peters Road; no phone) with 25 working machines—bring quarters. Shops in between showcase antiques and handmade jewelry; you might also stumble upon a yoga class or a wine-tasting session at **West Hanover Winery** (3416 St. Peters Road; 610-469-9540). One mile south of the village is **Glasslight** (610-469-9066), 3611 St. Peters Road; glasslightstudio.com), a glass-blowing studio with unique handmade gifts and weekend workshops. St. Peters Village seems like it's in the middle of nowhere, but it's a fairly easy back roads drive from Berks County, Valley Forge, and the Brandywine Valley. Keep in mind that some businesses might have limited, weekend-only hours.

THE INN AT ST. PETERS VILLAGE

deposit that spans 15 miles and dates back 350 million years. Tent sites $; cabins and cottages $$.

Christmas Pines Campground (610-570-366-8866; christmaspines .com), 450 Red Church Road, Auburn. About 10 miles east of Hawk Mountain

Sanctuary, this secluded property has tent and RV sites and lots of kid-friendly activities like disc golf, a pool, and catch-and-release fishing.

French Creek State Park (610-582-9680), 843 Park Road, Elverson. You'll find 201 wooded tent sites, 50 with electric hook-ups, near the east entrance of the state park. There are also several cabins and yurts, and cottages that sleep five, with a two-night minimum in summer and fall. (See Green Space.)

✻ Where to Eat

DINING OUT

READING

Ⴘ **Anthony's Trattoria** (610-370-2822; anthonystrattoriareading.com), 900 Byram Street. Family-run Italian eatery in a residential neighborhood east of downtown. The menu is as long as a Mario Puzo novel: There's everything from wood-fired pizza with artichokes and homemade ravioli to entrées such as veal saltimbocca and châteaubriand for two. The strip-mall exterior gives way to a soft-lit, burgundy-walled dining room and top-shelf service. There's a full bar with lounge singers on weekends.

Ⴘ **Frank and Diannah's Arbor Inn** (610-406-0126), 47 Bingaman Street. Open for dinner Tuesday–Saturday. A friendly American restaurant with a lively bar scene and a wood-paneled dining room. The Thursday burger nights are a big draw. $$–$$$.

Lang Restaurant (610-374-0434), 22 North Sixth Street. Long-running Vietnamese-Chinese BYO (formerly known as Hong Thanh) across from the county courthouse. Lunch Wednesday–Friday, dinner Wednesday–Sunday. Specialties include sautéed filet mignon over watercress; marinated duck; and chicken, pork, or beef stew with lemongrass, curry, and coconut. There's homemade ice cream for dessert. Expect crowds on the weekend. $$.

& Ⴘ **Judy's on Cherry** (610-374-8511), 332 Cherry Street, Reading. Lunch and dinner Tuesday–Friday, dinner Tuesday–Saturday. A Mediterranean-style downtown café serving simple yet creative dishes such as fig and prosciutto pizza,

double pork chop with house-cellared sauerkraut, and seafood cioppino. Next door is the **Speckled Hen Pub** (see Nightlife). $$–$$$.

NEARBY

♂ Ⴘ **Gracie's 21st Century Café** (610-323-4004; gracies21stcentury.com), 1534 Manatawny Road, Pine Forge. Dinner Wednesday–Saturday. It's doubtful you will find another restaurant like this in Pennsylvania or quite possibly anywhere. Owner and Chef Gracie Skiadas bought a decaying early-1800s building in the middle of nowhere more than 20 years ago and turned it into a hip Santa-Fe-meets-1776 hangout. The entrée prices are high for this area, but the good food and ambiance make it a perfect special-occasion place. The global fusion menu might include savory pear salad, grilled elk chop with homemade ravioli, and prosciutto-wrapped Scottish salmon. Don't miss the legendary Jamaican curried crab bisque or the "Ole Hippy" carrot cake for dessert. Extensive wine list. $$$.

& Ⴘ **Yellow House Hotel** (610-689-9410), 6743 Boyertown Pike, Douglassville. Lunch and dinner Monday–Saturday; brunch and dinner Sundays. Once a stagecoach stop and general store for travelers between Reading and Philadelphia, this country inn has three attractive dining rooms and a separate bar. The traditional menu offers many steak, chicken, and seafood entrées, as well as lighter fare such as burgers, stir fries, and salads. Specialties include BBQ spareribs and duck with Grand Marnier sauce. $$–$$$.

EATING OUT

READING

House of Jerk Dread (HOJD) (484-513-3165), 1034 Penn Street. Open Wednesday–Saturday. Baked mac 'n' cheese, mango wings, and smoked jerk pork with savory house-made sauces are some

RAPTOR REFUGE & HIKING HAVEN

Hawk Mountain Sanctuary (610-756-6961), 1700 Hawk Mountain Road, Kempton. Open dawn to dusk daily; sturdy shoes are recommended. One of the top bird-watching sites in North America, Hawk Mountain is also a quiet refuge of hiking trails, thick forest, and panoramic views. During fall migration, an average of 20,000 hawks, eagles, and falcons from 18 different species pass by daily, often at eye level, as they travel down the Appalachian corridor. The largest migration takes place between mid-August and December, though mid-September and October are considered the peak times and also usually mean spectacular leaf-peeping opportunities. First-timers will want to stop at the visitor center for trail maps, guides, and tickets (the $5–10 trail fees support raptor conservation). It also has an awesome display of hand-carved and painted model raptors. South Lookout, with rewarding views of mountains and valleys, is 200 yards from the visitor center and can be accessed by wheelchair or stroller. Most hikers and birders opt for the mile-long North Lookout trail, which leads to a boulder-strewn jetty that yields the clearest views of southbound birds.

From here, you can access the Appalachian Trail by continuing another 2.5 miles on the rugged, ridgetop Skyline Trail. If you're coming in from the east side, consider stopping at Wanamaker General Store (610-756-6609; 8888 Kings Highway, Kempton) for sandwiches to bring on the hike. There's not much commerce around the sanctuary itself, and let's hope it stays that way.

VIEWS AT HAWK MOUNTAIN SANCTUARY

highlights of this casual, music-filled BYO café near Santander Arena. $–$$.

♈ **Jimmie Kramer's Peanut Bar** (610-376-8500), 322 Penn Street. Lunch and dinner Monday–Saturday. Opened in the 1930s by the son of Russian immigrants, this legendary family-run haunt in downtown Reading serves hot and cold sandwiches, wings, fried seafood platters, and a small number of entrées such as filet mignon, schnitzel, and lemon Parmesan flounder. John Updike and other *Reading Eagle* staffers met sources here or unwound at the bar after putting the

JIMMIE KRAMER'S PEANUT BAR IS A READING INSTITUTION

paper to bed each night. Join the regulars at the long bar or settle in at a table; everyone gets a bowl of fresh peanuts—tossing the crushed shells on the floor is encouraged. $$.

♨ **Marvel Ranch** (610-373-3150), 361 Penn Street. Another Updike haunt that hasn't changed in 50 years. Its prices, comfort eats, and utterly unpretentious vibe draw crowds, especially on weekends. Try the Marvel Mess, a carb-fueled plate of homefries, ham, eggs, and onions. $

♨ **Mi Casa Su Casa** (610-375-1161), 320 Penn Street. Owner Johanny Cepeda-Freytiz infuses her casual Latino café with an upbeat vibe and a diverse menu that includes *pernil asado* (slow-roasted pork), shrimp in garlic sauce, and BBQ

ribs. There are also many breakfast options, from pancakes to *mangu con los tres golpes* (mashed plantains with fried eggs, salami, and queso blanco).

Ⓨ **Ugly Oyster** (610-373-6791), 21 South Fifth Street. Lunch and dinner Monday–Saturday. This red-walled Irish pub near the downtown convention center has a *Cheers*-like bar, a wide selection of beers and single malt Scotch, and very good food. There's a small selection of steak and seafood entrées at dinner, and a lunch and tavern menu (available all day) of crabcake sandwiches, cheesesteaks, salads, a raw bar, and excellent soups. There's live Celtic music every Thursday. $–$$.

KUTZTOWN

Ⓨ **Basin Street Hotel** (610-683-7900; basinstreethotel.com), 42 East Main Street. Open daily. This circa-1897 tavern and restaurant features hearty sandwiches with names such as Professor (sautéed veggies with mozzarella and tomato sauce) and Golden Bear (hot roast beef). Wings are a big draw here; choose from 25 different flavors and check the website for all-you-can-eat specials. There are also salads, fried appetizers, and reasonably priced entrées such as London broil and crabcakes. $–$$.

Letterman's Diner (610-683-3879), 242 Main Street. Cozy vintage diner with a long counter serving traditional breakfast and lunch fare. You won't leave hungry. $.

NEARBY

⚓ **Deitsch Eck** (610-562-8520; the-eck .com), Old US 22, Lenhartsville. Lunch and dinner Wednesday–Sunday. Hex signs welcome you to this highly regarded Pennsylvania Dutch restaurant just east of Hamburg on Old US 22. The service couldn't be friendlier, and the prices couldn't be more reasonable. Choose from dozens of sandwiches, from burgers to hot roast beef, or a long list of platters such as smoked pork chops, meat loaf, and grilled ham steak. $.

Hecky's Sub Shop (610-562-4500), 315 State Street, Hamburg. Great local hangout for hefty made-to-order sandwiches, cheesesteaks, and fried pierogi. $.

& ♪ **Jukebox Café** (610-369-7272), 535 South Reading Avenue (PA 562), Boyertown. Breakfast and lunch daily. A 1950s-style diner (with a real jukebox and black-and-white tile floors) known for its many vegetarian entrées and liberal use of fresh local produce. Try the vegetarian eggs Benedict (made with portobello mushrooms and sun-dried tomatoes) or the Boardwalk Wrap with Italian sausage, eggs, cheese, and salsa. Homemade soups might be corn on the cob or crab bisque. Good food and low prices keep the tables full most days, so there might be a wait. Cash only. $–$$.

Saville's Diner (610-369-1433), 830 East Philadelphia Avenue, Boyertown. Classic cash-only diner with low prices, large portions, savory homemade soups, and to-die-for desserts like graham cracker cream pie and funnel cake fries. $–$$.

St. Peter's Bakery (610-469-7501; saintpetersbakery.com), 3441 St. Peters Road, St. Peters. Marvelous house-made breads, pastries, and sandwiches, with a big deck overlooking French Creek. On Friday nights there's artisan pizza and live music until 9 p.m. $–$$.

The Other Farm and Forge (484-415-0741; theotherfarmbrewingcompany .com), 128 East Philadelphia Avenue, Boyertown. House brews and hard cider pair with wood-fired pizzas and shareable plates like homemade pierogi and roasted mushroom poutine. $$.

Wanamakers General Store (610-756-6609; wanamakersgeneralstore.com), 8888 Kings Highway, Kempton. Its sandwiches, wraps, and seasonal homemade soups are perfect for a picnic at Hawk Mountain Sanctuary, 7 miles down the road. Save time to browse the locally made crafts and wooden toys for sale in the retail store. $.

FARMERS' MARKETS Boscov's Fairgrounds Farmer's Market (610-929-3429), North Fifth Street at US 222, Reading. Open Thursday–Saturday; hours vary. The rather plain building near the Fairgrounds Mall hides a bonanza of tidy stalls selling fresh local produce, smoked meats, free-range chicken eggs, Longacre's Farm ice cream, and Amish baked goods such as cinnamon buns and cherry-top doughnuts. It's an ideal spot for a cheap, delicious lunch: Cajun crab cakes and jambalaya, Polish sausage sandwiches, piping hot pizza by the slice. **Monte Lauro Italian Gourmet** is a favorite for hoagies and lunch specials like zucchini risotto, and anyone who loves a bargain should seek out the bakery selling mini-doughnuts for $1 a dozen. Go early if you can; it's wildly popular at lunchtime.

Leesport Farmers' Market (610-926-1307; leesportmarket.com), 312 Gernants Church Road, Leesport. Open 8 a.m.–9 p.m. Wednesdays. Located 8 miles north of Reading, this indoor-outdoor market features a livestock auction plus a large selection of fresh local produce, baked goods, clothes, antiques, and garden items. There's even a barber shop. It also hosts huge crafts fairs and flea markets several times a year.

Stoudt's Wonderful Good Market (717-484-2757), Reading Road, Adamstown. Open Thursday–Saturday. A foodie haven within Stoudt's antiques mall: There's artisan cheese made from local cow's milk, fresh breads, plus a gourmet coffee roaster and a random assortment of other edibles. Prices are reasonable, and it's an easy walk across the street to the shops of Stoudtburg Village.

DESSERTS & SNACKS Longacre's Modern Dairy (610-845-7551; longacres icecream.com), 1445 PA 100, Barto. Open daily, but hours are cut back in fall and winter. The ice cream and milkshakes are freshly made in the adjacent dairy at this family-run ice cream parlor. The setting is old school: leather booths, wood paneling, and a list of flavors as long as your arm, from cherry vanilla to coconut custard and pumpkin.

✪ **The Shoppes of Premise Maid** (610-395-3221; premisemaid.com), 10860 Hamilton Boulevard (US 222), Breinigsville. Open daily. Look for the giant toy soldiers improbably guarding a Tudor-style building in the middle of lush, rolling farmland. Enjoy huge helpings of hand-dipped ice cream before or after a visit to Crystal Cave or Rodale Experimental Farm. Expect lines in the summer, but they move quickly. Sit indoors (they are generous with the air-conditioning) or eat in the courtyard surrounded by trees and wrought-iron tables. Separate areas also sell premium chocolates and pastries (torte cakes are a specialty). All goods are made on the premises, hence the name.

Tom Sturgis Pretzel Factory Store (610-775-0335), 2267 Lancaster Pike (at US 222), Shillington. Closed Sundays. There are no tours here, but you'll find pretzel bargains (and generous samples) by the barrelful. Chocolate-covered, cheese, and jalapeño are just a few of the flavors available—plus gift baskets at prices lower than the average grocery store. Don't leave without a photo of the kids in front of the giant pretzel out front. The factory in back has been producing pretzels for more than a century.

games and indoor football to Broadway shows and Eddie Money concerts.

Strand Theater (610-683-8775; kutztownstrand.com), 32 North White Oak Street, Kutztown. Historic old theater with two screens showing first-run movies.

NIGHTLIFE ⅋ **Speckled Hen Pub** (610-685-8511), Fourth and Cherry Streets, Reading. Adjacent to Judy's on Cherry restaurant, this comfortable neighborhood pub has tavern food, happy hour specials, and a nice selection of microbrews and ales on tap.

⅋ **Café Waldorf**, (610-373-7111; cafewaldorf.com), 658 North Sixth Street, Reading. Late hours, live music, and open-mic nights in a quaint and cozy space with a first-floor dining room and upstairs lounge. Check the website for the entertainment schedule.

Kutztown Tavern (610-683-9600; kutztowntavern.com) 272 West Main Street, Kutztown. Closed Sundays. Shorty's Bar has pool tables, plasma TVs, and a DJ on weekends. Try the house-made lager.

The Inn at St. Peters Village (610-469-2600; theinnatsaintpeters.com), 3471 St. Peters Road, St. Peters. This B&B anchors a charming former mining village. It has a full bar, seasonal deck, and restaurant serving standard American fare, and it hosts live performers most Friday and Saturday nights.

❋ Entertainment

MOVIES & THEATER **Boscov Film Theatre at GoggleWorks** (610-374-4600; goggleworks.org), 201 Washington Street, Reading. A 125-seat modern venue in the GoggleWorks art center showing independent films.

♿ **Santander Arena and Performing Arts Center** (610-898-7200; santanderarena.com), 700 Penn Street, Reading. This large downtown venue hosts everything from Reading Royals hockey

❋ Selective Shopping

ANTIQUES Adamstown, between Reading and Lancaster, might have more antiques shops and flea markets than Lancaster County has cows. Many of them line PA 272 and offer reasonable prices that experts say are tough to beat anywhere else on the East Coast. Pick up a free map and shopping guide to the area at just about any shop. For a more complete listing of shops, visit www.antiquescapital.com.

Renninger's Antiques and Collectors Market (717-336-2177; renningers.net), 2500 North Reading Road. Open 7:30–4 Sundays. The granddaddy of antiques marts, with more than 300 indoor and 200 outdoor vendors selling everything from farm tables to Chippendale desks to comic books and costume jewelry. Expect to see more Windsor chairs than you will ever see again in your lifetime. There are also plenty of food vendors selling everything from cream doughnuts to soft pretzels. The outdoor section opens at 5 a.m., weather permitting; bring a flashlight. Locals know that the produce stands sell some of the sweetest summer corn around. Renninger's also operates a market Saturdays in Kutztown.

Stoudt's Black Angus Antiques Mall (717-484-2757; stoudts.com/antiques), 2800 North Reading Road. Open 7:30–4 Sundays. Just down the street from Renninger's, this 400-vendor market is known for upscale offerings such as 19th-century Normandy farm tables, fine china and porcelain, rare books, gas chandeliers, and more. It shares a roof with Wonderful Good Market, a foodie haven of artisan cheese, breads, and micro-roasted coffee.

Adams Antiques (717-355-3166; adamsantiques.com), 2400 North Reading Road. Open Monday–Saturday 10–5, Sundays. 8–5. A fun-to-browse antiques mall featuring 85 booths selling vintage dollhouses, toys, beer steins, lawn ornaments, old postcards, and more. There's an outdoor setup on weekends as well.

Country French Collection (717-484-0200), 2887 North Reading Road. Open 1–4 Sundays and by appointment. Housed in an 18th-century stone barn full of exquisite (and expensive) armoires, chairs, farm tables, and copper cookware from France and England.

Merritt's Antiques (610-689-9541; merritts.com), 1860 Weavertown Road, Douglassville. A large warehouse full of hard-to-find antiques, clocks, and quirky treasures such as horsehead hitching posts, mechanical banks, tin signs, and weathervanes.

Fleetwood Antique Mall (610-207-2322; fleetwoodantiquemall.com), 14129 Kutztown Road/US 222, Fleetwood. There's a big market for life-sized resin farm animals in Pennsylvania, and many of them are made and sold here. Furniture and accessories from the former antiques complex are also for sale in a nearby barn.

Stoudtburg Village (stoudtburg village.com), Stoudtburg Road (at Reading Road), Adamstown. Local antiques-and-beer king Ed Stoudt came up with the idea for a faux European village after many visits to the motherland. Shopkeepers live above their stores and coffeehouses in a somewhat self-contained arrangement. It's not exactly thriving with stores and shoppers, but it's an interesting place to spend an hour.

SPECIAL SHOPS **Cabela's** (610-929-7000), 100 Cabela Drive (off I-78), Hamburg. Open daily. As much theme park as retail store, this outpost of the Nebraska-based outdoor adventure catalog has a café, a walk-through aquarium, and a mini-mountain full of taxidermied animals. Prices are comparable to the catalog's; there's also a bargain cave in the back. It's an easy destination to bundle with a trip to Hawk Mountain Sanctuary or Crystal Cave.

Country Seat (610-756-6124; countryseat.com), 1013 Old Philly Pike, Kempton. Closed Sundays; check the website for schedule on other days. Master weaver Donna Longenecker sells all kinds of basket- and seat-weaving supplies—wire handles, wooden bases, pine needles, Shaker tape, braided seagrass—plus woven ornaments, jewelry, silk scarves, and gourd art. It's a great place to buy a unique gift or just learn about a fascinating but dying craft. She also teaches weaving classes, from beginner to advanced, once a month.

Five and Divine (610-670-9700; fiveanddivine.com), 27 East Penn

Avenue, Wernersville. Closed Mondays. A haven for DIYers: vintage piggy banks, hand-painted glassware, recycled glass bowls, chalk paint, unique gifts.

Dixon's Muzzleloading Shop (610-756-6271), 9952 Kunkels Mill Road, Kempton. Muzzleloaders are firearms that are loaded from the front. This is one of the largest muzzle-loading supply shops in the country, and the owner is an expert on their manufacture and repair.

✳ Special Events

March/April: **Berks Jazz Fest**, Reading—10 days of master classes, workshops, and performances by top jazz and blues musicians at venues throughout Reading. Past performers have included Al Jarreau, the Dave Brubeck Quartet, Journey's Steve Smith. Info: berksjazzfest.com.

June/July: **Kutztown Folk Festival** (last weekend/first weekend), Kutztown University—the state's biggest Pennsylvania Dutch–themed party. Nine days of square dancing, agricultural demonstrations, hex sign painting, chair caning, folk arts-and-crafts fair, hay mazes, pony rides, and the country's largest quilt sale. Food options include funnel cakes, corn fritters, apple dumplings, ham and chicken dinners, and a 1,200-pound ox roasted on a spit. Info: kutztownfestival.com.

August: **Goschenhoppen Festival** (second weekend), Perkiomenville—preserved German homestead showcases 18th- and 19th-century Pennsylvania Dutch life with furniture-making and tinsmithing demonstrations, hand-churned ice cream and homemade summer sausage, and baking in a restored outdoor oven. It's smaller and lesser known than the Kutztown Folk Festival, but just as interesting and a little easier to manage. For information, visit goschenhoppen.org.

LOWER SUSQUEHANNA RIVER VALLEY

HARRISBURG & HERSHEY

GETTYSBURG

YORK COUNTY

HARRISBURG & HERSHEY

L ess than 15 miles apart from one another, Hershey and Harrisburg are close in distance but quite different in mood and offerings. Harrisburg is the state capital with grand old buildings, historical museums, expense-account steakhouses, and commanding views of the Susquehanna River. Once an important crossroads for Native Americans traveling to and from the Potomac and upper Susquehanna region, it is named for a later settler, John Harris. During the American Civil War, Harrisburg was a training center for the Union army and developed into a major rail center and link between the Atlantic coast and the Midwest. Today it's a city of about 49,500 with a reputation for shutting down on weekends and when the state legislature is out of session. But there is more going on than first meets the eye. The city boasts many beautiful parks, most notably downtown's City Island, historic sites such as Fort Hunter, good restaurants, and the best nightlife outside of Philadelphia and Baltimore. One could plan a trip based around a visit to the State Museum of Pennsylvania alone.

Meanwhile, chocolate, theme-park rides, and a man named Milton dominate the small town of Hershey. Mr. Hershey died in 1945 after spending decades building his successful candy empire, but his spirit lives on in this Willy Wonka–like realm of resort hotels, gardens, trolley rides, hot-chocolate lattes, and street lamps shaped like Hershey's Kisses. Recent worthwhile additions to the area include the huge Antique Auto Museum of America and the Hershey Museum's Chocolate Lab, a hands-on classroom that lets kids and adults play and create. You will have a chance to sample chocolate again and again during your visit: upon check-in at many hotels, in the chocolate fondue wraps at the Chocolate Spa, and as a gentle scent wafting throughout the town, especially around the main factory on Chocolate Avenue.

AREA CODE Harrisburg and Hershey are within the 717 area code.

GUIDANCE Contact the **Harrisburg-Hershey-Carlisle Tourism and Convention Bureau** (717-231-7788; 800-955-0969; www.visithhc.com), 415 Market Street, Harrisburg, for maps and a visitor guide. A welcome center is open weekdays from 8:30–4:30 in the east wing of the Capitol. In Hershey, Chocolate World and the Hershey Lodge have brochures and maps of the area.

GETTING THERE *By air:* **Harrisburg International Airport** (717-948-3900; 1-888-235-9442) is about 50 miles northeast of Gettysburg. **Philadelphia International** (215-937-6800) is about a two-hour drive.

By car: From Philadelphia, take the Pennsylvania Turnpike to Exit 266 (Lebanon-Lancaster), then US 322 west to Hershey. For Harrisburg, take the Pennsylvania Turnpike to Exit 247, then take I-83 south to Second Street.

By bus: **Greyhound** (800-231-2222) offers service between Harrisburg and dozens of major cities, operating out of a terminal at 411 Market Street, Harrisburg.

GETTING AROUND For Harrisburg, **Capital Area Transit** (717-238-8304; cattransit.com) offers bus service throughout the city.

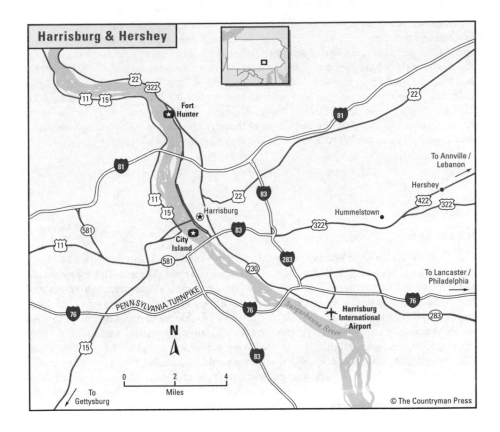

The Hershey Trolley (717-533-3000) is a great way for first-time visitors to learn the town's layout and history before heading to the park and other attractions. Guides are witty and generous with candy samples. Tours depart regularly in front of Chocolate World.

Milton S. Hershey Medical Center (717-531-8521), 500 University Drive, Hershey.

WHEN TO GO Hershey Park is a seasonal attraction open from May–Labor Day and some weekends in the fall. If you're looking for a bargain and don't mind skipping the theme park, plan to go anytime off-season and you will find that many area hotel rates drop significantly. There are still plenty of attractions that stay open year-round, including Hershey Gardens, ZooAmerica, and the State Museum of Pennsylvania and National Civil War Museum in Harrisburg. To see Harrisburg at its busiest, plan your visit for a weekday when the legislature is in session. January is also a great time to visit the state capital; the fabulous Farm Show kicks into gear toward the end of the month, and its huge indoor complex keeps you protected from inclement weather.

✳ Villages

Annville. A few miles east of Hershey, Annville has a classic American main street with a historic theater and beautifully preserved old homes. It's also home to Lebanon Valley College.

Hummelstown. Before the chocolate industry came along, this small town between Harrisburg and Hershey was the driving economic force in the area: supplying brownstone for buildings from Philadelphia to Chicago. Today you will find charming tree-lined streets anchored by a square with antiques shops, preserved old homes, and restaurants, including the wonderful Warwick Hotel. It is also home to Indian Echo Caverns, limestone caves that once served as a shelter for Native Americans, and the historic Middletown and Hummelstown Railroad. Its historical society operates a museum that has an extensive collection of Indian arrowheads collected between 1914 and 1940 by Philander Ward Hartwell, the town's newspaper editor.

✲ To See

MUSEUMS

HARRISBURG

✐ ♿ ☂ **State Museum of Pennsylvania** (717-787-4780; statemuseumpa.org), 300 North Street. Closed Mondays and Tuesdays; admission charged. There aren't many places that house a 12,000-year-old reconstructed mastodon, a planetarium, a re-created Susquehannock Indian village, and a Civil War museum, all under the same roof. Next to the Capitol, this rarely crowded attraction has four floors of exhibits and activities on Pennsylvania's role in history, geology, pop culture, industrial and technological innovations, and war. Highlights of the huge collection include the original Penn Charter of 1691, a set of golf clubs owned by Arnold Palmer, a 1910 cast-iron turnstile from Philadelphia's Shibe Park, and portraits of famous Pennsylvanians such as Marian Anderson. There's a hands-on play area for the under-5 set in the basement. The gift shop has a huge inventory of Pennsylvania-themed merchandise, from books on the Pittsburgh Steelers and Philadelphia Phillies to the usual assortment of coffee mugs and magnets.

THE BANK VAULT AT SUSQUEHANNA ART MUSEUM AYLEEN GONTZ

♿ ☂ **National Civil War Museum** (717-260-1861; nationalcivilwarmuseum.org), 1 Lincoln Circle at Reservoir Park. Open daily from April–August; Wednesday–Sunday from September–March; admission charged. This privately owned hilltop museum opened in 2001 with the goal of telling the entire story of the American Civil War "without bias to Union or Confederate causes." It covers each major battle of the Civil War, and many history buffs say its breadth and human-interest focus make a worthwhile complement to any trip to Gettysburg. Its dozen galleries are divided by theme and include slavery and battle artifacts, electronic battle maps, surgery demonstrations, and interactive displays that are interspersed with more than 24,000 artifacts, from Robert E. Lee's pocket Bible and Ulysses S. Grant's sword belt to lead bullets, complete with teeth marks, given to surgery-bound soldiers. It's not geared toward young children. Reenactments and other events are held in a large field behind the building.

✝ ✪ **Susquehanna Art Museum** (717-233-8668; susquehannaartmuseum.org), 1401 North Third Street. Closed Mondays. Admission charged; children under 12 are free. Established in 1970, the museum reclaimed the 1916 Keystone Bank Building in 2015, built a two-story addition, and created a permanent, 20,000-square-foot home here after more than 30 years of renting or borrowing space in downtown Harrisburg. Inside, the towering bank windows provide light for the lobby gallery, and the vault at the back of the room creates an intimate space for special exhibits. Upstairs, the 3,500-square-foot main exhibit space supports an amazing array of two-dimensional, three-dimensional, and cinematic artwork. The museum also hosts piano concerts, yoga classes, and other events in its multipurpose gallery spaces. Outside you'll find a sculpture garden and the VanGo! Museum on Wheels, a 31-foot Winnebago Sightseer repurposed for educational visits to school districts and area events.

✏ **Whitaker Center for Science and the Arts** (717-214-2787; whitakercenter.org), 222 Market Street; admission charged for science center. This 130,000-square-foot complex is home to a science museum geared toward younger kids, an IMAX theater, and a musical performance stage that has hosted string quartets and heavy metal bands. Check the website for performance and 3D movie schedules.

HERSHEY

Antique Automobile Club of America Museum (717-566-7100; aacamuseum.org), 161 Museum Drive; admission charged. A must for car buffs or anyone who appreciates a thoughtful, well-organized American history lesson. There are Ford Model Ts, mopeds, and Jeeps; vehicles dating from 1865 through the 1990s (a recent acquisition was Betty White's custom-made 1977 Cadillac Seville); and the country's largest collection of buses, including the Lakeland bus from *Forrest Gump*. Don't miss the detailed dioramas that put the car culture of different eras in context and the restored 1941 diner airlifted to Hershey from Wichita, Kansas. There's also a hands-on kids' activity area.

Hershey Derry Township Historical Society (717-520-0748; hersheyhistory.org), 40 Northeast Drive; small admission fee charged. Closed Tuesdays, Thursdays, and two Saturdays a month. Hershey wasn't always about chocolate; this old stone barn has exhibits on the early quarry industry, sports memorabilia, and Native American life. Of course, there's a room devoted to the man behind the chocolate bar.

✏ ♿ ✝ **Hershey Story** (717-534-3439; hersheystory.org), 63 West Chocolate Avenue. Open daily; admission charged, with extra fees for Chocolate Tastings and Chocolate Lab. This modern museum tells the history of Milton Hershey's boyhood, marketing genius, and philanthropy. The kid-friendly interactive exhibits include a re-creation of Hershey's first shop in Philadelphia, old promotional campaigns, and machines and panels that demonstrate the chocolate-making process (including one for wrapping Hershey's Kisses). A Chocolate Tastings section features "flights" of warm drinking chocolate sourced from around the world (there's a kid-friendly version too). The popular Chocolate Lab (for ages 4 and up) lets participants mold, dip, design, and taste their own chocolate creations; it's less expensive—but just as interesting—as the Create Your Own Candy Bar sessions over at Chocolate World.

HISTORIC SITES & GARDENS ✏ ♿ **Hershey Gardens** (717-534-3492; hersheygardens .org), 170 Hotel Road, Hershey. Open daily year-round; free to guests of any Hershey resort. You'll find Japanese, rock, and herb gardens; a fun children's garden

A CHOCOLATE ADVENTURE

Hershey Park and Chocolate World (717-534-3900; 800-437-7439; hersheypark.com), 100 West Hersheypark Drive. Open daily from mid-May–Labor Day and some weekends through October (hours vary); single and multi-day flex passes are available. Built in 1907 by Milton S. Hershey as picnic grounds for the employees of his candy company, this family-friendly amusement park now encompasses more than 100 acres with dozens of rides and attractions. There are 11 roller coasters that will soak, lift, terrify, and just plain thrill you; Skyrush, a megacoaster with winged seating, is one of the newest additions. Kiddie rides include a Dinosaur-Go-Round and a kid-sized pirate ship. Don't miss the Kissing Tower, which rises above the nearby stacks of the candy factory and gives way to a 360-degree view of the town and surrounding valley. In summer, East Coast Waterworks, a mammoth water-play structure, features four slides, a roller coaster, and multistory jungle gym. Modeled after Wildwood, New Jersey, and other Atlantic shore boardwalks, it also offers a pier for strolling, hermit crab sales, corn-dog carts, water balloon races, and a sandcastle area for toddlers. You will get wet, so bring a change of clothes if you plan to hit this area of the park.

A cost-saving tip: Many local businesses offer discount park tickets, and one of the best places to get them is at Giant Food (717-312-0725; 1250 Cocoa Avenue; open daily), where one-day tickets include a free parking pass if you buy two adult tickets. Another good value is the preview plan: arrive after 7:30 p.m. when the park closes at 10 or 11, buy a ticket for the following day, and your admission for the evening is free.

Within walking distance of the park and open year-round is Chocolate World (717-534-4900; hersheys.com/chocolateworld). Free to enter, but admission is charged for some attractions. Loyalists miss the old (read: less high-tech) factory-tour rides that ended in the 1980s, but the complex is still a great place to start your chocolate sojourn, with plenty of seats, sustenance, and a staffed information booth. It gets packed during peak hours; consider visiting when it first opens or later in the evening (it stays open until 11 p.m. on Saturdays and most nights in July and August). Take the free ride through a simulated Hershey factory, let the kids

and butterfly house; and more than 7,000 roses in bloom June–August on this lovely 23-acre property. In the spring, 45,000 tulips blanket the seasonal display garden.

    ♿ ⚲ **Pennsylvania State Capitol** (800-868-7672; pacapitol.org), North and Commonwealth Streets, Harrisburg. No trip to the Harrisburg area is complete without a visit to this domed downtown building, which was modeled after St. Peter's Basilica in Rome. Free guided tours include stops at the main rotunda and supreme court chambers and run every half hour on weekdays between 8:30 and 4. Walk-ins are welcome, or you can book ahead through the website.

    ⚭ **Fort Hunter** (717-599-5751; forthunter.org), 5300 North Front Street, Harrisburg. Built in 1756 at the beginning of the French and Indian War, this was one of a string of small forts constructed by the British along the Susquehanna River. Today, it's a beautiful place to spend an afternoon, with picnic pavilions, a playground, the pedestrian-only Everhart Covered Bridge, and a Federal-style mansion (built on the site of the old fort). Even on weekdays, you'll probably encounter locals enjoying the river views from strategically placed benches. Tours of the mansion are available, or pick up an informative walking tour brochure and wander the grounds.

❋ To Do

FOR FAMILIES ⚭ ♿ **ZooAmerica** (717-534-3860; zooamerica.com), 201 Park Avenue. Admission is included with a Hershey Park ticket, and the zoo can be accessed from

wrap their own Hershey's Kisses, then browse what is possibly the best and largest chocolate-themed gift shop around. It's a great opportunity to find new products that aren't yet available elsewhere. There's also a big and loud 3D show featuring singing and dancing candy bars and a Create Your Own Candy Bar experience. The first three hours of parking are free.

THE ENTRANCE TO THE TRAM TOUR AT HERSHEY'S CHOCOLATE WORLD

the park. A fee is charged for zoo-only visits. This small yet engaging zoo is home to more than 200 species of animals from North America (black bears, wild turkeys, reindeer, and black-footed ferrets, to name just a few) and can be covered in two hours or less. Watch for special events, like Creatures of the Night (part of Hersheypark in the Dark), which lets visitors bring flashlights to check out the animals after hours. Hershey Park ticketholders can enter the zoo via a bridge near the Kissing Tower. There is also a separate, year-round entrance to the zoo off Route 743.

🎣 **Indian Echo Caverns** (717-566-8131; indianechocaverns.com), 368 Middletown Road, Hummelstown. Admission charged. Open for tours since 1929, this small but popular attraction makes a nice side trip from Hershey. The 45-minute guided tours include up-close views of stalactites, stalagmites, cave coral, and even undergound lakes (it requires a long walk up and down steep steps to get there). During the summer, kids can pan for gemstones in a replica sluice near the gift shop. There's also a petting zoo with goats and alpacas, an arcade, and shaded public picnic areas.

🎣 **M&H Railroad** (717-944-4435; mhrailroad.com), 136 Brown Street, Middletown. Open May–October; admission charged. Kids will love this 11-mile vintage 1920s coach ride along pretty Swatara Creek and Union Canal; the conductor shares historical anecdotes and leads a sing-along on the way back. There's also a boarding platform at Indian Echo Caverns.

🎣 **City Island.** One of Harrisburg's best-known attractions, this 60-acre island in the middle of the Susquehanna River is an easy walk from downtown via Walnut Street Bridge, or you can drive onto the island via Market or Front Streets and pay to park in designated lots. It offers a long list of seasonal and year-round activities for locals and visitors: boat and train rides, minor league baseball games (the Senators are the Double-A affiliate of the Washington Nationals), seasonal swimming, mini-golf, and hiking and cycling trails with views of the Harrisburg skyline. At **City Island Beach** (717-238-9012) on the north end, you can sunbathe and swim every day but Wednesday from mid-June–Labor Day. The *Pride of the Susquehanna* (717-234-6500) is an authentic stern paddle-wheel riverboat that offers 45-minute rides daily from late May–August and weekends in October. Take the kids to **City Island Railroad** (717-232-2332), a scaled version of a Civil War–era steam train that offers rides around the island. Nearby, an antique carousel offers rides for a small fee. For more things to do here, see *Outdoor Activities.*

BREWERY TOURS **Tröeg's Independent Brewing** (717-232-1297; troegs.com), 200 East Hershey Park Drive. Two brothers from Mechanicsburg started this brewery near the Harrisburg waterfront in 1997. In 2011 it expanded to a 90,000-square-foot facility outside Hershey Park with a tasting room, snack bar, and daily brewery tours. Its scratch beers are brewed in limited small batches, and new releases are available in a concession-style tasting room and snack bar. Self-guided tours are free and available daily, though any serious beer drinker should consider the $10 guided tours (check the website for a daily schedule). They include visits to the mill room, hop cooler, brewhouse deck, and fermentation cellar, plus a welcome beer of your choice and samples.

✳ Green Space

Reservoir Park (717-255-3020), Walnut Street between 18th and 21st Streets. Built in 1872, this 85-acre park is home to the National Civil War Museum (see *Museums*), a

A WALKING PATH ALONG THE SUSQUEHANNA RIVER IN HARRISBURG AYLEEN GONTZ

restored 1898 mansion that houses several art galleries, a large playground, and a band shell that hosts summer concerts and an annual Shakespeare in the Park event. The Capital Area Greenbelt passes through here (see *Walks*).

Italian Lake (717-255-3020), Third and Division Streets. This 10-acre city park is a popular local gathering place and features formal gardens in the Italian Renaissance style, a Japanese harmony bridge, and two scenic man-made lakes. A paved walking path winds around the larger of the two lakes. Outdoor concerts are held here Sunday evenings in July and August.

Wildwood Lake Sanctuary and Nature Center (717-221-0292; wildwoodlake.org), 100 Wildwood Way. Grounds open daily dawn to dusk. Nestled in what looks like an industrial section of the city, this lake is home to all sorts of wildlife. Birding is popular along the paved pathway that circles the lake. There are several easy hiking trails and boardwalks that wind through marshes and bogs; bikes are permitted on some trails. Stop by the nature center for a detailed map.

WALKS **Capital Area Greenbelt** (717-921-4733; caga.org). This 20-mile trail laces its way around the city like a necklace and can be used for walking, biking, or skating. Start at the **Five Senses Garden** (717-564-0488) off PA 441 behind the Harrisburg East Mall.

✲ Outdoor Activities

AUTO RACING **Williams Grove Raceway** (717-697-5000; williamsgrove.com), PA 15 South, Mechanicsburg. Open Friday and Saturday from March–October. This half-mile track southwest of Harrisburg has been in operation since 1939.

BASEBALL Baseball in Harrisburg goes back as far as 1907, when the local team played in the Class D Tri-State League. Today the **Harrisburg Senators,** a farm team of the Washington Nationals, play at FNB Field (717-231-4444; milb.com/harrisburg) on City Island.

BICYCLING/RENTALS **Susquehanna Outfitters** (717-234-7879) rents canoes, kayaks, and stand-up paddleboards at the Wormleysburg Waterfront near Market Street bridge.

BOAT EXCURSIONS/RENTALS **Susquehanna River Trail** (susquehannarivertrail .org) is a 51-mile river trail with 25 access points between Harrisburg and Sunbury to the north.

Blue Mountain Outfitters (717-957-2413), US 11 and US 15, Marysville, rents canoes and kayaks starting at $45 a day.

GOLF **Iron Valley Golf Club** (717-279-7409), 201 Iron Valley Drive, Lebanon. Built on an abandoned iron mine, this challenging course offers 18 holes with significant elevation changes (11 of them are carved out of a mountain).

Royal Oaks Golf Club (717-274-2212), 3350 West Oak Street, Lebanon. This former cattle ranch has 18 holes featuring 6,730 yards of golf from the longest tees for a par of 71.

HUNTING **Fort Indiantown Gap** (717-861-2733), 1 Garrison Road, Annville. This National Guard training center is open for hunting from the first Saturday after Labor Day through February, and late April–May. All hunters must pay a $30 access fee and attend a safety briefing.

SKIING **Roundtop Mountain Resort** (717-432-9631; skiroundtop.com), 925 Roundtop Road, Lewisberry. About 20 miles south of Harrisburg, this resort has 16 ski trails (some winding), plus snowboarding, tubing, and year-round paintball.

❋ Lodging

HOTELS, LODGES & MOTELS Rates usually drop considerably in the Hershey area during the off-season of late fall, winter, and early spring. Many chains, including Days Inn, Howard Johnson, and Hampton Inn, line Chocolate Avenue east of the park.

HERSHEY

🐌 **White Rose Motel** (717-533-9876; whiterosemotel.com), 1060 East Chocolate Avenue. Simple family-owned two-story motel with tidy rooms and a small pool. Book online for the best rates. $$.

🔥 **Hotel Hershey** (717-533-2171; thehotelhershey.com), 100 Hotel Road. It was a bold endeavor to build a luxury Mediterranean-style hotel during the Depression, but that's exactly what Milton Hershey did when he returned home from a trip to Europe in the 1930s. It remains one of Pennsylvania's top special-occasion hotels, a grand lodge complete with 276 rooms and cottages, palatial gardens, indoor and outdoor pools, and commanding views of the Conewago Valley. Guest rooms have a sophisticated Victorian feel and feature original artwork, luxury linens, and chocolate soaps and bath foam. There are 20 suites, including the lavish Catherine Hershey Suite, which sleeps up to eight and features a garden theme, three bathrooms, two bedrooms, living and dining rooms, and a private balcony. Nearby is Hershey Gardens, to which hotel guests are admitted free. You don't have to be a hotel guest to take a free tour (offered Monday, Wednesday, and Friday at 10 a.m. in the registration lobby) of the premises or indulge in a chocolate fondue wrap or massage at the Chocolate Spa. $$$$.

🔥 **Hershey Lodge** (717-533-3311; hersheylodge.com), 325 University Drive. Part of the Hershey Resorts umbrella, this sprawling complex of 665 rooms may seem daunting on arrival, but it offers efficient and friendly service, spacious rooms, and a convenient location near Hershey Park and other attractions. It does a huge meetings and conventions business. Rooms are decorated in chocolate tones and have refrigerators, TVs, and chocolate-scented toiletries. A 30,000-square-foot indoor Water Works complex, open to guests, has slides, a Reese's Cup–themed obstacle course, tipping buckets, basketball hoops, and other kid-friendly features. Rates include passes to Hershey Gardens and Hershey Museum, discounted Hershey Park tickets, and shuttle service to the park. $$$.

Annville Inn (717-867-1991; annville inn.com), 4515 Hill Church Road, Annville. Looking for solace after a day of roller coaster rides? Consider this five-room B&B 6 miles east of Hershey. Meticulously cared for by innkeeper Rosalie George, it has five well-appointed rooms, some with Jacuzzi tubs, fireplaces, and private entrances. Other amenities include a large landscaped pool, game room, and screening room with stadium-style seating. $$–$$$.

HARRISBURG

Quality Inn Riverfront (717-233-1611), 525 South Front Street. This family- and pet-friendly hotel overlooking the Susquehanna is within walking distance of the Capitol and City Island. Its rooms have mini-fridges and microwaves; a small outdoor swimming pool is also open in season. $$, including breakfast.

BED & BREAKFASTS **Inn at Westwynd Farm** (717-533-6764; www.westwyndfarm

A COCOA-THEMED SPA DAY

I don't include many spas in this guide, but the **Chocolate Spa at the Hotel Hershey** (717-520-5888; 877-772-9988; chocolatespa.com) stands out for its stellar service and unique cocoa-themed treatments. Situated amid an elegant marble-floored setting overlooking the hotel's formal gardens, it offers such indulgences as chocolate hydrotherapy, chocolate-oil massages, and cocoa butter scrubs. There are also Cuban-themed treatments—a nod to Milton Hershey's ties to the island's sugar industry—featuring mojito sugar scrubs and ocean therapy wraps. For a truly indulgent day, start with a hot-chocolate latte at the hotel's Cocoa Beanery. Follow this with a whipped cocoa bath or a chocolate fondue wrap, a gentle body brushing and rinse that will leave you smelling sweetly, but not overwhelmingly, of cocoa. (For the more traditional spa-goer, there's also a roster of massage, facial, and mani-pedi treatments.) Spend the rest of the afternoon lounging in the spa's quiet areas (guests who partake of any treatment may stay as long as they like at the spa and nearby fitness center). Cap your day with a chocolate soufflé served with malted milk ball gelato in the hotel's Circular dining room. In town, **MeltSpa by Hershey** (855-500-2366; meltspa.com), 11 East Chocolate Avenue, also offers an array of signature chocolate treatments, as well as hair, makeup, and waxing services.

inn.com), 1620 Sand Beach Road, Hummelstown. This picturesque B&B is located on a 32-acre working horse farm 5 miles west of Hershey. The main house has nine cozy rooms (six with private baths and luxurious linens, some with Jacuzzi tubs and fireplaces), two living rooms, and an inviting wraparound porch with a view of the countryside. A spacious carriage house with sleeping loft is a good option for families. Owners Frank and Carolyn Troxell started a horse training and boarding operation in the 1980s and added the inn portion in 2002; goats, alpacas, cats, and dogs also live on the property, and benches provide front-row views of the riding rings. Breakfast (maybe pumpkin waffles or eggs baked in ham) is served on the sunporch or in the dining room; fresh-baked snacks, drinks, and candy are available day and night. $$; two-night minimum on weekends.

♂ **Canna Country Inn** (717-938-6077; cannainnbandb.com), 393 Valley Road, Etters. About 8 miles southeast of Harrisburg, this seven-room B&B is housed in a converted 18th-century barn surrounded by 3 acres of gardens and a picnic grove with hammocks and firepits. Rooms have king or queen beds, DVD players,

and WiFi; some have private entrances and whirlpool tubs. The 600-square-foot common living room invites lounging, with a fireplace and window seat overlooking the grounds. Breakfasts are huge and made to order. Skiers from nearby Roundtop fill the inn during winter; ask about lift discounts. $$–$$$.

Mt. Gretna Inn (717-964-3234; mtgretnainn.com), 16 Kauffman Avenue, Mount Gretna. This genteel Arts and Crafts–style inn offers seven unique rooms with private baths, some with fireplaces and whirlpool tubs. A three-course gourmet breakfast is served by candlelight in the elegant dining room. $$$.

CAMPGROUNDS **Elizabethtown/ Hershey KOA** (717-367-7718), 1980 Turnpike Road, Elizabethtown. Open April–October. About a 15-minute drive from Hershey off PA 743, this large campground and RV park wins raves for its private wooded sites and friendly staff. There's a seasonal pool and café and lots of activities, including mini-golf and a fish pond. Tent sites $; cabins $$.

Hershey Park Camping Resort (717-534-8999; hersheyparkcampingresort.com), 1200 Sweet Street, Hummelstown.

MOUNT GRETNA: OFF THE BEATEN TRACK

Nothing in the Harrisburg-Hershey area says "nostalgia" quite like a visit to Mount Gretna (mtgretna.com). For a relaxing day trip, head southwest out of town toward the hills that break up the valley floor. You'll soon find yourself on PA 117 surrounded by forested state game lands.

The lake that appears as you drive into town formed in the late 1800s when land owner Robert Habersham Coleman ordered a dam built across Conewago Creek. Today its sandy, lifeguarded beach (717-964-3130; mtgretnalake.com) is a popular spot open to the public for lake swimming and boating (day and season passes are available). Arrive early to grab a parking spot in the lot behind the lake and plan to stay all day. You can bring your own food and grill or eat at the snack bar; an in-and-out stamp at the gate allows for exploring the town between swims.

If you're here to stroll rather than swim, there's a lot to see. Park your car in the general lot off PA 117 at the Mount Gretna Roller Rink or at the Mount Gretna Fire Company lot off Boulevard Avenue. Mount Gretna has a number of beautiful shaded streets lined with stately homes, but only a few of them are drivable. Navigating the paved roads and pathways by foot is by far the best way to experience the town.

Head for the Tabernacle first, at Third Street and Glossbrenner Avenue. Built in 1899, this fabulous wooden structure marks the center of the United Brethren Campmeeting (mtgretnacampmeeting.com) cottages, erected in 1892 when the campmeeters abandoned their previous location in nearby Stoverdale.

Cross Pinch Road and you are headed for the Pennsylvania Chautauqua (pachautauqua.info). Mount Gretna's first Chautauqua, a type of summer camp that emphasized intellectual, physical, and religious pursuits for families, was held here in 1892. The lovely, modern-equipped houses that ring the open-air Mount Gretna Playhouse, another wooden marvel, still show

There are 300 tent sites (few with shade), rustic log cabins (deluxe and rustic), swimming pools, and a complimentary seasonal shuttle to Hershey Park, about five minutes away. Keep in mind that the campground is bordered by Swatara Creek on one side and freight train tracks that operate 24/7. Tent sites $; cabins $$; rates drop after Labor Day.

✳ Where to Eat

DINING OUT

HERSHEY

Devon Seafood + Steak (717-508-5460; devonseafood.com), 27 West Chocolate Avenue. Lunch daily; dinner Monday–Saturday; brunch Sundays. Small, upscale chain located in the Hershey Press building—specialties include seafood cioppino, linguine with clams and spicy cherry peppers, char-crusted Hawaiian ahi tuna, or bone-in rib eye with a side of roasted wild mushrooms. Save room for the fabulous three-layer Hershey's chocolate velvet cake. $$–$$$.

The Circular (717-534-8800), Hotel Hershey. Open for breakfast and dinner Monday–Saturday, lunch Friday and Saturday, Sunday brunch. The area's most elegant (and priciest) restaurant boasts wonderful views of the hotel's immaculate gardens and reflecting pools, and a menu that offers a sophisticated twist on the ubiquitous chocolate theme. The dinner menu might include cocoa-dusted scallops or more traditional offerings, such as grilled fillet of beef with corn custard, or Berkshire pork tenderloin with grits, charred zucchini, and baby leeks. Brunch is an extravaganza of cold seafood, carving and omelet stations, and dozens of fabulous chocolate desserts. Reservations recommended. $$$$.

their Victorian roots, and many are available for rent throughout the year. The Emporium, now a gift shop, and the Hall of Philosophy are also part of this National Historic District site. The only other place to stay in town is the Arts and Crafts–style Mt. Gretna Inn (717-964-3234; mtgretnainn.com), built in 1941 (see *Lodging*).

Culinary delights draw nearby residents to Mount Gretna on a regular basis. The Jigger Shop (717-964-9686; jiggershop.com), with its indoor and outdoor seating, reflects the summer resort nature of the Chautauqua. You won't find air-conditioning, but you will find a Jigger—a unique sundae topped with its namesake jigger nuts—and other specialty sundaes featuring local delights such as fastnachts and shoofly pie. For meals before treats, visit the Hide-A-Way Restaurant (717-675-7987; mtgretnahideaway.com), Porch and Pantry (717-964-3771; porchandpantry.com), and Mt. Gretna Pizzeria (717-964-1853). For a dinner and a show, try the Timbers (717-964-3601; gretnatimbers.com).

Popular with hikers, mountain bikers, and horse riders, the Pennsylvania State Game Lands surrounding Mount Gretna are ideal for an afternoon outing; the 18-mile Lebanon Valley Rail Trail also passes by here. The new Clarence Schock Memorial Park at Governor Dick (parkatgovernordick.org) holds educational programs and guided hikes and is a hot spot for bouldering on some of the oldest rocks in Pennsylvania. It also serves as a gateway to the iconic Governor Dick Observation Tower, a circular cement structure built in 1954, located just a short distance from the town. A climb to the top of the 66-foot-tall tower will reward you with stunning views of the valley, but be prepared: You'll be resting your back against a polished wooden board and using ladders to get to the top.

For maps and more information about Mount Gretna's unique history, stop by the Information and Visitor Center on Carnegie Avenue or the Mount Gretna Area Historical Society (717-964-1105; mtgretnahistory.org) on Pennsylvania Avenue. Both are open between Memorial Day and Labor Day, but year-round postings outside will tell you about upcoming events.

HARRISBURG

♈ **Bricco** (717-724-0222; briccopa.com), 31 South Third Street. Lunch and dinner Monday–Friday, dinner Saturday and Sunday. Bricco manages to stand out among the city's many fine-dining options by marrying local Pennsylvania produce with creative French and Tuscan-style cooking. Hand-tossed pizza comes with Kennett Square mushrooms, caramelized onions, and burrata. Roasted lobster and crab are served with root beer pork belly, fennel, apples, and vanilla-bourbon sauce. Dessert might feature pine nut gelato or strawberry rhubarb semifreddo. A truly memorable dining experience. $$$.

♪ **Millworks** (717-695-4888; millworks harrisburg.com), 340 Verbeke Street. A restaurant, craft brewery, artist studio, and beer garden all rolled into one unique space. Lumber left behind by the Stokes Millwork was incorporated into the tables, bar tops, and doorframes. The New American menu of wood-fired pizzas, sandwiches, and suppers features seasonal, locally sourced ingredients.

♈ **Sammy's** (717-221-0192; sammys italianrestaurant.com), 502 North Third Street. Lunch and dinner from Monday–Friday, dinner Saturdays. A two-story BYO bistro near the Capitol with a traditional Italian menu; try the shrimp scampi or eggplant rollatini stuffed with ricotta. The $6.95 all-you-can-eat lunch buffet is a great deal. Reservations recommended on weekends. $$–$$$.

EATING OUT **Broad Street Market** (717-236-7923), 1233 North Third Street (at Verbeke), Harrisburg. Open 7 a.m.–2 p.m. Wednesday (with limited vendors), 7 a.m.–5 p.m. Thursday and Friday, and 7 a.m.–5 p.m. Saturday. A good spot for

FOOD VENDORS AT HISTORIC BROAD STREET MARKET AYLEEN GONTZ

lunch near the Capitol and the State Museum of Pennsylvania. This market has been around since the Civil War and fills three city blocks. Its stalls are more varied than most food markets in the area: Offerings include fried and smoked chicken, crêpes, subs, and hand-rolled pretzels. Next door in the stone building, expect sushi, Indian curry dishes, sweet potato pie, and Haitian Creole cuisine. Local bands or singer-songwriters perform in the courtyard most Saturdays.

Brownstone Café (717-944-3301), 1 North Union Street, Middletown. Breakfast, lunch, and dinner daily. Terrific and unpretentious eatery in an old brownstone near the M&H Railroad station. Prices are very reasonable; for breakfast, try the hash-brown casserole or generous stack of pancakes. The hot ham and cheese on a pretzel roll is a lunchtime favorite; platters include ham loaf and stuffed cabbage. $.

Roxy's Café (717-232-9292), 274 North Street (at Third), Harrisburg. Breakfast and lunch daily. Friendly eatery near the Capitol, with hearty sandwiches, beer-battered onion rings, and salads. It's a popular local breakfast spot; don't

be surprised if you see a state politician or two drop in. $.

What If Café (717-238-1155), 3424 North Sixth Street, Harrisburg. Lunch and dinner Monday–Saturday. The rooms at this popular BYO eatery are bright and stylish, and the diverse menu includes Angus beef burgers, steamed clams, panko-crusted chicken over pasta, and veal Marsala. There's also a branch in Hershey. $$.

♈ ✿ **Wolfe's Diner** (717-432-2101), 625 North US 15, Dillsburg. Everything you'd want in an old-fashioned diner: low prices, a menu full of comfort food, and a tidy décor of stainless steel and linoleum. This makes a good stop for travelers between Harrisburg and Gettysburg. $.

HERSHEY & NEARBY

♈ **Fenicci's of Hershey** (717-533-7159), 102 West Chocolate Avenue. Open Monday–Friday for lunch and dinner; dinner only on Saturday and Sunday. The original home of the H. B. Reese Candy Co. (and the birthplace of Reese's Peanut Butter Cups), this dimly lit tavern has a wide selection of pastas, steaks, and seafood, but the pizzas draw the biggest raves. Toppings include buffalo chicken and bruschetta. It has live music and stays open late on weekends. $$.

Hershey Pantry (717-533-7505; hersheypantry.com), 801 East Chocolate Avenue. Open daily. It's not the best value in town, but the meals (especially breakfast) are reliably good at this cozy spot just east of Hershey Park. Try the cinnamon bread French toast or egg sandwich on a pretzel roll for breakfast. For lunch, there's a nice selection of salads and sandwiches, and dinner entrées include fish tacos, chicken carbonara, coconut shrimp, and filet mignon. Portions are ample, and kids are welcome. There's even an afternoon tea of scones, soup, sandwiches, and rich desserts from the in-house bakery. $$.

Lebanon Farmers' Market (717-274-3663; lebanonfarmersmarket.com), 35 Eighth Street, Lebanon. Open Thursday and Friday 8–7, Saturday 8–3. Grab a fresh-from-the-oven soft pretzel or a Lebanon bologna sandwich and take it upstairs to a dining room overlooking the entire market. Two of my favorite stops are S. Clyde Weaver for sweet Lebanon bologna and salt-and-vinegar potato chips, and Candy Rama, which sells caramels, fudge, and every type of wrapped sweet imaginable. The market is also now home to the beloved **Sirro's Italian Ice and Malt Shop** (717-274-9080), an old-school soda fountain known for its specialty water ices and thick milkshakes.

☿ **Warwick Hotel** (717-566-9124; thewarwickhotel.com), 12 West Main Street, Hummelstown. Open Monday–Saturday for breakfast, lunch, and dinner; dinner only on Sundays. Locals call it "The Wick," and it's a favorite gathering spot, with several dining rooms, an outdoor patio, full bar, and lots of old-fashioned charm. The 12-page menu features all kinds of burgers,

sandwiches, salads, pastas, steaks, and seafood. $$.

Backstage Café (717-867-3545), 36 East Main Street, Annville. This would be a good place to eat even if it weren't adjacent to a first-run movie theater. It shares a doorway with the Allen Theater, so you can grab a turkey sandwich and enjoy it with the movie or hang out in the laid-back, art-filled dining room. There's also free WiFi, and there's live jazz on Friday, Saturday, and the first Thursday of the month.

✳ Entertainment

MUSIC Many Harrisburg bars feature live music on Thursday, Friday, and Saturday nights. Pick up a copy of *Pennsylvania Musician*, available for free around town, or check out pamusician.net. The longtime highlights what's going on musicwise each week in the Harrisburg area and beyond.

☿ **Appalachian Brewing Company** (717-221-1080), 50 Cameron Street, Harrisburg. This cavernous microbrewery hosts top-notch acoustic acts and open-mic nights in the Abbey Bar. There's usually no cover, and there's free pool on Sunday and Tuesday. Brewery tours are given Saturday at 1 p.m.

Giant Center (717-534-3911; giant center.com), 550 West Hersheypark Drive, hosts Hershey Bears hockey games, Disney on Ice shows, and pop-music concerts.

Harrisburg Comedy Zone (717-920-5653; harrisburgcomedyzone.com), 110 Limekiln Road, New Cumberland. Open-mic nights, improv, and performances by local personalities like Raymond the Amish Comic.

☿ **Winner's Circle Saloon** (717-469-0661), 604 Station Road, Harrisburg. This "eatin', drinkin', and dancin' place" in the Grantville Holiday Inn features live country bands Wednesday–Saturday and line-dancing lessons on Tuesday and Thursday.

EXCURSIONS

A DAY IN MIDTOWN New yet old, energized yet laid-back, hip but definitely not square . . . this is Harrisburg's Midtown District. Officially, the area is bounded by Forester Street to the south, Seventh Street to the east, Kelker and Maclay Streets to the north, and the Susquehanna River to the west, but if you show up at the corner of Verbeke and North Third Streets, you'll be right in the heart of one of the most watched areas of the city.

Park in one of the angled spots that run up one side and down the other side of the Broad Street Market or in the lots by the Millworks restaurant, then start your day with a short walk to the **Midtown Scholar,** a book lover's dream with 200,000 used, rare, new, and discounted titles. Start by browsing the bookshelves outside, then grab an espresso or a cup of loose leaf tea at the café just inside the door. The three floors of stacks are organized by subject, with the new books at the front of the store and a large collection of rare books in the basement.

Assuming it's lunchtime when you're done at the bookstore, head across the street to the **Broad Street Market** (broadstreetmarket.org), the oldest continuously running market house in the United States. Established in 1860 and added to the National Register of Historic Places in 1974, the market was restored in 1996 and updated again in 1999. Today the market comprises two buildings and covers three city blocks. You'll find produce in the Stone Market that faces Third Street and food vendors in the Brick Market behind it. The open-air plaza between the two buildings has become a neighborhood gathering spot and a perfect place to enjoy a light meal or some live music.

When you're ready to move on, go north two blocks on Third Street until you hit Calder Street and spend the afternoon at the **Susquehanna Art Museum** (see *Museums*) in the 1916 Keystone Bank Building. The back vault hosts special exhibits, while the 3,500-square-foot main exhibit space upstairs supports an amazing array of 2D, 3D, and cinematic artwork.

For dinner, return to your starting point and enjoy an evening at **Millworks** (see *Dining Out*), a restaurant, craft brewery, artist studio, and beer garden all rolled into one unique space. While you're waiting to be seated, browse through the 30-plus art studios on-site or have a beer in the rooftop beer garden overlooking the city.

THEATER & MOVIES ♿ **Hershey Theater** (717-534-3405; hersheytheater.com), 15 East Caracas Avenue, Hershey. This renovated and gorgeous 1933 building hosts everything from Broadway musicals to classic films and children's shows. Tours are given on Fridays (year-round) and Sundays (summer only) for $10 a person. Call 717-533-6299 for times.

Allen Theatre and Backstage Café (717-867-4766; allentheatre.com), 36 Main Street, Annville. A beautifully restored art deco theater showing first-run films. The owner introduces most of the screenings, and local college students and aspiring musicians provide prescreen entertainment. The adjacent café serves sandwiches, pastries, and good coffee, and there is live music most weekends.

Haars Drive-In (717-432-3011), 185 Logan Road, Dillsburg. Open April–September. This 1950s-style drive-in off US 15 shows first-run movies on weekends.

✳ Selective Shopping

In downtown Harrisburg, the **Shops at Strawberry Square** (717-255-1020; closed Sundays), 11 North Third Street, offers a handful of boutiques, urban grocers, and a food court. Just off I-83 at Paxton Street, **Harrisburg East Mall** (717-564-0980) is another main shopping area, anchored by Macy's, Bass Pro Shops, and Boscov's.

The Midtown Scholar (717-236-1680; midtownscholar.com), 1301 North Third

MIDTOWN SCHOLAR, A BOOKSTORE AND CAFÉ IN DOWNTOWN HARRISBURG AYLEEN GONTZ

One last thing to round out your day: rent a bike at the self-serve Zagstar station near the entrance to Broad Street Market and pedal the six blocks along Verbeek Street to the bank of the Susquehanna River. Here you'll find the **Sunken Garden** at Riverfront Park. It offers not only a lovely view of the river, but also a glimpse into history. Created in 1924, the gardens mark the site of Harrisburg's Hardscrabble neighborhood, which supported the burgeoning lumbering efforts of the 19th century. The lower levels of the homes that once stood here in the 1800s now form the "sunken" part of the gardens.

Street. Once a movie theater in the 1920s and a department store in the 1950s, this place in Harrisburg's newly energized Midtown District is now a book lover's dream—with 200,000 used, rare, new, and discounted titles. Start by browsing the rolling bookshelves lining the street out front, then grab an espresso or a cup of loose leaf tea at the café just inside the door. The three floors of stacks are organized by subject, with the new books at the front of the store and rare books, including vellum-bound volumes and 19th-century prints, in the basement.

Old Sled Works Antiques and Craft Market (717-834-9333; sledworks.com), 722 North Market Street, Duncannon. Open Wednesday–Sunday. You'll find 125 vendors selling toys, cookbooks, jewelry,

baskets, and all kinds of furniture at this indoor market. Be sure to check out the old sleds on display (a nod to the building's former use) and the vintage penny arcade. An antique forest-fire lookout tower (no climbing) anchors the riverfront property.

West Shore Farmers' Market and Shoppes (717-737-9881; westshore farmersmarket.com), 900 Market Street, Lemoyne. Market open Tuesday, Friday, and Saturday, shops open Tuesday–Saturday. Indoor market with prepared foods, butcher, and produce stalls downstairs and crafts, used books, and clothes for sale upstairs. Kepler Seafood is renowned for its lump crabmeat and smoked salmon cream cheese. Fewer vendors show up on Tuesdays.

HUMMELSTOWN

Olde Factory (717-566-5685), 139 South Hanover Street. Three floors of antiques, folk art, quilts, and unusual crafts located in a former dress factory.

Rhoads Hallmark and Gift Shop (717-566-2525), 17 West Main Street. This old-fashioned multiservice store sells candles, beer steins, Boyds Bears, and other collectibles in addition to the usual drugstore inventory.

✻ Special Events

January: **Pennsylvania Farm Show** (second and third weeks), 2300 North Cameron Street, Harrisburg—the largest indoor agricultural event in America features more than a million square feet of farm equipment displays, cooking demos, animal beauty contests, and some of the best cuisine the state has to offer. A must-see is the life-sized butter sculpture designed in a different likeness each year. Food highlights include potato doughnuts from the state potato cooperative, honey ice cream from the beekeepers association, apple dumplings, chicken corn soup, deep-fried mushrooms, and every variation of beef and pork sandwich you can think of. Admission is free, but parking will cost you.

GETTYSBURG

One of Pennsylvania's top tourist attractions, the small town of Gettysburg sits west of Harrisburg and just north of the Maryland border, surrounded by the battlefield that made it famous. It was a tiny isolated farming community before the Union and Confederate armies arrived in 1863 and fought one of the bloodiest battles of the Civil War, with more than 50,000 casualties. Four months later, at the dedication of the Soldiers' National Cemetery, President Abraham Lincoln delivered the Gettysburg Address, considered one of the greatest speeches in American history, rededicating the nation to the war effort and to the ideal that no soldier here had died in vain. The war would continue for two more years.

Today's Gettysburg, without a doubt, remains steeped in its Civil War history. It is difficult to find a prewar building that didn't serve as a shelter for wounded soldiers or isn't full of bullet holes, or an attic that wasn't taken over by sharpshooters. Its main streets are lined with souvenir shops, hotels and B&Bs, all types of restaurants, and sightseeing attractions that range from fading kitsch to garish. Buses, RVs, and motorcycles crawl along the battlefield's one-way roads at any given time of day. Yet despite the crowds and touristy vibe, a visit to Gettysburg remains a soul-stirring experience. The force of the battle and the spirits of the dead soldiers stay with you at just about every turn and long after you've left town.

One of the most enjoyable things about Gettysburg is the people. Whether they grew up or elected to retire here, bought a bullet-pocked B&B, or became a guide after years of playing tourist, their fascination with the town's history is earnest and very contagious. Talk to them; they are often happy to share their stories and knowledge.

Another thing to keep in mind is that the area is a pleasant place to spend a few days even if you or your companions don't care much about cannonades and infantry positions. Adams County is a mecca of apple, peach, and pear orchards that is awash in harvest celebrations and gorgeous foliage in the fall. Nearby villages such as New Oxford and East Berlin have antiques shops and quaint inns; to the west, Michaux State Forest offers plenty of biking and hiking opportunities.

AREA CODE The Gettysburg area lies within the 717 area code.

GUIDANCE **Gettysburg Convention and Visitors Bureau** (717-334-6274; 800-337-5015), 35 Carlisle Street, located in the town's original railway station near Lincoln Square, has maps, brochures, and a central location. It also has a staffed desk at the military park's new visitor center.

GETTING THERE *By air:* **Harrisburg International Airport** (717-948-3900) is about 50 miles northeast of Gettysburg. **Baltimore-Washington International** (301-859-7111) is about 80 miles away.

By car: Gettysburg is about four and a half hours from New York City, about 90 minutes from Baltimore, and two hours from Philadelphia. From the Pennsylvania Turnpike, take Exit 17 to US 15 south.

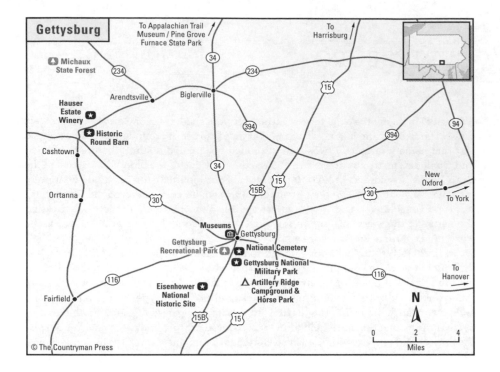

GETTING AROUND Lincoln Square, where US 30 and US 15 meet, is the center of downtown Gettysburg. Carlisle, Baltimore, Washington, and York Streets are main thoroughfares off or near the square.

Freedom Transit Trolley (717-334-6296) runs on four lines throughout town, with a hub near Lincoln Square. The tourist-friendly Lincoln Line stops at many major attractions, including the park visitor center and the American Civil War Museum. The Gold Line circulates between parking areas and the Gettysburg National Military Park Museum and Visitor Center. It operates morning to evening, Memorial Day weekend through Labor Day weekend and select weekends in October and November. Hours are limited from December–March. A one-way token costs $1, cash only and exact change required. It's a great way to circumvent parking hassles, especially during the busy summer months.

Self-guided historic walking tours begin at the **Lincoln Railroad Station,** 35 Carlisle Street. Pick up a map at the visitor center in the station.

PARKING Parking in Gettysburg can be a challenge. There is a two-hour limit on most of the metered downtown spaces. A small parking garage is located downtown behind Gallery 30 on Racehorse Alley. A handful of metered parking spaces that accept coins or payment through a parking app also are located here. A two-hour limit applies for either method of payment.

WHEN TO GO September is a good time to go if you're looking to find fewer people and decent weather—the summer crowds have left, and leaf-peeping season and Halloween are a few weeks away. Though hotels often fill up, another quiet time to visit the battlefield is the first week of July, when most people are attending the reenactment outside town. Spring brings wildflowers and thawed monuments, but it also means busloads of school groups.

✳ Villages

Biglerville. North of Gettysburg 6 miles, this rural town along PA 34 is home to a country store, a museum that chronicles and celebrates the history of the apple in Pennsylvania, and a couple of casual restaurants. Best of all, it's surrounded by good produce stands. There's no real downtown, but it's a good place to stock up on apples and other fruit on your way north out of town. Just down the road is Arendtsville, home to the popular apple harvest festival.

Cashtown. West of Gettysburg 8 miles, Cashtown dates back to 1797 and stems from the business practices of the village's first innkeeper, Peter Marck, who insisted on cash payments for the goods he sold and the highway tolls he collected. In June 1863, Confederate leaders met at the Cashtown Inn to discuss their course of action. Still in existence, the inn operates as a restaurant and B&B and is one of the few main commercial establishments in town.

Fairfield. During the Gettysburg Campaign in the American Civil War, the Battle of Fairfield played an important role in securing the Hagerstown Road, enabling Robert E. Lee's army to retreat through Fairfield toward the Potomac River. Lee and his officers stopped to eat at the Fairfield Inn, which still operates as a small hotel.

New Oxford. Anchored by an attractive town square (actually a circle) with brick sidewalks and tree-lined streets, this town of neat Victorian and Colonial homes north of Gettysburg is home to dozens of quaint shops, as well as a few B&Bs and restaurants. Every June it's the site of a huge antiques and crafts show.

Hanover. About 20 miles to the west of Gettysburg, Hanover is the county's second-largest city and the site of a small but significant Civil War battle. Though small hotels, big-box stores, and franchise food operations are prevalent along the main drag, its town center remains attractive, anchored by a large square and surrounded by historic homes and churches (see *York County*).

✳ To See

HISTORIC SITES **Gettysburg National Cemetery,** 97 Taneytown Road. Open daily dawn to dusk. Created after the war and dedicated on November 19, 1863, this solemn graveyard is the site of President Lincoln's Gettysburg Address and a reminder that the Battle of Gettysburg was a horrific and fatal event for many. Today American veterans of all the major wars are buried here. Take a guided walking tour or wander through on your own. Be sure to pause to read the passages

SIGN AT GETTYSBURG NATIONAL CEMETERY

GETTYSBURG NATIONAL CEMETERY

from Theodore O'Hara's stirring poem, "Bivouac of the Dead," located on stone tablets throughout the grounds.

♿ **David Wills House** (717-334-2499), 8 Lincoln Square. This is where you go to learn how the town coped in the aftermath of the battle. It was here that President Lincoln stayed on his postwar visit to Gettysburg and here that he completed the **Gettysburg Address** the night before he delivered it. Run by the National Park Service, the home has five rooms with original furnishings and photographs belonging to the Wills family (David Wills was a prominent local judge) and exhibits on the crafting of Lincoln's most famous speech.

Eisenhower National Historic Site (717-338-9114; nps.gov/eise), 250 Eisenhower Farm Drive; admission charged. Allow at least two hours for this worthwhile tour of Ike and Mamie Eisenhower's dairy farm and weekend retreat from Washington. Adjacent to the battlefield but a separate entity, it was the only home the Eisenhowers owned and remains much as it was when they retired here in 1967, right down to their TV-dinner trays and pink monogrammed towels. Guides start your tour with a short introduction in the formal living room (which has hosted Winston Churchill and other VIPs); afterward, visitors are free to stroll the house and grounds. Kids seven and up can partake in a Junior Secret Service Agent program and see Black Angus cows that roam the farm. You must buy tickets at the park's visitor center and take a shuttle bus to the farm. Buy your tickets early during the busy summer months; they sometimes sell out.

General Lee's Headquarters (717-334-3141), 401 Buford Avenue. Located near McPherson Ridge, this tiny stone house was the home of Gettysburg resident Mary Thompson and the impromptu headquarters of Confederate General Robert E. Lee. It underwent a $6 million renovation in 2016, and the property looks much as it did in July 1863, when Lee was defeated in a bloody three-day battle here. The grounds are available for self-guided tours, and plans are in the works to incorporate it into Gettysburg National Battlefield Park.

✎ ✋ **Gettysburg Diorama** (717-334-6408; gettysburgdiorama.com), 241 Steinwehr Avenue; admission charged. This 800-foot miniature re-creation of the 1863 battle is centrally located in the Gettysburg History Center. It's a good prop to help kids understand the logistics of the battle or just to see before setting out to tour the actual battlefield.

MUSEUMS ⚐ **Shriver House Museum** (717-337-2800), 308 Baltimore Street. Open daily from April–October, limited hours the rest of the year; admission charged. This restored 1860 house offers a rare glimpse into civilian life back then, thanks largely to the Shriver family's neighbor, Tillie Pierce, who kept a detailed diary of their experiences. The 30-minute tour, led by a costumed guide, includes a look at the bullet-riddled attic that was taken over by Confederate sharpshooters and the basement saloon of George Washington Shriver, who died before he could open it. The museum hosts a reenactment of Confederate soldiers occupying the home, which occurs annually during the anniversary weekend of the Battle at Gettysburg.

⚑ ⚐ **Rupp House History Center** (717-334-7292; gettysburgfoundation.org), 451 Baltimore Street. Open weekends from April–November; free. Another favorite Civil War attraction in the heart of downtown and a good place to stop before heading to the battlefield. It operated as a tannery during the battle, then later as a B&B until the nonprofit Friends of the National Parks of Gettysburg bought it in 2001 and turned the first floor into three rooms of interactive exhibits that use sight, sound, touch, and smell to show what life was like for civilians and soldiers of the time. You can build your own monument, carry the pack of a Civil War soldier, and take part in scavenger hunts and computer games, all designed to make the scope of the Civil War easy for anyone to digest.

Jennie Wade House (717-334-4100; jennie-wade-house.com), 548 Baltimore Street; admission charged. Jennie Wade was the only civilian killed during the Battle of Gettysburg, and it happened in this unassuming brick home near the Dobbin House. A stray bullet struck the 20-year-old while she was baking biscuits for Union soldiers. The self-guided tour begins in the kitchen, where Wade was struck, and recounts the

OUTSIDE THE GETTYSBURG NATIONAL MILITARY PARK MUSEUM AND VISITOR CENTER

NAVIGATING THE BATTLEFIELD

Gettysburg National Military Park (717-334-1124; nps.gov/gett). Park open 6 a.m.–10 p.m. daily from April–October, until 7 p.m. from November–March. Visitor center open daily 8 a.m.–6 p.m. from April–October, until 5 p.m. from November–March.

The Battle of Gettysburg was a crucial and devastating turning point in the Civil War. It ended General Robert E. Lee's most ambitious invasion of the North and was one of the war's bloodiest battles. Managed by the National Park Service since 1933, the battlefield where it all happened is the town's marquee attraction and should not be missed, no matter how short your stay.

In 2008, a bold and expanded Visitor Center opened just outside the battlefield boundaries at 1195 Baltimore Pike, 0.6 mile away from the old Taneytown Road center. Modeled after a 19th-century barn, it is an excellent place to start your tour. You'll find a bookstore, large dining area, a 20-minute film narrated by Morgan Freeman, and a museum with a dozen galleries devoted to each day of the 1863 battle. There's also the 377-foot Gettysburg Cyclorama, Paul Phillipoteaux's iconic 1884 painting of the battle that was restored to its original format and painstakingly moved to the new center in 2008. Unlike many other national parks, there is no cost or annual pass required to visit the battlefield or visitor center, but there is a charge for the film, museum, and Cyclorama. Tickets may be purchased online or at the visitor center. You may also buy tickets for the David Wills house here.

From the visitor center, many people choose to drive around the battlefield with the help of a self-guided map. Allow two to three hours or up to an entire day to cover all the monuments and key cannonade sites. Here are several other ways to view the battlefield:

By guided walking tour. They cover only a fraction of the field, but these free walks by knowledgeable guides are one of the best deals around. Mid-June–mid-August, the National Park Service offers more than 15 different themed walks across sections of the battlefield, lasting from 30 minutes to three hours. There is no need for reservations; just show up at the visitor center and join one. The walks are also offered occasionally in spring and fall.

By car with a licensed battlefield guide. This is a favorite choice of battlefield veterans. For $65 for one to six people, a rigorously trained Civil War buff will drive your car around the battlefield for two hours and vividly recount the battle with facts and anecdotes. The Gettysburg Foundation handles guide services at the visitor center, but keep in mind that a surcharge

scene through a talking mannequin dressed like a Confederate soldier. It's a popular stop for ghost lovers.

↑ **Battle Theatre** (717-334-6100), 571 Steinwehr Avenue; admission charged. This long-standing theater runs a 30-minute multimedia show on the Battle of Gettysburg in a complex also housing the tour bus–friendly General Pickett's Buffet and a very large souvenir shop.

✎ ↑ ♿ **Lincoln Train Museum** (717-334-5678), 571 Steinwehr Avenue. Admission charged. A narrow hallway lined with shadow boxes tells the story of the railroad's importance in Gettysburg, then gives way to a room filled with a jaw-dropping display of more than a thousand miniature trains and real train whistles. Admission includes a 15-minute simulated train ride that reenacts Lincoln's famous 1863 trip from Washington, DC, to Gettysburg.

↑ ♿ **Gettysburg Heritage Center Museum** (717-334-6245; gettysburgmuseum.com), 297 Steinwehr Avenue. Open daily from mid-March–December, weekends in winter; admission charged. Historical documents and artifacts combine with interactive displays and 3D photography to offer an easy-to-follow approach to the war's precursors and strategies behind the three-day battle. In the cellar, a 20-minute movie, *Gettysburg:*

of $10–15 per reservation is added to the fee. During busy times of the year, the tours often sell out before noon. You can also arrange for a guide directly (with no surcharge) by calling 717-337-1709 ahead of your visit.

By car with a GPS-guided smart phone app. At a cost of about $10, you can download an app onto your Android or Apple smart phones and follow along as the voice guides you through the National Park Service "auto tour" route. The route is marked by red and black signs with a white star in the middle and includes important monuments and highlights of the battle. As you drive, the audio guide will narrate highlights, prompt you to watch re-enactment videos and give you direction reminders.

WINTER DRIVING TOUR OF THE GETTYSBURG BATTLEFIELD   AYLEEN GONTZ

By bus with a tour guide (gettysburgfoundation.org). These tours cost less than a car tour and operate six times a day in summer (less often in spring and fall) and leave from the visitor center. A licensed battlefield guide leads the two-hour rides past all major monuments.

Other options for touring the battlefield include guided horse or bicycle, or hiking several trails that wind through the battlefield (see *Outdoor Activities*).

An Animated Map, highlights the major events of the battle with high-definition maps. The gift shop has one of the best selections of Civil War books around. Guided battlefield tours by horseback, scooter, and electric bicycles can be booked here; iPad rentals with GPS-triggered audio guides are also available.

✴ To Do

FOR FAMILIES ✐ **Explore and More Children's Museum** (717-337-1951; exploreandmore.com), 20 East High Street. Closed Wednesdays from October–March, closed Sundays from April–September; admission charged. When the kids are melting down at the prospect of another battlefield tour, take them here. The preschool teachers who created this play space for the under-8 set managed to squeeze in plenty of history lessons amid the train tables and building blocks. Kids can dress up as Civil War–era shopkeepers in the 1860s room, wash clothes on scrubbing boards, and step inside a giant bubble. It's housed in a historic brick home a few blocks from the square.

MUST SEE

ROUND BARN The ever-efficient Shakers believed the circle to be the most perfect shape because "the devil couldn't trap you in the corner." With this in mind, farmers built dozens of round barns in the late 18th and early 19th century. Only a few remain in the country today, and one of them is 8 miles outside Gettysburg. The **Historic Round Barn & Farm Market** (717-334-1984; 298 Cashtown Road, Biglerville) makes a nice respite from the in-town traffic and battlefield tours. The ground-floor farm market sells seasonal apples and peaches at fair prices, plus a wide selection of jams, soup mixes, and other giftable items. Be sure to climb the stairs to the second floor to gape at the huge spoked ceiling—built without machines by a local family in 1914. There's also a small petting farm with goats and donkeys, and there are seasonal events such as haunted barn tours on Friday and Saturday in October.

Just down the road from the barn is **Hauser Estate Winery** (717-334-4888; 410 Cashtown Road), whose magnificent hilltop views alone are worth a visit. Besides red and white wines, the Hauser Estate also makes several kinds of tasty hard ciders (a nod to the property's apple orchard history). Tastings are available, and there are regular events such as weekday happy hours and live concerts.

HISTORIC ROUND BARN IN BIGLERVILLE

Civil War Tails at the Homestead Diorama Museum (717-420-5273; civilwartails .com), 785 Baltimore Street. Closed Wednesdays and Sundays; admission charged. This has got to be the only war museum featuring soldiers in the form of clay cats. Twins Ruth and Rebecca Brown have been fashioning felines out of clay since they were kids. In 2016 they turned their hobby and scholarly Civil War knowledge into a museum of scale-model battle dioramas that include Fort Sumter, the Battle of the Ironclads, and Little Round Top (a work in progress). Housed in a former orphanage for the children of Civil War soldiers, it's a worthwhile educational stop for kids and adults alike. "Sure, the cat angle is fun," the sisters note on their website, "but we want you to learn about the men and women behind the cats."

⚘ **Land of Little Horses** (717-334-7259; landoflittlehorses.com), 125 Glenwood Drive. Open daily in summer, Friday–Sunday in spring and fall; admission fee charged. This farm park north of town stages several daily performances by trained Falabella miniature horses from Argentina in an enclosed arena. Kids of all ages will love the clever shows, which also star a posse of Jack Russell terriers, plus miniature donkeys, cows, and sheep. Check the website for showtimes and a schedule of special events, such as petting time with the animals, and hands-on activities like goat milking and horse grooming.

SCENIC DRIVE The countryside surrounding the town of Gettysburg is lush with fruit orchards, vineyards, and family farms. It's worth setting aside a few hours to explore it during your visit. Destination Gettysburg's scenic valley tour covers about 36 miles south, west, and north of Gettysburg. The route consists entirely of two-lane, paved secondary roads that are clearly marked with SCENIC VALLEY TOUR signs. The drive begins downtown at Lincoln Square and includes parts of the battlefield, peach and apple orchards, historic taverns and churches, and splendid hillside views. Upload a map at destinationgettysburg.com.

✳ Green Space

Pine Grove Furnace State Park (717-486-7174), 1100 Pine Grove Road, Gardners. Once the site of an iron furnace that made Revolutionary War–era kettles, stoves, and munitions, this 696-acre state park north of Gettysburg is now home to two man-made lakes (Laurel and Fuller), primitive campsites, picnic areas, and several miles of easy hiking trails. Swimming and fishing are allowed in both lakes; limited boating is allowed on Laurel. You can also access the Appalachian Trail here. Stop at the visitor center on Pine Grove Road for a map and info on overnight parking.

Strawberry Hill Nature Center and Preserve (717-642-5840; strawberryhill.org), 1537 Mount Hope Road, Fairfield. This 609-acre preserve about 8 miles west of town has three ponds, 10 miles of easy to moderate trails, picnic tables, and a nature center with hands-on wildlife and plant displays. Wildflowers cover the grounds in spring; great blue herons, great horned owls, wild turkeys, and other birds have been spotted here year-round.

✳ Outdoor Activities

BICYCLING Bikes are permitted on all paved roads within the battlefield; it's a great way to combine exercise with history lessons. **Healthy Adams Bicycle Pedestrian Inc.,** a nonprofit fitness group, has mapped out a variety of bike rides around town for all levels. Most begin at Gettysburg Recreational Park, a few blocks outside town. The routes can be found at habpi.org/pages/onroad.php.

GettysBike Tours (717-752-7752; gettysbike.com) rents bikes per hour or per day; you'll find them in the bus and RV lot at the visitor center at 1195 Baltimore Pike. It also offers three-hour battlefield tours led by licensed guides and other custom tours. Reservations recommended. **Gettysburg Bike and Fitness** (717-334-7791; gettysburgbicycle .com), 307 York Street, also rents bikes by the hour or day. Reserve ahead on weekends. Closed Sundays.

GOLF **Carroll Valley Golf Course** (717-642-8252; libertymountain resort.com), 78 Country Club Trail, Fairfield. A clear stream fronts a third of the 18 holes at this championship par-71 course.

EXCURSIONS

APPALACHIAN TRAIL MUSEUM Anyone who has set foot on the Appalachian National Scenic Trail—or anyone who simply enjoys being outdoors—should plan a foray into the mountains north of Gettysburg to the **Appalachian Trail Museum** (717-486-8126; atmuseum.org) in Pine Grove Furnace State Park. Located just 2 miles from the halfway point of the 2,190-mile hiking trail that

THE APPALACHIAN TRAIL MUSEUM SITS 2 MILES FROM THE FAMOUS TRAIL'S HALFWAY POINT AYLEEN GONTZ

The Links at Gettysburg (717-359-8000; thelinksatgettysburg.com), 601 Mason Dixon Road. Rated one of the top 10 public courses in Pennsylvania by *Golfweek*, this 18-hole course plays 6,979 yards from the tips, with a 73.9 rating and 140 slope.

Quail Valley Golf Course (717-359-8453), 901 Teeter Road, Littlestown, has 18 holes to 7,042 yards from the longest tees, with a par of 72 and a slope rating of 123.

HORSEBACK RIDING **Artillery Ridge Campground and Horse Park** (717-334-1288), 610 Taneytown Road. Offers one- and two-hour guided tours of the battlefield by horseback. It's especially nice in spring, when the dogwood and redbud are blooming, or during fall foliage season.

Hickory Hollow Horse Farm (717-253-6300; hickoryhollowfarm.com). Guided horse tours depart from the McMillan Woods Youth Campground. Choose from one- or two-hour scenic trail rides and two-hour historic tours with a licensed battlefield guide.

If you like horses but would rather ride in a carriage pulled by one, look for the **Victorian Carriage Company** (866-907-0633, victoriancarriagecompany.com), at 297 Steinwehr Avenue, which offers town and battlefield tours.

SKIING **Liberty Mountain Ski Resort** (717-642-8282; skiliberty.com), 78 Country Club Trail, Carroll Valley. Ski trails, terrain parks, and snow tubing during the winter. It's about 10 miles south of Gettysburg.

stretches from Mount Katahdin in Maine to Springer Mountain in Georgia, the museum offers a fascinating look at the trail's history and current use.

Sign in at the front desk guest book with your real name and address or your trail name and destination, then browse the detailed exhibits highlighting the trail's famous people and events, including the trail's inception in 1921, the first "thru-hike" by Earl Shaffer in 1948, and Congress's vote to make it a national scenic route in 1968. The top floor houses a research library with more than 1,700 books, magazines, and other items about the trail. Kids and adults alike will enjoy the museum's lower level, which features a pathway through large, colorful cutouts representing each state through which the trail passes. There are also interactive displays, like a lean-to at night and a chance to try on hiking boots.

STATE-THEMED DISPLAYS AT THE APPALACHIAN TRAIL MUSEUM AYLEEN GONTZ

Next door, the **General Store** (717-486-4920), at 1 Bendersville Road, is a destination for thru-hikers as well. Here, hikers who are making the full trek from Maine to Georgia stop in for ice cream—a rarity along the trail—and can indulge in the traditional "Half-Gallon Challenge" (winners get to keep the victory spoon). If the weather is warm enough, bring a swimsuit and picnic gear and spend the rest of the day on the lifeguarded beach at the park's scenic **Fuller Lake.**

✳ Lodging

Expect to pay state and local room taxes on top of regular hotel rates. You'll find large chain hotels scattered along US 30 west of town and near the outlets on PA 97. Downtown offers myriad choices for all other tastes.

HOTELS ♟ **Gettysburg Hotel** (717-337-2000; hotelgettysburg.com), 1 Lincoln Square. You can't beat the prime location or the guest list of this historic 1797 hotel: Carl Sandburg, Ulysses S. Grant, and Henry Ford are some of the VIPs who have stayed here. It's part of the Historic Hotels of America and has the efficient vibe of a business hotel with family-friendly amenities such as a rooftop swimming pool. Many of the 119 rooms and suites have Jacuzzis and fireplaces; the ones that face the square can be noisy. The town trolley stops out front, and a restaurant, One Lincoln, offers sophisticated entrées, pub fare, and cocktails in a handsome setting. $$$.

James Gettys Hotel (888-900-5275; jamesgettyshotel.com), 27 Chambersburg Street. This upscale 11-room inn is named after the town's founder and operated as a hotel before and after the 1863 battle. Centrally located a block west of Lincoln Square, it was restored to 1920s-style splendor in the 1990s and is known for its attention to detail. All rooms have full or queen beds and private baths, and feature Egyptian cotton linens and luxury toiletries. Expect some traffic noise in the front-facing rooms. A breakfast of pastries and orange juice is delivered daily to each room. Ask about special rates and packages if you're staying off-season. $$$.

⚲ **The Lodges at Gettysburg** (717-642-2500; 877-607-2442; gettysburg accommodations.com), 685 Camp Gettysburg Road. Spacious luxury cabins dot a quiet hillside southwest of town. It's a peaceful place to escape to after a day of sightseeing, and the view of the battlefield from many of the rooms is unmatched. Flat-screen TVs, WiFi, and iHome docking stations are just a few of the high-tech amenities. The property also includes a pretty lake (fishing poles available) and covered bridge. A continental breakfast is served in the main lodge for an extra fee. Studios with one or two queen or king beds $$$; two-bedroom suites with a full kitchen and living area $$$$.

Comfort Suites (717-334-6715; gettys burgcomfortsuites.com), 945 Baltimore Pike. The closest hotel to the park's visitor center has 70 modern suites with mini-fridges, flat-screen TVs, and living areas. Some of the rooms overlook a private cemetery. Amenities include a free hot breakfast buffet and an indoor pool. $$.

1863 Inn of Gettysburg (717-334-6211; 1863innofgettysburg.com), 516 Baltimore Street. If you want to stay in the thick of tourist action, this former Holiday Inn is a good choice. It's a mile from the visitor center and within walking distance of the Jennie Wade House and many other attractions. The clean and attractive rooms have two double beds or one queen or king bed with Jacuzzi tubs, and all have exterior entrances; request one in the back for the quietest experience. Breakfast is included, and pets are allowed in most rooms for an extra fee. $$$.

BED & BREAKFASTS ✪ **Baladerry Inn** (717-337-1342; baladerryinn.com), 40 Hospital Road. This elegant inn on 4 acres at the southeast edge of the battlefield will appeal to visitors looking for a peaceful escape at the end of a day of sightseeing. There are 10 attractive rooms, five in the main house and five in a separate carriage house (including a large suite that sleeps four). Elaborate breakfasts are served in a large dining area next to a wood fireplace. Owners Judy and Kenny Caudill are enthusiastic, accommodating hosts who will share stories about the inn's history of ghost sightings if you ask. $$$.

✎ ⚲ **Battlefield Bed and Breakfast Inn** (717-334-8804; gettysburgbattlefield .com), 2264 Emmitsburg Road. Civil War buffs love this comfortable 1809 farmhouse at the southern edge of the park. The eight rooms and suites are attractive and comfortable and the surrounding 30 acres bucolic, but it might be the daily history-themed breakfasts that make this a true standout. Mornings begin with an animated lecture by a Civil War expert and are followed by a lavish breakfast of fresh fruit and frittatas, French toast, or crêpes. Homemade cookies are served in the afternoon. Dogs of all sizes are welcome. There are also ghost stories on Friday nights and a kid-friendly menagerie of goats, sheep, horses, and donkeys on the premises. $$$.

Brickhouse Inn (717-338-9337; brick houseinn.com), 452 Baltimore Street. This charming three-story Victorian inn has 13 rooms and suites, a manicured garden with a koi pond, and a downtown location within walking distance of the military park's visitor center. Five of the rooms are located next door in the Welty House, a restored 1830 home that stood in the battle's firing line and still bears the scars. All rooms have queen beds, original wood floors, and satellite TV; a multicourse breakfast that may include shoofly pie is served on the patio during warm weather. The Kentucky Suite, with its private porch, skylight, and claw-foot tub, is a favorite; value seekers will want to book the cozy Virginia Room. No children under 10. $$–$$$.

Doubleday Inn (717-334-9119; doubledayinn.com), 104 Doubleday Avenue. This quiet house near Gettysburg College is located in a small neighborhood on the actual battlefield at Oak Ridge. Many of the comfortable rooms have splendid views of the battlefield, and breakfasts are ample and delicious, with fruits and produce sourced from local farms. $$$.

Farnsworth House Inn (717-334-8838; farnsworthhouseinn.com), 401 Baltimore Street. Named after a brigadier general, this Victorian inn revels in its status as one of the most haunted inns in America, hosting regular candlelight walks and other ghost-related events. Confederate sharpshooters took shelter here during the battle; the south wall is riddled with bullet holes, and one of the men is believed to have shot Jennie Wade (see *Museums*). Despite its central location, inside is relatively quiet, with common areas that include a trellised back garden and enclosed second-story porch; there's also a restaurant and tavern on the premises (see *Dining Out*). Each of the nine rooms has a private bath and antique furnishings; some have TVs and Jacuzzis. Rooms in the main house are on the small side and more susceptible to street noise than the ones off the back garden. No children under 16. Breakfast served by costumed employees. $$$, with a two-night minimum on weekends.

NEARBY

Fairfield Inn (717-642-5410 or 717-334-8868; thefairfieldinn.com), 15 West Main Street, Fairfield. An episode of HGTV's *If Walls Could Talk* chronicled its rich history as a field hospital for Confederate soldiers and a stop on the Underground Railroad. The antiques-filled rooms have private baths with whirlpool or clawfoot tubs; there's also a suite that sleeps four on the third floor, with a private balcony. $$$.

MOTELS

🐾 🍴 **Inn at Cemetery Hill** (717-334-9281; innatcemeteryhill.com), 613 Baltimore Street. Simple rooms and efficiency units in a central location within walking distance of many attractions and eateries. A breakfast buffet is included in the rate. $$.

🐾 **President Inn and Suites** (717-334-4274; presidentinnsuites.us), 606 York Street. The tidy, basic rooms at this simple inn on US 30 just east of town have TVs and coffeemakers; microwaves and fridges are available upon request. There's also a small indoor pool and a large parking lot. $.

CAMPGROUNDS 🐾 🍴 **Artillery Ridge Camping Resort and Horse Park** (717-334-1288; artilleryridge.com), 610 Taneytown Road. Open daily from April–October, weekends in November. This campground and equestrian center near the southern edge of the battlefield has more than 400 tent and RV sites and several air-conditioned one-room cabins that sleep up to four. Tents and cabins $.

🐾 **Granite Hill Camping Resort** (717-642-8749; granitehillcampingresort .com), 3340 Fairfield Road. Open April–November. The site of an annual bluegrass festival and Gettysburg's annual bike week, this scenic property about 8 miles south of town has 300 sites for tents and RVs, plus 5 two-room cabins and a small B&B inn with four rooms. It also has a swimming pool, fishing pond, mini-golf course, four playgrounds, and a packed activity schedule. $–$$.

🐾 **Round Top Campground** (717-334-9565; roundtopcamp.com), 180 Knight Road. One of the few campgrounds open year-round, it has 200 sites with full hook-ups and 60 sites with water and electricity. The campground also rents basic air-conditioned cabins and cottages. It also has a swimming pool, mini-golf course, and tennis court. Tents and cabins $; cottages $$.

HAUNTED GETTYSBURG

With more than 50,000 casualties, it's no surprise that ghosts and spirits have been sighted and felt all over Gettysburg. From May–November, you'll stumble upon dozens of nightly ghost tours offered in or around downtown. Most run twice nightly and last between one and two hours; kids under age 7 are often free. Keep in mind that the tours that center around Baltimore Street can get traffic and pedestrian noise. For storytelling at its most macabre, try the Farnsworth House's Civil War Mourning Theater (717-334-8838; farnsworthhouseinn.com)—a seated presentation in the cellar surrounded by coffins and vintage photos—in which a costumed guide relates the story of the Farnsworth House Inn and the many ghosts that reside in its walls. Ghosts of Gettysburg (717-337-0445; ghostsofgettysburg .com) offers several popular walking tours that combine history lessons with ghost lore based on paranormal investigator Mark Nesbitt's best-selling book series, *Ghosts of Gettysburg*. The Carlisle and Baltimore Street tours, led by candlelit lanterns, are favorites.

✳ Where to Eat

DINING OUT ❢ **Dobbin House** (717-334-2100; dobbinhouse.com), 89 Steinwehr Avenue. Dinner daily. The dining rooms can get quite loud, especially when bus tours descend upon the place, but this painstakingly restored colonial-era house has its charms. Its owner, the Reverend Alexander Dobbin, built the house in the 1770s, and its original stone walls and other nifty details remain; the basement was once a station for runaway slaves. Today, waiters dress in period breeches, bonnets, and petticoats, and some authentic 18th-century dishes such as hunter's chicken and William Penn's broiled pork tenderloin in an "outftand-ing rafpberry sauce" are on the menu. For a more casual and intimate experience, head downstairs to the Springhouse Tavern, where the meals are lighter (and cheaper), and the stone walls, roaring fireplaces, and well-stocked bar invite lingering. Reservations are recommended for the restaurant. $$–$$$.

❢ **Farnsworth House** (717-334-8838; farnsworthhouseinn.com), 401 Baltimore Street. Breakfast and dinner daily. Expect to be surrounded by Civil War–era paintings, photographs, and antiques when you dine in the candlelit rooms of one of Gettysburg's legendary haunted homes. The house specialty is game pie, a rich casserole of turkey, pheasant, and duck. Other menu highlights: peanut soup, Yankee pot roast, and sweet potato pudding; children may be placated with macaroni and cheese or chicken tenders. This unique Gettysburg experience should not be missed. A tavern menu is available in the outdoor garden. $$$.

Food 101 (717-334-6080; food101 gettysburg.com), 101 Chambersburg Street. A 1950s-style BYO bistro with big taste. The vegetarian-friendly menu includes artisan pizzas, savory sandwiches, and truffle fries. Look for their chef's specials after 4 p.m. $$.

Hoof, Fin, and Fowl (717-549-2160), 619 Baltimore Street. The rotating seasonal menu of this family-run newcomer features fresh steamed crabs and crabcakes, plus burgers and Wagyu steaks sourced from a local farm. $$–$$$.

❢ **Inn at Herr Ridge** (717-334-4332; innattheridge.com), 900 Chambersburg Road. This historic prewar building has been a tavern, an Underground Railroad stop, and a temporary Confederate hospital; today, it's a small inn and restaurant known for its superb food, service, and wine cellar. The dinner menu includes fresh seasonal oysters, dry-aged filet mignon in a port-wine veal reduction sauce, and braised New Zealand lamb shank with mint-parsley gremolata. Its high-ceilinged dining rooms and roof-top terrace overlook Herr Ridge, where Union General John Buford's cavalry camped the night before the Battle of Gettysburg. Reservations recommended. Extensive wine list. $$$.

NEARBY

Ŷ **Cashtown Inn** (717-334-9722; cashtown inn.com), 1325 Old US 30, Cashtown. Open for lunch and dinner Tuesday–Saturday. This small 18th-century inn west of town provides a nice escape, either overnight or for a couple of hours, from the downtown Gettysburg crowds. It served as headquarters for Confederate General A. P. Hill and was featured in the film *Gettysburg*. Jack and Maria Paladino are your genial hosts; they also operate a B&B upstairs. The seasonal American menu includes char-grilled filet mignon topped with blue cheese sauce, and a brown sugar– and bourbon-glazed pork chop with garlic mashed potatoes and sautéed herb-roasted brussels sprouts. Reservations are recommended for dinner. $$–$$$.

EATING OUT **Dunlap's Restaurant and Bakery** (717-334-4816; dunlapsrestaurant .com), 90 Buford Avenue. Closed Tuesdays. This family-owned diner near the north end of the battlefield is the perfect place for an inexpensive sit-down meal. Its wide-ranging menu includes filet mignon, honey-dipped fried chicken, and Maryland crabcakes; they also have daily specials like prime rib on Saturday, for $14 and a Friday night fish fry for $11. For breakfast, there are omelets, hot-cakes, and six different kinds of Danish. Save room for dessert. $–$$.

⌀ ⚲ **Ernie's Texas Lunch** (717-334-1970), 58 Chambersburg Street. Breakfast, lunch, and dinner daily. This always-crowded spot off Lincoln Square serves the best hot dogs in town; there are also breakfast sandwiches, hoagies, fried chicken, and homemade soups. The daily specials are a bargain. $.

Lincoln Diner (717-334-3900), 32 Carlisle Street. This 24-hour diner near the center of town is popular for breakfast and has an everything-but-the-kitchen-sink menu and wonderful baked desserts. $–$$.

Montezuma Mexican Restaurant (717-334-7750), 225 Buford Avenue (US 30). You'll find tasty fajitas, carnitas, and chiles rellenos in this unassuming building west of town.

General Pickett's Buffets (717-334-7580; generalpickettsbuffets.com), 571 Steinwehr Avenue. Lunch and dinner daily. Located next to the field where Confederate General George Pickett led his infamous doomed charge, this all-you-can-eat buffet elicits mixed reactions from those who have tried it. Its central location in the basement of the Battle Theater makes it very popular with bus tours; some say the food suffers as a result. It's tough to beat the value, though—meals include a huge soup and salad bar; hot

THE LINCOLN DINER AT DUSK

entrées such as roast beef, fried catfish, and baked chicken; and desserts.

The Pike (717-334-9227; thepike restaurant.com), 985 Baltimore Pike. The closest restaurant to the park's main entrance caters to big appetites and frugal wallets. Monday means $4 appetizer night, kids eat free on Wednesdays—you get the picture. Sports is on the TV, beer specials are plentiful, and there's a dog-friendly deck. There's also an all-you-can eat breakfast buffet on Sunday. $–$$.

Pub on the Square (717-334-7100; the-pub.com), 20–22 Lincoln Square. One of the few places in town that serves dinner late. If the dining room overlooking the square is packed, head to the friendly, tin-ceilinged pub next door and order off the main menu. There are huge sandwiches, salads, steak and pasta entrées, and tasty appetizers like soft-pretzel nuggets with dipping sauce. You can't go wrong with most items, but the Ritz cracker–crusted mahi-mahi and sweet potato waffle fries come highly recommended. $$.

Garryowen Irish Pub (717-337-2719; garryowenirishpub.net), 126 Chambersburg Street. This welcoming local haunt offers two floors and a courtyard where you can enjoy traditional Irish dishes, 100-plus Irish whiskeys, and the finest Irish beers. $$.

Mason Dixon Distillery (717-398-3385; masondixondistillery.com), 331 East Water Street. Small plates made from locally sourced produce that are perfect to share with two or a crowd. Pair with a craft cocktail from their own vodka, whiskey, and rum. $$.

CAFÉS & BAKERIES **Ragged Edge** (717-334-4464; raggededgehs.com), 110 Chambersburg Street. This hip art-filled coffeehouse has indoor and outdoor seating, a light breakfast and lunch menu, and a stay-as-long-as-you-like vibe. $.

Cannonball Old Tyme Malt Shop (717-334-9695), 11 York Street. The small but comfortable, old-fashioned shop on Lincoln Square offers superb ice cream, malts,

and handmade phosphate sodas, plus a selection of burgers and sandwiches. $.

✱ Entertainment

Much of Gettysburg's entertainment revolves around the battlefield; one of the most popular evening activities is the ghost tour (see *Haunted Gettysburg* on page 204). Also, more music venues, tasting rooms, and small-plate bistros have helped boost the nightlife scene in recent years (see *Apples . . . to Alcohol* on page 207).

Several convivial watering holes, including the **Pub on the Square** (717-334-7100; 20 Lincoln Square) and **The Parrot** (717-337-3739; 35 Chambersburg Street) also stay open late on weekends. **Garryowen Pub** (717-337-2719; 126 Chambersburg Street) is a festive spot to catch live music on weekends.

THEATER & MOVIES **Majestic Theater Performing Arts and Cultural Center** (717-337-8200; gettysburgmajestic.org), 29 Carlisle Street. Built in 1925, this gorgeously restored 850-seat theater hosts Broadway musicals, live bands, and more. It also has a two-screen cinema showing art films.

Gateway Theater at the Gettysburg Gateway Complex (717-334-5577; rctheatres.com), US 30 and US 15, shows first-run films and offers bargain shows all day on Tuesday.

✱ Selective Shopping

All stores are in downtown Gettysburg unless otherwise noted. Many of the shops stay open later in the summer. The **Outlet Shoppes at Gettysburg** (717-337-0091; 1863 Gettysburg Village Drive), a huge complex whose stores include Under Armour, Coach, Gap, Harry & David, and Tommy Hilfiger, is conveniently located down the road from

EXCURSIONS

APPLES TO . . . ALCOHOL Adams County, long known as the fourth-largest apple producer in the United States, is also home to a burgeoning market of vineyards, cideries, and even breweries. Their presence has added another layer of interest to Gettysburg as tasting rooms, outdoor music venues, and several small-plate restaurants now give tourists a reason to stay up late after a day of touring the battlefield.

North of town, **Adams County Winery** (717-334-4631; adamscountywinery.com; 251 Peach Tree Road, Orrtanna), **Hauser Estate Winery** (717-334-4888; jackshardcider.com; 410 Cashtown Road, Biglerville), and **Reid's Orchard and Winery** (717-677-7047; www.reidsorchardwinery.com; 2135 Buchanan Valley Road, Orrtanna) hold regular events at their vineyards and also offer tasting rooms in town. The deck of **Thirsty Farmer Brew Works** (717-334-3325; thirstyfarmer.com; 290 Cashtown Road, Biglerville) offers a view of its recently planted hops. The tasting room at **Boyer Cellars** (717-677-8558; boyercellars.com; 405 Boyer Nursery Road, Biglerville) overlooks the orchard where Great Shoals Winery sources fruit for its wines and ciders.

For live music outdoors in the summer, grab a seat in the Sweney's Tavern beer garden beside the historic **Farnsworth House Inn** (717-334-8838; farnsworthhouseinn.com; 401 Baltimore Street, Gettysburg), at the picnic tables behind **Reid's Winery Tasting Room and Cider House** (717-334-7537; reidsorchardwinery.com; 400 Baltimore Street, Gettysburg), or in the shaded area next to the **Appalachian Brewing Company** (717-334-2200; abcbrew.com; 259 Steinwehr Avenue, Gettysburg).

The **Mason Dixon Distillery** (see *Eating Out*) serves up unique small plates paired with house-made vodka, rum, and whiskey, and the **Battlefield Brew Works** (717-398-2907; battlefieldbreworks.com; 248 Hunterstown Road, Gettysburg) offers spirits and beer with dinner in a barn that served as a field hospital during the Battle of Gettysburg.

If you'd rather taste then eat, stop by the tasting room of **Knob Hall Winery** (717-420-5171; knobhallwinery.com;100 Chambersburg Street, Gettysburg) and pick a bottle of French-style wine, then cross the street to **Food 101** (see *Eating Out*). The wait staff has corkscrews and bottle openers on hand.

One way to see/taste more and drive less is to sign up for the **Adams County Pour Tour.** For $35 you can choose from a four-hour downtown trip or a shuttle through countryside vineyards. A gift and transportation are included, while food or drinks are purchased separately. Passports are available if you decide to explore the 30-plus locations on your own. Visit destinationgettysburg .com for details.

---

the park's visitor center. It also has a 10-screen movie theater.

GIFT SHOPS & GALLERIES **Adams County Arts Council** (717-334-5006; adamsarts.org), 125 South Washington Street. Rotating art exhibits and classes featuring local artists, plus First Friday opening receptions and cultural programs throughout the year. Check the website for an updated schedule.

Codori's Gifts (717-334-6371) 2 York Street. This long-running boutique carries nesting dolls, nutcrackers, and a fun assortment of gifts and collectibles from around the world.

Gallery 30 (717-334-0335; gallery30 .com), 26 York Street. A thoughtful selection of current books shares space with hand-carved duck decoys, unique jewelry, and paintings and sculpture by local artists.

Horse Soldier (717-334-0347; horse soldier.com), 777 Baltimore Street. Home to one of the largest collections of military antiques around, with items dating from the Revolutionary War through World War II. The emphasis, of course, is on the Civil War, and the shop guarantees that all its inventory, from firearms to discharge papers, is genuine. It also offers a genealogical research service that will help search for an ancestor's war records.

The Jeweler's Daughter (717-338-0770; jewelersdaughter.com), 49 Steinwehr Avenue. A huge collection of reproduction Victorian jewelry, from earrings and necklaces to pocket watches and hair ornaments.

Lark (717-334-5275; larkgifts.com), 17 Lincoln Square. A treasure trove of modern and delightful finds from handcrafted jewelry to bowls made from old records.

Lincoln into Art (203-770-3421; lincolnintoart.com), 329 Baltimore Street. Acclaimed artist Wendy Allen, who grew up in Mt. Lebanon, displays her unique oil-based portraits of the 16th president in a Civil War–era house in the heart of the Historic District.

The Crystal Wand (717-420-5637; crystalwandinpa), 529 Baltimore Street. A metaphysical shop with a robust selection of books, tarot cards, oils, stones, and charms.

✳ Special Events

May: **Gettysburg Bluegrass Festival** (mid-May and mid-August; gettysburgbluegrass.com), 3340 Fairfield Road—four days of music on two stages. Musicians present workshops for adults, and there's a bluegrass academy for kids. Camping packages are available.

June: **Adams County BarnART Show and Sale** (first weekend; hgaconline.org), G.A.R. Hall, 53 East Middle Street—in an effort to raise money and preserve historic barns, local artists display works featuring barns—or a detail of one—both abstract and realistic. An opening-night reception is followed by artist awards and sales.

July: **Annual Civil War Battle Reenactment** (first weekend), Table Rock Road north of town—costumed volunteers commemorate the famous battle with faux rifles and swords at this three-day ticketed spectator event. For more information, go to gettysburgreenactment.com. A week later, motorcycles from all over the country roar into town for **Gettysburg Bike Week** (800-374-7540; gettysburgbikeweek.com), three days of live music, fireworks, tattoo contests, and a "chrome parade." Tickets can be purchased online or at Battlefield Harley-Davidson, 21 Cavalry Field Road.

August: **Civil War Music Muster** (last weekend), Gettysburg National Military Park—brass bands, fife and drum groups, and individuals bring to life the band and parlor music of the Civil War period.

September: **Gettysburg Wine and Music Festival** (gettysburgwineandmusicfestival.com), Gettysburg Gateway Complex, 95 Presidential Circle—bring your chairs, portable tents, and blankets and spend the day sampling wines from more than 25 Pennsylvania wineries and listening to an eclectic lineup of live music.

October: **National Apple Harvest Festival** (first two weekends; appleharvest.com), Arendtsville—a popular country gathering of food, live music, crafts, and pony rides that seems to get bigger each year. The food alone (pumpkin funnel cake, caramel apples, sweet potato fries) is worth the trip.

November: **Remembrance Day** (third weekend)—this solemn event begins with a parade of living history and reenactment groups through town to the battlefield, is followed by the placement of candles at each Civil War grave, and ends with a recitation of Lincoln's Gettysburg Address.

December: **Gingerbread House Celebration and Holiday Mart** (last weekend of November/first weekend of December; adamsarts.org/gingerbread-celebration)—rows and rows of artful and tasty gingerbread houses. Awards, gift shopping, and children's activities. **Gettysburg Christmas Festival** (first weekend; agettysburgchristmasfestival.com)—a parade, holiday movies, arts and crafts, and more.

YORK COUNTY

York County likes to call itself the Snack Food Capital of the World. Spend some time here and you will find this to be a well-earned appellation. Potato chips, candy, ice cream, and pretzels are all made in the small towns and rural countryside that make up this county of more than 200,000. So are Pfaltzgraff pottery, Bluett Bros. violins, and the bulk of Harley-Davidson's Touring and Softail motorcycles.

Situated between Gettysburg and Amish Country, the region often gets squeezed out by its two more famous neighbors. The pace is a little slower here, the prices a little lower—it feels more like a 9-to-5 kind of place than a tourism destination. This is not to say that the region lacks history or amenities. You will find real farmers' markets, homey B&Bs, and free hands-on tours of Harley-Davidson, Utz Potato Chips, and a dozen other factories and farms. You will leave with newfound admiration for chocolate-covered pretzels and high-butterfat ice cream.

The small city of York, which anchors the county, was founded in 1741 and named for the English city of the same name. It served as the temporary capital of the Continental Congress during the Revolutionary War. The Articles of Confederation were drafted here in 1777. Several original 18th-century buildings are open for tours downtown, which also features many other colonial-era buildings, Gothic Revival churches, and wide sidewalks.

Surrounding York and Hanover are miles of rolling countryside, several golf courses, and small towns with mom-and-pop antiques shops, farmers' markets, and ice cream stands.

AREA CODE All towns in York County fall under the 717 area code.

GUIDANCE York County Convention & Visitors Bureau (717-852-9675; yorkpa.org) has an information center at 34 West Philadelphia Street at Central Market. It also operates a small one at the **Harley-Davidson plant** (717-852-6006; 1425 Eden Road) just off US 30. In Hanover, stop by the **Guthrie Memorial Library** (717-632-5183; 301 Carlisle Street) for maps and brochures.

GETTING THERE *By air:* **Harrisburg International Airport** (888-235-9442) is 30 miles north of downtown York.

By car: US 30 south from Lancaster; I-83 from Harrisburg and Maryland.

By bus: **Greyhound** (800-231-2222) and **rabbittransit** (717-846-7743) offer regular service between York and Harrisburg. **Capitol Trailways** has service through Lancaster to Philadelphia and New York.

GETTING AROUND Downtown York is walkable, especially the area around Market and George Streets, but you will need a car to get to most of the factories, including Harley-Davidson and Hope Acres. Also, **rabbittransit** operates bus routes in the city and surrounding area.

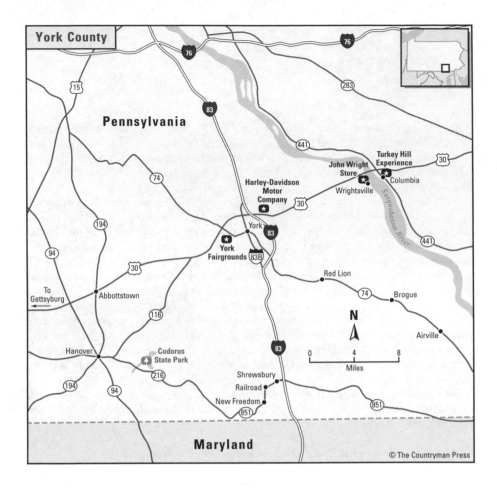

York County

Pennsylvania

Maryland

© The Countryman Press

WHEN TO GO Fall is particularly scenic in this rural part of the state, but most of the factories and museums here are open for tours year-round. Keep in mind that many of the factories aren't air-conditioned.

✳ Villages

Railroad. This tiny town of 300 people near the Maryland border is home to the Jackson House B&B, a popular crab shack, and not much else. It takes its name from the century-old North Central Railroad that passes through town on its way to and from Baltimore and York.

Red Lion. About 5 miles outside York, Red Lion is a quaint town of antiques shops, a B&B, and a few restaurants, and serves as a sort of gateway to the rural countryside east of York. Founded in 1880, it is named after one of its first taverns and was once a major manufacturer of cigars. (To this day, the town lowers a giant cigar on New Year's Eve instead of the traditional ball.)

Wrightsville. Named for one of the area's early settlers, John Wright, this sleepy town on the Susquehanna River is a pleasant place to stop if you're on your way to York from Lancaster or Philadelphia. It was once home to one of the longest covered bridges in the country, which unfortunately was burned during the Civil War to stop the eastern advance of Lee's army. A diorama, housed in a former barbershop, tells the story of the bridge and Wrightsville's role in the Civil War. Today, John Wright cast-iron products are made here and sold in a nearby warehouse.

✳ To See

MUSEUMS & HISTORIC SITES **York County History Center** (717-845-2951; yorkhistorycenter.org), 157 West Market Street, York. Admission charged. This complex of historic buildings includes the **Colonial Complex,** a 19th-century log cabin, a tavern, and a replica of the colonial courthouse where the Continental Congress met in 1777 and 1778. Don't miss the half-timbered Plough Tavern, where a plan to overthrow General Washington was derailed in 1778 by the visiting Marquis de Lafayette. A statue of Lafayette, wine glass raised in a toast to Washington, stands in his honor outside the tavern. Check the website for tour schedules.

 ⚲ ⛾ **Indian Steps Museum** (717-862-3948; indiansteps.org), 205 Indian Steps Road, Airville (south of Brogue). Open Thursday–Sunday from mid-April–mid-October; free. Eccentric local attorney John Vandersloot built this home on the Susquehanna River for the main purpose of displaying his huge collection of Indian artifacts. More than 10,000 artifacts are embedded in the masonry walls to form Indian patterns, birds, animals, and reptiles. A favorite stop is the kiva, a reproduction of a circular room used by the Hopi Indians for religious assemblies. A second-floor gallery traces the evolution of early Indians who lived by or passed along the nearby Susquehanna River. Outside there's plenty of open space for kids to run around.

 USA Weightlifting Hall of Fame (717-767-6481), 3300 Board Road, York. Closed Sundays. Look for the giant Instagrammable weightlifter on top of the building as proof you've arrived at York Barbell Co. Bob Hoffman, known as the Father of Modern Weightlifting, founded the business in 1932, and it still makes iron dumbbells, kettlebells, and other products in its factory. The first-floor museum is full of vintage barbells and virile statues of Hoffman and other professional bodybuilders. It won't take very long to peruse, but it does a decent job of tracing the sport's history, from its role in the Olympic Games to the accomplishments of famous strongmen such as Charles Atlas, Warren Lincoln Travis, and George Jowett.

✳ To Do

FACTORY TOURS All tours are free unless otherwise noted. Most require advance reservations; it's always a good idea to call ahead, as sometimes tours are canceled due to manufacturing schedules or weather.

 Bluett Bros. Violins (717-854-9064; bluettbros-violins.com), 122 Hill Street, York. Tours are available by appointment. Learn how master luthier Mark Bluett makes violins, mandolins, cellos, and other stringed instruments in his exquisitely old-fashioned shop.

 George's Furniture (800-799-1685; georgesfurniturepa.com), 9 Reichs Church Road, Marietta. See how quality furniture is made on tours held Monday–Friday.

 Martin's Potato Chips (800-272-4477; martinssnacks.com), 5847 Lincoln Highway (US 30), Thomasville. Tours Tuesdays by reservation only. No tours in April. This family-run chip factory is on the road between York and Gettysburg. The 45-minute guided tours provide an up-close look at the peeling, cutting, and frying processes. A small shop sells just about every flavor and type—from kettle-cooked jalapeño to BBQ waffle chips.

York County Resource Recovery (717-845-1066; ycswa.org), 2700 Blackbridge Road, York. Tours Monday–Friday; call two weeks ahead for reservations. See how tons of solid waste are converted daily into ash and electricity at this 130-acre facility north of town. Hard-hat tours begin with an orientation talk and include visits to the tipping floor, where trucks deposit trash into a huge storage pit, and the turbine generator room, where steam produced by the heat of burning garbage is used to produce electricity. It's one of York County's newest tours—fascinating, if not aromatic. No children under 6 are allowed.

HANOVER

🖉 ♿ **Revonah Pretzel** (717-630-2883), 507 Baltimore Street. This bakery specializes in handcrafted sourdough pretzels; free 20-minute tours of its small factory are given Tuesday–Thursday mornings. Reservations recommended. Don't leave without trying a fresh-baked soft pretzel or picking up a bag of hard pretzels with flavors such as pumpernickel and onion, honey whole wheat, and roasted garlic.

🖉 ♿ **Snyder's of Hanover** (800-233-7125; snydersofhanover.com/tour-snyders-of -hanover), 1350 York Street. Tours Tuesday, Wednesday, and Thursday; reservations required. You'll see some of the largest pretzel ovens in the world churning out 40 pretzels a second on this hour-long tour that covers the production process of pretzels and potato chips from start to finish. Leave time to shop at the outlet store, where the tours start and where you can find great bulk deals on many Snyder's products, plus hard-to-find products like caramel-dipped pretzels.

🖉 **Utz Potato Chips** (717-637-6644; utzsnacks.com/pages/tour), 900 High Street. Tours 10–3:30 Monday–Thursday; no reservations. Bill and Salie Utz started their company in 1925 in a small summer house behind their Hanover home. Now run by fourth-generation family members, it's still going strong and continues to offer self-guided tours that last 30 to 45 minutes and use videos and audio presentations to describe the process of making hand-cooked chips, flavored chips, and other products.

FOR FAMILIES **Painted Spring Alpaca Farm** (717-225-3941; paintedspring.com), 280 Roth Church Road, Spring Grove. Tours are available on weekends and early mornings, or by appointment. Owners Beth and Neal Lutz breed these gentle creatures on their peaceful farm between York and Abbottstown. A retail shop sells alpaca yarn and fleece and items that have been handwoven and knitted by local artisans. Check the website for open house and shearing events, which usually feature spinning and weaving demonstrations and plenty of hands-on contact with the animals.

Perrydell Farms (717-741-3485), 90 Indian Rock Dam Road, York. Kids will enjoy the free self-guided tour of this working dairy farm just south of town. Pick up a map in the retail store, then watch cows being milked (afternoons only), pet the calves, and see fresh milk being bottled. Afterward, return to the store for hand-dipped ice cream or the tastiest chocolate milk in town.

Sweet Willows Creamery (717-718-9219; sweetwillows.com), 2812 Prospect Road, York. Closed Mondays. Brent Lebouitz, a graduate of Penn State's Creamery, takes ice cream ingredients to new levels in his homey café: The ever-changing flavors might include midnight cappuccino crunch, Nutella, no-sugar-added strawberry, or Tahitian vanilla Grape-Nuts. Anyone can ask for a brief, free tour of the property. More

BIKER NIRVANA

Harley-Davidson Vehicle Operations Tour Center (414-343-7850; 877-883-1450; harley
-davidson.com/us/en/about-us/visit-us/yorkpa.html), 1425 Eden Road, York. Tours
are first-come, first-served and run 9–2 Monday–Friday, Monday–Saturday in the
summer. Children under 12 aren't allowed on the tour. One of four Harley-Davidson plants
to give tours (the others are in Wisconsin and Missouri), this plant just off US 30 is home to
the company's largest manufacturing facility, covering more than 200 acres and 1.5 million
square feet.

The hour-long tours take you right onto the factory floor, where the bikes are being formed,
welded, machined, polished, and painted, then to the end of the line, where you can watch
them inching along by color code on their way to Japan, Australia, and other destinations. The
bikers who come from all over to take the tour are just as interesting as the assembly line;
their passion for chrome is infectious. Not surprisingly, the gift shop sells plenty of Harley-
emblazoned gear, from shot glasses and T-shirts to helmets and heated hand grips.

informative guided tours (in which you witness an actual batch of ice cream being
made) are available for groups of 10 or more; $5 per person; reservations required.

✳ Green Space

Heritage Rail Trail County Park (717-840-7440; www.yorkcountyparks.org). Established in 1992, this 176-acre park has an excellent 21-mile hiking and biking trail that
follows the path of a historic railroad between the Mason-Dixon line and downtown
York near the Colonial Courthouse at 25 West Market Street. It's also popular with
horseback riders and cross-country skiers. The trail has many places to stop and
rest or explore, including two historic stations turned museums (New Freedom and
Hanover). Download a map from the website before you go, or pick one up at one of the
station stops.

Codorus State Park (717-637-2816), 2600 Smith Station Road, Hanover. The 3,300-
acre park is 3 miles southeast of Hanover and about an hour's drive from York. Its top
attraction is the 1,275-acre Lake Marburg, which has 26 miles of shoreline and offers
boating, sailing, and fishing opportunities. It also has a public swimming pool with
tube slides and several miles of hiking, biking, and equestrian trails. There's also a
campground with 190 tent and RV sites, most with electric hook-ups, plus a few cottages and yurts.

✳ Outdoor Activities

BICYCLING/RENTALS **Whistle Stop Bike Shop** (717-227-0737), right off the 21-mile
Heritage Rail Trail (see *Green Space*) in New Freedom, is a full-service shop that
rents bikes and does repairs. **Gung Ho Bikes** (717-852-9553; gunghobikes.com),
1815 Susquehanna Trail (at US 30), also rents bikes.

BOAT EXCURSIONS/RENTALS **AOS Marina** (717-632-7484; aosmarina.com) rents
canoes, kayaks, and pontoon and motorboats at the marina at Codorus State Park daily,
Memorial Day–Labor Day (see *Green Space*).

COUNTRYSIDE WINERIES

Naylor Wine Cellars (717-993-3370; naylorwine.com), 4069 Vineyard Road, Stewart-stown. Full-service winery in a rural country setting about 15 miles south of York near the Maryland border, with live music on Sunday afternoons.

Logan's View Winery (717-741-0300; logansviewwinery.com), 8892 Susquehanna Trail South, Loganville. Wine tastings on the grounds of Brown's Orchards and Farm Market, a family-friendly complex with a counter-order café, bakery, and events like summer concerts and hayrides. Check the website for dates and times.

In Wrightsville, **Shank's Mare Outfitters** (717-252-1616; shanksmare.com), 2092 Long Level Road) gives kayak lessons and rents single, double, and triple kayaks for trips along the Susquehanna River.

FISHING **Lake Marburg** in Codorus State Park (see *Green Space*) is a warm-water fishery stocked with yellow perch, bluegill, northern pike, crappie, largemouth bass, and catfish. A state fishing license is required; visit www.fish.state.pa.us for more information.

GOLF **Heritage Hills Golf Course** (717-755-0123), 2700 Mount Rose Avenue, York. Nestled in the rural countryside less than a mile from downtown, this 18-hole course has wide fairways; large, well-maintained greens; and a par of 71. A driving range and a mini-golf course are also on-site.

✳ Lodging

HOTELS **Yorktowne Hotel** (717-848-1111; yorktowne.com), 48 East Market Street, York. Scott and Zelda would be right at home mingling under the brass and crystal chandeliers in the high-ceilinged lobby of this 11-story 1920s-era hotel. The Fitzgeralds never stayed here, but Bill Clinton, Johnny Cash, and B. B. King did. It's also popular with business travelers and anyone performing at the nearby Strand-Capitol Theatre. All rooms and suites are spacious and handsomely decorated and come with king beds, sitting areas, writing desks, and coffeemakers. There are two restaurants on-site, plus a small fitness center and laundry room. You can walk to the city's historic sites and central market from here, though the neighborhood tends to be deserted at night. $$.

Glen Rock Mill Inn (717-235-5918), 50 Water Street, Glen Rock. This 19th-century water-powered mill was renovated and repurposed into an inn in the 1980s. It sits right off the Heritage Rail Trail and near several wineries and has 13 simple guest rooms, including two extended-stay suites. Many original mill artifacts are on display or have been repurposed into chandeliers, wine racks, and ceiling beams. There's also a farm-to-table restaurant and bar with live jazz on Friday nights. $$.

Heritage Hills Golf Resort and Conference Center (717-755-0123; heritagehillsresort.com), 2700 Mount Rose Avenue, York. This large resort on 150 acres east of downtown attracts golfers and families with its all-inclusive package deals. The 128 rooms and suites have luxury beds, flat-screen TVs, granite-top desks, mini-fridges, and microwaves. There are also four restaurants, a fitness center, a spa, a mini-golf course, a summer kids' camp, and a winter snow-tubing operation. $$$.

BED & BREAKFASTS **Grace Manor** (717-542-0787; gracemanorbandb.com), 258 West Market Street, York. Four elegant suites with international themes in a preserved 19th-century Beaux Arts home. The four-room French suite features 10-foot ceilings, a Toulouse Lautrec–inspired mural and a vintage claw-foot tub, while the Asian suite has geisha tapestries, a hand-carved Malaysian canopy bed, and a Japanese-style river rock shower. It's right off the Heritage Rail Trail (tie-in packages are available), and rates include a lavish breakfast. $$$.

Jackson House (717-227-2022; jacksonhousebandb.com), 6 East Main Street, Railroad. George and Jean Becker made this small B&B next to the Heritage Rail Trail hugely popular with bicyclists and motorcyclists. They retired in 2007 but left the place in the very hospitable hands of Pam Nicholson and Bob Wilhelm. The front of the 1859 red-shingled building abuts a busy Main Street intersection; the back features terraced gardens, a patio, and a hot tub. There are two small rooms with private baths, two large suites with private entrances and sitting areas (the Bordello Suite shows off a collection of vintage nude pinups from the 1930s and 1940s), and a separate one-room cottage. A lavish breakfast of eggs, coffee cake, fresh fruit, and more is served in the elegant stone-walled dining room. It's also pet friendly. $$.

Red Lion Bed & Breakfast (717-244-4739; 888-288-1701; redlionbandb.com), 101 South Franklin Street, Red Lion. A lovely turn-of-the-20th-century brick home just off the small town's main drag. Bedrooms are comfortable and simply decorated with antiques and hardwood floors; some have shared baths. Common rooms include a sunporch and well-stocked library. The inn holds murder mystery weekends and a big holiday craft show in November and December, when the house is filled with unique gift displays by 150 artisans and the aromas of apple cider and cookies. $$.

✳ Where to Eat

DINING OUT

YORK

♈ **Left Bank** (717-843-8010; leftbankyork.com), 120 North George Street. Lunch and dinner Tuesday–Friday, dinner only Saturdays. One of York's finest restaurants, serving creative American cuisine, such as cioppino in Old Bay–seasoned tomato broth, house-smoked Kurobuta pork belly, and a deconstructed Philly cheesesteak. Eat in the formal dining room or the smoking-allowed bistro. Desserts are grand; try the frozen s'mores tower. Reservations recommended. $$–$$$.

♈ **Roosevelt Tavern** (717-854-7725; roosevelttavern.com), 50 North Penn Street, York. Lunch and dinner daily. This casual downtown establishment was a cigar store/speakeasy in the 1930s. Today it's a convivial place to have a cocktail, listen to some jazz at the bar, and dig into comfort fare such as steaks, seafood, chicken, and salads. Crabcakes are a specialty. A choice of tasty sides such as corn pudding and sweet potatoes drenched in honey butter comes with every entrée. $$–$$$.

HANOVER

✐ ❦ **Bay City Seafood** (717-637-1217), 110 Eisenhower Drive. This local favorite offers a wide selection of steaks, seafood, and lobster in a casual fisherman-themed environment. Try the crabcakes any way, or the crab pretzel, a huge baked soft pretzel smothered with melted cheese and crabmeat. There's also a cocktail lounge and a seasonal deck with live music. $$.

NEARBY

Altland House Grill and Pub (717-259-9535), 20 West King Street, Abbottstown. The ground-floor restaurant of the Altland House B&B serves high-end comfort food such as chicken and waffles, crabcakes with house-made tartar, and meat loaf with red-skinned mashed potatoes. A rotating selection of craft beer from the in-house brewery is also available. $$–$$$.

EATING OUT 🍴🦀 **Captain Bob's Crabs** (717-235-1166), 1 Main Street, Railroad. Dinner daily from March–December. This casual outdoor eatery is known for its steamed Maryland crabs, but it also has clam strips, halibut, salmon cakes, Maine lobster tail, and other fresh seafood dishes. The all-you-can-eat crab fests draw big crowds. BYO. $$.

🍴 **Central Family Restaurant** (717-845-4478), 400 North George Street, York. Breakfast, lunch, and dinner daily. This down-home diner is up with the chickens and makes up in good food what it lacks in décor. Breakfast includes omelets, hotcakes, and creamed chipped beef on toast. For lunch or dinner, there are burgers, crab melts, fried chicken, hand-cut steaks, and homemade meat loaf. $–$$.

York City Pretzel Company (717-467-3556; yorkcitypretzelcompany.com), 39 West Market Street. Open daily 10–3. York's newest (and some say best) pretzel maker offers hand-twisted traditional pretzels, nuggets, and hearty sandwiches on pretzel rolls, like the Horse & Buggy (smoked ham, cheddar, apple butter, and sweet-hot mustard) and the Cumberland Parkway (turkey, provolone, and cranberry-Dijon spread).

Red Brick Bakery and Tea Room (717-332-7427), 55 North Main Street, Red Lion. Open Wednesday–Saturday. The best place in town for peaches and cream scones, cheesecake, or a light lunch. High tea is available by reservation. $.

Seven Sports Bar and Grill (717-759-8707), 14 East Franklin Street, New Freedom. This local haunt serves creative pub grub such as a baked crab soft pretzel and Asian tuna BLT, plus classic American entrées. There are daily food specials, such as 60-cent wings on Mondays.

HANOVER

Famous Hot Weiner (717-637-1282), 101 Broadway. This small diner serves everything from eggs to hamburgers, but it's best known for its hot dogs with mustard, chili sauce, and chopped onions. There's also two branches in Hanover. $.

Reader's Café (717-630-2524), 125 Broadway. Closed Sundays. The handwritten menu usually includes soup, coffee drinks, and several tasty sandwiches. Best of all, you get to eat surrounded by neatly arranged books and magazines (all for sale, of course). $.

WRIGHTSVILLE

John Wright Restaurant (717-252-2519), 234 North Front Street. You can't beat the setting in a former silk mill beside the Susquehanna River, but the seasonal cuisine at this multifaceted facility also stands out. The glass-enclosed dining room offers locally sourced seafood (Chesapeake Bay catfish nuggets, baked Maryland crab dip) and Hershey Farms filet mignon with mushroom brandy sauce. A separate "pizza patio," open May–September, features a bar and live music. Reservations are recommended on weekends.

ICE CREAM & FARMERS' MARKETS
Bonkey's (bonkeys.com), 28 East Franklin Street, New Freedom. Landmark local chain turning out sno-balls and homemade ice cream in a historic theater one block from the Heritage Rail Trail. There's also a branch in Stewartstown.

Central Market (717-848-2243), 34 West Philadelphia Street, York. Open Tuesday, Thursday, and Saturday. Saturday is the best day to visit this historic downtown market for local produce, fresh-cut flowers, and homemade peanut butter doughnuts. It's also good for

THE JOHN WRIGHT STORE AND RESTAURANT COMPLEX ON THE BANKS OF THE SUSQUEHANNA RIVER

a quick lunch. Try the Greek salads at Tina's or the seasoned potato wedges at Bair's Fried Chicken. There are a few tables and a public piano in the center.

New Eastern Market (717-755-5811), 201 Memory Lane, York. Open Friday 7 a.m.–6 p.m. Apple fritters flecked with raisins, Bair's Fried Chicken, cake pops, house-made pickles, and a robust selection of meats and produce are some of the highlights of this indoor market in East York.

Perrydell Farms (717-741-3485), 90 Indian Acres Farm, York. Open daily. This small working farm south of downtown sells delicious chocolate milk and hand-dipped ice cream. Self-guided tours are available (see *For Families*).

✳ Entertainment

MUSIC & THEATER **Appel Center for the Performing Arts** (717-846-1111; strandcapitol.org), 50 North George Street. This restored Italian Renaissance–style theater was once a vaudeville house and now features musicals, dance performances, film festivals, and other events.

The Belmont Theater (717-854-5715; thebelmont.org), 27 South Belmont Street, York. Crowd-pleasing musicals, dramas, and original children's plays in a former movie house.

Glen Rock Mill Inn (717-235-5918), 50 Water Street, Glen Rock. Live jazz on Friday nights.

✳ Selective Shopping

Markets at Shrewsbury (717-235-6611), 12025 Susquehanna Trail, Glen Rock. Open Thursday–Saturday. Shop for handcrafted Amish furniture, crafts, and quilts, then sample the wide selection of food offerings at this large indoor-outdoor market just off I-83 near the Maryland border. Sticky buns, soft pretzels, roast beef sandwiches, and local produce are just a few of the highlights.

✐ **Sunrise Soap Company** (717-843-7627; sunrisesoapco.com), 29 North Beaver Street, York. The scents of sandalwood vanilla or banana coconut might greet you at the door at this quaint little downtown shop. Owner Chris Clarke makes her own soaps, shampoos, facial

scrubs, and other bath products with olive oil, shea and cocoa butters, and other natural products. You can watch the soaps being made in the back of the store, or opt to make your own bath bombs and scent your own lotions (reservations are taken, but walk-ins are welcome). Call ahead to schedule a free tour.

York Emporium (717-846-2866; theyorkemporium.com), 343 West Market Street, York. Open Wednesday–Sunday. An extraordinarily good used bookstore near the downtown visitor center, with more than 250,000 titles in just about every category you can think of, from Gettysburg to flower arranging. Reasonable prices too. It also carries comics, videos and DVDs, and music, from CDs to eight-track tapes. Lingering is encouraged and you might be serenaded by live music while you browse.

Gardener of the Owl Valley (717-252-2519), 234 North Front Street. Perched on the west bank of the Susquehanna River in the John Wright Store and Restaurant complex, this garden boutique stocks terrariums, miniature gardens, and unique handcrafted gifts with a focus on nature.

✳ Special Events

June: **Made in America** (third weekend), throughout York County—dozens of area factories, including ones that don't usually offer public tours, open their doors during this three-day event. For more information, visit yorkpa.org/events/made-in-america-event. Past years have featured homing pigeon demonstrations, alpaca shearing, cheese-making opportunities, and even the chance to see how LED lights and model trains are made on high-speed assembly lines.

September: **York Fair** (second week), York Fairgrounds, 334 Carlisle Avenue—one of America's oldest town fairs, this 10-day event has the usual rides, games, and country food stands, but it is best known for attracting nationally known performers such as Willie Nelson, Gretchen Wilson, and Lynyrd Skynyrd.

Harley-Davidson Open House (last weekend), 425 Eden Road—three days of extended plant tours, demo rides, and a Saturday night parade through downtown York.

NORTHEASTERN PENNSYLVANIA

THE LEHIGH VALLEY

The Lehigh Valley is Pennsylvania's third most populous area behind Pittsburgh and Philadelphia. For nearly 150 years, it was dominated by Bethlehem Steel, one of the world's largest steel manufacturers and shipbuilders, which closed in 2003 and has now reopened as a large casino, hotel, and retail complex. Though the area has plenty to offer vacationers, including a large theme park and picture-postcard historic districts, it sometimes gets overshadowed by its neighbors, the Pocono Mountains to the north and Bucks County to the south.

Today, Allentown, Bethlehem, and Easton are the valley's largest towns. Allentown, the state's third-largest city, is home to Dorney Park and Wildwater Kingdom, a good art museum, and a revitalization effort that has helped bring a minor league baseball stadium and a high-tech transportation museum to the area.

Before steel came to Bethlehem, it was known as a haven for religious freedom. The area was settled by Moravian brethren, a denomination of German Protestant settlers who arrived here in 1740. The city was named a year later when Moravian patron Count Nikolaus Ludwig von Zinzendorf visited the settlement's first house on Christmas Eve and bestowed the name "Bethlehem" on the community. It's also home to Lehigh University, founded by railroad pioneer Asa Packer.

The town of Easton sits in the far east side of the Lehigh Valley near the New Jersey border. Anchored by a large historic square and the nearby Lehigh Canal, it is home to Lafayette College, the Crayola Experience, many good restaurants, and a waterfront park offering canal boat rides and picnic tables.

AREA CODE The entire Lehigh Valley falls within the 610 area code.

GUIDANCE Discover Lehigh Valley (610-882-9200; discoverlehighvalley.com), 840 Hamilton Street, Allentown. Open Monday–Friday. A small welcome center and a gift shop are in **Bethlehem's Historic District** (610-691-6055; bethlehempa.org), 505 Main Street. Guides lead walking tours from here every Saturday from April–December. The city also sponsors weekend walking tours along the Lehigh River about the rise and fall of Bethlehem Steel; they start at the SteelStacks facility.

GETTING THERE *By air:* Lehigh Valley is about an hour's drive from two major airports: **Philadelphia International** (215-937-6800) and New Jersey's **Newark International** (800-397-4636). **Lehigh Valley International Airport** (888-359-5842), between Allentown and Bethlehem, offers nonstop flights to Atlanta, Charlotte, Chicago, and a few other cities.

By car: The Lehigh Valley can be reached from the north or south via the Pennsylvania Turnpike. I-78 crosses it from east to west, with exits for Easton, Bethlehem, and Allentown.

GETTING AROUND The Lehigh Valley is quite spread out, so you'll need a car. That said, Bethlehem, Emmaus, and Easton all have attractive walking districts with shops, restaurants, and preserved historic buildings and churches.

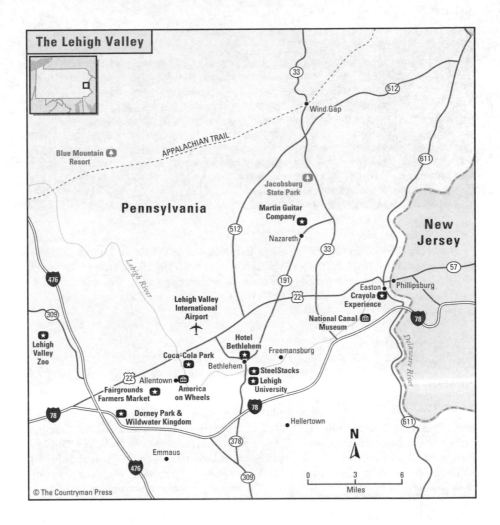

The Lehigh Valley

Wind Gap

Blue Mountain Resort

APPALACHIAN TRAIL

Pennsylvania

Jacobsburg State Park

Martin Guitar Company

Nazareth

New Jersey

Lehigh River

Easton

Phillipsburg

Crayola Experience

Lehigh Valley International Airport

National Canal Museum

Delaware River

Lehigh Valley Zoo

Hotel Bethlehem

Coca-Cola Park

Freemansburg

Bethlehem

Allentown

SteelStacks

Fairgrounds Farmers Market

America on Wheels

Lehigh University

Dorney Park & Wildwater Kingdom

Hellertown

N

Emmaus

0   3   6
Miles

© The Countryman Press

WHEN TO GO What better time to visit a place called Bethlehem than December? The town truly rises to the occasion, with daily concerts, walking tours, carriage rides, and Christkindlmarkt, a huge monthlong crafts bazaar. Summer is also a good time to be here; top attractions such as Dorney Park & Wildwater Kingdom and Crayola Experience are open daily, the canal boat rides are open for business, and the farmers' markets are brimming with local peaches and tomatoes.

✳ Towns & Villages

Emmaus. Founded as a closed community of the Moravian church in the 1700s, Emmaus couldn't be any quainter or more picturesque. Its charming downtown area has historic buildings, hip cafés, and mom-and-pop shops. About 6 miles west of Allentown, it was named one of the top 100 Best Places to Live in America in 2007 by *Money* magazine.

WIND CREEK CASINO

Bling came to the southern Lehigh Valley in May 2009 with the opening of a Las Vegas–style casino and hotel on former Bethlehem Steel property. Formerly known as the Sands, the Wind Creek Casino Resort (877-726-3777; windcreekbethlehem.com), 77 Sands Boulevard (PA 412 south), ranks among the state's top moneymakers, with slot machines, table games, and a 26-table poker room. There's also a hotel, shopping outlet, food court, and several restaurants, including steak and seafood houses from Emeril Lagasse and a more casual burger and milkshake joint, also from the celebrity chef. Expect plenty of tour-bus crowds from New York City and Philadelphia. There's free live music (bands, DJs) most nights in the Molten Lounge, which also draws big crowds. A 12,000-square-foot event hosts big events such as trade shows and rock concerts.

Nazareth. This town joins Bethlehem and Emmaus as towns in the Lehigh Valley named after famous biblical places. Also settled by Moravians, it is about 4 miles north of Bethlehem, with a pretty tree-lined main street of shops and cafés anchored by a circular plaza. It is home to the C. F. Martin Guitar Company, known for its quality acoustic guitars.

✳ To See

MUSEUMS

ALLENTOWN

🍴 ♿ ⬆ **Liberty Bell Museum** (610-435-4232; libertybellmuseum.org), 622 Hamilton Street. Closed for the month of January; small admission fee charged. The Old Zion Reformed Church served as a hiding place for the Liberty Bell and 11 other church bells while the British occupied Philadelphia in 1777 and 1778 (it was feared the Brits would melt the bells for musket and cannonballs). Today, in the church basement you'll find a full-size replica of the famous bell (which rings, unlike the real one), a multimedia light and sound show depicting scenes from the Revolutionary War, and a small exhibit of colonial artifacts and paintings.

⬆ **Allentown Art Museum** (610-432-4333; allentownartmuseum.org), 31 North Fifth Street, Allentown. Closed Mondays and Tuesdays. Free on Sundays and the third Thursday of the month from 4–8 p.m. This small but impressive facility has a collection that includes European Renaissance works and American art by Robert Motherwell, Gilbert Stuart, and local artists. Don't miss the Frank Lloyd Wright–designed library, which was dismantled from his Prairie-style Northome in Minnesota and reassembled here in 1973. Fun and unique special exhibits, too.

⬆ **America on Wheels** (610-432-4200; www.americanonwheels.org), 5 North Front Street. Closed Mondays; admission charged, but kids 12 and younger are free most weekends. This long-in-the-making museum chronicles the history of over-the-road transportation in the United States in a former meat-packing plant. Its impressive, rotating collection includes historic Mack trucks, bicycles and Segways, and cars powered by hydrogen, electricity, steam, and gasoline (including an 1891 Nadig). Also on display: one of four replicas of Pee-wee Herman's Schwinn and the lawnmower that won the 2007 US Lawn Mower Racing trophy (top speed: 65 mph). There's a holiday-themed model train display every December. The seasonal Hubcap Café serves milkshakes, egg creams, hot dogs, and other soda fountain staples.

⬆ **Mack Trucks Historical Museum** (610-351-8999; macktruckshistoricalmuseum .org), 2402 Lehigh Parkway. Open Monday, Wednesday, and Friday. The Mack brothers operated their truck company in Allentown from 1905 until 2009. Global headquarters moved to North Carolina, but a few facilities remain, and one of them houses a museum dedicated to the iconic heavy-duty trucks. Former employees lead informative tours every 30 minutes. You'll learn about the role of Mack Trucks in Hollywood, the World Wars, the making of the Hoover Dam and other projects and events that shaped America, and get up-close views of current and historic models, including the "Megatron" truck used in the film *Transformers*. Allow for at least an hour or more to best experience this hidden gem.

⬆ **Sigal Museum** (610-253-1222), 342 Northampton Street, Easton. Small admission fee charged; free on Sundays. Opened in 2010, this local history museum offers thoughtful displays of pre-European settlement artifacts, decorative arts, farming tools, and colonial furniture. There is also a gallery showcasing works by local artists and an exhibit on music and Martin guitars. Docents lead historic Easton walking tours on Sunday or by appointment.

✳ To Do

TOURS ⬆ **C. F. Martin Guitar Company and Museum** (610-759-2837), 510 Sycamore Street, Nazareth. This family-owned guitar maker has been producing high-quality acoustic guitars since the early 1800s. Johnny Cash, Paul McCartney, Eric Clapton, and Gene Autry are a few artists who have owned them. You don't have to be a serious musician to enjoy the free tours of its small plant north of Bethlehem, offered weekdays at 11 a.m. and 2:30 p.m. Led by enthusiastic guides, they last about an hour and walk you through the many steps involved in making a guitar. You can stand next to workers as they bend, shape, fit, sand, lacquer, and inspect, converting rough fine woods into a brand-new instrument. There's also a well-executed display of vintage Martin guitars (including Ricky Nelson's leather-covered one and clips of Elvis Presley playing his Martin in the 1950s) off the lobby and a gift shop that sells new and used Martin guitars, books, T-shirts, and other guitar-related items.

SteelStacks (610-297-7200; steelstacks .org), 711 First Street, Bethlehem. Guided walking tours of Bethlehem Steel's main plant, which closed in 1995, are available most weekends from the visitor center on the SteelStacks complex. Some of the guides worked for, or have relatives who once worked for, the steel behemoth. The hour-long "Rise and Fall of Bethlehem Steel" tour covers the history of the company, its contributions to the world's skyscrapers and military efforts, and which buildings housed which operation in the steelmaking process, while the "Hoover-Mason Trestle" tour takes you

THE STEELSTACKS COMPLEX OFFERS LIVE CONCERTS, ART SHOWS, TOURS, AND MORE

BLAST FURNACES AT BETHLEHEM STEELSTACKS

up close to view the giant blast furnaces that once produced up to 3,000 tons of iron a day. Check the website for times and availability.

Historic Bethlehem (610-882-0450; historicbethlehem.org) offers a variety of specialty walking tours, including visits to the remains of an 18th-century apothecary and one of the nation's largest dollhouse collections. On weekends, professionals sometimes lead a variety of blacksmithing workshops, where you'll learn things like how to make a cheese knife or a fireplace poker in a reconstructed smithy.

FOR FAMILIES **Crayola Experience** (610-515-8000; crayolaexperience.com/easton), 30 Centre Square, Easton. Open 10–6 daily; admission charged. Binney & Smith, the local company that makes Crayola crayons, opened this hands-on discovery center in 1996 after the demand for factory tours became overwhelming. It's more of an activity center aimed at kids 4–12 than a lesson on how crayons are manufactured, but kids will love the coloring stations, drawing on the giant glass walls, and making their own stationery at the printmaking exhibit. Plus, they distribute free crayons and markers here like the town of Hershey hands out chocolate kisses. Weekends can get quite crowded; also keep in mind that school groups flood the place weekdays in late April and May.

Dorney Park & Wildwater Kingdom (610-395-3724; dorneypark.com), 3830 Dorney Park Road, Allentown. Open daily from late May–August, Friday–Sunday in September and October; admission charged. Season passes are often a good value and include free parking, unlimited visits, and early access to the water park. Part of the Cedar Fair chain, Dorney Park has about a dozen thrill rides and roller coasters (including the Steel Force "hypercoaster" and the floorless Hydra), plus family-friendly rides such as the Tilt-a-Whirl, an antique carousel, and Planet Snoopy. Wildwater Kingdom, a large water park with speed slides, tubing rivers, wave pools, and a kids' area, is included in the price of admission. On 200 acres, it's not as big nor as famous as Hershey Park, but it's a beloved summertime diversion that rarely gets overcrowded. Fun fact: Dorney Park was the amusement park featured in the 1988 John Waters film *Hairspray* and the 1968 comedy *Where Angels Go, Trouble Follows* with Rosalind Russell.

Da Vinci Science Center (484-664-1002; davincisciencecenter.org), 3145 Hamilton Boulevard Bypass, Allentown. Open daily; admission charged. Kids can take a gyroscope ride, control a robotic dinosaur, and learn about earthquakes, smog, and nanotechnology at this sleek science lab. A preschool area includes a 72-foot maze tunnel and a water table with movable parts.

THUNDER HAWK, DORNEY PARK'S WOODEN ROLLER COASTER, HAS OPERATED SINCE 1923

Lehigh Valley Zoo (610-799-4171, lvzoo.org), 5150 Game Preserve Road, Schnecksville. This manageable zoo sits atop a mountain within the Trexler Nature Preserve. It may be the only zoo that requires driving across a covered bridge to reach. It's perfect for kids 10 and younger, with an easy loop trail, a large playground, and daily animal feedings. The African penguins are always entertaining, as are the lorikeets and river otters. There are often themed events on weekends to keep things interesting.

Lost River Caverns (610-838-8767; lostcave.com), 726 Durham Street, Hellertown. Open daily. These limestone caves are at the northern edge of Bucks County, about 20 miles south of Allentown. Five cavern chambers, discovered in 1883, have an

PENGUIN FEEDING TIME AT THE LEHIGH VALLEY ZOO

SCHLICHER'S COVERED BRIDGE IN THE LEHIGH VALLEY

abundance of stalactites, stalagmites, and other crystal formations; guided tours take 30 to 45 minutes. The adjacent free museum has rare fossils, minerals, and gems as well as a large collection of antique weapons.

✳ Green Space

Hoover-Mason Trestle (610-297-7100, steelstacks.org), 711 First Street, Bethlehem. This may be the coolest repurposed hunk of steel in the world. Once a narrow-gauge railway that shuttled raw materials from ore yards to Bethlehem Steel's giant furnaces, it's now an elevated park, four stories above street level, that sits at the foot of Bethlehem Steel's five giant blast furnaces. Interpretive signs explain a day in the life of a steelworker and how the decommissioned furnaces operated and produced up to 3,000 tons of iron a day between the late 1800s and the late 1990s. There are also benches, native plants artfully placed amid the machinery, and views of the entire SteelStacks complex. The park can be reached by elevator or stairs between the visitor center and Levitt Pavilion, or by stairs from the Wind Creek casino parking lot. It's open daily but may close due to inclement weather or private events.

    Hugh Moore Historical Park (610-559-6613; canals.org), Lehigh Drive, Easton. Named after the founder of the Dixie Cup Company, this 520-acre city-owned park parallels several miles of the Lehigh River and has picnic areas, flat biking trails, and mule-drawn canal boat rides in the summer. A canal boat ticket includes admission to the **National Canal Museum** (610-923-3548; canals.org), a terrific museum about America's towpath canals on the first floor of the Emrick Technology Center. Artifacts from the period combine with hands-on interactive displays that let visitors steer a canal boat, harness a mule, and build an aqueduct.

Jacobsburg State Park (610-746-2801), 835 Jacobsburg Road, Bushkill Township. This 1,200-acre state park near Nazareth is located on a historic site that once housed two 18th-century rifle factories and an iron furnace and forge. Bounded by Bushkill Creek, it has an environmental education center and 18 miles of well-maintained hiking and biking trails. Maps are available at the kiosk in the main parking lot on Belfast Road. The pedestrian-only Henry's Woods Trail, also accessible from here, is a 1.5-mile shaded loop that follows the creek downstream past hemlock and oak forest.

Lehigh Gap Nature Center (610-760-8889; lgnc.org), 884 Paint Mill Road, Slatington. You can access the Appalachian Trail from the well-marked Blue Trail in this 750-acre wildlife refuge and restored Superfund site. There's also access from here to the Delaware and Lehigh Trail, part of a national historic corridor that runs from Wilkes-Barre to Philadelphia. The Osprey House, open Friday–Monday, has trail maps along with an education lab, events, and photos chronicling the gap's transformation from toxic wasteland to environmental showcase.

Sand Island (610-865-7079), 56 River Street, Bethlehem. This 2-mile-long city park on the Lehigh River is near downtown and has tennis and basketball courts, a playground, a boat ramp, and a small cultural center. You'll also find access to the Lehigh Canal and towpath, a popular biking and running trail that follows the canal west to Allentown or east to Freemansburg and then on to Easton. The island can be accessed via car by a small bridge next to an old railroad station just under the Hill to Hill Bridge (PA 378).

✳ Outdoor Activities

BICYCLING/HIKING TRAILS **South Bethlehem Greenway Rail Trail** is a paved path for walkers, cyclers, and skateboarders that follows an old rail line on Bethlehem's south side. It's a chance to see the ruins of Bethlehem Steel from a unique vantage

HISTORIC LOCKTENDER'S HOUSE IN WALNUTPORT

TRIPLE-A BASEBALL IN ALLENTOWN

In 2008 the Lehigh Valley welcomed its first Major League–affiliated baseball team since 1960. The Triple-A team, called the Iron Pigs in a nod to the area's steelmaking days, is affiliated with the Philadelphia Phillies and plays at the 8,200-seat Coca-Cola Park on Allentown's east side. Lawn seats (bring your own blanket) are reasonably priced and great for kids. The Bacon Strip, designed to resemble the Green Monster seats at Fenway Park in Boston, is a two-level seating area with barstools and drink counters along the right field wall. For a schedule and more information, visit milb.com/lehigh-valley.

WATCHING THE IRON PIGS AT COCA-COLA PARK IS A LEHIGH VALLEY TRADITION

point. Other points of interest include a community garden, interesting artwork, and **Bonn Place Brewing,** a cozy English-style taproom at 310 Taylor Street.

BOAT EXCURSIONS Canal boat rides, narrated by costumed crew members, run regularly throughout the summer and weekends in September from **Hugh Moore Park** (see *Green Space*).

DIVING Dutch Springs Park (610-759-2270; dutchsprings.com), 4733 Hanoverville Road, Bethlehem. This former quarry is one of the largest freshwater diving facilities in the country, with an average visibility of 20 to 30 feet. It offers scuba diving daily from April–October and overnight tent camping on Friday and Saturday nights. Ocean kayaks and paddleboats are also available for rental.

FOOTBALL The **Lehigh Valley Steelhawks** joined the Indoor Football League in 2011; home games are played at Lehigh University's Stabler Arena. For more info, visit lvsteelhawks.com or call 610-292-3100.

GOLF Bethlehem Golf Club (610-691-9393), 400 Illicks Mill Road, Bethlehem. Built in 1965, this 18-hole municipal course has a mix of flat and hilly terrain and stretches to nearly 7,000 yards. An executive nine-hole course, a driving range, and mini-golf are available.

Center Valley Golf Club (610-791-5580), 3300 Center Valley Parkway, Center Valley. This 18-hole, par-72 course near I-78 and PA 309 is in excellent condition, with five tees ranging from 4,932 to 6,973 yards.

HOCKEY The **Leigh Valley Phantoms** are the National Hockey League affiliate of the Philadelphia Flyers and play at the PPL Center in Allentown (484-273-4490; phantomshockey.com). They have garnered a huge following since they started playing here in 2014 through their successes (they took the Atlantic Division Title in the 2017-18 season) and their strong presence within the community.

HUNTING Hunting of squirrels, pheasants, rabbits, and white-tailed deer is permitted on about 900 acres of **Jacobsburg State Park** (see *Green Space*). Hunters are expected to follow the rules and regulations of the Pennsylvania Game Commission (pgc.state.pa.us).

SKIING Bear Creek Ski & Recreation Area (610-682-7100; bcmountainresort.com), 101 Doe Mountain Lane, Macungie. Geared toward novice and intermediate skiers, it has 17 slopes, three terrain parks, and a snow-tubing park. There's a full-service resort at its base.

Blue Mountain Ski Area (610-826-7700; skibluemt.com), 1660 Blue Mountain Drive, Palmerton. About 17 miles north of Allentown, with 110 acres of skiing terrain and 30 slopes. There's also a half-pipe and snow-tubing area.

✳ Lodging

HOTELS & INNS Bear Creek Mountain Resort (866-754-2822; bcmountain resort.com), 101 Doe Mountain Lane, Macungie. Located in the far western reaches of the Lehigh Valley, this full-service resort attracts skiers and snow tubers in winter and hikers or couples in search of an uncomplicated getaway in summer. Its modern rooms are spacious and comfortable, though the layout is large and mazelike. A 5-acre fishing pond stocked with trout, two tennis courts, and a luxury spa are on-site. It's surrounded by quiet farmland, and chances are you won't want to leave once you check in.

🦌 **Glasbern** (610-285-4723; glasbern .com), 2141 Pack House Road, Fogelsville. Romance meets businesslike efficiency at this family farm turned country inn on 100 acres a few miles outside Allentown. Seven separately renovated buildings, once used to run the farm, now house 35 large rooms or suites, many with fireplaces and whirlpool tubs, and a lodge-style guest house. A fitness center, spa, and outdoor heated pool are available. Its fine restaurant is open to the public (see *Dining Out*). Rates are on the high side, but most folks looking for a luxury getaway find their expectations are met or exceeded here. $$$.

Grand Eastonian Suites Hotel (610-258-6350; grandeastoniansuiteshotel .com), 140 Northampton Street, Easton. Anchoring Easton's main square, this gorgeous turn-of-the-20th-century building was restored to its original grandeur in 2004 and, after a brief stint as condos, turned into a hotel in late 2008. It features one-, two-, and three-bedroom modern suites with full kitchens, all furnished in sleek beiges and whites. An indoor pool and fitness room, plus free high-speed Internet and flat-screen TVs are on-site. It's popular with relocating business folks, but families will want to ask about their package deals with the Crayola Experience, which is two blocks away. Pets are allowed. $$$–$$$$.

Hotel Bethlehem (610-625-5000; 800-607-2384; hotelbethlehem.com), 437 Main Street. What this busy urban hotel lacks in warmth it makes up for in rich historical background. Centrally located downtown, it was built in 1922 on the site of the area's first house, where a wealthy Moravian patron named Count Nikolaus Ludwig von Zinzendorf christened the town Bethlehem. The hotel underwent major renovations in the 1990s and has 125 rooms and suites with amenities such as a free airport shuttle, fitness center, and complimentary coffee and Moravian sugar cakes offered in the lobby each morning. Even if you don't stay here, be sure to check out the grand old lobby and the seven George Gray murals that have hung in the hotel since 1937, chronicling the town's history from religious settlement to industrial center. $$$.

BED & BREAKFASTS **Lafayette Inn** (610-253-4500; 800-509-6990; lafayetteinn.com), 525 West Monroe Street, Easton. Perched high on a hill overlooking the valley, this inn near Lafayette College is one of your best and friendliest options for lodging in the Easton area. Owners Paolo and Laura Di Liello were electrical engineers before joining the hospitality business. All 18 rooms and suites are tastefully furnished with antiques, desks, TVs, and private baths. Deluxe rooms can accommodate up to four people; standard rooms sleep two. The inn attracts a mix of business travelers, Lafayette College visitors, and general tourists. Breakfast (usually made-to-order omelets and waffles during the week and a feast of homemade granola, fruit, cereals, and stratas or French toast on weekends) is served on individual tables in the sunroom. Kids and pets (in some rooms) are welcome. $$–$$$.

Sayre Mansion (610-882-2100; sayremansion.com), 250 Wyandotte Street, Bethlehem. This Gothic Revival home once belonged to Robert Sayre, founder of the Lehigh Railroad. It's in a central location about a 5-minute drive or 25-minute walk to historic Bethlehem. The 18 spacious and attractive rooms have desks, flat-panel TVs, wing chairs, fireplaces, and luxurious feather beds. A four-course breakfast is served in the elegant dining room, or you may opt to have it delivered to your room. Home-baked cookies are offered in the afternoons, and port is available in the evening. The separate Carriage House has two large suites and a loft. It's a popular destination for weekend weddings. $$$–$$$$.

❋ Where to Eat

DINING OUT ❚ **Apollo Grill** (610-865-9600; apollogrill.com), 85 West Broad Street, Bethlehem. Lunch and dinner Tuesday–Saturday. Busy bistro near the Historic District specializing in innovative tapas such as shrimp limoncello, beef short-rib lettuce wraps, and cheesesteak spring rolls. There's also a selection of sandwiches (beef brisket, chipotle chicken) and simple pastas. It is always hopping, so reservations are recommended. $$.

❚ **Bay Leaf** (610-433-4211; allentownbayleaf.com), 935 Hamilton Street, Allentown. Lunch and dinner Monday–Friday, dinner Saturdays. A reliable, upscale dining option at the center of downtown. The lengthy French- and Asian-influenced menu includes wasabi sesame crust tuna with red wine sauce, lemongrass shrimp with spiced carrot sauce, fillet tips with oyster and béarnaise sauce, and many curry dishes. $$.

Glasbern (610-285-4723; glasbern.com), 2141 Pack House Road, Fogelsville. Dinner daily. This romantic restaurant showcases meats and produce raised and grown on its adjacent farm. Dinners

Sunday–Friday are à la carte and might include aged beef meat loaf with molasses BBQ, house-made ricotta gnocchi, and shrimp capellini with white wine and fresh herbs. The dining room is exquisite and welcoming, with stone walls, vaulted rafters, and a fireplace. A four-course prix fixe dinner is served on Saturdays. Reservations required. $$$$.

♀ **House and Barn** (610-967-6225; houseandbarn.net), 1449 Chestnut Street, Emmaus. You have two options here: Dine on innovative New American cuisine (crab and avocado spring rolls, seared scallops with focaccia bread pudding) in an elegant 19th-century farmhouse, or sample the pub menu (smoked pork shoulder sandwiches, curried cauliflower flatbreads) in the more casual (but no less charming) bank barn. Leave time for lingering over a local craft ale in the House's basement tavern. The Barn also has a creek-side patio and live music on weekends. $$–$$$.

♀ **Savory Grille** (610-845-2010; savorygrille.com), 2934 Seisholtzville Road, Macungie. Dinner Wednesday–Saturday; lunch and dinner Sundays. Husband and wife chefs Dorothy and Shawn Doyle serve simple yet creative fare in a historic former hotel south of Bear Creek Resort. The menu might feature coffee-dusted buffalo strip steak with caramelized Jack Daniels onions or grilled swordfish and coconut rice in an orange-ginger emulsion. Reservations recommended at dinner. $$$–$$$$.

EASTON

♀ **Pearly Baker's Ale House** (610-253-9949), 11 Centre Square. Lunch, dinner, and late-night menu daily; closed Mondays. Locals love to steer newcomers to this popular eatery and tavern on the square. Menu highlights include pear and Brie salad, a long list of burgers (from lamb to Impossible), and comfort dishes such as Stoudt-braised short ribs and duck confit. Dine outside overlooking the square in the summer or under the dining room's grand chandelier any other time. There's live music on weekends. $$–$$$.

Sette Luna (610-253-8888; setteluna .com), 219 Ferry Street. Small and bustling bistro near Easton's main square serving wood-burning-oven pizzas, homemade pastas, and excellent salads. The Sunday jazz brunch features homemade tomato juice, open-faced frittatas, and salmon Hollandaise. Wine and beer. $$.

EATING OUT Billy's Downtown Diner (610-867-0105), 10 East Broad Street, Bethlehem. Local celebrity chef Billy Kounoupis and his wife, Yanna, took over this former newsstand in 2000 and transformed it into a friendly and upscale noshing place. Breakfast menu includes specialty omelets such as smoked salmon or crispy bacon, stuffed French toast, and creamed chipped beef. For lunch, there's a long list of sandwiches, melts, and other diner items such as gravy boat fries, pierogi, and mozzarella sticks. There are also branches in Allentown and Easton. $.

Pete's Hot Dog Shop (610-866-6622), 400 Broadway, Bethlehem. Closed Sundays. The chili dogs are made to order, and the service is friendly and quick at this casual eatery, with crisp pierogi, locally made A-Treat soda, and omelets for breakfast. The prices, like the vibe, remain firmly rooted in the past. $.

ALLENTOWN

🍴 **Wert's Café** (610-439-0951; wertscafe .com), 515 North 18th Street. Closed Sundays. There are 15 types of Burgers with Personality on the menu of this family-owned restaurant near the Allentown Fairgrounds, but the one that gets well-deserved top billing is the Wert's Burger. It comes stuffed with mushrooms and onions and has something of a cult following. There are also crispy eggplant fries, batter-dipped pickles, onion rings (the stringy kind), homemade soups, and entrées such as chopped sirloin and

FROM STEEL PLANT TO ARTS & CULTURE HUB

SteelStacks (610-332-1300; steelstacks.org), 101 Founders Way, Bethlehem. The giant blast furnaces that were once part of the country's second-largest steel manufacturer loom large over just about every event at this 10-acre arts and cultural complex. The furnaces no longer produce the 2,500 to 3,000 tons of iron a day they once did in their 20th-century heydays, but the town found a clever way to keep them around and make sure no one forgets the essential role Bethlehem Steel played in supplying parts that built the nation's skyscrapers, bridges, and warships. It's a spectacularly unique way to enjoy a concert, comedy festival, or play. SteelStacks includes the ArtsQuest Center, which houses a bistro and several different venues for live music, plays, independent films, and children's theater, and the Banana Factory, home to artists' studios, galleries, and a monthly First Friday celebration featuring artist talks, demonstrations, and live music. The sleek outdoor Levitt Pavilion hosts free outdoor summer concerts, as well as performances for MusikFest, an August event that draws big crowds to the area (see *Special Events*). Rounding out the SteelStacks experience are guided tours (see *Activities*) and a large visitor center in the beautifully restored 1863 Stock House, which once stored the coal, iron ore, and limestone used to fuel those adjacent blast furnaces.

country ham. Rounding things out is a full bar and locally made white birch beer on tap. Check the website for special deals like Monday's package of burger, onion rings, and chocolate cake. $–$$.

Yocco's Hot Dogs (610-433-1950; yoccos.com), 2128 Hamilton Street. Don't be put off by the gritty white facade and sometimes indifferent service. Founded by the uncle of native son Lee Iacocca, Yocco's makes hot dogs that people drive miles for; the pierogi are tasty too. In addition to three Allentown locations, there are also branches in Emmaus, Fogelsville, and Trexlertown. $.

EASTON

Josie's New York Deli (610-252-5081), 14 Centre Square, Easton. A worthy lunch option near the Crayola Experience—the sandwiches are fresh, large, and cheap. People drive miles for the tasty chicken salad. The line to order can be long, but it moves fast. $.

EMMAUS

Trivet Diner (610-965-2838), 4102 Chestnut Street. Open daily. Huge portions, low prices, homemade pies, and authentic Pennsylvania Dutch cooking. There's also a location on Tilghman Street in Allentown. $.

ICE CREAM & DESSERT **Baked** (610-966-6100; bakedinemmaus.com), 228 Main Street, Emmaus. Hippest place in town for vegan pumpkin muffins, pear ginger scones, iced organic green tea, and La Colombe coffee. There's also a selection of gourmet sandwiches such as baked tofu and provolone or salami with olive relish and asiago.

Bank Street Creamery (610-252-5544), 14 South Bank Street, Easton. Formerly the Purple Cow Creamery, this family-run ice cream parlor serves Italian ice, milkshakes, real hot fudge sundaes, and delicious ice cream. Choose from tiramisu, toasted coconut, Black Forest cake, cotton candy, and other fun flavors. It is conveniently tucked in an alley around the corner from the Crayola Experience.

The Caramelcorn Shop (610-253-6461), 62 Centre Square, Easton. An old-time confectionary on the square known for its homemade caramel corn, fresh-roasted nuts, and fudge. There's also a large assortment of gummies, sugar-free candies, and swizzle sticks.

FARMS & FARMERS' MARKETS

Easton Farmers' Market (eastonfarmers market.com), Centre Square (next to the Crayola Experience). Open 9–1 Saturday from May–November. The oldest continuous open-air farmers' market in the country. Shop for grass-fed beef and pork, organic yogurt, Welsh tea cakes, and all sorts of fruits and vegetables. Homemade baby food, fair-trade coffee, tasty prepared foods, and locally made crafts and jellies are also available.

Emmaus Farmers' Market (emmausmarket.com), 235 Main Street (in the Keystone Nazareth Bank & Trust parking lot). Open 10–2 Sunday from May–November. More than 20 vendors sell seasonal local produce, fresh bison, goat's milk cheese, and pastries at this highly regarded outdoor market.

✪ **Fairgrounds Farmers' Market** (610-435-7469), 17th and Chew Streets, Allentown. Open Thursday–Saturday. You can get a haircut, shop for fondue forks and Avon products, hear Pennsylvania Dutch spoken, and eat some of the finest local specialties around at this large,

CHICKEN POTPIES AT ALLENTOWN FAIRGROUNDS FARMERS' MARKET

multifaceted indoor market. It is widely known for its meat selection: There's everything from ring bologna and Habbersett scrapple to Italian Braciole and stuffed pork chops ready for the oven. Other favorites include Dan's Bar-B-Que for chicken pies and ribs; Gdynia Polish Market for hand-shaped pierogi and

THE FARMERS' MARKET AT ALLENTOWN FAIRGROUNDS

kielbasa; Heckenberger's Seafood for fresh, reasonably priced salmon and lobster tails; and the Kiffle Kitchen for fruit-filled cookies. It gets more crowded as the day goes on, but there is plenty of free parking. Some vendors only take cash.

✳ Entertainment

⊙ **Eight Oaks Craft Distillers** (484-387-5287; eightoaksdistillers.com), 7189 PA 309, New Tripoli. This friendly small-batch maker of whiskey, bourbon, rum, and barrel-aged applejack sources its rye, grain, and herbs from local farms. The tasting room is open Thursday–Sunday, with live music every Saturday afternoon; a casual, seasonal dinner menu is offered on Friday and Saturday evenings, with "Brunch & Bloodys" on Sundays. Hour-long tours of the distillery are held on Saturdays for $20 a person.

The Bookstore Speakeasy (610-867-1100; bookstorespeakeasy.com), 336 Adams Street, Bethlehem. Ordering a Coors Light is immediate grounds for dismissal from this cozy and welcoming 1920s-style bar. The menu offers 50+ specialty cocktails and modern bar bites like house-made pickles and chickpea popcorn. There's live jazz Thursday–Sunday.

Social Still (610-625-4585), 530 East Third Street, Bethlehem. A tasting room and gastropub inside a historic bank building offering cocktails with house-distilled spirits and creative eats like a pastrami-cured BLT and crab-jalapeño hush puppies. Tours of the distillery are available (with advance reservations) on Saturdays, or you can request a basic tour anytime and they'll show you around if it isn't too busy.

Yergey's Brewing (484-232-7055; yergeybrewing.com), 518 Bank Street, Emmaus. Open Thursday–Sunday. Enjoy the nano-brewery's signature double IPA and other artisan brews surrounded by lagering tanks and an upbeat vibe. There's often a food truck or two parked outside and live music on weekends. It shares a building with **Triple Sun Spirits** (610-904-8082; triplesunspirits.com), a small-batch distillery with its own tasting room offering handcrafted cocktails and pickleback shots, as well as in-depth tours of its operations. **Miller Symphony Hall** (610-351-7990; millersymphonyhall .org), 23 North Sixth Street, Allentown. Home to the Allentown Symphony, the 1,200-seat concert hall also stages non-orchestral music and theatrical performances for adults and kids throughout the year.

State Theatre (610-252-3132; state theatre.org), 453 Northampton Street, Easton. Renovated in the 1990s, this historic theater hosts concerts by nationally known performers and comedians, animal shows, and off-Broadway hits.

Pines Dinner Theatre (610-433-2333; pinesdinnertheatre.com), 448 North 17th Street, Allentown. Crowd-pleasing musicals and multicourse comfort food.

✳ Selective Shopping

Historic Bethlehem Visitor Center Store (800-360-8687; historicbethlehem .org/visitor-center), 505 Main Street, Bethlehem. Lots of local handcrafted items, from jewelry to Kivka pottery and Moravian stars. This store is also a good source of information on the area, with maps and tour tickets available here.

Kemerer Museum Store (610-868-6868), 427 North New Street, Bethlehem. Part of the Kemerer Museum of Decorative Arts, this gift boutique sells decorative tiles, pottery, stationery, and children's clothes and toys.

Moravian Bookshop (610-866-5481), 428 Main Street, Bethlehem. Open daily except some holidays. Established in 1745 by the Moravian church, this charming retail complex near the Hotel Bethlehem claims to be the world's oldest bookseller. Besides a wide selection of books on the Moravian church and Lehigh Valley history, it also offers best-sellers and children's books, candles, pottery, and exquisite ornaments and gifts featuring the symbolic Moravian star. It was sold in 2018 to Moravian College, which vowed to continue the store's "Moravian legacy." In 2019 a local brewpub and deli/gelato shop opened within the store.

✳ Special Events

May: **Bethlehem Bach Festival** (first two weekends), around Bethlehem—the all-volunteer Bach Choir of Bethlehem ardently and lovingly performs works of the legendary composer during this century-old event. For more information, visit www.bach.org.

May–August: **Pennsylvania Shakespeare Festival,** DeSales University, Center Valley—the state's official summer celebration of the Bard and other master dramatists attracts a talented pool of actors from New York and Philadelphia. For details, visit pashakespeare.org.

August: **MusikFest** (first week), around Bethlehem—more than 300 musical acts, from polka bands to rock legends, perform at this popular 11-day event that brings more than a million people to indoor and outdoor venues around Bethlehem. Tickets for individual concerts are in the $20–50 range; many performances are free. For details, go to musikfest.org.

Great Allentown Fair (late August/ early September)—started as a small agricultural event in 1852 and has evolved into a week-long celebration with petting zoos, rides, and plenty of food and live entertainment (Hall & Oates, Keith Urban, and Brooks & Dunn are a few recent headliners).

ORNAMENTS FOR SALE AT CHRISTKINDLMARKT

September: **Celtic Fest** (last weekend), downtown Bethlehem—fiddling, poetry, and songwriting contests, as well as soda bread and whiskey tastings, beer tents, and a "Showing of the Tartan" parade. The National Highlands Athletic Championship games are also a highlight of this three-day event.

November/December: **Christkindlmarkt** (late November–December), Bethlehem—modeled after Germany's open-air Christmas markets, this popular holiday bazaar in the SteelStacks complex features unique handmade crafts, live music, ice sculpting, and more. Related events include trolley and carriage rides, walking tours of downtown Bethlehem, and holiday concerts. For details, go to christmascity.org.

INTRODUCTION TO THE POCONOS

A couple of decades ago, the Pocono Mountains region was widely regarded as an over-the-top honeymoon destination for couples who liked ceilings painted with cherubs and bathtubs shaped like champagne flutes. A few affordable rustic family lodges attracted vacationing city folk from New York and Philadelphia for a week or two in the summer. Candle shops were plentiful.

A handful of couples-only resorts still exist today, but the area has come a long, long way since then, turning itself into a major vacation destination for families and couples of all tastes. Golfers can take their pick of three dozen courses. Outdoor adventure types flock to the Lehigh Gorge area, where stellar white-water rafting and mountain-biking opportunities abound; there's even dogsledding for those who may want to try a new outdoor adventure sport. Families favor the water parks and affordable camping and cabin rental options. Meanwhile, couples can choose from a long list of upscale B&Bs and country inns that are more likely to have antique brass beds than the mirrored headboards of yore.

Though they are geologically a southwestern extension of the Catskill Mountains, the Pocono Mountains aren't really a mountain chain at all. They are a combination of deep forests, rolling hills, sparkling lakes, and limitless outdoor pastimes. The entire Pocono Mountains region encompasses more than 2,400 square miles and four counties: Carbon, Monroe, Pike, and Wayne. It is home to eight state and two national parks, 170 miles of rivers, 35 golf courses, 63 ski trails, summer camps, and more resorts than anywhere else in the state. The towns of Jim Thorpe, Blakeslee, Marshalls Creek, Stroudsburg, Milford, Hawley, and Honesdale are part of the Pocono Mountains region; the towns of Wilkes-Barre and Scranton are not, though they are within easy driving distance.

To make it more easily digestible, I have divided the region into two sections: the south region, which includes the Delaware Water Gap, Jim Thorpe, and the region's largest number of resorts; and the north region of Pike and Wayne Counties, which is less than 90 miles from New York City and known for its quaint towns, unique museums, and Green Acres–meets-Manhattan vibe.

Perhaps because it harks back to the region's heart-shaped tub days, tourism officials and current business owners tend to frown upon referring to the region by its nickname, the Poconos. I try to adhere to that in this guide, but I apologize in advance if I fall off the wagon occasionally and call it the Poconos. I spent many adolescent summers here, and the area's unpretentious beauty holds a special place in my heart.

THE POCONO MOUNTAINS SOUTH

AREA CODE The entire southern Pocono Mountain region lies within 570.

GUIDANCE The **Pennsylvania Welcome Center** (570-234-1180), just off I-80 near Delaware Water Gap, is a full-service rest facility with picnic tables, vending machines, maps, and information about attractions throughout the state, as well as the latest road and weather conditions. It's staffed daily 7 a.m.–7 p.m. In Stroudsburg, the **Pocono Mountains Vacation Bureau** (570-421-5791; poconomountains.com), 1004 Main Street, Stroudsburg, is a good spot for area maps and attractions; they will also send you materials by mail upon request. In **Jim Thorpe,** stop by the visitor center in the old railway station for maps and information on current activities.

GETTING THERE *By air:* **Philadelphia International** (215-937-6800) and **Newark Liberty International** (973-961-6000) are the closest major airports, each more than two hours away. **Lehigh Valley International** (888-359-5842) is about a 45-minute drive from Stroudsburg.

By car: From Philadelphia, take I-476 to Lehighton or Blakeslee for the western region. For Stroudsburg and Delaware Water Gap, pick up US 22 in Allentown, then follow PA 33 north. From New York or New Jersey, take I-80 west to Stroudsburg and points beyond.

By bus: **Martz Trailways** (570-421-3040; martztrailways.com) runs buses from New York City and Scranton to stations in Delaware Water Gap, Mount Pocono, and Marshalls Creek. **Greyhound** also has service to Scranton and Philadelphia from Delaware Water Gap.

GETTING AROUND Unless you have the Olympian stamina of Jim Thorpe, you'll need a car to get around the region. It can take as long as an hour to drive from Lehigh Gorge to Delaware Water Gap. The main streets of Stroudsburg and Jim Thorpe are pleasant for walking, with plenty of shops, restaurants, and historic architecture. Be sure to bring a good map and request very clear directions to your destinations, especially places without numbered addresses.

WHEN TO GO Summer is the most popular time to visit the Pocono Mountains, as it's the time when the lakes and rivers are warmest and most attractions are open and in full swing. The fall, however, is my favorite time to visit. The leaves are turning brilliant shades of gold and orange, the air is crisp, and you can't drive a mile without bumping into a pumpkin or harvest fest. Late March–June (and to a lesser extent September and October) is the best period for white-water rafting here because of scheduled dam releases along the Lehigh River.

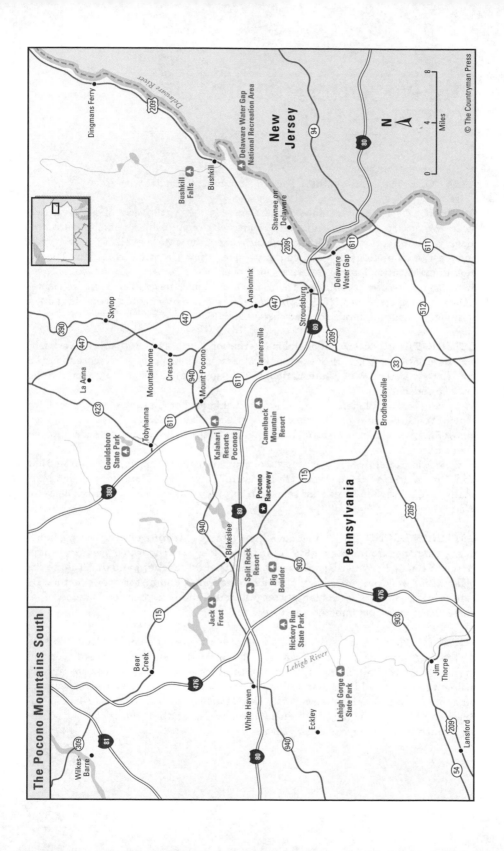

The Pocono Mountains South

✳ Villages

Delaware Water Gap. Not to be confused with the natural wonder of the same name, this sleepy town of 800 residents was once a thriving resort serving the many people visiting the nearby gorge, including Teddy Roosevelt. Some of its once-grand buildings and hotels are fading and in need of repair, but it still has several worthwhile attractions, such as the jazz performances at the Deer Head Inn. The Appalachian Trail crosses right through its main street (PA 611).

Mount Pocono. Home to many of the all-inclusive resorts and souvenir candle shops that first put the Pocono Mountains on the map, this central borough probably best epitomizes the Poconos as a honeymoon capital. It has been heavily developed in recent years and has a Walmart, freestanding casino, and several grocery stores and strip malls. Busy PA 940 cuts through its center, but there are still numerous forested country roads to its north that lead past old general stores, rustic inns, and bait and tackle shops. It's also home to the old-fashioned Casino Theater and Memorytown, a kitschy destination complex composed of a tavern, picnic area, game room, and a lake with a faux covered bridge and paddleboats.

Mountainhome. You could call this aptly named town the gateway to the central Poconos. You'll pass through it on your way to such destinations as Canadensis, Skytop, La Anna, and Buck Hill Falls. It's not a walkable kind of place, but it has several cafés, shops, and attractions such as the Pocono Playhouse and Callie's Candy Kitchen.

Shawnee. Golf. Ski. Swim. Kayak. Those are your main options in this small community next to the Delaware River. Its dominant resident is the Shawnee ski resort, but you will also find a well-regarded theater, several good B&Bs, and the lovely and regal Shawnee Inn and Golf Resort, once owned by Fred Waring and patronized by Arnold Palmer, Jackie Gleason, and other celebrities.

✳ To See

MUSEUMS Antoine Dutot Museum and Gallery (570-476-4240; dutotmuseum.com), Main Street (PA 611), Delaware Water Gap. Open 1–5 Saturday and Sunday from May–October; donation suggested. This 1850s-era school houses an art gallery, preserved classroom, and history exhibits that cover the area's early development by French plantation owner Antoine Dutot to its current role as a faded resort town.

Pocono Indian Museum (570-588-9338; poconoindianmuseum.com), 5425 Milford Road, East Stroudsburg. Open daily; small admission fee charged. Located in a white-columned mansion, this unsung, if dated, six-room museum is obviously a labor of love for its employees. Instead of just pinning up their collection of ancient artifacts, many of which were found in the Delaware River area, they present them in context with mannequins and other ways that let you see how they worked within the Lenape lifestyle. You will also find an 1843 Cree Indian scalp from the Dakotas and a full-sized wigwam among the displays. The gift shop is huge and fun to browse.

✳ To Do

FOR FAMILIES Bushkill Falls (570-588-6682; visitbushkillfalls.com), US 209 and Bushkill Falls Road, Bushkill. Open daily from April–October; fee charged. This series of eight scenic waterfalls has long been a popular destination for families.

Charles E. Peters started charging visitors a dime to see the falls in 1904. His descendants still run the place. Over the years, they have added a gift shop, Native American museum, small lake with paddleboats, and playground, but it all remains relatively rustic. The "hiking trails" that lead to the falls are actually well-maintained walkways flanked by locust-wood guardrails. You can take an easy path to reach the main falls, or spend as long as two hours hiking to the upper canyons and glens. Families with young kids might want to bring a back carrier. The place gets packed on summer weekends. Don't miss the Bushkill Story cabin, a small house displaying early marketing materials, photographs, souvenirs (like a Bushkill Falls handheld pinball game), and brochures.

Callie's Candy Kitchen (570-595-2280), PA 390, Mountainhome. A visit to this multiroom candy shop is a rite of passage for every school-age kid in the area. As you browse the store, you'll find that Callie's isn't afraid to dip anything in chocolate, including whole s'mores, crackers, whipped marshmallows, Oreos, and even cream cheese.

Callie's Pretzel Factory (570-595-3257), PA 191/PA 390, Cresco. Also owned by the Callie family and about 3 miles south of the candy store, this place is a must-stop for pretzel lovers. Show up right around opening at 10 a.m. and you can watch the day's batches being made by a huge machine in the back. Choose from garlic pretzels, pretzels stuffed with apples or cheddar cheese, hot dogs wrapped in pretzels, and even funnel cake pretzels. For some reason, there's also a gift shop for lefthanders in the back.

ANTIQUES ON DISPLAY AT CALLIE'S CANDY KITCHEN

✎ **Camelbeach Mountain Waterpark** (570-629-1661; camelbeach.com), 309 Resort Drive, Tannersville. Open late May–Labor Day; $35 adults, $25 ages 3–11; season passes also available. Every summer, Camelback Ski Area, adjacent to Camelback Lodge, transforms into a wild and wacky water park with a giant wave pool, a tubing "river," and 22 slides with names such as Vortex, Spin Cycle, and Triple Venom. It's popular with teenagers, but there are a few sedate activities such as chairlift rides, mini-golf, and a shallow pool for tots. A tip: Bring your own food and eat in the picnic area outside before or after your visit.

Lehigh Gorge Scenic Railway (570-325-8485; lgsry.com), 1 Susquehanna Street, Jim Thorpe. If you don't want to bike the Lehigh Gorge Rail Trail, this is a way to witness some of the same gorgeous scenery. Vintage coaches leave the downtown station for a 16-mile ride along the Lehigh River. Wave to the hikers, cyclists, and rafters while conductors describe the area's wildlife, plants, and history of the anthracite coal industry.

The ride is especially beautiful in October, when the leaves turn brilliant shades of orange, red, and gold.

GAMBLING The state's first freestanding slots parlor, **Mount Airy Casino Resort** (877-682-4791; mountairycasino.com), 312 Woodland Road, Mount Pocono, opened in late fall 2007 on the grounds of a former honeymooners' lodge. It features more than 2,400 slot machines, plus blackjack, craps, and roulette, and is one of the few casinos to offer a nonsmoking gambling area. A hotel, spa, and nightclub are adjacent.

Mohegan Sun Pocono (888-946-4672; mohegansunpocono.com), 1280 PA 315, Wilkes-Barre. Set on 400 acres, this sprawling complex has 82,000 feet of gaming space, including table games and 2,300 slot machines, plus a 238-room hotel, spa, and adjacent convention center. For nightlife, there's live music at Breakers and Bar Louie, and the many dining options include Ruth's Chris Steak House and an Irish pub.

SCENIC DRIVES **Buck Hill Falls,** north of Mountainhome, is home to the region's first golf course and some of the prettiest stone houses you'll ever see. Escape the tourist scene around Mount Pocono and head north on PA 191 for a peaceful 30-minute drive. On the way, you'll pass forested lands and meadows and a handful of antiques and gift shops and old general stores. Bear left onto Bush Mountain Road in Mountainhome, then drive several miles to Buck Hill Road and make a right. Once you get here, there's not much to do except gawk at the stately mansions and natural stone bridges or have a lemonade at the semiprivate **Buck Hills Tennis Club.** Before heading back, you can continue north a few miles on PA 191 to **Holley Ross Pottery** in the tiny village of LaAnna.

✳ Green Space

Big Pocono State Park (570-894-8336), Camelback Road, Tannersville. You can see much of northeastern Pennsylvania and stretches of New Jersey and New York from the summit of this 1,300-acre park, which is also home to Camelback Mountain. It has 7 miles of hiking trails, three picnic areas, and limited hunting grounds. The summit can be reached by foot or car up a steep and winding paved road.

Gouldsboro and Tobyhanna State Parks (570-894-8336). These two family-friendly parks are adjacent and anchored by two large lakes with swimming and boating opportunities and 19 miles of hiking trails for all levels. A park office at Tobyhanna just off PA 423 has maps and other information. The entrance to Gouldsboro is off PA 507.

Lehigh Gorge State Park (570-443-0400), White Haven. This 4,500-acre park follows the Lehigh River from Francis E. Walter Dam in White Haven down to Jim Thorpe in the south. It is dominated by its eponymous gorge, sheer rock walls, rock outcroppings, and dozens of waterfalls. It offers hunting, fishing, and plenty of scenic vistas, but its biggest draw is its white-water rafting and mountain-biking opportunities (see *Outdoor Activities*). The Lehigh Gorge Trail, which follows 26 miles of abandoned railroad grade along the river, is beloved by mountain bikers for its scenery, tree canopies, and slight downhill north-to-south grade; horseback riders and hikers may also use it. It can be accessed via White Haven, Tannery Rapid, Rockport, and Glen Onoko, where an iron railroad bridge was renovated in 2009 to provide welcome access into downtown Jim Thorpe. Many bike shops offer a shuttle ride that drops you at White Haven in the north and lets you take the trail downhill all the way back to Jim Thorpe. The upper portion of Lehigh Gorge links with **Hickory Run State**

JIM THORPE: A HAVEN FOR OUTDOORS ENTHUSIASTS

Located along the Lehigh River at the southwestern edge of the Pocono Mountains region, Jim Thorpe is a former railroad and coal-shipping town that was known as Mauch Chunk until 1955. That's when the famous Native American athlete died and his struggling widow struck a deal to have his remains buried there and the town renamed for the famous Olympian. Though Thorpe never set foot here, a large monument stands in his honor near a sign declaring the town THE SWITZERLAND OF AMERICA. Today, Jim Thorpe is one of those destinations that more than lives up to the expectations based on postcards or word of mouth. Anchored by a thriving little downtown, it is surrounded by miles of pristine forest, rivers, and a free and easy spirit. Just about every outdoor adventure and cycling magazine has ranked it as one of the top biking destinations in the state, if not the country; it is also a popular spot for paintball, hiking, and white-water rafting.

The nonathlete will also find things to do here. The opulent Asa Packer Mansion (570-325-3229; asapackermansion.com), home of the founder of the Lehigh Valley Railroad, sits on a hilltop overlooking the town and is open for tours daily June–October. The Old Jail Museum (570-325-5259) on West Broadway was built in 1871 and offers fascinating tours of original cells and tales about the Molly Maguires, a secret society of anthracite miners

JIM THORPE'S GRAVE ON THE OUTSKIRTS OF TOWN

Park (570-443-0400), a 15,500-acre park with plenty of recreational features such as a lake, swimming pool, playground, snack bar, visitor center, and dozens of hiking and snowmobile trails.

✳ Outdoor Activities

AUTO RACING **Pocono Raceway** (570-646-2300; 800-722-3929; poconoraceway .com), Long Pond. Many NASCAR racers consider this 2.5-mile tri-oval speedway to be one of the toughest tracks in the country. Located on a former spinach farm, it draws more than 100,000 fans twice a year to its annual cup races (see *Special Events*). It also has stock car racing and driving school programs.

who used terrorism to force mine owners to improve working conditions (seven were accused and hanged here). Call ahead for hours.

One can also easily spend a couple of hours poking around the frozen-in-time downtown, gawking at the varied styles of architecture and visiting the hip cafés, art galleries, and small shops. The **Mauch Chunk Opera House** (570-325-4439; mcohjt.com), 14 West Broadway, built in 1881, still hosts theatrical and music performances, films, and art exhibits. For kids, there's a model train display in the **Hooven Building** next to the train depot, along with rides on the **Lehigh Gorge Scenic Railway** (570-325-8485; lgsry.com). Sleeping options include the venerable **Inn at Jim Thorpe** and a handful of B&Bs and nearby campgrounds (see *Lodging*). I can't say enough good things about this town. Go.

THE HISTORIC INN AT JIM THORPE IN THE CENTER OF TOWN

Mahoning Valley Raceway (570-386-4900; mahoningvalley-speedway.com), PA 443, Lehighton. Open Saturday evenings from March–October. Nonstop action rules at this quarter-mile track, which runs modified and late-model stock cars and vintage Camaros and Monte Carlos. Family-friendly features include bring-your-own-picnic baskets, a no-alcohol policy, and free admission for kids under 10.

BICYCLING Once described by *Bicycling* magazine as Durango East, Jim Thorpe is for riders of all abilities.

By far the most popular trail around—and arguably one of the top bike rides in the country—is **Lehigh Gorge Rail Trail,** a 26-mile converted railroad bed between White Haven and Jim Thorpe. Several bike shops offer shuttle service to the northern entrance at White Haven, which takes you past waterfalls, sheer rock walls, and gorgeous scenic overlooks before dropping into Jim Thorpe. **Whitewater Rafting Adventures** (800-876-0285; adventurerafting.com/biking) and **Pocono Biking** (800-944-8392; poconobiking.com) offer bike rentals, shuttle service, and half- and full-day guided trips.

CANOEING & KAYAKING **Kittatinny Canoes** (800-356-2852), 102 Kittatinny Court, Dingmans Ferry. Guided canoe and kayak trips at five different points of the Delaware River. They also do tubing trips.

DOGSLEDDING Learn how to steer a sled pulled by Siberian and Alaskan huskies across snow-covered hills and paths (actually golf courses). The newest sport to arrive in northeast Pennsylvania teaches the exhilarating art of mushing between December and February. **Arctic Paws Dog Sled Tours** offers its very popular husky-led rides at the Inn at Pocono Manor (arcticpawsdogsledtours.com) between December and February, while **Skytop Lodge** (see *Lodging*) added dogsledding to its all-inclusive winter sports activities.

FISHING **Paradise Trout Preserve** (570-629-0422; paradisetrout.com), PA 191, Paradise, near Cresco. Home to the state's first fish hatchery, the property has two ponds stocked with bass and trout, plus picnic areas and a snack bar. No fishing license is required. There's a small entrance fee for adults.

Good fishing spots that require a license include **Tobyhanna Lake** in Tobyhanna State Park, a favorite for bass, brook trout, catfish, and perch. **Hickory Run State Park** has two stocked trout streams, and you'll find bass and trout in the nearby **Lehigh River.** In Jim Thorpe, you can fish for bass, pickerel, and trout in **Mauch Chunk Lake.**

GOLF **Split Rock Golf Club** (570-722-9901), Lake Harmony. This 27-hole public course at Split Rock Lodge has midsized greens, nice views, and a par of 72.

Taminent Golf Club (570-588-6652), Bushkill Falls Road, Taminent. Designed by Robert Trent Jones, this 18-hole mountaintop course has tree-lined fairways, undulating greens, and majestic views.

OUTSIDE THE LODGE AT CAMELBACK

DELAWARE WATER GAP

You don't need to be a geologist to appreciate this natural wonder. Millions of years ago, this area was a level plain; it is believed that over time moving water wore down and pushed through a weak spot in the mountain ridge to form a breathtaking gorge that separates two mountains, Minsi and Tammany. For a generation after the Civil War, the Delaware Water Gap was one of the top tourist destinations in existence (before the emergence of names such as Catskill, Disney, and Niagara). Today, it's a popular day trip for Pennsylvania and New Jersey residents, as well as outdoors types who come to kayak and canoe the river or hike the Appalachian Trail. The gorge is located at the southern edge of the Delaware Water Gap National Recreation Area (570-588-2451; nps.gov/dema), a national park that stretches along either side of the Delaware River from Delaware Water Gap north to Milford.

VIEWPOINT AT THE DELAWARE WATER GAP

The gap itself can be viewed from several parking overlooks around the town of Delaware Water Gap, including Point of Gap, off PA 611, where there's plenty of parking. There are nice views of the carved stone side of Mount Tammany (some say it looks like the profile of the Lenape Indian chief for whom the mountain is named). Another good place to stop is Kittatinny Point Visitor Center, just off I-80 across the state border in New Jersey, where you can pick up maps and speak to helpful park rangers. If you have the time and are in decent shape, consider hiking up Mount Tammany for gorgeous views of the entire gap and surrounding towns. From the New Jersey side, at the Dunnfield Creek parking area in Worthington State Forest, you can access a section of the Appalachian Trail that runs right over the top of Kittatinny Ridge to Sunfish Pond, a beautiful glacial lake surrounded by woods.

If you're short on time or aren't into hiking up a mountain, another good way to learn about the history of the area is via narrated trolley ride. **Water Gap Trolley** (570-476-9766; PA 611) runs tours four or five times a day from March–November. Guides are informative and funny, and the hour-long trip includes stops at several overlooks and historic buildings and tales about local celebrities such as Fred Waring, Jackie Gleason, and Mr. Green Jeans (of Captain Kangaroo fame).

WATER, WATER EVERYWHERE

Indoor water parks have taken on a whole new dimension in the past decade, and the Poconos area is home to some of the country's largest and best outfits. Big chains like Great Wolf Lodge and Kalahari operate resorts here, along with local stalwarts Camelback and Split Rock Resorts, which have transformed themselves from quaint lodges to year-round family entertainment centers. Here's a guide to navigating these giant amusement centers and finding the best fit:

Camelback Resort (855-515-1283; camelbackresort.com), 193 Resort Drive, Tannersville. This longtime ski resort added the 125,000-square-foot Aquatopia in 2015, with seven pools, 13 slides, a swim-up bar, and a very popular indoor/outdoor hot tub. It is the only indoor water park facility in the area that also operates as a ski resort, and it has a large outdoor adventure center with ziplining. Its 265 rooms are simple and modern, and some overlook the ski area. There's also a ground-floor arcade and many dining options all under one roof. Water park access is included in the room rate, but day passes are also usually available. The town of Tannersville is a mile away. In summer, Camelbeach is a hopping scene (see *Outdoor Activities*).

Great Wolf Lodge (800-768-9653; greatwolflodge.com/poconos), 1 Great Wolf Drive, Scotrun. This animal-themed resort draws families with young children, who like its whimsical suites with bunk beds and tented sleeping areas. The 79,000-square-foot water park has tandem tube slides, a wave pool, and a four-story treehouse fort. Even the spa is geared toward tots, with its ice cream theme, and costumed animal characters often roam the property. The water park is for resort guests only.

Kalahari Resort (570-580-6000; kalahariresorts.com/Pennsylvania), 250 Kalahari Boulevard, Pocono Manor. This African-themed resort caters to both families and couples, offering standard rooms, suites with bunk beds, and honeymoon suites with heart-shaped tubs. At 220,000 square feet, the water park is the largest in the Poconos (and maybe America). There are also adult and kid spas, mini-golf, escape rooms, and a seasonal outdoor pool. Limited day passes are available for the indoor park, and the park allows resort guests in an hour before it opens to the public.

HIKING A popular portion of the **Joseph McDade Recreational Trail** in the Delaware Water Gap National Recreation Area begins at the Hialeah Picnic Area north of Shawnee and follows the river for 5 scenic and flat miles north to Turn Farm. Along the way you'll pass **Smithfield Beach,** which offers roped-off swimming in the summer and stellar vistas of the river and mountain ridges. Biking and cross-country skiing are also allowed on this flat, well-maintained trail.

HORSEBACK RIDING **Bushkill Riding Stables** (570-588-5192; bushkillridingstable .com), 124 Golf Drive, East Stroudsburg. This facility in the Delaware Water Gap area offers 30- and 45-minute trail rides for all levels.

SKIING **Camelback** (570-629-1661; skicamelback.com), Camelback Road, Tannersville. This is the largest ski area in the region, with 38 trails, most of them easy and intermediate, plus 16 lifts, a terrain park, and tubing and half-pipe areas. There's a ski-in/ski-out restaurant at the base of the mountain; there's also a restaurant at the summit. It's part of a big resort that includes indoor and outdoor water parks. Lift ticket day passes start at $55.

Split Rock Resort (570-722-9111; splitrockresort.com), 428 Moseywood Road, Lake Harmony. This long-running lodge and former hunting retreat sits beside pretty Lake Harmony. Its water park, H2Oooohh!, is about a mile away in a newer resort complex. At 53,000 square feet, it's the smallest water park of the bunch, with three slides, a wave pool, and a play structure, and it only operates full time in the summer. It is open to the public and not included in the resort rate. Resort rooms are closest to the water park; lodge rooms are in the original inn closer to the lake.

AQUATOPIA INDOOR WATER PARK AT CAMELBACK LODGE

Jack Frost Big Boulder (570-443-8425; jfbb.com), 357 Big Boulder Drive, Lake Harmony. Known for its challenging terrain, Jack Frost has 20 trails, 12 lifts, and a 600-foot vertical drop. It shares facilities with nearby Big Boulder, which has 15 trails and a popular tubing park, allowing you to hit both areas on the same day on one ticket.

Shawnee Mountain (570-421-7231; shawneemt.com), Hollow Road, Shawnee. This family-friendly ski area is at the southernmost point of the Poconos region, with 23 trails for all levels, terrain and tubing parks, and a half-pipe area.

WHITE-WATER RAFTING The **Lehigh River** offers Class III white-water rafting, and many outfitters in the area run regular trips during summer and during spring and fall dam release weekends (see also *Green Space*.) Many also offer kayaking packages, bike rentals, and shuttles.

Pocono Whitewater Rafting (570-325-3655; 800-944-8392), 1519 PA 903, also known as Lehigh Gorge Outpost, runs rafting trips for all levels, plus kayaking, paintball, bike rentals, and shuttles to Lehigh Gorge. **Jim Thorpe River Adventures** (800-424-7238; www .jtraft.com), 1 Adventure Lane, off PA 903, offers guided rafting trips and bike rentals.

✳ Lodging

RESORTS **Skytop Lodge** (570-595-7401; 800-617-2389; skytop.com), PA 390, Skytop, 3 miles north of Canadensis. Built in the 1920s as a members-only hunting lodge, this secluded mountaintop resort ranks among the best all-inclusive destinations in the area. Sprawled on 5,500 acres of woods, streams, meadows, lakes, and waterfalls, it has an air of country elegance and more activities than you can possibly imagine: tennis, swimming, nighttime deer watching, stargazing, downhill skiing, fly-fishing, golf, massages, lawn bowling, and even high tea. You can stay in the original stone lodge, in a nearby modern 20-room inn, or in spacious cottages overlooking the stream, lodge, or golf course; meals are served in the lodge's grandiose dining room, a separate lake-view restaurant, or an English pub. $$$–$$$$.

INNS & GUEST HOUSES **Deer Head Inn** (570-424-2000; deerheadinn.com), 5 Main Street, Delaware Water Gap. Most people associate the Deer Head with terrific live jazz and don't realize there are eight comfortable rooms and suites upstairs. All rooms have private baths, crown molding, high ceilings, and top-of-the-line mattresses and linens; the suites have sitting areas. Ask about packages that include jazz and dinner for two (see *Entertainment*). $$–$$$.

Inn at Jim Thorpe (570-325-2599; innjt.com), 24 Broadway, Jim Thorpe. This historic hotel in the heart of downtown has beautiful wrought-iron balconies from which to take in all the action. The 34 rooms and nine suites are decorated in understated Victorian style and have private baths and wireless Internet access; some have fireplaces and Jacuzzi tubs. Rates include a voucher for the adjacent Broadway Grille. They also offer biking and rafting packages that include all equipment and bike shuttles to Lehigh Gorge. $$–$$$.

⚥ **Stroudsmoor Country Inn** (570-421-6431; stroudsmoor.com), Stroudsmoor Road, Stroudsburg. Just five minutes from town, it's surrounded by woodlands and feels like a quiet country getaway. The main house has 15 small and attractive rooms and junior suites. Newer suites with balconies overlooking the forest are just across the way, and there are also small cottages with front porches overlooking an outdoor pool. The rates include a full breakfast at the inn's restaurant. This is a popular spot for destination weddings, and sometimes it hosts several over a single weekend. $$–$$$.

BED & BREAKFASTS ⚘ **Bischwind** (570-472-3820; bischwind.com), 1 Coach Road, Bear Creek. Located just outside Wilkes-Barre and about a 20-minute drive from many western Pocono Mountains attractions, this eight-room hunting lodge turned B&B is a must for history buffs. A giant carved wooden bear greets you near the entrance in honor of one-time guest Theodore Roosevelt. Handsome and ornate is the best way to describe the living and dining areas, which are decorated with stuffed deer heads, rich red leather chairs, large fireplaces, and wood floors. The rooms have the same grand feel as the common areas but come with modern upgrades such as TVs, whirlpool tubs, and wireless Internet access; the two-room Teddy Roosevelt Suite is a favorite. Bear Creek is a stone's throw from the inn, and an exquisitely peaceful hour-long hiking trail loops around the lake. Other nice touches include an outdoor swimming pool and a lavish breakfast of poached salmon or filet mignon, sautéed potatoes, eggs, and cheesecake (though guests may opt for a lighter continental breakfast). $$$.

Gatehouse Country Inn (570-420-4553; gatehousecountry inn.com), River Road, Shawnee. Originally built circa 1900 as a stable and carriage house, the Gatehouse was turned into a summer home by bandleader and Pennsylvania native Fred Waring in the 1950s. Gordon and Cindy Way opened it as a B&B in 2001, offering three second-floor rooms with private baths and sitting areas. The upstairs game room, where Waring is believed to have entertained friends such as Jackie Gleason and Dwight Eisenhower, features comfy chairs, games, and the original pool table. Guests also have access to a back courtyard flanked by an old-fashioned icehouse, which the Ways have turned into a small antiques store. No children under 12. $$$.

Hill Home Forge (570-325-0216; hillhomeforge.com), 10 Flagstaff Road, Jim Thorpe. Eileen East runs this artistic mountain retreat about 2.5 miles west of town. The three rooms are spacious, quiet, and tastefully decorated. The Woodland Suite is large enough for three adults and one child. Breakfast is especially good; apple-stuffed French toast is a specialty. $$$.

Stony Brook Inn (570-424-1100; 888-424-5240; stonybrookinn.com), P.O. Box 240, River Road, Shawnee. Pete and Roseann Ferguson are the gregarious owners of this cozy 1850s inn next to the Shawnee Playhouse. The four themed rooms (Country Bear, Rose, Oak, and the Bridal Suite) have private baths, TVs, and nice individual touches such as clawfoot tubs or Victorian chaise lounges. There's also a swimming pool with a large patio out back. The Delaware River and access to the McDade Trail are two blocks away. $$–$$$.

CAMPGROUNDS & COTTAGES

⚓ 🏕 **Delaware Water Gap KOA** (570-223-8000; 800-562-0375; www.delaware watergapkoa.com), 233 Hollow Road, East Stroudsburg. Located just north of Shawnee a few miles off River Road, this year-round campground has over 140 tent sites, primitive and with hook-ups, plus five cabins and dozens of RV sites. Activities include miniature train rides, mini-golf, volleyball, horseshoes, and hayrides. Tent sites $; cabins $$.

RELAXING BY THE LAKE IS A POCONOS RITUAL

Mauch Chunk Lake County Park (570-325-3669), Jim Thorpe. Open mid-April–October. About 4 miles from downtown, this county park has more than 100 primitive tent sites and 12 two-room cabins with electricity. Many people love it for its access to 4-acre Mauch Chunk Lake and the Switchback Railroad Rail Trail, which crosses through the park. $–$$.

Magnolia Streamside Resort (570-595-2489; magnoliastreamside.com), 2518 PA 390 North, Canadensis. Remodeled in 2017, it's ideal for families with children, with a swimming pool and a pond with a slide and watercraft; a lovely stream runs right through the property. The eight rustic cottages sleep four to eight and have wraparound decks, full kitchens, and modern living rooms with fireplaces and TVs. Two suites above the main lodge have king beds, futons, gas fireplaces, and small refrigerators. Water comes from a local stream; it's a good idea to bring your own for cooking and drinking purposes. Cottages $$$. Suites $$.

Dingmans Campground (570-828-1551), 1006 US 209, Dingmans Ferry. Its primo riverfront location is what most campers love best about this rustic property about 10 miles north of Delaware Water Gap. Choose from 133 sites; the ones on the river go fast. $.

✳ Where to Eat

DINING OUT **Moya** (570-325-8957; jimthorpemoya.com), Race Street, Jim Thorpe. Closed Tuesdays and Wednesdays in fall and winter. Local B&B owners will (rightly) steer you toward this elegant restaurant at the center of town. Chef Heriberto Yunda infuses the cuisine with influences from his native Ecuador, such as corn and feta salad, pork tenderloin with balsamic-vinegar chutney, and shrimp with red curry, ginger, and coconut. His wife, Stephanie Yerme, is an artist whose colorful paintings brighten the walls. Beer and wine. $$.

EATING OUT **Barley Creek Brewing Company** (570-839-9678), 1774 Sullivan Trail, Tannersville. Lunch and dinner daily. Part Ye Olde Pub and part timbered ski lodge, this microbrewery near Camelback Resort is known for its handmade ales and tasty pub grub. Try the fish-and-chips or special Reuben of the day. If you happen to be here for lunch, you can join the free brewery tours that begin at 12:30 every day. $$–$$$.

⅃ ⌇ **The Gem and Keystone** (570-424-0990), River Road, Shawnee. The menu complements the local handcrafted beers on tap: cheddar ale dip with soft pretzels, baby back ribs, hand-cut rib eye steak, fish-and-chips, and vegetarian or beef chili. Many of the ingredients are locally sourced. In summer you can dine on a deck overlooking a pretty stream.

Weekday happy hours offer beer discounts and $5 appetizer specials. $$.

⅃ ⌇ **Jubilee Restaurant** (570-646-2377), PA 940, Pocono Pines. Breakfast, lunch, and dinner daily. A local favorite known for its large portions, juicy burgers, and friendly service. Breakfasts are legendary; try the chef's free-for-all Pocono Sampler or any of the omelets. After your meal, you can join in games of billiards, darts, and TV sports watching in the adjacent pub. $–$$.

Village Farmer and Bakery (570-476-9440; villagefarmerbakery.com), 52 Broad Street, Delaware Water Gap. Open daily at 8 a.m. This bakery doesn't have an address on its business card; it just describes its location as between the town's two traffic lights. It's tough to miss—just look for the giant red-lettered sign that says APPLE PIE AND A HOT DOG FOR JUST $1.49. If that sweet deal doesn't interest you, try any of the doughnuts, cookies, brownies, or other desserts that were made that day. They also sell whole pies—apple is the specialty, but they usually have at least a dozen other kinds.

JIM THORPE

Bear Appetit (570-732-4700), 29 Broadway. New York–style deli fare without the Manhattan prices. Stop here for a hearty breakfast before a day of hiking or cycling. $.

Broadway Grille & Pub (570-732-4343), 24 Broadway. Owned by the adjacent Inn at Jim Thorpe, this popular hangout serves inventive global fare such as fried cheese curd with Yuengling-infused honey, steak frites, miso cod, and shrimp po'boys. There's breakfast too. $$.

BYO Where to buy wine in the southern Pocono Mountains region:

You'll find **Wine & Spirits** stores in the Pocono Village Mall (570-839-9586), 87 PA 940, Mount Pocono; in the **Blakeslee Corners Shopping Plaza**

(570-646-8069), PA 115/PA 940; and in downtown **Stroudsburg** (570-424-3943), 761 Main Street.

✳ Entertainment

MUSIC **Deer Head Inn** (570-424-2000; deerheadinn.com), 5 Main Street, Delaware Water Gap. Dinner and live performances Wednesday–Sunday. Enjoy terrific live jazz and blues in one of the oldest jazz bars in the country.

Sarah Street Grill (570-424-9120; sarahstreetgrill.com), 550 Quaker Alley, Stroudsburg. One of the best places around to hear live original music. Wednesday open-mic nights are popular. For sports fans, there are 25 TVs, plus a pool table and a daily happy hour with food and drink deals.

Penn's Peak (610-826-9000; 866-605-7325; pennspeak.com), 325 Maury Road, Jim Thorpe. This large venue attracts a mix of country and western bands, tribute bands, and veteran acts like Willie Nelson and the Bay City Rollers. A dance floor, restaurant, and bar are on the premises, as well as a deck with views that stretch for 50 miles.

MOVIES **Pocono Cinema and Cultural Center** (570-421-6684; pococinema.org), 88 South Courtland Street, East Stroudsburg. This century-old theater was restored in the late 1990s and features four screens showing mainstream and independent films. An adjacent café serves specialty coffees, ice cream, and popcorn with real butter. It also runs a cinema book club and free family movies once a month.

Casino Theatre and Village Malt Shoppe (570-839-7831; casinotheatre .net), 1403 Pocono Boulevard (PA 611), Mount Pocono. Landmark two-screen theater shows first-run films and also has mini-golf, an arcade, and an ice cream parlor. It's a favorite evening destination for summer vacationers from all over the area. There are dinner specials on Monday and Tuesday, and they'll deliver the food on special trays right to your seats.

THEATER **Shawnee Playhouse** (570-421-5093; theshawneeplayhouse.com), River Road, Shawnee. This small, 200-seat theater stages musicals, comedies, and plays year-round, plus kids' shows and *The Nutcracker Ballet* in December.

✳ Selective Shopping

Crossing Premium Outlets (570-629-4650), PA 611 at I-80, Tannersville. This eight-building complex features more than 100 factory outlet stores (from Timberland and Reebok to Ann Taylor and Banana Republic) and draws huge weekend crowds.

Carroll & Carroll Booksellers (570-420-1516), 740 Main Street, Stroudsburg. Well-stocked and friendly store with a mix of new and used books and many first and rare editions.

Country Junction (610-377-5050; countryjunction.com), 6565 Interchange Road, Lehighton. More than a general store, this huge and kitschy retail complex sells everything from hand tools and garden supplies to local honey and ice cream. Plus, there's a petting zoo, escape room, and laser tag.

Holley Ross Pottery (570-676-3248; holleyross.com), PA 191, LaAnna. Open daily from May–mid-December. Surrounded by a pretty nature park above Cresco, this factory outlet sells Fiesta dinnerware, Robinson Ransbottom pottery, and other home décor items at steep discounts. They also make their own ceramic vases, centerpieces, and candle holders; free pottery demonstrations are given weekdays at 11 a.m. Picnic tables and nature trails are on the property, making it very easy to pass an afternoon here.

Olde Engine Works Marketplace (570-421-4340; oldeengineworks.com), 62

North Third Street, Stroudsburg. Open daily. This 1902 brick machine shop once made steam-powered winches used to pull nets from shrimp boats; today it's an antiques and collectibles co-op with 125 vendors. The ever-changing inventory ranges from circa-1900 toy pianos and Depression-era glass to Industrial Age spools and modern furniture.

Pocono Bazaar Flea Market (570-223-8640; poconobazaar.com), US 209, Marshalls Creek. Open Saturday and Sunday. A people-watcher's paradise with hundreds of indoor and outdoor stands selling antiques, produce, baked goods, miracle gadgets, rock 'n' roll T-shirts, housewares, and more. A food court offers a variety of casual eats—from pickles and funnel cakes to fried chicken and collard greens.

✳ Special Events

June: **Pocono 500 Nextel Cup Race** (first weekend), Pocono Raceway—a hugely popular event that draws NASCAR superstars to compete, plus 100,000 fans who come to watch them. There's a similar race in late July.

September: **Pocono Garlic and Harvest Festival** (Labor Day weekend), Shawnee Mountain Ski Area—this creative and fun event celebrates the region's love affair with the pungent bulb. Expect plenty of garlic-laced food, crafts, and entertainment by the Garlic-Eating Tuba Troubadours. Also in September is the **Celebration of the Arts Jazz Festival** (weekend after Labor Day), a nationally recognized four-day event that unites jazz musicians, chefs, and artists on outdoor stages throughout Delaware Water Gap.

October: **Stroudsburg Halloween Parade** (last weekend), Stroudsburg—Costumed kids, adults, and even dogs take over Main Street beginning at noon and march to Courthouse Square for more fun and games.

THE POCONO MOUNTAINS NORTH

GUIDANCE For a town map and other information on Milford and its outlying areas, visit the **Pike County Chamber of Commerce** (570-296-8700), 201 Broad Street, Milford. In Honesdale, the **Wayne County Visitor Center** (570-253-1960), 32 Commercial Street, has local maps and information; it's also the place to buy tickets for the adjacent Stourbridge Railway Excursions. A great starting point is the **Pocono Mountains Visitor Center** (570-226-3191) in Lake Wallenpaupack, just below the dam overlook on US 6/PA 507. It has helpful staffers, restrooms, and a deck out back overlooking the lake. There's also access to a short trail running along the edge of the lake.

GETTING THERE *By air:* **Newark International** (800-397-4636) is about an hour's drive from Milford. Alternatives include **Scranton/Wilkes-Barre Airport** in Avoca (877-235-9287) and **Lehigh Valley International** in Allentown (888-359-5842).

By car: From the Pennsylvania Turnpike: I-81 to I-84 east. From New York: I-80 west to Exit 34B (Sparta); then follow PA 15/US 206 north to Milford. Follow US 6 west to Hawley and Honesdale.

By train: **Metro-North** line from Manhattan to Port Jervis, New Jersey, across the river from Milford.

By bus: **Short Line** (800-631-8405; www.coachusa.com) runs daily bus service between New York's Port Authority and Milford, Hawley, and Honesdale.

GETTING AROUND While Hawley, Honesdale, and Milford are all pleasant walking towns, you'll need a car to get around up here.

WHEN TO GO If you don't ski, summer and fall are the best times to visit the northern Pocono Mountains. Many outdoor (and some indoor) attractions don't even open their doors until Memorial Day and stay open through October.

✻ Villages

Hawley. Named for the first president of the Pennsylvania Coal Company, this town of 1,300 was a thriving center for anthracite coal distribution in the mid-1800s. The coal and lumber industries were replaced by fine cut glass and silk and textile mills in the 1920s.

Also changing Hawley's identity in the 1920s was the Pennsylvania Power and Light Company's decision to dam a nearby creek to create hydroelectric power. This created Lake Wallenpaupack, the state's third-largest man-made lake. The town became known as a recreational destination for families from Pennsylvania, New Jersey, and New York, a reputation it still has today. Hawley is home to one of the state's top family resorts, Woodloch, as well as many well-regarded antiques shops and several upscale inns and mom-and-pop lakefront motels.

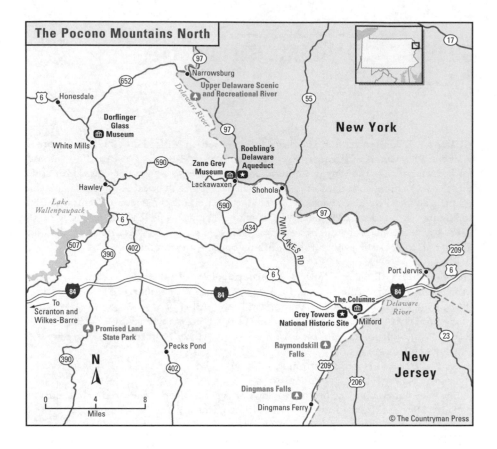

The Pocono Mountains North

Honesdale. Like Hawley, its neighbor to the north, Honesdale was named for a railroad VIP: Philip Hone, president of the Delaware and Hudson Canal Company and former mayor of New York City. It is the largest municipality in Wayne County and home to the Stourbridge Lion, the first steam locomotive to run on rails in the United States; rides on a full-scale replica run on a regular basis from the original station. Honesdale doesn't have many hotels or inns, but it makes a pleasant day trip from Hawley or Scranton. Its main street is a treasure trove of Victorian architecture and antiques shops. Detour to Church Street and you'll find many lovely historic churches that date to 1860. On its outskirts are a commercial district and the Dorflinger Glass Museum and Dorflinger-Suydam Wildlife Sanctuary.

Lackawaxen. This quiet village is named after the river that flows through it. It was once a major center for bluestone quarrying and is home to Roebling Bridge, the oldest existing wire suspension bridge in the country. Zane Grey lived here between 1905 and 1918 and wrote several novels from his home overlooking the river, now a museum run by the National Park Service. It's also a great place to spot eagles in January and February; there is an observation platform next to Roebling Bridge.

Milford. This sophisticated hamlet has a prime location along the Delaware River where Pennsylvania, New York, and New Jersey intersect. A few years ago, *New York* magazine dubbed it the New Hamptons, stemming from the influx of New Yorkers who have bought second homes here or use its upscale hotels and country inns for frequent getaways. Settled in 1796 and used as a setting in some of the earliest silent movies starring Mary Pickford and Lillian Gish, Milford has art galleries, antiques shops, preserved Victorian-era homes, upscale restaurants and cafés, and a bucolic get-away-from-it-all setting. You will also find Grey Towers, a French chateau–style estate that belonged to a leader of the US conservation movement, and a fascinating little museum, the Columns, which houses a piece of American history: the flag that cushioned Abraham Lincoln's head after he was shot at Ford's Theatre.

✳ To See

HISTORIC SITES **Grey Towers National Historic Site** (570-296-9630; greytowers .org), 122 Old Owego Turnpike, Milford. Grounds open daily; mansion tours Thursday–Monday from Memorial Day–October; small fee charged. Gifford Pinchot, a former governor of Pennsylvania and the founder and first chief of the US Forest Service, used this stunning French chateau–style home a mile outside of town as a summer retreat. If you have the time, join one of the hour-long tours of this fascinating home that show-cases Pinchot's quirky and conservation-conscious ways. Fun items on display include artifacts collected in his travels, such as a pair of terra-cotta camels from China's Tang dynasty and the family's infamous Finger Bowl, an outdoor dining table with a pool in the center that required guests to pass the salt by floating it to the recipient in a wooden bowl. The tour isn't for small children, but they will enjoy the broad sloping grounds, which include paved paths and a moat full of koi.

The Columns (570-296-8126; pikehistorical.org), 608 Broad Street, Milford. Open April–November; small fee charged. The marquee exhibit in this grand old building is the Lincoln flag, a bloodstained American flag that was used to cradle the president's head after he was shot at Ford's Theatre. It found its way to Milford via the daugh-ter of the stage manager who took the flag home that tragic night. She inherited it before moving to the area in 1888, then passed it on to her son, who donated it the county historical society. Members of the Pike County Historical Society have built an interesting little museum around the bloody flag, with exhibits on local history, a vintage clothing collection that includes two fedoras owned by William Jennings Bryan, and a Hiawatha stagecoach from the mid-1800s.

Zane Grey Museum (570-685-4871), 135 Scenic Drive, Lackawaxen. Open daily in summer and weekends in October; free. The prolific Western author wrote his first novel, *The Heritage of the Des-ert*, as well as *Riders of the Purple Sage,* in this decidedly eastern riverfront retreat near Roebling Bridge. It was turned into a museum in the 1970s and purchased by the National Park Service in 1989; Grey and his wife, Dollie, are buried nearby. Rangers lead 20-minute tours through Grey's old study, which includes original manuscripts and the Morris chair where he did much of his writing. There's also a gift shop that sells a wide selection of his

ZANE GREY'S FORMER HOME ON THE DELAWARE RIVER

SCRANTON & WILKES-BARRE

About 30 minutes apart, these are the two of the largest cities around, though they are not considered part of the Pocono Mountains. Both towns served as industrial centers for Pennsylvania's anthracite coal mining industry and offer live theater, art galleries, shopping, and nightlife options.

Scranton, with a population of 77,000, is the bigger of the two and about a 45-minute drive from Hawley in the northern Pocono Mountains. Its baseball team, the Scranton/Wilkes-Barre RailRiders, is a Triple-A affiliate of the New York Yankees; you can catch a game at PNC Field (570-969-2255), 235 Montage Mountain Road, Moosic. In recent years, Scranton has become famous as the main setting of *The Office*, the popular TV show starring Steve Carell. Steamtown mall, Lake Scranton, and the now-closed Farley's restaurant were a few of the existing sites mentioned on the NBC comedy. Two of the city's marquee attractions are the Lackawanna County Coal Mine Tour (see *Coal Mining* on page 258) and Steamtown National Historic Site (570-340-5200; www.nps.gov/stea), 150 South Washington Avenue, a huge and fascinating complex of authentic standard-gauge steam locomotives, freight and passenger cars, and historic exhibits located on an old railway yard; ask about their regular train excursions. Across the parking lot from Steamtown is the Electric City Trolley Museum (570-963-6590; ectma.org), home to a kid-friendly collection of authentic streetcars, hands-on displays that let you steer model trolleys and ring up fares, and exhibits that chronicle the history of the early electric trolley industry. Both Steamtown and the trolley museum are an easy walk to Steamtown Mall's shops and restaurants. For information on the Scranton area, contact the Lackawanna County Convention and Visitor Bureau (800-229-3526; visitnepa.org).

Between Scranton and Wilkes-Barre is the quaint town of Old Forge, which rightly bills itself as the Pizza Capital of the World. Old-fashioned Italian gravy joints line the sleepy main street. A favorite is Arcaro and Genell (570-457-5555; 433 South Main Street), whose rectangular pizza has been featured in *USA Today*. It really is that good.

Thirty minutes south of Scranton, Wilkes-Barre is home to five colleges, a population of 43,000, and more than 200 historic buildings, including a 1909 Beaux Arts courthouse that is the city's pride and joy. You'll also find Mohegan Sun Pocono (570-831-2100; mohegansunpocono

writings. Every July, the museum holds a Zane Grey Festival that celebrates the writer's link to the area.

Dorflinger Glass Museum (570-253-1185; dorflinger.org), 55 Suydam Drive, Honesdale. Open Wednesday–Sunday from mid-May–October, weekends in November; small fee charged. In the late 1800s and early 1900s, the factory that operated here produced some of the finest glass in the world and counted two presidents (Lincoln and Wilson) among its clientele. All sorts of cut, enameled, etched, and gilded glass are displayed among period antiques and artifacts from the glass factory. The gift shop sells phenomenal Christmas ornaments, as well as paperweights, jewelry, and a wide assortment of glassware. The museum is surrounded by the Dorflinger-Suydam Wildlife Sanctuary (see *Green Space*).

✷ To Do

Roebling's Delaware Aqueduct (570-729-7134) in Lackawaxen is the oldest existing wire suspension bridge in the country; it runs 535 feet from Minisink Ford, New York, to Lackawaxen, and is known locally as Roebling Bridge. Begun in 1847 as one of four

STEAMTOWN NATIONAL HISTORIC SITE IS ONE OF SCRANTON'S TOP ATTRACTIONS

.com; 1280 PA 315), one of a handful of racino complexes featuring slot machines and harness racing; the **Frederick Stegmaier Mansion** (570-823-9372; stegmaiermansion.com), an ornate 1870s mansion and hotel at 304 South Franklin Street; and **Seven Tubs Nature Area** (570-675-1312; 900 Bear Creek Boulevard), a peaceful, Walden-like nature park centered around a stream and seven tub-shaped glacial potholes. For more information about the area, contact the **Luzerne County Convention and Visitor Bureau** (888-905-2872; visitluzernecounty.com).

suspension aqueducts on the Delaware and Hudson Canal, it was designed by John A. Roebling, the future engineer of New York's Brooklyn Bridge. Its suspension design allowed more room for ice floes and river traffic than conventional bridges, and it was considered a huge time-saving success during its 50 years of operation. There is a small parking lot and information kiosks on the Pennsylvania side, and a pedestrian walkway affords terrific views of the river.

FOR FAMILIES ✺ **Claws 'N' Paws Wild Animal Park** (570-698-6154; clawsnpaws.com), PA 590, Hamlin. Open daily from May–October; admission fee charged. This private zoo is home to more than 120 species of animals, including a white tiger, snow leopard, and the usual allotment of monkeys, reptiles, and meerkats. There are lots of hands-on activities that let kids feed parrots and giraffes, mingle with turtles, and participate in a fossil dig.

Stourbridge Railway (570-470-2697; thestourbridgeline.net), 303 Commercial Street, Honesdale. On August 8, 1829, the Delaware & Hudson Railroad launched the first commercial locomotive on rails in the Western Hemisphere. Diesel passenger trains still leave from this spot on themed excursions from June to mid-September. Check the website for a schedule. They also run kid-friendly "Ice Cream Express" rides in summer.

COAL MINING

Northeast Pennsylvania was once a huge coal mining center that supplied nearly 80 percent of the country. The towns of Hawley and Honesdale were major distribution centers that funneled the coal to New York via boat or railroad. The areas around Scranton and Wilkes-Barre were among the few places in the world that harbored anthracite, or hard coal, beneath their surfaces. There are no remaining active deep mines left, but a few attractions allow you to get an up-close understanding of this once-mighty industry.

Lackawanna Coal Mine Tour (570-963-6463), McDade Park, Scranton. Open daily from April–November, except Easter and Thanksgiving; admission fee charged. Informative hour-long tours are led by former mine workers and take you via a yellow transport car 300 feet down into an underground city of offices, stables, and hundreds of rooms; be prepared to walk about 0.25 mile. Before or after your tour, stop by the adjacent **Pennsylvania Anthracite Heritage Museum** (570-963-4804) to round out your visit.

No. 9 Coal Mine and Museum (570-645-7074; no9mine.com), 9 Dock Street, Lansford. Open Wednesday–Sunday for museum and mine tours. About 10 miles southwest of Jim Thorpe, this deep mine produced coal for more than a century before closing in 1972. It reopened as a tourist attraction in the 1990s, offering hour-long underground tours by enthusiastic guides. The museum displays include an armored coal car and the mine's original elevator shaft.

Eckley Miners' Village Museum (570-636-2070; eckleyminersvillagemuseum.com), Freeland. Open daily except some holidays; small fee charged. About 30 minutes from either Jim Thorpe or Wilkes-Barre, Eckley is an authentic anthracite coal mining "patch town" and is worth the effort it takes to get here. The coal operation closed in 1971, but the town was saved from demolition by the 1970 Sean Connery film, *The Molly Maguires*, which filmed many scenes here and in Jim Thorpe; several movie props, such as a general store and a miniature coal breaker, remain. Exhibits in the visitor center demonstrate the dangers, misery, and class divisions endured by miners and their families; check these out and then stroll down the main street and see how the workers' homes were ranked by skill level and religion. About 50 descendants of the miners, mostly widows and offspring, still live in many of the homes. Guided tours are offered daily and included in the admission fee. Bring a map and detailed directions; this is definitely off the beaten path.

COAL MINING WAS ONCE A HUGE INDUSTRY IN NORTHEASTERN PENNSYLVANIA

SCENIC DRIVES For breathtaking scenery, head to NY 97, at the intersection of US 6 and US 209 in Port Jervis, and follow it north a few miles to the hamlet of **Sparrow Bush**. Continue on 97 to a dramatic section of the road known as **Hawk's Nest**, a stunning and winding road perched on rocky cliffs high above the Delaware that has been featured in many car commercials. Continue on to Barryville, New York, where you can cross back over the river to Pennsylvania and follow Twin Lakes Road to US 6 back to Milford.

✱ Green Space

Promised Land State Park (570-676-3428), PA 390, Promised Land Village. The early settlers who named the area mistakenly thought it would be great for farming, but once you see the place you'll realize the name isn't entirely off base. Located a few miles south of Lake Wallenpaupack, it has two large swimming and boating lakes with sand beaches, several camping areas, and some of the best hiking and cross-country ski trails in the region. Also within the park is **Bruce Lake Natural Area,** a 2,700-acre natural site with two lakes. The loop around Conservation Island is a popular easy trail; serious hikers can take the Bruce Lake Loop through hemlock and oak forest to a glacial lake, about 9.5 miles round-trip.

    Dorflinger-Suydam Wildlife Sanctuary (570-253-1185; dorflinger.org), White Mills. Acres of scenic forest and meadows surround the Dorflinger Glass Museum (see *Museums*). No picnicking or pets are allowed, but visitors may wander along any of the easy nature trails (pick up a map at the kiosk on the way in). The Wildflower Amphitheatre is the site of regular summer concerts and an annual wildflower festival.

WATERFALLS The Pocono Mountains region has more than two dozen named waterfalls. Here are a few favorites. There is no charge to see them. Swimming is prohibited.

    Dingmans Falls (570-828-7802), Johnny Bee Road, near the junction of US 209 and PA 739. Take the raised boardwalk trail past a slender but pretty cascade of water, then continue another 0.5 mile through a hemlock ravine to the base of the steep and stunning Dingmans Falls.

    Raymondskill Falls, Raymondskill Falls Road, off US 209. These exquisite cascades are only 3 miles south of Milford, and some feel that they are the state's most splendid (at 165 feet, they are definitely the highest). It's a very short hike to the Upper Falls, but the best views can be found at the Middle Falls, which require a steep 0.5-mile hike down uneven stairs.

    Shohola Falls, off US 6 between Milford and Hawley. Located on state game lands in the Shohola Recreation Area, these pretty falls are challenging to find. Look for the two parking lots on either side of a concrete bridge. It's a short but very steep walk past a scenic dammed lake to the falls.

✱ Outdoor Activities

BICYCLING Bicycling along the **Lackawaxen River** affords level terrain and a pretty river view on the lightly traveled road known as "The Towpath." **Lackawanna State Park** has 15 miles of singletrack trails with varying levels difficulty. **Sawmill Cycles** (570-352-3444; sawmillcycles.com) in Honesdale rents bikes (as well as kayaks, paddleboards and snowshoes) for a daily rate and is a good source of information for trails in the area.

VIEW OF LAKE WALLENPAUPACK

BOAT EXCURSIONS/RENTALS In **Promised Land State Park** (see *Green Space*), a boat concession off PA 390 (570-676-4117) offers rowboat, canoe, and kayak rentals. Electric motors are also available.

On the south end of Lake Wallenpaupack, **Pocono Action Sports Marina** (570-857-0779; poconoactionsports.com) rents powerboats, sailboats, canoes, paddleboards, and Jet Skis.

Wallenpaupack Scenic Boat Tour (717-226-6211; wallenpaupackboattour.com), near the observation dike on US 6, offers 50-minute cruises by patio boat daily mid-June–August and weekends in spring and fall.

Kittatiny Canoes (800-356-2852; kittatiny.com) has seven locations in the Poconos area, including Dingmans Ferry and Milford. It leads daily canoe, kayak, and tube trips on the Delaware River in season, and also offers paintball and dual racing ziplines.

FISHING The **Lackawaxen River** is stocked with rainbow, brook, and brown trout in the spring and fall. For condition updates and supplies, visit or call **Angler's Roost Sporting Goods** (570-685-2010; tworiverjunction.net), 106 Scenic Drive, Lackawaxen. They also run canoe and rafting trips for small and large groups.

Rivers Outdoor Adventures (570-943-3151; riversflyfishing.com) runs trips to the Upper Delaware River, where smallmouth bass, trout, shad, and walleye are popular catches. Fishing this region requires either a New York or a Pennsylvania license.

GOLF Cliff Park Golf Course (570-296-6491; cliffparkgolf.com), 155 Cliff Park Drive, Milford. The country's second-oldest golf course has nine challenging holes stretching over 3,153 yards.

Country Club at Woodloch Springs (570-685-8075), 1 Woodloch Drive, Hawley. Serious golfers love this challenging par-72, 18-hole course, though it's accessible only to guests of nearby Woodloch Pines and a few other resorts in the area.

Cricket Hill Golf Club (570-226-4366), US 6, Hawley. More than 10 ponds dot this 18-hole public course with tees to 5,790 yards.

HIKING **Promised Land State Park** has some of the region's best hiking trails, from easy to strenuous (see *Green Space*). In Milford, folks like to hike up to the **Knob,** an overlook with views of the entire town and surrounding valley. Access it via the Mott Street Bridge off Harford Street. For light exercise, there's the **Bingham Park River Walk** in Hawley.

HORSEBACK RIDING **Malibu Dude Ranch** (570-296-7281; malibududeranch.com) in Milford offers guided day trips through the countryside and pony rides for children.

SKIING For a comprehensive list of ski resorts in the region, contact the **Pocono Mountains Visitors Bureau** (570-421-5791; poconomountains.com).

Elk Mountain Ski Resort (570-679-4400; elkskier.com), Union Dale, north of Scranton. One of the largest ski areas in northeast Pennsylvania, with 27 trails and a terrain park on the east side of the mountain.

Ski Big Bear at Masthope (570-685-1400; www.ski-bigbear.com), 196 Karl Hope Road, Lackawaxen. This small facility near the New York border caters to families and groups. It has 18 trails, three lifts, snow tubing, and a terrain park. There's also a ski school for first-timers and kids.

SWIMMING **Lake Wallenpaupack** has a public beach where swimming is allowed; it's just south of the visitor center off US 6/PA 507; you can also swim at designated spots by the lakes in Promised Land State Park. In Milford, a favorite spot is **Milford Beach** (570-729-7134), a former farm overlooking the Delaware River that was spruced up by the National Park Service. There's no sand, but you will find lifeguards (in summer), comfort stations, and picnic areas. There's a small fee to park.

WALKING An easy lakefront walking trail can be accessed at the **Wallenpaupack Environmental Learning Center** (877-775-5253; 126 Lamberton Lane) or the **Lake Wallenpaupack Visitor Center** (570-226-2141) on US 6. It's about 1.5 miles long and leads to a waterfront overlook. Pick up a trail map at the visitor center.

✳ Lodging

BED & BREAKFASTS **Harrington House** (888-272-1234; harringtonhousemilford .com), 208 West Harford Road, Milford. Formerly the Hattree Inn, this popular B&B is pet friendly and within walking distance of downtown Milford. The four rooms with private baths are spacious and elegantly furnished with unique touches such as working fireplaces, Oriental rugs, and exposed brick walls.

Owner Adriane Wendell is a gracious and accommodating host (along with her dog, Spencer) who whips up gourmet breakfasts such as pumpkin spice waffles and herb-cheese soufflés. $$.

Roebling Inn (570-685-7900; roeblinginn.com), 155 Scenic Drive, Lackawaxen. This stately home two doors down from the Zane Grey Museum is nestled in an extraordinary setting overlooking the Lackawaxen River. Each of the five rooms has a private bath, TV, and queen bed; the corner rooms facing the river are especially nice and have fireplaces. A cute one-bedroom cottage (with a two-night minimum) sleeps three and allows children under 12. $$–$$$.

INNS & RESORTS

MILFORD

Hotel Fauchère (570-409-1212; hotelfauchere.com), 401 Broad Street. Step through the doors of this sophisticated 19th-century inn and you might think you've been transported to a boutique hotel in SoHo. New Yorkers love it here, perhaps because of its connection to the famous Delmonico's Restaurant (see *Dining Out*) or because owner Sean Strub is a tireless promoter of Milford's beauty and amenities. Luxuries abound: Kiehl's bath products, luxury Frette linens, heated bathroom floors and towel racks, and complimentary wine. The two second-floor rooms with large balconies are especially nice. Rates include breakfast and usually drop from November–April. $$$–$$$$.

Laurel Villa Inn (570-296-9940; laurelvilla.com), 210 Second Street, Milford. Ten quaint rooms and suites in a spacious 19th-century home near the center of town. An on-premises restaurant serves classic American meals and holds regular events like wine tastings. Breakfast is included in the rate. $$–$$$.

Malibu Dude Ranch (570-296-7281; malibududeranch.com), 401 Broad Street. Horse lovers and families will want to check out this all-inclusive dude ranch next to a pretty lake. Rates include all meals, clean and rustic accommodations (no TV or A/C), and all activities such as volleyball, swimming, and horseback and pony riding. New owners took over in 2010 and renovated rooms in the lodge. There are several buildings (the Boat House is a favorite) and 16 cabins on the property that sit apart from the main lodge; they tend to be quieter. Daily and weekly rates are available (kids 5–12 are half-price).

HAWLEY

The Ledges (570-226-1337; ledgeshotel.com), 120 Falls Avenue. Hawley's newest inn opened in a former silk mill complex in 2011. The rooms and suites are modern, comfortable, and environmentally friendly, but the standout attraction here is the views of the waterfall and river gorge out back. Multitiered decks and a welcoming great room provide the best vantage points; if the weather is good, you may never want to leave the grounds. A wine bar serves drinks and small dishes in the evening, and there's a breakfast café next door (see *Eating Out*). A trail out back leads to Lake Wallenpaupack, which is less than a mile away; ask the front desk for details. Getting to the hotel is the hardest part: Look for the unmarked road off US 6 that winds behind the Hawley Silk Mill complex. $$$.

Woodloch Resort (570-685-8000; 800-966-3562; woodloch.com), 731 Welcome Lake Road. This popular lakefront resort outside Hawley bills itself as being "like a cruise on land." Indeed, you'll never have to leave the complex; there are indoor and outdoor pools, a golf course, and plenty of morning-to-night organized activities, from movies and boat rides to bocce and scavenger hunts. It also helps that the lake-and-forest setting is gorgeous and shouts "getaway" from the tips of its blue spruce trees. Standard rooms in the main lodge sleep up to four, with small sitting areas and foldout couches. Deluxe lake-view rooms are spacious, with two queen beds, a pullout couch, and a small balcony. There are also large homes available for rent a few minutes' drive away in the Woodloch Springs golfing community. Rates vary, but most include three meals and plenty of activities.

The Lodge at Woodloch (800-966-3562; thelodgeatwoodloch), 2 miles from the resort, is a quieter, adults-only escape with a luxury spa (open to day visitors), private lake, and seasonal, healthy cuisine. $$$–$$$$.

The Settlers Inn (570-226-2993; thesettlersinn.com), 4 Main Avenue. First-class all the way, from the 20 stylish guest rooms to the attentive service and excellent on-site restaurant. Weather permitting, breakfast is served on the terrace and usually includes a choice of four different entrées, house-made granola, and fresh fruit. A restaurant and tavern offers one of the area's best dining experiences (*see Dining Out*). $$$.

MOTELS **Myer Country Motel** (570-296-7223; 800-764-6937; myermotel .com), 600 US 6 and 209, Milford. This 1940s-style cabin motel is one of the best values in Milford. Located just outside town near the New Jersey border, it has been in the same family for generations and features 19 separate cottage units. The rooms are tidy and charming, with TVs, refrigerators, and front porches. Coffee and juice are available in the office each morning. The place fronts a busy road but is surrounded by several acres of blue spruce and pine trees. Reserve early; these rooms go fast. $–$$.

East Shore Lodging (570-226-3293; eastshorelodging.com), US 6, Hawley. It doesn't look like much from the outside, but this friendly motel right on Lake Wallenpaupack is a terrific value. Rooms are bright and attractive, with one or two queen beds, private baths, and TVs. Breakfast is included in the rate. $$.

Ehrhardt's Waterfront Resort (800-678-5907; 570-226-4388; ehrhardts.com), 205 PA 507. This family-owned operation includes a motel, cottages, and popular restaurant—all framed by views of Lake Wallenpaupack. Don't expect luxury, but rooms are clean and have small fridges and microwaves. Rates include the use of paddleboats, canoes, two swimming pools, and boat slips, but my favorite amenity might be the many Adirondack chairs thoughtfully placed all over the property with prime views of the lake. Rates drop considerably in winter and fall. $$–$$$.

ENTRANCE TO THE SETTLERS INN IN HAWLEY

CAMPGROUNDS **Promised Land State Park** (570-888-7275; see also *Green Space*) offers nearly 500 campsites on its property. The centrally located Pickerel Point and Deerfield areas have more than 200 primitive tent sites; many walk-in sites overlook Promised Land Lake. Sites at Lower Lake Campground at the lake's western edge have hot showers and electricity hook-ups. Pickerel Point is open year-round.

Wilsonville Recreation and Camping Area (570-226-4382; wilsonville campground.com), 113 Ammon Drive, has 160 wooded tent and RV sites with electric and water hook-ups. It's right on Lake Wallenpaupack and within walking distance of the lake's only public beach.

✲ Where to Eat

DINING OUT

MILFORD

The Delmonico Room (570-409-1212), 401 Broad Street. Dinner Thursday–Sunday; Sunday jazz brunch. It's easy to picture Theodore Roosevelt or Mary Pickford enjoying frog legs in aioli or Alsatian country pâté in the grand formal dining room of the Hotel Fauchere. They were among the famous who patronized the hotel when it was owned by Louis Fauchere, a well-known chef at Delmonico's in New York. Today the dining room stays true to its haute cuisine roots, offering a prix fixe menu featuring items such as lamb osso bucco and lobster Newberg. For a more casual meal, try the downstairs Bar Louis, which serves brunch, sandwiches, and a delectable sushi pizza. Delmonico: $$$$; Bar Louis: $$–$$$.

Dimmick Inn & Steakhouse (570-296-4021), 101 East Harford Street. Lunch and dinner daily. The wide front porch of this 19th-century establishment is among the most coveted people-watching spots in town. The large menu includes flatbread pizzas, burgers, sandwiches, and a wide craft beer selection. Leave room for the cheesecake of the day. $$–$$$.

WaterWheel Café (570-296-2383; waterwheelcafe.com), 150 Water Street. Breakfast and lunch daily; dinner and bar menu Thursday–Saturday. Located in a beautiful creek-side location near Grey Towers, this multifaceted eatery features a café, restaurant, bakery, and a bar with live blues jams every Thursday night. It's a great spot for lunch; sit on the deck overlooking the creek and choose from a long list of specialty sandwiches including soft-shell crab and duck-liver mousse with port. Inside you can watch the three-story-high waterwheel in action behind a glass wall. Dinner specialties include crispy hazelnut pork chops and several tasty Vietnamese dishes. Reservations are recommended for dinner. $$.

SHOHOLA

Peter's Europa House (570-296-2624; peterseuropahouse.co), 1023 US 6, Shohola. The menu in this warm and welcoming dining room features traditional Italian and American fare such as jumbo shrimp, steak au poivre, and slow-braised lamb shank. Don't miss the signature garlic soup with roasted mushrooms and chopped tomato. $$$.

HAWLEY AREA

French Manor (877-720-6090; thefrenchmanor.com), 50 Huntingdon Drive, South Sterling. Many consider this to be the finest restaurant in the Pocono Mountains. Classic French cuisine is served in a candlelit dining room with a high-vaulted ceiling; specialties include coq au vin, grilled filet mignon and lobster tail, and pan-seared duck with fig- and pancetta-infused polenta cake. The cheese and dessert cart is a spectacular indulgence. Proper attire required. $$$–$$$$.

The Settlers Inn (570-226-2993; thesettlersinn.com), 4 Main Avenue, Hawley. Breakfast and dinner daily; call for lunch hours. One of the town's top restaurants, it has a farm-to-table menu that might include zucchini lavender soup, miso-glazed salmon with orange fennel salad, or black truffle chicken roulade. There's an extensive and thoughtful wine and beer selection. You can also opt for a more casual and inexpensive meal in the cozy tavern. $$–$$$.

EATING OUT **Trackside Grill** (570-253-2462), Honesdale. Breakfast and lunch Monday–Saturday. This small diner and local favorite near the Stourbridge Railway station serves tasty breakfast dishes and hearty sandwiches such as hot turkey and French dip, plus salads and homemade soups. $.

✨ **Mr. Yock's BBQ** (570-780-0735), 1387 Ledgedale Road, Lake Ariel. Closed Mondays. Smoked brisket, pulled pork, ribs, and homemade sides. Sit in the small dining room or outside at a picnic table. $.

Milford Diner (570-296-8611), 301 Broad Street, Milford. Classic diner with friendly service and hearty dishes such as pork and sauerkraut, beef goulash, and stuffed cabbage. Expect long waits for breakfast on weekends. $–$$.

HAWLEY

The Boat House (570-226-5027), 141 PA 507. Lunch and dinner daily. This nautical-themed bar and grill overlooks Lake Wallenpaupack and has a huge menu featuring appetizers, salads, hot and cold sandwiches, and burgers, plus grilled seafood and steak dinners. Reservations are recommended in summer. There's live music on Friday nights. $$.

Cocoon Coffeehouse (570-226-6130), 8 Silk Mill Drive, Hawley. Stop here for blueberry coffee cake, ginger peach iced tea, and savory sandwiches on the menu. You can also surf the web, lounge on the comfy couches, and admire the artwork on the walls. It's next door to the Ledges Hotel in the Hawley Silk Mill complex. $.

Cora's 1850 Bistro (570-226-8878), 525 Welwood Avenue. Lunch and dinner daily; Sunday brunch. Housed in a former hotel and run by two Culinary Institute of America graduates, this attractive yellow-walled eatery seems to have something for everyone on its menu, from burgers and salads to a long list of appetizers. Entrées include filet mignon, stuffed flounder, rack of lamb, and spicy Cajun pasta. There are also ciabatta sandwiches and a kids' menu. $$.

Hawley Diner (570-226-0523), 302 Main Avenue. Breakfast, lunch, and dinner Monday–Saturday, breakfast and lunch Sundays. Old-school diner that was serving good jumbo, Belgian waffles, and other typical diner fare long before tourists discovered the area. It fills up on weekends. $–$$.

BYO Where to buy wine in the northern Pocono Mountains region:

There are **Wine & Spirits** stores in Milford at 106 West Harford Street (570-296-7021) and in Hawley at the **Village Shopping Center** on PA 739 (570-775-5010).

❋ Entertainment

MUSIC If you're not staying at an all-inclusive resort like Woodloch Pines, your best bets for late-night action in this area are the bars and lounges of popular restaurants and hotels. **The Pub in the Apple Valley Restaurant** (570-296-6831; 104 US 6, Milford) hosts karaoke or live bands most weekends. **The WaterWheel Café** in Milford and the **Boat House** in Hawley also feature live music on weekends.

Ritz Company Playhouse (570-226-9752; ritzplayhouse.com), 512 Keystone Street, Hawley. A 1930s movie house, now a nonprofit community theater, stages five shows each summer, mostly comedies and children's plays.

❋ Selective Shopping

Antiques are the main inventory of stores around here. Hawley, Honesdale, and Milford all have a robust selection of shops selling furniture, crafts, and other items. The **Hawley Antique Exchange** (570-226-1711), 209 Bellemonte Avenue (US 6), is a multivendor antique mall and long-standing source for art, collectibles, vintage fashions, books, and every type of furniture imaginable. Hawley is also home to **Main Avenue Books and Bindery** (570-226-4777), 202 Main Avenue, a lovely shop that specializes in antiquarian, out-of-print, and used books obtained from private collections. In Milford, **Forest Hall Antiques** (570-296-4299), 214 Broad Street, occupies the upper floors of a French Normandy–style building that once housed Yale's School of Forestry, with wares such as Victorian chairs, pewter pitchers, porcelain china, and film posters. Milford also is home to the quaint Old Lumberyard Shops complex, which has a pizza café and **Old Lumberyard Antiques** (570-409-8636), 113 Seventh Street, a browser's paradise of furniture, quilts, toys, china, vintage advertisements, and more.

OLD LUMBERYARD ANTIQUES IN MILFORD

✳ Special Events

January: **Eagle Fest** (second or third weekend), Narrowsburg, New York, across from Beach Lake, Pennsylvania—winter is the best time to spot eagles here, and the area welcomes them with a festival featuring live birds of prey demonstrations, lectures, films, and staffed observation areas. Contact the Eagle Institute for more information: 570-685-5960.

February: **Crystal Cabin Fever** (last two weeks), PA 590, between Hawley and Hamlin—the area rids itself of winter cabin fever with detailed ice sculptures, a life-sized ice cabin, carving contests, and a giant ice slide that will thrill kids. There's also plenty of hot chocolate. For more info, visit crystalcabinfever.com.

June: **Milford Music Festival** (fourth weekend), Ann Street Park, Milford—a mix of jazz, blues, rock, and classical performers take the stage over three days during this popular celebration of live music.

August: **Festival of Wood** (second weekend), Grey Towers National Historic Site, Milford—wood-carving demonstrations, forestry walks, and live music.

October: **Black Bear Film Festival** (third weekend), Milford—independent films and lectures, plus displays of life-sized bear sculptures. Visit blackbearfilm.com.

INDEX